Acclaim for *Orhan Pamuk*'s

MY NAME IS RED

"Captures not just Istanbul's past and present contradictions, but also its terrible, timeless beauty. It's almost perfect, in other words." —*New Statesman*

"Enlightening.... Pamuk depicts [Ottoman Istanbul] with skill and linguistic energy.... A rich, cruel and claustrophobic world where art leads through dark alleyways, to murder." —*The Economist*

"A fabulously rich novel, highly compelling.... [*My Name Is Red*] could conclusively establish [Pamuk] as one of the world's finest living writers." —*The Independent*

"Draws the reader into [a] mental world where art is both sacred and profane, representational and abstract, innovative and traditional." —*The Washington Post Book World*

"[A] tour de force.... [A] remarkably original work of fiction ... [where] galaxies open ... [into] a world as rich as the illuminated manuscripts which form the basis of its plot." —*The Baltimore Sun*

"Magnificent.... Pamuk is the real thing, and this book might well be one of the few recent works of fiction that will be remembered at the end of this century." —*The Observer*

"[An] elegant and superbly plotted mystery ... with an engaging love story and a full canvas of memorable characters ... wonderful." —*The Orlando Sentinel*

Orhan Pamuk

MY NAME IS RED

Orhan Pamuk is the winner of the Nobel Prize in Literature for 2006. *My Name is Red* won the 2003 IMPAC Dublin Literary Award. His work has been translated into more than fifty languages. He lives in Istanbul.

A NOTE ABOUT THE TRANSLATOR

Erdağ M. Göknar is visiting assistant professor of Turkish language and culture at Duke University. He is also writing his first novel.

Also by Orhan Pamuk

The White Castle

The Black Book

The New Life

Snow

MY NAME IS RED

Orhan Pamuk

Translated from the Turkish by
Erdağ M. Göknar

VINTAGE INTERNATIONAL
VINTAGE BOOKS
A DIVISION OF RANDOM HOUSE, INC.
NEW YORK

FIRST VINTAGE INTERNATIONAL EDITION, SEPTEMBER 2002

Copyright © 2001 by Alfred A. Knopf, a division of Random House, Inc.

All rights reserved under International and Pan-American Copyright Conventions. Published in the United States by Vintage Books, a division of Random House, Inc., New York, and simultaneously in Canada by Random House of Canada Limited, Toronto. Originally published in Turkey as *Benim Adım Kırmızı* by İletişim, Istanbul, in 1998. Copyright © 1998 by Iletisim Yayinlari A.S. Subsequently published in the English language in hardcover in the United States by Alfred A. Knopf, a division of Random House, Inc., New York, in 2001.

Vintage is a registered trademark and Vintage International and colophon are trademarks of Random House, Inc.

The Library of Congress has cataloged the Knopf edition as follows:
Pamuk, Orhan, 1952–
[Benim adım Kırmızı. English]
My name is Red / Orhan Pamuk ;
translated from the Turkish by Erdağ M. Göknar.
p. cm.
ISBN 0-375-40695-6 (alk. paper)
I. Göknar, Erdağ M.
PL248.P34 B4613 2001
894'.3533—dc21   2001029866

Vintage ISBN: 0-375-70685-2

Book design by Ralph Fowler
Map by James Sinclair

www.vintagebooks.com

Printed in the United States of America
19

The translator would like to thank fellow translator and friend
Professor Walter G. Andrews for his incisive comments
and suggestions on the manuscript.   —E.M.G.

For Rüya

*You slew a man and then fell out
with one another concerning him.*

—KORAN, "THE COW," 72

The blind and the seeing are not equal.

—KORAN, "THE CREATOR," 19

To God belongs the East and the West.

—KORAN, "THE COW," 115

CONTENTS

MAP xiii

CHAPTER 1 I AM A CORPSE 3

CHAPTER 2 I AM CALLED BLACK 6

CHAPTER 3 I AM A DOG 10

CHAPTER 4 I WILL BE CALLED A MURDERER 15

CHAPTER 5 I AM YOUR BELOVED UNCLE 22

CHAPTER 6 I AM ORHAN 27

CHAPTER 7 I AM CALLED BLACK 31

CHAPTER 8 I AM ESTHER 35

CHAPTER 9 I, SHEKURE 38

CHAPTER 10 I AM A TREE 47

CHAPTER 11 I AM CALLED BLACK 51

CHAPTER 12 I AM CALLED "BUTTERFLY" 61

CHAPTER 13 I AM CALLED "STORK" 68

CHAPTER 14 I AM CALLED "OLIVE" 75

CHAPTER 15 I AM ESTHER 82

CHAPTER 16	I, SHEKURE	86
CHAPTER 17	I AM YOUR BELOVED UNCLE	91
CHAPTER 18	I WILL BE CALLED A MURDERER	96
CHAPTER 19	I AM A GOLD COIN	102
CHAPTER 20	I AM CALLED BLACK	107
CHAPTER 21	I AM YOUR BELOVED UNCLE	110
CHAPTER 22	I AM CALLED BLACK	115
CHAPTER 23	I WILL BE CALLED A MURDERER	120
CHAPTER 24	I AM DEATH	125
CHAPTER 25	I AM ESTHER	129
CHAPTER 26	I, SHEKURE	135
CHAPTER 27	I AM CALLED BLACK	149
CHAPTER 28	I WILL BE CALLED A MURDERER	154
CHAPTER 29	I AM YOUR BELOVED UNCLE	165
CHAPTER 30	I, SHEKURE	177
CHAPTER 31	I AM RED	185
CHAPTER 32	I, SHEKURE	188
CHAPTER 33	I AM CALLED BLACK	193
CHAPTER 34	I, SHEKURE	205
CHAPTER 35	I AM A HORSE	216

Contents

CHAPTER 36	I AM CALLED BLACK	219
CHAPTER 37	I AM YOUR BELOVED UNCLE	228
CHAPTER 38	IT IS I, MASTER OSMAN	232
CHAPTER 39	I AM ESTHER	240
CHAPTER 40	I AM CALLED BLACK	245
CHAPTER 41	IT IS I, MASTER OSMAN	249
CHAPTER 42	I AM CALLED BLACK	264
CHAPTER 43	I AM CALLED "OLIVE"	273
CHAPTER 44	I AM CALLED "BUTTERFLY"	275
CHAPTER 45	I AM CALLED "STORK"	277
CHAPTER 46	I WILL BE CALLED A MURDERER	279
CHAPTER 47	I, SATAN	287
CHAPTER 48	I, SHEKURE	291
CHAPTER 49	I AM CALLED BLACK	295
CHAPTER 50	WE TWO DERVISHES	306
CHAPTER 51	IT IS I, MASTER OSMAN	309
CHAPTER 52	I AM CALLED BLACK	324
CHAPTER 53	I AM ESTHER	339
CHAPTER 54	I AM A WOMAN	352
CHAPTER 55	I AM CALLED "BUTTERFLY"	356

CHAPTER 56	I AM CALLED "STORK"	367
CHAPTER 57	I AM CALLED "OLIVE"	374
CHAPTER 58	I WILL BE CALLED A MURDERER	383
CHAPTER 59	I, SHEKURE	405

CHRONOLOGY 415

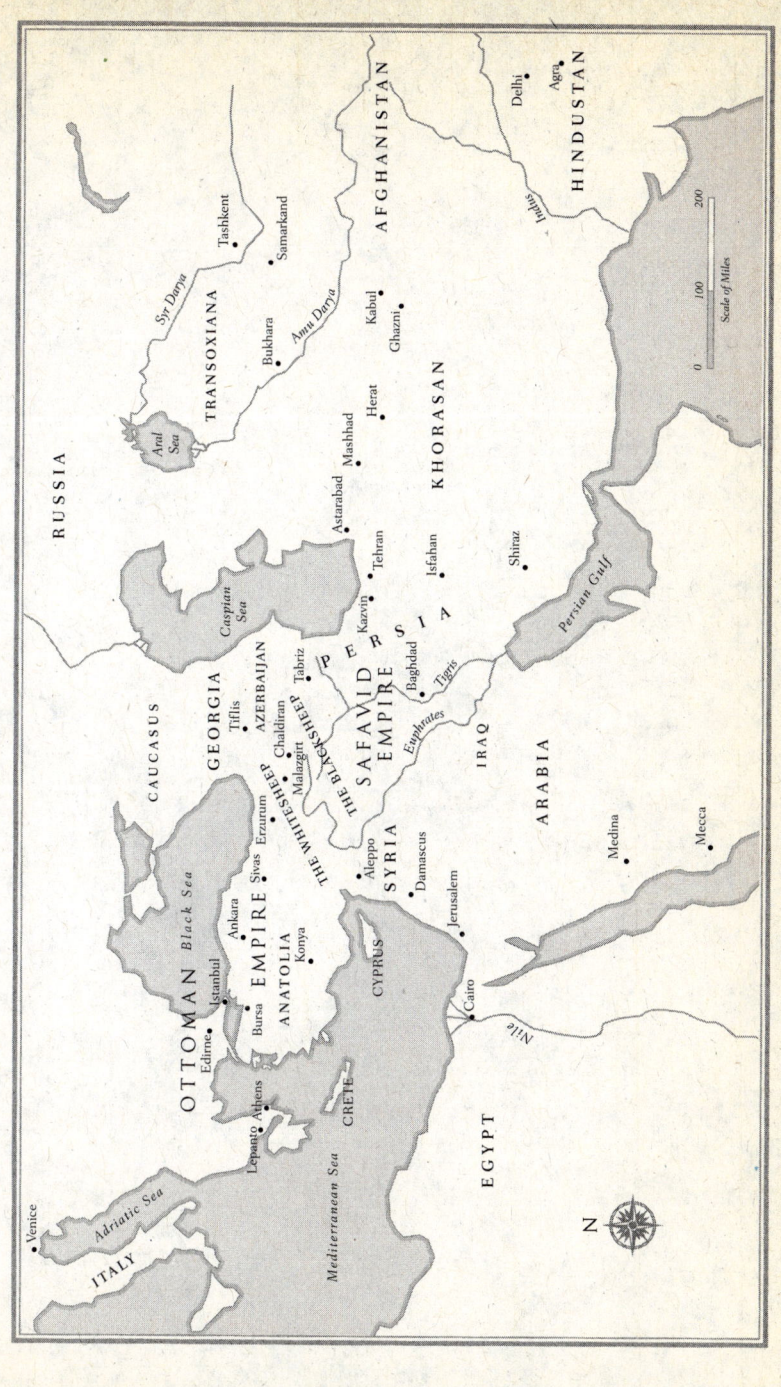

MY NAME IS RED

CHAPTER 1

I AM A CORPSE

I am nothing but a corpse now, a body at the bottom of a well. Though I drew my last breath long ago and my heart has stopped beating, no one, apart from that vile murderer, knows what's happened to me. As for that wretch, he felt for my pulse and listened for my breath to be sure I was dead, then kicked me in the midriff, carried me to the edge of the well, raised me up and dropped me below. As I fell, my head, which he'd smashed with a stone, broke apart; my face, my forehead and cheeks, were crushed; my bones shattered, and my mouth filled with blood.

For nearly four days I have been missing: My wife and children must be searching for me; my daughter, spent from crying, must be staring fretfully at the courtyard gate. Yes, I know they're all at the window, hoping for my return.

But, are they truly waiting? I can't even be sure of that. Maybe they've gotten used to my absence—how dismal! For here, on the other side, one gets the feeling that one's former life persists. Before my birth there was infinite time, and after my death, inexhaustible time. I never thought of it before: I'd been living luminously between two eternities of darkness.

I was happy; I know now that I'd been happy. I made the best illuminations in Our Sultan's workshop; no one could rival my mastery. Through the work I did privately, I earned nine hundred silver coins a month, which, naturally, only makes all of this even harder to bear.

I was responsible for painting and embellishing books. I illuminated the edges of pages, coloring their borders with the most lifelike designs of leaves, branches, roses, flowers and birds. I painted scalloped Chinese-style clouds, clusters of overlapping vines and forests of color that hid gazelles, galleys, sultans, trees, palaces, horses and hunters. In my youth, I would decorate a plate, or the back of a mirror, or a chest, or at times, the ceiling of a mansion or of a Bosphorus manor, or even, a wooden spoon. In later years, however, I only worked on manuscript pages because Our Sultan paid well for them. I can't say it seems insignificant now. You know the value of money even when you're dead.

After hearing the miracle of my voice, you might think, "Who cares what you earned when you were alive? Tell us what you see. Is there life after death? Where's your soul? What about Heaven and Hell? What's death like? Are you in pain?" You're right, the living are extremely curious about the Afterlife. Maybe you've heard the story of the man who was so driven by this curiosity that he roamed among soldiers in battlefields. He sought a man who'd died and returned to life amid the wounded struggling for their lives in pools of blood, a soldier who could tell him about the secrets of the Otherworld. But one of Tamerlane's warriors, taking the seeker for the enemy, cleaved him in half with a smooth stroke of his scimitar, causing him to conclude that in the Hereafter man gets split in two.

Nonsense! Quite the opposite, I'd even say that souls divided in life merge in the Hereafter. Contrary to the claims of sinful infidels who've fallen under the sway of the Devil, there is indeed another world, thank God, and the proof is that I'm speaking to you from here. I've died, but as you can plainly tell, I haven't ceased to be. Granted, I must confess, I haven't encountered the rivers flowing beside the silver and gold kiosks of Heaven, the broad-leaved trees bearing plump fruit and the beautiful virgins mentioned in the Glorious Koran—though I do very well recall how often and enthusiastically I made pictures of those wide-eyed houris described in the chapter "That Which Is Coming." Nor is there a trace of those rivers of milk, wine, fresh water and honey described with such flourish, not in the Koran, but by visionary dreamers like Ibn Arabi. But I have no intention of tempting the faith of those who live rightfully through their hopes and visions of the Otherworld, so let me declare that all I've seen relates specifically to my own very personal circumstances. Any believer with even a little knowledge of life after death would know that a malcontent in my state would be hard-pressed to see the rivers of Heaven.

In short, I, who am known as Master Elegant Effendi, am dead, but I have not been buried, and therefore my soul has not completely left my body. This extraordinary situation, although naturally my case isn't the first, has inflicted horrible suffering upon the immortal part of me. Though I cannot feel my crushed skull or my decomposing body covered in wounds, full of broken bones and partially submerged in ice-cold water, I do feel the deep torment of my soul struggling desperately to escape its mortal coil. It's as if the whole world, along with my body, were contracting into a bolus of anguish.

I can only compare this contraction to the surprising sense of release I felt during the unequaled moment of my death. Yes, I instantly understood that the wretch wanted to kill me when he unexpectedly struck me with a stone and cracked my skull, but I didn't believe he'd follow through. I suddenly realized I was a hopeful man, something I hadn't been aware of while living my life in the shadows between workshop and household. I clung passionately to life with my nails, my fingers and my teeth, which I sank into his skin. I won't bore you with the painful details of the subsequent blows I received.

When in the course of this agony I knew I would die, an incredible feeling of relief filled me. I felt this relief during the moment of departure; my arrival to this side was soothing, like the dream of seeing oneself asleep. The snow- and mud-covered shoes of my murderer were the last things I noticed. I closed my eyes as if I were going to sleep, and I gently passed over.

My present complaint isn't that my teeth have fallen like nuts into my bloody mouth, or even that my face has been maimed beyond recognition, or that I've been abandoned in the depths of a well—it's that everyone assumes I'm still alive. My troubled soul is anguished that my family and intimates, who, yes, think of me often, imagine me engaged in trivial dealings somewhere in Istanbul, or even chasing after another woman. Enough! Find my body without delay, pray for me and have me buried. Above all, find my murderer! For even if you bury me in the most magnificent of tombs, so long as that wretch remains free, I'll writhe restlessly in my grave, waiting and infecting you all with faithlessness. Find that son-of-a-whore murderer and I'll tell you in detail just what I see in the Afterlife—but know this, after he's caught, he must be tortured by slowly splintering eight or ten of his bones, preferably his ribs, with a vise before piercing his scalp with skewers made especially for the task by torturers and plucking out his disgusting, oily hair, strand by strand, so he shrieks each time.

Who is this murderer who vexes me so? Why has he killed me in such a surprising way? Be curious and mindful of these matters. You say the world is full of base and worthless criminals? Perhaps this one did it, perhaps that one? In that case let me caution you: My death conceals an appalling conspiracy against our religion, our traditions and the way we see the world. Open your eyes, discover why the enemies of the life in which you believe, of the life you're living, and of Islam, have destroyed me. Learn why one day they might do the same to you. One by one, everything predicted by the great preacher Nusret Hoja of Erzurum, to whom I've tearfully listened, is coming to pass. Let me say also that if the situation into which we've fallen were described in a book, even the most expert of miniaturists could never hope to illustrate it. As with the Koran—God forbid I'm misunderstood—the staggering power of such a book arises from the impossibility of its being depicted. I doubt you've fully comprehended this fact.

Listen to me. When I was an apprentice, I too feared and thus ignored underlying truths and voices from beyond. I'd joke about such matters. But I've ended up in the depths of this deplorable well! It could happen to you, be wary. Now, I've nothing left to do but hope for my thorough decay, so they can find me by tracing my stench. I've nothing to do but hope—and imagine the torture that some benevolent man will inflict upon that beastly murderer once he's been caught.

CHAPTER 2

I AM CALLED BLACK

After an absence of twelve years I entered Istanbul like a sleepwalker. "The earth called to him," they say of men who are about to die, and in my case, it was death that drew me back to the city where I'd been born and raised. When I first returned, I thought there was only death; later, I would also encounter love. Love, however, was a distant and forgotten thing, like my memories of having lived in the city. It was in Istanbul, twelve years ago, that I fell helplessly in love with my young cousin.

Four years after I first left Istanbul, while traveling through the endless steppes, snow-covered mountains and melancholy cities of Persia, carrying letters and collecting taxes, I admitted to myself that I was slowly forgetting the face of the childhood love I'd left behind. With growing panic, I tried desperately to remember her, only to realize that despite love, a face long not seen finally fades. During the sixth year I spent in the East, traveling or working as a secretary in the service of pashas, I knew that the face I imagined was no longer that of my beloved. Later, in the eighth year, I forgot what I'd mistakenly called to mind in the sixth, and again visualized a completely different countenance. In this way, by the twelfth year, when I returned to my city at the age of thirty-six, I was painfully aware that my beloved's face had long since escaped me.

Many of my friends and relatives had died during my twelve-year exile. I visited the cemetery overlooking the Golden Horn and prayed for my mother and for the uncles who'd passed away in my absence. The earthy smell of mud mingled with my memories. Someone had broken an earthenware pitcher beside my mother's grave. For whatever reason, gazing at the broken pieces, I began to cry. Was I crying for the dead or because I was, strangely, still only at the beginning of my life after all these years? Or was it because I'd come to the end of my life's journey? A faint snow fell. Entranced by the flakes blowing here and there, I became so lost in the vagaries of my life that I didn't notice the black dog staring at me from a dark corner of the cemetery.

My tears subsided. I wiped my nose. I saw the black dog wagging its tail in friendship as I left the cemetery. Sometime later, I settled into our neighborhood, renting one of the houses where a relative on my father's side once lived. It seems I reminded the landlady of her son who'd been killed by Safavid Persian soldiers at the front and so she agreed to clean the house and cook for me.

I set out on long and satisfying walks through the streets as if I'd settled not in Istanbul, but temporarily in one of the Arab cities at the other end of the world. The streets had become narrower, or so it seemed to me. In certain areas, on roads squeezed between houses leaning toward one another, I was forced to rub up against walls and doors to avoid being hit by laden packhorses. There were more wealthy people, or so it seemed to me. I saw an ornate carriage, a citadel drawn by proud horses, the likes of which couldn't be found in Arabia or Persia. Near the "Burnt Column," I saw some bothersome beggars dressed in rags huddling together as the smell of offal coming from the chicken-sellers market wafted over them. One of them who was blind smiled as he watched the falling snow.

Had I been told Istanbul used to be a poorer, smaller and happier city, I might not have believed it, but that's what my heart told me. Though my beloved's house was where it'd always been among linden and chestnut trees, others were now living there, as I learned from inquiring at the door. I discovered that my beloved's mother, my maternal aunt, had died, and that her husband, my Enishte, and his daughter had moved away. This is how I came to learn that father and daughter were the victims of certain misfortunes, from strangers answering the door, who in such situations are perfectly forthcoming, without the least awareness of how mercilessly they've broken your heart and destroyed your dreams. I won't describe all of this to you now, but allow me to say that as I recalled warm, verdant and sunny summer days in that old garden, I also noticed icicles the size of my little finger hanging from the branches of the linden tree in a place whose misery, snow and neglect now evoked nothing but death.

I Am Called Black 7

I'd already learned about some of what had befallen my relatives through a letter my Enishte sent to me in Tabriz. In that letter, he invited me back to Istanbul, explaining that he was preparing a secret book for Our Sultan and that he wanted my help. He'd heard that for a period while in Tabriz, I made books for Ottoman pashas, provincial governors and Istanbulites. What I did then was to use the money advanced by clients who'd placed manuscript orders in Istanbul to locate miniaturists and calligraphers who were frustrated by the wars and the presence of Ottoman soldiers, but hadn't yet left for Kazvin or another Persian city, and it was these masters—complaining of poverty and neglect—whom I commissioned to inscribe, illustrate and bind the pages of the manuscripts I would then send back to Istanbul. If it weren't for the love of illustrating and fine books that my Enishte instilled in me during my youth, I could have never involved myself in such pursuits.

At the market end of the street, where at one time my Enishte had lived, I found the barber, a master by trade, in his shop among the same mirrors, straight razors, pitchers of water and soap brushes. I caught his eye, but I'm not sure he recognized me. It delighted me to see that the head-washing basin, which hung by a chain from the ceiling, still traced the same old arc, swinging back and forth as he filled it with hot water.

Some of the neighborhoods and streets I'd frequented in my youth had disappeared in ashes and smoke, replaced by burnt ruins where stray dogs congregated and where mad transients frightened the local children. In other areas razed by fire, large affluent houses had been built, and I was astonished by their extravagance, by windows of the most expensive Venetian stained glass, and by lavish two-story residences with bay windows suspended above high walls.

As in many other cities, money no longer had any value in Istanbul. At the time I returned from the East, bakeries that once sold large one-hundred drachma loaves of bread for one silver coin now baked loaves half the size for the same price, and they no longer tasted the way they did during my childhood. Had my late mother seen the day when she'd have to spend three silver pieces for a dozen eggs, she'd say, "We ought to leave before the chickens grow so spoiled they shit on us instead of the ground." But I knew the problem of devalued money was the same everywhere. It was rumored that Flemish and Venetian merchant ships were filled with chests of counterfeit coin. At the royal mint, where five hundred coins were once minted from a hundred drachmas of silver, now, owing to the endless warring with the Persians, eight hundred coins were minted from the same amount. When Janissaries discovered that the coins they'd been paid actually floated in the Golden Horn like the dried beans that fell from the vegetable-sellers pier, they rioted, besieging Our Sultan's palace as if it were an enemy fortress.

A cleric by the name of Nusret, who preached at the Bayazid Mosque and claimed to be descended from Our Glorious Prophet Muhammad, had made a name for himself during this period of immorality, inflation, crime and theft. This hoja, who was from the small town of Erzurum, attributed the catastrophes that had befallen Istanbul in the last ten years—including the Bahçekapı and Kazanjılar district fires, the plagues that claimed tens of thousands, the endless wars with the Persians at a cost of countless lives, as well as the loss of small Ottoman fortresses in the West to Christians in revolt—to our having strayed from the path of the Prophet, to disregard for the strictures of the Glorious Koran, to the tolerance toward Christians, to the open sale of wine and to the playing of musical instruments in dervish houses.

The pickle seller who passionately informed me about the cleric from Erzurum said that the counterfeit coins—the new ducats, the fake florins stamped with lions and the Ottoman coins with their ever-decreasing silver content—that flooded the markets and bazaars, just like the Circassians, Abkhazians, Mingarians, Bosnians, Georgians and Armenians who filled the streets, were dragging us toward an absolute degradation from which it would be difficult to escape. I was told that scoundrels and rebels were gathering in coffeehouses and proselytizing until dawn; that destitute men of dubious character, opium-addicted madmen and followers of the outlawed Kalenderi dervish sect, claiming to be on Allah's path, would spend their nights in dervish houses dancing to music, piercing themselves with skewers and engaging in all manner of depravity, before brutally fucking each other and any boys they could find.

I didn't know whether it was the melodious sound of a lute that compelled me to follow, or if in the muddle of my memories and desires, I could simply no longer endure the virulent pickle seller, and seized upon the music as a way out of the conversation. I do, however, know this: When you love a city and have explored it frequently on foot, your body, not to mention your soul, gets to know the streets so well after a number of years that in a fit of melancholy, perhaps stirred by a light snow falling ever so sorrowfully, you'll discover your legs carrying you of their own accord toward one of your favorite promontories.

This was how I happened to leave the Farrier's Market and ended up watching the snow as it fell into the Golden Horn from a spot beside the Süleymaniye Mosque: Snow had already begun to accumulate on the rooftops facing north and on sections of the dome exposed to the northeasterly breeze. An approaching ship, whose sails were being lowered, greeted me with a flutter of canvas. The color of its sails matched the leaden and foggy hue of the surface of the Golden Horn. The cypress and plane trees, the rooftops, the heartache of dusk, the sounds coming from the neighborhood below, the calls of hawkers and the cries of children playing in mosque courtyards mingled in my head and announced emphatically that, hereafter, I wouldn't be able to live anywhere but in their city. I had the sensation that my beloved's face, which had escaped me for years, might suddenly appear to me.

I began to walk down the hill and melded into the crowds. After the evening prayer was called, I filled my stomach at a liver shop. In the empty shop, I listened carefully to the owner, who fondly watched me eat each bite as if he were feeding a cat. Taking his cue and following his directions, I found myself turning down one of the narrow alleys behind the slave market—well after the streets had become dark—and located the coffeehouse.

Inside, it was crowded and warm. The storyteller, the likes of whom I had seen in Tabriz and in Persian cities and who was known thereabouts as a "curtain-caller," was perched on a raised platform beside the woodburning stove. He had unfolded and hung before the crowd a picture, the figure of a dog drawn on rough paper hastily but with a certain elegance. He was giving voice to the dog, and pointing, from time to time, at the drawing.

CHAPTER 3

I AM A DOG

As you can doubtless tell, dear friends, my canines are so long and pointed they barely fit into my mouth. I know this gives me a menacing appearance, but it pleases me. Noticing the size of my teeth, a butcher once had the gall to say, "My God, that's no dog at all, it's a wild boar!"

I bit him so hard on the leg that my canines sank right through his fatty flesh to the hardness of his thighbone. For a dog, you see, nothing is as satisfying as sinking his teeth into his miserable enemy in a fit of instinctual wrath. When such an opportunity presents itself, that is, when my victim, who deserves to be bitten, stupidly and unknowingly passes by, my teeth twinge and ache in anticipation, my head spins with longing and without even meaning to, I emit a hair-raising growl.

I'm a dog, and because you humans are less rational beasts than I, you're telling yourselves, "Dogs don't talk." Nevertheless, you seem to believe a story in which corpses speak and characters use words they couldn't possibly know. Dogs do speak, but only to those who know how to listen.

Once upon a time, long, long ago, in a faraway land, a brash cleric from a provincial town arrived at one of the largest mosques in a capital city; all right, let's call it the Bayazid Mosque. It'd be appropriate to withhold his name, so let's refer to him as "Husret Hoja." But why should I cover up anything more: This man was one boneheaded cleric. He made up for the modesty of his intellect with the power of his tongue, God bless it. Each Friday, he so animated his congregation, so moved them to tears that some would cry until they fainted or dried up and withered away. Don't get me wrong, unlike other clerics with the gift of preaching, he himself didn't weep. On the contrary, while everyone else cried, he intensified his oration without a blink as if to chastise the congregation. In all probability, the gardeners, royal pages, halva makers, riffraff and clerics like himself became his lackeys because they enjoyed the tongue lashing. Well, this man was no dog after all, no sir, he was a human being—to be human is to err—and before those enthralled crowds, he lost himself when he saw that intimidating throngs of people was as pleasurable as bringing them to tears. When he understood that there was much more bread to be made in this new venture, he went over the top and had the nerve to say the following:

"The sole reason for rising prices, plague and military defeat lies in our forgetting the Islam of the time of our Glorious Prophet and falling sway to falsehoods. Was the Prophet's birth epic read in memory of the dead back then? Was the fortieth-day ceremony performed, where sweets like halva and fried dough are offered to honor the dead? When Muhammad lived, was the Glorious Koran recited melodically, like a song? Were the prayers called haughtily and pompously to show how close one's Arabic was to an Arab's? Was there such a thing as reciting the call to prayer coyly, with the flourish of a man imitating a woman? Today, people plead before gravesites, begging for amends. They hope for the intervention of the dead on their behalf. They visit the tombs of saints and worship at graves like pagans before pieces of stone. They tie votive pieces of cloth everywhere, and make promises of sacrifice in return for atonement. Were there dervish sectarians who spread such beliefs in Muhammad's time? Ibn Arabi, the intellectual mentor of these sectarians, became a sinner by swearing that the infidel Pharaoh had died a believer. These dervishes, the Mevlevis, the Halvetis, the Kalenderis and those who sing the Koran to musical accompaniment or justify dancing with children and juveniles by saying 'we pray together anyway, why not?' are all kaffirs. Dervish lodges ought to be destroyed, their foundations excavated to a depth of seven ells and the collected earth cast into the sea. Only then might ritual prayers be performed there again."

I heard tell that this Husret Hoja, taking matters even further, declared with spittle flying from his mouth, "Ah, my devoted believers! The drinking of coffee is an absolute sin! Our Glorious Prophet did not partake of coffee because he knew it dulled the intellect, caused ulcers, hernia and sterility; he understood that coffee was nothing but the Devil's ruse. Coffeehouses are places where pleasure-seekers and wealthy gadabouts sit knee-to-knee, involving themselves in all sorts of vulgar behavior; in fact, even before the dervish houses are closed, coffeehouses ought to be banned. Do the poor have enough money to drink coffee? Men frequent these places, become besotted with coffee and lose control of their mental faculties to the point that they actually listen to and believe what dogs and mongrels have to say. But those who curse me and our religion, it is they who are the true mongrels."

With your permission, I'd like to respond to this last comment by the esteemed cleric. Of course, it is common knowledge that hajis, hojas, clerics, and preachers despise us dogs. In my opinion, the whole matter concerns our revered Prophet Muhammad, peace and blessings be upon him, who cut off a piece of his robe upon which a cat lay sleeping rather than wake the beast. By pointing out this affection shown to the cat, which has incidentally been denied to us dogs, and due to our eternal feud with this feline beast, which even the stupidest of men recognizes as an ingrate, people have tried to intimate that the Prophet himself disliked dogs. They're convinced that we'll defile those who have performed ritual ablutions, and the result of this erroneous and slanderous belief is that we've been barred from mosques for centuries and have suffered beatings in their courtyards from broomstick-wielding caretakers.

Allow me to remind you of "The Cave," the most beautiful of the Koran's chapters. I'm reminding you not because I suspect there may be those who never read the Koran among us in this good coffeehouse, but because I want to refresh your memories: This chapter recounts the story of the seven youths who grow tired of living among pagans and take refuge in a cave where they enter a deep sleep. Allah then seals their ears and causes them to doze off for exactly three hundred and nine years. When they awake, they learn just how many years have passed only after one of them enters the society of men and tries to spend an outdated silver coin. All of them are stunned to learn what has happened. This chapter subtly describes man's attachment to Allah, His miracles, the transitory nature of time and the pleasure of deep sleep, and though it's not my place, allow me to remind you of the eighteenth verse, which makes mention of a dog resting at the mouth of this cave where the seven youths have fallen asleep. Obviously, anyone would be proud to appear in the Koran. As a dog, I take pride in this chapter, and through it I intend to bring the Erzurumis, who refer to their enemies as dirty mongrels, to their senses.

So then, what's the actual reason for this animosity toward dogs? Why do you persist in saying that dogs are impure, and cleaning and purifying your homes from top to bottom if a dog happens to enter? Why do you believe that those who touch us spoil their ablutions? If your caftan brushes against our damp fur, why do you insist on washing that caftan seven times like a frenzied woman? Only tinsmiths could be responsible for the slander that a pot licked by a dog must be thrown away or retinned. Or perhaps, yes, cats . . .

When people left their villages for the sedentary life of the city, shepherd dogs remained in the provinces; that's when rumors of the filthiness of dogs like me began to spread. Yet before the advent of Islam, two of the twelve months of the year were "months of the dog." Now, however, a dog is considered a bad omen. I don't want to burden you with my own problems, my dear friends who have come to hear a story and ponder its moral—to be honest, my anger arises out of the esteemed cleric's attacks upon our coffeehouses.

What would you think if I said that this Husret of Erzurum was of dubious birth? But they've also said of me, "What kind of dog do you think you are? You're attacking the venerable cleric because your master is a picture-hanging storyteller who tells tales at a coffeehouse and you want to protect him. Go on, scat!" God forbid, I'm not denigrating anyone. But I'm a great admirer of our coffeehouses. You know, I have no problem with the fact that my portrait was drawn on such cheap paper or that I'm a four-legged beast, but I do regret that I can't sit down like a man and have a cup of coffee with you. We'd die for our coffee and our coffeehouses—what's

I Am a Dog

this? See, my master is pouring coffee for me from a small coffeepot. A picture can't drink coffee, you say? Please! See for yourselves, this dog is happily lapping away.

Ah, yes, that hit the spot, it's warmed me up, sharpened my sight and quickened my thoughts. Now listen to what I have to tell you: Besides bolts of Chinese silks and Chinese pottery adorned with blue flowers, what did the Venetian Doge send to Nurhayat Sultan, the esteemed daughter of our respected Sultan? A soft and cuddly Venetian she-dog with a coat of silk and sable. I heard that this bitch is so spoiled she has a red silk dress as well. One of our friends actually fucked her, that's how I know, and she can't even engage in the act without her dress. In that Frankish land of hers, all dogs wear outfits like that anyway. I've heard tell that over there a so-called elegant and well-bred Venetian woman saw a naked dog—or maybe she saw its thing, I'm not sure—anyway, she screamed, "My dear God, the dog is naked!" and fainted dead away.

In the lands of the infidel Franks, the so-called Europeans, every dog has an owner. These poor animals are paraded on the streets with chains around their necks, they're fettered like the most miserable of slaves and dragged around in isolation. These Franks force the poor beasts into their homes and even into their beds. Dogs aren't permitted to walk with one another, let alone sniff and frolic together. In that despicable state, in chains, they can do nothing but gaze forlornly at each other from a distance when they pass on the street. Dogs who roam the streets of Istanbul freely in packs and communities, the way we do, dogs who threaten people if necessary, who can curl up in a warm corner or stretch out in the shade and sleep peacefully, and who can shit wherever they want and bite whomever they want, such dogs are beyond the infidels' conception. It's not that I haven't thought that this might be why the followers of the Erzurumi oppose praying for dogs and feeding them meat on the streets of Istanbul in exchange for divine favors and even why they oppose the establishment of charities that perform such services. If they intend both to treat us as enemies and make infidels of us, let me remind them that being an enemy to dogs and being an infidel are one and the same. At the, I hope, not too distant executions of these disgraceful men, I pray our executioner friends invite us to take a bite, as they sometimes do to set a deterring example.

Before I finish, let me say this: My previous master was a very just man. When we set out at night to thieve, we'd cooperate: I'd begin to bark, and he'd cut the throat of our victim whose screams would be drowned out by my barking. In return for my help, he'd cut up the guilty men that he'd punished, boil them and feed them to me. I don't like raw meat. God willing, the would-be executioner of that cleric from Erzurum will take this into account so I won't upset my stomach with that scoundrel's raw flesh.

CHAPTER 4

I WILL BE CALLED A MURDERER

Nay, I wouldn't have believed I could take anyone's life, even if I'd been told so moments before I murdered that fool; and thus, my offense at times recedes from me like a foreign galleon disappearing on the horizon. Now and again, I even feel as if I haven't committed any crime at all. Four days have passed since I was forced to do away with hapless Elegant, who was a brother to me, and only now have I, to some extent, accepted my situation.

I would've preferred to resolve this unexpected and awful dilemma without having to do away with anybody, but I knew there was no other choice. I handled the matter then and there, assuming the burden of responsibility. I couldn't let the false accusations of one foolhardy man endanger the entire society of miniaturists.

Nevertheless, being a murderer takes some getting used to. I can't stand being at home, so I head out to the street. I can't stand my street, so I walk on to another, and then another. As I stare at people's faces, I realize that many of them believe they're innocent because they haven't yet had the opportunity to snuff out a life. It's hard to believe that most men are more moral or better than me simply on account of some minor twist of fate. At most, they wear somewhat stupider expressions because they haven't yet killed, and like all fools, they appear to have good intentions. After I took care of that pathetic man, wandering the streets of Istanbul for four days was enough to confirm that everyone with a gleam of cleverness in his eye and the shadow of his soul cast across his face was a hidden assassin. Only imbeciles are innocent.

Tonight, for example, while warming up with a steaming coffee at the coffeehouse located in the back streets of the slave market, gazing at the sketch of a dog hanging on the back wall, I was gradually forgetting my plight and laughing with the rest of them at everything the dog recounted. Then, I had the sensation that one of the men beside me was a common murderer like myself. Though he was simply laughing at the storyteller as I was, my intuition was sparked, either by the way his arm rested near mine or by the way he restlessly rapped his fingers on his cup. I'm not sure how I knew, but I suddenly turned and looked him directly in the eye. He gave a start and his face contorted. As the crowd dispersed, an acquaintance of his took him by the arm and said, "Nusret Hoja's men will surely raid this place."

Raising an eyebrow, he signaled the man quiet. Their fear infected me. No one trusted anyone, everyone expected to be done in at any moment by the man next to him.

It had become even colder, and snow had accumulated on street corners and at the bases of walls. In the blindness of night, I could find my way along the narrow streets only by groping with my hands. At times, the dim light of an oil lamp still burning somewhere inside a wooden house filtered out from behind blackened windows and drawn shutters, reflecting on the snow; but mostly, I could see nothing, and found my way by listening for the sounds of watchmen banging their sticks on stones, for the howling of mad dogs, or the sounds coming from houses. At times the narrow and dreadful streets of the city seemed to be lit up by a wondrous light coming from the snow itself; and in the darkness, amid the ruins and trees, I thought I spotted one of those ghosts that have made Istanbul such an ominous place for thousands of years. From within houses, now and again, I heard the noises of miserable people having coughing fits or snorting or wailing as they cried out in their dreams, or I heard the shouts of husbands and wives as they tried to strangle each other, their children sobbing at their feet.

For a couple of nights in a row, I came to this coffeehouse to relive the happiness I'd felt before becoming a murderer, to raise my spirits and to listen to the storyteller. Most of my miniaturist friends, the brethren with whom I'd spent my entire life, came here every night. Since I'd silenced that lout with whom I'd made illustrations since childhood I didn't want to see any of them. Much embarrasses me about the lives of my brethren, who can't do without gossiping, and about the disgraceful atmosphere of joviality in this place. I even sketched a few pictures for the storyteller so they wouldn't accuse me of conceit, but that failed to put an end to their envy.

They're justified in being jealous. Not one of them could surpass me in mixing colors, in creating and embellishing borders, composing pages, selecting subjects, drawing faces, arranging bustling war and hunting scenes and depicting beasts, sultans, ships, horses, warriors and lovers. Not one could approach my mastery in imbuing illustrations with the poetry of the soul, not even in gilding. I'm not bragging, but explaining this to you so you might fully understand me. Over time, jealousy becomes an element as indispensable as paint in the life of the master artist.

During my walks, which grow increasingly longer due to my restlessness, I come face-to-face occasionally with one of our most pure and innocent religious countrymen, and a strange notion suddenly enters my head: If I think about the fact that I'm a murderer, the man before me will read it on my face. Therefore, I force myself to think of different things, just as I forced myself, writhing in embarrassment, to banish thoughts of women when performing prayers as an adolescent. But unlike those days of youthful fits when I couldn't get the act of copulation out of my thoughts, now, I can indeed forget the murder that I've committed.

You realize, in fact, that I'm explaining all these things because they relate to my predicament. But if I were to divulge even one detail related to the killing itself, you'd figure it all out and this would relieve me from being a nameless, faceless murderer roaming among you like an apparition and relegate me to the status of an ordinary, confessed criminal who has given himself up, soon to pay for his crime with his head. Give me the license not to dwell on every single detail, allow me to keep some clues to myself: Try to discover who I am from my choice of words and colors, as attentive people like yourselves might examine footprints to catch a thief. This, in turn, brings us to the issue of "style," which is now of widespread interest: Does a miniaturist, ought a miniaturist, have his own personal style? A use of color, a voice all his own?

Let's consider a piece by Bihzad, the master of masters, patron saint of all miniaturists. I happened across this masterpiece, which also nicely pertains to my situation because it's a depiction of murder, among the pages of a flawless ninety-year-old book of the Herat school. It emerged from the library of a Persian prince killed in a merciless battle of succession and recounts the story of Hüsrev and Shirin. You, of course, know the fate of Hüsrev and Shirin, I refer to Nizami's version, not Firdusi's:

The two lovers finally marry after a host of trials and tribulations; however, the young and diabolical Shiruye, Hüsrev's son by his previous wife, won't give them any peace. The prince has his eye on not only his father's throne but also his father's young wife, Shirin. Shiruye, of whom Nizami writes, "His breath had the stench of a lion's mouth," by hook or crook imprisons his father and succeeds to the throne. One night, entering the bedchamber of his father and Shirin, he feels his way in the dark, and on finding the pair in bed, stabs his father in the chest with his dagger. Thus, the father's blood flows till dawn and he slowly dies in the bed that he shares with the beautiful Shirin, who remains sleeping peacefully beside him.

This picture by the great master Bihzad, as much as the tale itself, addresses a grave fear I've carried within me for years: The horror of waking in the black of night to realize there's a stranger making faint sounds as he creeps about the blackness of the room! Imagine that the intruder wields a dagger in one hand as he strangles you with the other. Every detail, the finely wrought wall, window and frame ornamentation, the curves and circular designs in the red rug, the color of the silent scream emanating from your clamped throat and the yellow and purple flowers embroidered with incredible finesse and vigor on the magnificent quilt upon which the bare and vile foot of your murderer mercilessly steps as he ends your life, all of these details serve the same purpose: While augmenting the beauty of the painting, they remind you just how exquisite are the room in which you will soon die and the world you will soon leave. The indifference of the painting's beauty and of the world to your death, the fact of your being totally alone in death despite the presence of your wife, this is the inescapable meaning that strikes you.

"This is by Bihzad," the aging master said twenty years ago as we examined the book I held in my trembling hands. His face was illuminated not by the nearby candle, but by the pleasure of observation itself. "This is so Bihzad that there's no need for a signature."

Bihzad was so well aware of this fact that he didn't hide his signature anywhere in the painting. And according to the elderly master, there was a sense of embarrassment and a feeling of shame in this decision of his. Where there is true art and genuine virtuosity the artist can paint an incomparable masterpiece without leaving even a trace of his identity.

Fearing for my life, I murdered my unfortunate victim in an ordinary and crude manner. As I returned to this fire-ravaged area night after night to ascertain whether I'd left behind any traces that might betray me, questions of style increasingly arose in my head. What was venerated as style was nothing more than an imperfection or flaw that revealed the guilty hand.

I could've located this place even without the brilliance of the falling snow, for this spot, razed by fire, was where I'd ended the life of my companion of twenty-five years. Now, snow covered and erased all the clues that might have been interpreted as signature, proving that Allah concurred with Bihzad and me on the issue of style and signature. If we actually committed an unpardonable sin by illustrating that book—as that half-wit had maintained four days ago—even if we had done so unawares, Allah wouldn't have bestowed this favor upon us miniaturists.

That night, when Elegant Effendi and I came here, the snow hadn't yet begun to fall. We could hear the howling of mongrels echo in the distance.

"Pray, for what reason have we come here?" the unfortunate one had asked. "What do you plan to show me out here at this late hour?"

"Just ahead lies a well, twelve paces beyond which I've buried the money I've been saving for years," I said. "If you keep everything I've explained to you secret, Enishte Effendi and I will see that you are happily rewarded."

"Am I to understand that you admit you knew what you were doing from the beginning?" he said in agitation.

"I admit it," I lied obligingly.

"You acknowledge the picture you've made is in fact a desecration, don't you?" he said innocently. "It's heresy, a sacrilege that no decent man would have the gall to commit. You're going to burn in the pits of Hell. Your suffering and pain will never diminish—and you've made me an accomplice."

As I listened to him, I sensed with horror how his words had such strength and gravity that, willingly or not, people would heed them, hoping that they would prove true about miserable creatures other than themselves. Many rumors like this about Enishte Effendi had begun to fly due to the secrecy of the book he was making and the money he was willing to pay—and because Master Osman, the Head Illuminator, despised him. It occurred to me that perhaps my brother gilder, Elegant, had with sly intent used these facts to buttress his false accusations. To what degree was he being honest?

I had him repeat the claims that pitted us against each other, and as he spoke, he didn't mince his words. He seemed to be provoking me to cover up a mistake, as during our apprentice years, when the goal was to avoid a beating by Master Osman. Back then, I found his sincerity convincing. As an apprentice, his eyes would widen as they did now, but back then they hadn't yet dimmed from the labor of embellishing. But finally I hardened my heart; he was prepared to confess everything to everyone.

"Do listen to me," I said with forced exasperation. "We make illuminations, create border designs, draw frames onto pages, we brightly ornament page after page with lovely tones of gold, we make the greatest of paintings, we adorn armoires and boxes. We've done nothing else for years. It is our calling. They commission paintings from us, ordering us to arrange a ship, an antelope or a sultan within the borders of a particular frame, demanding a certain style of bird, a certain type of figure, take this particular scene from the story, forget about such-and-such. Whatever it is they demand, we do it. 'Listen,' Enishte Effendi said to me, 'here, draw a horse of your own imagining, right here.' For three days, like the great artists of old, I sketched hundreds of horses so I might come to know exactly what 'a horse of my own imagining' was. To accustom my hand, I drew a series of horses on a coarse sheet of Samarkand paper."

I took these sketches out and showed them to Elegant. He looked at them with interest and, leaning close to the paper, began to study the black and white horses in the faint moonlight. "The old masters of Shiraz and Herat," I said, "claimed that a miniaturist would have to sketch horses unceasingly for fifty years to be able to truly depict the horse that Allah envisioned and desired. They claimed that the best picture of a horse should be drawn in the dark, since a true miniaturist would go blind working over that fifty-year period, but in the process, his hand would memorize the horse."

The innocent expression on his face, the one I'd also seen long ago, when we were children, told me that he'd become completely absorbed in my horses.

"They hire us, and we try to make the most mysterious, the most unattainable horse, just as the old masters did. There's nothing more to it. It's unjust of them to hold us responsible for anything more than the illustration."

"I'm not sure that's correct," he said. "We, too, have responsibilities and our own will. I fear no one but Allah. It was He who provided us with reason that we might distinguish Good from Evil."

It was an appropriate response.

"Allah sees and knows all . . ." I said in Arabic. "He'll know that you and I, we've done this work without being aware of what we were doing. Who will you notify about Enishte Effendi? Aren't you aware that behind this affair rests the will of His Excellency Our Sultan?"

Silence.

I wondered whether he was really such a buffoon or whether his loss of composure and ranting had sprung out of a sincere fear of Allah.

We stopped at the mouth of the well. In the darkness, I vaguely caught sight of his eyes and could see that he was scared. I pitied him. But it was too late for that. I prayed to God to give me one more sign that the man standing before me was not only a dim-witted coward, but an unredeemable disgrace.

"Count off twelve steps and dig," I said.

"Then, what will you do?"

"I'll explain it all to Enishte Effendi, and he'll burn the pictures. What other recourse is there? If one of Nusret Hoja's followers hears of such an allegation, nothing will remain of us or the book-arts workshop. Are you familiar with any of the Erzurumis? Accept this money so that we can be certain you won't inform on us."

"What is the money contained in?"

"There are seventy-five Venetian gold pieces inside an old ceramic pickle jar."

The Venetian ducats made good sense, but where had I come up with the ceramic pickle jar? It was so foolish it was believable. I was thereby reassured that God was with me and had given me a sign. My old companion apprentice, who'd grown greedier with each passing year, had already started excitedly counting off the twelve steps in the direction I indicated.

There were two things on my mind at that moment. First of all, there were no Venetian coins or anything of the sort buried there! If I didn't come up with some money this buffoon would destroy us. I suddenly felt like embracing the oaf and kissing his cheeks as I sometimes did when we were apprentices, but the years had come between us! Second, I was preoccupied with figuring out how we were going to dig. With our fingernails? But this contemplation, if you could call it that, lasted only a wink in time.

Panicking, I grabbed a stone that lay beside the well. While he was still on the seventh or eighth step, I caught up to him and struck him on the back of his head with all my strength. I struck him so swiftly and brutally that I was momentarily startled, as if the blow had landed on my own head. Aye, I felt his pain.

Instead of anguishing over what I'd done, I wanted to finish the job quickly. He'd begun thrashing about on the ground and my panic deepened further.

Long after I'd dropped him into the well, I contemplated how the crudeness of my deed did not in the least befit the grace of a miniaturist.

I Will Be Called a Murderer

CHAPTER 5

I AM YOUR BELOVED UNCLE

I am Black's maternal uncle, his *enishte,* but others also call me "Enishte." There was a time when Black's mother encouraged him to address me as "Enishte Effendi," and later, not only Black, but everyone began referring to me that way. Thirty years ago, after we'd moved to the dark and humid street shaded by chestnut and linden trees beyond the Aksaray district, Black began to make frequent visits to our house. That was our residence before this one. If I were away on summer campaign with Mahmut Pasha, I'd return in the autumn to discover that Black and his mother had taken refuge in our home. Black's mother, may she rest in peace, was the older sister of my dearly departed wife. There were times on winter evenings I'd come home to find my wife and his mother embracing and tearfully consoling each other. Black's father, who could never maintain his teaching posts at the remote little religious schools where he taught, was ill-tempered, angry and had a weakness for drink. Black was six years old at the time; he'd cry when his mother cried, quiet down when his mother fell silent and regarded me, his Enishte, with apprehension.

It pleases me to see him before me now, a determined, mature and respectful nephew. The respect he shows me, the care with which he kisses my hand and presses it to his forehead, the way, for example, he said, "Purely for red," when he presented me with the Mongol inkpot as a gift, and his polite and demure habit of sitting before me with his knees mindfully together; all of this not only announces that he is the sensible grown man he aspires to be, but it reminds me that I am indeed the venerable elder I aspire to be.

He shares a likeness with his father, whom I've seen once or twice: He's tall and thin, and makes slightly nervous yet becoming gestures with his arms and hands. His custom of placing his hands on his knees or of staring deeply and intently into my eyes as if to say, "I understand, I'm listening to you with reverence" when I tell him something of import, or the way he nods his head with a subtle rhythm matching the measure of my words are all quite appropriate. Now that I've reached this age, I know that true respect arises not from the heart, but from discrete rules and deference.

During the years Black's mother brought him frequently to our house under every pretense because she anticipated a future for him here, I understood that books pleased him, and this brought us together. As those in the house used to put it, he would serve as my "apprentice." I explained to him how miniaturists in Shiraz had created a new style by raising the horizon line clear to the top of the border, and that while everyone depicted Mejnun in a wretched state in the desert, crazed with love for his Leyla, the great master Bihzad was better able to convey Mejnun's loneliness by portraying him walking among groups of women cooking, attempting to ignite logs by blowing on them or walking between tents. I remarked how absurd it was that most of the illustrators who depicted the moment when Hüsrev spied the naked Shirin bathing in a lake at midnight had whimsically colored the lovers' horses and clothes without having read Nizami's poem, my point being that a miniaturist who took up a brush without the care and diligence to read the text he was illustrating was motivated by nothing more than greed.

I'm delighted now to see that Black has acquired another essential virtue: To avoid disappointment in art, one mustn't treat it as a career. Despite whatever great artistic sense and talent a man might possess, he ought to seek money and power elsewhere to avoid forsaking his art when he fails to receive proper compensation for his gifts and efforts.

Black recounted how he'd met one by one all of the master illustrators and calligraphers of Tabriz by making books for pashas, wealthy Istanbulites and patrons in the provinces. All these artists, I learned, were impoverished and overcome by the futility of their lot. Not only in Tabriz, but in Mashhad and Aleppo, many miniaturists had abandoned working on books and begun making odd single-leaf pictures—curiosities that would please European travelers—even obscene drawings. Rumor has it that the illuminated manuscript Shah Abbas presented to Our Sultan during the Tabriz peace treaty has already been taken apart so its pages could be used for another book. Supposedly, the Emperor of Hindustan, Akbar, was throwing so much money around for a large new book that the most gifted illustrators of Tabriz and Kazvin quit what they were doing and flocked to his palace.

As he told me all of this, he pleasantly interjected other stories as well; for example, he described with a smile the entertaining story of a Mehdi forgery or the frenzy that erupted among the Uzbeks when the idiot prince sent to them by the Safavids as a hostage to peace fell feverishly ill and dropped dead within three days. Even so, I could tell from the shadow that fell across his face that the dilemma to which neither of us referred, but which troubled us both, had yet to be resolved.

Naturally, Black, like every young man who frequented our house or heard what others had to say about us, or who knew about my beautiful daughter, Shekure, from hearsay, had fallen in love with her. Perhaps I didn't consider it dangerous enough to warrant my attention back then, but everyone—including many who'd never laid eyes on her—fell in love with my daughter, that belle of belles. Black's affliction was the overwhelming passion of an ill-fated youth who had free access to our house, who was accepted and well liked in our home and who had the opportunity actually to see Shekure. He did not bury his love, as I hoped he would, but made the mistake of revealing his extreme passion to my daughter.

As a result, he was forced to quit our house completely.

I assumed that Black now also knew how three years after he'd left Istanbul, my daughter married a spahi cavalryman, at the height of her loveliness, and that this soldier, having fathered two boys but still bereft of any common sense, had gone off on a campaign never to return again. No one had heard from the cavalryman in four years. I gathered he was aware of this, not only because such gossip spreads fast in Istanbul, but because during the silences that passed between us, I felt he'd learned the whole story long ago, judging by the way he looked into my eyes. Even at this moment, as he casts an eye at the *Book of the Soul,* which stands open on the folding X-shaped reading stand, I know he's listening for the sounds of her children running through the house; I know he's aware that my daughter has returned here to her father's house with her two sons.

I've neglected to mention the new house I had built in Black's absence. Most likely, Black, like any young fellow who'd set his mind to becoming a man of wealth and prestige, considered it quite discourteous to broach such a subject. Still, when we entered, I told him on the staircase that the second floor was always less humid, and that moving upstairs had served to ease the pains in my joints. When I said "the second floor," I felt oddly embarrassed, but let me tell you: Men with much less money than I, even simple spahi cavalrymen with tiny military fiefs, will soon be able to build two-story houses.

We were in the room with the blue door that I used as the painting workshop in winter, and I sensed that Black was aware of Shekure's presence in the adjacent room. I at once disclosed to him the matter that inspired the letter I'd sent to Tabriz, inviting him to Istanbul.

"Just as you did in concert with the calligraphers and miniaturists of Tabriz, I, too, have been preparing an illustrated manuscript," I said. "My client is, in fact, His Excellency Our Sultan, the Foundation of the World. Because this book is a secret, Our Sultan has disbursed payment to me under cover of the Head Treasurer. And I have come to an understanding with each of the most talented and accomplished artists of Our Sultan's atelier. I have been in the process of commissioning one of them to illustrate a dog, another a tree, a third I've charged with making border designs and clouds on the horizon, and yet another is responsible for the horses. I wanted the things I depicted to represent Our Sultan's entire world, just as in the paintings of the Venetian masters. But unlike the Venetians, my work would not merely depict material objects, but naturally the inner riches, the joys and fears of the realm over which Our Sultan rules. If I ended up including the picture of a gold coin, it was to belittle money; I included Death and Satan because we fear them. I don't know what the rumors are about. I wanted the immortality of a tree, the weariness of a horse and the vulgarity of a dog to represent His Excellency Our Sultan and His worldly realm. I also wanted my cadre of illustrators, nicknamed 'Stork,' 'Olive,' 'Elegant' and 'Butterfly,' to select subjects of their own choosing. On even the coldest, most forbidding winter evenings, one of my Sultan's illustrators would secretly visit to show me what he'd prepared for the book.

"What kind of pictures were we making? Why were we illustrating them in that way? I can't really answer you at present. Not because I'm withholding a secret from you, and not because I won't eventually tell you. It's as though I myself don't quite know what the pictures mean. I do, however, know what kind of paintings they ought to be."

Four months after I sent my letter, I heard from the barber located on the street where we used to live that Black had returned to Istanbul, and, in turn, I invited him to our house. I was fully aware that my story bore a promise of both sorrow and bliss that would bind the two of us together.

"Every picture serves to tell a story," I said. "The miniaturist, in order to beautify the manuscript we read, depicts the most vital scenes: the first time lovers lay eyes on each other; the hero Rüstem cutting off the head of a devilish monster; Rüstem's grief when he realizes that the stranger he's killed is his son; the love-crazed Mejnun as he roams a desolate and wild Nature among lions, tigers, stags and jackals; the anguish of Alexander, who, having come to the forest before a battle to divine its outcome from the birds, witnesses a great falcon tear apart his woodcock. Our eyes, fatigued from reading these tales, rest upon the pictures. If there's something within the text that our intellect and imagination are at pains to conjure, the illustration comes at once to our aid. The images are the story's blossoming in color. But painting without its accompanying story is an impossibility.

"Or so I used to think," I added, as if regretfully. "But this is indeed quite possible. Two years ago I traveled once again to Venice as the Sultan's ambassador. I observed at length the portraits that the Venetian masters had made. I did so without knowing to which scene and story the pictures belonged, and I struggled to extract the story from the image. One day, I came across a painting hanging on a palazzo wall and was dumbfounded.

"More than anything, the image was of an individual, somebody like myself. It was an infidel, of course, not one of us. As I stared at him, though, I felt as if I resembled him. Yet he didn't resemble me at all. He had a full round face that seemed to lack cheekbones, and moreover, he had no trace of my marvelous chin. Though he didn't look anything like me, as I gazed upon the picture, for some reason, my heart fluttered as if it were my own portrait.

"I learned from the Venetian gentleman who was giving me a tour through his palazzo that the portrait was of a friend, a nobleman like himself. He had included whatever was significant in his life in his portrait: In the background landscape visible from the open window there was a farm, a village and a blending of color which made a realistic-looking forest. Resting on the table before the nobleman were a clock, books, Time, Evil, Life, a calligraphy pen, a map, a compass, boxes containing gold coins, bric-a-brac, odds and ends, inscrutable yet distinguishable things that were probably included in many pictures, shadows of jinns and the Devil and also, the picture of the man's stunningly beautiful daughter as she stood beside her father.

"What was the narrative that this representation was meant to embellish and complete? As I regarded the work, I slowly sensed that the underlying tale was the picture itself. The painting wasn't the extension of a story at all, it was something in its own right.

"I never forgot the painting that bewildered me so. I left the palazzo, returned to the house where I was staying as a guest and pondered the picture the entire night. I, too, wanted to be portrayed in this manner. But, no, that wasn't appropriate, it was Our Sultan who ought to be thus portrayed! Our Sultan ought to be rendered along with everything He owned, with the things that represented and constituted His realm. I settled on the notion that a manuscript could be illustrated according to this idea.

"The Venetian virtuoso had made the nobleman's picture in such a way that you would immediately know which particular nobleman it was. If you'd never seen that man, if they told you to pick him out of a crowd of a thousand others, you'd be able to select the correct man with the help of that portrait. The Venetian masters had discovered painting techniques with which they could distinguish any one man from another—without relying on his outfit or medals, just by the distinctive shape of his face. This was the essence of 'portraiture.'

"If your face were depicted in this fashion only once, no one would ever be able to forget you, and if you were far away, someone who laid eyes on your portrait would feel your presence as if you were actually nearby. Those who had never seen you alive, even years after your death, could come face-to-face with you as if you were standing before them."

We remained silent for a long time. A chilling light the color of the iciness outside filtered through the upper part of the small hallway window facing the street; this was the window whose lower shutters were never opened, which I'd recently paned over with a piece of cloth dipped in beeswax.

"There was a miniaturist," I said. "He would come here just like the other artists for the sake of Our Sultan's secret book, and we would work together till dawn. He did the best of the gilding. That unfortunate Elegant Effendi, he left here one night never to arrive at home. I'm afraid they might have done him in, that poor master gilder of mine."

CHAPTER 6

I AM ORHAN

Black asked: "Have they indeed killed him?"

This Black was tall, skinny and a little frightening. I was walking toward them where they sat talking in the second-floor workshop with the blue door when my grandfather said, "They might have done him in." Then he caught sight of me. "What are you doing here?"

He looked at me in such a way that I climbed onto his lap without answering. Then he put me back down right away.

"Kiss Black's hand," he said.

I kissed the back of his hand and touched it to my forehead. It had no smell.

"He's quite charming," Black said and kissed me on my cheek. "One day he'll be a brave young man."

"This is Orhan, he's six. There's also an older one, Shevket, who's seven. That one's quite a stubborn little child."

"I went back to the old street in Aksaray," said Black. "It was cold, everything was covered in snow and ice. But it was as if nothing had changed at all."

"Alas! Everything has changed, everything has become worse," my grandfather said. "Significantly worse." He turned to me. "Where's your brother?"

"He's with our mentor, the master binder."

"So, what are you doing here?"

"The master said, 'Fine work, you can go now' to me."

"You made your way back here alone?" asked my grandfather. "Your older brother ought to have accompanied you." Then he said to Black: "There's a binder friend of mine with whom they work twice a week after their Koran school. They serve as his apprentices, learning the art of binding."

"Do you like to make illustrations like your grandfather?" asked Black.

I gave him no answer.

"All right then," said my grandfather. "Leave us be, now."

The heat from the open brazier that warmed the room was so nice that I didn't want to leave. Smelling the paint and glue, I stood still for a moment. I could also smell coffee.

"Yet does illustrating in a new way signify a new way of seeing?" my grandfather began. "This is the reason why they've murdered that poor gilder despite the fact that he worked in the old style. I'm not even certain he's been killed, only that he's missing. They're illustrating a commemorative story in verse, a *Book of Festivities,* for Our Sultan by order of the Head Illuminator Master Osman. Each of the miniaturists works at his own home. Master Osman, however, occupies himself at the palace book-arts workshop. To begin with, I want you to go there and observe everything. I worry that the others, that is, the miniaturists, have ended up falling out with and slaying one another. They go by the workshop names that Head Illuminator Master Osman gave them years ago: 'Butterfly,' 'Olive,' 'Stork' . . . You're also to go and observe them as they work in their homes."

MY NAME IS RED

Instead of heading downstairs, I spun around. There was a noise coming from the next room with the built-in closet where Hayriye slept. I went in. Inside there was no Hayriye, just my mother. She was embarrassed to see me. She stood half in the closet.

"Where have you been?" she asked.

But she knew where I'd been. In the back of the closet there was a peephole through which you could see my grandfather's workshop, and if its door were open, the wide hallway and my grandfather's bedroom across the hall by the staircase—if, of course, his bedroom door were open.

"I was with grandfather," I said. "Mother, what are you doing in here?"

"Didn't I tell you that your grandfather had a guest and that you weren't to bother them?" She scolded me, but not very loud, because she didn't want the guest to hear. "What were they doing?" she asked afterward, in a sweet voice.

"They were seated. Not with the paints though. Grandfather spoke, the other listened."

"In what manner was he seated?"

I dropped to the floor and imitated the guest: "I'm a very serious man now, Mother, look. I'm listening to my grandfather with knit eyebrows, as if I were listening to the birth epic being recited. I'm nodding my head in time now, very seriously like that guest."

"Go downstairs," my mother said, "call for Hayriye at once."

She sat down and began writing on a small piece of paper on the writing board she'd taken up.

"Mother, what are you writing?"

"Be quick, now. Didn't I tell you to go downstairs and call for Hayriye?"

I went down to the kitchen. My brother, Shevket, was back. Hayriye had put before him a plate of the pilaf meant for the guest.

"Traitor," my brother said. "You just went off and left me with the Master. I did all the folding for the bindings myself. My fingers are bruised purple."

"Hayriye, my mother wants to see you."

"When I'm done here, I'm going to give you such a beating," my brother said. "You'll pay for your laziness and treachery."

When Hayriye left, my brother stood and came after me threateningly, even before he'd finished his pilaf. I couldn't get away in time. He grabbed my arm at the wrist and began twisting it.

"Stop, Shevket, don't, you're hurting me."

"Are you ever going to shirk your duties again and leave?"

I Am Orhan

"No, I won't ever leave."

"Swear to it."

"I swear."

"Swear on the Koran."

". . . on the Koran."

He didn't let go of my arm. He dragged me to the large copper tray that we used as a table for eating and forced me to my knees. He was strong enough to eat his pilaf as he continued to twist my arm.

"Quit torturing your brother, tyrant," said Hayriye. She covered herself and was heading outside. "Leave him be."

"Mind your own affairs, slave girl," my brother said. He was still twisting my arm. "Where are you off to?"

"To buy lemons," Hayriye said.

"You're a liar," my brother said. "The cupboard is full of lemons."

As he had eased up on my arm, I was suddenly able to free myself. I kicked him and grabbed a candleholder by its base, but he pounced on me, smothering me. He knocked the candleholder away, and the copper tray fell over.

"You two scourges of God!" my mother said. She kept her voice lowered so the guest wouldn't hear. How had she passed before the open door of the workshop, through the hallway, and come downstairs without being seen by Black?

She separated us. "You two just continue to disgrace me, don't you?"

"Orhan lied to the master binder," Shevket said. "He left me there to do all the work."

"Hush!" my mother said, slapping him.

She'd hit him softly. My brother didn't cry. "I want my father," he said. "When he returns he's going to take up Uncle Hasan's ruby-handled sword, and we're going to move back with Uncle Hasan."

"Shut up!" said my mother. She suddenly became so angry that she grabbed Shevket by the arm and dragged him through the kitchen, passed the stairs to the room that faced the far shady side of the courtyard. I followed them. My mother opened the door. When she saw me, she said, "Inside, the both of you."

"But I haven't done anything," I said. I entered anyway. Mother closed the door behind us. Though it wasn't pitch-black inside—a faint light fell through the space between the shutters facing the pomegranate tree in the courtyard—I was scared.

"Open the door, Mother," I said. "I'm cold."

"Quit whimpering, you coward," Shevket said. "She'll open it soon enough."

Mother opened the door. "Are you going to behave until the visitor leaves?" she said. "All right then, you'll sit in the kitchen by the stove until Black takes his leave, and you're not to go upstairs, do you understand?"

"We'll get bored in there," Shevket said. "Where has Hayriye gone?"

"Quit butting into everyone's affairs," my mother said.

We heard a soft whinnying from one of the horses in the stable. The horse whinnied again. It wasn't our grandfather's horse, but Black's. We were overcome with mirth, as if it were a fair day. Mother smiled, wanting us to smile as well. Taking two steps forward, she opened the stable door that faced us off the stairwell outside the kitchen.

"Drrsss," she said into the stable.

She turned around and guided us into Hayriye's greasy-smelling and mice-ridden kitchen. She forced us to sit down. "Don't even consider standing until our guest leaves. And don't fight with each other or else people will think you're spoiled."

"Mother," I said to her before she closed the kitchen door. "I want to say something, Mother: They've done our grandfather's gilder in."

CHAPTER 7

I AM CALLED BLACK

When I first laid eyes on her child, I knew at once what I'd long and mistakenly recalled about Shekure's face. Like Orhan's face, hers was thin, though her chin was longer than what I remembered. So, then the mouth of my beloved was surely smaller and narrower than I imagined it to be. For a dozen years, as I ventured from city to city, I'd widened Shekure's mouth out of desire and had imagined her lips to be more pert, fleshy and irresistible, like a large, shiny cherry.

Had I taken Shekure's portrait with me, rendered in the style of the Venetian masters, I wouldn't have felt such loss during my long travels when I could scarcely remember my beloved, whose face I'd left somewhere behind me. For if a lover's face survives emblazoned on your heart, the world is still your home.

Meeting Shekure's youngest son and speaking with him, seeing his face up close and kissing him, aroused in me a restlessness peculiar to the luckless, to murderers and to sinners. An inner voice urged me on, "Be quick now, go and see her."

For a while, I considered silently quitting my Enishte's presence and opening each of the doors along the wide hallway—I'd counted them out of the corner of my eye, five dark doors, one of which, naturally, opened onto the staircase—until I found Shekure. But, I'd been separated from my beloved for twelve years because I recklessly revealed what lay in my heart. I decided to wait discreetly, listening to my Enishte while admiring the objects that Shekure had touched and the large pillow upon which she'd reclined who knows how many times.

He recounted to me that the Sultan wanted to have the book completed in time for the thousandth-year anniversary of the Hegira. Our Sultan, Refuge of the World, wanted to demonstrate that in the thousandth year of the Muslim calendar He and His state could make use of the styles of the Franks as well as the Franks themselves. Because He was also having a *Book of Festivities* made, the Sultan granted that the master miniaturists, whom He knew were quite busy, be permitted to sequester themselves at home to work in peace instead of among the crowds at the workshop. He was, of course, also aware that they all regularly paid clandestine visits to my Enishte.

"You shall visit Head Illuminator Master Osman," said my Enishte. "Some say he's gone blind, others that he's lost his senses. I think he's blind and senile both."

Despite the fact that my Enishte didn't have the standing of a master illustrator and that this wasn't his field of artistic expertise at all, he did have control over an illustrated manuscript. This, in fact, was with the permission and encouragement of the Sultan, a situation that, of course, strained his relationship with the elderly Master Osman.

Thinking of my childhood, I allowed my attention to be absorbed by the furniture and objects within the house. From twelve years ago, I still remembered the blue kilim from Kula covering the floor, the copper ewer, the coffee set and tray, the copper pail and the delicate coffee cups that had come all the way from China by way of Portugal, as my late aunt had boasted numerous times. These effects, like the low X-shaped reading desk inlaid with mother-of-pearl, the stand for a turban nailed to the wall, the red velvet pillow whose smoothness I recalled as soon as I touched it, were from the house in Aksaray where I'd passed my childhood with

Shekure, and they still carried something of the bliss of my days of painting in that house.

Painting and happiness. I would like my dear readers who have given close attention to my story and my fate to bear these two things in mind, as they are the genesis of my world. At one time, I was contented here, among these books, calligraphy brushes and paintings. Then, I fell in love and was banished from this Paradise. In the years I endured my amorous exile, I often thought how I was in fact deeply indebted to Shekure and my love for her, because they had enabled me to adapt optimistically to life and the world. Since I had, in my childlike naïveté, no doubt that my love would be reciprocated, I grew exceedingly assured and came to regard the world as a good place. You see, it was with this same earnestness that I involved myself with books and came to love them, to love the reading my Enishte required of me back then, my religious school lessons and my illustrating and painting. But as much as I owed the sunny, festive and more fertile first half of my education to the love I felt for Shekure, I owed the dark knowledge that poisoned the latter time to being rejected; my desire on icy nights to sputter out and vanish like the dying flames in the iron stoves of a caravansary, repeatedly dreaming after a night of love that I was plunging into a desolate abyss along with whichever woman lay beside me, and the notion that I was simply worthless—all of it was furnished by Shekure.

"Were you aware," my Enishte said much later, "that after death our souls will be able to meet with the spirits of men and women in this world who are peacefully asleep in their beds?"

"No, I was not."

"We take a long journey after death, so I'm not afraid of dying. What I fear is dying before I finish Our Sultan's book."

Part of me felt I was stronger, more reasonable and more reliable than my Enishte, and part of me was dwelling on the cost of the caftan that I'd purchased on my way here to meet with this man who'd denied me his daughter's hand and on the silver bridle and hand-worked saddle of the horse which, soon after going downstairs, I'd take out of the stable and ride away.

I told him I'd apprise him of everything I learned during my visits to the various miniaturists. I kissed his hand and brought it to my forehead. I walked down the stairs, entered the courtyard, and sensing the snowy cold upon me, accepted that I was neither a child nor an old man: I joyously felt the world upon my skin. As I shut the stable door, a breeze began to stir. I led my white horse by the bridle over the stone walkway to the earthen part of the courtyard, and we both shuddered: I felt as if his strong, large-veined legs, his impatience and his stubbornness were my own. As soon as we entered the street, I was about to swiftly mount my steed and disappear down the narrow way like a fabled horseman, never to return again, when an enormous woman, a Jewess dressed all in pink and carrying a bundle, appeared out of nowhere and accosted me. She was as large and wide as an armoire. Yet she was boisterous, lively and even coquettish.

"My brave man, my young hero, I see you're truly as handsome as they say you are," she said. "Might you be married? Or might you be a bachelor? Would you deign to buy a silk handkerchief for your secret lover from Esther, Istanbul's premier peddler of fine cloth?"

"Nay."

"A red sash of Atlas silk?"

"Nay."

"Don't go on piping 'nay' at me like that! How could a brave heart like you not have a fiancée or a secret lover? Who knows how many teary-eyed maidens are burning with desire for you?"

Her body lengthened like the slender form of an acrobat and she leaned toward me with an elegant gesture. At the same time, with the skill of a magician who plucks objects out of thin air, she caused a letter to appear in her hand. I stealthily grabbed it, and as if I'd been training for this moment for years, I hastily and artfully placed it into my sash. It was a thick letter and felt like fire against the icy skin of my side, between my belly and back.

"Ride at an amble," said Esther the clothes peddler. "Turn right at the corner, following the curve of the wall without breaking stride, but when you get to the pomegranate tree turn and look at the house you've just left, at the window to your right."

She went on her way and vanished in an instant.

I mounted the horse, but like a novice doing so for the first time. My heart was racing, my mind was overcome by excitement, my hands had forgotten how to control the reins, but when my legs tightly gripped the horse's body, sound reason and skill took control of my horse and me, and as Esther had instructed, my wise horse ambled steadily and, how lovely, we turned right onto the sidestreet!

It was then that I felt I might in truth be handsome. As in fairy tales, from behind every shutter and every latticed window, a coy woman was watching me and I felt I might burn once again with that same fire that had once consumed me. Is this what I desired? Was I succumbing anew to the illness from which I'd suffered for so many years? The sun suddenly broke through the clouds, startling me.

Where was the pomegranate tree? Was it this thin, melancholy tree here? Yes! I turned slightly to the right in my saddle. I saw a window behind the tree, but there was nobody there. I'd been duped by that wench Esther!

Just as I was thinking such thoughts, the window's iced-over shutters opened with a loud burst, as if they'd exploded, and after twelve years, I saw my beloved's stunning face among snowy branches, framed by the window whose icy trim shone brightly in the sunlight.

Was my dark-eyed beloved looking at me or at another life beyond me? I couldn't tell whether she was sad or smiling or smiling sadly. Foolish horse, heed not my heart, slow down! I calmly twisted in my saddle again, fixing my desirous stare for as long as possible, until her gaunt, elegant and mysterious face disappeared behind the branches.

Much later, after opening her letter and seeing the illustration within, I thought how my visit to her at the window on horseback closely resembled that moment, pictured a thousand times, in which Hüsrev visits Shirin beneath her window—only in our case, there was that melancholy tree between us. When I recognized this similarity, oh how I burned with a love such as they describe in those books we so cherish and adore.

CHAPTER 8

I AM ESTHER

All of you, I know, are wondering what Shekure penned in that letter I presented to Black. As this was also a curiosity of mine, I learned everything there was to know. If you would, then, pretend you're flipping back through the pages of the story and let me tell you what occurred before I delivered that letter.

Now, it's getting on toward evening, I've retired to our house in the quaint little Jewish quarter at the mouth of the Golden Horn with my husband Nesim, two old people huffing and puffing, trying to keep warm by feeding logs into the stove. Pay no mind to my calling myself "old." When I load my wares—items cheap and precious alike, certain to lure the ladies, rings, earrings, necklaces and baubles—into the folds of silk handkerchiefs, gloves, sheets and the colorful shirt cloth sent over in Portuguese ships, when I shoulder that bundle, Esther's a ladle and Istanbul's a kettle, and there's nary a street I don't visit. There isn't a word of gossip or letter that I haven't carried from one door to the next, and I've played matchmaker to half the maidens of Istanbul, but I didn't begin this recital to brag. As I was saying, we were taking our ease in the evening, and "rap, rap" someone was at the door. I went and opened it to discover Hayriye, that idiot slave girl, standing before me. She held a letter in her hand. I couldn't tell whether it was from the cold or from excitement, but she was trembling as she explained Shekure's wishes.

At first, I assumed this letter was to be taken to Hasan, that's why I was so astonished. You know about pretty Shekure's husband, the one who never returned from the war—if you ask me, he's long since had his hide pierced. Well you see, that never-to-return soldier-husband also has an eager, lovesick brother by the name of Hasan. So imagine my surprise when I saw that Shekure's letter wasn't meant for Hasan, but for someone else. What did the letter say? Esther was mad with curiosity, and in the end, I did succeed in reading it.

But alas, we don't know each other that well, do we? To be honest, I was overcome with embarrassment and worry. How I read the letter you'll never know. Maybe you'll shame and belittle me for my meddling—as if you yourselves aren't as nosy as barbers. I'll just relate to you what I learned from reading the letter. This is what sweet Shekure had written:

Black Effendi, you're a visitor to my house thanks to your close relations with my father. But don't expect a nod from me. Much has happened since you left. I was wed, and have two strong and spirited sons. One of them is Orhan, he's the one whom you saw just now come to the workshop. While I've been awaiting the return of my husband these four years, little else has entered my thoughts. I might feel lonely, hopeless and weak living with my two children and an elderly father. I miss the strength and protection of a man, but let no one assume he might take advantage of my situation. Therefore, it would please me if you ceased calling on us. You did embarrass me once before, and afterward, I had to endure much suffering to regain my honor in my father's eyes! Along with this letter, I'm also returning the picture you painted and sent to me when you were an impulsive youth with his wits not yet about him. I do this so you won't harbor any false hopes or misread any signs. It's a mistake to believe that one could fall in love gazing at a picture. It'd be best if you stopped coming to our house completely.

My poor Shekure, you're neither a nobleman nor a pasha with a fancy seal to stamp your letter! At the bottom of the page, she signed the first letter of her name, which looked like a small, frightened bird. Nothing more.

I said "seal." You're probably wondering how I open and close these wax-sealed letters. But in fact the letters aren't sealed at all. "That Esther is an illiterate Jew," my dear Shekure had assumed. "She'll never understand my writing." True, I can't read what's written, but I can always have someone else read it. And as for what's not written, I can quite readily "read" that myself. Confused, are you?

Let me put it this way, so even the most thick-headed of you will understand:

A letter doesn't communicate by words alone. A letter, just like a book, can be read by smelling it, touching it and fondling it. Thereby, intelligent folk will say, "Go on then, read what the letter tells you!" whereas the dull-witted will say, "Go on then, read what he's written!" Listen, now, to what else Shekure said:

1. Though I've sent this letter in secret, by relying on Esther, who's made letter-delivery a matter of commerce and custom, I'm signifying that I don't intend to conceal that much at all.

2. That I've folded it up like a French pastry implies secrecy and mystery, true. But the letter isn't sealed and there's a huge picture enclosed. The apparent implication is, "Pray, keep our secret at all costs," which more befits an invitation to love than a letter of rebuke.

3. Furthermore, the smell of the letter confirms this interpretation. The fragrance was faint enough to be ambiguous—did she intentionally perfume the letter?—yet alluring enough to fire readers' curiosity—is this the aroma of attar or the smell of her hand? And a fragrance, which was enough to enrapture the poor man who read the letter to me, will surely have the same effect on Black.

4. I am Esther, who knows neither how to read nor write, but this I do know: Although the flow of the script and the handwriting seems to say "Alas, I am rushed, I am writing carelessly and without paying serious attention," these letters that twitter

elegantly as if caught in a gentle breeze convey the exact opposite message. Even her phrase "just now come" when referring to Orhan, implying that the letter was written at that very moment, betrays a ploy no less obvious than care taken in each line.

5. The picture sent along with the letter depicts pretty Shirin gazing at handsome Hüsrev's image and falling in love, as told in the story that even I, Esther the Jewess, know well. All the lovelorn ladies of Istanbul adore this story, but never have I known someone to send an illustration relating to it.

It happens all the time to you fortunate literate people: A maiden who can't read begs you to read a love letter she's received. The letter is so surprising, exciting and disturbing that its owner, though embarrassed at your becoming privy to her most intimate affairs, ashamed and distraught, asks you all the same to read it once more. You read it again. In the end, you've read the letter so many times that both of you have memorized it. Before long, she'll take the letter in her hands and ask, "Did he make that statement there?" and "Did he say that here?" As you point to the appropriate places, she'll pore over those passages, still unable to make sense of the words there. As she stares at the curvy letters of the words, sometimes I am so moved I forget that I myself can't read or write and feel the urge to embrace those illiterate maidens whose tears fall to the page.

Then there are those truly accursed letter-readers; pray, don't you turn out to be like one of them: When the maiden takes the letter in her own hands to touch it again, desiring to look at it without understanding which words were spoken where, these beasts will say to her, "What are you trying to do? You can't read, what more do you want to look at?" Some of them won't even return the letter, treating it henceforth as if it belonged to them. At times, the task of accosting them and retrieving the letter falls to me, Esther. That's the kind of good woman I am. If Esther likes you, she'll come to your aid as well.

CHAPTER 9

I, SHEKURE

Oh, why was I there at the window just when Black rode by on his white steed? Why did I open the shutters intuitively at that exact moment and stare at him so long from behind the snowy branches of the pomegranate tree? I can't tell you for sure. I'd sent word to Esther by way of Hayriye. I was, of course, well aware that Black would take that route. Meanwhile, I'd gone up alone to the room with the built-in closet and the window facing the pomegranate tree to inspect the sheets in the chest. On a whim, and at just the right moment, I pushed the shutters open with all my strength and sunlight flooded the room: Standing at the window, I came face-to-face with Black, who, like the sun, dazzled me. Oh, it was quite lovely.

He'd grown and matured and, having lost his awkward youthful lankiness, he turned out to be a comely man. Listen Shekure, my heart did tell me, he's not only handsome, look into his eyes, he possesses the heart of a child, so pure, so alone: Marry him. I, however, sent him a letter wherein I'd given him quite the opposite message.

Though he was twelve years my elder, when I was twelve, I was more mature than he. Back then, instead of standing straight and tall before me in a fashion befitting a man and announcing that he was going to do this or that, jump from this spot or climb onto that thing, he'd just bury his face in some book or picture, hiding as if everything embarrassed him. In time, he also fell in love with me. He made a painting declaring his love. We'd both matured by then. When I turned twelve, I sensed that Black could no longer look into my eyes, as if he were afraid I'd discover he loved me. "Hand me that ivory-handled knife," he'd say, for example, looking at the knife but unable to look at me. If I asked him, for instance, "Is the cherry sherbet to your liking?" he couldn't simply indicate so with a delicate smile or nod, as we do when our mouths are full, you see. Instead, he'd scream "Yes" at the top of his lungs, as if trying to communicate with a deaf man. He feared looking me in the face. I was a maiden of striking beauty then. Any man who caught sight of me even once, from afar, or from between parted curtains or yawning doors, or even through the layers of my modest head coverings, immediately became enamored of me. I'm not being a braggart, I'm explaining this so you'll understand my story and be better able to share in my grief.

In the well-known tale of Hüsrev and Shirin, there's a moment that Black and I had discussed at length. Hüsrev's friend, Shapur, intends to make Hüsrev and Shirin fall in love. One day Shirin embarks on a countryside outing with her ladies of the court, when she sees a picture of Hüsrev that Shapur has secretly hung from the branch of one of the trees beneath which the outing party has stopped to rest. Beholding this picture of the handsome Hüsrev in that beautiful garden, Shirin is stricken by love.

Many paintings depict this moment—or "scene" as the miniaturists would have it—consisting of Shirin's look of adoration and bewilderment as she gazes upon the image of Hüsrev. While Black was working with my father, he'd seen this picture many times and had twice made exact copies by eyeing the original as he painted. After falling in love with me, he made a copy for himself. But this time in place of Hüsrev and Shirin, he portrayed himself and me, Black and Shekure. If it weren't for the captions beneath the figures, only I would've known who the man and maiden in the picture were, because sometimes when we were joking around, he'd depict us in the same manner and color: I all in blue, he all in red. And if this weren't indication enough, he'd also written our names beneath the figures. He'd left the painting where I would find it and run off. He watched me to see what my reaction to his composition would be.

I was well aware that I wouldn't be able to love him like a Shirin, so I feigned ignorance. On the evening of that summer's day when Black gave me his painting, during which we'd tried to cool ourselves with sour-cherry sherbets made with ice said to have been brought all the way from snow-capped Mount Ulu, I told my father that he'd made a declaration of love. At that time, Black had just graduated from the religious school. He taught in remote neighborhoods and, more out of my father's insistence than his own desire, Black was attempting to obtain the patronage of the powerful and esteemed Naim Pasha. But according to my father, Black didn't yet have his wits about him. My father, who'd taken great pains to win Black a place in Naim Pasha's circle, at least as a clerk to begin, complained that he wasn't doing much to further his own cause; in other words, Black was being an ignoramus. And that very night in reference to Black and me, my father declared, "I think he's set his sights very high, this impoverished nephew," and without regard for my mother's presence, he added, "he's smarter than we'd supposed."

I remember with misery what my father did in the following days, how I kept my distance from Black and how he ceased to visit our house, but I won't explain all of this for fear that you'll dislike my father and me. I swear to you, we had no other choice. You know how in such situations reasonable people immediately sense that love without hope is simply hopeless, and understanding the limits of the illogical realm of the heart, make a quick end of it by politely declaring, "They didn't find us suitably matched. That's just the way it is." But, I'll have you know that my mother said several times, "At least don't break the boy's heart." Black, whom my mother referred to as a "boy," was twenty-four, and I was half his age.

Because my father considered Black's declaration of love an act of insolence, he wouldn't humor my mother's wishes.

Though we hadn't forgotten him altogether by the time we received news that he'd left Istanbul, we'd let him slip completely out of our affections. Because we hadn't received news about him from any city for years, I deemed it appropriate to save the picture he'd made and shown me, as a token of our childhood memories and friendship. To prevent my father, and later my soldier-husband, from discovering the picture and getting upset or jealous, I expertly concealed the names "Shekure" and "Black" beneath the figures by making it appear as if someone had dribbled my father's Hasan Pasha ink onto them, in an accident later to be disguised as flowers. Since I've returned that picture to him today, maybe those among you inclined to take a dim view of how I revealed myself to him at the window will feel ashamed and reconsider your prejudices somewhat.

Having exposed my face to him, I remained for a while there at the window, showered in the crimson hue of the evening sun, and gazed in awe at the garden bathed in reddish-orange light, until I felt the chill of the evening air. There was no breeze. I didn't care what someone passing in the street would've said upon seeing me at the open window. One of Ziver Pasha's daughters, Mesrure, who always laughed and enjoyed herself saying the most surprising things at the most inopportune times when we went merrily and playfully to the public baths each week, once told me that a person never knows exactly what she herself is thinking. This is what I know: Sometimes I'll say something and realize upon uttering it that it is of my own thinking; but no sooner do I arrive at that realization than I'm convinced the very opposite is true.

I was sorry when poor Elegant Effendi, one of the miniaturists my father often invited to the house—and I won't pretend I haven't spied on each of them—went missing, much like my unfortunate husband. "Elegant" was the ugliest among them and the most impoverished of spirit.

I closed the shutters, left the room and went down to the kitchen.

"Mother, Shevket didn't listen to you," Orhan said. "While Black was taking his horse out of the stable, Shevket left the kitchen and spied on him from the peephole."

"What of it!" Shevket said, waving his hand in the air. "Mother spied on him from the hole in the closet."

"Hayriye," I said. "Fry some bread in a little butter and serve it to them with marzipan and sugar."

Orhan jumped up and down with joy though Shevket was silent. But as I walked back upstairs, they both caught up to me, screaming, pushing and shoving by me excitedly. "Be slow, slow down," I said with a laugh. "You rascals." I patted them on their delicate backs.

How wonderful it is to be home with children as evening approaches! My father had quietly given himself over to a book.

"Your guest has departed," I said. "I hope he didn't trouble you much?"

"On the contrary," he said. "He entertained me. He's as respectful as ever of his Enishte."

"Good."

"But now he's also measured and calculating."

He'd said that less to observe my reaction than to close the subject in a manner that made light of Black. On any other occasion, I would've answered him with a sharp tongue, as I am wont to do. This time, though, I just thought of Black making ground on his white horse, and I shuddered.

I'm not sure how it happened, but later in the room with the closet, Orhan and I found ourselves hugging each other. Shevket joined us; there was a brief skirmish between them. As they tussled we all rolled over onto the floor. I kissed them on the backs of their necks and their hair, I pressed them to my bosom and felt their weight on my breasts.

"Ahhh," I said. "Your hair stinks. I'm going to send you to the baths tomorrow with Hayriye."

"I don't want to go to the baths with Hayriye anymore," Shevket said.

"Why? Are you too grown-up?" I said.

"Mother, why did you wear your fine purple blouse?" Shevket said.

I went into the other room and removed my purple blouse. I pulled on the faded green one that I usually wear. As I was changing, I felt cold and shivered, but I could sense that my skin was aflame, my body vibrant and alive. I'd rubbed a bit of rouge onto my cheeks, which probably smudged while I was rolling around with the children, but I evened it out by licking my palm and rubbing my cheeks. Are you aware that my relatives, the women whom I meet at the baths and everyone who sees me, swear that I look more like a sixteen-year-old maiden than a twenty-four-year-old mother of two past her prime? Believe them, truly believe them, or I shan't tell you any more.

Don't be surprised that I'm talking to you. For years I've combed through the pictures in my father's books looking for images of women and great beauties. They do exist, if few and far between, and always look shy, embarrassed, gazing only at one another, as if apologetically. Never do they raise their heads, stand straight and face the people of the world as soldiers and sultans would. Only in cheap, hastily illustrated books by careless artists are the eyes of some women trained not on the ground or on some thing in the illustration—oh, I don't know, let's say a lover or a goblet—but directly at the reader. I've long wondered about that reader.

I shudder in delight when I think of two-hundred-year-old books, dating back to the time of Tamerlane, volumes for which acquisitive giaours gleefully relinquish gold pieces and which they carry all the way back to their own countries: Perhaps one day someone from a distant land will listen to this story of mine. Isn't this what lies behind the desire to be inscribed in the pages of a book? Isn't it just for the sake of this delight that sultans and viziers proffer bags of gold to have their histories written? When I feel this delight, just like those beautiful women with one eye on the life within the book and one eye on the life outside, I, too, long to speak with you who are observing me from who knows which distant time and place. I'm an attractive and intelligent woman, and it pleases me that I'm being watched. And if I happen to tell a lie or two from time to time, it's so you don't come to any false conclusions about me.

Maybe you've noticed that my father adores me. He had three sons before me, but God took them one by one and left me, his daughter. My father dotes on me, though I married a man not of his choosing. I went to a spahi cavalry soldier whom I'd noticed and fancied. If it were left to my father, my husband would not only be the greatest of scholars, he'd also have an appreciation for painting and art, be possessed of power and authority, and be as rich as Karun, the wealthiest of men in the Koran. The inkling of such a man couldn't even be found in the pages of my father's books, and so I would've been forced to pine away at home forever.

My husband's handsomeness was legendary, and I gave him the nod through intermediates. He found the opportunity to appear before me as I was returning from the public baths. His eyes were as brilliant as fire, and I immediately fell in love. He was a dark-haired, fair-skinned, green-eyed man with strong arms; but at heart, he was innocent and quiet like a sleepy child. Nevertheless, it seemed, to me at least, that he also had the tang of blood about him, perhaps because he expended all his strength slaying men in battle and amassing booty, even though at home he was as gentle and quiet as a lady. This man—whom my father looked upon as a penniless soldier, and hence, disapproved of—was later allowed to marry me because I threatened to kill myself otherwise. And after they gave him a military fief worth ten thousand silver coins, a reward for his heroism in battle after battle wherein he performed the greatest acts of bravery, truly, everyone envied us.

Four years ago when he failed to return with the rest of the army from warring against the Safavids I wasn't worried at first. For the more experience he had on the battlefield, the more adept and clever he became in creating opportunities for himself, in bringing home greater spoils, in winning larger fiefs, and in enlisting more soldiers of his own. There were witnesses who said he fled to the mountains with his own men after he became separated from a division of the army. In the beginning, I suspected a scheme and hoped he'd return, but after two years, I slowly grew accustomed to his absence; and when I realized how many lonely women like me with missing soldier-husbands there were in Istanbul, I resigned myself to my fate.

At night, in our beds, we'd hug our children and mope and cry. To quiet their tears, I'd tell them hopeful lies; for example, that so-and-so had proof their father would return before spring. Afterward, when my lie would circulate, changing and spreading until it found its way back to me, I'd be the first to believe the good news.

When the main support of the household vanished, we fell upon hard times. We were living in a rented house in Charshıkapı with my husband's gentlemanly Abkhazian father, who'd never lived an easy life, and his brother, who had green eyes as well. My father-in-law, who left his mirror-making business after his oldest son made his fortune soldiering, returned to take up his trade at a late age. Hasan, my husband's bachelor brother, worked in customs, and as he prospered he made plans to assume the role of "man of the house." One winter, fearing they wouldn't be able to pay rent, they hastily took the slave who saw to the household chores to the slave market and sold her, after which they wanted me to do the kitchen work, wash the clothes and even go out to the bazaars to do the shopping in her stead. I didn't protest by saying, "Am I the type of woman to take on such drudgery?" I swallowed my pride and went to work. But when that brother-in-law of mine Hasan, now without his slave girl to take into his room at night, began forcing my door, I didn't know what to do.

Of course, I could've immediately come back here to the home of my father, but according to the kadi judge my husband was legally alive, and were I to anger my in-laws, they might not stop at forcing my children and me back to my husband's home, but humiliate us further by having me and my father, who had "detained" me, punished. To tell the truth, I could've loved Hasan, whom I found to be more humane and reasonable than my husband, and who was obviously very much in love with me. But if I were to do this without careful thought, I might find myself, God forbid, his slave instead of his wife. In any event, because they were afraid

MY NAME IS RED

that I would demand my portion of the inheritance and then abandon them and return to my father with the children, they, too, weren't eager for a judge's decision proclaiming my husband's death. If, in the eyes of the judge, my husband wasn't dead, I naturally couldn't wed Hasan, nor could I marry anyone else. Because this dilemma bound me to that house and that marriage, my in-laws preferred my having a "missing" husband, and the continuation of this vague situation. For lest you forget, I saw to all their household chores, I did everything from their cooking to their laundry, and furthermore, one of them was madly in love with me.

When my father-in-law and Hasan grew dissatisfied with this arrangement and decided it was time for me to marry Hasan, it was necessary first to arrange for the witnesses to convince the judge of my husband's death. Thus, if my missing husband's closest kin, his father and brother, accepted his death, if there was no longer anyone who objected to declaring my husband dead, and if, for the price of a few silver coins, witnesses would testify that they'd seen the man's corpse in the field of battle, the judge would also oblige. It would be most difficult to convince Hasan once I was declared a widow that I wouldn't leave the household, demand my inheritance rights or ask for money to marry him; and moreover, that I'd marry him of my own free will. Naturally, I knew that to gain his trust in this regard, I'd have to sleep with him in a very convincing manner so he'd be completely assured I was giving myself to him, not to get his permission to divorce my husband, but because I was sincerely in love with him.

With some effort, I could've fallen in love with Hasan. He was eight years younger than my missing husband, and when my husband was at home, Hasan was like my little brother, and this sentiment endeared him to me. I liked his humble and passionate demeanor, his pleasure in playing with my children and even the way he desirously looked at me as though he were dying of thirst and I were a glass of cold sour-cherry sherbet. On the other hand, I also knew I'd really have to force myself to fall in love with a man who made me wash clothes and didn't mind my having to wander through markets and bazaars like a common slave. During those days when I'd go to my father's house and cry endlessly as I stared at the pots, pans, bowls and cups, during those nights when the children and I would sleep cuddled up together in solidarity, Hasan never gave me cause for a change of heart. He had no faith that I could love him or that this essential and mandatory precondition for our marriage would manifest itself; and because he had no confidence in himself, he acted inappropriately. He tried to corner me, kiss me and fondle me. He declared that my husband would never return, that he would kill me. He threatened me, cried like a baby, and in his haste and fluster, never allowed time for a true and noble love to be born. I knew I could never wed him.

One night, when he tried to force the door of the room where I slept with the children, I rose immediately, and without a thought that I might frighten them, screamed at the top of my lungs that evil jinns had entered the house. This fit of jinn-panic and screaming awakened my father-in-law and thereby exposed Hasan, whose excited violence was still visible, to his father. Amid my ridiculous howls and inane rantings about jinns, the staid old man to his embarrassment acknowledged the awful truth: His son was besotted and had inappropriately approached his brother's wife, a mother of two. My father-in-law made no reply when I said I wouldn't sleep a wink till morning, keeping watch at the door to protect my children against "the jinns." The following day, I announced that I'd be returning to my father's home with my children for an extended stay to care for him in his time of illness; thus did Hasan accept his defeat. I returned to my father's house, taking with me as mementos of my married life the clock with bells plundered from Hungarian lands by my husband (who'd never succumbed to the temptation to sell it), the whip made from the sinews of the most explosive of Arab steeds, the Tabriz-made ivory chess set whose pieces the children used to play war and the silver candlesticks (booty from the Battle of Nahjivan), which I'd fought so desperately to keep when money was short.

As I expected, quitting my absent husband's house turned Hasan's obsessive and disrespectful love into a hopeless inferno. Knowing full well that his father wouldn't stand behind him, instead of threatening me, he sought my pity by sending me love letters in whose corners he drew forlorn birds, teary-eyed lions and sad gazelles. I won't hide from you the fact that I've recently begun to read them anew, those letters that reveal Hasan's rich imagination, of which I wasn't aware when we lived together under the same roof—assuming he didn't enlist one of his more artistic or poetic friends to write and embellish them. In his last letter, Hasan pledged that I would no longer be a slave to housework, and that he'd made a lot of money. This disclosure in his sweet, respectful and humorous tone, compounded by the endless fights and demands of the children, and my father's complaints, turned my head into a veritable kettledrum. Indeed, it was in order to heave a sigh of relief to the world that I'd opened the shutters of that window.

Before Hayriye set the dinner table, I prepared a draught of bitters from the best Arabian date palm flower; I mixed in a spoonful of honey and a little lemon juice, then quietly entered my father's company as he was reading the *Book of the Soul,* and like a spirit myself, placed it before him without making my presence known, as he preferred.

"Is it snowing?" he asked in such a faint and melancholy voice that I understood at once this would be the last snowfall my poor father would ever see.

CHAPTER 10

I AM A TREE

I am a tree and I am quite lonely. I weep in the rain. For the sake of Allah, listen to what I have to say. Drink down your coffee so your sleep abandons you and your eyes open wide. Stare at me as you would at jinns and let me explain to you why I'm so alone.

1. They allege that I've been hastily sketched onto nonsized, rough paper so the picture of a tree might hang behind the master storyteller. True enough. At this moment, there are no other slender trees beside me, no seven-leaf steppe plants, no dark billowing rock formations which at times resemble Satan or a man and no coiling Chinese clouds. Just the ground, the sky, myself and the horizon. But my story is much more complicated.

2. As a tree, I need not be part of a book. As the picture of a tree, however, I'm disturbed that I'm not a page within some manuscript. Since I'm not representing something in a book, what comes to mind is that my picture will be nailed to a wall and the likes of pagans and infidels will prostrate themselves before me in worship. May the followers of Erzurumi Hoja not hear that I secretly take pride in this thought—but then I'm overcome with the utmost fear and embarrassment.

3. The essential reason for my loneliness is that I don't even know where I belong. I was supposed to be part of a story, but I fell from there like a leaf in autumn. Let me tell you about it:

Falling from My Story Like a Leaf Falls in Fall

Forty years ago, the Persian Shah Tahmasp, who was the archenemy of the Ottomans as well as the world's greatest patron-king of the art of painting, began to grow senile and lost his enthusiasm for wine, music, poetry and painting; furthermore, he quit drinking coffee, and naturally, his brain stopped working. Full of the suspicions of a long-faced, dark-spirited old geezer, he transferred his capital from Tabriz, which was then Persian territory, to Kazvin so it would be farther from the Ottoman armies. One day when he had grown even older, he was possessed by a jinn, had a nervous fit, and begging God's forgiveness, completely swore off wine, handsome young boys and painting, which is proof enough that after this great shah lost his taste for coffee, he also lost his mind.

This was why the divinely inspired bookbinders, calligraphers, gilders and miniaturists, who created the greatest masterpieces in the world over a twenty-year period in Tabriz, scattered like a covey of partridges to other cities. Shah Tahmasp's nephew and son-in-law, Sultan Ibrahim Mirza, invited the most gifted among them to Mashhad, where he served as provincial governor, and settled them in his miniaturists' workshop to copy out a marvelous illuminated and illustrated manuscript of all seven fables of the *Seven Thrones* of Jami—the greatest poet in Herat during the reign of Tamerlane. Shah Tahmasp, who both admired and envied his intelligent and handsome nephew, and regretted having given his daughter to him, was consumed by jealousy when he heard about this magnificent book and angrily ousted his nephew from the post of Governor of Mashhad, banishing him to the city of Kain, before sending him off to the smaller town of Sebzivar in a renewed fit of anger. The calligraphers and illuminators of Mashhad thereupon dispersed to other cities and regions, to the book-arts workshops of other sultans and princes.

Miraculously, however, Sultan Ibrahim Mirza's marvelous volume did not remain unfinished, for in his service he had a devoted librarian. This man would travel on horseback all the way to Shiraz where the best master gilders lived; then he'd take a couple pages to Isfahan seeking the most elegant calligraphers of Nestalik script; afterward he'd cross great mountains till he'd made it all the way to Bukhara where he'd arrange the picture's composition and have the figures drawn by the great master painter who worked under the Uzbek Khan; next he'd go down to Herat to commission one of its half-blind old masters to paint from memory the sinuous curves of plants and leaves; visiting another calligrapher in Herat, he'd direct him to inscribe, in gold Rika script, the sign above a door within the picture; finally, he'd be off again to the south, to Kain, where displaying the half-page he had finished during his six months of traveling, he'd receive the praises of Sultan Ibrahim Mirza.

At this pace, it was clear that the book would never be completed, so mounted Tatar couriers were hired. In addition to the manuscript leaf, which was to receive artwork and scripted text, each horseman was given a letter describing the desired work in question to the artist. Thus, messengers carrying manuscript pages passed over the roads of Persia, Khorasan, the Uzbek territory and Transoxania. The creation of the book sped up with the fleet messengers. At times, on a snowy night, page 59 and 162, for example, would cross paths in a caravansary wherein the howlings of wolves could be heard, and as they struck up a friendly conversation, they'd discover that they were working on the same book project and would try to determine between themselves where and in which fable the prospective pages, retrieved from their rooms for this purpose, actually belonged.

I was meant to be among the pages of this illustrated manuscript that I sadly heard was completed today. Unfortunately, on a cold winter's day, the Tatar courier who was carrying me as he crossed a rocky mountain pass was ambushed by thieves. First they beat the poor Tatar, then they robbed him and raped him in a manner befitting thieves before mercilessly killing him. As a result, I know nothing about the page I've fallen from. My request is that you look at me and ask: "Were you perhaps meant to provide shade for Mejnun disguised as a shepherd as he visited Leyla in her tent?" or "Were you meant to fade into the night, representing the darkness in the soul of a wretched and hopeless man?" How I would've wanted to complement the happiness of two lovers who fled from the whole world, traversing oceans to find solace on an island rich with birds and fruit! I would've wanted to shade Alexander during the final moments of his life on his campaign to conquer Hindustan as he died from a persistent nosebleed brought on by sunstroke. Or was I meant to symbolize the strength and wisdom of a father offering advice on love and life to his son? Ah, to which story was I meant to add meaning and grace?

Among the brigands who'd killed the messenger and taken me with them, dragging me headlong from mountain to mountain and city to city, there was a thief who occasionally understood my worth, and had the refinement to realize that looking at the drawing of a tree is more pleasant than looking at a tree; but because he didn't know to which story I belonged, he quickly tired of me. After dragging me from city to city, this rogue didn't tear me apart and dispose of me as I'd feared he might, but sold me to a cultivated man in a caravansary for a jug of wine. Sometimes at night this unfortunate delicate-spirited man would stare at me by candlelight and cry. In time, he died of grief and they sold his belongings.

Thanks to the master storyteller who purchased me, I've come all the way to Istanbul. Now, I'm most happy, and honored to be here tonight among you, the Ottoman Sultan's miraculously inspired, eagle-eyed, iron-willed, elegant-wristed, sensitive-spirited miniaturists and calligraphers—and for Heaven's sake, I beg of you not to believe those who claim I've been hastily sketched onto coarse paper by some master miniaturist as a wall prop.

But hear yet what other lies, slander and brazen untruths are being spread! You might remember how last night my master nailed the picture of a dog here on the wall and recounted the adventures of this crass beast; and how at the same time he told of the adventures of Husret Hoja of Erzurum! Well now, the admirers of His Excellency Nusret Hoja have completely misunderstood this story; they think he was the target of our account. Could we have possibly said that the great preacher, His Esteemed Excellency, was of uncertain birth? God forbid! Would it have even crossed our minds? What mischief, what a crude lie! Clearly, Husret of Erzurum is being confused with Nusret of Erzurum, so let me proceed to tell you the story of Cross-Eyed Nedret Hoja of Sivas and the Tree.

Besides denouncing the wooing of pretty boys and the art of painting, this Cross-Eyed Nedret Hoja of Sivas maintained that coffee was the Devil's work and that coffee drinkers would go to Hell. Hey, you from Sivas, have you forgotten how this enormous branch of mine was bent? Let me tell you about it, then, but swear you won't tell anyone, and may Allah protect you from baseless slander. One morning, I awoke to find that a giant of a man—God protect him, he was as tall as a minaret with hands like a lion's claws—had climbed up onto this branch of mine and hidden beneath my lush leaves together with the aforementioned Hoja and, excuse the expression, they were going at it like dogs in heat. While the giant, whom I later realized was the Devil, attended to his business with our hero, he was compassionately kissing his lovely ear and whispering into it, "Coffee is a sin, coffee is a vice . . ." Accordingly, those who believe in the harmful effects of coffee, believe not in the commandments of our good religion, but in the Devil himself.

And finally, I shall make mention of Frank painters, so if there are degenerates among you who have pretensions to be like them, may you heed my warning and be deterred. Now, these Frank painters depict the faces of kings, priests, noblemen and even women in such a manner that after gazing upon the portrait, you'd be able to identify that person on the street. Their wives roam freely on the streets anyway—now, just imagine the rest. As if this weren't enough, they've taken matters even further. I don't mean in regard to pimping, but in regard to painting.

MY NAME IS RED

A great European master miniaturist and another great master artist are walking through a Frank meadow discussing virtuosity and art. As they stroll, a forest comes into view before them. The more expert of the two says to the other: "Painting in the new style demands such talent that if you depicted one of the trees in this forest, a man who looked upon that painting could come here, and if he so desired, correctly select that tree from among the others."

I thank Allah that I, the humble tree before you, have not been drawn with such intent. And not because I fear that if I'd been thus depicted all the dogs in Istanbul would assume I was a real tree and piss on me: I don't want to be a tree, I want to be its meaning.

CHAPTER 11

I AM CALLED BLACK

The snow began to fall at a late hour and continued till dawn. I spent the night reading Shekure's letter again and again. I paced in the empty room of the empty house, occasionally leaning toward the candlestick; in the flickering light of the dim candle, I watched the tense quivering of my beloved's angry letters, the somersaults they turned trying to deceive me and their hip-swinging right-to-left progression. Abruptly, those shutters would open before my eyes, and my beloved's face and her sorrowful smile would appear. And when I saw her real face, I forgot all of those other faces whose sour-cherry mouths had increasingly matured and ripened in my imagination.

In the middle of the night I lost myself in dreams of marriage: I had no doubts about my love or that it was reciprocated—we were married in a state of great contentment—but, my imaginary happiness, set in a house with a staircase, was dashed when I couldn't find appropriate work and began arguing with my wife, unable to make her heed my words.

I knew I'd appropriated these ominous images from the section on the ills of marriage in Gazzali's *The Revival of Religious Science*, which I'd read during my nights as a bachelor in Arabia; at the same time, I recalled that there was actually advice on the benefits of marriage in that same section, though now I could remember only two of these benefits: first, having my household kept in order (there was no such order in my imagined house); second, being spared the guilt of self-abuse and of dragging myself—an even deeper sense of guilt—behind pimps leading me through dark alleyways to the lairs of prostitutes.

The thought of salvation at this late hour brought masturbation to mind. With a simple-minded desire, and to rid my mind of this irrepressible urge, I retired to a corner of the room, as was my wont, but after a while I realized I couldn't jack off—proof well enough that I'd fallen in love again after twelve years!

This struck such excitement and fear into my heart that I walked around the room nearly atremble like the flame of the candle. If Shekure meant to present herself at the window, then why this letter, which put the opposite belief into play? Why did her father call for me? As I paced, I sensed that the door, wall and squeaky floor, stuttering as I myself did, were trying to creak their responses to my every question.

I looked at the picture I'd made years ago, which depicted Shirin stricken with love upon gazing at Hüsrev's image hanging from a branch. It didn't embarrass me as it would each time it came to mind in subsequent years, nor did it bring back my happy childhood memories. Toward morning, my mind had mastered the situation: By returning the picture, Shekure had made a move in an amatory chess game she was masterfully luring me into. I sat in the candlelight and wrote her a letter of response.

In the morning, after sleeping for a spell, I went out and walked a long way through the streets, carrying the letter upon my breast and my light pen-and-ink holder, as was my custom, in my sash. The snow widened Istanbul's narrow streets and freed the city of its crowds. All was quieter and slower, as it'd been in my childhood. Crows seemed to have beset Istanbul's roofs, domes and gardens just as they had on the snowy winter days of my youth. I walked swiftly, listening to my steps in the snow and watching the fog of my breath. I grew excited, expecting the palace workshop that my Enishte wanted me to visit to be as silent as the streets. Before I entered the Jewish quarter, I sent word by way of a little street urchin to Esther, who'd be able to deliver my letter to Shekure, telling her where to meet me before the noontime prayers.

I arrived early at the royal artisans' workshop located behind the Hagia Sophia. Except for the icicles hanging from the eaves, there was no change in the building where I'd often visited my Enishte and for a time worked as a child apprentice.

Following a handsome young apprentice, I walked past elderly master binders dazed from the smell of glue and bookbinder's paste, master miniaturists whose backs had hunched at an early age and youths who mixed paints without even looking into the bowls perched on their knees, so sorrowfully were they absorbed by the flames of the stove. I saw an old man meticulously painting an ostrich egg on his lap, an elder enthusiastically embellishing a drawer and a young apprentice graciously watching them both. Through an open door, I witnessed young students being reprimanded as they leaned forward, their noses almost touching the pages spread before their reddened faces, as they tried to understand the mistakes they'd made. In another room, a mournful and melancholy apprentice, having forgotten momentarily about colors, papers and painting, stared into the street I'd just now eagerly walked down.

We climbed the icy staircase. We walked through the portico, which wrapped around the inner second floor of the building. Below, in the inner courtyard covered with snow, two young students, obviously trembling from the cold despite their thick capes of coarse wool, were waiting—perhaps for an imminent beating. I recalled my early youth and the beatings given to students who were lazy or who wasted expensive paints, and the blows of the bastinado, which landed on the soles of their feet until they bled.

We entered a warm room. I saw two novices who'd recently finished their apprenticeships. Since the great masters, whom Master Osman had given workshop names, now worked at home, this room, which once aroused excessive reverence and delight in me, no longer seemed like the workshop of a great and wealthy sultan but merely a largish room in some secluded caravansary in the remote mountains of the East.

Immediately off to the side, before a long counter, I saw the Head Illuminator, Master Osman, for the first time in fifteen years; he seemed like an apparition. Whenever I contemplated illustrating and painting during my travels, the great master would appear in my mind's eye as if he were Bihzad himself; now, in his white outfit and in the snow-white light falling through the window facing the Hagia Sophia, he looked as though he'd long become one of the spirits of the Otherworld. I kissed his hand, which I noticed was mottled, and I introduced myself. I explained how my Enishte had enrolled me here as a youth, but that I'd preferred a bureaucratic post and left. I recounted my years on the road, my time spent in Eastern cities in the service of pashas as a clerk or treasurer's secretary. I told him how, working with Serhat Pasha and others, I'd met calligraphers and illuminators in Tabriz and produced books; how I'd spent time in Baghdad and Aleppo, in Van and Tiflis, and how I'd seen many battles.

"Ah, Tiflis!" the great master said, as he gazed at the light from the snow-covered garden filtering through the oilskin covering the window. "Is it snowing there now?"

befitted those old Persian masters who grew blind per-
[...]stry; who, after a certain age, lived half-saintly, half-senile
[...]ut whom endless legends were told. I straightaway saw in
[...]yes that he despised my Enishte vehemently and that he was
[...]re suspicious of me. Even so, I explained how in the Arabian
[...] snow didn't simply fall to the Earth, as it was now falling onto the
Hagi[a] Sophia, but onto memories as well. I spun a yarn: When it snowed
on the fortress of Tiflis, the washerwomen sang songs the color of flowers
and children hid ice cream under their pillows for summer.

"Do tell me what those illuminators and painters illustrate in the countries you've visited," he said. "What do they depict?"

A dreamy-eyed young painter who was ruling out pages in the corner, lost in revery, raised his head from his folding work desk along with the others in the room and gave me a look that said, "Let this be your most honest answer." Many of these craftsmen didn't know the corner grocer in their own neighborhood, or how much an oke's worth of bread cost, but they were very curious about the latest gossip East of Persia, where armies clashed, princes strangled one another and plundered cities before burning them to the ground, where war and peace were contested each day, where the best verses were written and the best illustrations and paintings were made for centuries.

"Shah Tahmasp reigned for fifty-two years. In the last years of his life, as you know, he abandoned his love of books, illustrating and painting, turned his back on poets, illustrators and calligraphers, and resigning himself to worship, passed away, whereupon his son, Ismail, ascended to the throne," I said. "Shah Tahmasp had been well aware of his son's disagreeable and antagonistic nature, so he kept him, the shah-to-be, behind locked doors for twenty years. As soon as Ismail assumed the throne, in a mad frenzy, he had his younger brothers strangled—some of whom he'd blinded beforehand. In the end, however, Ismail's enemies succeeded in plying him with opium and poisoning him, and after being liberated from his worldly presence, they placed his half-witted older brother Muhammad Khodabandeh on the throne. During his reign, all the princes, brothers, provincial governors and Uzbeks, in short everyone, started to revolt. They went after each other and our Serhat Pasha with such martial ferocity that all of Persia turned to smoke and dust and was left in disarray. Indeed, the present shah, bereft of money and intelligence and half-blind, is not fit to sponsor the writing and illustration of illuminated manuscripts. Thus, these legendary illustrators of Kazvin and Herat, all these elderly masters, along with their apprentices, these artisans who made masterpieces in Shah Tahmasp's workshops, painters and colorists whose brushes made horses gallop at full speed and whose butterflies fluttered off the page, all of these master binders and calligraphers, every last one was left without work, penniless and destitute, homeless and bereft. Some migrated to the North among the Uzbeks, some West to India. Others took up different types of work, wasting themselves and their honor, and still others entered the service of insignificant princes and provincial governors, all sworn enemies of each other, to begin working on palm-size books containing at most a few leaves of illustration. Rapidly transcribed, hastily painted, cheap books appeared everywhere, matching the tastes of common soldiers, boorish pashas and spoiled princes."

"How much would they go for?" asked Master Osman.

"I hear that the great Sadiki Bey illustrated a copy of *Strange Creatures*, commissioned by an Uzbek spahi cavalryman, for only forty gold pieces. In the tent of a vulgar pasha who was returning from his Eastern campaign to Erzurum, I beheld an album consisting of lewd pictures including paintings by the virtuoso Siyavush. A few great masters who hadn't abandoned illustrating were making and selling individual pieces, which weren't part of any story at all. By examining such single leaves, you couldn't tell which scene or which story it represented; rather, you would admire it for its own sake, for the pleasure of beholding alone. For example, you might comment, 'This is the exact likeness of a horse, how beautiful,' and you'd pay the artist on this basis. Scenes of combat or fucking are quite common. The price for a bustling battle has fallen to three hundred silver coins, and there are hardly any interested clients. To sell pieces on the cheap and to better lure a buyer, some simply draw in black ink on nonsized, unfinished paper with nary a brushstroke of color."

"There was a gilder of mine who was content as content could be and talented as talent would allow," said Master Osman. "He saw to his work with such elegance that we referred to him as 'Elegant Effendi.' But he has abandoned us. It's been six days, and he's not to be found anywhere. He's plain disappeared."

"How could anyone quit such a workshop as this, such a joyous hearth?" I said.

"Butterfly, Olive, Stork and Elegant, the four young masters whom I've trained since they were apprentices, now work at home at Our Sultan's behest," said Master Osman.

This apparently came about so they could work more comfortably on the *Book of Festivities* with which the entire workshop was involved. This time, the Sultan hadn't arranged for a special workspace for His master miniaturists in the palace courtyard; rather, He decreed that they work on this special book at home. When it occurred to me that this order was probably issued for the sake of my Enishte's book, I fell silent. To what degree was Master Osman making insinuations?

"Nuri Effendi," he called to a pale and hunched painter, "present Our Master Black with a 'survey' of the workshop!"

The "survey" was a regular ritual of Our Sultan's bimonthly visits to the miniaturists' atelier during that exciting time when His Excellency had intently followed what transpired at the workshop. Under the auspices of Hazım, the Head Treasurer; Lokman, the Head Poetic Chronicler and Master Osman, the Head Illuminator, Our Sultan would be apprised of which pages in which books the masters were working on at any given moment: who did which gilding, who colored which picture, and one by one, how the colorists, the page rulers, the gilders and the master miniaturists, whose talent allowed them to accomplish miracles, were engaged. It saddened me that they were holding a fake ceremony in place of the one that was no longer performed because age and ill health bound the Head Poetic Chronicler Lokman Effendi, who wrote most of the books which were illustrated, to his home; because Master Osman often disappeared in a cloud of indignation and wrath; because the four masters known as Butterfly, Olive, Stork and Elegant worked at home; and because Our Sultan no longer waxed enthusiastic like a child in the workshop. As happened to many miniaturists, Nuri Effendi had grown old in vain, without having fully experienced life or become a master of his art. Not in vain, however, did he spend those years over his worktable becoming hunchbacked: He always paid close attention to what happened in the workshop, to who made which exquisite page.

And so I eagerly beheld for the first time the legendary pages of the *Book of Festivities,* which recounted the circumcision ceremonies of Our Sultan's prince. When I was still in Persia, I heard stories about this fifty-two-day circumcision ceremony wherein people from all occupations and all guilds, all of Istanbul, had participated, indeed at a time when the book that memorialized the great event was yet being prepared.

In the first picture placed before me, fixed in the royal enclosure of late Ibrahim Pasha's palace, Our Sultan, the Refuge of the World, gazed upon the festivities in the Hippodrome below with a look that bespoke His satisfaction. His face, even though not so detailed as to permit one to distinguish Him from others by features alone, was drawn adeptly and with reverence. As for the right side of the double-leaf picture showing Our Sultan on the left, there were viziers, pashas, Persian, Tatar, Frankish and

Venetian ambassadors standing in the arched colonnades and windows. Because they were not sultans, their eyes were drawn hastily and carelessly and focused on nothing in particular besides the general commotion in the square. Later, I noticed in other pictures that the same arrangement and page composition repeated—even though the wall ornamentation, the trees and terra-cotta shingles were depicted in different styles and colors. Once the text was written out by scribes, the illustrations completed and the book bound; the reader, turning pages, would each time see completely different activities in completely different colors in the Hippodrome which remained under the same watchful gazes of the Sultan and His crowd of guests—who always stood identically, forever gazing at the same area below.

There before me I saw people scrambling for hundreds of bowls of pilaf that were placed in the Hippodrome; I saw the live rabbits and birds emerge out of the roast ox and startle the crowd that had descended upon it. I saw the master coppersmiths' guild riding in a wheeled cart before Our Sultan, its members hammering away at copper but never striking the one among them lying in the cart with the anvil balanced on his bare chest. I saw glaziers embellishing glass with carnations and cypresses as they paraded before Our Sultan in a wagon; confectioners reciting sweet poems as they drove camels laden with sacks of sugar and displayed cages holding sugar-parrots; and aged locksmiths who showed off a variety of hanging locks, padlocks, dead bolts and gearlocks as they complained of the evils of new times and new doors. Butterfly, Stork and Olive had worked on the picture that depicted the magicians: One of them was causing eggs to march down a pole without dropping them—as if on a broad slab of marble—to the beat of a tambourine played by another. In one wagon I saw precisely how Sea-Captain Kılıç Ali Pasha had forced the infidels he'd captured at sea to make an "infidels' mountain" out of clay; he'd then loaded all the slaves into the cart, and when he was right before the Sultan, he exploded the powder within the "mountain" to demonstrate how he'd made infidel lands wail and moan with cannon fire. I saw cleanshaven butchers wielding cleavers, wearing rose- and purple-colored uniforms and smiling at the pink carcasses of skinned sheep hanging from hooks. The spectators applauded lion tamers who'd brought a chained lion before Our Sultan, provoking and enraging it until its eyes shone blood-red with rage; and on the next page, I saw the lion, representing Islam, chase away a gray-and-pink pig, symbolizing the cunning Christian infidel. I indulged my eyes at length on a picture of a barber suspended upside down from the ceiling of a shop built onto a cart, as he shaved a customer

I Am Called Black

while his assistant, dressed in red, held a mirror and a silver bowl containing fragrant soap, waiting for baksheesh; I inquired after the identity of the magnificent miniaturist responsible for the piece.

"It is indeed important that a painting, through its beauty, summon us toward life's abundance, toward compassion, toward respect for the colors of the realm which God created, and toward reflection and faith. The identity of the miniaturist is not important."

Was Nuri the Miniaturist, who was much more subtle in thought than I'd assumed, being reserved because he understood that my Enishte sent me here to investigate, or was he merely parroting Head Illuminator Master Osman?

"Is Elegant the one responsible for all this gilding work?" I asked. "Who's doing the gilding now, in his stead?"

The shouts and screams of children could now be heard through the open door that faced the inner courtyard. Below, one of the division heads had started administering the bastinado to apprentices who'd most likely been caught with red ink powder in their pockets or gold leaf hidden away in a fold of paper; probably the two whom I'd seen trembling as they waited in the cold. Young painters, seizing an opportunity to mock them, ran to the door to watch.

"By the time the apprentices paint the ground of the Hippodrome here a rose color, finishing it off as our Master Osman has dictated," said Nuri Effendi cautiously, "our brother Elegant Effendi, God willing, will have returned from wherever he's gone and will complete the gilding on these two pages. Our master, Osman the Miniaturist, wanted Elegant Effendi to color the dirt floor of the Hippodrome differently in each scene. Rose pink, Indian green, saffron yellow or the color of goose shit. Whosoever beholds the picture will realize in the first rendering this is a dirt square and should be earth-colored, but in the second and third pictures, he'll want other colors to keep himself amused. Embellishing ought to bring merriment to the page."

I noticed some pictures on a sheet of paper that an assistant left in a corner. He was working on a single-leaf picture for a *Book of Victories*, the depiction of a naval fleet heading off to battle, but it was obvious that the screams of his friends whose soles were being severely beaten, provoked the illustrator to run off and watch. The fleet he made by repeatedly tracing identical ships with a block pattern didn't even seem to float in the sea; yet, this artificiality, the lack of wind in the sails, had less to do with the block pattern than the young painter's lack of skill. I saw with sorrow that the pattern had been cut violently out of an old book which I couldn't identify, perhaps a collage album. Obviously, Master Osman was overlooking quite a lot.

When we came to his own worktable, Nuri Effendi proudly stated that he finished a gilded royal insignia for Our Sultan, which he'd been working on for three weeks. I respectfully admired Nuri Effendi's gold inlay and the insignia, which had been made on an empty sheet to ensure that its recipient and the reason for its being sent would remain secret. I knew well enough that many impetuous pashas in the East had refrained from rebellion upon seeing the noble and potent splendor of the Sultan's royal insignia.

Next, we saw the last masterpieces that Jemal the Calligrapher had transcribed, completed and left behind; but we passed over them hastily to avoid giving credence to opponents of color and decoration who maintained that true art consisted of calligraphy alone and that decorative illumination was simply a secondary means of adding emphasis.

Nasır the Limner was making a mess of a plate he intended to repair from a version of the *Quintet* of Nizami dating back to the era of Tamerlane's sons; the picture depicted Hüsrev looking at a naked Shirin as she bathed.

A ninety-two-year-old former master who was half blind and had nothing to say besides claiming that sixty years ago he kissed Master Bizhad's hand in Tabriz and that the great master of legend was blind and drunk at the time, showed us with trembling hands the ornamentation on the pen box he would present as a holiday gift to Our Sultan when it was completed three months hence.

Shortly a silence enveloped the whole workshop where close to eighty painters, students and apprentices worked in the small cells which constituted the lower floor. This was a postbeating silence, the likes of which I'd experienced many times; a silence which would be broken at times by a nerve-wracking chuckle or a witticism, at times by a few sobs or the suppressed moan of the beaten boy before his crying fit would remind the master miniaturists of the beatings they themselves received as apprentices. But the half-blind ninety-two-year-old master caused me to sense something deeper for a moment, here, far from all the battles and turmoil: the feeling that everything was coming to an end. Immediately before the end of the world, there would also be such silence.

Painting is the silence of thought and the music of sight.

As I kissed Master Osman's hand to bid him farewell, I felt not only great respect toward him, but a sentiment that plunged my soul into turmoil: pity mixed with the adoration befitting a saint, a peculiar feeling of guilt. This, perhaps, because my Enishte—who wanted painters, openly or secretly, to imitate the methods of the Frankish masters—was his rival.

I suddenly sensed, as well, that I was perhaps seeing the great master alive for the last time, and in the fluster of wanting to please and hearten him, I asked a question:

"My great master, my dear sir, what separates the genuine miniaturist from the ordinary?" I assumed the Head Illuminator, who was accustomed to such fawning questions, would give me a dismissive response, and that he was presently in the midst of forgetting who I was altogether.

"There is no single measure that can distinguish the great miniaturist from the unskilled and faithless one," he said in all seriousness. "This changes with time. Yet the skills and morality with which he would face the evils that threaten our art are of significance. Today, in order to determine just how genuine a young painter is, I'd ask him three questions."

"And what would they be?"

"Has he come to believe, under the sway of recent custom as well as the influence of the Chinese and the European Franks, that he ought to have an individual painting technique, his own style? As an illustrator, does he want to have a manner, an aspect distinct from others, and does he attempt to prove this by signing his name somewhere in his work like the Frankish masters? To determine precisely these things, I'd first ask him a question about 'style' and 'signature.'"

"And then?" I asked respectfully.

"Then, I'd want to learn how this illustrator felt about volumes changing hands, being unbound, and our pictures being used in other books and in other eras after the shahs and sultans who'd commissioned them have died. This is a subtle issue demanding a response beyond one's being simply upset or pleased by it. Thus, I'd ask the illustrator a question about 'time'—an illustrator's time and Allah's time. Do you follow me, my child?"

Nay. But that's not what I said. Instead, I asked, "And the third question?"

"The third would be 'blindness'!" said the great master Head Illuminator Osman, who then fell silent as if this required no explication.

"What is it about 'blindness'?" I said with embarrassment.

"Blindness is silence. If you combine what I've just now said, the first and the second questions, 'blindness' will emerge. It's the farthest one can go in illustrating; it is seeing what appears out of Allah's own blackness."

I said no more. I walked outside. I descended the icy stairs without hurrying. I knew that I would ask the great master's three great questions of Butterfly, Olive and Stork, not only for the sake of conversation, but to better understand these living legends who were contemporaries of mine.

I did not, however, go to the master illuminators' houses immediately. I met with Esther near the Jewish quarter at a new bazaar that had an elevated view of the confluence of the Golden Horn and the Bosphorus. Esther was all atwitter in the pink dress she was forced to wear as a Jew, with her large and lively body, her mouth which never stopped moving, and her eyebrows and eyes which twitched madly and signaled to me; indeed, this is how she was among the shopping slave women, the women wearing the faded and loose caftans of poor neighborhoods and among the crowds that had lost themselves amid carrots, quinces and small bundles of onions and turnips.

She stuffed the letter I gave her into her shalwar pants with an adept and mysterious gesture, as if the whole market were spying upon us. She told me that Shekure was thinking of me. She took her baksheesh and when I said, "Please, make haste and deliver it straightaway," she indicated that she still had quite a lot of work to do by gesturing toward her bundle and said that she only could deliver the letter to Shekure toward midday. I asked her to tell Shekure that I'd gone to pay visits to the three young and renowned master miniaturists.

CHAPTER 12

I AM CALLED "BUTTERFLY"

The midday prayers had yet to be called. A knock at the door: I opened it to find Black Effendi, who was among us for a while during our apprenticeships. We embraced and kissed on the cheeks. I was wondering whether he'd brought some word from his Enishte, when he said that he wanted to look at the pages I'd been illustrating and at my paintings, that he'd called in friendship, and was going to direct a question to me in the name of Our Sultan. "Very well," I said, "what's the question I'm to answer?"

He told me. Very well, then!

Style and Signature

"As long as the number of worthless artists motivated by money and fame instead of the pleasure of seeing and a belief in their craft increases," I said, "we will continue to witness much more vulgarity and greed akin to this preoccupation with 'style' and 'signature.'" I made this introduction because this was the way it is done, not because I believed what I said. True ability and talent couldn't be corrupted even by the love of gold or fame. Furthermore, if truth be told, money and fame are the inalienable rights of the talented, as in my case, and only inspire us to greater feats. But if I were to say this openly, the mediocre illustrators in the miniaturists' division, rabid with envy, would pounce upon me, so, to prove that I love this work more than they themselves do, I'll paint the picture of a tree on a grain of rice. I'm well aware that this lust for 'style,' 'signature' and 'character' has come to us all the way from the East by way of certain unfortunate Chinese masters who've been led astray under the influence of the Europeans, by pictures brought there from the West by Jesuit priests. Nevertheless, let me tell you three parables that comprise a recital on this topic."

Three Parables on Style and Signature

ALIF

Once upon a time, to the North of Herat, in a mountain castle, there lived a young Khan who was fascinated with illuminating and painting. This Khan loved only one of the women in his harem, and this striking Tatar woman, whom he loved madly, loved him in return. They engaged in such bouts of lovemaking, sweating until morning, and lived in such ecstasy that their only wish was to live eternally. They soon discovered the best way to realize their wish was by opening books and gazing, for hours and hours and days on end, upon the astounding and flawless pictures of the old masters. As they stared at these perfect renderings, unfalteringly reproduced, they felt as though time would stop and their own felicity would mingle with the bliss of the golden age revealed in the stories. In the royal bookmaker's workshop, there was a miniaturist, a master of masters, who made the same flawless pieces over and over for the same pages of the same books. As was his custom, the master depicted the anguish of Ferhad's love for Shirin, or the loving and desirous glances between Leyla and Mejnun, or the duplicitous, suggestive looks Hüsrev and Shirin exchanged in that fabled heavenly garden—with one slight alteration however: In place of these legendary lovers, the artist would paint the Khan and his Tatar beauty. Beholding these pages, the Khan and his beloved were thoroughly convinced that their rapture would never end, and they showered the master miniaturist with praises and gold. Eventually, however, this adulation caused the miniaturist to stray from good sense; incited by the Devil, he dismissed the fact that he was beholden to the old masters for the perfection of his pictures, and haughtily assumed that a touch of his own genius would make his work even more appealing. The Khan and his beloved, considering these innovations—the personal stylistic touches of the master miniaturist—nothing but imperfections, were deeply disturbed by them. In the paintings, which the Khan observed at length, he felt that his former bliss had been disrupted in numerous ways, and he grew increasingly jealous of his Tatar beauty who was depicted with the individual touch of the painter. So, with the intention of making his pretty Tatar jealous, he made love with another concubine. His beloved was so bereft upon learning of this betrayal from the harem gossips that she silently hanged herself from a cedar tree in the harem courtyard. The Khan, understanding the mistake he'd made and realizing that the miniaturist's own fascination with style lay behind this terrible incident, immediately blinded this master artist whom the Devil had tempted.

BA

Once upon a time in a country in the East there was an elderly Sultan, a lover of illustrations, illuminations and miniatures, who lived happily with his Chinese wife of unsurpassed beauty. Alas, it soon happened that the Sultan's handsome son from a previous marriage and the Sultan's young wife had become enamored of each other. The son, who lived in terror of his treachery against his father, and ashamed of his forbidden love, sequestered himself in the bookmaker's workshop and gave himself over to painting. Since he painted out of the sorrow and strength of his love, each of his paintings was so magnificent that admirers couldn't distinguish them from the work of the old masters. The Sultan took great pride in his son, and his young Chinese wife would say, "Yes, magnificent!" as she looked upon the paintings. "Yet, time will surely pass, and if he doesn't sign his work, no one will know that he was the one responsible for this majesty." The Sultan responded, "If my son signs his paintings, won't he be unjustly taking credit for the techniques and styles of the old masters, which he has imitated? Moreover, if he signs his work, won't he be saying 'My paintings bear my imperfections'?" The Chinese wife, seeing that she wouldn't be able to convince her elderly husband on this issue of signature, was, however, eventually successful in persuading his young son, confined, as always, in the bookmaker's workshop. Humiliated at having to conceal his love, persuaded by his pretty young stepmother's ideas and with the Devil's coercion, the son signed his name in a corner of a painting, between wall and grass, in a spot he assumed was beyond notice. This, the first picture he signed, was a scene from *Hüsrev and Shirin*. You know the one: After Hüsrev and Shirin are wed, Shiruye, Hüsrev's son from his first marriage, falls in love with Shirin. One night, entering their bedchamber through the window, Shiruye swiftly sinks his dagger into his father's chest. When the Sultan saw his son's depiction of this scene, he was overcome with the sense that the painting embodied some flaw; he'd seen the signature, but wasn't consciously aware of it, and he simply reacted to the picture with the thought, "This painting bears a flaw." And since one would never expect any such thing from the old masters, the Sultan was seized by a kind of panic, suspecting that this volume he was reading recounted not a story or a legend, but what was most unbefitting a book: reality itself. When the elderly man sensed this, he was overcome with terror. His illustrator son had entered through the window, as in the painting, and without even looking twice at his father's bulging eyes, swiftly drove his dagger—as large as the one in the painting—into his father's chest.

DJIM

In his *History*, Rashiduddin of Kazvin merrily writes that 250 years ago in Kazvin, manuscript illumination, calligraphy and illustration were the most esteemed and beloved arts. The reigning Shah in Kazvin at that time ruled over forty countries from Byzantium to China—perhaps the love of book arts was the secret of this great power—but alas, he had no male heir. To prevent the lands he'd conquered from being divided up after his death, the Shah decided to find a bright miniaturist husband for his beautiful daughter, and toward this end, arranged a competition among the three great young masters of his atelier, all of whom were bachelors. According to Rashiduddin's *History*, the object of the competition was very simple: Whoever made the most remarkable painting would be the victor! Like Rashiduddin himself, the young miniaturists knew that this meant painting in the manner of the old masters, and thus, each of the three made a rendition of the most widely liked scene: In a garden reminiscent of Heaven itself, a young and beautiful maiden stood amid cypress and cedar trees, among timid rabbits and anxious swallows, immersed in lovelorn grief, staring at the ground. Unknowingly, the three miniaturists had rendered the same scene exactly as the old masters would have; yet, the one who wanted to distinguish himself and thereby take responsibility for the painting's beauty had hidden his signature among the narcissus flowers in the most secluded spot in the garden. And on account of this brazen act, by which the artist broke with the humility of the old virtuosos, he was immediately exiled from Kazvin to China. Thus, the competition was begun anew between the two remaining miniaturists. This time, both painted a picture lovely as a poem, depicting a beautiful maiden mounted on her horse in a magnificent garden. But one of the miniaturists—whether by a slip of his brush or by intent, no one knew—had depicted strangely the nostrils of the white horse belonging to the maiden with Chinese eyes and high cheekbones, and this was straightaway perceived as a flaw by the Shah and his daughter. True, this miniaturist hadn't signed his name, but in his splendid painting, he'd apparently included a masterful variation in the horse's nostrils to distinguish the work. The Shah, declaring that "Imperfection is the mother of style," exiled this illustrator to Byzantium. Yet there was one last significant event according to the weighty *History* by Rashiduddin of Kazvin, which occurred when preparations were being made for the wedding between the Shah's daughter and the talented miniaturist, who painted exactly like the old masters without any signature or variation: For the entire day before the wedding, the Shah's daughter gazed grief-stricken at the painting made by the young and handsome great master who was to become her husband on the morrow. As darkness fell that evening, she presented herself to her father: "It is true, yes, that the old masters, in their exquisite paintings, would depict beautiful maidens as Chinese, and this is an unalterable rule come to us from the East," she said. "But when they loved someone, the painters would include an aspect of their beloved in the rendering of the beautiful maiden's brow, eye, lip, hair, smile, or even eyelash. This secret variation in their illustrations would be a sign that could be read by the lovers and the lovers alone. I've stared at the beautiful maiden mounted on her horse for the whole day, my dear father, and there's no trace of me in her! This miniaturist is perhaps a great master, he's young and handsome, but he does not love me." Thereupon, the Shah canceled the wedding at once, and father and daughter lived out the remainder of their lives together.

"Thus, according to this third parable, imperfection gives rise to what we call 'style,'" said Black quite politely and respectfully. "And does the fact that the miniaturist is in love become apparent from the hidden 'sign' in the image of the beauty's face, eye or smile?"

"Nay," I said in a manner that bespoke my confidence and pride. "What passes from the maiden, the focus of the master miniaturist's love, to his picture is not ultimately imperfection or flaw but a new artistic rule. Because, after a time and through imitation, everyone will begin to depict the faces of maidens just like that particular beautiful maiden's face."

We fell silent. I saw that Black, who'd listened intently to the three parables I recounted, had now focused his attentions upon the sounds my attractive wife made as she roamed the hallway and the next room. I glared at him menacingly.

"The first story established that 'style' is imperfection," I said. "The second story established that a perfect picture needs no signature, and the third marries the ideas of the first and the second, and thus demonstrates that 'signature' and 'style' are but means of being brazenly and stupidly self-congratulatory about flawed work."

How much did this man, to whom I'd just given an invaluable lesson, understand of painting? I said: "Have you understood who I am from my stories?"

"Certainly," he said, without conviction.

So you don't try to discern who I am through his eyes and perceptions, allow me to tell you directly. I can do anything. Like the old masters of Kazvin, I can draw and color with pleasure and glee. I say this with a smile: I'm better than everybody. I have nothing whatsoever to do with the reason for Black's visit, which—if perchance my intuition serves me correctly—is the disappearance of Elegant Effendi the Gilder.

Black asked me about the mixing of marriage and art.

I work a lot and I enjoy my work. I recently married the most beautiful maiden in the neighborhood. When I'm not illuminating, we make love like mad. Then I set to working again. That's not how I answered. "It's a serious issue," I said. "If masterpieces issue from the brush of a miniaturist, when it comes to issuing it to his wife, he'll be at a loss to bestir the same joy," I said. "The opposite holds true as well: If a man's reed satisfies the wife, his reed of artistry will pale in comparison," I added. Like everyone who envies the talent of the miniaturist, Black, too, believed these lies and was heartened.

He said he wanted to see the last pages I'd illustrated. I seated him at my worktable, among the paints, inkwells, burnishing stones, brushes, pens and reed-cutting boards. Black was examining the double-leaf painting I was in the process of completing for the *Book of Festivities*, which portrayed Our Prince's circumcision ceremony, and I sat beside him on the red cushion whose warmth reminded me that my beautiful wife with her gorgeous thighs had been sitting here recently; indeed, I had used my reed pen to draw the sorrow of the unfortunate prisoners before Our Sultan, as my intelligent wife clung to the reed of my manhood.

The two-page scene I was painting depicted the deliverance of condemned and imprisoned debtors and their families by the grace of Our Sultan. I'd situated the Sultan on the corner of a carpet covered in bags full of silver coins, as I'd personally witnessed during such ceremonies. Behind Him, I'd located the Head Treasurer holding and reading out of the debt ledger. I'd portrayed the condemned debtors, chained to each other by the iron shackles around their necks, in their misery and pain with knit brows, long faces and some with teary eyes. I'd painted the lute players in shades of red with beatific faces as they accompanied the joyous prayers and poems that followed the Sultan's presentation of His benevolent gift: sparing the condemned from prison. To emphasize deliverance from the pain and embarrassment of debt—though I had no such plan at the outset—beside the last of the miserable prisoners, I'd included his wife, wearing a purple dress in the wretchedness of destitution, along with his longhaired daughter, sorrowful yet beautiful, clad in a crimson mantle. So that this man Black, with his furrowed brows, might understand how illustrating equaled love-of-life, I was going to explain why the chained gang of debtors was extended across two pages; I was going to tell him about the hidden logic of red within the picture; I was going to elucidate the things my wife and I had laughingly discussed while admiring the piece, such as how I'd lovingly colored—something the old masters never did—the dog resting off to the side in precisely the same hue as the Sultan's caftan of atlas silk, but he asked me a very rude, discourteous question:

Would I, perchance, have any idea where unfortunate Elegant Effendi might be?

What did he mean "unfortunate"! I didn't say that Elegant Effendi was a worthless plagiarist, a fool who did his gilding for money alone with nary a hint of inspiration. "Nay," I said, "I do not know."

Had I ever considered that the aggressive and fanatical followers of the preacher from Erzurum might've done Elegant Effendi harm?

I maintained my composure and refrained from responding that Elegant Effendi himself was no doubt one of their lot. "Nay," I said. "Why?"

The poverty, plague, immorality and scandal we are slave to in this city of Istanbul can only be attributed to our having distanced ourselves from the Islam of the time of Our Prophet, Apostle of God, to adopting new and vile customs and to allowing Frankish, European sensibilities to flourish in our midst. This is all that the Preacher Erzurumi is saying, but his enemies attempt to persuade the Sultan otherwise by claiming that the Erzurumis are attacking dervish lodges where music is played, and that they're defacing the tombs of saints. They know I don't share their animosity toward His Excellency Erzurumi, so they're making polite insinuations: "Are you the one who has taken care of our brother Elegant Effendi?"

It suddenly dawned on me that these rumors had long been spreading among the miniaturists. That group of uninspired, untalented incompetents was gleefully alleging that I was nothing but a beastly murderer. I felt like lowering an inkpot onto the Circassian skull of this buffoon Black purely because he took the slander of this jealous group of miniaturists seriously.

Black was examining my workshop, committing everything he saw to memory. He was intently observing my long paper scissors, ceramic bowls filled with yellow pigment, bowls of paint, the apple I occasionally nibbled as I worked, the coffeepot resting on the edge of the stove in the back, my diminutive coffee cups, the cushions, the light filtering through the half-opened window, the mirror I used to check the composition of a page, my shirts and, over there, my wife's red sash caught like a sin in the corner where she'd dropped it as she quickly quit the room upon hearing Black's knock at the front door.

Despite the fact that I've concealed my thoughts from him, I've surrendered the paintings I've made and this room I live in to his bold and aggressive gaze. I sense this hubris of mine will be a shock to you all, but I am the one who earns the most money, and therefore, I am the best of all miniaturists! Yes, God must've wanted the art of illumination to be ecstasy so He could demonstrate how the world itself is ecstasy to those who truly see.

CHAPTER 13

I AM CALLED "STORK"

At about the time of midday prayer I heard a knock at the door. It was Black from long ago, from our childhood. We embraced. He was chill and I invited him inside. I didn't even ask how he'd found his way to the house.

His Enishte must have sent him to question me about Elegant Effendi's absence and his whereabouts. Not only that, he also brought word from Master Osman. "Allow me to ask you a question," he said. "According to Master Osman, 'time' separates a true miniaturist from others: The time of the illustration." What were my thoughts? Listen closely.

Painting and Time

Long ago, as is common knowledge, the illustrators of our Islamic realm, including, for example, the old Arab masters, perceiving the world the way Frankish infidels do today, would regard everything and depict it from the level of a vagabond, mutt or clerk at work in his shop. Unaware of today's perspectival techniques, of which the Frankish masters haughtily boast, their world remained dull and limited, restricted to the simple perspective of the mutt or the shop clerk. Then a great event came to pass and our entire world of illustration changed. Let me begin here.

Three Stories on Painting and Time

ALIF

Three hundred fifty years ago, when Baghdad fell to the Mongols and was mercilessly plundered on a cold day in the month of Safar, Ibn Shakir was the most renowned and proficient calligrapher and scribe not only of the whole Arab world but of all Islamdom; despite his youth, he had transcribed twenty-two volumes, most of which were Korans and could be found in the world-famous libraries of Baghdad. Ibn Shakir believed these books would last until the end of the world, and, therefore, lived with a deep and infinite notion of time. He'd toiled heroically all through the night by flickering candlelight on the last of those legendary books, which are unknown to us today because in the span of a few days, they were one by one torn up, shredded, burned and tossed into the Tigris River by the soldiers of the Mongol Khan Hulagu. Just as the master Arab calligraphers, commited to the notion of the endless persistence of tradition and books, had for five centuries been in the habit of resting their eyes as a precaution against blindness by turning their backs to the rising sun and looking toward the western horizon, Ibn Shakir ascended the minaret of the Caliphet Mosque in the coolness of morning, and from the balcony where the muezzin called the faithful to prayer, witnessed all that would end a five-centuries-long tradition of scribal art. First, he saw Hulagu's pitiless soldiers enter Baghdad, and yet he remained where he was atop the minaret. He watched the plunder and destruction of the entire city, the slaughter of hundreds of thousands of people, the killing of the last of the Caliphs of Islam who'd ruled Baghdad for half a millennium, the rape of women, the burning of libraries and the destruction of tens of thousands of volumes as they were thrown into the Tigris. Two days later, amid the stench of corpses and cries of death, he watched the flowing waters of the Tigris, turned red from the ink bleeding out of the books, and he thought about how all those volumes he'd transcribed in beautiful script, those books that were now gone, hadn't in the least served to stop this horrifying massacre and devastation, and in turn, he swore never to write again. Furthermore, he was struck with the desire to express his pain and the disaster he'd witnessed through painting, which until that day, he'd belittled and deemed an affront to Allah; and so, making use of the paper he always carried with him, he depicted what he saw from the top of the minaret. We owe the happy miracle of the three-hundred-year renaissance in Islamic illustration following the Mongol invasion to that element which distinguished it from the artistry of pagans and Christians; that is, to the truly agonizing depiction of the world from an elevated Godlike position attained by drawing none other than a horizon line. We owe this renaissance to the horizon line, and also to Ibn Shakir's going north after the massacre he witnessed—in the direction the Mongol armies had come from—carrying with him his paintings and the ambition for illustration in his heart; in brief, we owe much to his learning the painting techniques of the Chinese masters. Thereby, it is evident that the notion of endless time that had rested in the hearts of Arab calligrapher-scribes for five hundred years would finally manifest itself not in writing, but in painting. The proof of this resides in the fact that the illustrations in manuscripts and volumes that had been torn apart and vanished have passed into other books and other volumes to survive forever in their revelation of Allah's worldly realm.

BA

Once upon a time, not so very long ago yet not so recently, everything imitated everything else, and thus, if not for aging and death, man would've never been the wiser about the passage of time. Yes, when the worldly realm was repeatedly presented through the same stories and pictures, as if time did not flow, Fahir Shah's small army routed Selahattin Khan's soldiers—as Salim of Samarkand's concise *History* attests. After the victorious Fahir Shah captured Selahattin Khan and tortured him to death, his first task in asserting his sovereignty, according to custom, was to visit the library and the harem of the vanquished khan. In the library, the late Selahattin Khan's experienced binder pulled apart the dead shah's books, and rearranging the pages, began to assemble new volumes. His calligraphers replaced the epithet of "Always Victorious Selahattin Khan" with that of "Victorious Fahir Shah" and his miniaturists set about replacing the late Selahattin Khan—masterfully portrayed on the most beautiful of manuscript pages—who was, as of that moment, starting to fade from people's memories, with the portrait of the younger Fahir Shah. Upon entering the harem, Fahir Shah had no difficulty in locating the most beautiful woman there, yet instead of forcing himself upon her, because he was a refined man versed in books and artistry, and resolving to win her heart, he engaged her in conversation. Consequently, Neriman Sultan, the late Selahattin Khan's belle of beauties, his teary-eyed wife, made but one request of Fahir Shah: that the illustration of her husband in a version of the romance *Leyla and Mejnun*, wherein Leyla was depicted as Neriman Sultan and Mejnun as Selahattin Khan, not be altered. In at least this one page, she maintained, the immortality that her husband had tried to attain over the years through books should not be denied. The victorious Fahir Shah bravely granted this simple request and his masters of the book left that one picture alone. Thereby, Neriman and Fahir immediately made love and within a short period, forgetting the horrors of the past, came to truly love each other. Still, Fahir Shah could not forget that picture in *Leyla and Mejnun*. Nay, it wasn't jealousy that made him uneasy or that his wife was portrayed with her old husband. What gnawed at him was this: Since he wasn't painted in the old legend in that splendid book, he wouldn't be able to join the ranks of the immortals with his wife. This worm of doubt ate at Fahir Shah for five years, and at the end of a blissful night of copious lovemaking with Neriman, candlestick in hand, he entered the library like a common thief, opened the volume of *Leyla and Mejnun*, and in place of the face of Neriman's late husband, drew his own. Like many khans who had a love for illustrating and painting, however, he was an amateur artist and couldn't portray himself very well. In the morning, when his librarian opened the book on a suspicion of tampering and beheld another figure in place of the late Selahattin Khan, next to Neriman-faced Leyla, rather than identifying it as Fahir Shah, he announced that it was Fahir Shah's archenemy, the young and handsome Abdullah Shah. This gossip provoked Fahir Shah's soldiers and emboldened Abdullah Shah, the young and aggressive new ruler of the neighboring country, who, subsequently, in his first campaign, defeated, captured and killed Fahir Shah, established his own sovereignty over his enemy's library and harem and became the new husband of the eternally beautiful Neriman Sultan.

DJIM

The miniaturists of Istanbul recount the legend of Tall Mehmet—known as Muhammad Khorasani in Persia—mostly as an example of long life and blindness. However, the legend of Tall Mehmet is essentially a parable of painting and time. The primary distinction of this master, who, having begun his apprenticeship at the age of nine, illustrated for more or less 110 years without going blind, was his lack of distinction. I'm not being witty here, but expressing my sincere admiration. Tall Mehmet drew everything, as everyone else did, in the style of the great masters of old, but even more so, and for this reason, he was the greatest of all masters. His humbleness and complete devotion to illustration and painting, which he deemed a service to Allah, set him above both the disputes within the book-arts workshops where he worked and the ambition to become head miniaturist, though he was of appropriate age and talent. As a miniaturist, for 110 years, he patiently rendered every trivial detail: grass drawn to fill up the edges of the page, thousands of leaves, curly wisping clouds, horse manes of short repetitive strokes, brick walls, never-ending wall ornamentation and the slant-eyed, delicate-chinned tens of thousands of faces that were each an imitation of one another. Tall Mehmet was quite content and reserved and he never presumed to distinguish himself or insisted about style or individuality. He considered whichever khan's or prince's workshop he happened to be working in at the time his house and regarded himself as but a fixture in that home. As khans and shahs strangled one another and miniaturists moved from city to city like the women of the harem to assemble under the auspices of new masters, the style of the new book-arts workshop would first be defined in the leaves Tall Mehmet drew, in his grass, in the curves of his rocks and in the hidden contours of his own patience. When he was eighty years old, people forgot that he was mortal and began to believe that he lived within the legends he illustrated. Perhaps for this reason, some maintained that he existed outside time and would never grow old and die. There were those who attributed his not going blind—despite living without a home of his own, sleeping in the rooms or tents which constituted miniaturists' workshops and spending most of his time staring at manuscript pages—to the miracle of time having ceased to flow for him. Some claimed that he was actually blind, and no longer had any need to see since he painted from memory.

At the age of 119, this legendary master who'd never married and had never even made love, met the flesh-and-blood ideal of the beautiful slant-eyed, sharp-chinned, moon-faced boy he'd depicted for a century: a part-Chinese part-Croatian sixteen-year-old apprentice in Shah Tahmasp's miniaturists' workshop, with whom quite abruptly and understandably, he fell in love. In order to seduce this boy-apprentice of unimaginable beauty, as a true lover would do, he schemed and joined in power struggles between miniaturists; he gave himself over to lying, deception and trickery. At first, the master miniaturist of Khorasan was invigorated by his attempts to catch up to the artistic fashions he'd successfully avoided for one hundred years, but this effort also divorced him from the eternal legendary days of old. Late one afternoon, staring dreamily at the beautiful apprentice before an open window, he caught cold in the icy Tabriz wind. The following day, during a fit of sneezing, he went completely blind. Two days later, he fell down the lofty stone workshop stairs and died.

"I've heard the name of Tall Mehmet of Khorasan, but I've never heard this legend," Black said.

He delicately offered this comment to show he knew the story was finished and his mind was occupied with what I'd related. I fell silent for a time so he could stare at me to his heart's content. Since it bothers me when my hands are not occupied, just after beginning the second story, I started to paint again, picking up where I'd left off when Black knocked on the door. My comely apprentice Mahmut, who always sat at my knee and mixed my paints, sharpened my reed pens and sometimes erased my errors, silently sat beside me, listening and staring; from within the house the sounds of my wife's movements could be heard.

"Aahaa," said Black, "the Sultan has arisen."

He stared at the painting with awe, and I pretended the reason for his awe was insignificant, but let me tell you candidly: Our Exalted Sultan appears seated in all two hundred of our circumcision ceremony pictures in the *Book of Festivities,* watching for fifty-two days the passing of the merchants, guilds, spectators, soldiers and prisoners from the window of the royal enclosure erected for the occasion. Only in one picture of mine is He shown on foot, tossing money from florin-filled pouches to the crowds in the square. My aim was to capture the surprise and excitement of the crowds punching, kicking and strangling one another as they scrambled to grab coins off the ground, their asses jutting toward the sky.

"If love is part of the subject of the painting, the work ought to be rendered with love," I said. "If there's pain involved, pain should issue from the painting. Yet the pain ought to emerge from the at first glance invisible yet discernible inner harmony of the picture, not from the figures in the illustration or from their tears. I didn't depict surprise, as it has been shown for centuries by hundreds of master miniaturists, as a figure with his index finger inserted into the circle of his mouth, but made the whole painting embody surprise. This, I accomplished by inviting the Sovereign to rise to His feet."

I was intrigued and bothered by how he scrutinized my possessions and illustrating tools, nay my whole life, looking for a clue; and then, I began to see my own house through his eyes.

You know those palace, hamam and castle pictures that were made in Tabriz and Shiraz for a time; so that the picture might replicate the piercing gaze of Exalted Allah, who sees and understands all, the miniaturist would depict the palace in cross-section as though having cut it in half with a huge, magical straight razor, and he'd paint all the interior details—which could otherwise never be seen from outside—down to the pots and pans, drinking glasses, wall ornamentation, curtains, caged parrots, the most private corners, and the pillows on which reclined a lovely maiden such as had never seen the light of day. Like a curious awestruck reader, Black was examining my paints, my papers, my books, my lovely assistant, the pages of a *Book of Costumes* and the collage album that I'd made for a Frankish traveler, scenes of fucking and other indecent pages I'd secretly dashed off for a pasha, my inkpots of variously colored glass, bronze and ceramic, my ivory penknives, my gold-stemmed brushes, and yes, the glances of my handsome apprentice.

"Unlike the old masters, I've seen a lot of battle, a lot," I said to fill the silence with my presence. "War machines, cannonballs, armies, corpses; it was I who embellished the ceilings of the tents of Our Sultan and our generals. After a military campaign, upon returning to Istanbul, it was I who recorded in pictures the scenes of battle that everyone would otherwise have forgotten, corpses sliced in two, the clash of opposing armies, the soldiers of the miserable infidels quaking before our cannon, the troops defending the crenellated towers of besieged castles, rebels being decapitated and the fury of horses attacking at full gallop. I commit everything I behold to memory: a new coffee grinder, a style of window grating that I've never seen before, a cannon, the trigger of a new style of Frankish rifle, who wore what color robe during a feast, who ate what, who placed his hand where and how . . ."

"What are the morals of the three stories you've told?" asked Black in a manner that summed everything up and ever so slightly called me to account.

"Alif," I said. "The first story with the minaret demonstrates that no matter how talented a miniaturist might be, it is time that makes a picture 'perfect.' 'Ba,' the second story with the harem and the library, reveals that the only way to escape time is through skill and illustrating. As for the third story, you proceed to tell me, then."

"Djim!" said Black confidently, "the third story about the one-hundred-and-nineteen-year-old miniaturist unites 'Alif' and 'Ba' to reveal how time ends for the one who forsakes the perfect life and perfect illuminating, leaving nothing but death. Indeed, this is what it demonstrates."

CHAPTER 14

I AM CALLED "OLIVE"

After the midday prayers, I was ever so swiftly yet pleasurably drawing the darling faces of boys when I heard a knock at the door. My hand jerked in surprise. I put down my brush. I carefully placed the workboard that was on my knees off to the side. Rushing like the wind, I said a prayer before opening the door. I won't withhold anything from you, because you, who can hear me from within this book, are much nearer to Allah than we in this filthy and miserable world of ours. Akbar Khan, the Emperor of Hindustan and the world's richest shah, is preparing what will one day become a legendary book. To complete his project, he sent word to the four corners of Islamdom inviting the world's greatest artists to join him. The men he'd sent to Istanbul visited me yesterday, inviting me to Hindustan. This time, I opened the door to find, in their place, my childhood acquaintance Black, about whom I'd forgotten entirely. Back then he wasn't able to keep our company, he was jealous of us. "Yes?"

He said he'd come to converse, to pay a friendly visit, to have a look at my illustrations. I welcomed him so he might see it all. I learned he'd just today visited Head Illuminator Master Osman and kissed his hand. The great master, he explained, had given him wise words to ponder: "A painter's quality becomes evident in his discussions of blindness and memory," he'd said. So let it be evident:

Blindness and Memory

Before the art of illumination there was blackness and afterward there will also be blackness. Through our colors, paints, art and love, we remember that Allah had commanded us to "See"! To know is to remember that you've seen. To see is to know without remembering. Thus, painting is remembering the blackness. The great masters, who shared a love of painting and perceived that color and sight arose from darkness, longed to return to Allah's blackness by means of color. Artists without memory neither remember Allah nor his blackness. All great masters, in their work, seek that profound void within color and outside time. Let me explain to you what it means to remember this darkness, which was revealed in Herat by the great masters of old.

Three Stories on Blindness and Memory

ALIF

In Lami'i Chelebi's Turkish translation of the Persian poet Jami's *Gifts of Intimacy*, which addresses the stories of the saints, it is written that in the bookmaker's workshop of Jihan Shah, the ruler of the Blacksheep nation, the renowned master Sheikh Ali Tabrizi had illustrated a magnificent version of *Hüsrev and Shirin*. According to what I've heard, in this legendary manuscript, which took eleven years to complete, the master of master miniaturists, Sheikh Ali, displayed such talent and skill and painted such wonderful pictures that only the greatest of the old masters, Bihzad, could have matched him. Even before the illuminated manuscript was half finished, Jihan Shah knew that he would soon possess a spectacular book without equal in all the world. He thus lived in fear and jealousy of young Tall Hasan, the ruler of the Whitesheep nation, and declared him his archenemy. Moreover, Jihan Shah quickly sensed that though his prestige would grow immensely after the book was completed, an even better version of the manuscript could be made for Tall Hasan. Being one of those truly jealous men who poisoned his own contentment with the thought "What if others come to know such bliss?" Jihan Shah sensed at once that if the virtuoso miniaturist made another copy, or even a better version, it would be for his archenemy Tall Hasan. Thus, in order to prevent anyone besides himself from owning this magnificent book, Jihan Shah decided to have the master miniaturist Sheikh Ali killed after he'd completed the book. But a good-hearted Circassian beauty in his harem advised him that blinding the master miniaturist would suffice. Jihan Shah forthwith adopted this clever idea, which he passed on to his circle of sycophants, until it ultimately reached the ears of Sheikh Ali. Even so, Sheikh Ali didn't leave the book half finished and flee Tabriz as other, mediocre illustrators might've done. He didn't resort to games like slowing down the progress of the manuscript or making inferior illustrations so it wouldn't be "perfect" and thereby forestalling his imminent blinding. Indeed, he worked with even more ardor and conviction. In the house where he lived alone, he'd begin working after the morning prayers and continue illustrating the same horses, cypresses, lovers, dragons and handsome princes by candlelight in the middle of the night again and again until bitter tears streamed from his eyes. Much of the time, he'd gaze for days at an illustration by one of the great old masters of Herat as he made an exact copy on another sheet. In the end, he completed the book for Jihan Shah the Blacksheep, and as the master miniaturist had expected, he was at first praised and showered with gold pieces, before being blinded with a sharp plume needle used to affix turban plumes. Before his pain had even subsided, Sheikh Ali left Herat and went to join Tall Hasan the Whitesheep. "Yes, indeed, I am blind," he explained to Tall Hasan, "yet I remember each of the splendors of the manuscript I've illuminated for the last eleven years, down to each mark of the pen and each stroke of the brush, and my hand can draw it again from memory. My Excellency, I could illustrate the greatest manuscript of all time for you. Since my eyes will no longer be distracted by the filth of this world, I'll be able to depict all the glories of Allah from memory, in their purest form." Tall Hasan believed the great master miniaturist; and the master miniaturist, keeping his promise, illustrated from memory the most magnificent of books for the ruler of the Whitesheep. Everyone knew the spiritual power provided by the new book was what lay behind Tall Hasan's subsequent defeat of the Blacksheep and the victorious Khan's execution of Jihan Shah during a raid near Bingöl. This magnificent book, along with the one Sheikh Ali Tabrizi made for the late Jihan Shah, entered Our Sultan's treasury in Istanbul when the ever-victorious Tall Hasan was defeated at the Battle of Otlukbeli by Sultan Mehmet Khan the Conqueror, may he rest in peace. Those who can truly see, know.

BA

Since the Denizen of Paradise, Sultan Süleyman Khan the Lawgiver, favored calligraphers over illustrators, unfortunate miniaturists of the day would recount the present story as an example of how illustrating surpasses calligraphy. However, as anyone who pays close attention will realize, this tale is actually about blindness and memory. After the death of Tamerlane, Ruler of the World, his sons and grandchildren set to attacking and mercilessly battling one another. In the event that one of them succeeded in conquering another's city, his first action was to mint his own coins and have a sermon read at the mosque. His second act as victor was to pull apart the books that had come into his possession; a new dedication would be written, boasting of the conqueror as the new "ruler of the world," a new colophon added, and it would all be bound together again so that those who laid eyes on the conqueror's book would believe that he truly was a world ruler. When Abdüllatif, the son of Tamerlane's grandson Uluğ Bey, captured Herat, he mobilized his miniaturists, calligraphers and binders with such haste, and so pressured them to make a book in honor of his father, a connoisseur of book arts, that as volumes were in the midst of being unbound and the scripted pages destroyed and burned, the corresponding pictures became mixed up. Since it did not befit the honor of Uluğ Bey for his son to arrange and bind albums without a care for which picture belonged to which story, he assembled all the miniaturists in Herat and requested that they recount the stories so as to put the illustrations in proper order. From each miniaturist's mouth, however, came a different account, and so the correct order of the plates was confused all the more. Thereupon, the oldest surviving head miniaturist was sought out. He was a man who'd extinguished the light of his eyes in painstaking labor on the books of all the shahs and princes who'd ruled over Herat for the last fifty-four years. A great commotion ensued when the men realized that the old master now peering at the pictures was indeed blind. Some laughed. The elderly master requested that an intelligent boy, who had not yet reached the age of seven and who couldn't read or write, be brought forward. Such a child was found and taken to him. The old miniaturist placed a number of illustrations before him. "Describe what you see," he instructed. As the boy described the pictures, the old miniaturist, raising his blind eyes to the sky, listened carefully and responded: "Alexander cradling the dying Darius from Firdusi's *Book of Kings* . . . the account of the teacher who falls in love with his handsome student from Sadi's *Rosegarden* . . . the contest of doctors from Nizami's *Treasury of Secrets* . . ." The other miniaturists, vexed by their elderly and blind colleague, said, "We could've told you that as well. These are the best-known scenes from the most famous stories." In turn, the aged and blind miniaturist placed the most difficult illustrations before the child and again listened intently. "Hürmüz poisoning the calligraphers one by one from Firdusi's *Book of Kings*," he said, again facing the sky. "A cheap rendition of the terrible account of the cuckold who catches his wife and her lover in a pear tree, from Rumi's *Masnawi*," he said. In this fashion, relying on the boy's descriptions, he identified all of the pictures, none of which he could see, and thereby succeeded in having the books properly bound together again. When Uluğ Bey entered Herat with his army, he asked the old miniaturist by what secret he, a blind man, could identify those stories that other master illustrators couldn't determine even by looking at them. "It isn't, as one might assume, that my memory compensates for my blindness," replied the old illustrator. "I have never forgotten that stories are recollected not only through images, but through words as well." Uluğ Bey responded that his own miniaturists knew those words and stories, but still couldn't order the pictures. "Because," said the old miniaturist, "they think quite well when it comes to painting, which is their skill or their art, but they don't comprehend that the old masters made these pictures out of the memories of Allah Himself." Uluğ Bey asked how a child could know such things. "The child doesn't know," said the old miniaturist. "But I, an elderly and blind miniaturist, know that Allah created this worldly realm the way an intelligent seven-year-old boy would want to see it; what's more, Allah created this earthly realm so that, above all, it might be seen. Afterward, He provided us with words so we might share and discuss with one another what we've seen. We mistakenly assumed that these stories arose out of words and that illustrations were painted in service of these stories. Quite to the contrary, painting is the act of seeking out Allah's memories and seeing the world as He sees the world."

DJIM

Two hundred fifty years ago, Arab miniaturists were in the custom of staring at the western horizon at daybreak to alleviate the understandable and eternal anxieties about going blind shared by all miniaturists; likewise, a century later in Shiraz, many illustrators would eat walnuts mashed with rose petals on an empty stomach in the mornings. Again, in the same era, the elder miniaturists of Isfahan who believed sunlight was responsible for the blindness to which they succumbed one by one, as if to the plague, would work in a half-dark corner of the room, and most often by candlelight, to prevent direct sunlight from striking their worktables. At day's end, in the workshops of the Uzbek artists of Bukhara, master miniaturists would wash their eyes with water blessed by sheikhs. But of all of these precautions, the purest approach to blindness was discovered in Herat by the miniaturist Seyyit Mirek, mentor to the great master Bihzad. According to master miniaturist Mirek, blindness wasn't a scourge, but rather the crowning reward bestowed by Allah upon the illuminator who had devoted an entire life to His glories; for illustrating was the miniaturist's search for Allah's vision of the earthly realm, and this unique perspective could only be attained through recollection after blindness descended, only after a lifetime of hard work and only after the miniaturist's eyes tired and he had expended himself. Thus, Allah's vision of His world only becomes manifest through the memory of blind miniaturists. When this image comes to the aging miniaturist, that is, when he sees the world as Allah sees it through the darkness of memory and blindness, the illustrator will have spent his lifetime training his hand so it might transfer this splendid revelation to the page. According to the historian Mirza Muhammet Haydar Duglat, who wrote extensively about the legends of Herat miniaturists, the master Seyyit Mirek, in his explication of the aforementioned notion of painting, used the example of the illustrator who wanted to draw a horse. He reasoned that even the most untalented painter—one whose head is empty like those of today's Venetian painters—who draws the picture of a horse while looking at a horse will still make the image from memory; because, you see, it is impossible, at one and the same time, to look at the horse and at the page upon which the horse's image appears. First, the illustrator looks at the horse, then he quickly transfers whatever rests in his mind to the page. In the interim, even if only a wink in time, what the artist represents on the page is not the horse he sees, but the memory of the horse he has just seen. Proof that for even the most miserable illustrator, a picture is possible only through memory. The logical extension of this concept, which regards the active worklife of a miniaturist as but preparation for both the resulting bliss of blindness and blind memory, is that the masters of Herat regarded the illustrations they made for bibliophile shahs and princes as training for the hand—as an exercise. They accepted the work, the endless drawing and staring at pages by candlelight for days without break, as the pleasurable labor that delivered the miniaturist to blindness. Throughout his whole life, the master miniaturist Mirek constantly sought out the most appropriate moment for this most glorious of approaching eventualities, either by purposely hurrying blindness through the painstaking depiction of trees and all their leaves on fingernails, grains of rice and even on strands of hair, or by cautiously delaying the imminent darkness by the effortless drawing of pleasant, sunfilled gardens. When he was seventy, in order to reward this great master,

Sultan Hüseyin Baykara allowed him to enter the treasury containing thousands of manuscript plates that the Sultan had collected and secured under lock and key. There, in the treasury that also contained weapons, gold and bolt upon bolt of silk and velvet cloth, by the candlelight of golden candelabra, Master Mirek stared at the magnificent leaves of those books, each a legend in its own right, made by the old masters of Herat. And after three days and nights of continuous scrutiny, the great master went blind. He accepted his condition with maturity and resignation, the way one might greet the Angels of Allah, and he never spoke or painted again. Mirza Muhammet Haydar Duglat, the author of the *History of Rashid,* ascribed this turn of events as follows: "A miniaturist united with the vision and landscape of Allah's immortal time can never return to the manuscript pages meant for ordinary mortals"; and he adds, "Wherever the blind miniaturist's memories reach Allah there reigns an absolute silence, a blessed darkness and the infinity of a blank page."

Certainly it was less out of desire to hear my answer to Master Osman's question on blindness and memory than to put himself at ease that Black asked me the question while he pored over my possessions, my room and my pictures. Yet again, I was pleased to see that the stories I recounted affected him. "Blindness is a realm of bliss from which the Devil and guilt are barred," I said to him.

"In Tabriz," said Black, "under Master Mirek's influence, some of the miniaturists of the old style still look upon blindness as the greatest virtue of Allah's grace, and they're embarrassed about growing old but not blind. Even today, fearing that others will consider this proof of a lack of talent and skill, they pretend to be blind. As a result of this moral conviction which bears the influence of Jemalettin of Kazvin, some of them sit for weeks in the darkness amid mirrors, in the dim light of an oil lamp, without eating or drinking and stare at illustrated pages painted by the old masters of Herat in order to learn how to perceive the world like a blind man despite not truly being blind."

Somebody knocked. I opened the door to find a handsome apprentice from the workshop whose lovely almond eyes were opened wide. He said that the body of our brother, the gilder Elegant Effendi, had been discovered in an abandoned well and that his funeral procession would commence at the Mihrimah Mosque during the afternoon prayer. He then ran off to deliver the news to others. Allah, may you protect us all.

CHAPTER 15

I AM ESTHER

Tell me then, does love make one a fool or do only fools fall in love? I've been a clothes peddler and matchmaker for years, and I don't have the slightest clue. How it'd thrill me to become acquainted with men—or couples—who grew more intelligent and became more cunning and devious as they fell deeper in love. I do know this much though: If a man resorts to wiles, guile and petty deceptions, it means he's nowhere near being in love. As for Black Effendi, it's obvious that he's already lost his composure—when he even talks about Shekure he loses all self-control.

At the bazaar, I fed him by rote all the well-rehearsed refrains that I tell everyone: Shekure is always thinking of him, she asked me about his response to her letter, I'd never seen her like this and so on. He gave me such a look that I pitied him. He told me to take the letter to Shekure straightaway. Every idiot assumes there's a pressing circumstance about his love that necessitates particular haste, and thereby lays bare the intensity of his love, unwittingly putting a weapon into the hands of his beloved. If his lover is smart, she'll postpone the answer. The moral: Haste delays the fruits of love.

Had lovesick Black known that I first took a detour while carrying the letter he'd charged me to deliver "posthaste," he'd thank me. In the market square, I nearly froze to death waiting for him. After he left, I thought I'd visit one of my "daughters" to warm up. I call the maidens whose letters I've delivered, the ones I've married off through the sweat of my brow, my "daughters." This ugly maiden of mine was so thankful and beholden to me that at my every visit, beyond waiting on me hand and foot, flitting about like a moth, she'd press a few silver coins into my palm. Now she was pregnant and in good humor. She put linden tea on the boil. I savored each sip. When she left me alone, I counted the coins Black Effendi had given me. Twenty silver pieces.

I set out on my way again. I passed through side streets and through ominous alleyways that were frozen, muddy and nearly impassable. As I was knocking on the door, mirth took hold of me and I began to shout.

"The clothier is here! Clothierrr!" I said. "Come and see the best of my ruffled muslin fit for a sultan. Come get my stunning shawls from Kashmir, my Bursa velvet sash cloth, my superb silk-edged Egyptian shirt cloth, my embroidered muslin tablecloths, my mattress and bedsheets, and my colorful handkerchiefs. Clothierrr!"

The door opened. I entered. As always, the house smelled of bedding, sleep, frying oil and humidity, that terrible smell peculiar to aging bachelors.

"Old hag," he said. "Why are you shouting?"

I silently removed the letter and handed it to him. In the half-lit room, he stealthily and quietly approached me and snatched it from my hand. He passed into the next room where an oil lamp always burned. I waited at the threshold.

"Isn't your dear father home?"

He didn't answer. He'd lost himself in the letter. I left him alone so he could read. He stood behind the lamp, and I couldn't see his face. After finishing the letter, he read it anew.

"Yes," I said, "and what has he written?"

Hasan read:

My Dearest Shekure, as I too have for years now sustained myself through my dreams of one single person, I respectfully understand your waiting for your husband without considering another. What else could one expect from a woman of your stature besides honesty and virtue? [Hasan cackled!] *My coming to visit your father for the sake of painting, however, does not amount to harassing you. This would never even cross my mind. I make no claim at having received a sign from you or any other encouragement. When your face appeared to me at the window like divine light, I considered it nothing but an act of God's grace. The pleasure of seeing your face is all I need.* ["He took that from Nizami," Hasan interrupted, annoyed.] *But you ask me to keep my distance; tell me then, are you an angel that approaching you should be so terrifying? Listen to what I have to say, listen: I used to try to sleep watching the moonlight fall onto the naked mountains from remote and godforsaken caravansaries where nobody but a desperate han keeper and a few thugs fleeing the gallows lodged, and there, in the middle of the night, listening to the howling of wolves even lonelier and more unfortunate than myself, I used to think that one day you would suddenly appear to me, just as you did at the window.*

Read closely: Now that I've returned to your father for the sake of the book, you've sent back the picture I made in my childhood. I know this is not a sign of your death but a sign that I've found you again. I saw one of your children, Orhan. That poor fatherless boy. One day I will become his father!

"God protect him, he's written well," I said, "this one has become quite the poet."

"'Are you an angel that approaching you should be so terrifying?'" he repeated. "He stole that line from Ibn Zerhani. I could do better." He took his own letter out of his pocket. "Take this and deliver it to Shekure."

For the first time, accepting money along with the letters disturbed me. I felt something like disgust toward this man and his mad obsession, his unrequited love. Hasan, as if to confirm my hunch, for the first time in a long while set aside his good etiquette and said quite rudely:

"Tell her that if we so desire, we'll force her back here under pressure of the judge."

"You really want me to say that?"

Silence. "Nay," he said. The light from the oil lamp illuminated his face, allowing me to see him lower his head like a guilty child. It's because I know this side of Hasan's character as well that I have some respect for his feelings and deliver his letters. It's not only for the money, as you might think.

I was leaving the house, and he stopped me at the door.

"Do you let Shekure know how much I love her?" he asked me excitedly and foolishly.

"Don't you tell her so in your letters?"

"Tell me how I might convince her and her father? How might I persuade them?"

"By being a good person," I said and walked to the door.

"At this age, it's too late . . ." he said with sincere anguish.

"You've begun to earn a lot of money, Customs Officer Hasan. This makes one a good person . . ." I said and fled.

The house was so dark and melancholy that the air outside seemed warmer. The sunlight hit my face. I wished for Shekure's happiness. But I also felt something for that poor man in that damp, chilly and dark house. On a whim, I turned into the Spice Market in Laleli thinking the smells of cinnamon, saffron and pepper would restore my spirits. I was mistaken.

At Shekure's house, after she took up the letters, she immediately asked after Black. I told her that the fire of love had mercilessly engulfed his entire being. This news pleased her.

"Even lonely spinsters busy with their knitting are discussing why Elegant Effendi might've been killed," I said later, changing the subject.

"Hayriye, make some halva as a present of condolence and take it over to Kalbiye, poor Elegant Effendi's widow," said Shekure.

"All the Erzurumis and quite a crowd of others will be attending his funeral service," I said. "His relatives swear they'll avenge his spilt blood."

Shekure had already begun to read Black's letter. I looked into her face intently and angrily. This woman was probably such a fox that she could control how her passions were reflected in her face. As she read I sensed that my silence pleased her, that she regarded it as my approval of the special import she gave to Black's letter. Shekure finished the letter and smiled at me; to meet with her satisfaction, I felt forced to ask, "What has he written?"

"Just as in his childhood . . . He's in love with me."

"What are your thoughts?"

"I'm a married woman. I'm waiting for my husband."

Contrary to your expectations, the fact that she'd lie to me after asking me to get involved in her affairs didn't anger me. Actually, this comment relieved me. If more of the young maidens and women I've carried letters for and advised in the ways of the world attended to details the way Shekure did, they would've lessened the work for us both by half. More importantly, they would've ended up in better marriages.

"What does the other one write?" I asked anyway.

"I don't intend to read Hasan's letter right now," she answered. "Does Hasan know that Black's returned to Istanbul?"

"He doesn't even know he exists."

"Do you speak with Hasan?" she asked, opening wide her beautiful black eyes.

"As you've requested."

"Yes?"

"He's in agony. He's deeply in love with you. Even if your heart belongs to another, it'll be difficult ever to be free of him now. By accepting his letters you've greatly encouraged him. Be wary of him, however. For not only does he want to make you return there, but by establishing that his older brother has died, he's preparing to marry you." I smiled to soften the

I Am Esther 85

weight of these words and so as not to be reduced to being that malcontent's mouthpiece.

"What's the other one say, then?" she asked, but did she herself know whom she was inquiring after?

"The miniaturist?"

"My mind's all ajumble," she said suddenly, perhaps afraid of her own thoughts. "It seems that matters will become even more confused. My father's growing older. What'll become of us, of these fatherless children? I sense an evil approaching, that the Devil is preparing some mischief for us. Esther, tell me something that will hearten me."

"Don't you fret in the slightest, my dearest Shekure," I said as emotion welled up within me. "You're truly intelligent, you're very beautiful. One day you'll sleep in the same bed with your handsome husband, you'll cuddle with him, and having forgotten all your worries, you'll be happy. I can read this in your eyes."

Such affection rose within me that my eyes filled with tears.

"Fine, but which one will become my husband?"

"Isn't that wise heart of yours giving you an answer?"

"It's because I don't understand what my heart is saying that I'm dispirited."

For a moment it occurred to me that Shekure didn't trust me at all, that she was masterfully concealing her distrust in order to learn what I knew, that she was trying to arouse my pity. When I saw she wouldn't be writing a response to the letters at present, I grabbed my sack, entered the courtyard and slipped away—but not before saying something I told all my maids, even those who were cross-eyed:

"Fear not, my dear, if you keep those beautiful eyes of yours peeled, no misfortune, no misfortune at all will befall you."

CHAPTER 16

I, SHEKURE

If truth be told, it used to be that each time Esther the clothier paid a visit, I'd fantasize that a man stricken with love would finally be roused to write a letter that could stir the heart of an intelligent woman like myself—beautiful, well-bred and widowed, yet with her honor still intact—and set it pounding. And to discover that the letter was from one of the usual suitors, would, at the very least, fortify my resolve and forbearance to await my husband's return. But these days, every time Esther leaves, I become confused and feel all the more wretched.

I listened to the sounds of my world. From the kitchen came the bubbling sound of boiling water and the smell of lemons and onions. Hayriye was boiling zucchini. Shevket and Orhan were frolicking and playing "swordsman" in the courtyard beneath the pomegranate tree, I heard their shouts. My father was sitting silently in the next room. I opened and read Hasan's letter and was reassured that there was no cause for alarm. Still, I grew a little more frightened of him, and congratulated myself for withstanding his efforts to make love to me when we shared the same house. Next, I read Black's letter, holding it gently as if it were some delicate and sensitive bird, and my thoughts became muddled. I didn't read the letters again. The sun broke through the clouds and it occurred to me that if I'd entered Hasan's bedchamber one night and made love with him, no one, except Allah, would've been the wiser. He did resemble my missing husband; it'd be the same thing. Sometimes a strange thought like this entered my head. As the sun quickly warmed me, I could feel my body: my skin, my neck, even my nipples. Orhan slipped inside as the sunlight struck me through the open door.

"Mama, what are you reading?" he said.

All right then, remember how I said that I didn't reread the letters Esther had just delivered? I lied. I was in the midst of reading them again. This time, I truly did fold them up and tuck them away in my blouse.

"Come here, you, onto my lap," I said to Orhan. He did so. "Oh my, you're so heavy. May God protect you, you've gotten quite big," I said and kissed him. "You're as cold as ice . . ."

"You're so warm, Mama," he interrupted, leaning back onto my bosom.

We were leaning tight against each other, enjoying sitting that way in silence. I smelled the nape of his neck and kissed him. I hugged him even more tightly. We were still.

"I'm feeling ticklish," he said later.

"Tell me then," I said in my serious voice. "If the Sultan of the Jinns came and said he'd grant you a wish, what would you want most of all?"

"I'd want Shevket to go away."

"What besides? Would you want to have a father?"

"No, when I grow up I'm going to marry you myself."

It wasn't aging, losing one's beauty or even being bereft of husband and money that was the worst of all calamities, what was truly horrible was not having anyone to be jealous of you. I lowered Orhan's warming body from my lap. Thinking that a wicked woman like myself ought to wed someone with a good soul, I went up to see my father.

"His Excellency Our Sultan will reward you after seeing for Himself that His book has been completed," I said. "You'll go to Venice again."

"I cannot be certain," said my father. "This murder has distressed me. Our enemies are apparently quite powerful."

"I know, as well, that my own situation has emboldened them, giving rise to misunderstandings and unfounded hopes."

"How do you mean?"

"I ought to be wed as soon as possible."

"What?" said my father. "To whom? But you are married. Where did this notion come from?" he asked. "Who's asked for your hand? Even if we were to find a reasonable and appealing prospect," said my reasonable father, "I doubt we'd be able to take him, not like that, you understand." He summed up my unfortunate situation as follows: "You're aware that there are weighty and complicated matters we must settle before you can marry again." After a protracted silence, he added, "Is it that you want to leave me, my dear daughter?"

"Last night I dreamed that my husband had died," I said. I didn't cry the way a woman who'd actually seen such a dream would have.

"Like those who know how to read a picture, one should know how to read a dream."

"Would you consider it appropriate for me to describe my dream?"

There was a pause: We smiled at each other, quickly inferring—as intelligent people do—all possible conclusions from the matter at hand.

"By interpreting your dream, I might be convinced of his death, yet your father-in-law, your brother-in-law and the judge, who is obligated to listen to them, will demand more proof."

"Two years have passed since I returned here with the children and my in-laws haven't been able to force me back . . ."

"Because they very well realize that they have their own misdeeds to answer for," said my father. "This doesn't mean that they'll be willing to let you petition for a divorce."

"If we were followers of the Maliki or the Hanbeli sects," I said, "the judge, acknowledging that four years have passed, would grant me a divorce in addition to securing a support allowance for me. But since we are, many thanks to Allah, Hanefis, this option is not open to us."

"Don't mention the Üsküdar judge's Shafiite stand-in to me. That's not a sound venture."

"All the women of Istanbul whose husbands are missing at the front go to him with their witnesses to get divorced. Since he's a Shafiite, he simply asks, 'Is your husband missing?' 'How long has he been missing?' 'Are you having trouble making ends meet?' 'Are these your witnesses?' and immediately grants the divorce."

"My dear Shekure, who's planted such schemes in your head?" he said. "Who's stripped you of your reason?"

"After I'm divorced once and for all, if there is a man who can truly strip me of my reason, you will, of course, tell me who that might be and I shall never question your decision about my husband."

My shrewd father, realizing that his daughter was as shrewd as he, began to blink. My father would blink rapidly like this for three reasons: 1. because he was in a tight spot and his mind was racing to find a clever way out; 2. because he was on the verge of tears of hopelessness and sorrow; 3. because he was in a tight spot, cunningly combining reasons 1 and 2 to give the impression that he might soon cry out of sorrow.

"Are you taking the children and abandoning your old father? Do you realize that on account of our book"—yes, he said "our book"—"I was afraid of being murdered, but now that you want to take the children and leave, I welcome death."

"My dear father, wasn't it you who always said that only a divorce could save me from that good-for-nothing brother-in-law?"

"I don't want you to abandon me. One day your husband might return. Even if he doesn't, there's no harm in your being married—so long as you live in this house with your father."

"I want nothing more than to live in this house with you."

"Darling, weren't you just now saying that you wanted to get married as soon as possible?"

This is the dead end you reach by arguing with your father: In due course, you too will be convinced that you're in the wrong.

"I was," I said, gazing at the ground in front of me. Then, holding back my tears and encouraged by the truth of what came to mind, I said:

"All right then, shall I never be married again?"

"There's a special place in my heart for the son-in-law who won't take you far from me. Who is your suitor, would he be willing to live here with us in this house?"

I fell silent. We both knew, of course, that my father would never respect a son-in-law willing to live here together with us, and would gradually demean and stifle him. And as Father's underhanded and expert

I, Shekure 89

belittling of the man who'd moved in with his bride's family proceeded I would soon want to be that wife no more.

"Without a father's approval, in your situation, you know that getting married is practically impossible, don't you? I don't want you to get married, and I refuse to grant you permission to do so—"

"I don't want to get married, I want a divorce."

"—because some thoughtless beast of a man who cares about nothing but his own concerns might hurt you. You know how much I love you, don't you, my dear Shekure? Besides, we must finish this book."

I said nothing. For if I were to speak—prompted by the Devil, who was aware of my anger—I would tell my father right to his face that I knew he slept with Hayriye at night. But would it befit a woman like me to admit that she knew that her elderly father slept with a slave girl?

"Who is it that wants to marry you?"

I gazed at the ground before me and was quiet, not out of embarrassment, but out of anger. And recognizing the extent of my anger, but not being able to respond in some manner made me even more furious. At that juncture, I imagined my father and Hayriye in bed in that ridiculous and disgusting position. I was on the verge of tears when I said:

"There's zucchini on the stove, I don't want it to burn."

I crossed to the room beside the staircase, the one with the always-closed window that looked out onto the well. In the dark, quickly locating the roll-up mattress with my hands, I spread it open and lay down: Ah, what a wonderful feeling, to lie down and fall asleep in a fit of tears like a child who's been wrongly chastised! And what agony it is to know that I'm the only person in the world who likes me. As I cry in my solitude, only you, who hear my sobs and moans, can come to my aid.

A while later, I found that Orhan had stretched out upon my bed. He placed his head between my breasts. I saw that he was sighing, and crying too. Pulling him close to me, I held him.

"Don't cry, Mother," he said later. "Father will return from the war."

"How do you know?"

He didn't answer. I loved him so, and pressed him to my bosom so that I forgot my own worries entirely. Before I cuddle up with my fine-boned, delicate Orhan and fall asleep, let me confess my only pressing concern: I regret having just now told you, out of spite, about the matter between my father and Hayriye. No, I wasn't lying, but I'm still so embarrassed that it would be best if you forgot about it. Pretend I never mentioned anything, as if my father and Hayriye weren't thus involved, please?

CHAPTER 17

I AM YOUR BELOVED UNCLE

Alas, it's difficult having a daughter, difficult. As she wept in the next room, I could hear her sobs, but I could do nothing but look at the pages of the book I held in my hands. On a page of the volume I was trying to read, the *Book of the Apocalypse,* it was written that three days after death, one's soul, receiving permission from Allah, visited the body it formerly inhabited. Upon beholding the piteous state of its body, bloodied, decomposing and oozing, as it rested in the grave, the soul would sorrowfully, tearfully and mournfully grieve, "Lo, my miserable mortal coil, my dear wretched old body." At once, I thought of Elegant Effendi's bitter end at the bottom of the well, and how upset his soul naturally must have been upon visiting, and finding his body not at his grave, but in the well.

When Shekure's sobs died down, I put aside the book on death. I donned an extra woolen undershirt, wound my thick wool sash tightly around my waist so as to warm my midriff, pulled on my shalwar pants lined with rabbit fur and, as I was leaving the house, turned to discover Shevket in the doorway.

"Where are you going, Grandfather?"

"You get back inside. To the funeral."

I passed through snow-covered streets, between poor rotting houses leaning this way and that way, barely able to stand, and through fire-ravaged neighborhoods. I walked for a long time, taking the cautious steps of an aging man trying not to slip and fall on the ice. I passed through out-of-the-way neighborhoods and gardens and fields. I walked by shops that dealt in carriages and wheels and passed iron smiths, saddlers, harness makers and farriers on my way toward the walls of the city.

I'm not sure why they decided to start the funeral procession all the way at the Mihrimah Mosque near the city's Edirne Gate. At the mosque, I embraced the big-headed and bewildered brothers of the deceased, who looked angry and obstinate. We miniaturists and calligraphers embraced each other and wept. As I was performing my prayers within a leaden fog that had suddenly descended and swallowed everything, my gaze fell on the coffin resting atop the mosque's stone funeral block, and I felt such anger toward the miscreant who'd committed this crime, believe me, even the Allahümme Barik prayer became muddled in my mind.

After the prayers, while the congregation shouldered the coffin, I was still among all the miniaturists and calligraphers. Stork and I had forgotten that on some nights, when we sat in the dim light of oil lamps working until morning on my book, he'd tried to convince me of the inferiority of Elegant Effendi's gilding work and of the lack of balance in his use of colors—he colored everything navy blue so it would look richer! We'd both forgotten that I'd actually given him credence, by allowing "But no one else is qualified to do this work," and we embraced each other anyway, sobbing once more. Later, Olive gave me a friendly and respectful look before hugging me—a man who knows how to embrace is a good man—and these gestures so pleased me that I was reminded how of all the workshop artists, he was the one who most believed in my book.

On the stairs of the courtyard gate I found myself beside Head Illuminator Master Osman. We were both at a loss for words, a strange and tense moment. One of the deceased's brothers began to cry and sob, and someone pompously shouted, "God is great."

"To which cemetery?" Master Osman asked me for the sake of asking something.

To respond "I don't know" seemed hostile for some reason. Flustered, and without thinking, I asked the same question of the man standing next to me on the stairs, "To which cemetery? The one by the Edirne Gate?"

"Eyüp," said an ill-tempered, bearded and young dolt.

"Eyüp," I said turning to the master, but he'd heard what the ill-tempered dolt had said anyway. Then, he looked at me as if to say, "I understand" in a way that let me know he didn't want our encounter to last a moment longer than it already had.

Without mentioning my influence on Our Sultan's growing interest in Frankish styles of painting, Master Osman was of course annoyed that Our Sultan had ordered me to oversee the writing out, embellishment and illustration of the illuminated manuscript, which I've described as "secret." On one occasion, the Sultan forced the great Master Osman to copy a portrait of His Highness, which had been commissioned from a Venetian. I know Master Osman holds me responsible for having to imitate that painter, for having to make that strange painting, which he did with disgust, referring to the experience as "torture." His wrath was justified.

Standing in the middle of the staircase for a while, I looked at the sky. When I was convinced that I'd been left quite behind, I continued down the icy stairs. I'd barely descended—ever so slowly—two steps when a man took me by the arm and embraced me: Black.

"The air is freezing," he said. "You must be cold."

I hadn't the slightest doubt that this was the one who'd muddled Shekure's mind. The self-confidence with which he took my arm was proof enough. There was something in his demeanor that announced, "I've worked for twelve years and have truly grown up." When we came to the bottom of the stairs, I told him that I'd expect an account later of what he'd learned at the workshop.

"You go ahead, my child," I said. "Go ahead and catch up to the congregation."

He was taken aback, but didn't let on. The way he let go of my arm with reservation and walked ahead of me pleased me, even. If I gave Shekure to him, would he agree to live in the same house with us?

We'd left the city through the Edirne Gate. I saw the coffin on the verge of disappearing into the fog along with the crowd of illustrators, calligraphers and apprentices shouldering it as they quickly descended the hill toward the Golden Horn. They were walking so fast, they'd already traveled half of the muddy road that led down the snow-covered valley to Eyüp. In the silent fog, off to the left, the chimney of the Hanım Sultan Charity candleworks shop happily piped up its smoke. Under the shadow of the walls, there were tanneries and the bustling slaughterhouses that served the Greek butchers of Eyüp. The smell of offal coming from these places had wafted over the valley, which extended to the vaguely discernible domes of the Eyüp Mosque and its cypress-lined cemetery. After walking for a while longer, I heard from below the shouts of children at play coming from the new Jewish quarter in Balat.

When we reached the plain where Eyüp was located, Butterfly approached me, and in his usual fiery manner, abruptly broached his subject:

"Olive and Stork are the ones behind this vulgarity," he said. "Like everyone else, they knew I had a bad relationship with the deceased. They knew everyone was aware of this. There was jealousy between us, even open animosity and antagonism, over who would assume leadership of the workshop after Master Osman. Now they expect the guilt to fall on my shoulders, or at the least, that the Head Treasurer, and under his influence, Our Sultan, will distance themselves from me, nay, from us."

"Who is this 'us' of which you speak?"

"Those of us who believe that the old morality ought to persist at the workshop, that we should follow the path laid by the Persian masters, that an artist shouldn't illustrate just any scene for money alone. In place of weapons, armies, slaves and conquests, we believe that the old myths, legends and stories ought to be introduced anew into our books. We shouldn't forgo the old models. Genuine miniaturists shouldn't loiter at the shops in the bazaar and paint any old thing, depictions of indecency, for a few extra kurush from anybody who happens by. His Excellency Our Sultan would find us justified."

"You're incriminating yourself senselessly," I said so he might be done with his ranting. "I'm convinced that the atelier could not harbor anybody capable of committing such a crime. You're all brethren. There's no great harm in illustrating a few subjects that haven't been depicted previously, at least no harm so great as to be an occasion for enmity."

As happened when I first heard the horrid news, I had an epiphany of sorts. Elegant Effendi's murderer was one of the premier masters in the palace workshop and he was a member of the crowd before me, climbing the hill that led to the cemetery. I was also convinced that the murderer would continue with his devilry and sedition, that he was an enemy of the book I was making, and most probably, that he'd visited my house to pick up some work illustrating and painting. Had Butterfly, too, like most of the artists who frequented my house, fallen in love with Shekure? As he made his assertions, had he forgotten the times when I'd requested that he paint pictures that were contrary to his point of view, or was he just needling me with expert skill?

Nay, I thought a little while later, he couldn't be needling me. Butterfly, like the other master illustrators, obviously owed me a debt of gratitude: With money and gifts to miniaturists dwindling, due to the wars and lack of interest on the part of Our Sultan, the sole significant source of extra income had for some time been what they earned working for me. I knew they were jealous of one another over my attentions, and for this reason—but not only for this reason—I met with them individually at my house, hardly a basis for hostility toward me. All of my miniaturists were mature enough to behave intelligently, to sincerely find a reason to admire a man to whom they were obliged for their own profit.

To relieve the silence and ensure that the previous topic of conversation wouldn't be revisited, I said, "Oh, will His wonders never cease! They're able to take the coffin up that hill as fast as they brought it down."

Butterfly smiled sweetly showing all his teeth: "Due to the cold."

Could this one actually kill a man, I wondered, for example, out of envy? Might he kill me? He had the following excuse: This man was debasing my religion. Nay, but he's a great master, a perfect embodiment of talent, why should he resort to murder? Age means not only straining oneself climbing hills, but also, I gather, not being so afraid of death. It means a lack of desire, entering into a slave girl's bedchamber, not in a fit of excitement, but out of custom. In a burst of intuition, I told him to his face the decision I'd made:

"I'm not continuing with the book any longer."

"What?" said Butterfly as his expression changed.

"There's some kind of ill-fortune in it. Our Sultan has cut off the funding. You're to tell Olive and Stork, as well."

Perhaps he would have inquired further, but we found ourselves on the slopes of the graveyard amid tightly spaced towering cypresses, high ferns and tombstones. As the great crowd encircled the grave site, my only clue that the body was at that very moment being lowered into the grave was the increasing intensity of the weeping and sobbing and the exclamations of *bismillahi* and *ala milleti Resulullah*.

"Uncover his face completely," someone said.

They were removing the white shroud, and they must've been eye to eye with the corpse if indeed there was an eye remaining in that smashed head. I was in the back and I couldn't see anything. I'd once gazed into the eyes of Death, not at a grave site, in an entirely different place . . .

A memory: Thirty years ago, Our Sultan's grandfather, Denizen of Paradise, decided once and for all to take Cyprus from the Venetians. Sheikhulislam Ebussuut Effendi, recalling that this island was once designated a commissariat for Mecca and Medina, issued a fatwa which more or less stated that it was inappropriate for an island which had helped sustain holy sites to remain under Christian infidel control. In turn, the difficult task of informing the Venetians of this unforeseen decision, that they must surrender their island, fell to me. As a result, I was able to tour the cathedrals of Venice. Though I marveled at their bridges and palazzos, I was most enchanted by the pictures hanging in Venetian homes. Nevertheless, in the midst of this bewilderment, trusting in the hospitality displayed by the Venetians, I delivered the menacing correspondence, informing them in a haughty, supercilious fashion that Our Sultan desired Cyprus. The Venetians were so angry that in their congress, which had been hastily convened, it was decided that even to discuss such a letter was unacceptable. Furious mobs had forced me to confine myself to the Doge's palazzo. And when some rogues managed to get past the guards and doorkeepers and had set to strangling me, two of the Doge's personal musketeers succeeded in escorting me out one of the secret passageways to an exit that opened onto the canal. There, in a fog not unlike this one, I thought for an instant that the tall and pale gondolier dressed in white, who'd taken me by the arm, was none other than Death. I caught sight of my reflection in his eyes.

Longingly, I dreamed of finishing my book in secret and returning to Venice. I approached the grave, which had been carefully covered with dirt: At this moment, angels are interrogating him above, asking him whether he is male or female, his religion and whom he recognizes as his prophet. The possibility of my own death came to mind.

A crow alighted beside me. I gazed lovingly into Black's eyes and asked him to take my arm and accompany me on the way back. I told him I expected him at the house early the next morning to continue working on the book. I had indeed imagined my own death, and realized, once again, that the book must be completed, whatever the cost.

CHAPTER 18

I WILL BE CALLED A MURDERER

They threw cold, muddy earth onto the battered and disfigured corpse of ill-fated Elegant Effendi and I wept more than any of them. I shouted, "I want to die with him!" and "Let me share his grave!" and they held me by the waist so I wouldn't fall in. I gasped for air and they pressed their palms to my forehead, drawing my head back so I might breathe. By the glances of the deceased's relatives, I sensed I might have exaggerated my sobs and wailing; I pulled myself together. Based upon my excessive sorrow the workshop gossips might suppose that Elegant Effendi and I had been in love.

I hid behind a plane tree until the funeral ended to avoid drawing more attention to myself. A relative of the oaf I'd sent to Hell—an even bigger idiot than the deceased—discovered me behind the tree and stared deep into my eyes with a look he assumed was meaningful. He held me in his embrace for a while, then the ignoramus said the following: "Were you 'Saturday' or 'Wednesday'?"

"'Wednesday' was the workshop name of the dearly departed for a time," I said. He fell silent.

The story behind these workshop names, which bound us to one another like a secret pact, was simple: During our apprenticeships, when Osman the miniaturist had newly graduated from assistant master to the level of master, we all shared a great respect, admiration and love for him. He was a virtuoso and he taught us everything, for God had blessed him with an enchanting artistic gift and the intellect of a jinn. Early each morning, as was demanded of apprentices, one of us would go to the master's home, and following respectfully behind him on the way to the workshop, carry his pen and brush box, his bag and his portfolio full of papers. So desperate were we to be near him that we'd argue and fight among ourselves to determine who would go that day.

Master Osman had a favorite. But if he were always to go, it would fan the flames of the never-ending gossip and tasteless jokes that inevitably filled the workshop, and so the great master decided that each of us would be assured a specified day of the week. The great master worked on Fridays and stayed at home Saturdays. His son, whom he loved dearly—who later betrayed him and us by quitting the trade—would accompany his father on Mondays like a common apprentice. There was also a tall thin brother of ours known as "Thursday," a miniaturist more gifted than any of us, who passed away at a young age, succumbing to the fever brought on by a mysterious illness. Elegant Effendi, may he rest in peace, would go on Wednesdays, and was therefore known as "Wednesday." Later, our great master meaningfully and lovingly changed our names from "Tuesday" to "Olive," from "Friday" to "Stork," and from "Sunday" to "Butterfly," renaming the dearly departed as "Elegant" in allusion to the finesse of his gilding work. The great master must have said, "Welcome 'Wednesday,' how are you this morning?" to the late Elegant just as he used to greet all of us back then.

When I recalled how he would address me, I thought my eyes might fill with tears: Master Osman admired us, and his own eyes would tear when he beheld the beauty of our work; he'd kiss our hands and arms, and despite the beatings, we felt as if we were in Heaven as apprentices; and so our talent blossomed with his love. Even jealousy, which cast its shadow over those happy years, had a different hue then.

Now I am completely divided, just like those figures whose head and hands are drawn and painted by one master while their bodies and clothes are depicted by another. When a God-fearing man like myself unexpectedly becomes a murderer, it takes time to adjust. I've adopted a second voice, one befitting a murderer, so that I might still carry on as though my old life continued. I am speaking now in this derisive and devious second

I Will Be Called a Murderer

voice, which I keep out of my regular life. From time to time, of course, you'll hear my familiar, regular voice, which would've remained my only voice had I not become a murderer. But when I speak under my workshop name, I'll never admit to being "a murderer." Let no one try to associate these two voices, I have no individual style or flaws in artistry to betray my hidden persona. Indeed, I believe that style, or for that matter, anything that serves to distinguish one artist from another, is a flaw—not individual character, as some arrogantly claim.

I do admit that in my own situation, this presents a problem. For though I might speak through my workshop name, lovingly given to me by Master Osman and used by Enishte Effendi, who also admired it, in no wise do I want you to figure out whether I am Butterfly, Olive or Stork. For if you do you won't hesitate to turn me over to the torturers of the Sultan's Commander of the Imperial Guard.

And, I must mind what I think about and say. Actually, I know that you're listening to me even when I'm mulling over matters in private. I can't afford careless contemplation of my frustrations or the incriminating details of my life. Even when recounting the "Alif," "Ba" and "Djim" stories, I was always mindful of your gaze.

One side of the warriors, lovers, princes and legendary heroes that I've illustrated tens of thousands of times faces whatever is depicted there, in that mythical time—the enemies they're battling, for example, or the dragons they're slaying, or the beautiful maidens over whom they weep. But another aspect, and another side of their bodies, faces the book lover who happens to be gazing at the magnificent painting. If I do have style and character, it's not only hidden in my artwork, but in my crime and in my words as well! Yes, try to discover who I am from the color of my words!

I, too, know that if you catch me, it'll bring consolation to unfortunate Elegant Effendi's miserable soul. They're shoveling dirt on him as I stand here beneath trees, amid chirping birds, watching the gilded waters of the Golden Horn and the leaden domes of Istanbul, and discovering anew how wonderful it is to be alive. Pathetic Elegant Effendi, soon after he joined the circle of that fierce-browed preacher from Erzurum, he stopped liking me completely; yet, in the twenty-five years that we illustrated books for Our Sultan, there were times when we felt very close to each other. Twenty years ago, we became friends while working on a royal history in verse for the late father of our present sultan. But we were never closer than when working on the eight illustrated plates that were to accompany a collection of Fuzuli poems. One summer evening back then, as a concession to his understandable but illogical desires—apparently a miniaturist ought to feel in his soul the text he's illustrating—I came here and patiently listened to him pretentiously recite lines from Fuzuli's collected works as flocks of swallows fluttered above us in a frenzy. I still recall a line recited that evening: "I am not me but eternally thee." I've always wondered how one might illustrate this line.

I ran to his house as soon as I learned that his body had been found. There, the diminutive garden where we once sat and recited poetry, now covered in snow, seemed diminished, just like any garden revisited after a period of years. His house was that way, too. From the next room, I could hear the wails of women, and their exaggerated exclamations, mounting as if they were competing with each other. When his eldest brother spoke, I listened intently: The face of our forlorn brother Elegant was practically destroyed, and his head was smashed. After he was removed from the bottom of the well where he'd lain for four days, his brothers scarcely knew him, and his poor wife, Kalbiye, whom they'd brought from the house, was forced to identify the unrecognizable body in the dark of night by its torn and tattered clothing. I was reminded of a depiction of the Midian merchants pulling Joseph from the pit into which he'd been cast by his jealous brothers. I quite enjoy painting this scene from the romance of *Joseph and Zuleyha*, for it reminds us that envy is the prime emotion in life.

There was a sudden lull. I sensed their eyes upon me. Should I cry? I caught Black's eye. That vile scoundrel, he's peering at us, like someone who's been sent here by Enishte Effendi to uncover the truth.

"Who could've perpetrated such a horrendous crime?" cried the oldest brother. "What kind of heartless beast could've slaughtered our brother, our brother who wouldn't dare harm an ant?"

He answered this question with his own tears, and I joined him, feigning grief while I sought my own answer: Who were Elegant's enemies? If it hadn't been me, who else could've murdered him? I recalled that some time ago—I believe it was when the *Book of Skills* was being prepared—he would get involved in arguments with certain artists inclined to dismiss the techniques of the old masters and ruin the pages we illustrators had labored extensively over; thus they would spoil the borders with the horrid colors used to embellish more cheaply and quickly. Who were they? Later, however, rumors began to spread that the enmity had arisen not for this reason, but out of competition for the affections of a handsome binder's apprentice who worked on the ground floor; but this was an old story. And there were those who were annoyed by Elegant's dignity, his refinement and his erudite feminine demeanor, but this had to do with another matter entirely: Elegant was slavishly bound to the old style, a fanatic about the coordination of color between gilding and illustration, and in the presence of Master Osman, he would, for instance, point out the nonexistent faults of other miniaturists—mine in particular—with gentle conceit. His last quarrel had to do with an issue about which Master Osman had, in past years, grown quite sensitive: royal miniaturists who moonlighted, secretly accepting trivial commissions outside the auspices of the palace. In recent years, after Our Sultan's interest had begun to wane and, along with it, the money coming from the Head Treasurer, all the miniaturists started paying visits to the two-story houses of the crass young pashas—and the best of the artists would go late at night to visit Enishte.

I wasn't at all bothered by Enishte's decision to stop working on his—on our—book or his excuse that it was ill-omened. He had, of course, guessed that the murderer who did away with brainless Elegant Effendi was one of us who were embellishing his book. Put yourself in his shoes: Would you invite a murderer to your house each fortnight to work on illustrations after dark? Wouldn't you first determine the identities of the murderer and the best illustrator? I have no doubt that he'll quickly deduce which of the miniaturists was the most talented and the most skilled in color selection, gilding, page ruling, illustration, face drawing and page composition; and having done so, he'll continue working with me alone. I can't imagine he'll be so petty as to think of me as a common murderer rather than a genuinely talented miniaturist.

Out of the corner of my eye I am watching that fool Black Effendi whom Enishte brought with him. When these two broke away from the cemetery crowd presently dispersing, and walked down to the Eyüp quay, I followed them. They boarded a four-oared longboat, and afterward, I got into a six-oar along with a few young apprentices who'd forgotten about the deceased and the funeral and were making merry. Within sight of the Phanar Gate, our boats momentarily came so near each other that they were about to lock oars, and I could see clearly that Black was earnestly whispering to Enishte. I thereupon thought how easy it was to end a life. My dear God, you've given each of us this unbelievable power, but you've also made us afraid to exercise it.

Still, if a man but once overcomes this fear and acts, he straightaway becomes an entirely different person. There was a time when I was terrified not only of the Devil, but of the slightest trace of evil within me. Now,

MY NAME IS RED

however, I have the sense that evil can be endured, and moreover, that it's indispensable to an artist. After I killed that miserable excuse of a man, discounting the trembling in my hands which lasted only a few days, I drew better, I made use of brighter and bolder colors, and most important, realized that I could conjure up wonders in my imagination. But, this begs the question how many men in Istanbul can truly appreciate the magnificence of my illustrations?

Off the waterfront near Jibali, from all the way in the middle of the Golden Horn, I gazed spitefully at Istanbul. The snow-capped domes shone bright in the sunlight that broke abruptly through the clouds. The larger and more colorful a city is, the more places there are to hide one's guilt and sin; the more crowded it is, the more people there are to hide behind. A city's intellect ought to be measured not by its scholars, libraries, miniaturists, calligraphers and schools, but by the number of crimes insidiously committed on its dark streets over thousands of years. By this logic, doubtless, Istanbul is the world's most intelligent city.

At the Unkapanı quay, I left my longboat a little after Black and his Enishte had left theirs. I was behind them as they leaned on one another and mounted the hill. At the site of a recent fire in the shadow of the Sultan Mehmet Mosque, they stopped and exchanged parting words. Enishte Effendi was alone, and he appeared for an instant like a helpless old man. I was tempted to run to him and tell him what that barbarian, from whose funeral we were returning, had slanderously confided in me; I was going to confess what I'd done to protect us, and to ask him: "Is it true what Elegant Effendi had claimed? Are we abusing Our Sultan's trust through the illustrations we've made? Are our painting techniques traitorous and an affront to our religion? And have you finished that last large painting?"

I stood in the middle of the snowy street as evening fell and gazed down the dark road which had been abandoned along with me to jinns, fairies, brigands, thieves, to the grief of fathers and children returning home and to the sorrow of snow-covered trees. At the end of the street, inside Enishte Effendi's grandiose two-story house, beneath the roof, which I can now see through the bare branches of the chestnut trees, there lives the most beautiful woman in the world. But, no, why should I drive myself mad?

CHAPTER 19

I AM A GOLD COIN

Behold! I am a twenty-two-carat Ottoman Sultani gold coin and I bear the glorious insignia of His Excellency Our Sultan, Refuge of the World. Here, in the middle of the night in this fine coffeehouse overcome with funereal melancholy, Stork, one of Our Sultan's great masters, has just finished drawing my picture, though he hasn't yet been able to embellish me with gold wash—I'll leave that to your imagination. My image is here before you, yet I myself can be found in the money purse of your dear brother, Stork, that illustrious miniaturist. He's rising now, removing me from his purse and showing me off to each of you. Hello, hello, greetings to all the master artists and assorted guests. Your eyes widen as you behold my glimmer, you thrill as I shimmer in the light of the oil lamp, and finally, you bristle with envy at my owner, Master Stork. You're justified in behaving so, for there's no better measure of an illustrator's talent than I.

In the past three months, Master Stork has earned exactly forty-seven gold pieces like myself. We're all in this money-purse and Master Stork, see for yourself, isn't hiding us from anyone; he knows there's none among the miniaturists of Istanbul who earns more than he does. I take pride in being recognized as a measure of talent among artists and in putting an end to unnecessary disagreements. In the past, before we got used to coffee and our minds sharpened, these dim-witted miniaturists weren't satisfied with spending their evenings arguing about who was the most talented or who had the best sense of color, who could draw the best tree or who was most expert in the depiction of clouds; no, they'd also come to blows over such issues, knocking out each other's teeth in the process. Now that my judgment decides everything, there's a sweet harmony in the workshop, and what's more, an air that would suit the old masters of Herat.

In addition to noting the harmony and ambience brought about by my judgment, let me list for you the various things I might be exchanged for: the foot of a young and beautiful slave girl, which amounts to about one-fiftieth of her person; a good-quality walnut-handled barber's mirror, edges inlaid with bone; a well-painted chest of drawers decorated with sunburst designs and silver leaf worth ninety silver pieces; 120 fresh loaves of bread; a grave site and coffins for three; a silver armband; one-tenth of a horse; the legs of an old and fat concubine; one buffalo calf; two high-quality pieces of china; the monthly wage of Persian miniaturist Mehmet the Dervish of Tabriz and the majority of those of his like who work in Our Sultan's workshop; one good hunting falcon with cage; ten jugs of Panayot's wine; a heavenly hour with Mahmut, one of those young boys world-renowned for his beauty, and many other opportunities too numerous to specify.

Before I arrived here, I spent ten days in the dirty sock of a poor shoemaker's apprentice. Each night the unfortunate man would fall asleep in his bed, naming the endless things he could buy with me. The lines of this epic poem, sweet as a lullaby, proved to me that there was no place on Earth a coin couldn't go.

Which reminds me. If I recited all that happened to me before I came here, it'd fill volumes. There are no strangers among us, we're all friends; as long as you promise not to tell anyone, and as long as Stork Effendi won't take offense, I'll tell you a secret. Do you swear not to tell?

All right then, I confess. I'm not a genuine twenty-two-carat Ottoman Sultani gold coin minted at the Chemberlitash Mint. I'm counterfeit. They made me in Venice using adulterated gold and brought me here, passing me off as twenty-two-carat Ottoman gold. Your sympathy and understanding are much obliged.

Based on what I could gather from being in the mint in Venice, this business has been going on for years. Until recently, the debased gold pieces that the Venetian infidels brought to the East and spent were Venetian ducats which they minted in that same mint. We Ottomans, forever respectful of whatever is written, paid no heed to the amount of gold in each ducat—so long as the inscription remained the same—and these fake Venetian gold pieces flooded Istanbul. Later, noting that coins with less gold and more copper were harder, we began to distinguish the coins by biting them. For example, you're burning with love; you go running to Mahmut, that youth of unsurpassed beauty, beloved by all; first, he takes into his soft mouth the coin—not the other thing—and biting it, declares it counterfeit. As a consequence, he'll take you to Heaven for only half an hour instead of one full hour. The Venetian infidels, realizing that their counterfeit coins presented such disadvantages, decided that they might as well counterfeit Ottoman coins, reasoning that the Ottomans would be fooled again.

I Am a Gold Coin

Now, let me draw your attention to something quite bizarre: When these Venetian infidels paint, it's as if they're not making a painting but actually creating the object they're painting. When it comes to money, however, rather than making the real thing, they make its counterfeit.

We were loaded into iron chests, hauled onto ships and pitching to and fro traveled from Venice to Istanbul. I found myself in a money changer's shop, in the garlicky mouth of its proprietor. We waited for a while, and a simple-minded peasant entered, hoping to exchange some gold. The master money changer, who was a genuine trickster, declared that he needed to bite the gold piece to see if it was counterfeit. So he took the peasant's coin and tossed it into his mouth.

When we met inside his mouth, I realized that the peasant's coin was a genuine Ottoman Sultani. He saw me within that stench of garlic and said, "You're nothing but a counterfeit." He was right, but his arrogant manner offended my pride and I lied to him: "Actually, my brother, you're the one who's counterfeit."

Meanwhile, the peasant was proudly insisting, "How could my gold coin possibly be counterfeit? I buried it in the ground twenty years ago, did a vice like counterfeiting exist back then?"

I was wondering what the outcome would be when the money changer took me out of his mouth instead of the peasant's gold coin. "Take your gold coin, I don't want any vile Venetian infidel's fake money," he said, "have you no shame?" The peasant responded with some biting words of his own, then took me with him out the door. After hearing the same pronouncement from other money changers, the peasant's spirit broke and he exchanged me as a debased coin for only ninety silver pieces. This is how my seven-year saga of endless wandering from hand to hand began.

Allow me to admit proudly that I've spent most of my time in Istanbul wandering from purse to purse, and from sash to pocket, as befits an intelligent coin. My worst nightmare is to be stored in a jug and languish for years beneath a rock, buried in some garden; not that it hasn't happened to me, but for whatever reason, these periods have never lasted long. Many of the people who hold me want to be rid of me as soon as possible, especially if they discover I'm fake. Nonetheless, I have yet to come across someone who'll warn an unsuspecting buyer that I'm counterfeit. A broker, not recognizing that I'm counterfeit, who has counted out 120 silver coins in exchange for me, will berate himself in fits of anger, sorrow and impatience as soon as he learns he's been cheated, and these fits won't subside until he rids himself of me by cheating another. During this crisis,

MY NAME IS RED

even as he attempts to repeatedly swindle others, failing each time on account of his haste and anger, he'll continue all the while to curse the "immoral" person who had originally conned him.

Over the last seven years in Istanbul, I've changed hands 560 times, and there's not a house, shop, market, bazaar, mosque, church or synagogue I haven't entered. As I've roamed about, I've learned that much more gossip has been spread, many more legends told and lies spun in my name than I'd ever suspected. I've constantly had my nose rubbed in it: Nothing's considered valuable anymore besides me, I'm merciless, I'm blind, I myself am even enamored of money, the unfortunate world revolves around, not God, but me, and there's nothing I can't buy—all this is to say nothing of my dirty, vulgar and base nature. And those who know that I'm fake are given to even harsher judgments. As my actual value drops, however, my metaphorical value increases—proof that poetry is consolation to life's miseries. But despite all such heartless comparison and thoughtless slander, I've realized that a large majority do sincerely love me. In this age of hatred, such heartfelt—even impassioned—affection ought to gladden us all.

I've seen every square inch of Istanbul, street by street and district by district; I've known all hands from Jews to Abkhazians and from Arabs to Mingerians. I once left Istanbul in the purse of a preacher from Edirne who was going to Manisa. On the way, we happened to be attacked by thieves. One of them shouted, "Your money or your life!" Panicking, the miserable preacher hid us in his asshole. This spot, which he assumed was the safest, smelled worse than the mouth of the garlic lover and was much less comfortable. But the situation quickly grew worse when instead of "Your money or your life!" the thieves began to shout "Your honor or your life!" Lining up, they took him by turns. I don't dare describe the agony we suffered in that cramped hole. It's for this reason that I dislike leaving Istanbul.

I've been well received in Istanbul. Young girls kiss me as if I were the husband of their dreams; they hide me beneath their pillows, between their huge breasts, and in their underwear; they even fondle me in their sleep to make certain I'm still there. I've been stored next to the furnace in a public bath, in a boot, at the bottom of a small bottle in a wonderful-smelling musk seller's shop and in the secret pocket sewn into a chef's lentil sack. I've wandered through Istanbul in belts made of camel leather, jacket linings made from checkered Egyptian cloth, in the thick fabric of shoe lining and in the hidden corners of multicolored shalwars. The master watchmaker Petro hid me in a secret compartment of a grandfather clock, and a Greek grocer stuck me directly into a wheel of kashari cheese. I hid together with jewelry, seals and keys wrapped in pieces of thick cloth stowed away in chimneys, in stoves, beneath windowsills, inside cushions stuffed with rough straw, in underground chambers and in the hidden compartments of chests. I've known fathers who frequently stood up from the dinner table to check whether I was still where I was supposed to be, women who sucked on me like candy for no reason, children who sniffed at me as they stuck me up their noses and old people with one foot in the grave who couldn't relax unless they removed me from their sheepskin purses at least seven times a day. There was a meticulous Circassian woman who, after spending the whole day cleaning the house, took us coins out of her purse and scrubbed us with a coarse brush. I remember the one-eyed money changer who constantly stacked us up into towers; the porter who smelled of morning glories and who, along with his family, watched us as if looking out over a stunning landscape; and the gilder, no longer among us—no need to name names—who spent his evenings arranging us into various designs. I've traveled in mahogany skiffs; I've visited the Sultan's palace; I've hidden within Herat-made bindings, in the heels of rose-scented shoes and in the covers of packsaddles. I've known hundreds of hands: dirty, hairy, plump, oily, trembling and old. I've been redolent of opium dens, candle-makers' shops, dried mackerel and the sweat of all of Istanbul. After experiencing such excitement and commotion, a base thief who had slit his victim's throat in the blackness of night and tossed me into his purse, once back in his accursed house, spat in my face and grunted, "Damn you, it's all because of you." I was so offended, so hurt, that I wanted nothing more than to disappear.

If I didn't exist, however, no one would be able to distinguish a good artist from a bad one, and this would lead to chaos among the miniaturists; they'd all be at each other's throats. So I haven't vanished. I've entered the purse of the most talented and intelligent of miniaturists and made my way here.

If you think you're better than Stork, then by all means, get hold of me.

CHAPTER 20

I AM CALLED BLACK

I wondered whether Shekure's father was aware of the letters we exchanged. If I were to consider her tone, which bespoke a timid maiden quite afraid of her father, I'd have to conclude that not a single word about me had passed between them. Yet, I sensed that this was not the case. The slyness in Esther's looks, Shekure's enchanting appearance at the window, the decisiveness with which my Enishte sent me to his illustrators and his despair when he ordered me to come this morning—all of it made me quite uneasy.

In the morning, as soon as my Enishte asked me to sit before him, he began to describe the portraits he saw in Venice. As the ambassador of Our Sultan, Refuge of the World, he'd visited quite a number of palazzos, churches and the houses of prosperous men. Over a period of days, he stood before thousands of portraits. He saw thousands of framed faces depicted on stretched canvas or wood or painted directly onto walls. "Each one was different from the next. They were distinctive, unique human faces!" he said. He was intoxicated by their variety, their colors, the pleasantness—even severity—of the soft light that seemed to fall on them and the meaning emanating from their eyes.

"As if a virulent plague had struck, everyone was having his portrait made," he said. "In all of Venice, rich and influential men wanted their portraits painted as a symbol, a memento of their lives and a sign of their riches, power and influence—so they might always be there, standing before us, announcing their existence, nay, their individuality and distinction."

His words were belittling, as if he were speaking out of jealousy, ambition or greed. Though, at times, as he talked about the portraits he'd seen in Venice, his face would abruptly light up like a child's, invigorated.

Portraiture had become such a contagion among affluent men, princes and great families who were patrons of art that even when they commissioned frescoes of biblical scenes and religious legends for church walls, these infidels would insist that their own images appear somewhere in the work. For instance, in a painting of the burial of St. Stephan, you'd suddenly see, ah yes, present among the tearful graveside mourners, the very prince who was giving you the tour—in a state of pure enthusiasm, exhilaration and conceit—of the paintings hanging on his palazzo walls. Next, in the corner of a fresco depicting St. Peter curing the sick with his shadow, you'd realize with an odd sense of disillusionment that the unfortunate one writhing there in pain was, in fact, the strong-as-an-ox brother of your polite host. The following day, this time in a piece depicting the Resurrection of the Dead, you'd discover the guest who'd stuffed himself beside you at lunch.

"Some have gone so far, just to be included in a painting," said my Enishte, fearfully as though he were talking about the temptations of Satan, "that they're willing to be portrayed as a servant filling goblets in the crowd, or a merciless man stoning an adulteress, or a murderer, his hands drenched in blood."

Pretending not to understand, I said, "Exactly the way we see Shah Ismail ascending the throne in those illustrated books that recount ancient Persian legends. Or when we come across a depiction of Tamerlane, who actually ruled long afterward, in the story of *Hüsrev and Shirin*."

Was there a noise somewhere in the house?

"It's as if the Venetian paintings were made to frighten us," said my Enishte later. "And it isn't enough that we be in awe of the authority and money of these men who commission the works, they also want us to know that simply existing in this world is a very special, very mysterious event. They're attempting to terrify us with their unique faces, eyes, bearing and with their clothing whose every fold is defined by shadow. They're attempting to terrify us by being creatures of mystery."

He explained how once he'd gotten lost in the exquisite portrait gallery of a lunatic collector whose opulent estate was perched on the shores of Lake Como; the proprietor had collected the portraits of all the great personages in Frankish history from kings to cardinals, and from soldiers to poets: "When my hospitable host left me alone to roam as I wished throughout his palazzo, which he'd proudly given me a tour of, I saw that these supposedly important infidels—most of whom appeared to be real and some of whom looked me straight in the eye—had attained their importance in this world solely on account of having their portraits made. Their likenesses had imbued them with such magic, had so distinguished them, that for a moment among the paintings I felt flawed and impotent. Had I been depicted in this fashion, it seemed, I'd better understand why I existed in this world."

MY NAME IS RED

He was frightened because he suddenly understood—and perhaps desired—that Islamic artistry, perfected and securely established by the old masters of Herat, would meet its end on account of the appeal of portraiture. "However, it was as if I too wanted to feel extraordinary, different and unique," he said. As if prodded by the Devil, he felt himself strongly drawn to what he feared. "How should I say it? It's as if this were a sin of desire, like growing arrogant before God, like considering oneself of utmost importance, like situating oneself at the center of the world."

Thereafter, this idea dawned on him: These methods which the Frankish artists made use of as if playing a prideful child's game, could be more than simply magic associated with Our Exalted Sultan—but could in fact become a force meant to serve our religion, bringing under its sway all who beheld it.

I learned that the idea of preparing an illuminated manuscript had arisen then: my Enishte, who'd returned to Istanbul from Venice, suggested it would be excellent indeed for Our Sultan to be the subject of a portrait in the Frankish style. But after His Excellency took exception, a book containing pictures of Our Sultan and the objects that represented Him was agreed upon.

"It is the story that's essential," our wisest and most Glorious Sultan had said. "A beautiful illustration elegantly completes the story. An illustration that does not complement a story, in the end, will become but a false idol. Since we cannot possibly believe in an absent story, we will naturally begin believing in the picture itself. This would be no different than the worship of idols in the Kaaba that went on before Our Prophet, peace and blessings be upon him, had destroyed them. If not as part of a story, how would you propose to depict this red carnation, for example, or that insolent dwarf over there?"

"By exposing the carnation's beauty and uniqueness."

"In the arrangement of your scene, then, would you situate the flower at the precise center of the page?"

"I was afraid," my Enishte said. "I panicked momentarily when I realized where Our Sultan's thoughts were taking me."

What filled my Enishte with fear was the notion of situating at the center of the page—and thereby, the world—something other than what God had intended.

"Thereafter," Our Sultan had said, "you'll want to exhibit a picture in whose center you've situated a dwarf." It was as I had assumed. "But this picture could never be displayed: after a while, we'd begin to worship a picture we've hung on a wall, regardless of the original intentions. If I believed, heaven forbid, the way these infidels do, that the Prophet Jesus was also the Lord God himself, then I'd also hold that God could be observed in this world, and even, that He could manifest in human form; only then might I accept the depiction of mankind in full detail and exhibit such images. You do understand that, eventually, we would unthinkingly begin worshiping any picture that is hung on a wall, don't you?"

My Enishte said: "I understood it quite well, and because I did, I was afraid of what we both were thinking."

"For this reason," Our Sultan remarked, "I could never allow my portrait to be displayed."

"Though this is exactly what he wanted," whispered my Enishte, with a devilish titter.

It was my turn to be frightened now.

"Nonetheless, it is my desire that my portrait be made in the style of the Frankish masters," Our Sultan went on. "Such a portrait will, of course, have to be concealed within the pages of a book. Whatever that book might be, you shall be the one to tell me."

"In an instant of surprise and awe, I considered his statement," said my Enishte, then grinning more devilishly than before, he seemed, suddenly, to become someone else.

"His Excellency Our Sultan ordered me to start working on His book posthaste. My head spun with joy. He added that it ought to be prepared as a present for the Venetian Doge, whom I was to visit once again. Once the book was completed, it would become a symbol of the vanquishing power of the Islamic Caliph Our Exalted Sultan, in the thousandth year of the Hegira. He requested that I prepare the illuminated manuscript in utmost secrecy, primarily to conceal its purpose as an olive branch extended to the Venetians, but also to avoid aggravating workshop jealousies. And in a state of great elation and sworn to secrecy, I embarked upon this venture."

CHAPTER 21

I AM YOUR BELOVED UNCLE

And so it was on that Friday morning, I began to describe the book that would contain Our Sultan's portrait painted in the Venetian style. I broached the topic to Black by recounting how I'd brought it up with Our

Sultan and how I'd persuaded him to fund the book. My hidden purpose was to have Black write the stories—which I hadn't even begun—that were meant to accompany the illustrations.

I told him I'd completed most of the book's illustrations and that the last picture was nearly finished. "There's a depiction of Death," I said, "and I had the most clever of miniaturists, Stork, illustrate the tree representing the peacefulness of Our Sultan's worldly realm. There's a picture of Satan and a horse meant to spirit us far far away. There's a dog, always cunning and wily, and also a gold coin . . . I had the master miniaturists depict these things with such beauty," I told Black, "that if you saw them but once, you'd know straightaway what the corresponding text ought to be. Poetry and painting, words and color, these things are brothers to each other, as you well know."

For a while, I pondered whether I should tell him I might marry off my daughter to him. Would he live together with us in this house? I told myself not to be taken in by his rapt attention and his childlike expression. I knew he was scheming to elope with my Shekure. Still, I could rely on nobody else to finish my book.

Returning together from the Friday prayers, we discussed "shadow," the greatest of innovations manifest in the paintings of the Venetian masters. "If," I said, "we intend to make our paintings from the perspective of pedestrians exchanging pleasantries and regarding their world; that is, if we intend to illustrate from the street, we ought to learn how to account for—as the Franks do—what is, in fact, most prevalent there: shadows."

"How does one depict shadow?" asked Black.

From time to time, as my nephew listened, I perceived impatience in him. He'd begin to fiddle with the Mongol inkpot he'd given me as a present. At times, he'd take up the iron poker and stoke the fire in the stove. Now and then I imagined that he wanted to lower that poker onto my head and kill me because I dared to move the art of illustrating away from Allah's perspective; because I would betray the dreams of the masters of Herat and their entire tradition of painting; because I'd duped Our Sultan into already doing so. Occasionally, Black would sit dead still for long stretches and fix his eyes deeply into mine. I could imagine what he was thinking: "I'll be your slave until I can have your daughter." Once, as I would do when he was a child, I took him out into the yard and tried to explain to him, as a father might, about the trees, about the light falling onto the leaves, about the melting snow and why the houses seemed to shrink as we moved away from them. But this was a mistake: It proved only that our former filial relationship had long since collapsed. Now patient sufferance of the rantings of a demented old man had taken the place of Black's childhood curiosity and passion for knowledge. I was just an old man whose daughter was the object of Black's love. The influence and experience of the countries and cities that my nephew had traveled through for a dozen years had been fully absorbed by his soul. He was tired of me, and I pitied him. And he was angry, I assumed, not only because I hadn't allowed him to marry Shekure twelve years ago—after all, there was no other choice then—but because I dreamed of paintings whose style transgressed the precepts of the masters of Herat. Furthermore, because I raved about this nonsense with such conviction, I imagined my death at his hands.

I was not, however, afraid of him; on the contrary, I tried to frighten him. For I believed that fear was appropriate to the writing I'd requested of him. "As in those pictures," I said, "one ought to be able to situate oneself at the center of the world. One of my illustrators brilliantly depicted Death for me. Behold."

Thus I began to show him the paintings I'd secretly commissioned from the master miniaturists over the last year. At first, he was a tad shy, even frightened. When he understood that the depiction of Death was inspired by familiar scenes that could be found in many *Book of Kings* volumes—from the scene of Afrasiyab's decapitation of Siyavush, for example, or Rüstem's murder of Suhrab without realizing this was his son—he quickly became interested in the subject. Among the pictures that depicted the funeral of the late Sultan Süleyman was one I'd made with bold but sad colors, combining a compositional sensibility inspired by the Franks with my own attempt at shading—which I'd added later. I pointed out the diabolic depth evoked by the interplay of cloud and horizon. I reminded him that Death was unique, just like the portraits of infidels I had seen hanging in Venetian palazzos; all of them desperately yearned to be rendered distinctly. "They want to be so distinct and different, and they want this with such passion that," I said, "look, look into the eyes of Death. See how men do not fear Death, but rather the violence implicit in the desire to be one-of-a-kind, unique and exceptional. Look at this illustration and write an account of it. Give voice to Death. Here's paper and pen. I shall give what you write to the calligrapher straightaway."

He stared at the picture in silence. "Who painted this?" he asked later.

"Butterfly. He's the most talented of the lot. Master Osman had been in love with and awed by him for years."

"I've seen rougher versions of this depiction of a dog at the coffeehouse where the storyteller performs," Black said.

"My illustrators, most of whom are spiritually bound to Master Osman and the workshop, take a dim view of the labors performed for my book. When they leave here at night I imagine they have their vulgar fun over these illustrations which they draw for money and ridicule me at the coffeehouse. And who among them will ever forget the time Our Sultan had the young Venetian artist, whom He'd invited from the embassy at my behest, paint His portrait. Thereafter, He had Master Osman make a copy of that oil painting. Forced to imitate the Venetian painter, Master Osman held me responsible for this unseemly coercion and the shameful portrait that came of it. He was justified."

All day long, I showed him every picture—except the final illustration that I cannot, for whatever reason, finish. I prodded him to write. I discussed the temperaments of the miniaturists, and I enumerated the sums of money I meted out to them. We discussed "perspective" and whether the diminutive objects in the background of Venetian pictures were sacrilegious, and equally, we talked about the possibility that unfortunate Elegant Effendi had been murdered for excessive ambition and out of jealousy over his wealth.

As Black returned home that night, I was confident he'd come again the next morning as promised and that he'd once again listen to me recount the stories that would constitute my book. I listened to his footsteps fading beyond the open gate; there was something to the cold night that seemed to make my sleepless and troubled murderer stronger and more devilish than me and my book.

I closed the courtyard gate tightly behind him. I placed the old ceramic water basin that I used as a basil planter behind the gate as I did each night. Before I reduced the stove to smoldering ashes and went to bed, I glanced up to see Shekure in a white gown looking like a ghost in the blackness.

"Are you absolutely certain that you want to marry him?" I asked.

"No, dear Father. I've long since forgotten about marriage. Besides, I am married."

"If you still want to marry him, I'm willing to give you my blessing now."

"I wish not to be wed to him."

"Why?"

"Because it's against your will. In all sincerity, I desire nobody that you do not want."

I Am Your Beloved Uncle

I noticed, momentarily, the coals in the stove reflected in her eyes. Her eyes had aged, not out of unhappiness, but anger; yet there was no trace of offense in her voice.

"Black is in love with you," I said as if divulging a secret.

"I know."

"He listened to all I had to say today not out of his love of painting, but out of his love for you."

"He will complete your book, this is what matters."

"Your husband might return one day," I said.

"I'm not certain why, perhaps it's the silence, but tonight I've realized once and for all that my husband will never return. What I've dreamt seems to be the truth: They must've killed him. He's long since turned to dust." She whispered the last statement lest the sleeping children hear. And she said it with a peculiar tinge of anger.

"If they happen to kill me," I said, "I want you to finish this book to which I've dedicated everything. Swear that you will."

"I give my word. Who will be the one to complete your book?"

"Black! You can ensure that he does so."

"You are already ensuring that he does so, dear Father," she said. "You have no need for me."

"Agreed, but he's giving in to me because of you. If they kill me, he might be afraid to continue on."

"In that case, he won't be able to marry me," said my clever daughter, smiling.

Where did I come up with the detail about her smiling? During the entire conversation, I noticed nothing except an occasional glimmer in her eyes. We were standing tensely facing one another in the middle of the room.

"Do you communicate with each other, exchange signals?" I asked, unable to contain myself.

"How could you even think such a thing?"

A long agonizing silence passed. A dog barked in the distance. I was slightly cold and shuddered. The room was so black now that we could no longer see each other; we could each only sense the other's presence. We abruptly embraced with all our might. She began to cry, and said that she missed her mother. I kissed and stroked her head, which indeed smelled like her mother's hair. I walked her to her bedchamber and put her to bed next to the children who were sleeping side by side. And as I reflected back over the last two days, I was certain that Shekure had corresponded with Black.

CHAPTER 22

I AM CALLED BLACK

When I returned home that night, ably evading my landlady—who was beginning to act like my mother—I sequestered myself in my room and lay on my mattress, giving myself over to visions of Shekure.

Allow me the amusement of describing the sounds I'd heard in Enishte's house. On my second visit after twelve years, she didn't show herself. She did succeed, however, in so magically endowing me with her presence that I was certain of being, somehow, continually under her watch, while she sized me up as a future husband, amusing herself all the while as if playing a game of logic. Knowing this, I also imagined I was continually able to see her. Thus was I better able to understand Ibn Arabi's notion that love is the ability to make the invisible visible and the desire always to feel the invisible in one's midst.

I could infer that Shekure was continually watching me because I'd been listening to the sounds coming from within the house and to the creaking of its wood boards. At one point, I was absolutely certain she was with her children in the next room, which opened onto the wide hallway-cum-anteroom; I could hear the children pushing, shoving and sparring with each other while their mother, perhaps, tried to quiet them with gestures, threatening glances and knit brows. Once in a while I heard them whispering quite unnaturally, not as one would whisper to avoid disturbing someone's ritual prayers, but affectedly, as one would before erupting in a fit of laughter.

Another time, as their grandfather was explaining to me the wonders of light and shadow, Shevket and Orhan entered the room, and with careful gestures obviously rehearsed beforehand, proffered a tray and served us coffee. This ceremony, which should've been Hayriye's concern, was arranged by Shekure so they could observe the man who might soon become their father. And so, I paid a compliment to Shevket: "What nice eyes you have." Then, I immediately turned to his younger brother, Orhan—sensing that he might grow jealous—and added, "Yours are as well." Next, I placed a faded red carnation petal, which I'd fast produced from the folds of my robe, onto the tray and kissed each boy on the cheeks. Later still, I heard laughter and giggling from within.

Frequently, I grew curious to know from which hole in the walls, the closed doors, or perhaps, the ceiling, and from which angle, her eye was peering at me. Staring at a crack, knot or what I took to be a hole, I'd imagine Shekure situated just behind it. Suddenly, suspecting another black spot, and to determine whether I was justified in my suspicion—even at the risk of being insolent toward my Enishte as he continued his endless recital—I'd stand up. Affecting all the while the demeanor of an attentive disciple, quite enthralled and quite lost in thought, in order to demonstrate how intent I was upon my Enishte's story, I'd begin pacing in the room with a preoccupied air, before approaching that suspicious black spot on the wall.

When I failed to find Shekure's eye nesting in what I had taken to be a peephole, I'd be overcome by disappointment, and then by a strange feeling of loneliness, by the impatience of a man uncertain where to turn next.

Now and then, I'd experience such an abrupt and intense feeling that Shekure was watching me, I'd be so absolutely convinced I was within her gaze, that I'd start posing like a man trying to show he was wiser, stronger and more capable than he really was so as to impress the woman he loved. Later, I'd fantasize that Shekure and her boys were comparing me with her husband—the boys' missing father—before my mind would focus again upon whichever variety of famous Venetian illustrator about whose painting techniques my Enishte was waxing philosophic at the moment. I longed to be like these newly famed painters solely because Shekure had heard so much about them from her father; illustrators who had earned their renown—not through suffering martyrdom in cells like saints, or through severing the heads of enemy soldiers with a mighty arm and a sharp scimitar, as that absent husband had done—but on account of a manuscript they'd transcribed or a page they'd illuminated. I tried very hard to imagine the magnificent pictures created by these celebrated illustrators, who were, as my Enishte explained, inspired by the power of the world's mystery and its visible blackness. I tried so hard to visualize them—those masterpieces my Enishte had seen and was now attempting to describe to one who had never laid eyes on them—that, finally, when my imagination failed me, I felt only more dejected and demeaned.

I looked up to discover that Shevket was before me again. He approached me decisively, and I assumed—as was customary for the oldest male child among certain Arab tribes in Transoxiana and among

Circassian tribes in the Caucasus mountains—that he would not only kiss a guest's hand at the beginning of a visit, but also when that guest left. Caught off guard, I presented my hand for him to kiss. At that moment, from somewhere not too far away, I heard her laughter. Was she laughing at me? I became flustered and to remedy the situation, I grabbed Shevket and kissed him on both cheeks as though this were what was really expected of me. Then I smiled at my Enishte as though to apologize for interrupting him and to assure him that I meant no disrespect, while carefully drawing the child near to check whether he bore his mother's scent. By the time I understood that the boy had placed a crumpled scrap of paper into my hand, he'd long since turned his back and walked some distance toward the door.

I clutched the scrap of paper in my fist like a jewel. And when I understood that this was a note from Shekure, out of elation I could scarcely keep from grinning stupidly at my Enishte. Wasn't this proof enough that Shekure passionately desired me? Suddenly, I imagined us engaged in a mad frenzy of lovemaking. So profoundly convinced was I that this incredible event I'd conjured was imminent that my manhood inappropriately began to rise—there in the presence of my Enishte. Had Shekure witnessed this? I focused intently on what my Enishte was explaining in order to redirect my concentration.

Much later, while my Enishte came near to show me another illustrated plate from his book, I discreetly unfolded the note, which smelled of honeysuckle, only to discover that she'd left it completely blank. I couldn't believe my eyes and senselessly turned the paper over and over, examining it.

"A window," said my Enishte. "Using perspectival techniques is like regarding the world from a window—what is that you are holding?"

"It's nothing, Enishte Effendi," I said. When he looked away, I brought the crumpled paper to my nose and deeply inhaled its scent.

After an afternoon meal, as I did not want to use my Enishte's chamber pot, I excused myself and went to the outhouse in the yard. It was bitter cold. I had quickly seen to my concern without freezing my buttocks too much when I saw that Shevket had slyly and silently appeared before me, blocking my way like a brigand. In his hands he held his grandfather's full and steaming chamber pot. He entered the outhouse after me and emptied the pot. He exited and fixed his pretty eyes on mine as he puffed out his plump cheeks, still holding the empty pot.

"Have you ever seen a dead cat?" he asked. His nose was exactly like his mother's. Was she watching us? I looked around. The shutters were closed on the enchanted second-floor window in which I'd first seen Shekure after so many years.

"Nay."

"Shall I show you the dead cat in the house of the Hanged Jew?"

He went out to the street without waiting for my response. I followed him. We walked forty or fifty paces along the muddy and icy path before entering an unkempt garden. Here, it smelled of wet and rotting leaves, and faintly of mold. With the confidence of a child who knew the place well, taking firm, rhythmic steps, he entered through the door of a yellow house, which stood before us almost hidden behind somber fig and almond trees.

The house was completely empty, but it was dry and warm, as if somebody were living there.

"Whose house is this?" I asked.

"The Jews'. When the man died, his wife and kids went to the Jewish quarter over by the fruit-sellers' quay. They're having Esther the clothier sell the house." He went into a corner of the room and returned. "The cat's gone, it's disappeared," he said.

"Where would a dead cat go?"

"My grandfather says the dead wander."

"Not the dead themselves," I said. " Their spirits wander."

"How do you know?" he said. He was holding the chamber pot tightly against his lap in all seriousness.

"I just know. Do you always come here?"

"My mother comes here with Esther. The living dead, risen from the grave, come here at night, but I'm not afraid of this place. Have you ever killed a man?"

"Yes."

"How many?"

"Not many. Two."

"With a sword?"

"With a sword."

"Do their souls wander?"

"I don't know. According to what's written in books, they must wander."

"Uncle Hasan has a red sword. It's so sharp it'll cut you if you just touch it. And he has a dagger with a ruby-studded handle. Are you the one who killed my father?"

I nodded indicating neither "yes" nor "no." "How do you know that your father is dead?"

"My mother said so yesterday. He won't be returning. She saw him in her dream."

If presented with the opportunity, we would choose to do in the name of a greater goal whatever awful thing we've already prepared to do for the sake of our own miserable gains, for the lust that burns within us or for the love that breaks our hearts; and so, I resolved once more to become the father of these forsaken children, and, when I returned to the house, I listened more intently to Shevket's grandfather as he described the book whose text and illustrations I had to complete.

Let me begin with the illustrations that my Enishte had shown me, the horse for example. On this page there were no human figures and the area around the horse was empty; even so, I couldn't say it was simply and exclusively the painting of a horse. Yes, the horse was there, yet it was apparent that the rider had stepped off to the side, or who knows, perhaps he was on the verge of emerging from behind the bush drawn in the Kazvin style. This was immediately apparent from the saddle upon the horse, which bore the marks and embellishments of nobility: Maybe, a man with his sword at the ready was about to appear beside the steed.

It was obvious that Enishte commissioned this horse from a master illustrator whom he'd secretly summoned from the workshop. Because the illustrator, arriving at night, could draw a horse—ingrained in his mind like a stencil—only if it were the extension of a story, that's exactly how he'd begin: by rote. As he was drawing the horse, which he'd seen thousands of times in scenes of love and war, my Enishte, inspired by the methods of the Venetian masters, had probably instructed the illustrator; for example, he might have said, "Forget about the rider, draw a tree there. But draw it in the background, on a smaller scale."

The illustrator, who came at night, would sit before his work desk together with my Enishte, eagerly drawing by candlelight an odd, unconventional picture that didn't resemble any of the usual scenes to which he was accustomed and had memorized. Of course, my Enishte paid him handsomely for each drawing, but frankly, this peculiar method of drawing also had its charms. However, as with my Enishte, after a while, the illustrator could no longer determine which story the illustration was intended to enhance and complete. What my Enishte expected of me was that I examine these illustrations made in half-Venetian, half-Persian mode and write a story suitable to accompany them on the opposite page. If I hoped to get Shekure, I absolutely had to write these stories, but all that came to mind were the stories the storyteller told at the coffeehouse.

I Am Called Black

CHAPTER 23

I WILL BE CALLED A MURDERER

Ticking away, my windup clock told me it was evening. The prayers had yet to be called, but long before, I'd lit the candle resting beside my folding worktable. I quickly completed drawing an opium addict from memory, having dipped my reed pen into black Hasan Pasha ink and skated it over well-burnished and beautifully sized paper, when I heard that voice calling me out to the street as it did every night. I resisted. I was so determined not to go, but to stay at home and work, I even tried nailing my door shut for a time.

This book I was hastily completing was commissioned by an Armenian who'd come all the way from Galata, knocking on my door this morning before anyone had risen. The man, an interpreter and guide, though he stuttered, hunted me down whenever a Frank or Venetian traveler wanted a "book of costumes" and engaged me in a bout of vicious bargaining. Having agreed that morning upon a lesser-quality book of costumes for a price of twenty silver pieces, I proceeded to illustrate a dozen Istanbulites in a single sitting around the time of the evening prayer, paying particular attention to the detail of their outfits. I drew a Sheikhulislam, a palace porter, a preacher, a Janissary, a dervish, a cavalryman, a judge, a liver seller, an executioner—executioners in the act of torture sold quite well—a beggar, a woman bound for the hamam, and an opium addict. I'd done so many of these books just to earn a few extra silver pieces that I began to invent games for myself to fight off boredom while I drew; for example, I forced myself to draw the judge without lifting my pen off the page or to draw the beggar with my eyes closed.

All brigands, poets and men of constant sorrow know that when the evening prayer is called the jinns and demons within them will grow agitated and rebellious, urging in unison: "Out! Outside!" This restless inner voice demands, "Seek the company of others, seek blackness, misery and disgrace." I've spent my time appeasing these jinns and demons. I've painted pictures, which many regard as miracles that have issued from my hands, with the help of these evil spirits. But for seven days now after dusk, since I murdered that disgrace, I'm no longer able to control the jinns and demons within me. They rage with such violence that I tell myself they might calm down if I go out for a while.

After saying so, as always without knowing how, I found myself roaming through the night. I walked briskly, advancing through snowy streets, muddy passages, icy slopes and deserted sidewalks as if I would never stop. As I walked, descending into the dark of night, into the most remote and abandoned parts of the city, I'd ever so gradually leave my soul behind, and walking along the narrow streets, my footsteps echoing off the walls of stone inns, schools and mosques, my fears would subside.

Of their own accord, my feet brought me to the abandoned streets of this neighborhood on the outskirts of the city, where I came each night and where even specters and jinns would shudder to roam. I heard tell that half the men in this neighborhood had perished in the wars with Persia and that the rest had fled, declaring it ill-omened, but I don't believe such superstition. The only tragedy that has befallen this good quarter on account of the Safavid wars was the closing of the Kalenderi dervish house forty years ago because it was suspected of harboring the enemy.

I meandered behind the mulberry bushes and the bay-leaf trees, which had a pleasant aroma even in the coldest weather, and with my usual fastidiousness, I straightened up the wall boards between the collapsed chimney and the window with its dilapidated shutters. I entered and drew the lingering scent of one-hundred-year-old incense and mold deep into my lungs. It made me so blissful to be here, I thought tears would fall from my eyes.

If I haven't already said so, I'd like to say that I fear nothing but Allah and the punishment meted out in this world has no import whatsoever in my opinion. What I fear are the various torments that murderers like myself will have to endure on Judgment Day, as is clearly described in the Glorious Koran, in the "Criterion" chapter, for example. In the ancient books, that I quite rarely lay hold of, whenever I see this punishment in all its colors and violence, recalling the simple, childish, yet terrifying scenes of Hell illustrated on calfskin by the old Arab miniaturists, or, for whatever reason, the torments of demons depicted by Chinese and Mongol master artists, I can't keep myself from drawing this analogy and heeding its logic: What does "The Night Journey" chapter state in its thirty-third verse? Is it not written that one should not, without justification, take the life of another whose murder God forbids? All right then: The miscreant I've sent to Hell was not a believer, whose murder God had forbidden; and besides, I had excellent justification for shattering his skull.

This man had slandered those of us who'd worked on that book Our Sultan had secretly commissioned. If I hadn't silenced him, he would've denounced as unbelievers Enishte Effendi, all the miniaturists and even Master Osman, letting the rabid followers of the Hoja of Erzurum have their way with them. If someone succeeded in announcing that the miniaturists were committing blasphemy, these followers of Ezurumi—who are looking for any excuse to exercise their strength—wouldn't just be satisfied with doing away with the master miniaturists, they'd destroy the entire workshop and Our Sultan would be helpless to do anything but watch without a peep.

As I did every time I came here, I cleaned up with the broom and some rags I kept hidden in a corner. As I cleaned, I was heartened and felt like a dutiful servant of Allah again. So that He wouldn't deprive me of this blessed feeling, I prayed for a long time. The cold, which was enough to make a fox shit copper, drove into my bones. I began to feel that sinister ache at the back of my throat. I stepped outside.

Soon afterward, again in the same strange state of mind, I found myself in a completely different neighborhood. I don't know what had happened, what I'd thought between the deserted neighborhood of the dervish house and here. I didn't know how I'd arrived on these roads lined with cypress trees.

However much I walked, a pestering thought wouldn't leave me be, and it ate at me like a worm. Maybe if I tell you it'll ease the burden: Call him a "vile slanderer" or "poor Elegant Effendi"—either way it's the same thing—a short time before the dearly departed gilder had left this world, he was making vehement accusations against our Enishte, but when he saw that I wasn't that affected by his declaration that Enishte Effendi made use of the perspectival techniques of the infidels, that beast divulged the following: "There's one final picture. In that picture Enishte desecrates everything we believe in. What he's doing is no longer an insult to religion, it's pure blasphemy." Furthermore, three weeks after this accusation by that scoundrel, Enishte Effendi had actually asked me to illustrate a number of unrelated things, such as a horse, a coin and Death, in various random spots on a page and in shockingly inconsistent scales; indeed, it was what one would expect of a Frankish painting. Enishte always took the trouble to cover large portions of the ruled section of the page he wanted me to illustrate as well as the places ill-fated Elegant Effendi had guilded, as though he wanted to conceal something from me and the other miniaturists.

I want to ask Enishte what he's illustrating in this large, final painting, but there's much holding me back. If I ask him, he'll of course suspect that I murdered Elegant Effendi and make his suspicions known to all. But there's something else that unsettles me as well. If I ask him, Enishte might declare that Elegant Effendi was in fact justified in his beliefs. Occasionally, I tell myself I should ask him, pretending as if this suspicion hadn't passed to me from Elegant Effendi, but had simply occurred to me. In the end, it's no comfort either way.

My legs, which have always been quicker than my head, had taken me of their own accord to Enishte Effendi's street. I crouched in a secluded spot, and for a long time observed the house as best I could in the blackness. I watched for a long time: Nestled among trees was the large and odd-looking two-story house of a rich man! I couldn't tell on which side Shekure's room was located. As is the case in some of the pictures made in Tabriz during the reign of Shah Tahmasp, I imagined the house in cross-section—as if it were cut in half with a knife—and I tried to illustrate in my mind's eye where I would find my Shekure, behind which shutter.

The door opened. I saw Black leaving the house in the darkness. Enishte gazed at him with affection from behind the courtyard gate for a moment before closing it.

Even my mind, which had given itself over to idiotic fantasies, quickly, and painfully, drew three conclusions based on what I had seen:

One: Since Black was cheaper and less dangerous, Enishte Effendi would have him complete our book.

Two: The beautiful Shekure would marry Black.

Three: What the unfortunate Elegant Effendi had said was true, and so, I'd killed him for naught.

In situations such as this, as soon as our merciless intellects draw the bitter conclusion that our hearts refuse, the entire body rebels against the mind. At first, half my mind violently opposed the third conclusion, which indicated that I was nothing but the vilest of murderers. My legs, once again, acting quicker and more rationally than my head, had already put me in pursuit of Black Effendi.

We'd passed down a few side streets when I thought how very easy it would be to murder him, so contentedly and self-assuredly walking before me, and how such a crime would save me from having to confront the first two vexing conclusions established by my mind. Furthermore, I wouldn't have cracked Elegant Effendi's skull for no reason at all. Now, if I run ahead eight or ten paces, catch up to Black and land a blow onto his head with all my might, everything will go on as usual. Enishte Effendi will invite me to finish our book. But meanwhile my more honest (what

I Will Be Called a Murderer

was honesty if not fear?) and prudent side continued to tell me that the monster I'd murdered and tossed into a well was truly a slanderer. And if this were the case, I hadn't killed him for naught, and Enishte, who no longer had anything to hide with respect to the book he was making, would most certainly invite me back to his home.

As I watched Black walking before me, however, I knew with utmost certainty that none of this would happen. It was all illusion. Black Effendi was more real than I. It happens to us all: In reaction to being overly logical we'll feed fantasies for weeks and years on end, and one day we'll see something, a face, an outfit, a happy person, and suddenly realize that our dreams will never come true; thus, we come to understand that a particular maiden won't be permitted to marry us or that we'll never reach such-and-such a station in life.

I was watching the rise and fall of Black's shoulders, his head and his neck—the incredibly annoying way that he walked, as though his every step were a gift to the world—with a profound hatred that coiled cozily around my heart. Men like Black, free from pangs of conscience and with promising futures before them, assume that the entire world is their home; they open every door like a sultan entering his personal stable and immediately belittle those of us crouched inside. The urge to grab a stone and run up behind him was almost too great to resist.

We were two men in love with the same woman; he was in front of me and completely unaware of my presence as we walked through the turning and twisting streets of Istanbul, climbing and descending, we traveled like brethren through deserted streets given over to battling packs of stray dogs, passed burnt ruins where jinns loitered, mosque courtyards where angels reclined on domes to sleep, beside cypress trees murmuring to the souls of the dead, beyond the edges of snow-covered cemeteries crowded with ghosts, just out of sight of brigands strangling their victims, passed endless shops, stables, dervish houses, candle works, leather works and stone walls; and as we made ground, I felt I wasn't following him at all, but rather, that I was imitating him.

CHAPTER 24

I AM DEATH

I am Death, as you can plainly see, but you needn't be afraid, I'm just an illustration. Be that as it may, I read terror in your eyes. Though you know very well that I'm not real—like children who give themselves over to a game—you're still seized by horror, as if you'd actually met Death himself. This pleases me. As you look at me, you sense that you'll soil yourselves out of fear when that unavoidable last moment is upon you. This is no joke. When faced with Death, people lose control of their bodily functions—particularly the majority of those men who are known to be bravehearted. For this reason, the corpse-strewn battlefields that you've depicted thousands of times reek not of blood, gunpowder and heated armor as is assumed, but of shit and rotting flesh.

I know this is the first time you've seen a depiction of Death.

One year ago, a tall, thin and mysterious old man invited to his house the young master miniaturist who would soon enough illustrate me. In the half-dark workroom of the two-story house, the old man served an exquisite cup of silky, amber-scented coffee to the young master, which cleared the youth's mind. Next, in that shadowy room with the blue door, the old man excited the master miniaturist by flaunting the best paper from Hindustan, brushes made of squirrel hair, varieties of gold leaf, all manner of reed pens and coral-handled penknives, indicating that he would be able to pay handsomely.

"Now then, draw Death for me," the old man said.

"I cannot draw a picture of Death without ever, not once in my entire life, having seen a picture of Death," said the miraculously sure-handed miniaturist, who would shortly, in fact, end up doing the drawing.

"You do not always need to have seen an illustration of something in order to depict that thing," objected the refined and enthusiastic old man.

"Yes, perhaps not," said the master illustrator. "Yet, if the picture is to be perfect, the way the masters of old would've made it, it ought to be drawn at least a thousand times before I attempt it. No matter how masterful a miniaturist might be, when he paints an object for the first time, he'll render it as an apprentice would, and I could never do that. I cannot put my mastery aside while illustrating Death; this would be equivalent to dying myself."

"Such a death might put you in touch with the subject matter," quipped the old man.

"It's not experience of subject matter that makes us masters, it's never having experienced it that makes us masters."

"Such mastery ought to be acquainted with Death then."

In this manner, they entered into an elevated conversation with double entendre, allusions, puns, obscure references and innuendos, as befit miniaturists who respected both the old masters as well as their own talent. Since it was my existence that was being discussed, I listened intently to the conversation, the entirety of which, I know, would bore the distinguished miniaturists among us in this good coffeehouse. Let me just say that there came a point when the discussion touched upon the following:

"Is the measure of a miniaturist's talent the ability to depict everything with the same perfection as the great masters or the ability to introduce into the picture subject matter which no one else can see?" said the sure-handed, stunning-eyed, brilliant illustrator, and although he himself knew the answer to this question, he remained quite reserved.

"The Venetians measure a miniaturist's prowess by his ability to discover novel subject matter and techniques that have never before been used," insisted the old man arrogantly.

"Venetians die like Venetians," said the illustrator who would soon draw me.

"All our deaths resemble one another," said the old man.

"Legends and paintings recount how men are distinct from one another, not how everybody resembles one another," said the wise illustrator. "The master miniaturist earns his mastery by depicting unique legends as if we were already familiar with them."

In this manner, the conversation turned to the differences between the deaths of Venetians and Ottomans, to the Angel of Death and the other angels of Allah, and how they could never be appropriated by the artistry of the infidels. The young master who is presently staring at me with his beautiful eyes in our dear coffeehouse was disturbed by these weighty words, his hands grew impatient, he longed to depict me, yet he had no idea what kind of entity I was.

The sly and calculating old man who wanted to beguile the young master caught the scent of the young man's eagerness. In the shadowy room, the old man bore his eyes, which glowed in the light of the idly burning oil lamp, into the miracle-handed young master.

"Death, whom the Venetians depict in human form, is to us an angel like Azrael," he said. "Yes, in the form of a man. Just like Gabriel, who appeared as a person when he delivered the Sacred Word to Our Prophet. You do understand, don't you?"

I realized that the young master, whom Allah had endowed with astonishing talent, was impatient and wanted to illustrate me, because the devilish old man had succeeded in arousing him with this devilish idea: What we essentially want is to draw something unknown to us in all its shadowiness, not something we know in all its illumination.

"I am not, in the least, familiar with Death," said the miniaturist.

"We all know Death," said the old man.

"We fear it, but we don't know it."

"Then it falls to you to draw that fear," said the old man.

He was about to create me just then. The great master miniaturist's nape was tingling; his arm muscles were tensing up and his fingers yearned for a reed pen. Yet, because he was the most genuine of great masters, he restrained himself, knowing that this tension would further deepen the love of painting in his soul.

The wily old man understood what was happening, and aiming to inspire the youth in his rendition of me, which he was certain would be completed before long, he began to read passages about me from the books before him: El-Jevziyye's *Book of the Soul*, Gazzali's *Book of the Apocalypse* and Suyuti.

And so, as the master miniaturist with the miracle touch was making this portrait, which you now so fearfully behold, he listened to how the Angel of Death had thousands of wings which spanned Heaven and Earth, from the farthest point in the East to the farthest point in the West. He heard how these wings would be a great comfort to the truly faithful yet for sinners and rebels as painful as a spike through the flesh. Since a majority of you miniaturists are bound for Hell, he depicted me laden with spikes. He listened to how the angel sent to you by Allah to take your lives would carry a ledger wherein all your names appeared and how, some of your names would be circled in black. Only Allah has knowledge of the exact moment of death: When this moment arrives, a leaf falls from the tree located beneath His throne and whoever lays hold of this leaf can read for whom Death has come. For all these reasons, the miniaturist depicted me as a terrifying being, but thoughtful, too, like one who understands accounts. The mad old man continued to read: when the Angel of Death, who appeared in human form, extended his hand and took the soul of the person whose time on Earth had ended, an

I Am Death

all-encompassing light reminiscent of the light of the sun shone, and thus, the wise miniaturist depicted me bathed in light, for he also knew that this light wouldn't be visible to those who had gathered beside the deceased. The impassioned old man read from the *Book of the Soul* about ancient grave robbers who had witnessed, in place of bodies riddled with spikes, only flames and skulls filled with molten lead. Hence, the wondrous illustrator, listening intently to such accounts, depicted me in a manner that would terrify whoever laid eyes on me.

Later, he regretted what he'd done. Not due to the terror with which he'd imbued his picture, but because he dared to make the illustration at all. As for me, I feel like someone whose father regards him with embarrassment and regret. Why did the miniaturist with the gifted hands regret having illustrated me?

1. Because I, the picture of Death, had not been drawn with enough mastery. As you can see, I am not as perfect as what the great Venetian masters or the old masters of Herat drew. I, too, am embarrassed by my wretchedness. The great master has not depicted me in a style befitting the dignity of Death.

2. Upon being cunningly duped by the old man, the master illustrator who drew me found himself, suddenly and unwittingly, imitating the methods and perspectives of the Frankish virtuosos. It disturbed his soul because he felt he was being disrespectful and, he sensed for the first time, oddly dishonorable toward the old masters.

3. It must've even dawned on him, as it does now on some of the imbeciles who have tired of me and are smiling: Death is no laughing matter.

The master miniaturist who made me now roams the streets endlessly each night in fits of regret; like certain Chinese masters, he believes he's become what he has drawn.

CHAPTER 25

I AM ESTHER

Ladies from the neighborhoods of Redminaret and Blackcat had ordered purple and red quilting from the town of Bilejik; so, early in the morning, I loaded up my makeshift satchel—the large cloth that I'd fill up and tie into a bundle. I removed the green Chinese silk that had recently arrived by way of the Portuguese trader but wasn't selling, substituting the more alluring blue. And given the persistent snows of this endless winter, I carefully folded plenty of colorful socks, thick sashes and heavy vests, all of wool, arranging them in the center of the bundle: When I spread open my blanket a bouquet of color would bloom to make even the most indifferent woman's heart leap. Next, I packed some lightweight, but expensive, silk handkerchiefs, money purses and embroidered washcloths especially for those ladies who called for me not to make a purchase but to gossip. I lifted the tote. My goodness, this is much too heavy, it'll break my back. I put it down and opened it. As I stared at it, trying to determine what to leave out, I heard knocking at the door. Nesim opened it and called to me.

It was that concubine Hayriye, all flushed and blushing. She held a letter in her hand.

"Shekure sent it," she hissed. This slave was so flustered that you'd think she was the one who'd fallen in love and wanted to get married.

With dead seriousness, I grabbed the letter. I warned the idiot to return home without being seen by anyone and she left. Nesim cast a questioning eye at me. I took up the larger, yet lighter decoy satchel I carried whenever I was out delivering my letters.

"Shekure, the daughter of Master Enishte, is burning with love," I said. "She's gone clear out of her mind, the poor girl."

I cackled and stepped outside, but then was gripped by pangs of embarrassment. If truth be told, I longed to shed a tear for Shekure's sorrows instead of making light of her dalliances. How beautiful she is, that dark-eyed melancholy girl of mine!

I ever so quickly strode past the run-down homes of our Jewish neighborhood, which looked even more deserted and pitiful in the morning cold. Much later, when I caught sight of that blind beggar who always took up his spot on the corner of Hasan's street, I shouted as loud as I could, "Clothierrr!"

"Fat witch," he said. "Even if you hadn't shouted I would've recognized you by your footsteps."

"You good-for-nothing blind man," I said. "You ill-fated Tatar! Blind men like you are scourges forsaken by Allah. May He give you the punishment you deserve."

In the past, such exchanges wouldn't have angered me. I wouldn't have taken them seriously. Hasan's father opened the door. He was an Abkhazian, a noble gentleman and polite.

"Let's have a look, then, what have you brought with you this time?" he said.

"Is that slothful son of yours still asleep?"

"How could he be sleeping? He's waiting, expecting news from you."

This house is so dark that each time I visit, I feel as if I've entered a tomb. Shekure never asks what they're up to, but I always make a point of carping about the place so she won't even consider returning to this crypt. It's hard to imagine that lovely Shekure was once mistress of this house and that she lived here with her rascally boys. Within, it smelled of sleep and death. I entered the next room, moving farther into the blackness.

You couldn't see your hand before your face. I didn't even have the chance to present the letter to Hasan. He appeared out of the darkness and snatched it from my hand. As I always did, I left him alone to read the letter and satisfy his curiosity. He soon raised his head from the page.

"Isn't there anything else?" he said. He knew there was nothing else. "This is a brief note," he said and read

> *Black Effendi, you pay visits to our home, and spend your days here. Yet I've heard that you haven't written even a single line of my father's book. Don't get your hopes up without first completing that manuscript.*

Letter in hand, he glared accusingly into my eyes, as if all this was my fault. I'm not fond of these silences in this house.

"There's no longer any word of her being married, of her husband returning from the front," he said. "Why?"

"How should I know why?" I said. "I'm not the one who writes the letters."

"Sometimes I wonder even about that," he said, handing back the letter along with fifteen silver.

"Some men grow stingier the more they earn. You're not that way," I said.

There was such an enchanting, intelligent side to this man that despite all his dark and evil traits, one could see why Shekure would still accept his letters.

"What is this book of Shekure's father?"

"You know! Our Sultan is funding the whole project they say."

"Miniaturists are murdering each other over the pictures in that book," he said. "Is it for the money or—God forbid—because the book desecrates our religion? They say one glance at its pages is enough to bring on blindness."

He said all this, smiling in such a way that I knew I shouldn't take any of it seriously. Even if it were a matter to take to heart, at the very least, there was nothing for him to take seriously about me taking the matter seriously. Like many of the men who depended on my services as a letter courier and mediator, Hasan lashed out at me when his pride was hurt. I, as part of my job, pretended to be upset to hearten him. Maidens, on the contrary, hugged me and cried when their feelings were hurt.

"You're an intelligent woman," said Hasan in order to soothe my pride, which he believed he'd injured. "Deliver this posthaste. I'm curious about that fool's response."

For a moment, I felt like saying, "Black is not so foolish." In such situations, making rival suitors jealous of each other will earn Esther the matchmaker more money. But I was afraid he'd have a sudden tantrum.

"You know the Tatar beggar at the end of the street?" I said. "He's very vulgar, that one."

To avoid getting into it with the blind man, I walked down the other end of the street and thus happened to pass through the Chicken Market early in the morning. Why don't Muslims eat the heads and feet of chickens? Because they're so strange! My grandmother, may she rest in peace, would tell me how chicken feet were so inexpensive when her family arrived here from Portugal that she'd boil them for food.

At Kemeraralık, I saw a woman on horseback with her slaves, sitting bolt upright like a man. She was proud as proud could be, maybe the wife of a pasha or his rich daughter. I sighed. If Shekure's father hadn't been so absentmindedly devoted to books, if her husband had returned from the

I Am Esther 131

Safavid war with his plunder, Shekure might've lived like this haughty woman. More than anyone, she deserved it.

When I turned onto Black's street, my heart quickened. Did I want Shekure to marry this man? I've succeeded both in keeping Shekure involved with Hasan and, at the same time, in keeping them apart. But what about this Black? He seems to have both feet on the ground in all respects except with regard to his love for Shekure.

"Clothierrrrr!"

There's nothing I'd trade for the pleasure of delivering letters to lovers addled by loneliness or the lack of wife or husband. Even if they're certain of receiving the worst news, when they're about to read the letter, a shudder of hope overcomes them.

By not mentioning anything about her husband's return, by tying her warning "Don't get your hopes up" to one condition alone, Shekure had, of course, given Black more than just cause to be hopeful. With great pleasure, I watched him read the letter. He was so happy he was distraught, afraid even. When he withdrew to write his response, I, being a sensible clothes peddler, spread open my decoy "delivery" satchel and withdrew from it a dark money purse, which I attempted to sell to Black's nosy landlady.

"This is made of the best Persian velvet," I said.

"My son died at war in Persia," she said. "Whose letters do you deliver to Black?"

I could read from her face that she was making plans to set up her own wiry daughter, or who knows whose daughter, with lionhearted Black. "No one's," I said. "A poor relative of his who's on his deathbed in the Bayrampasha sickhouse and needs money."

"Oh my," she said, unconvinced, "who is the unfortunate man?"

"How did your son die in the war?" I asked stubbornly.

We began to glare at each other with hostility. She was a widow and all alone. Her life must've been quite difficult. If you ever happen to become a clothier-cum-messenger like Esther, you'll soon learn that only wealth, might and legendary romances stir people's curiosity. Everything else is but worry, separation, jealousy, loneliness, enmity, tears, gossip and never-ending poverty. Such things never change, just like the objects that furnish a home: a faded old kilim, a ladle and small copper pan resting on an empty baking sheet, tongs and an ash box resting beside the stove, two worn chests—one small, one large—a turban stand maintained to conceal the widow's solitary life and an old sword to scare thieves off.

Black hastily returned with his money purse. "Clothier woman," he said, making himself heard to the meddling landlady rather than myself. "Take this and bring it to our suffering patient. If he has any response for me, I'll be waiting. You can find me at Master Enishte's house, where I'll spend the rest of the day."

There's no need for all of these games. No cause for a young braveheart like Black to hide his amatory maneuvers, the signals he receives, the handkerchiefs and letters he sends in pursuit of a maiden. Or does he truly have his eye on his landlady's daughter? At times, I didn't trust Black at all and was afraid that he was deceiving Shekure terribly. How is it that, despite spending his entire day with Shekure in the same house, he's incapable of giving her a sign?

Once I was outside, I opened the purse. It contained twelve silver coins and a letter. I was so curious about the letter that I nearly ran to Hasan. Vegetable-sellers had spread out cabbage, carrots and the rest in front of their shops. But I didn't even have it in me to touch the plump leeks that were crying out to me to fondle them.

I turned onto the side street, and saw that the blind Tatar was there waiting to heckle me again. "Tuh," I spat in his direction; that was all. Why doesn't this biting cold freeze these vagrants to death?

As Hasan silently read the letter, I could barely maintain my patience. Finally, unable to restrain myself, I suddenly said "Yes?" and he began reading aloud:

My Dearest Shekure, you've requested that I complete your father's book. You can be certain that I have no other goal. I visit your house for this reason; not to pester you, as you'd earlier indicated. I'm quite aware that my love for you is my own concern. Yet, due to this love, I'm unable properly to take up my pen and write what your father—my dear Uncle—has requested for his book. Whenever I sense your presence in the house, I seize up and am of no service to your father. I've mulled this over extensively and there can be but one cause: After twelve years, I've seen your face only once, when you showed yourself at the window. Now, I quite fear losing that vision. If I could once more see you close-up, I'd have no fear of losing you, and I could easily finish your father's book. Yesterday, Shevket brought me to the abandoned house of the Hanged Jew. No one will see us there. Today, at whatever time you see fit, I'll go there and wait for you. Yesterday, Shevket mentioned that you dreamt your husband had died.

Hasan read the letter mockingly, in places raising his already high-pitched voice even higher like a woman's, and in places, emulating the trembling supplication of a lover who'd lost all reason. He made light of Black's having written his wish "to see you just once" in Persian. He added, "As soon as Black saw that Shekure had given him some hope, he quickly began to negotiate. Such haggling isn't something a genuine lover would resort to."

"He's genuinely in love with Shekure," I said naively.

"This comment proves that you've taken Black's side," he said. "If Shekure has written that she dreamt my older brother was dead, it means she accepts her husband's death."

"That was just a dream," I said like an idiot.

"I know how smart and cunning Shevket is. We lived together for many years! Without his mother's permission and prodding, he'd never have taken Black to the house of the Hanged Jew. If Shekure thinks she's through with my older brother—with us—she's terribly mistaken! My older brother is still alive and he'll return from the war."

Before he had a chance to conclude, he went into the next room where he intended to light a candle, but succeeded only in burning his hand. He let out a howl. All the while licking the burn, he finally lit the candle and placed it beside a folding worktable. He produced a reed pen from its case, dipped it into an inkwell and began furiously writing on a small piece of paper. I sensed his pleasure at my watching him, and to show that I wasn't afraid, I smiled exaggeratedly.

"Who is this Hanged Jew, you must know?" he asked.

"Just beyond these houses there's a yellow one. They say that Moshe Hamon, the beloved doctor of the previous Sultan and the wealthiest of men, had for years hidden his Jewish mistress from Amasya and her brother there. Years ago in Amasya, on the eve of Passover, when a Greek youth supposedly 'disappeared' in the Jewish quarter, people claimed that he'd been strangled so unleavened bread could be made from his blood. When false witnesses were brought forward, an execution of Jews began; however, the Sultan's beloved doctor helped this beautiful woman and her brother escape, and hid them with the permission of the Sultan. After the Sultan died, His enemies couldn't find the beautiful woman, but they hanged her brother, who'd been living alone."

"If Shekure doesn't wait for my brother to come back from the front, they'll punish her," said Hasan, handing me the letters.

No anger or wrath could be seen on his face, just the misfortune and sorrow particular to the love-stricken. I suddenly saw in his eyes how fast love had aged him. The money he'd begun to earn working in customs hadn't made him more youthful at all. After all his offended grimaces and threats, it dawned on me that he might once again ask me how Shekure could be won over. But he'd come so close to becoming thoroughly evil that he could no longer ask. Once one accepts evil—and rejection in love is a significant cause for doing so—cruelty follows quickly. I became afraid of my thoughts and that terrible red sword the boys talked about, which severed whatever it touched; in my desperation to leave, in a near frenzy, I stumbled outside onto the street.

This was how I fell unwitting victim to the curses of the Tatar beggar. But I immediately pulled myself together. I softly dropped a small stone I'd picked off the ground into his handkerchief and said, "There you go, mangy Tatar."

Without laughing, I watched his hand reach hopefully for the stone he thought was a coin. Ignoring his curses, I headed toward one of my "daughters," whom I'd married off to a good husband.

That sweet "daughter" of mine served me a piece of spinach pie, a leftover, but still crisp. For the afternoon meal she was preparing lamb stew in a sauce heavy with beaten eggs and spiced with sour plum, just the way I like it. So as not to disappoint her, I waited and ate two full ladles with fresh bread. She'd also made a nice compote of stewed grapes. Without any hesitation, I requested some rose-petal jam, a spoonful of which I stirred into the compote before topping off my meal. Afterward, I went on to deliver the letters to my melancholy Shekure.

CHAPTER 26

I, SHEKURE

I was in the midst of folding and putting away the clothes that had been washed and hung out to dry yesterday when Hayriye announced Esther had come . . . or, this was what I planned to tell you. But why should I lie? All right then, when Esther arrived, I was spying on my father and Black through the closet peephole, impatiently waiting for the letters from Black and Hasan, and thus, my mind was preoccupied with her. Just as I sensed that my father's fears of death were justified, I also knew Black's interest in me wasn't eternal. He was in love insofar as he wanted to be married, and because he wanted to be married, he easily fell in love. If not me, he'd love. If not me, he'd marry another, taking care to fall in love with her beforehand.

In the kitchen, Hayriye sat Esther in a corner and handed her a glass of rosewater sherbet, as she gave me a guilty look. I realized that since Hayriye had become my father's mistress, she might be reporting to him everything she sees. I'm afraid that this may indeed be the case.

"My black-eyed girl, my dark-fortuned beauty, my stunning beauty of beauties, I was delayed because Nesim, my pig of a husband, kept me occupied with all sorts of nonsense," said Esther. "You have no husband senselessly haranguing you, and I hope you know the value of this."

She took out the letters; I snatched them from her hand. Hayriye withdrew to a corner where she wouldn't be in the way, but could still hear everything that passed between us. So Esther wouldn't be able to see my expression, I turned my back on her and read Black's letter first. When I thought about the house of the Hanged Jew, I shuddered for a moment. "Don't be afraid, Shekure, you can manage in any situation," I said to myself and began reading Hasan's letter. He was on the verge of madness:

> Shekure, I'm burning with desire, yet I know you're not in the least concerned. In my dreams, I see myself chasing you over deserted hilltops. Every time you leave one of my letters—that I know you read—unanswered, a three-feathered arrow pierces my heart. I'm writing in hopes that you'll respond this time. The word is out, everyone's spreading the news, even your children are saying it: You've dreamed that your husband has died, and now you claim that you're free. I cannot say whether or not it's true. What I do know is that you're still married to my older brother and bound to this household. Now that my father finds me justified, we're both going to the judge to have you returned here. We'll be coming with a group of men we've assembled; so let your father be forewarned. Collect your things, you're to come back to this house. Send your response with Esther immediately.

After reading the letter a second time, I pulled myself together and gazed at Esther with questioning eyes, but she told me nothing new about Hasan or Black.

I pulled out the reed pen that I kept hidden in a corner of the pantry, placed a sheet of paper on the breadboard and was about to begin writing a letter to Black when I froze.

Something came to mind. I turned toward Esther: She'd fallen upon the rosewater sherbet with the joy of a chubby child and so it seemed ridiculous to me that she could be aware of what was going through my mind.

"See how sweetly you're smiling, my dear," she said. "Don't worry, in the end everything will be all right. Istanbul is rife with rich gentlemen and pashas who'd give their souls to be wed to a stunning beauty, possessed of so many talents like yourself."

You understand what I'm talking about: Sometimes you'll say something you're convinced of, but no sooner do the words leave your mouth than you ask yourself, "Why did I say this so halfheartedly, even though I believe it through and through?" That was what happened when I said the following:

"But Esther, who'd want to marry a widow with two kids, for Heaven's sake?"

"A widow like you? Plenty, a slew of men," she said, conveying them all with a hand gesture.

I looked into her eyes. I was thinking I did not like her. I fell so silent that she knew I wasn't going to give her a letter and even that it would be better if she left. After Esther had gone, I withdrew to my own corner of the house as though I could feel my silence—how should I put it—in my soul.

Leaning on the wall, for a long while I stood still in the blackness. I thought of myself, of what I should do, of the fear that was growing within me. All the while I could hear Shevket and Orhan chattering upstairs.

"And you're as timid as a girl," said Shevket. "You only attack from behind."

"My tooth is loose," said Orhan.

At the same time, another part of my mind was concentrating on what was transpiring between my father and Black.

The blue door of the workshop was open, and I could easily hear them: "After beholding the portraits of the Venetian masters, we realize with horror," said my father, "that, in painting, eyes can no longer simply be holes in a face, always the same, but must be just like our own eyes, which reflect light like a mirror and absorb it like a well. Lips can no longer be a crack in the middle of faces flat as paper, but must be nodes of expression—each a different shade of red—fully expressing our joys, sorrows and spirits with their slightest contraction or relaxation. Our noses can no longer be a kind of wall that divides our faces, but rather, living and curious instruments with a form unique to each of us."

Was Black as surprised as I was that my father referred to those infidel gentlemen who had their pictures made as "we"? When I looked through the peephole, I found Black's face to be so pale that I was momentarily alarmed. My dark beloved, my troubled hero, were you unable to sleep for thinking of me the whole night? Is that why the blush has left your face?

Perhaps you aren't aware that Black is a tall, thin and handsome man. He has a broad forehead, almond-shaped eyes and a strong, straight, elegant nose. As in his childhood, his hands are long and thin and his fingers are jittery and agile. He's wiry, and stands straight and tall, with shoulders on the broad side, but not as broad as those of a water carrier. When he was younger, his body and his face hadn't yet settled. Twelve years later, when I first laid eyes on him from this dark refuge of mine, I immediately saw that he'd attained a kind of perfection.

Now, when I bring my eye right up to the hole, I see on his face the worry that plagues him. I felt at once guilty and proud that he'd suffered so on my account. Black listened to what my father said, gazing upon an illustration made for the book, with a look completely innocent and childlike. Just then, when I saw that he'd opened his pink mouth as a child would have, I unexpectedly felt, yes, like putting my breast into it. With my fingers on his nape and tangled in his hair, Black would place his head between my breasts, and as my own children used to do, he'd roll his eyes back into his head with pleasure as he sucked on my nipple: After understanding that only through my compassion would he find peace, he'd become completely bound to me.

I perspired faintly and imagined Black marveling at the size of my breasts with surprise and intensity—rather than studying the illustration of the Devil that my father was actually showing him. Not only my breasts, but as if drunk with the vision of me, he was gazing at my hair, my neck, at all of me. He was so attracted to me that he was giving voice to those sweet nothings he couldn't summon as a youth; from his glances, I realized how he was in awe of my proud demeanor, my manners, my upbringing, the way I waited patiently and bravely for my husband, and the beauty of the letter I'd written him.

I felt anger toward my father, who was setting things up so I wouldn't be able to marry again. I was also fed up with those illustrations he was having the miniaturists make in imitation of the Frankish masters, and I was sick of his recollections of Venice.

When I closed my eyes again—Allah, it wasn't my own desire—in my thoughts, Black had approached me so sweetly that in the dark I could feel him beside me. Suddenly, I sensed that he'd come up from behind me, he was kissing the nape of my neck, the back of my ears, and I could feel how strong he was. He was solid, large and hard, and I could lean on him. I felt secure. My nape tingled, my nipples were stiffening. It seemed as if there in the dark, with my eyes closed, I could feel his enlarged member behind me, close to me. My head spun. What was Black's like? I wondered.

At times in my dreams, my husband in his agony shows his to me. I come to the awareness that my husband is struggling to keep his bloody body, lanced and shot with Persian arrows, walking upright as he approaches. But sadly, there is a river between us. As he calls to me from the opposite bank, covered in blood and suffering terribly, I notice that he has become erect. If it's true what the Georgian bride said at the public bath, and if there's truth to what the old hags say, "Yes, it grows that large," then my husband's wasn't so big. If Black's is bigger, if that enormous thing I saw under Black's belt when he took up the empty piece of paper I'd sent by Shevket yesterday; if that was actually it—and it surely was—I'm afraid I'll suffer great pain, if it even fits inside me at all.

"Mother, Shevket is mocking me."

I left the black corner of the closet, quietly passing into the room across the hall, where I removed the red broadcloth vest from the chest and put it on. They'd spread out my mattress and were shouting and frolicking on it.

"Didn't I warn you that when Black visits you aren't to shout, did I not?"

"Mama, why did you put that red vest on?" Shevket asked.

"But Mother, Shevket was mocking me," Orhan said.

"Didn't I tell you not to mock him? And what's this foul thing doing here?" Off to the side there was a piece of animal hide.

"It's a carcass," Orhan said. "Shevket found it on the street."

"Quick, take it and throw it back where you found it, now."

"Let Shevket do it."

"I said now!"

As I would do before I slapped them, I bit my lower lip angrily, and seeing how serious I really was, they fled in fright. I hope they return soon so they don't catch cold.

Of all the miniaturists, I liked Black the best. He liked me more than the others did and I understood his soul. I took out pen and paper, and in one sitting, without having to think, I wrote the following:

All right then, before the evening prayer is called, I'll meet you at the house of the Hanged Jew. Finish my father's book as soon as possible.

I, Shekure 139

I did not reply to Hasan. Even if he was actually going to the judge today, I didn't believe that the men he and his father were assembling would raid our house immediately. If he were indeed ready to take such action he'd have done so without writing a letter or awaiting my reply. He's surely awaiting my response, and, when it doesn't arrive, it'll drive him mad. Only then will he begin assembling people and prepare to abduct me. Don't think I'm not afraid of him at all. But, I'm counting on Black to protect me. Anyway, let me tell you what's going on in my heart just now: I believe I'm not so afraid of Hasan because I love him as well.

If you object and think to yourselves, "Now what is this love about?" I'd find you justified. It's not that I failed to notice during the years we waited under the same roof for my husband's return, how pitiful, weak and selfish this man was. But now that Esther tells me he earns a lot of money—and I can always tell when she's being truthful from her raised eyebrows—since he has money, and with it self-confidence, the overbearing Hasan has surely disappeared, exposing the dark, jinnlike peculiarity that attracts me to him. I discovered this side of him through the letters he stubbornly sent to me.

Both Black and Hasan have suffered for their love of me. Black disappeared, traveling for twelve years. The other, Hasan, sent me letters every day, in the corners of which he'd illustrated birds and gazelles. At first I was frightened of him, but later, I loved to read his letters again and again.

As I well knew that Hasan was thoroughly curious about everything having to do with me, I wasn't surprised that he knew I'd seen my husband's corpse in a dream. What I suspected was that Esther was letting Hasan read the letters I'd sent to Black. That's why I sent no response to Black by way of Esther. You know better than I whether my suspicions are justified.

"Where were you?" I said to the children when they returned.

They quickly understood that I wasn't really angry. Discreetly, I pulled Shevket aside, to the edge of the darkened closet. I lifted him onto my lap. I kissed his head and the nape of his neck.

"You're cold, my dear," I said. "Give me those pretty hands of yours so Mother can warm them up . . ."

His hands had a foul smell, but I didn't comment. Pressing his head to my bosom, I gave him a long hug. In a short time he warmed up, relaxing like a kitten, sweetly mewling with pleasure.

"So then, you love your mother quite a lot, don't you?"

"Ummmhmmm."

"Is that a 'yes'?"

MY NAME IS RED

"Yes."

"More than anybody else?"

"Yes."

"Then I'm going to tell you something," I said as if divulging a secret. "But you won't tell anyone, all right?" I whispered in his ear: "I love you more than anyone, you know that?"

"More than Orhan, even?"

"More than Orhan, even. Orhan's young, like a small bird, he doesn't understand anything. You're smarter, you're able to understand." I kissed and smelled his hair. "So, I'm going to ask you a favor. Remember how you secretly brought Black a blank piece of paper yesterday? You'll do the same today, all right?"

"He's the one who killed Father."

"What?"

"He killed my father. He himself said so yesterday in the house of the Hanged Jew."

"What did he say?"

"'I killed your father,' he said. 'I've killed plenty of men,' he said."

Suddenly something happened. Shevket slid down my lap and began to cry. Why was this child crying now? All right then, I confess, I must've been unable to control myself just then, and I slapped him. I wouldn't want anyone to think I was hard-hearted. But how could he say such nonsense about a man I'd been making arrangements to marry—and that, with the well-being of these boys in mind.

My poor little fatherless boy was still crying, and all at once, this upset me greatly. I, too, was on the verge of tears. We hugged each other. He hiccuped occasionally. Did this slap merit so much crying? I stroked his hair.

This is how it all began: The previous day, as you know, I'd told my father in passing that I'd dreamed my husband had died. Actually, as happened quite frequently over these four years during which my husband never returned from battling the Persians, I dreamed of him fleetingly, and there was also a corpse, but was he the corpse? This was a mystery to me.

Dreams are always used as a means to other ends. In Portugal, from where Esther's grandmother had emigrated, it seems dreams were used as an excuse to prove heretics met with the Devil and made love. For example, even if Esther's forebears denied their Jewishness by declaring, "We've become Catholics like you," the Jesuit torturers of the Portuguese Church, unconvinced, would torture them, forcing them to describe the jinns and demons of their dreams, as well as burdening them with dreams they never had. Then they'd force the Jews to confess these dreams so in

I, Shekure

the end they could burn them at the stake. In this way, dreams could be manipulated over there, to show that people were having sex with the Devil and to accuse and condemn Jews.

Dreams are good for three things:

ALIF: You want something but you just can't ask for it. So you'll say that you've dreamed about it. In this manner, you can ask for what you want without actually asking for it.

BA: You want to harm someone. For example, you want to slander a woman. So, you'll say that such-and-such woman is committing adultery or that such-and-such pasha is pilfering wine by the jug. I dreamed it, you'll say. In this fashion, even if they don't believe you, the mere mention of the sinful deed is almost never forgotten.

DJIM: You want something, but you don't even know what it is. So, you'll describe a confusing dream. Your friends or family will immediately interpret the dream and tell you what you need or what they can do for you. For example, they'll say: You need a husband, a child, a house . . .

The dreams we recount are never the ones we actually see in our sleep. When people say they've "seen it," they simply describe the dream that is "dreamed" during the day, and there's always an underlying purpose. Only an idiot would describe his actual nighttime dreams exactly as he's had them. If you do, everyone will make fun of you or, as always, interpret the dream as a bad omen. No one takes real dreams seriously, including those who dream them. Or, pray tell, do you?

Through a dream that I half-heartedly recounted, I hinted that my husband might truly be dead. Though my father at first wouldn't accept this as an indication of the truth, after returning from the funeral, he was suddenly persuaded by the evidence of the dream, and concluded that my husband was indeed dead. Thus, everyone not only believed that my husband, who was virtually immortal these past four years, had died in a dream, they couldn't have been more certain of his death had it been officially announced. It was only then that the boys truly realized that they'd been left fatherless. It was then that they truly began to grieve.

"Do you ever have dreams?" I asked Shevket.

"Yes," he said smiling. "My father doesn't return home, and I end up marrying you."

MY NAME IS RED

His narrow nose, dark eyes and broad shoulders resemble me more than his father. Occasionally, I feel guilty that I wasn't able to pass on to my children their father's high, broad forehead.

"Go on then, play 'swordsman' with your brother."

"Can we use father's old sword?"

"Yes."

For some time, I gazed at the ceiling, listening to the sounds of the boys' swords striking each other, as I struggled to quell the fear and anxiety that was brewing within me. I went down to the kitchen and said to Hayriye: "My father's been asking for fish soup for quite some time now. Maybe I ought to send you to Galleon Harbor. Why don't you take a few strips of that dried fruit pulp that Shevket likes out of its hiding place and let the kids have some."

While Shevket was eating in the kitchen, Orhan and I went upstairs. I lifted him onto my lap and kissed his neck.

"You're covered in sweat," I said. "What happened here?"

"Shevket hit me with our uncle's red sword."

"It's bruised," I said and touched the spot. "Does it hurt? How thoughtless our Shevket is. Listen to what I have to say. You're very smart and sensitive. I have a request to make of you. If you do what I say, I'll tell you a secret that I won't tell Shevket or anyone else."

"What is it?"

"Do you see this piece of paper? You're to go to your grandfather, and without letting him see, you're to place this in Black Effendi's hand. Do you understand?"

"I understand."

"Will you do it?"

"What's the secret?"

"Just take him the paper," I said. I once again kissed his neck, which smelled fragrantly. And while we're on the subject of fragrance, it's been so very long since Hayriye has taken these boys to the public bath. They haven't gone since Shevket's thing began to rise in front of the women there. "I'll tell you the secret later." I kissed him. "You're very bright and very pretty. Shevket's a nuisance. He'd even have the audacity to lift a hand against his mother."

"I'm not going to deliver this," he said. "I'm afraid of Black Effendi. He's the one who killed my father."

"Shevket told you this, didn't he?" I said. "Quick, go downstairs and tell him to come here."

I, Shekure 143

Orhan could see the rage in my face. Terrified, he slid off my lap and ran out of the room. Maybe he was even slightly pleased that Shevket was in trouble. A while later, both of them returned flushed and blushing. Shevket was holding a strip of dried fruit in one hand and a sword in the other.

"You've told your brother that Black was the one who killed your father," I said. "I don't ever want you to say such a thing in this house again. You should both show respect and affection to Black. Do we understand each other? I won't allow you to live your entire lives without a father."

"I don't want him. I'd rather return to our house, where Uncle Hasan lives, and wait for my father," Shevket said brazenly.

This made me so irate that I slapped him. He hadn't put the sword down; it fell from his hand.

"I want my father," he said through his tears.

But I was crying more than he was.

"You have no father anymore, he won't be coming back," I said tearfully. "You're fatherless, don't you understand, you bastards." I was crying so much that I was afraid they'd heard me from within.

"We aren't bastards," said Shevket, crying.

We all cried long and hard. Weeping softened my heart and I sensed that I was crying because it made me a better person. In our communal fit of tears, we embraced each other and lay upon the roll-up mattress. Shevket had snuggled his head down between my breasts as if to nap. Sometimes, he'd cuddle up with me like this, as if we were stuck together, but I could sense that he wasn't sleeping. I might've dozed off with them, except that my mind was preoccupied with what was going on downstairs. I could smell the sweet aroma of boiling oranges. I abruptly sat up in bed and made such a sound that the boys awoke.

"Go downstairs, have Hayriye fill your stomachs."

I was alone in the room. Snow had begun to fall outside. I begged for Allah's help. Then I opened the Koran, and after once again reading the section in the "Family of Imran" chapter which stated that those who were killed in battle, who were killed on the path of Allah, would join Him, I put myself at ease with regard to my deceased husband. Had my father shown Black Our Sultan's as yet unfinished portrait? My father claimed that this portrait would be so lifelike that whoever beheld it would avert his eyes out of fear, as happened to those who tried to look directly into Our Glorious Sultan's eyes.

I called for Orhan, and without lifting him onto my lap, kissed him at length on the forehead, crown and cheeks. "Now then, without being scared, and without letting your grandfather see, you're to give this paper to Black. Do you understand?"

"My tooth is loose."

"When you get back, if you want, I'll pull it out," I said. "You're to sidle up to him. He'll be at a loss for what to do and he'll hug you. Then you'll secretly place the paper into his hand. Am I understood?"

"I'm afraid."

"There's nothing to be afraid of. If it weren't for Black, do you know who wants to become your father in his stead? Uncle Hasan! Do you want Uncle Hasan to become your father?"

"No."

"All right then, let's see you go, my pretty and smart Orhan," I said. "If not, watch out, I'll be really angry . . . And if you cry, I'll get even angrier."

I folded my letter several times, then stuck it into his small hand now stretched out in hopelessness and resignation. Allah, come to my aid so that these fatherless children aren't left to fend for themselves. I escorted him to the door, holding his hand. At the threshold he looked at me fearfully one last time.

I watched him through the peephole as he took his uncertain steps toward the sofa, approached my father and Black, stopped, and momentarily hesitated—unsure what to do. He glanced back at the peephole looking for me. He began to cry. But with one final effort he succeeded in surrendering himself to Black's lap. Black, clever enough to have earned the right to be father to my children, didn't panic to find Orhan crying unaccountably on his lap and he checked to see if there was anything in the boy's hands.

Orhan returned beneath the startled gaze of my father, and I ran to meet him and took him onto my lap, kissing him at length. I brought him downstairs to the kitchen, and filled his mouth with the raisins he liked so much.

"Hayriye, take the boys to Galleon Harbor and buy some gray mullet suitable for soup from Kosta's place. Take these silver coins and with the change from the fish, buy Orhan some dried yellow figs and cherries on the way back. Buy Shevket roasted chickpeas and sweetmeat sausage with walnuts. Walk them around to wherever they want to go until the evening prayers are called, but be careful they don't catch cold."

After they'd bundled up and left, the quiet in the house pleased me. I went upstairs and took out the little mirror that my father-in-law had made and my husband had given me as a gift. I kept it hidden away between pillowcases that smelled of lavender. I hung it up. If I looked at myself in the mirror from a distance, and moved oh so delicately, I could see my whole body. My vest of red broadcloth suited me, but I also wanted to don my mother's purple blouse which had been part of her trousseau. I took out the long pistachio-colored robe my grandmother had embroidered with flowers, and tried it on, but it didn't please me. As I was trying it on under the purple blouse, I felt a chill; I shuddered, and the candle flame trembled with me. Over it all, of course, I was going to wear my fox fur–lined street robe, but at the last minute I changed my mind, and silently crossing the hall, I removed the very long and loose azure-colored woolen robe that my mother had given me and put it on. Just then I heard a noise at the door and fell into a panic: Black was leaving! I quickly removed my mother's old robe and put on the fur-lined red one: It was tight around the bustline, but I liked it. I then donned the softest and whitest veil, lowering it over my face.

Black Effendi hadn't left yet, of course; I'd let my apprehension deceive me. If I go out now, I can tell my father that I went to buy fish with the children. I padded down the stairs like a cat.

I closed the door—click—like a ghost. I quietly passed through the courtyard and when I was out on the street, momentarily turned and looked back at the house. From behind my veil it seemed as if it wasn't our house at all.

There was no one in the street, not even any cats. Flakes of snow danced in the air. With a shudder, I entered the abandoned garden where sunlight never fell. It smelled of rotten leaves, dampness and death; yet, when I entered the house of the Hanged Jew, I felt as though I were in my own home. They say that jinns meet here at night, light the stove and make merry. I was startled to hear my footsteps in the empty house. I waited, stock-still. I heard a sound in the garden, but then everything was overcome by silence. I heard a dog bark nearby. I recognize all the dogs in our neighborhood from their barks, but I couldn't place this one.

During the next silence I sensed that there was somebody else in the house and I stood dead still so he wouldn't hear my footsteps. Strangers talked as they passed on the street. I thought of Hayriye and the children. I hoped to God that they wouldn't catch cold. In the silence that followed, I was gradually overcome by regret. Black wasn't coming. I'd made a mistake, and I ought to return home before my pride was damaged even further. Terrified, I imagined that Hasan was watching me, and then I heard movement in the garden. The door opened.

I abruptly changed my position. I didn't know why I did so, but when I stood to the left of the window through which a faint light from the garden was filtering, I realized that Black would be able to see me, to borrow a phrase from my father, "within the mysteries of shadow." I covered my face with my veil and waited, listening to his footsteps.

Black passed through the doorway and saw me, then took a few more steps and stopped. We stood five paces apart and beheld each other. He looked healthier and stronger than he'd appeared through the peephole. There was a silence.

"Remove your veil," he said in a whisper. "Please."

"I'm married. I'm awaiting my husband's return."

"Remove your veil," he said in the same tone. "Your husband won't ever come back."

"Have you arranged to meet me here to tell me this?"

"Nay, I've done so to be able to see you. I've been thinking of you for twelve years. Remove your veil, my darling, let me look at you just once."

I removed it. I was pleased as he silently studied my face and stared at length into the depths of my eyes.

"Marriage and motherhood have made you even more beautiful. And your face has become entirely different than what I remembered."

"How had you remembered me?"

"With agony, because when I thought of you, I couldn't help but think that what I was remembering wasn't you but a fantasy. In our childhood, you remember how we used to discuss Hüsrev and Shirin, who fell in love after seeing images of each other, don't you? Why was it that Shirin hadn't fallen in love with handsome Hüsrev when first she saw his picture hanging from a tree branch but had to see that image three times before falling in love? You used to say that in fairy tales everything happens thrice. I would argue that love ought to have blossomed when she first saw the picture. But who could have depicted Hüsrev realistically enough for her to fall in love with him, and precisely enough that she would recognize him? We never talked about this. Over these last twelve years, if I had such a realistic portrait of your matchless face, perhaps I wouldn't have suffered so."

He said some quite lovely things in this vein, stories of looking at an illustration and falling in love and of how he'd suffered desperately for me. I noticed the way he slowly approached; and his every word flitted through my conscious mind and alighted somewhere in my memory.

I, Shekure 147

Later, I would muse over these words one by one. But at the time my appreciation of the magic of what he said was purely visceral and it bound me to him. I felt guilty for having caused him such pain for twelve years. What a honey-tongued man! What a good person this Black was! Like an innocent child! I could read all of this from his eyes. The fact that he loved me so much made me trust him.

We embraced. This so pleased me that I felt no guilt. I let myself be borne away by sweet emotion. I hugged him tighter. I let him kiss me, and I kissed him back. And as we kissed, it was as if the entire world had entered a gentle twilight. I wished everybody could embrace each other the way we did. I faintly recalled that love was supposed to be like this. He put his tongue into my mouth. I was so content with what I was doing, it was as if the whole world were engulfed in blissful light; I could think of nothing bad.

Let me describe for you how our embrace might've been depicted by the master miniaturists of Herat, if this tragic story of mine were one day recorded in a book. There are certain amazing illustrations that my father has shown me wherein the thrill of the script's flow matches the swaying of the leaves, the wall ornamentation is echoed in the design of the border gilding and the joy of the swallow's matchless wings piercing the picture's border suggests the elation of the lovers. Exchanging glances from afar and tormenting each other with suggestive phrases, the lovers would be depicted so small, so far in the distance, that for a moment it'd seem like the story wasn't about them at all, but had to do with the starry night, the dark trees, the exquisite palace where they met, its courtyard and its wonderful garden whose every leaf was lovingly and particularly rendered. If, however, one paid very close attention to the secret symmetry of the colors, which the miniaturist could only convey with total resignation to his art, and to the mysterious light infusing the entire painting, the careful observer would immediately see that the secret behind these illustrations is that they're created by love itself. It's as if a light were emanating from the lovers, from the very depths of the illustration. And when Black and I embraced, well-being flooded the world in the very same manner.

Thank God I've seen enough of life to know that such well-being never lasts for long. Black sweetly took my large breasts into his hands. This felt good and, forgetting all, I longed for him to suck on my nipples. But he couldn't quite manage it, because he wasn't all that sure of what he was doing, though his uncertainty didn't prevent him from wanting more. Gradually, fear and embarrassment came between us the longer we embraced. But when he grabbed my thighs to pull me close, pressing his large hardened manliness against my stomach, I liked it at first; I was curious. I wasn't embarrassed. I told myself that an embrace such as we'd had would naturally lead to another such as this. And though I turned my head away, I couldn't take my widening eyes off its size.

Later still, when he abruptly tried to force me to perform that vulgar act that even Kipchak women and concubines who tell stories at the public baths wouldn't do, I froze in astonishment and indecision.

"Don't furrow your brow, my dear," he begged.

I stood up, pushed him away and began shouting at him without paying the slightest mind to his disappointment.

CHAPTER 27

I AM CALLED BLACK

Within the darkness of the house of the Hanged Jew, Shekure furrowed her brow and began raving that I might easily stick the monstrosity I held in my hands into the mouths of Circassian girls I'd met in Tiflis, Kipchak harlots, poor brides sold at inns, Turkmen and Persian widows, common prostitutes whose numbers were increasing in Istanbul, lecherous Mingerians, coquettish Abkhazians, Armenian shrews, Genoese and Syrian hags, thespians passing as women and insatiable boys, but it would not go into hers. She angrily accused me of having lost all sense of decorum and self-control by sleeping with all manner of cheap, pathetic riffraff—from Persia to Baghdad and from the alleyways of small hot Arabian towns to the shores of the Caspian—and of having forgotten that some women still took pains to maintain their honor. All my words of love, she charged, were insincere.

I respectfully listened to my beloved's outburst, which caused the guilty member in my hand to fade, and though I was thoroughly embarrassed by the situation and the rejection I was suffering, two things pleased me: 1. that I refrained from lowering myself to match Shekure's wrath with a response of similar hue, as I often had reacted viciously to other women in similar situations, and 2. that I discovered Shekure's particular awareness of my travels, proof that she'd thought of me much more than I'd assumed.

Seeing how downcast I'd become at being unable to carry out my desires, she'd already begun to pity me.

"If you truly loved me, passionately and obsessively," she said as if trying to excuse herself, "you'd try to control yourself like a gentleman. You wouldn't try to offend the honor of the woman toward whom you entertained serious intentions. You're not the only man who's making motions to marry me. Did anyone see you on your way here?"

"Nay."

As if she heard someone walking in the dark and snow-covered garden, she turned her sweet face, which for twelve years I hadn't been able to recall, toward the door and gave me the pleasure of seeing her profile. When we heard a momentary clattering, we both waited in silence, but nobody entered. I recalled how even when she was only twelve, Shekure had aroused in me an odd feeling because she knew more than I did.

"The ghost of the Hanged Jew haunts this place," she said.

"Do you ever come here?"

"Jinns, phantoms, the living dead . . . they come with the wind, possess objects and make sounds out of silence. Everything speaks. I don't have to come all the way here. I can hear them."

"Shevket brought me here to show me the dead cat, but it was gone."

"I understand you told him that you killed his father."

"Not exactly. Is that the way my words were twisted? Not that I killed his father, rather that I'd like to become his father."

"Why did you say that you'd killed his father?"

"He'd asked me first if I'd ever killed a man. I told him the truth, that I'd killed two men."

"In order to boast?"

"To boast, and to impress a child whose mother I love, because I realized that this mother comforted those two little brigands by exaggerating the wartime heroics of their father and by showing off the remnants of his plunder in the house."

"Go on boasting then! They don't like you."

"Shevket doesn't like me, but Orhan does," I said, in the prideful glow of having caught my beloved's error. "Yet, I shall become father to them both."

We shuddered anxiously and trembled in the half-light as though the shadow of some nonexistent thing had passed between us. I pulled myself together and saw that Shekure was crying with tiny sobs.

"My ill-fated husband has a brother named Hasan. As I waited for my husband's return, I lived two years in the same house with him and my father-in-law. He fell in love with me. Lately, he's suspicious of what might be going on. He's furious imagining that I might marry somebody else, you perhaps. He sent word declaring that he wants to take me back to their house by force. They say that since I'm not a widow in the eyes of the judge, they're going to force me back there in the name of my husband. They might raid our house at any time. My father doesn't want me to be declared a widow by verdict of the judge either. If I am granted a divorce, he thinks I'll find myself a new husband and abandon him. By returning home with my children, I brought him great happiness in the loneliness he suffered after the death of my mother. Would you agree to live with us?"

"How do you mean?"

"If we were wed, would you live with my father, together with us?"

"I don't know."

"Think about this as soon as possible. You don't have much time, believe me. My father senses that some evil is coming our way, and I think he's right. If Hasan and his men raid our home with a handful of Janissaries and bring my father before the judge, would you testify that you'd in fact seen my husband's corpse? You've recently come from Persia, they would believe you."

"I would testify, but I wasn't the one who killed him."

"All right, then. Together with another witness, in order that I be declared a widow, would you testify before the judge that you saw my husband's bloody corpse on the battlefield in Persia?"

"I didn't actually see it, my dear, but for your sake I would testify so."

"Do you love my children?"

"I do."

"Tell me, what is it about them that you love?"

"I love Shevket's strength, decisiveness, honesty, intelligence and stubbornness," I said. "And I love Orhan's sensitive and delicate demeanor and his astuteness. I love the fact that they're your children."

My black-eyed beloved smiled slightly and shed a few tears. Then, in the calculated fluster of a woman hoping to accomplish a lot in a short time, she changed the subject:

"My father's book ought to be completed and presented to Our Sultan. This book is the source of the bad luck that plagues us."

"What devilry has plagued us besides the murder of Elegant Effendi?"

This question displeased her. Appearing insincere in her attempt to be sincere, she said:

"The followers of Nusret Hoja are spreading rumors that my father's book is a desecration and bears the marks of Frankish infideldom. Have the miniaturists who frequent our house grown jealous of each other to the degree that they're hatching plans? You've been among them, you would know best!"

"Your late husband's brother," I said, "does he have any association with these miniaturists, your father's book or the followers of Nusret Hoja, or does he keep to himself?"

"He's not involved in any of that, but he doesn't keep to himself at all," she said.

A mysterious and strange quiet passed.

"When you lived in the same house with Hasan wasn't there any way you could get away from him?"

"As much as possible in a two-room house."

A few dogs, not too far away, giving themselves over completely to whatever they were up to, began barking excitedly.

I couldn't bring myself to ask why Shekure's late husband, a man who'd emerged victorious from so many battles and had become the proprietor of a fief, saw fit to have his wife live together with his brother in a two-room house. Timidly and hesitantly, I asked my childhood beloved the following question: "Why did you see fit to marry him?"

"I was, of course, certain to be married off to someone," she said. This was true, and it succinctly and cleverly explained her marriage in a way that avoided praising her husband and upsetting me. "You'd left, perhaps never to return. Disappearing in a sulk might be a symptom of love, yet a sulking lover is also tiresome and holds no promise of a future." This was true as well, but it wasn't cause enough to marry that rogue. It wasn't too difficult to deduce from her coy expression alone that a short time after I'd abandoned Istanbul, Shekure had forgotten about me, like everyone else had. She'd told me this blatant lie to mend my broken heart, if only a little, and I considered it a sign of her good intentions, which demanded my gratitude. I began to explain how during my travels I couldn't get her out of my thoughts, how at night her image haunted me like a specter. This was the most secret, most profound agony I'd suffered and I assumed I'd never be able to share it with another; the agony was quite real, but as I realized with surprise at that instant, it wasn't the least bit sincere.

So that my feelings and desires might be rightfully understood, I must presently lay bare the meaning of this distinction between truth and sincerity that I've come to know for the first time: How expressing one's reality in words, as truthful as they might be, goads one to insincerity. Perhaps, the best example might be made of us miniaturists, who've grown edgy of late due to the murderer in our midst. Consider a perfect painting—the image of a horse, for instance—no matter how well it represents a real horse, the horse meticulously conceived by Allah or the horses of the great master miniaturists, it might still fail to match the sincerity of the talented miniaturist who drew it. The sincerity of the miniaturist, or of us humble servants of Allah, doesn't emerge in moments of talent and perfection; on the contrary, it emerges through slips of the tongue, mistakes, fatigue and frustration. I say this for the sake of those young ladies who will become disillusioned when they see that there was no difference between the strong desire I felt for Shekure at that moment—as she too could tell—and, say, the dizzying lust I'd felt for a delicately featured, copper-complexioned, burgundy-mouthed Kazvin beauty during my travels. With her profound God-given savvy and jinnlike intuition, Shekure understood both my being able to withstand twelve years of pure torture for love's sake as well as my behaving like a miserable thrall of lust who thought of nothing but the quick satisfaction of his dark desires the first time we were alone. Nizami had compared the mouth of that beauty of beauties, Shirin, to an inkwell filled with pearls.

When the eager dogs began barking with renewed fervor, a restless Shekure said, "I ought to go now." It was at that moment we both realized that the house of the Jew's ghost had indeed become quite dark, although there was still time before nightfall. My body sprung up of its own volition, to hug her once again, but like a wounded sparrow, she quickly hopped away.

"Am I still beautiful? Answer me quickly."

I told her. How beautifully she listened to me, believing and agreeing with what I said.

"And my clothes?"

I told her.

"Do I smell nice?"

Of course, Shekure also knew that what Nizami referred to as "love chess" did not consist of such rhetorical games, but of the hidden emotional maneuvers between lovers.

"What kind of living do you expect to earn?" she asked. "Will you be able to care for my fatherless children?"

As I talked about my more than twelve years of governmental and secretarial experience, the vast knowledge I'd acquired in battle and witnessing death and my luminous prospects, I embraced her.

"How beautifully we embraced each other just now," she said. "And already everything has lost its primal mystery."

To prove how sincere I was, I hugged her even tighter. I asked her why, after having kept it for twelve years, she'd had Esther return the painting I'd made for her. In her eyes I read surprise at my weariness and an affection that welled up within her. We kissed. This time I didn't find myself immobilized by a staggering yoke of lust; both of us were stunned by the fluttering—like a flock of sparrows—of a powerful love that had entered our hearts, chests and stomachs. Isn't lovemaking the best antidote to love?

As I palmed her large breasts, Shekure pushed me away in an even more determined and sweeter way than before. She implied that I wasn't a mature-enough man to maintain a trustworthy marriage with a woman that I'd sullied beforehand. I was careless enough to forget that the Devil would get involved in any hasty deeds and too inexperienced to know how much patience and quiet suffering underlie happy marriages. She'd escaped my arms and was walking toward the door, her linen veil having fallen around her neck. I caught sight of the snow falling onto the streets, which always succumbed to the darkness first, and forgetting that we'd been whispering here, perhaps to avoid disturbing the spirit of the Hanged Jew, I cried out:

"What are we to do now?"

"I don't know," she said, minding the rules of "love chess." Walking through the old garden, she left delicate footprints in the snow—certain to be erased by the whiteness—and disappeared quietly.

CHAPTER 28

I WILL BE CALLED A MURDERER

Doubtless, you too have experienced what I'm about to describe: At times, while walking through the infinite and winding streets of Istanbul, while spooning a bite of vegetable stew into my mouth at a public kitchen or squinting with fixed attention on the curved design of a reed-style border illumination, I feel I'm living the present as if it were the past. That is, when I'm walking down a street whitewashed with snow, I'll have the urge to say that I was walking down it.

The extraordinary events I will relate occurred at once in the present and in the past. It was evening, the twilight gave way to blackness and a very faint snow fell as I walked down the street where Enishte Effendi lived.

Unlike other evenings, I'd come here knowing precisely what I wanted. On other evenings, my legs would take me here as I absentmindedly thought about other things: how I'd told my mother I earned seven hundred silver pieces for a single book, about the covers of Herat volumes with ungilded ornamental rosettes dating from the time of Tamerlane, about the continued shock of learning that others still painted under my name or about my tomfoolery and transgressions. This time, however, I'd come here with forethought and intent.

The large courtyard gate—that I feared no one would open for me—opened on its own when I went to knock, reassuring me that Allah was with me. The shiny stone-paved portion of the courtyard that I walked through on those nights when I came to add new illustrations to Enishte Effendi's magnificent book was empty. To the right beside the well rested the bucket, and perched on it a sparrow apparently oblivious to the cold; a bit farther on sat the open-air stone stove, which for some reason wasn't lit even at this late hour; and to the left, the stable for visitors' horses which made up part of the house's ground floor. Everything was as I expected it to be. I entered through the unlocked door beside the stable, and as an uninvited guest might do to avoid happening upon an inappropriate scene, I stamped my feet and coughed as I climbed the wooden staircase to the living quarters.

My coughing elicited no response. Nor did the noise of stamping my muddy shoes, which I removed and left next to those lined up at the entrance of the wide hall which was also used as an anteroom. As had become my custom whenever I visited, I searched for what I assumed to be Shekure's elegant green pair among the others, but for naught, and the possibility that no one was home crossed my mind.

I walked to the right into the room—there was one in each corner of the second floor—where I imagined Shekure slept cuddled with her children. I groped for beds and mattresses, and opened a chest in the corner and a tall armoire with a very light door. While I thought the delicate almond scent in the room must be the scent of Shekure's skin, a pillow, which had been stuffed into the cabinet, fell onto my dim-witted head and then onto a copper pitcher and cups. You hear a noise and suddenly realize the room is dark; well, I realized it was cold.

"Hayriye?" Enishte Effendi called from within another room, "Shekure? Which of you is it?"

I swiftly exited the room, walking diagonally across the wide hall, and entered the room with the blue door where I had labored with Enishte Effendi on his book this past winter.

"It's me, Enishte Effendi," I said. "Me."

I Will Be Called a Murderer 155

"Who might you be?"

At that instant, I understood that the workshop names Enishte Effendi had selected had less to do with secrecy then with his subtle mockery of us. As a haughty scribe might write in the colophon on the last leaf of a magnificently illustrated manuscript, I slowly pronounced the syllables of my full name, which included my father's name, my place of birth and the phrase "your poor sinful servant."

"Hah?" he said at first, then added, "Hah!"

Just like the old man who meets Death in the Assyrian fable I heard as a child, Enishte Effendi sank into a very brief silence that lasted forever. If there are those among you who believe, since I've just now mentioned "Death," that I've come here to involve myself in such an affair, you've completely misunderstood the book you're holding. Would someone with such designs knock on the gate? Take off his shoes? Come without a knife?

"So, you've come," he said, again like the old man in the fable. But then he assumed an entirely different tone: "Welcome, my child. Tell me then, what is it that you want?"

It had grown quite dark by now. Enough light entered through the narrow beeswax-dipped cloth windowpane—which, when removed in springtime, revealed a pomegranate and plane tree—to distinguish the outlines of objects within the room, enough light to please a humble Chinese illustrator. I could not fully see Enishte Effendi's face as he sat, as usual, before a low, folding reading desk, so that the light fell to his left side. I tried desperately to recapture the intimacy between us when we'd painted miniatures together, gently and quietly discussing them all night by candlelight amid these burnishing stones, reed pens, inkwells and brushes. I'm not sure if it was out of this sense of alienation or out of embarrassment, but I was ashamed and held back from openly confessing my misgivings; at that moment, I decided to explain myself through a story.

Perhaps you've also heard of the artist Sheikh Muhammad of Isfahan? There was no painter who could surpass him in choice of color, in his sense of symmetry, in depicting human figures, animals and faces, in painting with an effusiveness bespeaking poetry, and in the application of an arcane logic reserved for geometry. After achieving the status of master painter at a young age, this virtuoso with a divine touch spent a full thirty years in pursuit of the most fearless innovation of subject matter, composition and style. Working in the Chinese black-ink style—brought to us by the Mongols—with skill and an elegant sense of symmetry, he was the one who introduced the terrifying demons, horned jinns, horses with large testicles, half-human monsters and giants into the devilishly subtle and sensitive Herat style of painting; he was the first to take an interest in and be influenced by the portraiture that had come by Western ships from Portugal and Flanders; he reintroduced forgotten techniques dating back to the time of Genghis Khan and hidden in decaying old volumes; before anybody else, he dared to paint cock-raising scenes like Alexander's peeping at naked beauties swimming on the island of women and Shirin bathing by moonlight; he depicted Our Glorious Prophet ascending on the back of his winged steed Burak, shahs scratching themselves, dogs copulating and sheikhs drunk with wine and made them acceptable to the entire community of book lovers. He'd done it, at times secretly, at times openly, drinking large quantities of wine and taking opium, with an enthusiasm that lasted for thirty years. Later, in his old age, he became the disciple of a pious sheikh, and within a short time, changed completely. Coming to the conclusion that every painting he'd made over the previous thirty years was profane and ungodly, he rejected them all. What's more, he devoted the remaining thirty years of his life to going from palace to palace, from city to city, searching through the libraries and the treasuries of sultans and kings, in order to find and destroy the manuscripts he'd illuminated. In whichever shah's, prince's or nobleman's library he found a painting he'd made in previous years, he'd stop at nothing to destroy it; gaining access by flattery or by ruse, and precisely when no one was paying attention, he'd either tear out the page on which his illustration appeared, or, seizing an opportunity, he'd spill water on the piece, ruining it. I recounted this tale as an example of how a miniaturist could suffer great agony for unwittingly forsaking his faith under the spell of his art. This was why I mentioned how Sheikh Muhammad had burned down Prince Ismail Mirza's immense library containing hundreds of books that the sheikh himself had illustrated; so many books that he couldn't cull his own from the others. With great exaggeration, as if I'd experienced it myself, I told how the painter, in profound sorrow and regret, had burned to death in that terrible conflagration.

"Are you afraid, my child?" said Enishte Effendi compassionately, "of the paintings we've made?"

The room was black now, I couldn't see for myself, but I sensed that he'd said this with a smile.

"Our book is no longer a secret," I answered. "Perhaps this isn't important. But rumors are spreading. They say we've underhandedly committed blasphemy. They say that, here, we've made a book—not as Our Sultan had commissioned and hoped for—but one meant to entertain our own

I Will Be Called a Murderer

whims; one that ridicules even Our Prophet and mimics infidel masters. There are those who believe it even depicts Satan as amiable. They say we've committed an unforgivable sin by daring to draw, from the perspective of a mangy street dog, a horsefly and a mosque as if they were the same size—with the excuse that the mosque was in the background—thereby mocking the faithful who attend prayers. I cannot sleep for thinking about such things."

"We made the illustrations together," said Enishte Effendi. "Could we have even considered such ideas, let alone committed such an offense?"

"Not at all," I said expansively. "But they've heard about it somehow. They say there's one final painting in which, according to the gossip, there's open defiance of our religion and what we hold sacred."

"You yourself have seen the final painting."

"Nay, I made pictures of whatever you requested in various places on a large sheet, which was to be a double-leaf illustration," I said with a caution and precision that I hoped would please Enishte Effendi. "But I never saw the completed illustration. If I had seen the entire painting, I'd have a clear conscience about denying all this foul slander."

"Why is it that you feel guilty?" he asked. "What's gnawing at your soul? Who has caused you to doubt yourself?"

". . . to worry that one has attacked what he knows to be sacred, after spending months merrily illustrating a book . . . to suffer the torments of Hell while living . . . if I could only see that last painting in its entirety."

"Is this what troubles you?" he said. "Is this why you've come?"

Suddenly panic seized me. Could he be thinking something horrendous, like I was the one who'd killed the ill-fated Elegant Effendi?

"Those who want Our Sultan dethroned and replaced by the prince," I said, "are furthering this insidious gossip, saying that He secretly supports the book."

"How many really believe that?" he asked wearily. "Every cleric with any ambition who's met with some favor and whose head has swollen as a result will preach that religion is being ignored and disrespected. This is the most reliable way to ensure one's living."

Did he suppose I'd come solely to inform him of a rumor?

"Poor old Elegant Effendi, God rest his soul," I said, my voice quavering. "Supposedly, we killed him because he saw the whole of the last painting and was convinced that it reviled our faith. A division head I know at the palace workshop told me this. You know how junior and senior apprentices are, everyone gossips."

Maintaining this line of reasoning and growing increasingly impassioned, I went on for quite some time. I didn't know how much of what I said I myself had indeed heard, how much I fabricated out of fear after doing away with that wicked slanderer, or how much I improvised. Having devoted much of the conversation to flattery, I was anticipating that Enishte Effendi would show me the two-page illustration and put me at ease. Why didn't he realize this was the only way I might overcome my fears about being mired in sin?

Intending to startle him, I defiantly asked, "Might one be capable of making blasphemous art without being aware of it?"

In place of an answer, he gestured very delicately and elegantly with his hand—as if to warn me there was a child sleeping in the room—and I fell completely silent. "It has become very dark," he said, almost in a whisper, "let's light the candle."

After lighting the candlestick from the hot coals of the brazier which heated the room, I noticed in his face an expression of pride, one to which I was unaccustomed, and this displeased me greatly. Or was it an expression of pity? Had he figured everything out? Was he thinking that I was some sort of a base murderer or was he frightened by me? I remember how suddenly my thoughts spiraled out of control and I was stupidly listening to what I thought as if somebody else was thinking. The carpet beneath me, for example: There was a kind of wolflike design in one corner, but why hadn't I noticed it before?

"The love all khans, shahs and sultans feel for paintings, illustrations and fine books can be divided into three seasons," said Enishte Effendi. "At first they are bold, eager and curious. Rulers want paintings for the sake of respect, to influence how others see them. During this period, they educate themselves. During the second phase, they commission books to satisfy their own tastes. Because they've learned sincerely to enjoy paintings, they amass prestige while at the same time amassing books, which, after their deaths, ensure the persistence of their renown in this world. However, in the autumn of a sultan's life, he no longer concerns himself with the persistence of his worldly immortality. By 'worldly immortality' I mean the desire to be remembered by future generations, by our grandchildren. Rulers who admire miniatures and books have already acquired an immortality through the manuscripts they've commissioned from us—upon whose pages they've had their names inserted, and, at times, their histories written. Later, each of them comes to the conclusion that painting is an obstacle to securing a place in the Otherworld, naturally

I Will Be Called a Murderer 159

something they all desire. This is what bothers and intimidates me the most. Shah Tahmasp, who was himself a master miniaturist and spent his youth in his own workshop, closed down his magnificent atelier as his death approached, chased his divinely inspired painters from Tabriz, destroyed the books he had produced and suffered interminable crises of regret. Why did they all believe that painting would bar them from the gates of Heaven?"

"You know quite well why! Because they remembered Our Prophet's warning that on Judgment Day, Allah will punish painters most severely."

"Not painters," corrected Enishte Effendi. "Those who make idols. And this not from the Koran but from Bukhari."

"On Judgment Day, the idol makers will be asked to bring the images they've created to life," I said cautiously. "Since they'll be unable to do so their lot will be to suffer the torments of Hell. Let it not be forgotten that in the Glorious Koran, 'creator' is one of the attributes of Allah. It is Allah who is creative, who brings that which is not into existence, who gives life to the lifeless. No one ought to compete with Him. The greatest of sins is committed by painters who presume to do what He does, who claim to be as creative as He."

I made my statement firmly, as if I, too, were accusing him. He fixed his gaze into my eyes.

"Do you think this is what we've been doing?"

"Never," I said with a smile. "However, this is what Elegant Effendi, may he rest in peace, began to assume when he saw the last painting. He'd been saying that your use of the science of perspective and the methods of the Venetian masters was nothing but the temptation of Satan. In the last painting, you've supposedly rendered the face of a mortal using the Frankish techniques, so the observer has the impression not of a painting but of reality; to such a degree that this image has the power to entice men to bow down before it, as with icons in churches. According to him, this is the Devil's work, not only because the art of perspective removes the painting from God's perspective and lowers it to the level of a street dog, but because your reliance on the methods of the Venetians as well as your mingling of our own established traditions with that of the infidels will strip us of our purity and reduce us to being their slaves."

"Nothing is pure," said Enishte Effendi. "In the realm of book arts, whenever a masterpiece is made, whenever a splendid picture makes my eyes water out of joy and causes a chill to run down my spine, I can be certain of the following: Two styles heretofore never brought together have come together to create something new and wondrous. We owe Bihzad and the splendor of Persian painting to the meeting of an Arabic illustrating sensibility and Mongol-Chinese painting. Shah Tahmasp's best paintings marry Persian style with Turkmen subtleties. Today, if men cannot adequately praise the book-arts workshops of Akbar Khan in Hindustan, it's because he urged his miniaturists to adopt the styles of the Frankish masters. To God belongs the East and the West. May He protect us from the will of the pure and unadulterated."

However soft and bright his face might have appeared by candlelight, his shadow, cast on the wall, was equally as black and frightening. Despite finding what he said to be exceedingly reasonable and sound, I didn't believe him. I assumed he was suspicious of me, and thus, I grew suspicious of him; I sensed that he was listening at times for the courtyard gate below, that he was hoping someone would deliver him from my presence.

"You yourself told me how Sheikh Muhammad the Master of Isfahan burned down the great library containing the paintings he had renounced, and how he also immolated himself in a fit of bad conscience," he said. "Now let me tell you another story related to that legend that you don't know. It's true, he'd spent the last thirty years of his life hunting down his own works. However, in the books he perused, he increasingly discovered imitations inspired by him rather than his original work. In later years, he came to realize that two generations of artists had adopted as models of form the illustrations he himself had renounced, that they'd ingrained his pictures in their minds—or more accurately, had made them a part of their souls. As Sheikh Muhammad attempted to find his own pictures and destroy them, he discovered that young miniaturists had, with reverence, reproduced them in countless books, had relied on them in illustrating other stories, had caused them to be memorized by all and had spread them over the world. Over long years, as we gaze at book after book and illustration after illustration, we come to learn the following: A great painter does not content himself by affecting us with his masterpieces; ultimately, he succeeds in changing the landscape of our minds. Once a miniaturist's artistry enters our souls this way, it becomes the criterion for the beauty of our world. At the end of his life, as the Master of Isfahan burned his own art, he not only witnessed the fact that his work, instead of disappearing, actually proliferated and increased; he understood that everybody now saw the world the way he had seen it. Those things which did not resemble the paintings he made in his youth were now considered ugly."

Unable to rein in the awe stirring within me and to control my desire to please Enishte Effendi, I fell before his knees. As I kissed his hand, my eyes filled with tears and I felt I had relinquished to him the place in my soul that had always been reserved for Master Osman.

"A miniaturist," said Enishte Effendi in the tone of a self-satisfied man, "creates his art by heeding his conscience and by obeying the principles in which he believes, fearing nothing. He pays no attention to what his enemies, the zealots and those who envy him have to say."

But it occurred to me that Enishte Effendi wasn't even a miniaturist as I kissed his aged and mottled hand through my tears. I was embarrassed by my thought. It was as if another had forced this devilish, shameless notion into my head. Even so, you too know how true this statement is.

"I'm not afraid of them," Enishte said, "because I'm not afraid of death."

Who were "they"? I nodded as if I understood. Yet annoyance began to mount within me. I noticed that the old volume immediately beside Enishte was El-Jevziyye's *Book of the Soul*. All dotards who seek death share a love for this book that recounts the adventures that await the soul. Since I'd been here last, I saw only one new item among the objects collected in trays, resting on the chest, among the pen cases, penknives, nib-cutting boards, inkwells and brushes: a bronze inkpot.

"Let's establish, once and for all, that we do not fear *them*," I said boldly. "Take out the last illustration. Let's show it to them."

"But wouldn't this prove that we minded their slander, at least enough to take it seriously? We've done nothing of which we ought to be afraid. What could justify your being so frightened?"

He stroked my hair like a father. I was afraid that I might burst into tears again; I embraced him.

"I know why that unfortunate gilder Elegant Effendi was killed," I said excitedly. "By slandering you, your book and us, Elegant Effendi was planning to set Nusret Hoja of Erzurum's men upon us. He was convinced that we'd fallen sway to the Devil. He'd begun spreading such rumors, trying to incite the other miniaturists working on your book to rebel against you. I don't know why he suddenly began to do this. Perhaps out of jealousy, perhaps he'd come under Satan's influence. And the other miniaturists also heard how determined Elegant Effendi was to destroy us all. You can imagine how each of them grew frightened and succumbed to suspicions as I myself had. Because one of their lot was cornered, in the middle of the night, by Elegant Effendi—who had incited him against you, us, our book, as well as against illustrating, painting and all else we

MY NAME IS RED

believe in—that artist fell into a panic, killing that scoundrel and tossing his body into a well."

"Scoundrel?"

"Elegant Effendi was an ill-natured, ill-bred traitor. Villain!" I shouted as if he were before me in the room.

Silence. Did he fear me? I was afraid of myself. It was as if I'd succumbed to somebody else's will and thoughts; yet, this was not wholly unpleasant.

"Who was this miniaturist who fell into a panic like you and the illustrator from Isfahan? Who killed him?"

"I don't know," I said.

Yet I wanted him to infer from my expression that I was lying. I realized that I'd made a grave error in coming here, but I wasn't going to succumb to feelings of guilt and regret. I could see that Enishte Effendi was growing suspicious of me and this pleased and fortified me. If he became convinced that I was a murderer and this knowledge struck terror throughout his soul, then he wouldn't dare refuse to show me the final painting. I was so curious about that picture, not because of any sin I'd committed on its account—I genuinely wanted to see how it'd turned out.

"Is it important who killed that miscreant?" I said. "Is it not possible that whoever rid us of him has done a good deed?"

I was encouraged when I saw he could no longer look me directly in the eye. Magnanimous men, who think themselves better and morally superior to others, cannot look you in the eye when they are embarrassed on your behalf, perhaps because they are contemplating reporting you and abandoning you to a fate of torture and execution.

Outside, just in front of the courtyard gate, the dogs began a frenzied howling.

"It's begun to snow again," I said. "Where has everyone gone at this late hour? Why have they left you here all alone? They haven't even lit a candle for you."

"It's quite strange, indeed," he said. "I don't understand it myself."

He was so sincere that I believed him completely, and despite ridiculing him just as the other miniaturists did, I once again knew that I actually loved him profoundly. But how had he so quickly sensed my sudden and great flood of respect and affection, to which he responded by stroking my hair with irresistible fatherly concern? I began to see that Master Osman's style of painting, and the legacy of the old masters of Herat, had no future whatsoever. And this abominable thought frightened me yet again. After some tragedy, we all feel the same way: In one last desperate hope, and without caring how comic and foolish we might appear, we pray that everything might continue as it always has.

"Let's continue to illustrate our book," I said. "Let everything continue as it always has."

"There's a murderer among the miniaturists. I am continuing my work with Black Effendi."

Was he provoking me to kill him?

"Where is Black now?" I asked. "Where is your daughter and her children?"

I sensed that some other power had placed these words into my mouth, yet I couldn't restrain myself. There was no longer any way for me to be happy and hopeful. I could only be smart and sarcastic. Behind these two always entertaining jinns—intelligence and sarcasm—I sensed the presence of the Devil, who controlled them, overcoming me. At the same moment, the accursed dogs beyond the gate began to howl madly as if they'd tracked the scent of blood.

Had I lived this exact moment long ago? In a distant city, at a time which now seemed far from me, as a snow that I couldn't see fell, by the light of a candle, I was attempting to explain through tears that I was entirely innocent to a crotchety old dotard, who'd accused me of stealing paint. Back then, just as now, dogs began to howl as if they'd smelled blood. And I understood from Enishte Effendi's great chin, befitting an evil old man, and from his eyes, which he was finally able to fix mercilessly into mine, that he intended to crush me. I recalled this tattered memory from when I was a ten-year-old miniaturist's apprentice like a picture whose outlines are clear but whose colors have faded. Thus was I living the present as though it were a distinct but faded memory.

So, as I arose and circled behind Enishte Effendi, lifting that new, huge and heavy bronze inkpot from among the familiar glass, porcelain and crystal ones that rested on his worktable, the hardworking miniaturist within me—that Master Osman had instilled in us all—was illustrating what I did and what I saw in distinct yet faded colors, not as something I was experiencing now but as if it were a memory from long ago. You know how in dreams we shudder to see ourselves as if from the outside, with the same sensation, holding the large yet small-mouthed bronze inkpot, I said:

"When I was a ten-year-old apprentice, I saw just such an inkpot."

"It's a three-hundred-year-old Mongol inkpot," said Enishte Effendi. "Black brought it all the way from Tabriz. It's for red."

At that very moment, it was of course the Devil prodding me to drive that inkpot down with all my might onto this conceited old man's faulty brain. But I didn't give in to the Devil, and with false hope, I said, "It is I, I'm the one who murdered Elegant Effendi."

You understand why I said this hopefully, don't you? I trusted that Enishte would understand, and in turn, forgive me—that he would fear and help me.

CHAPTER 29

I AM YOUR BELOVED UNCLE

A silence filled the room when he confessed he'd murdered Elegant Effendi. I assumed he'd kill me as well. My heart quickened. Had he come here to end my life or to confess and terrify me? Did he himself know what he wanted? I was afraid, realizing how absolutely unacquainted I was with the inner world of this magnificent artist whose splendid lines and magical use of color had been familiar to me for years. I could sense him standing stiffly behind me, there at the nape of my neck, holding that large inkpot reserved for red, but I didn't turn to face him. I knew my silence would make him uneasy. "The dogs haven't yet quieted down," I said.

We fell silent again. This time, I knew that my death, or my somehow avoiding this misfortune, would depend on what I told him. All I knew aside from his work was that he was quite intelligent, and if you grant that an illustrator must never reveal his soul in his work, intelligence is, of course, an asset. How had he cornered me at home when no one else was here? My aged mind was furiously preoccupied with this question, but I was too confused to see myself out of this game. Where was Shekure?

"You knew it was me, didn't you?" he asked.

I hadn't known at all, not until he told me. In the back of my mind, I was even wondering whether he hadn't done well by killing Elegant Effendi, and that the late miniaturist might've actually succumbed to his anxieties and made trouble for the rest of us.

I was ever so slightly grateful to this murderer, with whom I was alone in the empty house.

"I'm not surprised you killed him," I said. Men like us who live with books and dream eternally of their pages fear only one thing in this world.

What's more, we're struggling with something more forbidden and dangerous; that is, we're struggling to make pictures in a Muslim city. As with Sheikh Muhammad of Isfahan, we miniaturists are inclined to feel guilty and regretful, we're the first to blame ourselves before others do, to be ashamed and beg pardon of God and the community. We make our books in secret like shameful sinners. I know too well how submission to the endless attacks of hojas, preachers, judges and mystics who accuse us of blasphemy, how the endless guilt both deadens and nourishes the artist's imagination."

"You don't fault me for murdering that idiotic miniaturist, do you then?"

"What attracts us to writing, illustrating and painting is bound up in this fear of retribution. It's not only for money and favor that we kneel before our work from morning to evening, continuing by candlelight through the night to the point of blindness and sacrifice ourselves for pictures and books, it's to escape the prattle of others, to escape the community, but in contrast to this passion to create, we also want those we've forsaken to see and appreciate the inspired pictures we've made—and if they should call us sinners? Oh, the suffering this brings upon the illustrator of genuine talent! Yet, genuine painting is hidden in the agony no one sees and no one creates. It's contained in the picture, which on first sight, they'll say is bad, incomplete, blasphemous or heretical. A genuine miniaturist knows he must reach that point, yet at the same time, he fears the loneliness that awaits him there. Who would accede to such a frightful, nerve-wracking existence? By blaming himself before anyone else does, the artist believes he'll be spared what he's feared for years. Others listen to him and believe him only when he admits his guilt, for which he is then condemned to burn in Hell—the illustrator of Isfahan lit these hellfires himself."

"But you're not a miniaturist," he said. "I didn't kill him out of fear."

"You murdered him because you wanted to paint as you wished, without fear."

For the first time in a long while, the miniaturist who aspired to be my murderer said something quite intelligent: "I know you're explaining all this to distract me, to dupe me, to get yourself out of this situation," and he added, "but what you've just said is the truth. I want you to understand, listen to me."

I looked into his eyes. He'd completely forgotten the formality customary between us as he spoke: He'd been carried away by his own thoughts. But to where?

"Never fear, I won't offend your honor," he said. He laughed bitterly as he circled around to face me. "Even now," he said, "as I'm doing this, it doesn't seem to be me. It's as if there's something writhing within me compelling me to do its evil bidding. Yet I need that thing nonetheless. It's that way with painting, too."

"These are old wives' tales about the Devil."

"You think I'm lying, then?"

He didn't have enough courage to murder me, so he wanted me to enrage him. "Nay, you're not lying but you're not acknowledging what you feel either."

"I acknowledge very well what I feel. I'm suffering the torments of the grave without having died. Unawares, we've sunk to our necks in sin because of you, and now you're preaching 'more courage.' You're the one who's made me a murderer. Nusret Hoja's rabid henchmen will kill us all."

The less confident he became, the more he raised his voice and the more fiercely he gripped the inkpot. Would somebody passing down the snowy street hear his shouting and enter the house?

"How did you kill him?" I asked, more to buy time than out of curiosity. "How did you chance to meet at the mouth of that well?"

"The night Elegant Effendi left your house, he came to me," he said, with an unexpected desire to confess. "He said he'd seen the final double-leaf painting. I tried at length to dissuade him from making an issue out of it. I got him to walk over to the area ravaged by the fire. I told him I had money buried near the well. When he heard that, he believed me... What better proof that an illustrator is motivated by greed alone? That's another reason I'm not sorry. He was a talented, but mediocre artist. The greedy oaf was ready to dig into the frozen earth with his fingernails. You see, if I truly had gold pieces buried beside that well, I wouldn't have had to do away with him. Yes, you hired yourself quite a miserable wretch to do your gilding. The dearly departed had finesse, but his choice of color and application was ordinary, and his illuminations were uninspired. I didn't leave a trace... Tell me, then, what is the essence of 'style'? Today, both the Franks and the Chinese talk about the character of a painter's talent, what they call 'style.' Should style distinguish a good artist from others or not?"

"Fear not," I said, "a new style doesn't spring from a miniaturist's own desire. A prince dies, a shah loses a battle, a seemingly never-ending era ends, a workshop is closed and its members disband, searching for other homes and other bibliophiles to become their patrons. One day, a compassionate sultan will assemble these exiles, these bewildered but talented refugee miniaturists and calligraphers, in his own tent or palace and begin to establish his own book-arts workshop. Even if these artists, unaccustomed to one another, continue at first in their respective painting styles, over time, as with children who gradually become friends by roughhousing on the street, they'll quarrel, bond, struggle and compromise. The birth of a new style is the result of years of disagreements, jealousies, rivalries and studies in color and painting. Generally, it'll be the most gifted member of the workshop who fathers this form. Let's also call him the most fortunate. To the rest of the miniaturists falls the singular duty of perfecting and refining this style through perpetual imitation."

Unable to look me straight in the eye, he assumed an unexpected gentle manner, and begging my compassion as much as my honesty, he asked me, trembling like a maiden:

"Do I have a style of my own?"

I thought tears would flow from my eyes. With all the gentleness, sympathy and kindness I could muster, I hastened to tell him what I believed to be the truth:

"You are the most talented, divinely inspired artist with the most enchanted touch and eye for detail that I've seen in all my sixty years. If you put a painting before me which had seen the combined work of a thousand miniaturists, I'd still be able to recognize instantly the God-given magnificence of your pen."

"Agreed, but I know you're not wise enough to appreciate the mystery of my skill," he said. "You're lying, now, because you're afraid of me. Describe, once again, the character of my methods."

"Your pen selects the right line seemingly of its own accord, as if without your touch. What your pen draws is neither truthful nor frivolous! When you portray a crowded gathering, the tension emerging from the glances between figures, their positioning on the page and the meaning of the text metamorphose into an elegant eternal whisper. I return to your paintings again and again to hear that whisper, and each time, I realize with a smile that the meaning has changed, and how shall I put it, I begin to read the painting anew. When these layers of meaning are taken together, a depth emerges that surpasses even the perspectivism of the European masters."

"Fine and well. Forget about the European masters. Start from the beginning."

"You have such a truly magnificent and forceful line, that the observer believes in what you've painted rather than in reality itself. And just as your talent could create a picture that would force the most devout man to renounce his faith, it could also bring the most hopeless, unrepentant unbeliever to Allah's path."

"True, but I'm not sure that amounts to praise. Try again."

"There's no miniaturist who knows the consistency of paint and its secrets as well as you do. You always prepare and apply the glossiest, most vibrant, most genuine colors."

"Yes, and what else?"

"You know you're the greatest of painters after Bihzad and Mir Seyyid Ali."

"Yes, I'm aware of this. If you are too, why are you making the book with that model of mediocrity Black Effendi?"

"First, the work he does doesn't require a miniaturist's skill," I said. "Second, unlike yourself, he's not a murderer."

He smiled sweetly under the influence of my joke. With this, I thought I might be able to escape this nightmare thanks to a new expression—this word "style." Upon my broaching the subject, we began a pleasant discussion concerning the bronze Mongol inkpot he held, not like father and son, but like two curious and experienced old men. The weight of the bronze, the balance of the inkpot, the depth of its neck, the length of old calligraphy reed pens and the mysteries of red ink, whose consistency he could feel as he gently swung the inkpot before me . . . We agreed that if the Mongols hadn't brought the secrets of red paint—which they'd learned from Chinese masters—to Khorasan, Bukhara and Herat, we in Istanbul couldn't make these paintings at all. As we talked, the consistency of time, like that of the paint, seemed to change, to flow ever more quickly. In a corner of my mind I was wondering why no one had yet returned home. If only he'd put down that weighty object.

With our customary workaday ease, he asked me, "When your book is finished, will those who see my work appreciate my skill?"

"If we can, God willing, finish this book without interference, Our Sultan will look it over, of course, checking first to see whether we used enough gold leaf in the appropriate places. Then, as if reading a description of Himself, as any sultan would, He'll stare at his own portrait, struck by His own likeness rather than by our magnificent illustrations; thereafter, if He takes the time to examine the spectacle we've painstakingly and devotedly created at the expense of the light of our eyes, so much the better. You know, as well as I, that barring a miracle, He'll lock the book away in His treasury without even asking who made the frame or the gilded illuminations, who painted this man or that horse—and like all skillful artisans, we'll go back to painting, ever hopeful that one day a miracle of acknowledgment will find us."

We were silent for a while, as if patiently waiting for something.

"When will that miracle happen?" he asked. "When will all those paintings we've worked on until we could no longer see straight truly be appreciated? When will they give me, give us, the respect we deserve?"

"Never!"

"How so?"

"They'll never give you what you want," I said. "In the future, you'll be even less appreciated."

"Books last for centuries," he said proudly but without confidence.

"Believe me, none of the Venetian masters have your poetic sensibility, your conviction, your sensitivity, the purity and brightness of your colors, yet their paintings are more compelling because they more closely resemble life itself. They don't paint the world as seen from the balcony of a minaret, ignoring what they call perspective; they depict what's seen at street level, or from the inside of a prince's room, taking in his bed, quilt, desk, mirror, his tiger, his daughter and his coins. They include it all, as you know. I'm not persuaded by everything they do. Attempting to imitate the world directly through painting seems dishonorable to me. I resent it. But there's an undeniable allure to the paintings they make by those new methods. They depict what the eye sees just as the eye sees it. Indeed, they paint what they see, whereas we paint what we look at. Beholding their work, one comes to realize that the only way to have one's face immortalized is through the Frankish style. And it's not only the inhabitants of Venice who are captured by this notion, but all the tailors, butchers, soldiers, priests and grocers in all the Frankish lands . . . They all have their portraits made this way. Just a glance at those paintings and you too would want to see yourself this way, you'd want to believe that you're different from all others, a unique, special and particular human being. Painting people, not as they are perceived by the mind, but as they are actually seen by the naked eye, painting in the new method, allows for this possibility. One day everyone will paint as they do. When 'painting' is mentioned, the world will think of their work! Even a poor foolish tailor who understands nothing of illustrating will want such a portrait so he might be convinced, upon seeing the unique curve of his nose, that he's not an ordinary simpleton, but an extraordinary man."

"So? We can make that portrait, as well," quipped the witty assassin.

"We won't!" I replied. "Haven't you learned from your victim, the late Elegant Effendi, how afraid we are of being labeled imitators of the

Franks? Even if we venture bravely to paint like them, it'll amount to the same thing. In the end, our methods will die out, our colors will fade. No one will care about our books and our paintings, and those who do express interest will ask with a sneer, with no understanding whatsoever, why there's no perspective—or else they won't be able to find the manuscripts at all. Indifference, time and disaster will destroy our art. The Arabian glue used in the bindings contains fish, honey and bone, and the pages are sized and polished with a finish made from egg white and starch. Greedy, shameless mice will nibble these pages away; termites, worms and a thousand varieties of insect will gnaw our manuscripts out of existence. Bindings will fall apart and pages will drop out. Women lighting their stoves, thieves, indifferent servants and children will thoughtlessly tear out the pages and pictures. Child princes will scrawl over the illustrations with toy pens. They'll blacken people's eyes, wipe their runny noses on the pages, doodle in the margins with black ink. And religious censors will blacken out whatever is left. They'll tear and cut up our paintings, perhaps use them to make other pictures or for games and such entertainment. While mothers destroy the illustrations they consider obscene, fathers and older brothers will jack off onto the pictures of women and the pages will stick together, not only because of this, but also due to being smeared with mud, water, bad glue, spit and all manner of filth and food. Stains of mold and dirt will blossom like flowers where the pages have stuck together. Rain, leaky roofs, floods and dirt will ruin our books. Of course, together with the tattered, faded and unreadable pages, which water, humidity, bugs and neglect will have reduced to pulp, the one last volume to emerge intact, like a miracle, from the bottom of a bone-dry chest will also one day disappear, swallowed up in the flames of a merciless fire. Is there a neighborhood in Istanbul that hasn't been burned to the ground at least once every twenty years that we might expect such a book to survive? In this city, where every three years more books and libraries disappear than those the Mongols burned and plundered in Baghdad, what painter could possibly imagine that his masterpiece might last more than a century, or that one day his pictures might be seen, and he revered like Bihzad? Not only our own art, but every single work made in this world over the years will vanish in fires, be destroyed by worms or be lost out of neglect: Shirin proudly watching Hüsrev from a window; Hüsrev delightfully spying on Shirin as she bathes by moonlight; lovers gazing at each other with grace and subtlety; Rüstem's wrestling a white demon to death at the bottom of a well; the anguished state of a lovelorn Mejnun befriending a white tiger and a mountain goat in the desert; the capture and hanging of a deceitful shepherd dog who presents a sheep from his flock to the she-wolf he mates with each night; the flower, angel, leafy twig, bird and teardrop border illuminations; the lute players that embellish Hafiz's enigmatic poems; the wall ornamentations that have ruined the eyes of thousands, nay tens of thousands of miniaturist apprentices; the small plaques hung above doors and on walls; the couplets secretly written between the embedded borders of illustrations; the humble signatures hidden at the bases of walls, in corners, in façade embellishments, under the soles of feet, beneath shrubbery and between rocks; the flower-covered quilts covering lovers; the severed infidel heads patiently awaiting Our Sultan's late grandfather as he victoriously marches upon an enemy fortress; the cannon, guns and tents that even in your youth you helped illustrate and that appeared in the background as the ambassador of the infidels kissed the feet of Our Sultan's great-grandfather; the devils, with and without horns, with and without tails, with pointed teeth and with pointed nails; the thousands of varieties of birds including Solomon's wise hoopoe, the jumping swallow, the dodo and the singing nightingale; the serene cats and restless dogs; fast-moving clouds; the small charming blades of grass reproduced in thousands of pictures; the amateurish shadows falling across rocks and tens of thousands of cypress, plane and pomegranate trees whose leaves were drawn one after another with the patience of Job; the palaces—and their hundreds of thousands of bricks—which were modeled on palaces from the time of Tamerlane or Shah Tahmasp but accompanied stories from much earlier eras; the tens of thousands of melancholy princes listening to music played by beautiful women and boys sitting on magnificent carpets in fields of flowers and beneath flowering trees; the extraordinary pictures of ceramics and carpets that owe their perfection to the thousands of apprentice illustrators from Samarkand to Islambol beaten to the point of tears over the last one hundred fifty years; the sublime gardens and the soaring black kites that you still depict with your old enthusiasm, your astounding scenes of death and war, your graceful hunting sultans, and with the same finesse, your startled fleeing gazelles, your dying shahs, your prisoners of war, your infidel galleons and your rival cities, your shiny dark nights that glimmer as if night itself had flowed from your pen, your stars, your ghostlike cypresses, your red-tinted pictures of love and death, yours and all the rest, all of it will vanish . . ."

    Raising the inkpot, he struck me on the head with all his strength.
    I tottered forward under the force of the blow. I felt a horrible pain that I could never even hope to describe. The entire world was wrapped in

my pain and faded to yellow. A large portion of my mind assumed that this attack was intentional; yet, along with the blow—or perhaps because of it—another, faltering part of my mind, in a sad show of goodwill, wanted to say to the madman who aspired to be my murderer: "Have mercy, you've attacked me in error."

He raised the inkpot again and brought it down upon my head.

This time, even the faltering part of my mind understood that this was no mistake, but madness and wrath that might very well end in my death. I was so terrified by this state of affairs that I began to raise my voice, howling with all my strength and suffering. The color of this howl would be verdigris, and in the blackness of evening on the empty streets, no one would be able to hear its hue; I knew I was all alone.

He was startled by my wail and hesitated. We momentarily came eye to eye. I could tell from his pupils that, despite his horror and embarrassment, he'd resigned himself to what he was doing. He was no longer the master miniaturist I knew, but an unfamiliar and ill-willed stranger who didn't speak my language, and this sensation protracted my momentary isolation for centuries. I wanted to hold his hand, as if to embrace this world; it was of no use. I begged, or thought I did: "My child, my dear child, please do not end my life." As if in a dream, he seemed not to hear.

He lowered the inkpot onto my head again.

My thoughts, what I saw, my memories, my eyes, all of it, merging together, became fear. I could see no one color and realized that all colors had become red. What I thought was my blood was red ink; what I thought was ink on his hands was my flowing blood.

How unjust, cruel, and merciless I found it to be dying at that instant. Yet, this was the conclusion that my aged and bloody head was slowly coming to. Then I saw it. My recollections were stark white, like the snow outside. My heart ached as it throbbed as if within my mouth.

I shall now describe my death. Perhaps you've understood this long ago: Death is not the end, this is certain. However, as it is written everywhere in books, death is something painful beyond comprehension. It was as if not only my shattered skull and brain but every part of me, merging together, was burning and racked with torment. Withstanding this boundless suffering was so difficult that a portion of my mind reacted—as if this were its only option—by forgetting the agony and seeking a gentle sleep.

Before I died, I remembered the Assyrian legend that I heard as an adolescent. An old man, living alone, rises from his bed in the middle of the night and drinks a glass of water. He places the glass upon the end

I Am Your Beloved Uncle

table to discover the candle that had been there is missing. Where had it gone? A fine thread of light is filtering from within. He follows the light, retracing his steps back to his bedroom to find that somebody is lying in his bed holding the candle. "Who might you be?" he asks. "I am Death," says the stranger. The old man is overcome by a mysterious silence. Then he says, "So, you've come." "Yes," responds Death haughtily. "No," the old man says firmly, "you're but an unfinished dream of mine." The old man abruptly blows out the candle in the stranger's hand and everything vanishes in blackness. The old man enters his own empty bed, goes to sleep and lives for another twenty years.

I knew this was not to be my fate. He brought the inkpot down onto my head once again. I was in such a state of profound torment that I could only vaguely discern the impact. He, the inkpot and the room illuminated faintly by the candle had already begun to fade.

Yet, I was still alive. My desire to cling to this world, to run away and escape him, the flailing of my hands and arms in an attempt to protect my face and bloody head, the way, I believe, I bit his wrist at one time, and the inkpot striking my face made me aware of this.

We struggled for a while, if you can call it that. He was very strong and very agitated. He laid me out flat on my back. Pressing his knees onto my shoulders, he practically nailed me to the ground while he raved on in a very disrespectful tone, accosting me, a dying old man. Perhaps because I could neither understand nor listen to him, perhaps because I took no pleasure in looking into his bloodshot eyes, he struck my head once more. His face and his entire body had become bright red from the ink splattering out of the inkpot, and I suppose, from the blood splattering out of me.

Saddened that the last thing I'd ever see in this world was this man who would be my enemy, I closed my eyes. Thereupon, I saw a soft, gentle light. The light was as sweet and enticing as the sleep I thought would straightaway ease all my pains. I saw a figure within the light and as a child might, I asked, "Who are you?"

"It is I, Azrael, the Angel of Death," he said. "I am the one who ends man's journey in this world. I am the one who separates children from their mothers, wives from their husbands, lovers from each other and fathers from their daughters. No mortal in this world avoids meeting me."

When I knew death was unavoidable, I wept.

My tears made me profoundly thirsty. On the one hand there was the stupefying agony of my face and eyes drenched in blood; on the other hand there was the place where frenzy and cruelty ceased, yet that place was strange and terrifying. I knew it to be that illumined realm, the Land of the Dead, to which Azrael beckoned me, and I was frightened. Even so, I knew I couldn't long remain in this world that caused me to writhe and howl in agony. In this land of frightful pain and torment, there was no place for me to take solace. To stay, I'd have to resign myself to this unbearable torment and this was impossible in my elderly condition.

Just before I died, I actually longed for my death, and at the same time, I understood the answer to the question that I'd spent my entire life pondering, the answer I couldn't find in books: How was it that everybody, without exception, succeeded in dying? It was precisely through this simple desire to pass on. I also understood that death would make me a wiser man.

Nonetheless, I was overcome with the indecision of a man about to take a long journey and unable to refrain from taking one last glance at his room, at his belongings and his home. In a panic I wished to see my daughter one last time. I wanted this so badly I was prepared to grit my teeth for a while longer and endure the pain and my increasing thirst, to wait for Shekure's return.

And thus, the deathly and gentle light before me faded somewhat, and my mind opened itself up to the sounds and noises of the world in which I lay dying. I could hear my murderer roaming around the room, opening the cabinet, rifling through my papers and searching intently for the last picture. When he came up empty-handed, I heard him pry open my paint set and kick the chests, boxes, inkpots and folding worktable. I sensed that I was groaning now and then and making odd twitching gestures with my old arms and tired legs. And I waited.

My pain was not abating in the least. I grew increasingly silent and could no longer stand to grit my teeth, but again, I held on, waiting.

Then it occurred to me, if Shekure came home, she might encounter my ruthless murderer. I didn't want to even think about this. At that instant, I sensed that my murderer had exited the room. He'd probably found the last painting.

I'd become excessively thirsty but still I waited. Come now, dear daughter, my pretty Shekure, show yourself.

She did not come.

I no longer had strength to withstand the suffering. I knew I would die without seeing her. This seemed so bitter I wanted to die of misery. Afterward, a face I'd never seen before appeared to my left, and smiling all the while, he kindly offered me a glass of water.

Forgetting all else, I greedily reached for the water.

He pulled the glass back: "Denounce the Prophet Muhammad as a liar," he said. "Deny all that he has said."

It was Satan. I didn't answer, I wasn't even afraid of him. Since I never once believed that painting amounted to being duped by him, I waited confidently. I dreamed of the endless journey that awaited me and of my future.

Meanwhile, as I was approached by the illuminated angel whom I'd just seen, Satan vanished. Part of me knew that this glowing angel who had caused Satan to flee was Azrael. But another rebellious part of my mind remembered that in the *Book of the Apocalypse* it was written that Azrael was an angel with one thousand wings spanning East and West and that he held the whole world in his hands.

As I grew more confused, the angel bathed in light approached as if coming to my aid, and yes, just as Gazzali had stated in *Pearls of Magnificence*, he sweetly said:

"Open your mouth so that your soul might leave."

"Nothing but the *besmele* prayer ever leaves my mouth," I answered him.

This was just one last excuse however. I knew I could no longer resist, that my time had now come. For a moment I was embarrassed at having to leave my bloodied and ugly body in this miserable condition for my daughter, whom I'd never see again. But I wanted to leave this world, shedding it like some tight-fitting garment that pinched.

I opened my mouth and abruptly all was color just as in the pictures of Our Prophet's Miraj journey, during which he visited Heaven. Everything was flooded in exquisite brightness as if generously painted with gold wash. Painful tears flowed from my eyes. A strained exhalation passed from my lungs through my mouth. All was subsumed in wondrous silence.

I could see now that my soul had left my body and that I was cupped in Azrael's hand. My soul, the size of a bee, was bathed in light, and it shuddered as it left my body and continued to tremble like mercury in Azrael's palm. My thoughts were not of this, however, but of the unfamiliar new world I'd just been born into.

After so much suffering, a calm overcame me. Death did not cause me the pain I'd feared; on the contrary, I relaxed, quickly realizing that my present situation was a permanent one, whereas the constraints I'd felt in life were only temporary. This was how it would be from now on, for century upon century, until the end of the universe. This neither upset nor gladdened me. Events I'd once endured briskly and sequentially were now spread over infinite space and existed simultaneously. As in one of those large double-leaf paintings wherein a witty miniaturist has painted a number of unrelated things in each corner—many things were happening all at once.

CHAPTER 30

I, SHEKURE

It was snowing so hard that snowflakes occasionally passed right through my veil into my eyes. I picked my way through the garden covered in rotting grass, mud and broken branches, then quickened my pace once I'd exited onto the street. I know you're all wondering what I'm thinking. How much do I trust Black? Let me be frank with you, then. I myself don't know what to think. You do understand, don't you? I'm confused. This much, however, I do know: As always, I'll fall into the routine of meals, children, my father and errands, and before long my heart, without even having to be asked, will whisper the truth to me of its own accord. Tomorrow, before noon, I'll know whom I am to marry.

I want to share something with you before I arrive home. No! Come off it, now, it's not about the size of that monstrosity Black showed me. If you want we can talk about that later. What I was going to discuss was Black's haste. It's not that he seems to think only of satisfying his lust. To be honest, it'd make no difference if he did. What surprises me is his stupidity! I suppose it never crossed his mind that he could frighten and abduct me, play with my honor and put me off, or open the door to even more dangerous outcomes. I can tell from his innocent expression how much he loves and desires me. But after waiting twelve years, why can't he play the game according to the rules and wait another twelve days?

Do you know I have the sinking feeling I've fallen in love with his incompetence and his melancholy childlike glances? At a time when it would've been more appropriate to be irate with him, instead, I pitied him. "Oh, my poor child," a voice inside me said, "you suffer such torment and are still so utterly incompetent." I felt so protective of him that I might've even made a mistake, I might've actually given myself to that spoiled little boy.

Thinking of my unfortunate children, I quickened my steps. Just then, in the early darkness and blinding snow, I thought a phantom of a man would run right over me. Ducking my head, I slipped by him.

Upon entering through the courtyard gate, I knew that Hayriye and the children hadn't yet returned. Very well then, I'd come back in time, the evening prayers hadn't yet been called. I climbed the stairs, the house smelled of orange jam. My father was in his darkened room with the blue door; my feet were freezing. I entered my room to the right beside the stairs holding a lamp, and when I saw that the cabinet had been opened, that the cushions had fallen out and the room had been ransacked, I assumed it was the naughty work of Shevket and Orhan. There was a silence in the house, not unusual, yet unlike the usual silence. I donned my house clothes and sat alone in the darkness, and as I gave myself over to momentary daydreaming, my mind registered a noise coming from below, directly below me, not from the kitchen but from the large room next to the stable, used in summertime as the illustrating workshop. Had my father gone down there, in this cold? I didn't remember seeing the light of an oil lamp there; suddenly, I heard the squeak of the front door between the stone walkway and the courtyard, and afterward, the cursed and ominous barking of the pesky dogs roaming past the courtyard gate—I was alarmed, to put it mildly.

"Hayriye," I shouted. "Shevket, Orhan . . ."

I felt a cold draft. My father's brazier must be burning; I ought to sit with him and warm up. As I went to be with him, holding an oil lamp aloft, my thoughts weren't with Black any longer, but with the children.

I crossed the wide hall diagonally, wondering if I should set water to boil on the downstairs brazier for the gray mullet soup. I entered the room with the blue door. Everything was in shambles. Without thinking, I was about to say, "What has my father done?"

Then I saw him on the floor.

I screamed, overcome with horror. Then I screamed again. Gazing at my father's body, I fell silent.

Listen, I can tell by your tight-lipped and cold-blooded reaction that you've known for some time what's happened in this room. If not everything, then quite a lot. What you're wondering about now is my reaction to what I've seen, what I feel. As readers sometimes do when studying a picture, you're trying to discern the pain of the hero and thinking about the events in the story leading up to this agonizing moment. And then, having considered my reaction, you'll take pleasure in trying to imagine, not my pain, but what you'd feel in my place, had it been your father murdered like this. I know this is what you're so craftily trying to do.

Yes, I returned home in the evening to discover that someone had killed my father. Yes, I tore out my hair. Yes, as I would do in my childhood, I hugged him with all my might and smelled his skin. Yes, I trembled and I couldn't breathe. Yes, I begged Allah to raise him up and have him sit silently in his corner among his books as he always did. Get up, Father, get up, don't die. His bloodied head was crushed. More than the torn papers and books, more than the breaking and tossing about of the end tables, paint sets and inkpots, more than the wild destruction of cushions, worktables and writing boards, and the ransacking of everything, more even than the anger that had killed my father, I feared the hatred that had destroyed the room and everything within it. I was no longer crying. A couple passed down the street outside, laughing and talking in the blackness; meanwhile, I could hear the infinite silence of the world in my mind; with my hands I wiped my running nose and the tears off my cheeks. For a long long time I thought about the children and our lives.

I listened to the silence. I ran, I grabbed my father by the ankles and dragged him into the hallway. For whatever reason, he felt heavier out there, but without paying any mind to this, I began to pull him down the stairs. Halfway down, my strength gave out and I sat on a step. I was on the verge of tears again when I heard a noise that made me assume that Hayriye and the children had returned. I grabbed my father by the ankles, and pressing them into my armpits, I continued to descend, faster this time. My dear father's head had been so crushed and was so soaked in blood that it made the sound of a wrung-out mop as it struck each step. At the base of the stairs, I turned his body, which now seemed to have grown lighter, and with one great effort, dragging him across the stone floor, I took him into the summer painting room. In order to see within the pitch-black room, I hastened back out to the stove in the kitchen. When I returned with a candle I saw how thoroughly the room where I'd dragged my father had been pillaged. I was dumbstruck.

Who is it, my God, which one of them?

My mind was churning. Closing the door tightly, I left my father in the demolished room. I grabbed a bucket from the kitchen, and filled it with water from the well. I climbed the stairs, and by the light of an oil lamp, I quickly wiped away the blood in the hallway, on the staircase and everywhere else. I went back upstairs to my room, removed my bloodied clothes and put on clean clothes. Carrying the bucket and rag, I was about to enter the room with the blue door when I heard the courtyard gate swing open. The evening call to prayer had begun. I mustered all my strength, and holding the oil lamp in my hand, I waited for them at the top of the stairs.

"Mother, we're back," Orhan said.

"Hayriye! Where have you been!" I said forcefully, but as if I were whispering, not shouting.

"But Mother, we didn't stay out past the evening call to prayer . . ." Shevket had begun to say.

"Quiet! Your grandfather is ill, he's sleeping."

"Ill?" said Hayriye from below. She could tell from my silence that I was angry: "Shekure, we waited for Kosta. After the gray mullet arrived, without tarrying, we picked bay leaves, then I bought the dried figs and cherries for the children."

I had the urge to go down and admonish Hayriye in a whisper, but I was afraid that as I was going downstairs, the oil lamp I carried would illuminate the wet steps and the drops of blood I'd missed in my haste. The children noisily climbed the stairs and then removed their shoes.

"Ah-ah-ah," I said. Guiding them toward our bedroom, "Not that way, your grandfather's sleeping, don't go in there."

"I'm going into the room with the blue door, to be by the brazier," Shevket said, "not to Grandfather's room."

"Your grandfather fell asleep in that room," I whispered.

But I noticed that they hesitated for a moment. "Let's be certain that the evil jinns that've possessed your grandfather and made him sick don't set upon the both of you as well," I said. "Go to your room, now." I grabbed both of them by their hands and put them into the room where we slept together. "Tell me then, what were you doing out on the streets till this hour?" "We saw some black beggars," said Shevket. "Where?" I asked. "Were they carrying flags?" "As we were climbing the hill. They gave Hayriye a lemon. Hayriye gave them some money. They were covered in snow." "What else?" "They were practicing shooting arrows at a target in the square." "In this snow?" I said. "Mother, I'm cold," said Shevket. "I'm going into the room with the blue door." "You're not to leave this room," I said. "Otherwise you'll die. I'll bring you the brazier." "Why do you say we're going to die?" said Shevket. "I'm going to tell you something," I said, "but you're not to tell anyone, are we understood?" They swore not to tell. "While you were out, a completely white man who'd died and lost his color came here from a faraway country and spoke to your grandfather. It turns out he was a jinn." They asked me where the jinn came from.

MY NAME IS RED

"From the other side of the river," I said. "Where our father is?" asked Shevket. "Yes, from there," I said. "The jinn came to take a look at the pictures in your grandfather's books. They say that a sinner who looks at those pictures immediately dies."

A silence.

"Listen, I'm going downstairs to be with Hayriye," I said. "I'm going to carry the brazier in here, as well as the dinner tray. Don't even think of leaving the room or you'll die. The jinn is still in the house."

"Mama, Mama, don't go," Orhan said.

I squared myself to Shevket. "You're responsible for your brother," I said. "If you leave the room and the jinn doesn't get you, I'll be the one who kills you." I put on the frightening expression that I made before slapping them. "Now pray that your ill grandfather doesn't die. If you're good, God will grant you your prayers and no one will be able to harm you." Without giving themselves over to it too much, they began to pray. I went downstairs.

"Somebody knocked over the pot of orange jam," said Hayriye. "The cat couldn't have done it, not strong enough; a dog couldn't have gotten into the house . . ."

She abruptly saw the terror on my face and stopped: "What's the matter, then," she said, "what happened? Has something happened to your dear father?"

"He's dead."

She shrieked. The knife and onion she was holding fell from her hands and hit the cutting board with such force that the fish she was preparing flopped. She shrieked again. We both noticed that the blood on her left hand had come, not from the fish, but from her index finger, which she'd sliced accidentally. I ran upstairs, and as I was searching for a piece of muslin in the room opposite the one the children were in, I heard their noises and shouts. Holding the piece of cloth I'd torn off, I entered the room to find that Shevket had climbed onto his younger brother, pinning Orhan's shoulders down with his knees. He was choking him.

"What are you two doing!" I shouted at the top of my lungs.

"Orhan was leaving the room," Shevket said.

"Liar," said Orhan. "Shevket opened the door and I told him not to leave." He began to cry.

"If you don't sit up here quietly, I'll kill both of you."

"Mama, don't go," Orhan said.

Downstairs, I bound Hayriye's finger, stopping the bleeding. When I told her that my father hadn't died a natural death, she grew frightened

I, Shekure 181

and recited some prayers asking for Allah's protection. She stared at her injured finger and began crying. Was her affection for my father great enough to unleash such a fit of crying? She wanted to go upstairs and see him.

"He's not upstairs," I said. "He's in the back room."

She gazed at me suspiciously. But when she realized I couldn't bear another look at him, she was overcome by curiosity. She grabbed the lamp and left. She took four or five steps beyond the entrance of the kitchen, where I stood, and with respect and apprehension, she slowly pushed open the door of the room, and by the light of the lamp she was holding, looked inside. Unable at first to see my father, she raised the lamp even higher, trying to illuminate the corners of the large rectangular room.

"Aaah!" she screamed. She'd caught sight of my father where I'd left him just beside the door. Frozen, she gazed at him. The shadow she cast along the floor and stable wall was motionless. As she looked, I imagined what she was seeing. When she returned, she wasn't crying. I was relieved to see that she still had her wits about her, enough to be able to register completely what I was prepared to tell her.

"Now listen to me, Hayriye," I said. As I spoke, I waved the fish knife, which my hand had grabbed seemingly on its own. "The upstairs has been ransacked too; the same accursed demon has destroyed all, he's made a shambles of everything. That's where he crushed my father's face and skull; that's where he killed him. I brought him down here so the children wouldn't see and so I might have a chance to caution you. After you three left, I also went out. Father was home by himself."

"I was not aware of that," she said insolently. "Where were you?"

I wanted her to take careful note of my silence. Then I said, "I was with Black. I met with Black in the house of the Hanged Jew. But you won't breathe a word of this to anyone. Nor, for the time being, will you mention that my father has been killed."

"Who was it that murdered him?"

Was she truly such an idiot or was she trying to corner me?

"If I knew, I wouldn't hide the fact that he was dead," I said. "I don't know. Do you?"

"How should I know anything?" she said. "What are we going to do now?"

"You're going to behave as if nothing whatsoever has happened," I said. I felt the urge to wail, to burst out crying, but I restrained myself. We both were quiet.

Much later, I said, "Forget about the fish for now, set out the dishes for the children."

She objected and started to cry, and I put my arms around her. We hugged each other tightly. I loved her then, momentarily pitying, not only myself and the children, but all of us. But even as we embraced, a worm of doubt was anxiously gnawing at me. You know where I was while my father was being murdered. To further my own designs, I'd cleared the house of Hayriye and the children. You know that leaving my father alone in the house was an unforeseen coincidence... But did Hayriye know? Did she comprehend what I'd explained to her, will she understand? Indeed, yes, she'd quickly understand and grow suspicious. I hugged her even tighter; but I knew that with her slave girl's mind she'd assume I was doing this to cover up my wiles, and before long even I felt as if I were deceiving her. While my father was being murdered here, I was with Black engaged in an act of lovemaking. If it were only Hayriye who knew this, I wouldn't feel as guilty, but I suspect that you might make something of it as well. So, admit it, you believe that I'm hiding something. Alas, poor woman! Could my fate be any darker? I began to cry, then Hayriye cried, and we embraced again.

I pretended to satisfy my hunger at the table we'd set upstairs. From time to time, with the excuse of "checking on Grandfather," I would step into the other room and burst into tears. Later because the children were scared and agitated, they snuggled up tightly next to me in bed. For a long while they were unable to sleep for fear of jinns, and as they tossed and turned they kept asking, "I heard a noise, did you hear it?" To lull them to sleep, I promised to tell them a love story. You know how words take wing in the darkness.

"Mother, you're not going to get married are you?" said Shevket.

"Listen to me," I said. "There was a prince who, from afar, fell in love with a strikingly beautiful maiden. How did this happen? I'll tell you how. Before laying eyes on the pretty maiden, he'd seen her portrait, that's how."

As I would often do when I was upset and troubled, I recounted the tale not from memory, but improvising according to how I felt at that time. And since I colored it using a palette of my own memories and worries, what I recounted became a kind of melancholy illustration to accompany all that had happened to me.

After both children fell asleep, I left the warm bed and, together with Hayriye, cleaned up what that vile demon had scattered about. We picked up ruined chests, books, cloth, ceramic cups, earthenware pots, plates and inkpots that had been thrown about and shattered;

we cleared away a demolished folding worktable, paint boxes and papers that had been torn up with furious hatred; and while doing so one of us, periodically, would stop and break down crying. It was as though we were more distraught over the wreckage of the rooms and their furnishings and the savage violation of our privacy, than we were over my father's death. I can tell you from experience, unfortunates who've lost loved ones are comforted by the unchanged presence of objects in the house; they're lulled by the sameness of the curtains, blankets and daylight, which, in turn, allows them occasionally to forget that Azrael has carried away their beloved or kin. The house that my father looked after with patience and love, whose nooks and doors he had meticulously embellished, had been mercilessly vandalized; thus, we were not only devoid of comfort and pleasant memories but, reminded of the pitilessness of the culprit's damned soul, we were terrified as well.

When, for example, at my insistence we went downstairs, drew fresh water from the well, performed our ablutions and were reciting from the "Family of Imran" chapter—which my dearly departed father said he loved so much because it mentioned hope and death—out of his most cherished Herat-bound Koran, we were under sway of this terror and alarmed that the courtyard gate had begun to creak. It was nothing. But, after we checked that the latch was locked, and barricaded the gate by moving with our combined strength the planter of sweet basil that my father would water on spring mornings with freshly drawn well water, we reentered the house in the dead of night, and it suddenly seemed that the elongated shadows we were casting by the light of the oil lamp belonged to others. Most frightening of all was the horror that overcame us like a silent act of piety, as we solemnly washed his bloodied face and changed his clothes so that I might deceive myself into believing that my father had died at his appointed time; "Hand me his sleeve from underneath," Hayriye had whispered to me.

As we removed his bloody clothes and undergarments, what aroused our amazement and awe was the vitality and whitish color of my father's skin illuminated by candlelight. Because there were many more threatening things to frighten us, neither of us was shy about looking at my father's sprawling naked body covered with moles and wounds. When Hayriye went back upstairs to fetch clean undergarments and his green silk shirt, unable to restrain myself, I looked down there and was immediately quite ashamed at what I'd done. After I'd dressed my father in fresh clothes and carefully cleaned the blood off his neck, face and hair, I embraced him with all my strength, and burying my nose in his beard, I inhaled his scent and cried at length.

For those of you who would accuse me of lacking feeling, or even of being guilty, let me hasten to tell of two further instances when I broke down crying: 1. When I was tidying the upstairs room so the children wouldn't discover what had happened and I brought a seashell he'd used as a paper burnisher to my ear, as I'd done as a child, only to discover that the sound of the sea had diminished. 2. When I saw that the red velvet cushion my father sat upon often over the last twenty years—so much so it'd become part of his rear end—had been torn apart.

When everything in the house, excluding the damage that was beyond repair, was put back in order, I mercilessly denied Hayriye's request to spread her roll-up mattress out in our room. "I don't want the children to get suspicious in the morning," I explained to her. But, to be honest, I was as eager to be alone with my children as I was to punish her. I entered my bed but was unable to sleep for a long while, not because I was preoccupied with the horror of what had happened, but because I was considering all that yet lay in store.

CHAPTER 31

I AM RED

I appeared in Ghazni when *Book of Kings* poet Firdusi completed the final line of a quatrain with the most intricate of rhymes, besting the court poets of Shah Mahmud, who ridiculed him as being nothing but a peasant. I was there on the quiver of *Book of Kings* hero Rüstem when he traveled far and wide in pursuit of his missing steed; I became the blood that spewed forth when he cut the notorious ogre in half with his wondrous sword; and I was in the folds of the quilt upon which he made furious love with the beautiful daughter of the king who'd received him as a guest. Verily and truly, I've been everywhere and am everywhere. I emerged as Tur traitorously decapitated his brother Iraj; as legendary armies, spectacular as a dream, clashed on the steppes; and as Alexander's lifeblood shimmered brightly from his handsome nose after he suffered sunstroke. Yes, Shah Behram Gür spent every night of the week with a different beauty beneath domes of varying color from distant lands, listening to the story she recounted, and I was upon the outfit of the striking maiden he visited on a Tuesday, whose picture he'd fallen in love with, just as I appeared from the crown to the caftan of Hüsrev, who'd fallen in love with Shirin's picture. Verily, I was visible upon the military banners of armies besieging fortresses, upon the tablecloths covering tables set for feasts, upon the velvet caftans of ambassadors kissing the feet of sultans, and wherever the sword, whose legends children loved, was depicted. Yes, handsome almond-eyed apprentices applied me with elegant brushes to thick paper from Hindustan and Bukhara; I embellished Ushak carpets, wall ornamentation, the combs of fighting cocks, pomegranates, the fruits of fabled lands, the mouth of Satan, the subtle accent lines within picture borders, the curled embroidery on tents, flowers barely visible to the naked eye made for the artist's own pleasure, blouses worn by stunning women with outstretched necks watching the street through open shutters, the sour-cherry eyes of bird statues made of sugar, the stockings of shepherds, the dawns described in legends and the corpses and wounds of thousands, nay, tens of thousands of lovers, warriors and shahs. I love engaging in scenes of war where blood blooms like poppies; appearing on the caftan of the most proficient of bards listening to music on a countryside outing as pretty boys and poets partake of wine; I love illuminating the wings of angels, the lips of maidens, the death wounds of corpses and severed heads bespeckled with blood.

I hear the question upon your lips: What is it to be a color?

Color is the touch of the eye, music to the deaf, a word out of the darkness. Because I've listened to souls whispering—like the susurrus of the wind—from book to book and object to object for tens of thousands of years, allow me to say that my touch resembles the touch of angels. Part of me, the serious half, calls out to your vision while the mirthful half soars through the air with your glances.

I'm so fortunate to be red! I'm fiery. I'm strong. I know men take notice of me and that I cannot be resisted.

I do not conceal myself: For me, delicacy manifests itself neither in weakness nor in subtlety, but through determination and will. So, I draw attention to myself. I'm not afraid of other colors, shadows, crowds or even of loneliness. How wonderful it is to cover a surface that awaits me with my own victorious being! Wherever I'm spread, I see eyes shine, passions increase, eyebrows rise and heartbeats quicken. Behold how wonderful it is to live! Behold how wonderful to see. Behold: Living is seeing. I am everywhere. Life begins with and returns to me. Have faith in what I tell you.

MY NAME IS RED

Hush and listen to how I developed such a magnificent red tone. A master miniaturist, an expert in paints, furiously pounded the best variety of dried red beetle from the hottest climes of Hindustan into a fine powder using his mortar and pestle. He prepared five drachmas of the red powder, one drachma of soapwort and a half drachma of lotor. He boiled the soapwort in a pot containing three okkas of water. Next, he mixed thoroughly the lotor into the water. He let it boil for as long as it took to drink an excellent cup of coffee. As he enjoyed his coffee, I grew as impatient as a child about to be born. The coffee had cleared the master's mind and given him the eyes of a jinn. He sprinkled the red powder into the kettle and carefully mixed the concoction with one of the thin, clean sticks reserved for this task. I was ready to become genuine red, but the issue of my consistency was of utmost importance: The liquid shouldn't be permitted to just boil away. He drew the tip of his stirring stick across the nail of his thumb (any other finger was absolutely unacceptable). Oh, how exquisite it is to be red! I gracefully painted that thumbnail without running off the side in watery haste. In short, I was the right consistency, but I still contained sediment. He took the pot off the stove and strained me through a clean piece of cheesecloth, purifying me even further. Next, he heated me up again, bringing me to a frothy boil twice more. After adding a pinch of crushed alum, he left me to cool.

A few days passed and I sat there quietly in the pan. In the anticipation of being applied to pages, of being spread everywhere and onto everything, sitting still like that broke my heart and spirit. It was during this period of silence that I meditated upon what it meant to be red.

Once, in a Persian city, as I was being applied by the brush of an apprentice to the embroidery on the saddle cloth of a horse that a blind miniaturist had drawn by heart, I overheard two blind masters having an argument:

"Because we've spent our entire lives ardently and faithfully working as painters, naturally, we, who have now gone blind, know red and remember what kind of color and what kind of feeling it is," said the one who'd made the horse drawing from memory. "But, what if we'd been born blind? How would we have been truly able to comprehend this red that our handsome apprentice is using?"

"An excellent issue," the other said. "But do not forget that colors are not known, but felt."

"My dear master, explain red to somebody who has never known red."

"If we touched it with the tip of a finger, it would feel like something between iron and copper. If we took it into our palm, it would burn. If we tasted it, it would be full-bodied, like salted meat. If we took it between our lips, it would fill our mouths. If we smelled it, it'd have the scent of a horse. If it were a flower, it would smell like a daisy, not a red rose."

One hundred and ten years ago Venetian artistry was not yet threat enough that our rulers would bother themselves about it, and the legendary masters believed in their own methods as fervently as they believed in Allah; therefore, they regarded the Venetian method of using a variety of red tones for every ordinary sword wound and even the most common sackcloth as a kind of disrespect and vulgarity hardly worth a chuckle. Only a weak and hesitant miniaturist would use a variety of red tones to depict the red of a caftan, they claimed—shadows were not an excuse. Besides, we believe in only one red.

"What is the meaning of red?" the blind miniaturist who'd drawn the horse from memory asked again.

"The meaning of color is that it is there before us and we see it," said the other. "Red cannot be explained to he who cannot see."

"To deny God's existence, victims of Satan maintain that God is not visible to us," said the blind miniaturist who'd rendered the horse.

"Yet, He appears to those who can see," said the other master. "It is for this reason that the Koran states that the blind and the seeing are not equal."

The handsome apprentice ever so delicately dabbed me onto the horse's saddle cloth. What a wonderful sensation to fix my fullness, power and vigor to the black and white of a well-executed illustration: as the cat-hair brush spreads me onto the waiting page, I become delightfully ticklish. Thereby, as I bring my color to the page, it's as if I command the world to "Be!" Yes, those who cannot see would deny it, but the truth is I can be found everywhere.

CHAPTER 32

I, SHEKURE

Before the children awoke, I wrote Black a brief note telling him to hurry to the house of the Hanged Jew and pressed it into Hayriye's hand so that she might rush to Esther. As Hayriye took the letter, she looked into my eyes with more fearlessness than usual despite worrying what was to become of us; and I, who no longer had a father to fear, returned her glare with newfound temerity. This exchange would determine the tone of our relationship in the future. Over the last two years, I suspected Hayriye might even have a child by my father, and forgetting her status as slave, maneuver to become lady of the house. I visited my unfortunate father, respectfully kissing his now stiffened hand, which, oddly, hadn't lost its softness. I hid my father's shoes, quilted turban and purple cloak, then explained to the children once they awoke that their grandfather had gotten better and had left for the Mustafa Pasha district early in the morning.

Hayriye returned from her morning errand. As she was laying out the low table for breakfast, and I was placing a portion of orange jam in the middle of it, I imagined how Esther was now calling at Black's door. The snow had stopped and the sun had begun to shine.

In the garden of the Hanged Jew, I encountered a familiar scene. The icicles hanging from the eaves and window casings were quickly shrinking, and the garden that smelled of mold and rotting leaves was eagerly absorbing the sun. I found Black waiting in the spot where I'd first seen him last night—it seemed so long ago, as if weeks had passed. I raised my veil and said:

"You can be glad, if you feel the urge. My father's objections and doubts will not come between us anymore. While you were craftily trying to lay your hands on me here last night, a devil-of-a-man broke into our empty house and murdered my father."

Rather than wondering about Black's reaction, you're probably puzzling over why I spoke so coldly and somewhat insincerely. I don't quite know the answer myself. Maybe I thought I'd cry otherwise, provoking Black to embrace me, and I'd become intimate with him sooner than I wanted.

"He destroyed our home with a thoroughness that clearly reveals anger and hatred. I don't think his work is done either, I don't expect this devil will calmly retire to some corner now. He stole the final picture. I'm calling on you to protect me—protect us—and keep my father's book from him. Now tell me, under what arrangement and conditions will you see to our safety? This is what we have to resolve."

He made an overture to speak, but I easily silenced him with a look—as though this were something I'd done countless times before.

"In the eyes of the judge, it is my husband and his family who succeed my father as my guardians. This was the case even before his death, for according to the judge my husband is still alive. It was only because Hasan

I, Shekure 189

tried to take advantage of me during his older brother's absence, a failed assault that embarrassed my father-in-law, that I was allowed to return to my father's home though not officially a widow. But now that my father is dead and I am without even a brother, there is no question that my only possible guardians are my husband's brother and my father-in-law. They've already been scheming to have me returned to their home, coercing my father, and threatening me. Once they hear my father is dead, they won't hesitate to take official action. My only hope to prevent this is to conceal my father's death. Perhaps in vain, for they may be the ones behind the crime."

At that very moment, a thin beam of light gracefully filtered through the broken shutters and fell between Black and me, illuminating the ancient dust inside the room.

"This isn't the only reason I'm hiding my father's death," I said, fixing my gaze into Black's eyes, in which I was gladdened to see attentiveness more than love. "I'm also afraid of being unable to prove my whereabouts at the time of my father's murder. Though she's a slave and her word might be discounted, I'm afraid that Hayriye is involved in these machinations, if not against me, then against my father's book. And as long as I remain without a protector, the announcement of my father's murder, while initially simplifying matters at home, might well, solely for the reasons I've enumerated, cause me great misfortune at her hand; for instance, what if Hayriye is aware that my father didn't want me to marry you?"

"Your father didn't want you to marry me?" asked Black.

"No, he didn't, he was worried that you'd take me away from him. Since there's no longer any danger of you doing such evil to him, let's assume my dear unfortunate father has no further objection. Do you have any?"

"None at all, my darling."

"Fine, then. My guardian has no claims of money or gold on you. Please excuse the impropriety of my discussing marital circumstances on my own behalf, but I have certain prerequisites that I must, unfortunately, explain to you."

As I fell silent for a while, Black said, "Yes," in a manner that suggested an apology for his hesitation.

"First," I began, "you must swear before two witnesses that if you behave badly toward me in our marriage, to a degree that I find unbearable, or if you take a second wife, you will grant me a divorce with alimony. Second, you must swear before two witnesses that if for whatever reason you are absent from the house for more than a six-month period without a visit, I will also be granted a divorce with alimony. Third, after we are married, you will of course move into my home; however, until the villain who has murdered my father has been caught or until you find him—how I'd love to torture him myself!—and until Our Sultan's book, completed under the guidance of your talents and efforts, has been honorably presented to Him, you will not share my bed. Fourth, you will love my sons, who do share my bed with me, as if they were your own children."

"I agree."

"Good. If all of the obstacles that still lie before us disappear this quickly, we'll soon be wed."

"Yes, wed, but not in the same bed."

"The first step is marriage," I said. "Let's see to that first. Love comes after marriage. Don't forget: Marriage douses love's flame, leaving nothing but a barren and melancholy blackness. Of course, after marriage, love itself will vanish anyway; but happiness fills the void. Still, there are those hasty fools who fall in love before marrying and, burning with emotion, exhaust all their feeling, believing love to be the highest goal in life."

"What, then, is the truth of the matter?"

"The truth is contentment. Love and marriage are but a means to obtaining it: a husband, a house, children, a book. Can't you see that even in my state, with a missing husband and a deceased father, I'm better off than you in your isolation? I'd die without my sons, with whom I spend my days laughing, tussling and loving. Moreover, since you long for me even in my present predicament, since you secretly ache to spend the night with me—even if not in the same bed—under the same roof with my father's body and my unruly children, you're compelled to listen with all your heart to what I now have to say."

"I'm listening."

"There are various ways that I might secure a divorce. False witnesses could swear that before my husband set out on campaign, they witnessed him grant me a conditional divorce; for example, that he'd pledged that if he didn't return within two years, I should be considered free. Or, more simply, they might swear they'd seen my husband's corpse in the field of battle, citing various convincing and descriptive details. But taking my father's body and the objections of my in-laws into consideration, to rely on false witnesses would be an unsound way to proceed, as no judge of any intelligence or caution would be persuaded. Considering that my husband left me without alimony and hasn't returned from war for four years, even judges of our Hanefi creed couldn't grant me a divorce. The Üsküdar judge, however, knowing how the number of women in my situation is increasing each day, is more sympathetic and so—with a nod from Our Excellency the Sultan and the Sheikhulislam—the judge occasionally allows his proxy of the Shafii creed to rule in his place, thereby granting divorces left and right to women like me, including conditions of alimony. Now, if you can find two witnesses to testify openly to my predicament, pay them off, cross the Bosphorus with them to the Üsküdar side, arrange for the judge, making certain that his proxy will sit in for him so the divorce might be granted by virtue of the witnesses, register the divorce in the judge's ledger, obtain a certificate testifying to the proceeding, obtain written permission for my immediate remarriage, and if you can accomplish all of this and get back to this side of the Bosphorus by the afternoon, then—assuming no difficulty in finding a preacher who might marry us this evening—then, as my husband, you could spend this night with me and my children. Thereby, you'll also spare us a sleepless night of hearing in every creaking of the house the steps of that devilish murderer. Moreover, you'll save me from the wretchedness of being a poor unprotected woman when we announce the death of my father in the morning."

"Yes," said Black with good humor and somewhat childishly. "Yes. I agree to make you mine."

You remember how only recently I declared I didn't know why I was speaking to Black in such a high-handed and insincere manner. Now I know: I've come to realize that only by assuming such a tone might I convince Black—who has yet to outgrow his childhood muddleheadedness—to believe in the possibility of events that even I have a hard time believing will come to pass.

"We have a lot to do in fighting our enemies, those who would obstruct the completion of my father's book and those who could contest my divorce and our marriage ceremony—which will be performed tonight, God willing. But I suppose I shouldn't further confuse you, since you are already even more confused than I."

"You aren't confused at all," said Black.

"Perhaps, but only because these aren't my own ideas, I learned them from my father over the years." I said this so he wouldn't dismiss what I said, assuming that these plans had sprung from my feminine mind.

Next, Black said what I'd heard from every man who wasn't afraid to admit he found me very intelligent:

"You're very beautiful."

"Yes," I said, "it pleases me to be praised for my intelligence. When I was a child, my father would often do so."

I was about to add that once I'd grown up my father ceased to praise my intelligence, but I began to weep. As I cried, it was as if I'd left myself and was becoming another, entirely separate woman. Like some reader troubled by a sad picture in the pages of a book, I saw my life from the outside and pitied what I saw. There's something so innocent in crying over one's troubles, as though they were another's, that when Black embraced me, a sense of well-being spread over us both. Yet, this time, as we hugged, this sense of comfort remained there between us, unable to affect the adversaries circling us.

CHAPTER 33

I AM CALLED BLACK

Widowed, abandoned and aggrieved, my beloved Shekure fled with featherlike steps, and I stood as if stunned in the stillness of the house of the Hanged Jew, amid the aroma of almonds and dreams of marriage she'd left in her wake. I was bewildered, but my mind was churning so fast it almost hurt. Without even a chance to grieve properly over my Enishte's death, I swiftly returned home. On the one hand, a worm of doubt was gnawing at me: Was Shekure using me as a pawn in a grand scheme, was she duping me? On the other hand, fantasies of a blissful marriage stubbornly played before my eyes.

After making conversation with my landlady who interrogated me at the front door as to where I'd gone and whence I was coming at this morning hour, I went to my room and removed the twenty-two Venetian gold pieces from the lining of the sash I'd hidden in my mattress, placing them in my money purse with trembling fingers. When I returned to the street, I knew immediately I'd see Shekure's dark, teary, troubled eyes for the rest of the day.

I changed five of the Venetian Lions at a perpetually smiling Jewish money changer. Next, deep in thought, I entered the neighborhood whose name I've yet to mention because I'm not fond of it: Yakutlar, where my deceased Enishte and Shekure, along with her children, awaited me at their house. As I made my way along the streets almost running, a tall plane tree seemed to reproach me for being overjoyed by dreams and plans of marriage on the very day my Enishte had passed away. Next, as the ice had melted, a street fountain hissed into my ear: "Don't take matters too seriously, see to your own affairs and your own happiness." "That's all fine and good," objected an ill-omened black cat licking himself on the corner, "but everybody, yourself included, suspects you had a hand in your uncle's murder."

The cat left off licking himself as I suddenly caught sight of its bewitching eyes. I don't have to tell you how brazen these Istanbul cats get when the locals spoil them.

I found the Imam Effendi, whose droopy eyelids and large black eyes gave him a perpetually sleepy look, not at his house, but in the courtyard of the neighborhood mosque, and there I asked him quite a trivial legal question: "When is one obligated to testify in court?" I raised my eyebrows as I listened to his haughty answer as if I were hearing this information for the first time. "Bearing witness is optional if other witnesses are present," explained the Imam Effendi, "but, in situations where there was only one witness, it is the will of God that one bear witness."

"That's just the predicament I find myself in now," I said, taking up the conversation. "In a situation everyone knows about, all the witnesses have shirked their responsibilities and avoided going to court with the excuse that 'it's only voluntary,' and as a result the pressing concerns of those I'm trying to help are being completely disregarded."

"Well," said the Imam Effendi, "why don't you loosen your purse-strings a little more?"

I took out my pouch and showed him the Venetian gold pieces huddled within: The broad space of the mosque courtyard, the face of the preacher, everything was suddenly illuminated by the glimmer of gold. He asked me what my dilemma was all about.

I explained who I was. "Enishte Effendi is ill," I confided. "Before he dies, he wants his daughter's widowhood certified and an alimony to be instituted."

I didn't even have to mention the proxy of the Üsküdar judge. The Imam Effendi understood at once and said the entire neighborhood had long been troubled over the fate of hapless Shekure, adding that the situation had already persisted too long. Instead of searching for a second witness required for a legal separation at the door of the Üsküdar judge, the Imam Effendi suggested his brother. Now, if I were to offer an additional gold piece to the brother, who lived in the neighborhood and was familiar with the predicament of Shekure and her darling children, I'd be doing a good pious turn. After all, for only two gold coins the Imam Effendi was giving me a deal on the second witness. We immediately agreed. The Imam Effendi went to fetch his brother.

The rest of our day rather resembled the "cat-and-mouse" stories that I'd watched storytellers in Aleppo coffeehouses act out. Because of all the adventure and trickery, such stories written up as narrative poems and bound were never taken seriously even if presented in fine calligraphy; that is, they were never illustrated. I, on the other hand, was quite pleased to divide our daylong adventure into four scenes, imagining each in the illustrated pages of my mind.

In the first scene, the miniaturist ought to depict us amid mustachioed and muscled oarsmen, forging our way across the blue Bosphorus toward Üsküdar in the four-oared red longboat we'd boarded in Unkapanı. The preacher and his skinny dark-complexioned brother, pleased with the surprise voyage, are engaging the oarsmen in friendly chatter. Meanwhile, amid blithe dreams of marriage that play ceaselessly before my eyes, I stare deep into the waters of the Bosphorus, flowing clearer than usual on this sunny winter morning, on guard for an ominous sign within its currents. I'm afraid, for example, that I might see the wreck of a pirate ship below. Thus, no matter how joyously the miniaturist colors the sea and clouds, he ought to include something equivalent to the darkness of my fears and as intense as my dreams of happiness—a terrifying-looking fish, for example—in the depths of the water so the reader of my adventure won't assume all is rosy.

Our second picture ought to show the palaces of sultans, the meetings of the Divan Council of State, the reception of European ambassadors, and detailed and carefully composed crowded interiors of a subtlety worthy of Bihzad; that is, the picture ought to partake of playful tricks and irony. Thereby, while the Kadi Effendi apparently makes an open-handed "halt" gesture indicating "never" or "no" to my bribe, with his other hand he ought to be shown obligingly pocketing my Venetian gold coins, and the ultimate result of this bribe should be depicted in the same picture: Shahap Effendi, the Shafii proxy presiding in place of the Üsküdar judge. The simultaneous depiction of sequential events could only be achieved through an intelligent miniaturist's cunning facility in page composition. Thus, when the observer, who first sees me giving a bribe, notices elsewhere in the painting that the man sitting cross-legged on the judge's cushion is the proxy, he'll realize, even if he hasn't read the story, that the honorable judge has temporarily given up his office so his proxy might grant Shekure a divorce.

The third illustration should show the same scene, but this time the wall ornamentation should be darker and rendered in the Chinese style, the curly branches being more intricate and dense, and colorful clouds should appear above the judge's proxy so the chicanery in the story might be apparent. Though the Imam Effendi and his brother have actually testified separately before the judge's proxy, in the illustration they are shown together explaining how the husband of anguished Shekure hasn't returned from war for four years, how she is in a state of destitution without a husband to look after her, how her two fatherless children are perpetually in tears and hungry, how there is no prospect for remarriage because she's still considered married, and how in this state she can't even receive a loan without permission from her husband. They're so convincing that even a man as deaf as a stone would grant her a divorce through a cascade of tears. The heartless proxy, however, having none of it, asks about Shekure's legal guardian. After a moment of hesitation, I immediately interrupt, declaring that her esteemed father, who has served as herald and ambassador for Our Sultan, is still alive.

"Until he testifies in court, I'll never grant her a divorce!" said the proxy.

Thereupon, thoroughly flustered, I explained how my Enishte Effendi was ill, bed-ridden and struggling for his life, how his last wish to God was to see his daughter divorced, and how I was his representative.

"What does she want with a divorce?" asked the proxy. "Why would a dying man want to see his daughter divorced from her husband who's long vanished at war anyway? Listen, I'd understand if there were a good, trustworthy candidate for son-in-law, because then he wouldn't pass away with his wish unfulfilled."

"There is a prospect, sir," I said.

"Who might that be?"

"It is I!"

"Come now! You're the guardian's representative!" said the judge's proxy. "What line of work are you in?"

"In the eastern provinces, I served as secretary, chief secretary and assistant treasurer to various pashas. I completed a history of the Persian wars that I intend to present to Our Sultan. I'm a connoisseur of illustrating and decoration. I've been burning with love for this woman for twenty years."

"Are you a relative of hers?"

I was so embarrassed at having fallen so abruptly and unexpectedly into groveling meekness before the judge's proxy, at having bared my life like some dull object devoid of any mystery, that I fell completely silent.

MY NAME IS RED

"Instead of turning beet red, give me an answer, young man, lest I refuse to grant her a divorce."

"She's the daughter of my maternal aunt."

"Hmmm, I see. Will you be able to make her happy?"

When he asked the question he made a vulgar hand gesture. The miniaturist should omit this indelicacy. It'd be enough for him to show how much I blushed.

"I make a decent living."

"As I belong to the Shafii sect, there is nothing contrary to the Holy Book or my creed in my granting the divorce of this unfortunate Shekure, whose husband has been missing at the front for four years," said the Proxy Effendi. "I grant the divorce. And I rule that her husband no longer has any superceding rights should he return."

The subsequent illustration, that is, the fourth, ought to depict the proxy recording the divorce in the ledger, unleashing obedient armies of black-ink letters, before presenting me with the document declaring that my Shekure is now a widow and there is no obstacle to her immediate remarriage. Neither by painting the walls of the courtroom red, nor by situating the picture within bloodred borders could the blissful inner radiance I felt at that moment be expressed. Running back through the crowd of false witnesses and other men gathering before the judge's door seeking divorces for their sisters, daughters or even aunts, I set out on my return journey.

After I crossed the Bosphorus and headed directly to the Yakutlar neighborhood, I dismissed both the considerate Imam Effendi, who wanted to perform the marriage ceremony, and his brother. Since I suspected everyone I saw on the street of hatching some mischief out of jealousy over the incredible happiness I was on the verge of attaining, I ran straight to Shekure's street. How had the ominous crows divined the presence of a body in the house and taken to hopping around excitedly on the terra-cotta shingles? I was overcome by guilt because I hadn't been able to grieve for my Enishte or even shed a single tear; even so, I knew from the tightly closed shutters and door of the house, from the silence, and even from the look of the pomegranate tree that everything was proceeding as planned.

I was acting intuitively in a great haste. I tossed a stone at the courtyard gate but missed! I tossed another at the house. It landed on the roof. Frustrated, I began pelting the house with stones. A window opened. It was the second-story window where four days ago, on Wednesday, I'd first seen Shekure through the branches of the pomegranate tree. Orhan appeared, and from the gap in the shutters I could hear Shekure scolding him. Then I saw her. For a moment, we gazed hopefully at each other, my fair lady and I. She was so beautiful and becoming. She made a gesture that I took to mean "wait" and shut the window.

There was still plenty of time before evening. I waited hopefully in the empty garden, awestruck by the beauty of the world, the trees and the muddy street. Before long, Hayriye came in, dressed and covered not like a servant, but rather, like a lady of the house. Without nearing each other, we removed ourselves to the cover of the fig trees.

"Everything is progressing as planned," I said to her. I showed her the document I'd obtained from the proxy. "Shekure is divorced. As for the preacher from another neighborhood . . ." I was going to add, "I'll see to that," but instead blurted out, "He's on his way. Shekure should be ready."

"No matter how small, Shekure wants a bride's procession, followed by a neighborhood reception with a wedding repast. We've prepared a stewpot of pilaf with almonds and dried apricots."

In her excitement, she seemed prepared to tell me everything else she'd cooked but I cut her off. "If the wedding is going to be such an elaborate affair," I cautioned, "Hasan and his men will hear of it; they'll raid the house, disgrace us, have the marriage nullified and we'll be able to do nothing about it. All our efforts will have been in vain. We need to protect ourselves not only from Hasan and his father, but from the devil who murdered Enishte Effendi as well. Aren't you afraid?"

"How could we not be?" she said and began to cry.

"You're not to tell anyone a thing," I said. "Dress Enishte in his nightclothes, spread out his mattress and lay him upon it, not as a dead man, but as though he were sick. Arrange glasses and bottles of syrup by his head, and draw the shutters closed. Make certain there are no lamps in his room so that he can act as Shekure's guardian, her sick father, during the ceremony. There's no place now for a bride's procession. You can invite a handful of neighbors at the last minute, that's all. While you're inviting them, say that this was Enishte Effendi's last wish . . . It won't be a joyous wedding, but a melancholy one. If we don't see ourselves through this affair, they'll destroy us, and they'll punish you as well. You understand, don't you?"

She nodded as she wept. Mounting my white horse, I said I'd secure the witnesses and return before long, that Shekure ought to be ready, that hereafter, I would be master of the house, and that I was going to the barber. I hadn't thought through any of this beforehand. As I spoke, the details came to me, and just as I'd felt during battles from time to time, I had the conviction that I was a cherished and favored servant of God and He was protecting me; thus, everything was going to turn out fine. When you feel this trust, do whatever comes to mind, follow your intuition and your actions will prove correct.

I rode four blocks toward the Golden Horn from the Yakutlar neighborhood to find the black-bearded, radiant-faced preacher of the mosque in Yasin Pasha, the adjacent neighborhood broom in hand, he was shooing shameless dogs out of the muddy courtyard. I told him about my predicament. By the will of God, I explained, my Enishte's time was upon him, and according to his last wish, I was to marry his daughter, who, by decision of the Üsküdar judge, had just been granted a divorce from a husband lost at war. The preacher objected that by the dictates of Islamic law a divorced woman must wait a month before remarrying, but I countered by explaining that Shekure's former husband had been absent for four years; and so, there was no chance she was pregnant by him. I hastened to add that the Üsküdar judge granted a divorce this morning to allow Shekure to remarry, and I showed him the certifying document. "My exalted Imam Effendi, you may rest assured that there's no obstacle to the marriage," I said. True, she was a blood relation, but being maternal cousins is not an obstacle; her previous marriage had been nullified; there were no religious, social or monetary differences between us. And if he accepted the gold pieces I offered him up front, if he performed the ceremony at the wedding scheduled to take place before the entire neighborhood, he'd also be accomplishing a pious act before God for the fatherless children of a widowed woman. Did the Imam Effendi, I inquired, enjoy pilaf with almonds and dried apricots?

He did, but he was still preoccupied with the dogs at the gate. He took the gold coins. He said he'd don his wedding robes, straighten up his appearance, see to his turban and arrive in time to perform the nuptials. He asked the way to the house and I told him.

No matter how rushed a wedding might be—even one that the groom has dreamed about for twelve years—what could be more natural than his forgetting his worries and troubles and surrendering to the affectionate hands and gentle banter of a barber for a prenuptial shave and haircut? The barber's, where my feet took me, was located near the market, on the street of the run-down house in Aksaray, which my late Enishte, my aunt and fair Shekure had quitted years after our childhood. This was the barber I'd faced five days ago, my first day back. When I entered he embraced me and as any good Istanbul barber would do,

I Am Called Black

rather than asking where the last dozen years had gone, launched into the latest neighborhood gossip, concluding the conversation with an allusion to the place we would all go at the end of this meaningful journey called life.

The master barber had aged. The straight-edged razor he held in his freckled hand trembled as he made it dance across my cheek. He'd given himself over to drinking and had taken on a pink-complexioned, full-lipped, green-eyed boy-apprentice—who looked upon his master with awe. Compared with twelve years ago, the shop was cleaner and more orderly. After filling the hanging basin, which hung from the ceiling on a new chain, with boiling water, he carefully washed my hair and face with water from the brass faucet at the bottom of the basin. The old broad basins were newly tinned with no signs of rust, the heating braziers were clean, and the agate-handled razors were sharp. He wore an immaculate silk waistcoat, something he was loath to wear twelve years ago. I assumed that the elegant apprentice, tall for his age and of slender build, had helped bring some order to the shop and its owner, and surrendering myself to the soapy, rose-scented and steamy pleasures of a shave, I couldn't help thinking how marriage not only brought new vitality and prosperity to a bachelor's home, but to his work and his shop as well.

I'm not certain how much time had passed. I melted into the warmth of the brazier that gently heated the small shop and the barber's adept fingers. With life having suddenly presented me the greatest of gifts today, as if for free, and after so much suffering, I felt a profound thanks toward exalted Allah. I felt an intense curiosity, wondering out of what mysterious balance this world of His had emerged, and I felt sadness and pity for Enishte, who lay dead in the house where, a while later, I would become master. I was readying myself to spring into action when there was a commotion at the always-open door of the barbershop: Shevket!

Flustered, but with his usual self-confidence, he held out a piece of paper. Unable to speak and expecting the worst, my insides were chilled as if by an icy draft as I read:

> *If there isn't going to be a bride's procession, I'm not getting married—Shekure.*

Grabbing Shevket by the arm, I lifted him onto my lap. I would've liked to have responded to my dear Shekure by writing, "As you wish, my love!" but what would pen and ink be doing in the shop of an illiterate barber? So, with a calculated reserve, I whispered my response into the boy's ear: "All right." Still whispering, I asked him how his grandfather was doing.

MY NAME IS RED

"He's sleeping."

I now sense that Shevket, the barber and even you are suspicious about me and my Enishte's death (Shevket, of course, suspects other things as well). What a pity! I forced a kiss upon him, and he quickly left, displeased. During the wedding, dressed in his holiday clothes, he glared at me with hostility from a distance.

Since Shekure wouldn't be leaving her father's house for mine, and I would be moving into the paternal home as bridegroom, the bridal procession was only fitting. Naturally, I was in no position to bedeck my wealthy friends and relatives and have them wait at Shekure's front gate mounted on their horses as others might have done. Even so, I invited two of my childhood friends whom I'd run into during my six days back in Istanbul (one had become a clerk like myself and the other was running a bath house) as well as my dear barber, whose eyes had watered as he wished me happiness during my shave and haircut. Mounted upon my white horse, which I'd been riding that first day, I knocked at my beloved Shekure's gate as if poised to take her to another house and another life.

To Hayriye, who opened the gate, I presented a generous tip. Shekure, dressed in a bright-red wedding gown with pink bridal streamers flowing from her hair to her feet, emerged amid cries, sobs, sighs (a woman scolded the children), outbursts, and shouts of "May God protect her," and gracefully mounted a second white horse which we'd brought with us. As a hand-drummer and shrill zurna piper, kindly arranged by the barber for me at the last minute, began to play a slow bride's melody, our poor, melancholy, yet proud procession set out on its way.

As our horses began to saunter, I understood that Shekure, with her usual cunning, had arranged this spectacle for the sake of safeguarding the nuptials. Our procession, having announced our wedding to the entire neighborhood, even if only at the last moment, had essentially secured everyone's approval, thereby neutralizing any future objections to our marriage. Nevertheless, announcing that we were on the verge of marriage, and having a public wedding—as if to challenge our enemies, Shekure's former husband and his family—further endangered the whole affair. Had it been left to me, I'd have held the ceremony in secret, without telling a soul, without a wedding celebration; I'd have preferred becoming her husband first and defending the marriage afterward.

I led the parade astride my fickle white fairy-tale horse, and as we moved through the neighborhood, I nervously watched for Hasan and his men, whom I expected to ambush us from an alleyway or a shadowy courtyard gate. I noticed how young men, the elders of the neighborhood and strangers stopped and waved from door fronts, without completely understanding all that was transpiring. In the small market area we'd unintentionally entered, I figured out that Shekure had masterfully activated her grapevine, and that her divorce and marriage to me was quickly winning acceptance in the neighborhood. This was evident from the excitement of the fruit-and-vegetable seller, who without leaving his colorful quinces, carrots and apples for too long, joined us for a few strides shouting "Praise be to God, may He protect you both," and from the smile of the woeful shopkeeper and from the approving glances of the baker, who was having his apprentice scrape away the burnt residue in his pans. Still, I was anxious, maintaining my vigil against a sudden raid, or even a word of vulgar heckling. For this reason, I wasn't at all disturbed by the commotion of the crowd of money-seeking children that had formed behind us as we left the bazaar. I understood from the smiles of women I glimpsed behind windows, bars and shutters that the enthusiasm of this noisy throng of children protected and supported us.

As I gazed at the road along which we'd advanced and were now, thank God, finally winding our way back toward the house, my heart was with Shekure and her sorrow. Actually, it wasn't her misfortune in having to wed within a day of her father's murder that saddened me, it was that the wedding was so unadorned and meager. My dear Shekure was worthy of horses with silver reins and ornamented saddles, mounted riders outfitted in sable and silk with gold embroidery, and hundreds of carriages laden with gifts and dowry; she deserved to lead an endless procession of pasha's daughters, sultans and carriages full of elderly harem women chattering about the extravagances of days bygone. But Shekure's wedding lacked even the four pole bearers to hold aloft the red silk canopy that ordinarily protected rich maidens from prying eyes; for that matter, there wasn't even one servant to lead the procession bearing large wedding candles and tree-shaped decorations ornamented with fruit, gold, silver leaf and polished stones. More than embarrassment, I felt a sadness that threatened to fill my eyes with tears each time the disrespectful hand-drum and zurna players simply stopped playing when our procession got swallowed up in crowds of market-goers or servants fetching water from the fountain in the square because we had no one clearing the way with shouts of "Here comes the bride." As we were nearing the house, I mustered the courage to turn in my saddle and gaze at her, and was relieved that beneath her pink bride's tinsel and red veil, far from being saddened by all these pitiful shortcomings, she seemed heartened to know that we'd concluded our procession and our journey with neither accident nor mishap. So, like all grooms, I lowered my beautiful bride, whom I would shortly wed, from her horse, took her by the arm, and handful by handful, slowly emptied a bag of silver coins over her head before the gleeful crowd. While the children who'd followed behind our meager parade scrambled for the coins, Shekure and I entered the courtyard and crossed the stone walkway, and as soon as we entered the house, we were struck not only by the heat, but the horror of the heavy smell of decay.

While the throng from the procession was making itself comfortable in the house, Shekure and the crowd of elders, women and children (Orhan was glaring suspiciously at me from the corner) carried on as if nothing were amiss, and momentarily I doubted my senses; but I knew how corpses left under the sun after battle, their clothes tattered, boots and belts stolen, and their faces, their eyes and lips ravaged by wolves and birds smelled. It was a stench that had so often filled my mouth and lungs to the point of suffocation that I could not mistake it.

Downstairs in the kitchen, I asked Hayriye about Enishte Effendi's body, aware that I was speaking to her for the first time as master of the house.

"As you asked, we laid out his mattress, dressed him in his nightclothes, drew his quilt over him and placed bottles of syrup beside him. If he's giving off an unpleasant smell, it's probably due to the heat from the brazier in the room," the woman said through tears.

One or two of her tears fell, sizzling into the pot she was using to fry the mutton. From the way she was crying, I supposed that Enishte Effendi had been taking her into his bed at night. Esther, who was quietly and proudly sitting in a corner of the kitchen, swallowed what she was chewing and stood.

"Make her happiness your foremost concern," she said. "Recognize her worth."

In my thoughts I heard the lute I'd heard on the street the first day I'd come to Istanbul. More than sadness, there was vigor in its melody. I heard the melody of that music again later, in the half-darkened room where my Enishte lay in his white nightgown, as the Imam Effendi married us.

Because Hayriye had furtively aired out the room beforehand and placed the oil lamp in a corner so its light was dimmed, one could scarcely tell that my Enishte was sick let alone dead. Thus, he served as Shekure's legal guardian during the ceremony. My friend the barber, along with a know-it-all neighborhood elder, served as witnesses. Before the ceremony ended with the hopeful blessings and advice of the preacher and the prayers of all in attendance, a nosy old man, concerned about the state of my Enishte's health, was about to lower his skeptical head toward the deceased; but as soon as the preacher completed the ceremony, I leapt from my spot, grabbed my Enishte's rigid hand and shouted at the top of my voice:

"Put your worries to rest, my sir, my dear Enishte. I'll do everything within my power to care for Shekure and her children, to see they're well clothed and well fed, loved and untroubled."

Next, to suggest that my Enishte was trying to whisper to me from his sickbed, I carefully and respectfully pressed my ear to his mouth, pretending to listen to him intently and wide-eyed, as young men do when an elder they respect offers one or two words of advice distilled from an entire lifetime, which they then imbibe like some magic elixir. The Imam Effendi and the neighborhood elder appeared to appreciate and approve of the loyalty and eternal devotion I showed my father-in-law. I hope that nobody still thinks I had a hand in his murder.

I announced to the wedding guests still in the room that the afflicted man wished to be left alone. They abruptly began to leave, passing into the next room where the men had gathered to feast on Hayriye's pilaf and mutton (at this point I could scarcely distinguish the smell of the corpse from the aroma of thyme, cumin and frying lamb). I stepped into the wide hallway, and like some morose patriarch roaming absentmindedly and wistfully through his own house, I opened the door to Hayriye's room, paying no mind to the women who were horrified to have a man in their midst, and gazing sweetly at Shekure, whose eyes beamed with bliss to see me, said:

"Your father's calling for you, Shekure. We're married now, you're to kiss his hand."

The handful of neighborhood women to whom Shekure had sent last-minute invitations and the young maidens I assumed were relatives motioned to collect themselves and cover their faces, all the while scrutinizing me to their heart's content.

Not long after the evening call to prayer the wedding guests dispersed, having heartily partaken of the walnuts, almonds, dried fruit leather, comfits and clove candy. In the women's quarters, Shekure's incessant crying and the bickering of the unruly children had dampened the festivity. Among the men, my stony-faced silence in response to the mirthful wedding-night gibes of the neighbors was attributed to my preoccupation with my father-in-law's illness. Amid all the distress, the scene most clearly ingrained in my memory was my leading Shekure to Enishte's room before dinner. We were alone at last. After both of us kissed the dead man's cold and rigid hand with sincere respect, we withdrew to a dark corner of the room and kissed each other as if slaking a great thirst. Upon my wife's fiery tongue, which I'd successfully taken into my mouth, I could taste the hard candies that the children greedily ate.

CHAPTER 34

I, SHEKURE

The last guests of our woeful wedding veiled and covered themselves, put on their shoes, dragged off their children, who were tossing a last piece of candy into their mouths, and left us to a penetrating silence. We were all in the courtyard, nothing could be heard but the faint noise of a sparrow gingerly drinking water from the half-filled well bucket. This sparrow, whose tiny head feathers gleamed in the light of the stone hearth, abruptly vanished into the blackness, and I felt the insistent presence of the corpse in my father's bed within our emptied house, now swallowed by night.

"Children," I said in the cadence Orhan and Shevket recognized as the one I used to announce something, "come here, the both of you."

They did so.

"Black is now your father. Let's see you kiss his hand."

They did so, quietly and docilely. "Since they've grown up without a father, my unfortunate children know nothing of obeying one, of heeding his words while looking into his eyes, or of trusting in him," I said to Black. "Thus, if they behave disrespectfully, wildly, immaturely or childishly toward you, I know that you'll show them tolerance at first, understanding that they've been raised without ever once obeying their father, whom they do not even remember."

"I remember my father," said Shevket.

"Hush . . . and listen," I said. "From now on Black's word carries more weight than even my own." I faced Black. "If they refuse to listen to you, if they are disobedient or show even the slightest sign of being rude, spoiled or ill-mannered, first warn them, but forgive them," I said, forgoing the mention of beatings that was on the tip of my tongue. "Whatever space I occupy in your heart, they shall share that space, too."

"I didn't marry you solely to be your husband," said Black, "but also to be father to these dear boys."

"Did you two hear that?"

"Oh my Lord, I pray you never neglect to shine your light down upon us," Hayriye interjected from a corner. "My dear God, I pray you protect us, my Lord."

"You two did hear, didn't you?" I said. "Good for you, my pretty young men. Since your father loves you like this, should you suddenly lose control and disregard his words, he will have forgiven you for it beforehand."

"And I'll forgive them afterward, as well," said Black.

"However, if you two defy his warning a third time . . . then, you'll have earned the right to a beating," I said. "Are we understood? Your new father, Black, has come here from the vilest, the worst of battles, from wars that were the very wrath of God and from which your late father did not return; yes, he's a hardened man. Your grandfather has spoiled you and indulged you. Your grandfather is now very ill."

"I want to go and be with him," Shevket said.

"If you're not going to listen, Black will teach you what it means to get a beating from Hell. Your grandfather won't be able to save you from Black the way he used to protect you from me. If you don't want to suffer your father's wrath, you're not to fight anymore, you're to share everything, tell no lies, perform your prayers, not go to bed before memorizing your lessons and you're not to speak roughly to Hayriye or tease her . . . Are we understood?"

In one movement, Black crouched down and took Orhan up in his arms. Shevket kept his distance. I had the fleeting urge to embrace him and weep. My poor forlorn and fatherless son, my poor solitary Shevket, you're so alone in this immense world. I thought of myself as a small child, like Shevket, a child all alone in the world, and remembered how once I'd been held in my dear father's arms the way Orhan was now being held by Black. But unlike Orhan, I wasn't awkward in my father's embrace, like a fruit unaccustomed to its tree. I was delighted; I recalled how my father and I would often embrace, sniffing each other's skin. I was on the verge of tears, but restrained myself. Though I hadn't planned to say anything of the sort, I said:

"Come now, let's hear you call Black 'Father.'"

The night was so cold and our courtyard was so very silent. In the distance dogs were barking and howling pitifully and sorrowfully. A few more minutes passed. The silence bloomed and spread secretly like a black flower.

"All right, children," I said much later. "Let's go inside so we all don't catch cold out here."

It wasn't only Black and I who felt the timidity of a bride and groom left alone after the wedding, but Hayriye and the children, all of us, entered our home hesitantly as though it were the darkened house of a stranger. We were met with the smell of my father's corpse, but nobody seemed to be aware of it. We silently climbed the stairs, and the shadows cast onto the ceiling by our oil lamps, as always, spun and merged, now expanding, now shrinking, yet seemed somehow to be doing so for the first time. Upstairs, as we were removing our shoes in the hall, Shevket said:

"Before I go to sleep can I kiss my grandfather's hand?"

"I checked in on him just now," Hayriye said. "Your grandfather is in such pain and discomfort it's clear that evil spirits have taken hold of him. The fever of the illness has consumed him. Go to your room so I can prepare your bed."

Hayriye herded them into the room. As she laid out the mattress and spread out the sheets and quilts, she was going on as if every object she held was a marvel unique to the world, and muttering about how sleeping here in a warm room between clean sheets and under warm down quilts would be like spending the night in a sultan's palace.

"Hayriye, tell us a story," said Orhan as he sat on his chamber pot.

"Once upon a time there was a blue man," said Hayriye, "and his closest companion was a jinn."

"Why was the man blue?" said Orhan.

"For goodness sake, Hayriye," I said. "Tonight at least don't tell a story about jinns and ghosts."

"Why shouldn't she?" said Shevket. "Mother, after we fall asleep do you leave the bed and go to be with Grandfather?"

"Your grandfather, Allah protect him, is gravely ill," I said. "Of course I go to his bedside at night to look after him. Then, I return to our bed, don't I?"

"Have Hayriye look after Grandfather," said Shevket. "Doesn't Hayriye look after my grandfather at night anyway?"

"Are you finished?" Hayriye asked of Orhan. As she wiped Orhan's behind with a wet rag, his face was overcome with a sweet lethargy. She glanced into the pot and wrinkled up her face, not due to the smell, but as if what she saw wasn't sufficient.

"Hayriye," I said. "Empty the chamber pot and bring it back. I don't want Shevket to leave the room in the middle of the night."

"Why shouldn't I leave the room?" asked Shevket. "Why shouldn't Hayriye tell us a story about jinns and fairies?".

"Because there are jinns in the house, you idiot," Orhan said, not so much out of fear, but with the dumb optimism I always noticed in his expression after he'd relieved himself.

"Mother, are there jinns here?"

"If you leave the room, if you attempt to see your grandfather, the jinn will catch you."

"Where will Black lay out his bed?" said Shevket. "Where will he sleep tonight?"

"I'm not sure," I said. "Hayriye will be preparing his bed."

"Mother, you're still going to sleep with us, aren't you?" said Shevket.

"How many times do I have to tell you? I'll sleep together with you two as before."

"Always?"

Hayriye left carrying the chamber pot. From the cabinet where I'd hidden them, I removed the remaining nine illustrations left behind by the unspeakable murderer and sat on the bed. By the light of a candle, I stared at them for a long time trying to fathom their secret. These illustrations were beautiful enough that you might mistake them for your own forgotten memories; and as with writing, as you looked at them, they spoke.

I'd lost myself in the pictures. I understood from the scent of Orhan's beautiful head, upon which I'd rested my nose, that he, too, was looking at that odd and suspicious Red. As occasionally happened, I had the urge to take out my breast and nurse him. Later, when Orhan was frightened by the terrifying picture of Death, gently and sweetly breathing through his reddish lips, I suddenly wanted to eat him.

"I'll eat you up, do you understand me?"

"Mama, tickle me," he said and threw himself down.

"Get off there, get up you beast," I screamed and slapped him. He'd lain across the pictures. I checked the illustrations; apparently no harm had come to them. The image of the horse in the topmost picture was faintly, yet unnoticeably, crumpled.

Hayriye entered with the empty chamber pot. I gathered the pictures and was about to leave the room when Shevket began to cry:

"Mother? Where are you going?"

"I'll be right back."

I crossed the freezing hallway. Black was seated across from my father's empty cushion, in the same position that he'd spent four days discussing painting and perspective with him. I laid out the illustrations on the folding bookstand, the cushion and on the floor before him. Color abruptly suffused the candlelit room with a warmth and an astonishing liveliness, as if everything had been set in motion.

Utterly still, we looked at the pictures at length, silently and respectfully. When we made even the slightest movement, the still air, which bore the scent of death from the room across the wide hall, would make the candle flame flicker and my father's mysterious illustrations seemed to move too. Had the paintings taken on such significance for me because they were the cause of my father's death? Was I mesmerized by the peculiarity of the horse or the uniqueness of Red, by the misery of the tree or the sadness of the two wandering dervishes, or was it because I feared the murderer who'd killed my father and perhaps others on account of these illustrations? After a while, Black and I fully understood that the silence between us, as much as it might've been caused by the paintings, was also due to our being alone in the same room on our wedding night. Both of us wanted to speak.

"When we wake tomorrow morning, we should tell everybody that my hapless father has passed away in his sleep," I said. Although what I'd said was correct, it appeared as if I were being insincere.

"Everything will be fine in the morning," said Black in the same peculiar manner, unable to believe in the truth of what he'd spoken.

When he made a nearly imperceptible gesture to draw closer to me, I had the urge to embrace him and, as I did with the children, to take his head into my hands.

Just at that moment, I heard the door to my father's room open and, springing up in terror, I ran over, opened our door and looked out: By the light that filtered into the hallway, I was shocked to see my father's door half open. I stepped into the icy hallway. My father's room, heated by the still-lit brazier, reeked of decay. Had Shevket or somebody else come here? His body, dressed in his nightgown, rested peacefully, bathed in the faint light of the brazier. I thought about the way, on some nights, I'd say, "Have a good night, dear Father," while he read the *Book of the Soul* by candlelight before going to sleep. Raising himself slightly, he'd take the glass I'd brought him out of my hand and say, "May the water bearer never want for anything," before kissing me on the cheek and looking into my eyes as he used to do when I was a girl. I stared down at my father's horrid face and, in short, I was afraid. I wanted to avoid looking at him, while at the same time, goaded by the Devil, I wanted to see how gruesome he'd become.

I timidly returned to the room with the blue door whereupon Black made an advance on me. I pushed him away, more unthinkingly than out of anger. We struggled in the flickering light of the candle, though it wasn't really a struggle but rather the imitation of a struggle. We were enjoying bumping into each other, touching one another's arms, legs and chests. The confusion I felt resembled the emotional state that Nizami had described with regard to Hüsrev and Shirin: Could Black, who'd read Nizami so thoroughly, sense that, like Shirin, I also meant "Continue" when I said, "Don't bruise my lips by kissing them so hard"?

"I refuse to sleep in the same bed with you until that devil-of-a-man is found, until my father's murderer is caught," I said.

As I fled the room, I was seized by embarrassment. I'd spoken in such a shrill voice it must've seemed I wanted the children and Hayriye to hear what I'd said—perhaps even my poor father and my late husband, whose body had long decayed and turned to dust on who knows what barren patch of earth.

As soon as I was back with the children, Orhan said, "Mama, Shevket went out into the hallway."

"Did you go out?" I said, and made as if to slap him.

"Hayriye," said Shevket and hugged her.

"He didn't go out," said Hayriye. "He was in the room the entire time."

I shuddered and couldn't look her in the eyes. I realized that after my father's death was announced, the children would thenceforth seek refuge in Hayriye, tell her all our secrets, and that this lowly servant, taking advantage of this opportunity, would try to control me. She wouldn't stop there either, but would try to place the onus of my father's murder onto me, then she'd have the guardianship of the children passed on to Hasan! Yes, indeed she would! All this shameless scheming because she'd slept with my father, may he rest in divine light. Why should I hide all this from you any longer? She was, in fact, doing this, of course. I smiled sweetly at her. Then, I lifted Shevket onto my lap and kissed him.

"I'm telling you, Shevket went out into the hallway," Orhan said.

"Get into bed, you two. Let me get between you so I can tell you the story of the tailless jackal and the black jinn."

"But you told Hayriye not to tell us a story about jinns," said Shevket. "Why can't Hayriye tell us the story tonight?"

"Will they visit the City of the Forsaken?" asked Orhan.

"Yes they will!" I said. "None of the children in that city have a mother or a father. Hayriye, go downstairs and check the doors again. We'll probably be asleep by the middle of the story."

"I won't fall asleep," said Orhan.

"Where is Black going to sleep tonight?" said Shevket.

MY NAME IS RED

"In the workshop," I said. "Snuggle up tight to your mother so we can warm up nicely under the quilt. Whose icy little feet are these?"

"Mine," said Shevket. "Where will Hayriye sleep?"

I'd begun telling the story, and as always, Orhan fell asleep first, after which I lowered my voice.

"After I fall asleep, you're not going to leave the bed, right, Mama?" said Shevket.

"No, I won't leave."

I really didn't intend to leave. After Shevket fell asleep, I was musing about how pleasurable it was to fall asleep cuddled up with my sons on the night of my second wedding—with my handsome, intelligent and desirous husband in the next room. I'd dozed off with such thoughts, but my sleep was fitful. Later, this is what I remembered about that strange restless realm between dreaming and wakefulness: First I settled accounts with my deceased father's angry spirit, then I fled the specter of that disgraceful murderer who wanted to send me off to be with my father. As he pursued me, the unyielding murderer, even more terrifying than my father's spirit, began making a clattering ruckus. In my dream, he tossed stones at our house. They struck the windows and landed on the roof. Later, he tossed a rock at the door, at one point even trying to force it open. Next, when this evil spirit began to wail like some ungodly animal, my heart began to pound.

I awoke covered in sweat. Had I heard those sounds in my dream or had I been awakened by sounds from somewhere in the house? I couldn't decide, and so snuggled up with the children, and without moving, I waited. I'd nearly assured myself that the noises were only in my sleep when I heard the same wail. Just then, something large landed in the courtyard with a bang. Was this also a rock, perhaps?

I was paralyzed with terror. But the situation immediately got worse: I heard noises from within the house. Where was Hayriye? In which room had Black fallen asleep? In what state was my father's pitiful corpse? My God, I prayed, protect us. The children were deep asleep.

Had this happened before I was married, I'd have risen from bed, and taking charge of the situation like the man of the house, I'd have suppressed my fears and scared away the jinns and spirits. In my present condition, however, I cowered and hugged the children. It was as if there were no one else in the world. Nobody was going to come to the aid of the children and me. Expecting something awful to happen, I prayed to Allah for deliverance. As in my dreams, I was alone. I heard the courtyard gate open. It was the courtyard gate, wasn't it? Yes, absolutely.

I, Shekure

I rose abruptly, grabbed my robe and quitted the room without even knowing myself what I was doing.

"Black!" I hissed from the top of the stairs.

After hastily donning shoes, I descended the stairs. The candle I'd lit at the brazier blew out as soon as I stepped out onto the courtyard's stone walkway. A strong wind had begun to blow, though the sky was clear. As soon as my eyes adjusted, I saw that the half-moon was flooding the courtyard with moonlight. My dearest Allah! The courtyard gate was open. I stood stunned, atremble in the cold.

Why hadn't I brought a knife with me? Neither did I have a candlestick or even a piece of wood. For a moment, in the blackness, I saw the gate move of its own accord. Later, after it appeared to have stilled, I heard it squeal. I remember thinking, This seems like a dream.

When I heard a noise from within the house, as if from just beneath the roof, I understood that my father's soul was struggling to leave his body. Knowing my father's soul was in such torment both put me at ease and plunged me into agony. If Father is the cause of these noises, I thought, then no evil will befall me. On the other hand, his tormented soul, frantically fluttering about, trying to escape and ascend, so troubled me that I prayed to Allah to comfort him. But when it occurred to me that his soul would protect me and the children, a feeling of great relief washed over me. If there were truly some demon contemplating evil just beyond the gate, let him fear my father's restless soul.

Just then, I worried that perhaps it was Black that was upsetting my father so much. Would my father bring evil upon Black? Where was he? Just then, outside the courtyard gate, on the street, I noticed him and froze. He was speaking with somebody.

A man was talking to Black from the trees in the empty yard on the far side of the street. I was able to infer that the howling I'd heard as I lay in bed had come from this man whom I straightaway knew to be Hasan. There was a plaintive strain, a weeping in his voice, but also a threatening overtone. I listened to them from a distance. Within the silent night they'd given themselves over to settling accounts.

I understood that I was all alone in the world with my children. I was thinking that I loved Black, but to tell the truth, what I wanted was to love only Black—for Hasan's melancholy voice singed my heart.

"Tomorrow, I'll return with the judge, Janissaries and witnesses who'll swear that my older brother is alive and still fighting in the mountains of Persia," he said. "Your marriage is illegitimate. You're committing adultery in there."

"Shekure wasn't your wife, she was your late brother's wife," Black said.

"My older brother's still alive," Hasan said with conviction. "There are witnesses who have seen him."

"This morning, based on the fact that he hasn't returned after four years campaigning, the Üsküdar judge granted Shekure a divorce. If he is alive, have your witnesses tell him that he's now a divorced man."

"Shekure is restricted from remarrying for a month," said Hasan. "Otherwise it's a sacrilege contrary to the Koran. How could Shekure's father consent to such disgraceful nonsense?"

"Enishte Effendi," Black said, "is very sick. He's on his death bed . . . and the judge sanctified our marriage."

"Did you work together to poison your Enishte?" said Hasan. "Did you plan this out with Hayriye?"

"My father-in-law is deeply distressed by what you've done to Shekure. Your brother, if he's really still alive, could also call you to account for your dishonor."

"These are all lies, each one!" said Hasan. "These are only excuses cooked up by Shekure so she could leave us."

There came a cry from within the house; it was Hayriye who'd screamed. Next, Shevket screamed. They shouted to each other. Unwitting and afraid, without being able to restrain myself, I shouted too and ran into the house without knowing what I was doing.

Shevket ran down the stairs and fled out into the courtyard.

"My grandfather is as cold as ice," he cried. "My grandfather has died."

We hugged each other. I lifted him up. Hayriye was still shouting. Black and Hasan heard the shouts and everything that was said.

"Mother, they've killed grandfather," Shevket said this time.

Everyone heard this, too. Had Hasan heard? I squeezed Shevket tightly, and calmly walked with him back inside. At the top of the stairs, Hayriye was wondering how the child had awoken and sneaked out.

"You promised you wouldn't leave us," said Shevket, who began to cry.

My mind was preoccupied now with Black. Because he was busy with Hasan, he didn't think to close the gate. I kissed Shevket on either cheek and hugged him even tighter, taking in the scent of his neck, consoling him and, finally handing him over to Hayriye, I whispered, "You two go upstairs."

They went upstairs. I returned and stood a few steps behind the gate. I assumed Hasan couldn't see me. Had he changed his position in the

I, Shekure 213

darkened garden across the way, perhaps moving behind the trees that lined the street? As it happened, however, he could see me, and as he spoke he addressed me, too. It was unnerving to convene in the dark with somebody whose face I couldn't see, but it was even worse, as Hasan accused me, accused us, to realize deep down that he was justified. With him, as with my father, I always felt guilty, always in the wrong. And now, moreover, I knew with great sadness that I was in love with the man who was incriminating me. My beloved Allah please help me. Love isn't suffering for the sake of suffering, but a means to reach You, is it not?

Hasan claimed that I'd killed my father in league with Black. He said he'd heard what Shevket had said, adding that everything had been laid bare and that we'd committed an unpardonable sin deserving of the torments of Hell. Come morning he'd go to the judge to explain it all. If I were found to be innocent, if my hands weren't red with my father's blood, he swore to have me and the children returned to his house where he'd serve as father until his older brother came back. If, however, I were found guilty, a woman like me, who'd mercilessly abandoned her husband—a man willing to make the highest sort of sacrifice—for her no punishment was too severe. We patiently listened to his fury, then noticed that there was an abrupt silence amid the trees.

"If you return of your own free will to the home of your true husband, now," said Hasan, assuming a completely different tone, "if you silently pitter-patter back with your children without being seen by anyone, I'll forget the fake wedding ploy, the crimes you've committed, all of it, I'll forgive it all. And, we'll wait together, Shekure, year after year, patiently, for my brother's return."

Was he drunk? There was something so infantile in his voice and what he was now proposing to me in front of my husband that I feared it might cost him his life.

"Do you understand?" he called out from among the trees.

I couldn't determine exactly where he was in the blackness. My dear God, come to our aid, to us, Your sinning servants.

"Because you won't be able to live under the same roof with the man who killed your father, Shekure. This I know."

I momentarily thought that he could've been the one who killed my father, and that he was now mocking us, perhaps. This Hasan was the Devil incarnate. But I couldn't be certain of anything.

"Listen to me, Hasan Effendi," Black called out to the darkness. "My father-in-law was murdered, this much is true. The most despicable of men killed him."

"He'd been murdered before the wedding, isn't that so?" said Hasan. "You two killed him because he opposed this marriage sham, this fake divorce, the false witnesses and all your deceits. If he'd considered Black to be appropriate, he'd have given his daughter to him years ago."

Having lived for years with my late husband, with us, Hasan knew our past as well as we ourselves did. And with the passion of a spurned lover, he remembered every last detail of everything I'd discussed with my husband at home, but had subsequently forgotten, or now wanted to forget. Over the years, we'd shared so many memories—he, his brother and I— that I worried how strange, new and distant Black would seem to me if Hasan were to begin recounting the past.

"We suspect that you were the one who killed him," Black said.

"On the contrary, you were the ones who killed him so you could marry. This is evident. As for me, I have no motive."

"You killed him so we wouldn't get married," said Black. "When you learned that he'd permitted Shekure's divorce and our marriage, you lost your mind. Besides, you were furious with Enishte Effendi because he'd encouraged Shekure to return home to live with him. You wanted revenge. As long as he remained alive, you knew you'd never get your hands on Shekure."

"Be done with your stalling," Hasan said decisively. "I refuse to listen to this prattle. It's very cold here. I froze out here trying to get your attention with the rocks—didn't you hear them?"

"Black had lost himself in my father's illustrations," I said.

Had I done wrong in saying this?

Hasan spoke in precisely the same false tone that I sometimes resorted to with Black: "Shekure, as you are my brother's wife, your best course of action is to return now with your children to the house of the hero spahi cavalryman to whom you're still wed according to the Koran."

"I refuse," I said, as if hissing into the heart of the night. "I refuse, Hasan. No."

"Then, my responsibility and devotion to my brother forces me to alert the judge first thing tomorrow morning of what I've heard here. Otherwise, they'll call me to account."

"They're going to call you to account anyway," said Black. "The moment you go to the judge, I'll reveal that you're the one who murdered Our Sultan's cherished servant, Enishte Effendi. This very morning."

"Very well," said Hasan calmly. "Make that revelation."

I shrieked. "They'll torture the both of you!" I shouted. "Don't go to the judge. Wait. Everything will become clear."

I, Shekure

"I have no fear of torture," Hasan said. "I've been tortured twice before, and both times I understood it was the only way the guilty could be culled from the innocent. Let the slanderers fear torture. I'm going to tell the judge, the captain of the Janissaries, the Sheikhulislam, everybody about poor Enishte Effendi's book and its illustrations. Everybody is talking about those illustrations. What is it about them? What's in those pictures?"

"There's nothing in them," Black said.

"Which means you examined them at the first opportunity."

"Enishte Effendi wants me to finish the book."

"Very well. I hope, God willing, that they'll torture the both of us."

The two of them fell silent. Next, Black and I heard footsteps in the empty yard. Were they leaving or approaching us? We could neither see Hasan nor tell what he was doing. It would've been senseless for him to push through the thorns, shrubs and brambles lining the far end of the garden in the pitch-blackness. He could've easily left without being seen, had he passed through the trees and wound his way before us, but we didn't hear any footsteps nearing us. I boldly shouted, "Hasan!" There was no response.

"Hush," said Black.

We were both trembling from the cold. Without hesitating too long, we closed the gate and the doors tightly behind us. Before entering my bed warmed by the children, I checked on my father again. Meanwhile, Black once again seated himself before the pictures.

CHAPTER 35

I AM A HORSE

Ignore the fact that I'm standing here placid and still; if truth be told, I've been galloping for centuries; I've passed over plains, fought in battles, carried off the melancholy daughters of shahs to be wed; I've galloped tirelessly page by page from story to history, from history to legend and from book to book; I've appeared in countless stories, fables, books and battles; I've accompanied invincible heroes, legendary lovers and fantastic armies; I've galloped from campaign to campaign with our victorious sultans, and as a result, I've appeared in countless illustrations.

How does it feel, you ask, to be painted so often?

Of course, I'm proud of myself. Yet, I also question whether, indeed, it is I being depicted in all cases. It is evident from these pictures that I'm perceived differently by everyone. Still, I have the strong sense that there's a commonality, a unity to the illustrations.

My miniaturist friends were recounting a story recently, and from it, I learned the following: The king of the Frankish infidels was considering marriage to the daughter of the Venetian Doge. He was considering it, but then he was plagued with the thought, "What if this Venetian is poor and his daughter ugly?" To reassure himself, he ordered his best artist to paint the Venetian Doge's daughter, possessions, property and belongings. The Venetians could care less about gross indecency: They'll expose not only their daughters to the prying eyes of the artist, but their horses and palazzos, as well. The gifted infidel artist could depict a maiden or a horse in such a way that you'd be able to pick either out of a crowd. Back in his courtyard, as the Frankish king examined the pictures from Venice, pondering whether he should take the maiden as his wife, his stallion, suddenly aroused, attempted to mount the attractive mare in the painting, and the horse grooms were hard pressed to bring the ferocious animal under control before he destroyed the picture and its frame with his huge member.

They say that it wasn't the beauty of the Venetian mare that had aroused the Frankish stallion—though she was indeed striking—but the act of taking a particular mare and painting a picture in her exact likeness. Now, the question arises: Is it sinful to be depicted as that mare had been, that is, like a real mare? In my case, as you can see, there is very little difference between my image and other pictures of horses.

Actually, those of you who pay particular attention to the grace of my midsection, the length of my legs and the pride of my bearing will understand that I am indeed unique. But these excellent features point to the uniqueness of the miniaturist who illustrated me, not to my uniqueness as a horse. Everyone knows that there's no horse exactly like me. I'm simply the rendering of a horse that exists in a miniaturist's imagination.

Looking at me, observers frequently say, "Good God, what a gorgeous horse!" But they're actually praising the artist, not me. All horses are in fact distinct, and the miniaturist, above all, ought to know this.

Take a close look, even a given stallion's organ doesn't resemble another's. Don't be afraid, you can examine it up close, and even take it in your hands: My God-given marvel has a shape and curve all its own.

I Am a Horse

Now then, all miniaturists illustrate all horses from memory in the same way, even though we've each been uniquely created by Allah, Greatest of all Creators. Why do they take pride in simply rendering thousands and tens of thousands of horses in the same way without ever truly looking at us? I'll tell you why: Because they're attempting to depict the world that God perceives, not the world that they see. Doesn't that amount to challenging God's unity, that is—Allah forbid—isn't it saying that I could do the work of God? Artists who are discontent with what they see with their own eyes, artists who draw the same horse a thousand times asserting that what rests in their imagination is God's horse, artists who claim that the best horse is what blind miniaturists draw from memory, aren't they all committing the sin of competing with Allah?

The new styles of the Frankish masters aren't blasphemous, quite the opposite, they're the most in keeping with our faith. I pray that my Erzurumi brethren don't misunderstand me. It displeases me that Frankish infidels parade their women around half naked, indifferent to pious modesties, that they don't understand the pleasures of coffee and handsome boys, and that they roam about with clean-shaven faces, yet with hair as long as women's, claiming that Jesus is also the Lord God—Allah protect us. I become so aggravated by these Franks that if I ever came across one, I'd give him a good mule kick.

Still, I'm sick of being incorrectly depicted by miniaturists who sit around the house like ladies and never go off to war. They'll depict me at a gallop with both of my forelegs extended at the same time. There isn't a horse in this world that runs like a rabbit. If one of my forelegs is forward, the other is aft. Contrary to what's depicted in battle illustrations, there isn't a horse in this world that extends one foreleg like a curious dog, leaving the other firmly planted on the ground. There is no spahi cavalry division in existence whose horses saunter in unison, as if traced with an identical stencil twenty times back to back. We horses scrounge for and eat the green grass at our feet when nobody is looking. We never assume a statuesque stance and wait around elegantly, the way we're shown in paintings. Why is everybody so embarrassed about our eating, drinking, shitting and sleeping? Why are they afraid to depict this wondrous God-given and unique implement of mine? On the sly, women and children, in particular, love to stare at it, and what's the harm in this? Is the Hoja from Erzurum against this as well?

They say that once upon a time there was a feeble and nervous shah in Shiraz. He was in mortal fear that his enemies would have him deposed so his son could assume the throne; rather than sending the prince to Isfahan as provincial governor, he imprisoned him in the most out of the way room of his palace. The prince grew up and lived in this makeshift cell, which looked onto neither courtyard nor garden, for thirty-one years. After his father's allotted time on Earth ran out, the prince, who'd lived alone with his books, ascended the throne and declared: "I command that you bring me a horse. I've always seen pictures of them in books, and am curious about them." They brought him the most beautiful gray steed in the palace, but when the new king saw that the horse had nostrils like mineshafts, a shameless ass, a coat duller than in the illustrations and a brutish rump, he was so disenchanted that he had all the horses in his kingdom massacred. After this brutal slaughter, which lasted forty days, all the kingdom's rivers flowed a somber red. But Exalted Allah did not refrain from meting out His justice: The king now had no cavalry whatsoever, and when faced with the army of his archenemy, the Turkmen Bey of the Blacksheep clan, he was routed and, in the end, hacked apart. Let there be no doubt: As all the histories will reveal, the nation of horses had taken its revenge.

CHAPTER 36

I AM CALLED BLACK

Shekure shut herself into the room with the children, and I listened at length to the sounds within the house and to its incessant creaking. Shekure and Shevket began whispering to each other and she anxiously quieted them with an abrupt "shush!" I heard a rattling coming from the stone-paved area near the well, but it didn't last. Later, my attention was caught by a squawking seagull that had alighted on the roof. Then it, too, fell silent along with everything else. Afterward, I heard a low moan from the other side of the hallway: Hayriye was crying in her sleep. Her moans dissolved into coughing which ended as suddenly as it had begun, giving way once again to that deep, dreadful silence. A while later, I imagined that an intruder was roaming around the room where my dead Enishte lay, and I froze completely.

During each span of silence, I examined the pictures before me, contemplating how the passionate Olive, the beautiful Butterfly and the deceased gilder had dabbed paint onto the page. I had the urge to confront each of the images by shouting "Satan!" or "Death!" as my Enishte used to do some nights, but fear restrained me. Besides, these illustrations had vexed me plenty because I couldn't write an appropriate story to accompany them despite my Enishte's insistence. Since I was slowly growing certain that his death was linked to these images, I felt fretful and impatient. I'd already scrutinized the illustrations endlessly while listening to Enishte's stories, all for a chance to be near Shekure. Now that she was my lawfully wedded wife, why should I preoccupy myself with them? A merciless inner voice answered: "Because even after her children have fallen asleep, Shekure refuses to leave her bed and join you." I waited for a long while gazing at the pictures by candlelight, hoping that my black-eyed beauty would come to me.

In the morning, stirred from my sleep by Hayriye's shrieks, I grabbed the candle-holder and rushed into the hallway. I thought Hasan had raided the house with his men, and I considered hiding the illustrations, but quickly realized that Hayriye had begun screaming upon Shekure's command, as a way to announce Enishte Effendi's death to the children and neighbors.

When I met Shekure in the hall, we embraced fondly. The children, who'd leapt out of bed when they'd heard Hayriye's shouts, stood motionless.

"Your grandfather has died," Shekure said to them. "I don't want you to enter that room anymore under any circumstances."

She freed herself from my arms and, going to her father's side, began to weep.

I herded the children back into their room. "Change out of your bedclothes, you'll catch cold," I said and sat on the edge of the bed.

"Grandfather didn't die this morning. He died last night," Shevket said.

A long loose strand of Shekure's gorgeous hair had coiled into an Arabic script "vav" on her pillow. Her warmth hadn't yet dissipated from beneath the quilt. We could hear her sobbing and wailing along with Hayriye. Her ability to shriek as though her father had actually died unexpectedly was so shockingly disingenuous that I felt as if I didn't know Shekure at all, like she'd been possessed by a strange jinn.

"I'm frightened," said Orhan with a glance that was also a request for permission to cry.

"Don't be afraid," I said. "Your mother is crying so the neighbors will know of your grandfather's death and pay their respects."

"What difference does it make if they come?" Shevket asked.

"If they come, they'll be sad and mourn with us over his death. That way we can share the burden of our pain."

"Did you kill my grandfather?" shouted Shevket.

"If you're going to upset your mother, don't expect any affection from me!" I shouted back.

We didn't shout at each other like stepfather and stepson, but like two men talking by the banks of a loud rushing river. Shekure stepped out into the hallway and was forcing the wooden slats of the window trying to throw open the shutters so her shouts could be better heard throughout the neighborhood.

I left the room to join her. We both tried to force the window. With a final combined effort, the shutters came loose and fell into the courtyard. Sunlight and cold struck our faces and we were stunned momentarily. Shekure screamed, crying her heart out.

Enishte Effendi's death, once announced by her cries, turned into a much more tragic and agonizing pain. Whether sincere or feigned, my wife's crying tormented me. Unexpectedly, I began to weep. I didn't even know if I was crying sincerely out of grief or was merely pretending for fear of being held responsible for my Enishte's death.

"He's gone, gone, gone, my dear father's gone!" cried Shekure.

My sobs and laments mimicked hers, though I didn't exactly know what I was saying. I was worried about how I looked to the neighbors staring at us from their houses, from behind cracked doors and between shutter slats, and wondered how fitting my behavior was. As I cried, I felt purged of doubts about whether my agony was genuine, of apprehensions about being accused of murder and of the fear of Hasan and his men.

Shekure was mine and it was as if I were celebrating with shouts and tears. I drew my sobbing wife close to me, and without paying any heed to the tearful children approaching us, I lovingly kissed her cheek and inhaled the scent of the almond trees of our youth.

Together with the children, we walked back to where the body lay. I said, *La ilahe illallah,* there is no God but Allah" as though addressing not a reeking two-day-old corpse but a dying man whom I wanted to reaffirm the words of witness; I wanted my Enishte to go to Heaven with these words on his lips. We pretended that he'd repeated them, and smiled for a moment as we gazed at his nearly destroyed face and battered head. I opened my palms to Heaven and recited from the "Ya Sin" chapter while the others listened quietly. With a clean piece of gauze that Shekure

I Am Called Black

brought into the room, we carefully bound my Enishte's mouth shut, tenderly closed his ravaged eyes and gently rolled him over onto his right side, arranging his head so it faced Mecca. Shekure spread a clean white sheet over her father.

I was pleased that the children were watching everything so intensely and by the quiet that followed the wailing. I felt like somebody with a real wife and children, with a hearth and home.

One by one, I collected the pictures into a portfolio, donned my heavy caftan and hastily fled the house. I headed directly for the neighborhood mosque, pretending not to see one of the neighbors—an elderly woman with a snot-nosed grandchild who was clearly jubilant about all the sudden activity: They'd heard our cries and had eagerly come to enjoy our pain.

The tiny hole in the wall that the preacher called his "house" was embarrassingly small next to the ostentatious structure with its enormous domes and expansive courtyard, typical of the mosques that were being constructed lately. The preacher, in what I'd observed as a custom of increasing frequency, was extending the boundaries of his cold, little rat hole of a "home," and had usurped the entire mosque, without the least concern over the faded and dingy wash his wife had hung between two chestnut trees at the edge of the courtyard. We avoided the attacks of two brutish dogs that had claimed the courtyard, just like the Imam Effendi and his family, and after the preacher's sons chased the beasts away with sticks and excused themselves, the preacher and I retired to a private corner.

After yesterday's divorce proceedings, and in light of the fact that we hadn't asked him to perform the wedding ceremony, which I was certain had upset him, I could read a "For goodness sake, what brings you here now?" upon his face.

"Enishte Effendi passed away this morning."

"May God have mercy upon him. May he find a home in Heaven!" he said benevolently. Why had I senselessly implicated myself by tacking the words "this morning" onto my statement? I dropped another gold piece into his hand, identical to the ones I'd given him yesterday. I requested that he recite the death prayer before the azan and appoint his brother as crier to go around announcing the death to the entire neighborhood.

"My brother has a dear friend who is half blind; together, we are expert at carrying out the final ablutions of the deceased," he said.

What could be more suitable than having a blind man and a half-wit wash Enishte Effendi's body? I explained to him that the ritual funeral prayer would be performed in the afternoon and that notables and crowds from the palace, the guilds and theological schools would be attending. I didn't attempt to explain the state of Enishte Effendi's face and battered head, having long decided that the matter needed to be addressed at a higher level.

Since Our Sultan had entrusted the balance of the funds for the book that He'd commissioned from my Enishte to the Head Treasurer, I had to report the death to him before anyone else. To this end, I sought out an upholsterer, a relative on my late father's side, who'd worked in the tailors' work stalls opposite Coldfountain Gate ever since I was a child. When I found him, I kissed his mottled hand and explained imploringly that I needed to see the Head Treasurer. He had me wait among his balding apprentices who were sewing curtains, doubled over the multicolored silk spread over their laps; then, he had me follow a head tailor's assistant who, I learned, was going to the palace to take measurements. When we climbed up to the Parade Square through Coldfountain Gate I knew I'd be able to avoid passing the workshop opposite the Hagia Sophia; and thus, I was spared from announcing the crime to the other miniaturists.

The Parade Square seemed abustle now, whereas it usually seemed empty to me. Though there wasn't a single person at the Petitioner's Gate, before which petitioners would line up on days when the Divan convened, nor anyone in the vicinity of the granaries, it was as if I could hear a continuous din emanating from the windows of the sick house, from the carpenters' workshop, the bakery, the stables, the grooms with their horses before the Second Gate (whose spires I looked upon with awe) and from among the cypresses. I attributed my sense of alarm to the fear of passing through the Gate of Salutation, or Second Gate, which I would soon be doing for the first time in my life.

At the gate, I could neither focus my attention on the spot where the executioners were said to be ever at the ready, nor could I hide my agitation from the keepers of the gate who glanced inquiringly at the bolt of upholstery cloth I carried as a prop so onlookers would assume I was assisting my tailor-cum-guide.

As soon as we entered the Divan Square, a deep silence enveloped us. I felt my heart pounding even in the veins of my forehead and neck. This area, so often described by my Enishte and others who visited the palace, lay before me like a heavenly garden of unequaled beauty. Yet, I didn't feel the elation of a man who'd entered Heaven, just trepidation and pious reverence; I felt myself to be a simple servant of Our Sultan, who, as I now thoroughly understood, was indeed the foundation of this worldly realm. I stared at the peacocks roaming through the greenery, the gold cups chained to splashing fountains and the Grand Vizier's heralds robed in silk (who seemed to move about without touching the ground), and I felt the thrill of serving my Sovereign. There was no doubt that I would complete Our Sultan's secret book, whose unfinished illustrations I carried under my arm. Without knowing exactly what I was doing, I trailed behind the tailor, my eyes fixed on the Divan Tower, spellbound by fear more than awe now at its proximity.

Accompanied by a royal page who'd attached himself to us, we fearfully and silently, as in a dream, passed the Divan building and the Treasury; I felt that I'd seen this place before and knew it well.

We entered through a wide door into a room that was referred to as the Old Divan Chamber. Beneath its huge dome, I saw master artisans holding cloth, pieces of leather, silver scabbards and mother-of-pearl inlaid chests. I inferred that these men were from Our Sultan's craftsmen's guilds: mace makers, boot makers, silversmiths, master velvet makers, ivory engravers, and luthiers. They were all waiting outside the Head Treasurer's door with various petitions concerning payments, the acquisition of materials and requests to enter the Sultan's forbidden private quarters to take measurements. I was pleased to discover no illuminators among them.

We withdrew to one side and began to wait as well. Occasionally, we heard the raised voice of the treasurer's clerk, suspecting an error in accounts, request clarification; this would be met by a polite response, from a locksmith, for example. Voices rarely rose above a whisper; the flutter of the courtyard pigeons echoing in the dome above us were louder than the petty requests of the humble artisans.

When my turn came, I entered the Head Treasurer's small domed chamber to find it occupied by a single clerk. I quickly explained that there was an important matter to be submitted to the Head Treasurer's attention: A book project that Our Sultan had commissioned and that was of utmost importance to Him. Intrigued by what I was holding, the clerk raised his eyes. I showed him the illustrations from my Enishte's book. I noticed that the peculiarity of the pictures, their striking eccentricity, boggled his mind. I hastened to inform him of my Enishte's name, his sobriquet and his vocation, adding that he'd died on account of these pictures. I spoke quickly, well aware that if I returned from the palace without reaching Our Sultan, I'd be accused of having put Enishte into that dreadful state myself.

When the clerk left to apprise the Head Treasurer, I broke into a cold sweat. Would the Head Treasurer, who, as my Enishte once informed me, never left Our Sultan's side, who on occasion even spread out His prayer rug for Him, and who was frequently His confidant—would he ever leave the restricted Enderun quarters of the palace to see me? The fact that a messenger had been dispatched to the heart of the palace on my behalf was unbelievable enough. I wondered where Our Excellency the Sultan Himself might be: Had He retired to one of the kiosks near the shore? Was He in the harem? Was the Head Treasurer in His company?

Much later, I was summoned. Let me put it this way: I was taken so unawares I had no time to be afraid. Even so, I panicked when I saw the respect and astonishment in the expression of the master velvet maker standing at the door. I stepped inside and was at once terrified; I thought I'd be unable to speak. He wore the gold embroidered headdress that only he and the Grand Viziers wore; yes, I was in the presence of the Head Treasurer. He was gazing upon the illustrations that rested on a reading table where the clerk had placed them after taking them from me. I felt as if I were the one who'd made the paintings. I kissed the hem of his robe.

"My dear child," he said. "I haven't misunderstood, have I, your Enishte has passed away?"

I couldn't answer out of excitement, or perhaps guilt, and simply nodded. At the same time the completely unexpected happened: There before the sympathetic and surprised gaze of the Head Treasurer, a teardrop slid ever so slowly down my cheek. I was at a loss; I was oddly affected by being in the palace, by the Head Treasurer having taken leave of Our Sultan to speak to me and by being so near to Him. Tears began to stream from my eyes, but I didn't feel the slightest tinge of embarrassment.

"Cry to your heart's content, my dear son," said the Head Treasurer.

I sobbed and whimpered. Though I'd assumed the past twelve years had matured me, being this close to the Sultan, to the heart of the Empire, one fast realizes he is but a child. I cared not whether the silversmiths and velvet makers outside heard my sobbing. I knew I'd confess to the Head Treasurer.

Yes, I told him all, just as it came to me. As I once again saw my dead Enishte, my marriage to Shekure, Hasan's threats, the difficulties relating my Enishte's book and the secrets borne by the illustrations, I regained my composure. I felt certain that the only way to extricate myself from the trap I'd fallen into was to put myself at the mercy of the infinite justice and affection of Our Sultan, Refuge of the World, and so I withheld nothing. Before digesting all that I said and handing me over to the torturers and executioners, would the Head Treasurer convey my story directly to Our Sultan?

"Let Enishte Effendi's death be announced in the workshop without delay," said the Head Treasurer. "I want the entire artists' guild to attend his funeral."

He looked at me to ascertain whether I might have any objections. Emboldened by his interest, I expressed my concerns about the culprit, and the possible motive behind the deaths of my Enishte and the gilder Elegant Effendi. I hinted that the followers of the preacher from Erzurum and those who were targeting dervish houses where music was played and men danced might be involved. When I saw the doubtful expression of the Head Treasurer, I eagerly shared my other suspicions: I informed him that the monetary rewards and honor involved in being invited to illustrate and illuminate Enishte Effendi's book had likely led to unavoidable competition and jealousy among the masters. The secrecy of the project alone could very well have instigated these hatreds, grudges and intrigues. As the words left my mouth, I sensed nervously that the Head Treasurer had somehow grown suspicious of me—the way you have as well. My dear Allah, let justice be done, that is all I ask, nothing more.

Within the ensuing silence, the Head Treasurer cast his glance away from me, as if embarrassed on my behalf for my words and my destiny, and fixed his attention on the pictures resting on the folding table.

"There are nine plates here," he said. "The arrangement had been for a book with ten illustrations. Enishte Effendi took more gold leaf from us than has been used here."

"That murdering heretic must have stolen the last illustration, upon which much of the gold was applied," I said.

"You haven't told us who the calligrapher-scribe might be."

"My late Enishte hadn't yet completed the book's text. He was anticipating my help in its completion."

"My dear child, you've just explained how you're newly arrived in Istanbul."

"It's been one week. I arrived three days after Elegant Effendi was killed."

"You mean to say that your Enishte Effendi has been illustrating an unwritten—a nonexistent—manuscript for an entire year?"

"Yes, sir."

"Had he, then, revealed to you what the book was to recount?"

"Precisely what Our Sultan stated He wanted: A book that depicted the thousandth year of the Muslim calendar, which would strike terror into the heart of the Venetian Doge by showing the military strength and pride of Islam, together with the power and wealth of the Exalted House of Osman. This was intended to be a book recounting and depicting the most valuable, most vital aspects of our realm; and just as with the *Treatises on Physiognomy,* a portrait of Our Sultan would be situated at the heart of the book. Furthermore, since the illustrations were made in the Frankish style using Frankish methods, they would arouse the awe of the Venetian Doge and his desire for friendship."

"I'm aware of all that, but are these dogs and trees the most valuable and vital aspects of the Exalted House of Osman?" he said, gesturing wildly at the illustrations.

"My Enishte, may he rest in peace, insisted that the book show not Our Sultan's wealth alone, but His spiritual and moral strength along with His hidden sorrows."

"And Our Sultan's portrait?"

"I haven't seen it. It's probably wherever that heretic murderer has hidden it. Who knows, it's probably in his house at this very moment."

My late Enishte had been diminished to the status of a man who'd commissioned a menagerie of odd pictures that the Head Treasurer deemed worthless, rather than one who'd struggled to complete a book worthy of the gold he'd been paid. Was the Head Treasurer thinking I'd murdered an inept and untrustworthy man in order to marry Enishte's daughter, or for some other reason—perhaps to sell off the gold leaf? From his glances, I read that my case was about to be closed, so speaking nervously and with the last of my strength, I tried to clear my name: I told him that my Enishte had confided to me that one of the master miniaturists he hired might've murdered poor Elegant Effendi. Keeping my declaration brief, I told him how my Enishte suspected Olive, Stork or Butterfly. I neither had much proof nor felt much self-confidence. Afterward, I sensed that the Head Treasurer considered me nothing but a base slanderer and a foolish gossip.

Finally, I was elated when the Head Treasurer said we must conceal the details of Enishte's mysterious death from the workshop; I took this as a sign that he believed my story. The pictures remained with the Head Treasurer and I passed through the Gate of Salutation—which had earlier felt like the Gate of Heaven. After exiting under the scrutiny of the guards, I immediately relaxed, like a soldier returned home after an absence of many years.

CHAPTER 37

I AM YOUR BELOVED UNCLE

My funeral was splendid, exactly as I'd wanted. It made me proud that everybody I'd wished would attend came. Of the viziers who were in Istanbul at the time of my death, Haji Hüseyin Pasha of Cyprus and Baki Pasha the Lame loyally remembered that I'd rendered extensive services to them at one time or another. The presence of the Minister of Accounts, Red Melek Pasha, who, at the time of my death was both in high favor and much criticized, enlivened the humble courtyard of our neighborhood mosque. Had I lived and continued an active political life, I would've been promoted to the same rank as Mustafa Agha, the Sultan's Chief Herald, whose presence especially delighted me. The mourners constituted a large, dignified and impressive group that included the Divan Secretary Kemalettin Effendi, Chief Secretary Salim Effendi the Austere, the heralds of the Divan—each of whom was either a dear friend or an archenemy—a group of former Divan councillors who'd resigned early from active political life, my school friends, others who'd somehow learned of my death—I cannot imagine how or where—and various other relatives, in-laws and youths.

I also took pride in the congregation, its seriousness and its grief. The presence of the Head Treasurer Hazım Agha and the Commander of the Imperial Guard made clear to all in attendance that His Excellency Our Sultan was sincerely aggrieved by my untimely death. I was, indeed, very pleased by this. I don't know whether the sorrow of Our Glorious Sultan means great efforts will be made to catch my rogue murderer, including the mobilization of torturers, but I do know this: that accursed man is now in the courtyard, among the other miniaturists and calligraphers, wearing a dignified and exceedingly tormented expression as he gazes at my coffin.

Pray, don't think that I'm infuriated by my murderer or that I'm set on a path of revenge, or even that my soul is restless because I've been treacherously and cruelly slain. I am, at present, on a completely different plane of being, and my soul is quite at peace, having returned to its former glory after years of suffering on Earth.

My soul temporarily quitted my body, which was writhing in pain as it lay covered in blood from the blows of the inkpot, and quivered for a while within an intense light; afterward, two beautiful and smiling angels with faces bright as the sun—such as I'd read about countless times in the *Book of the Soul*—slowly approached me within this ethereal brilliance, grabbed me by my arms, as if I were still a body, and began their ascent. Ever so serenely and gently, ever so quickly we ascended as if in a blissful dream! We passed through forests of fire, forded rivers of light and forged dark seas and mountains of snow and ice. Each crossing took us thousands of years, though it seemed no more than the blink of an eye.

We ascended through the seven Heavens, passing varieties of gatherings, peculiar creatures, marshes and clouds swarming with an infinite variety of insects and birds. At each level of Heaven, the angel who led the way would knock on a portal, and when the question, "Who goes there?" came from beyond, the angel would describe me including all my names and attributes, summing up by saying, "An obedient servant of Exalted Allah!"—which would bring tears of joy to my eyes. I knew, however, that there were yet thousands of years before the Day of Judgment when those destined for Heaven would be separated from those destined for Hell.

My ascension, except for a few minor differences, happened just the way Gazzali, El Jevziyye and other legendary scholars described in their passages on death. Eternal puzzles and dark enigmas that only the dead might understand were now being revealed and illuminated, bursting forth brilliantly one by one in thousands of colors.

Oh, how might I adequately describe the hues I saw during this exquisite journey? The whole world was made up of color, everything was color. Just as I sensed that the force separating me from all other beings and objects consisted of color, I now knew that it was color itself that had affectionately embraced me and bound me to the world. I saw orange-hued skies, beautiful leaf-green bodies, brown eggs and legendary sky-blue horses. The world was faithful to the illustrations and legends that I'd avidly scrutinized over the years. I beheld Creation with awe and surprise as if for the first time, but also as if it'd somehow emerged from my memory. What I called "memory" contained an entire world: With time spread out infinitely before me in both directions, I understood how the world as I first experienced it could persist afterward as memory. As I died surrounded by this festival of color, I also discovered why I felt so relaxed, as if I'd been liberated from a straitjacket: From now on, nothing was restricted, and I had unlimited time and space in which to experience all eras and all places.

As soon as I realized this freedom, with fear and ecstasy I knew I was close to Him; at the same time, I humbly felt the presence of an absolutely matchless red.

Within a short period, red imbued all. The beauty of this color suffused me and the whole universe. As I approached His Being in this manner, I had the urge to cry out in jubilation. I was suddenly ashamed to be taken into His presence, drenched in blood as I was. Another part of my mind recalled what I'd read in books on death, that He would enlist Azrael and His other angels to summon me to His presence.

Would I be able to see Him? I wasn't able to breathe out of excitement.

The red approaching me—the omnipresent red within which all the images of the universe played—was so magnificent and beautiful that it quickened my tears to think I would become part of it and be so close to Him.

But I also knew He'd come no closer to me than He already had; He'd inquired about me from His angels and they'd praised me; He saw me as a loyal servant bound to His commandments and prohibitions; and He loved me.

My mounting joy and flowing tears were abruptly poisoned by a nagging doubt. Guilt-ridden and impatient in my uncertainty, I asked Him:

"Over the last twenty years of my life, I've been influenced by the infidel illustrations that I saw in Venice. There was even a time when I wanted my own portrait painted in that method and style, but I was afraid. Instead, I later had Your World, Your Subjects and Our Sultan, Your Shadow on Earth, depicted in the manner of the infidel Franks."

I didn't remember His voice, but I recalled the answer He gave me in my thoughts.

"East and West belong to me."

I could barely contain my excitement.

"All right then, what is the meaning of it all, of this . . . of this world?"

"Mystery," I heard in my thoughts, or perhaps, "mercy," but I wasn't certain of either.

By the way the angels had come near me, I knew some sort of decision had been made about me at this height of the heavens, but I'd have to wait in the divine balance of Berzah with the mass of other souls who'd died over the last tens of thousands of years until the Day of Judgment, when the final decision about us would be made. That everything transpired the way it was recorded in books pleased me. I recalled from my readings as I descended that I'd be reunited with my body during my burial.

But I quickly understood that the phenomenon of "reentering my lifeless body" was just a figure of speech, thank goodness. Despite their sorrow, the dignified funeral congregation that filled me with pride was astonishingly organized as it shouldered my coffin after the prayers and descended into the little Hillock Cemetery beside the mosque. From above, the procession appeared like a thin and delicate length of string.

Let me clarify my situation: As might be inferred from the well-known legend of Our Prophet—which states "The soul of the faithful is a bird that feeds from the trees of Heaven"—after death, the soul roams the firmament. As claimed by Abu Ömer bin Abdülber, the interpretation of this legend doesn't mean that the soul will possess a bird or even become a bird itself, but as the learned El Jevziyye aptly clarifies, it means that the soul can be found where birds gather. The spot from which I was observing things, what the Venetian masters who love perspective would call my "point of view," confirmed El Jevziyye's interpretation.

From where I was, for example, I could both see the threadlike funeral procession entering the cemetery, and with the pleasure of analyzing a painting, watch a sailboat gaining speed, its sails gorging on wind as it tacked toward Palace Point, where the Golden Horn met the Bosphorus. Looking down from the height of a minaret, the whole world resembled a magnificent book whose pages I was examining one by one.

Still, I could see much more than a man who'd simply ascended to such heights without his soul having left his body, and furthermore, I could see it all at once: On the other side of the Bosphorus, beyond Üsküdar, among gravestones in an empty yard, children playing leapfrog; the graceful progression of the Vizier of Diplomatic Affair's caïque propelled by seven pairs of oarsmen twelve years and seven months ago, when we accompanied the Venetian ambassador from his seaside mansion to be received by the Grand Vizier, Bald Ragip Pasha; a portly woman in the new Langa bazaar holding a huge head of cabbage like a child she was about to nurse; my elation when the Divan Herald Ramazan Effendi died, opening the way for my own advancement; how I stared as a child from my grandmother's lap at red shirts while my mother hung the laundry to dry in the courtyard; how I ran to distant neighborhoods in search of the midwife when Shekure's mother, may she rest in peace, had gone into labor; the location of the red belt I'd lost over forty years ago (I know now that Vasfi stole it); the splendid garden in the distance that I'd dreamed about once twenty-one years ago, which I pray Allah will one day confirm is

I Am Your Beloved Uncle

Heaven; the severed heads, noses, and ears sent to Istanbul by Ali Bey, the Governor-General of Georgia, who suppressed the rebels in the fortress of Gori; and my beautiful, dear Shekure, who separated herself from the neighborhood women mourning over me in the house and stared into the flames of the brick stove in our courtyard.

As is recorded in books and confirmed by scholars, the soul dwells in four realms: 1. the womb; 2. the terrestrial world; 3. Berzah, or divine limbo, where I now await Judgment Day; and 4. Heaven or Hell, where I will arrive after the Judgment.

From the intermediate state of Berzah, past and present time appear at once, and as long as the soul remains within its memories, limitations of place do not obtain. Only when one escapes the dungeons of time and space does it becomes evident that life is a straitjacket. However blissful it is being a soul without a body in the realm of the dead, so too is being a body without a soul among the living; what a pity nobody realizes this before dying. Therefore, during my lovely funeral, as I grievously watched my dear Shekure wear herself out weeping in vain, I begged of Exalted Allah to grant us souls-without-bodies in Heaven and bodies-without-souls in life.

CHAPTER 38

IT IS I, MASTER OSMAN

You know about those ornery old men who've charitably devoted their lives to art. They'll attack anyone who gets in their way. They're usually gaunt, bony and tall. They'll want the dwindling number of days before them to be just like the long period they've left behind. They're short-tempered, and they complain about everything. They'll try to grab the reins in all situations, causing everyone around them to throw up their hands in frustration; they don't like anyone or anything. I know, because I'm one of them.

The master of masters Nurullah Selim Chelebi, with whom I had the honor of making illustrations knee to knee in the same workshop, was this way in his eighties, when I was but a sixteen-year-old apprentice (though he wasn't as peevish as I am now). Blond Ali, the last of the great masters, laid to rest thirty years ago, was also this way (though he wasn't as thin and tall as I am). Since the arrows of criticism aimed at these legendary masters, who directed the workshops of their day now frequently strike me in the back, I want you to know that the hackneyed accusations leveled at us are entirely unfounded. These are the facts:

1. The reason we don't like anything innovative is that there is truly nothing new worth liking.
2. We treat most men like morons because, indeed, most men are morons, not because we're poisoned by anger, unhappiness or some other flaw in character. (Granted, treating these people better would be more refined and sensible.)
3. The reason I forget and confuse so many names and faces—except those of the miniaturists I've loved and trained since their apprenticeships—is not senility, but because these names and faces are so lackluster and colorless as to be hardly worth remembering.

During the funeral of Enishte, whose soul was prematurely taken by God because of his own foolishness, I tried to forget that the deceased had at one time caused me unmentionable agony by forcing me to imitate the European masters. On the way back, I had the following thoughts: blindness and death, those gifts bestowed by God, are not so far from me now. Of course, I will be remembered only so long as my illustrations and manuscripts cause your eyes to prance and flowers of bliss to bloom in your hearts. But after my death let it be known that in my old age, at the very end of my life, there was still plenty that made me smile. For instance:

1. Children—They represent what is vital in the world.
2. Sweet memories of handsome boys, beautiful women, painting well and friendships.
3. Seeing the masterpieces of the old masters of Herat—this cannot be explained to the uninitiated.

The simple meaning of all of this: In Our Sultan's workshop, which I direct, magnificent works of art can no longer be made as they once were—and the situation will only get worse, everything will dwindle and disappear. I am painfully aware that we quite rarely reach the sublime level of the old masters of Herat, despite having lovingly sacrificed our entire lives to this work. Humbly accepting this truth makes life easier. Indeed, it is precisely because it makes life easier that modesty is such a highly prized virtue in our part of the world.

With an air of such modesty I was touching up an illustration in the *Book of Festivities,* which described the circumcision ceremonies of our prince, wherein was depicted the Egyptian Governor-General's presentation of the following gifts: a gold-chased sword decorated with rubies, emeralds, and turquoise on a swatch of red velvet and one of the Governor-General's proud, lightning fast and spirited Arabian horses with a white blaze on its nose and a silvery, gleaming coat, fully appointed with a gold bit and reins, stirrups of pearl and greenish-yellow chrysoberyl, and a red velvet saddle embellished with silver thread and ruby rosettes. With a flick of my brush, here and there, I was touching up the illustration, whose composition I had arranged while delegating the rendering of the horse, the sword, the prince and the spectator-ambassadors to various apprentices. I applied purple to some of the leaves of the plane tree in the Hippodrome. I dabbed yellow upon the caftan-buttons of the Tatar Khan's ambassador. As I was brushing a sparse amount of gold wash onto the horse's reins, somebody knocked at the door. I quit what I was doing.

It was an imperial pageboy. The Head Treasurer had summoned me to the palace. My eyes ached ever so mildly. I placed my magnifying lens in my pocket, and left with the boy.

Oh, how nice it is to walk through the streets after having worked without a break for so long! At such times, the whole world strikes one as original and stunning, as if Allah had created it all the day before.

I noticed a dog, more meaningful than all the pictures of dogs I'd ever seen. I saw a horse, a lesser creation than what my master miniaturists might make. I spied a plane tree in the Hippodrome, the same tree whose leaves I'd just now accented with tones of purple.

Strolling through the Hippodrome, whose parades I'd illustrated over the last two years, was like stepping into my own painting. Let's say we were to turn down a street: In a Frankish painting, this would result in our stepping outside both the frame and the painting; in a painting made following the example of the great masters of Herat, it'd bring us to the place from which Allah looks upon us; in a Chinese painting, we'd be trapped, because Chinese illustrations are infinite.

The pageboy, I discovered, wasn't taking me to the Divan Chamber where I often met with the Head Treasurer to discuss one of the following: the manuscripts and ornamented ostrich eggs or other gifts my miniaturists were preparing for Our Sultan; the health of the illustrators or the Head Treasurer's own constitution and peace of mind; the acquisition of paint, gold leaf or other materials; the usual complaints and requests; the desires, delights, demands and disposition of the Refuge of the World, Our Sultan; my eyesight, my looking glasses or my lumbago; or the Head Treasurer's good-for-nothing son-in-law or the health of his tabby cat.

Silently, we entered the Sultan's Private Garden. As if committing a crime, but with great delicacy, we serenely descended toward the sea through the trees. "We're nearing the Sea-Side Kiosk," I thought, "this means I will see the Sultan. His Excellency must be here." But we turned off the path. We walked ahead a few steps through the arched doorway of a stone building behind the rowboat and caïque sheds. I could smell the scent of baking bread wafting from the guard's bakery before catching sight of the Imperial Guard themselves in their red uniforms.

The Head Treasurer and the Commander of the Imperial Guard were together in one room: Angel and Devil!

The Commander, who performed executions in the name of Our Sultan on the palace grounds—who tortured, interrogated, beat, blinded and administered the bastinado—smiled sweetly at me. It was as if some piddling lodger, with whom I was forced to share a caravansary cell, were going to recount a heart-warming story.

The Head Treasurer diffidently said, "Our Sultan, one year prior, charged me with having an illuminated manuscript prepared under conditions of the utmost privacy, a manuscript that would be included among the gifts meant for an ambassadorial delegation. In light of the secrecy of the book, His Excellency did not deem it appropriate that Master Lokman the Royal Historian be enlisted to write the manuscript. Similarly, He did not venture to involve you, whose artistry He quite admires. Indeed, He supposed that you were already fully engaged with the *Book of Festivities*."

Upon entering this room I had abruptly assumed that some wretch had slandered me, claiming that I was committing heresy in such-and-such an illustration and that I'd lampooned the Sovereign in another; I imagined with horror that this tattler had been able to convince the Sovereign of my guilt and that I was about to be laid out for torture with no consideration for my age. And so to hear that the Head Treasurer was simply trying to make amends for Our Sultan's having commissioned a manuscript from an outsider—these words were sweeter than honey indeed. Without learning anything new, I listened to an account of the manuscript, about which I was already well aware. I was privy to the rumors about Nusret Hoja of Erzurum, and naturally, to the intrigues within the workshop.

"Who is responsible for preparing the manuscript?" I asked.

"Enishte Effendi, as you know," said the Head Treasurer. Fixing his gaze into my eyes, he added, "You were aware that he died an untimely death, that is to say, that he was murdered, weren't you?"

"Nay," I said simply, like a child, and fell quiet.

"Our Sultan is quite furious," the Head Treasurer said.

That Enishte Effendi was a dunce. The master miniaturists always mocked him for being more pretentious than knowledgeable, more ambitious than intelligent. I knew something was rotten at the funeral anyway. How was he killed, I wondered?

The Head Treasurer explained exactly how. Appalling. Dear God protect us. Yet who could be responsible?

"The Sultan has decreed," said the Head Treasurer, "that the book in question should be finished as soon as possible, as with the *Book of Festivities* manuscript . . ."

"He has also made a second decree," said the Commander of the Imperial Guard. "If, indeed, this unspeakable murderer is one of the miniaturists, He wants the black-hearted devil found. He intends to sentence him to a punishment such as will stand as a deterrent to one and all."

An expression of such excitement appeared on the face of the Commander as if to suggest he already knew the monstrous punishment Our Sultan had decreed.

I knew that Our Sultan had only recently charged these two men with this task, thereby forcing them to cooperate—on which account they couldn't hide their distaste even now. Seeing this inspired in me a love for the Sultan that went beyond mere awe. A servant boy served coffee and we sat for a while.

I was told that Enishte Effendi had a nephew named Black Effendi whom he'd cultivated, a man trained in illumination and book arts. Had I met him? I remained silent. A short while ago, upon the invitation of his Enishte, Black had returned from the Persian front, where he was under Serhat Pasha's command—the Commander shot me a look of suspicion. Here, in Istanbul, he worked himself into his Enishte's good graces and learned the story of the book whose creation Enishte was overseeing. Black claimed that after Elegant Effendi was killed, Enishte suspected one of the master miniaturists who visited him at night to work on this manuscript. He'd seen the illustrations these masters had made and said that Enishte's murderer—the selfsame painter who stole the Sultan's illustration with the lion's share of gold leaf—was one of them. For two days, this young Black Effendi had concealed the death of Enishte from the palace and the Head Treasurer. Within that very two-day period, he'd rushed ahead with a marriage to Enishte's daughter, an ethically and religiously dubious affair, and settled into Enishte's house; thus, both the men before me considered Black a suspect.

"If their houses and workplaces are searched and the missing page turns up with one of my master miniaturists, Black's innocence will be established at once," I said. "Frankly, however, I can tell you that my dearest children, my divinely inspired miniaturists, whom I've known since they were apprentices, are incapable of taking the life of another man."

"As for Olive, Stork and Butterfly," said the Commander, mockingly using the nicknames I'd affectionately given to them, "we intend to comb their homes, haunts, places of work and, if applicable, shops, leaving no stone unturned. And that includes Black . . ." His expression bespoke resignation: "Given such troublesome circumstances, thank God, the judge has granted us permission to resort to torture if necessary during the interrogation of Black Effendi. Torture was deemed lawfully permissible because a second murder had been committed against someone with a link to the miniaturists guild, making suspects of them all, from apprentice to master."

I mulled this over silently: 1. The phrase "lawfully permissible" made clear that Our Sultan wasn't the one who'd granted the permission for torture. 2. Because all the miniaturists were under suspicion of double murder in the eyes of the judge, and because I, though Head Illuminator, had been unable to identify the criminal in our midst, I, too, was suspect. 3. I understood that they wanted my explicit or implicit approval to go ahead with the torture of my beloved Butterfly, Olive, Stork and the others, all of whom, in recent years, had betrayed me.

"Since Our Sultan desires both the satisfactory completion of the *Book of Festivities* and this book—which is evidently only half finished," said the Head Treasurer, "we're worried that torture might damage the masters' hands and eyes, destroying their agility." He faced me. "Isn't this so?"

"There was similar worry over another incident recently," said the Commander brusquely. "A goldsmith and a jeweler who did repairs fell sway to the Devil. They were childishly enchanted with a ruby-handled coffee cup belonging to Our Sultan's younger sister Nejmiye Sultan, and ended up stealing it. Since the theft of the cup, which overwhelmed Our Sultan's sister with grief—she was quite fond of the piece—occurred in the Üsküdar Palace, the Sovereign appointed me to investigate. It became apparent that both Our Sultan and Nejmiye Sultan wanted no harm to come to the eyes and fingers of the master gold- and jewelry smiths lest their skills be affected. So, I had all the master jewelry smiths stripped naked and thrown into the freezing pool in the yard among pieces of ice and frogs. Periodically, I'd have them taken out and lashed forcefully, taking care that their faces and hands remained unharmed. Within a short period, the jeweler who'd been duped by the Devil confessed and accepted his punishment. Despite the ice-cold water, the frozen air and all the lashings, no lasting injury came to the eyes and fingers of the master jewelers because they were pure of heart. Even the Sultan mentioned that His sister was quite pleased with my work and that the jewelers were working with more zeal now that the bad apple was out of the barrel."

I was certain that the Commander would treat my master illustrators more severely than he had the jewelers. Though he had respect for Our Sultan's enthusiasm for illuminated manuscripts, like many others, he deemed calligraphy the only respectable art form, belittling embellishment and illustration as flirtations with heresy, fit for women and deserving of nothing but rebuke. In order to provoke me, he said, "While you've been absorbed in your work, your beloved miniaturists have already begun scheming to see who'll become Head Miniaturist upon your death."

Was this gossip I hadn't already heard? Had he informed me of something new? Restraining myself, I didn't respond. The Head Treasurer was more than aware of the fury I felt toward him for commissioning a manuscript from that deceased half-wit behind my back, and toward my ingrate miniaturists, who'd secretly prepared these illustrations to curry favor and earn a few extra silver coins.

I caught myself pondering the methods of torture that might be inflicted. They wouldn't resort to flaying during the interrogation, because that inevitably leads to death. They wouldn't impale anyone, either, as they do with rebels, because that's used as a deterrent. Cracking and splintering the fingers, arms or legs of these miniaturists was also out of the question. Of course, the removal of an eye—which I gathered was a measure of increasing frequency these days, to judge by the growing numbers of one-eyed people on the streets of Istanbul—would be inappropriate for master artists. So, as I imagined my dear miniaturists in a secluded corner of the Royal Private Garden, there in the ice-cold pool among the water lilies, shivering violently and glaring hatefully at one another, I had the passing urge to laugh. Nevertheless, it caused me agony to imagine how Olive would shriek when his hindquarters were branded with a hot iron and how dear Butterfly's skin would pale when he was shackled. I couldn't bear to conjure the scene of dear Butterfly—whose skill and love for illumination brought tears to my eyes—as he was given the bastinado like a common thieving apprentice. I just stood there dumbfounded and hollow.

My elderly mind was mute under the spell of its own internal silence. There was a time when we'd paint together with a passion that made us forget everything.

"These men are the most expert miniaturists serving Our Sultan," I said. "Make certain no harm befalls them."

Pleased, the Head Treasurer rose, grabbed a number of pages from the worktable at the other end of the room and arranged them in front of me. Next, as if the room were dark, he placed beside me two large candle holders whose portly tapers burned with bobbing and twittering flames so I could study the paintings in question.

How might I explain what I saw as I moved the magnifying lens over them? I felt like laughing—and not because they were humorous. I was incensed—it seemed that Enishte Effendi had instructed my masters as follows: "Don't paint like yourselves, paint as if you were someone else." He'd forced them to recall nonexistent memories, to conjure and paint a future, which they'd never want to live. What was even more incredible was that they were killing each other over this nonsense.

"By looking at these illustrations, can you tell me which miniaturist worked on which picture?" asked the Head Treasurer.

"Yes," I said angrily. "Where did you find these paintings?"

"Black brought them of his own accord and left them with me," said the Head Treasurer. "He's bent on proving that he and his late Enishte are innocent."

"During the interrogation, torture him," I said. "That way we'll learn what other secrets our late Enishte was harboring."

"We've sent for him," said the Commander of the Imperial Guard. "Afterward, we'll thoroughly search the house of that newlywed."

Both their faces were strangely illuminated, a flicker of fear and awe overcame them, and they snapped to their feet.

Without having to turn around I knew we were in the presence of His Excellency, Our Sultan, the Refuge of the World.

CHAPTER 39

I AM ESTHER

Oh, how wonderful it is to cry along with the rest of them! While the men were at the funeral of my dear Shekure's father, the women, kith and kin, spouses and friends, gathered in the house and shed their tears, and I, too, beat my chest in mourning and wept with them. Now wailing in unison with the pretty maiden beside me, leaning on her and swaying back and forth; now crying in a completely different frame of mind, I was deeply touched by my own woes and pitiful life. If I could cry like this just once a week, I thought, I might forget how I had to roam the streets all day just to make ends meet, forget being mocked for my weight and my Jewishness and be reborn an even more chattermouth Esther.

I like social gatherings because I can eat to my heart's content, and, at the same time, forget that I'm the black sheep of the crowd. I love the baklava, mint candy, marzipan bread and fruit leather of holidays; the pilaf with meat and the tea-cup pastries of circumcision ceremonies; drinking sour-cherry sherbet at celebrations held by the Sultan in the Hippodrome; eating everything at weddings; and tossing down the sesame, honey or variously flavored condolence halvas sent by the neighbors at wakes.

I quietly slipped into the hallway, put on my shoes and went downstairs. Before I turned into the kitchen, I grew curious about an odd noise coming through the half-open door of the room next to the stable. I took a few steps in that direction and glanced inside to discover that Shevket and Orhan had tied up the son of one of the women mourners and were in the midst of painting his face with their late grandfather's paints and brushes. "If you try to escape, we'll hit you like this," Shevket said and slapped the boy.

"My dear child, play nice and gentle now, don't hurt each other, all right?" I said in a voice as velvety as I could muster.

"Mind your own affairs!" Shevket shouted.

I noticed the small, frightened, blond-haired sister of the boy they were tormenting standing beside them, and for whatever reason, I felt for her completely. Forget about it, now, Esther!

In the kitchen, Hayriye peered at me suspiciously.

"I've cried myself dry, Hayriye," I said. "For God's sake, pour me a glass of water."

She did so, silently. Before I drank it, I stared into her eyes, swollen from weeping.

"Poor Enishte Effendi, they say he was already dead before Shekure's wedding," I commented. "People's mouths aren't like bags that can be cinched up, some even claim there was foul play involved."

In an exaggerated gesture, she looked down at her toes. Then she lifted her head and without looking at me said, "May God protect us from baseless slander."

Her first gesture confirmed what I'd said, and moreover the cadence of her words conveyed that they were spoken under duress—to hide the truth.

"What's going on?" I asked abruptly, whispering as if I were her confidant.

Indecisive Hayriye had of course understood that there was no hope of claiming any authority over Shekure after Enishte Effendi's death. And a short while ago, she was the one mourning with the most heartfelt tears.

"What's to become of me, now?" she said.

"Shekure holds you in high regard," I said in my habit of giving news. Lifting up the lids of the pots of halva lined up between the large clay jar of grape molasses and the pickle jar, sneaking a fingerful from one or simply leaning over to smell another, I asked who'd sent each of them.

Hayriye was rattling off who'd sent which pot: "This one's from Kasım Effendi of Kayseri; this one, the assistant from the miniaturists division who lives two streets over; that's from the locksmith, Left-Handed Hamdi; that one, the young bride from Edirne—" when Shekure interrupted her.

"Kalbiye, the late Elegant Effendi's widow, didn't come to offer her condolences, didn't send word and didn't send any halva either!"

She was heading from the kitchen door to the foot of the stairs. I followed her, knowing that she wanted to have a word with me in private.

"There was no ill-will between Elegant Effendi and my father. On the day of Elegant's funeral, we prepared our halva and sent it to them. I want to know what's going on," Shekure said.

"I'll go right away and find out," I said, anticipating Shekure's thoughts.

Since I kept our chat brief, she kissed me on the cheek. As the cold of the courtyard bit into us, we embraced and stood there without moving. Afterward, I stroked my beautiful Shekure's hair.

I Am Esther

"Esther, I'm afraid," she said.

"My dear, don't be afraid," I said. "Every cloud has a silver lining. Look, you're finally married."

"But I'm not sure I did the right thing," she said. "That's why I haven't let him get near me. I spent the night beside my unfortunate father."

She opened her eyes wide and looked at me in a way that said, You understand what I mean.

"Hasan claims that your wedding is null in the eyes of the judge," I said. "He sent this to you."

Though she said, "No more," she immediately opened the small note and read, but this time she didn't tell me what it contained.

She was right to be discreet; we weren't alone in the courtyard where we'd stood embracing: Above us, a smirking carpenter, reattaching the shutter of the hall window, which fell and broke for some unknown reason that morning, was also eyeing both us and the women mourning inside. Meanwhile, Hayriye came out of the house and rushed to open the door for the son of a loyal neighbor who'd called out, "the halva's here," as he knocked on the courtyard gate.

"It's been quite some time since we buried him," said Shekure. "I can now sense that my poor father's soul is leaving his body for good and rising into the heavens."

She removed herself from my arms, and gazing up at the bright sky, recited a long prayer.

I suddenly felt so distant and estranged from Shekure that it wouldn't have surprised me if I were the cloud she was gazing at. As soon as she finished her prayer, pretty Shekure kissed me affectionately on both cheeks.

"Esther," she said, "so long as my father's murderer roams free, there'll be no peace in this world for me or my children."

It pleased me that she didn't mention her new husband's name.

"Go to Elegant Effendi's house, talk casually to his widow and learn why they didn't send us any halva. Let me know immediately what you find out."

"Do you have any messages for Hasan?" I said.

I felt embarrassed, not because I'd asked this question, but because I couldn't look her in the eye as I did so. To cover up my embarrassment, I stopped Hayriye and opened the lid of the pot she was holding. "Ohh," I said, "semolina halva with pistachios," as I had a taste. "And they've added oranges, too."

It made me happy to see Shekure smile sweetly as if everything were happening as planned.

MY NAME IS RED

I grabbed my bundle and left. I'd taken no more than two steps when I saw Black at the end of the street. He'd just come from the burial of his father-in-law, and I could tell from his beaming face that this new husband was quite pleased with his life. In order not to dampen his spirits, I left the street, entered the vegetable rows and passed through the garden of the house where the brother of the lover of the famous Jewish doctor Moshe Hamon had lived before he was hanged. This garden, which recalled death, always brought such great sadness upon me when I walked through it that I invariably forgot I'd been charged to find a buyer for the property.

The air of death was also in Elegant Effendi's house, though for me it provoked no sadness. I was Esther, a woman who went in and out of thousands of homes and was acquainted with hundreds of widows; I knew that women who lost their husbands early were spellbound either by defeat and misery or anger and rebellion (although Shekure had suffered all these afflictions). Kalbiye had partaken of the poison of anger and I fast realized that this would serve to hasten my work.

As with all conceited women to whom life has been cruel, Kalbiye quite rightly suspected that all her visitors came to pity her in her darkest hour, or even worse, to witness her agony and secretly rejoice in their own better situations; thus, she engaged in no pleasantries with her guests, but went straight to the heart of the matter forgoing any flowery small talk. Why had Esther come this afternoon, just as Kalbiye was about to take a consoling nap with her grief? Well aware she'd take no interest in the latest silks from China or handkerchiefs from Bursa, I didn't even pretend to open my bundle, but came right to the point and described teary-eyed Shekure's concern. "It has heightened Shekure's misery to think that she has somehow hurt your feelings, with whom she shares the same sorrow," I said.

Arrogantly, Kalbiye confirmed that she hadn't asked after Shekure's well-being, hadn't visited to express her condolences or mourn with her, nor could she bring herself to prepare and send any halva. Behind her pride, there also lurked a glee that she couldn't conceal: The delight that her resentment had been recognized. It was from this point of entry that your sharp-witted Esther attempted to discover the reasons for and circumstances of Kalbiye's anger.

It didn't take long for Kalbiye to admit that she'd been upset with the late Enishte Effendi due to the illustrated manuscript he was preparing. She said her husband, may he rest in peace, hadn't agreed to work on the book for the sake of a handful of extra silver coins, but because

Enishte Effendi convinced him the project was authorized by the Sultan. However, when her late husband became aware that the illuminations Enishte Effendi hired him to gild were slowly evolving from simple ornamented pages into full-blown illustrations, pictures moreover that bore the marks of Frankish blasphemy, atheism and even heresy, he grew uneasy and began to lose sight of right and wrong. Being a much more reasonable and prudent person than Elegant Effendi, she cautiously added that all these doubts arose gradually rather than at once, and since poor Elegant Effendi never found anything that would be considered blatant sacrilege, he was able to dismiss his worries as unfounded. Besides, he comforted himself by never missing a sermon given by Nusret Hoja of Erzurum, and if he skipped one of his five daily prayers it unsettled him. Just as he knew that certain scoundrels at the workshop ridiculed his complete devotion to the faith, so he understood very well that their brazen jokes arose out of envy of his talent and artistry.

A large, glimmering tear slid from Kalbiye's gleaming eye down her cheek, and at the first opportunity, your good-hearted Esther decided to find Kalbiye a better husband than the one she'd recently lost.

"My late husband didn't often share these concerns of his with me," Kalbiye said cautiously. "Based on whatever I could remember and piece together I've concluded that everything happened on account of the illustrations that took him to Enishte Effendi's house on his very last night."

This was some manner of apology. In response, I reminded her how her fate and Shekure's, not to mention their enemies, were the same if one considered that Enishte Effendi had perhaps been killed by the same "scoundrel." The two large-headed fatherless waifs staring at me from the corner suggested another similarity between the two women. But my merciless matchmaker's logic quickly reminded me that Shekure's situation was much more beautiful, rich and mysterious. I let Kalbiye know exactly what I felt:

"Shekure told me to tell you that if she has wronged you, she's sorry," I said. "She wants to say that she loves you as a sister and as a woman who shares her fate. She wants you to think about this and help her. When the late Elegant Effendi left here on his last night, did he mention he'd be seeing anyone besides Enishte Effendi? Did you ever consider that he might've been going to meet somebody else?"

"This was found on his person," she said.

She removed a folded piece of paper from a lidded wicker box, which contained embroidery needles, pieces of cloth and a large walnut.

When I took up the crumpled piece of rough paper and examined it, I saw a variety of shapes drawn in ink that had run and smudged in the well water. I'd just determined what the forms were when Kalbiye voiced my thoughts.

"Horses," she said. "But late Elegant Effendi only did gilding work. He never drew horses. And no one would've ever asked him to render a horse."

Your elderly Esther was looking at the horses which had been quickly sketched, but she couldn't quite make anything of them.

"If I were to take this piece of paper to Shekure, she'd be quite pleased," I said.

"If Shekure desires to see these sketches, let her come get them herself," said Kalbiye with no small hint of conceit.

CHAPTER 40

I AM CALLED BLACK

Maybe you've understood by now that for men like myself, that is, melancholy men for whom love, agony, happiness and misery are just excuses for maintaining eternal loneliness, life offers neither great joy nor great sadness. I'm not saying we can't relate to other souls overwhelmed by these feelings, on the contrary, we sympathize with them. What we cannot fathom is the odd disquiet our souls sink into at such times. This silent turmoil dims our intellects and dampens our hearts, usurping the place reserved for the true joy and sadness we ought to experience.

I had buried her father, thank God, hurried home from the funeral, and in a gesture of condolence, embraced my wife, Shekure; then suddenly, in a fit of tears she collapsed onto a large cushion with her children, who were glaring at me with spite, and I didn't know what to do. Her misery coincided with my victory. In one fell swoop, I had wed the dream of my youth, freed myself from her father who belittled me, and become master of the house. Who would ever believe the sincerity of my tears? But believe me, it wasn't like that. I truly wanted to grieve, but couldn't: Enishte had always been more of a father to me than my real father. But since the meddlesome preacher who'd performed Enishte's final ablution never stopped babbling, the rumor that my Enishte died under mysterious circumstances spread among the neighbors during the funeral—as I could sense standing in the courtyard of the mosque. I didn't want my inability to cry to be interpreted negatively; I don't have to tell you how real the fear of being branded "stonehearted" is.

You know how some sympathetic aunt will always attest that "he's crying on the inside" to prevent someone like me from being banished from the group. I did in fact cry on the inside as I tried to hide in a corner from the busybody neighbors and distant relatives with their astonishing abilities to summon a downpour of tears; I thought about being the master of the house and whether I should somehow take charge of the situation, but just then there came a knock at the door. A moment of panic. Was it Hasan? Regardless, I wanted to save myself from this hell of whimpering at whatever cost.

It was a royal page, summoning me to the palace. I was stunned.

As I exited the courtyard, I found a mud-covered silver coin on the ground. Was I afraid to go to the palace? Yes, but I was also happy to be outside in the cold among the horses, dogs, trees and people. I thought I'd befriend the pageboy like those hopeless daydreamers who, believing they might sweeten the world's cruelty before facing the executioner, attempt a lighthearted conversation with the dungeon guard about this and that, the beauties of life, the ducks afloat on the pond, or the strangeness of a cloud in the sky; but alas he disappointed me, proving a rather morose, pimply, tight-lipped youth. As I passed the Hagia Sophia, noticing with awe the slender cypresses delicately stretching into the hazy sky, it wasn't the horror of dying right after marrying Shekure after all these years that made my hair stand on end. It was the injustice of dying at the hands of the palace torturers without having shared one good session of lovemaking with her.

We didn't walk toward the terrifying spires of the Middle Gate, beyond which the torturers and the quick-handed executioners saw to their work, but toward the carpentry shops. As we headed between the granaries, a cat cleaning itself in the mud between the legs of a chestnut horse with steaming nostrils turned but didn't look at us: The cat was preoccupied with its own filth, much as we were.

Behind the granaries, two figures, whose rank and affiliation I couldn't determine from their green and purple uniforms, relieved the pageboy, and locked me into the dark room of a small house, which I could tell was new by the smell of fresh lumber. I knew locking a man up in a dark room was meant to arouse fear before torture; hoping they'd begin with the bastinado, I thought about the lies I could tell to save my hide. A crowd in the adjoining room seemed to be raising quite a ruckus.

There are most certainly those of you who can't attribute my mocking and mirthful tone to that of a man on the verge of torture. But haven't I mentioned I consider myself one of God's luckier servants? And if the birds of fortune that alighted upon my head these last two days after years of deprivation aren't proof enough, surely the silver coin I found outside the courtyard gate must be some indication.

Awaiting my torture, I was comforted by the silver coin and had complete faith it would protect me; I palmed it, rubbed it and repeatedly kissed this token of good fortune that Allah had sent me. But at whatever time they removed me from the darkness and brought me into the next room where I saw the Commander of the Imperial Guard and his bald-headed Croatian torturers, I knew the silver coin was worthless. The pitiless voice within me was absolutely correct: The coin in my pocket hadn't come from God, but was one of those that I'd showered Shekure with two days ago—that the children overlooked. Hence, in the hands of my torturers, I had nothing in which to take refuge.

I didn't even notice that tears began to fall from my eyes. I wanted to beg, but as in a dream, no sound issued from my mouth. I knew from wars, deaths and political assassination and torture (which I'd witnessed from afar) that life could be extinguished instantaneously, but I'd never experienced it this closely. They were going to strip me from this world just as they'd stripped off my garments.

They took off my vest and shirt. One of the executioners sat on me, driving his knees into my shoulders. Another placed a cage over my head with all the practiced elegance of a woman preparing food and began slowly turning the screw at its front. Nay, it wasn't a cage, but rather a vise that gradually squeezed my head.

I screamed at the top of my lungs. I begged, but incoherently. I cried, mostly because my nerves had given out.

They stopped momentarily and asked: "Were you the one who killed Enishte Effendi?"

I took a deep breath: "Nay."

They began to tighten the vise again. It was excruciating.

They asked again.

"Nay."

"Who then?"

"I don't know!"

I Am Called Black 247

I wondered if I should just tell them I'd killed him. The world spun pleasantly about my head. I was overcome with reluctance. I asked myself if I were growing accustomed to the pain. My executioners and I stayed still for a moment. I felt no pain, I was simply terrified.

Just as I decided from the silver coin in my pocket that they weren't going to kill me, they suddenly released me. They removed the viselike contraption that had actually done little damage to my head. The executioner who'd pinned me down stood up without even a hint of apology. I donned my shirt and vest.

There passed a very long silence.

At the other end of the room, I saw Head Illuminator Osman Effendi. I went to him and kissed his hand.

"Don't be concerned, my child," he said to me. "They were just testing you."

I knew at once that I'd found a new father to replace Enishte, may he rest in peace.

"Our Sultan has ordered that you not be tortured at this time," said the Commander. "He deemed it appropriate for you to help Head Illuminator Master Osman find the rogue who's been killing His miniaturists and the loyal servants preparing His manuscripts. You have three days in which to interrogate the miniaturists, scrutinize the illuminated pages they've made and find the sly culprit. The Sovereign is quite appalled by the rumors being spread by mischief makers about His miniaturists and illuminated manuscripts. Both the Head Treasurer Hazım Agha and I will help you find this scoundrel, as the Sultan has decreed. One of you has been very close to Enishte Effendi, and has thus heard his recitations and knows about the miniaturists who visited him at night and the story behind the book. The other is a great master who takes pride in knowing all the miniaturists of the workshop like the back of his hand. Within three days, if you fail to produce that swine along with the missing page he stole—about which much gossip is flying—it is Our Just Sultan's express desire that you, my child Black Effendi, be the first to undergo torture and interrogation. Afterward, let there be no doubt, each of the other master miniaturists will have his turn."

I could detect no secret gestures or signs between these two old friends, who'd worked together for years: Head Treasurer Hazım Agha, who commissioned the work, and Head Illuminator Master Osman Effendi, who received the funds and materials through him from the treasury.

"Everyone knows, whenever a crime is committed within Our Sultan's wards, regiments and divisions, that the entire group is considered guilty until one among them is identified and turned in. A section that fails to name the murderer in its midst goes down in the judicial records as a 'division of murderers,' including its officer or master, and is punished accordingly," said the Commander. "Therefore, our Head Illuminator Master Osman will keep a sharp watch, scrutinize each of the illustrations with his penetrating gaze, uncover the devilry, ruse, mischief and instigation that has set the innocent miniaturists at each other's throats, and remand the guilty party to the unwavering justice of the Refuge of the World, Our Sultan, thereby clearing the good name of his guild. To this end, we've ordered that whatsoever Master Osman may require be granted to him. My men are at this moment confiscating each of the manuscript pages that the master miniaturists have been illuminating in the privacy of their homes."

CHAPTER 41

IT IS I, MASTER OSMAN

The Commader of the Imperial Guard and the Head Treasurer reiterated Our Sultan's decrees before leaving the two of us alone. Of course, Black was exhausted by fear, crying and the ruse of torture. He fell quiet like a boy. I knew I would come to like him, and I didn't disturb his peace.

I had three days to examine the pages that the Commander's men collected from the homes of my calligraphers and master miniaturists, and to determine who had worked on them. You all know how disgusted I was when I first laid eyes on the paintings prepared for Enishte Effendi's book, and how Black had given them to the Head Treasurer Hazım Agha to clear his name. Granted, there must be something to those pages for them to arouse such violent disgust and hatred in a miniaturist like myself who's devoted his life to artistry; merely bad art wouldn't provoke such a reaction. So, with newfound curiosity, I began to reexamine the nine pages that the deceased fool had commissioned from the miniaturists who came to him under cover of night.

I saw a tree in the middle of a blank page, situated within poor Elegant's border design and gilding work, which gracefully framed every page. I tried to conjure the scene and story to which the tree belonged. If I had told my illustrators to draw a tree, dear Butterfly, wise Stork and wily Olive would have begun by conceiving of this tree as part of a story so they might draw the image with confidence. If I were then to scrutinize that tree, I'd be able to determine which tale the illustrator had in mind based on its branches and leaves. This, however, was a miserable, solitary tree; behind it, there was a quite high horizon line that hearkened back to the style of the oldest masters of Shiraz and accentuated the feeling of isolation. There was nothing at all, however, filling the area created by raising the horizon. The desire to depict a tree simply as such, as the Venetian masters did, was here combined with the Persian way of seeing the world from above, and the result was a miserable painting that was neither Venetian nor Persian. This was how a tree at the edge of the world would look. Attempting to combine two separate styles, my miniaturists and the barren mind of that deceased clown had created a work devoid of any skill whatsoever. But it wasn't that the illustration was informed by two different worldviews so much as the lack of skill that incurred my wrath.

I felt the same way as I looked at the other pictures, at the perfect dream horse and the woman with the bowed head. The choice of subject matter also iritated me, whether it was the two wandering dervishes or Satan. It was obvious that my illustrators had coyly inserted these inferior pictures into Our Sultan's illuminated manuscript. I felt renewed awe at exalted Allah's judgment in taking Enishte's life before the book had been finished. Needless to say, I had no desire whatsoever to complete this manuscript.

Who wouldn't be annoyed by this dog, drawn from above but staring at me from just beneath my nose as if it were my brother? On the one hand, I was astounded by the plainness of the dog's positioning, the beauty of its threatening sidelong glance, head lowered to the ground, and the violent whiteness of its teeth, in short, by the talent of the miniaturists who'd depicted it (I was on the verge of determining precisely who'd worked on the picture); on the other hand, I couldn't forgive the way this talent had been harnessed by the absurd logic of an inscrutable will. Neither the desire to imitate the Europeans nor the excuse that the book Our Sultan had commissioned as a present for the Doge ought to make use of techniques familiar to the Venetians was adequate to explain the fawning pretension in these pictures.

I was terrified by the passion of red in one bustling picture, wherein I at once recognized the touch of each of my master miniaturists in each corner. An artist's hand that I couldn't identify had applied a peculiar red to the painting under the guidance of an arcane logic, and the entire world revealed by the illustration was slowly suffused by this color. I spent some time hunched over this crowded picture pointing out to Black which of my miniaturists had drawn the plane tree (Stork), the ships and houses (Olive), and the kite and flowers (Butterfly).

"Of course, a great master miniaturist like yourself, who's been head of a book-arts division for years, could distinguish the craft of each of his illustrators, the disposition of their lines and the temperament of their brush strokes," Black said. "But when an eccentric book lover like my Enishte forces these same illustrators to paint with new and untried techniques, how can you determine the artists responsible for each design with such certainty?"

I decided to answer with a parable: "Once upon a time there was a shah who ruled over Isfahan; he was a lover of book arts, and lived all alone in his castle. He was a strong and mighty, intelligent, but merciless shah, and he had love only for two things: the illustrated manuscripts he commissioned and his daughter. So devoted was this shah to his daughter that his enemies could hardly be faulted for claiming he was in love with her—for he was proud and jealous enough to declare war on neighboring princes and shahs in the event that one sent ambassadors to ask for her hand. Naturally, there was no husband worthy of his daughter, and he confined her to a room, accessible only through forty locked doors. In keeping with a commonly held belief in Isfahan, he thought that his daughter's beauty would fade if other men laid eyes on her. One day, after an edition of *Hüsrev and Shirin* that he'd commissioned was inscribed and illustrated in the Herat style, a rumor began to circulate in Isfahan: The pale-faced beauty who appeared in one bustling picture was none other than the jealous shah's daughter! Even before hearing the rumors, the shah, suspicious of this mysterious illustration, opened the pages of the book with trembling hands and in a flood of tears saw that his daughter's beauty had indeed been captured on the page. As the story goes, it wasn't actually the shah's daughter, protected by forty locked doors, who emerged to be portrayed one night, but her beauty which escaped from her room like a ghost stifled by boredom, reflecting off a series of mirrors and passing beneath doors and through keyholes like a ray of light or wisp of smoke to reach the eyes of an illustrator working through the night. The masterful young miniaturist, unable to restrain himself, depicted the beauty, which he couldn't bear to behold, in the illustration he was in the midst of completing. It was the scene that showed Shirin gazing upon a picture of Hüsrev and falling in love with him during the course of a countryside outing."

"My beloved master, my good sir, this is quite a coincidence," said Black. "I, too, am quite fond of that scene from *Hüsrev and Shirin*."

"These aren't fables, but events that actually happened," I said. "Listen, the miniaturist didn't depict the shah's beautiful daughter as Shirin, but as a courtesan playing the lute or setting the table, because that was the figure he was in the midst of illustrating at the time. As a result, Shirin's beauty paled beside the extraordinary beauty of the courtesan standing off to the side, thus disrupting the painting's balance. After the shah saw his daughter in the painting, he wanted to locate the gifted miniaturist who'd depicted her. But the crafty miniaturist, fearing the shah's wrath, had rendered both the courtesan and Shirin, not in his own style, but in a new way so as to conceal his identity. The skillful brush strokes of quite a few other miniaturists had gone into the work as well."

"How had the shah discovered the identity of the miniaturist who portrayed his daughter?"

"From the ears!"

"Whose ears? The ears of the daughter or her picture?"

"Actually, neither. Following his intuition, he first laid out all the books, pages and illustrations that his own miniaturists had made and inspected all the ears therein. He saw what he'd known for years in a new light: Regardless of the level of talent, each of the miniaturists made ears in his own style. It didn't matter if the face they depicted was the face of a sultan, a child, a warrior, or even, God forbid, the partially veiled face of Our Exalted Prophet, or even, God forbid again, the face of the Devil. Each miniaturist, in each case, always drew the ears the same way, as if this were a secret signature."

"Why?"

"When the masters illustrated a face, they focused on approaching its exalted beauty, on the dictates of the old models of form, on the expression, or on whether it should resemble somebody real. But when it came time to make the ears, they neither stole from others, imitated a model nor studied a real ear. For the ears, they didn't think, didn't aspire to anything, didn't even stop to consider what they were doing. They simply guided their brushes from memory."

"But didn't the great masters also create their masterpieces from memory without ever even looking at real horses, trees or people?" said Black.

"True," I said, "but those are memories acquired after years of thought, contemplation and reflection. Having seen plenty of horses, illustrated and actual, over their lifetimes, they know that the last flesh-and-blood horse they see before them will only mar the perfect horse they hold in their thoughts. The horse that a master miniaturist has drawn tens of thousands of times eventually comes close to God's vision of a horse, and the artist knows this through experience and deep in his soul. The horse that his hand draws quickly from memory is rendered with talent, great effort, and insight, and it is a horse that approaches Allah's horse. However, the ear that is drawn before the hand has accumulated any knowledge, before the artist has weighed and considered what it is doing, or before paying attention to the ears of the shah's daughter, will always be a flaw. Precisely because it is a flaw, or imperfection, it will vary from miniaturist to miniaturist. That is, it amounts to a signature."

There was a commotion. The Commander's men were bringing into the old workshop the pages they'd collected from the homes of the miniaturists and the calligraphers.

"Besides, ears are actually a human flaw," I said, hoping Black would smile. "They're at once distinct and common to everyone: a perfect manifestation of ugliness."

"What happened to the miniaturist who'd been caught by the authorities through his style of painting ears?"

I refrained from saying, "He was blinded," to keep Black from becoming even more downcast. Instead, I responded, "He married the shah's daughter, and this method, which has been used to identify miniaturists ever since, is known by many khans, shahs and sultans who fund book-arts workshops as the 'courtesan method.' Furthermore, it is kept secret so that if one of their miniaturists makes a forbidden figure or a small design that conceals some mischief and later denies having done so, they can quickly determine who was responsible—genuine artists have an instinctive desire to draw what's forbidden! Sometimes their hands make mischief on their own. Uncovering these transgressions involves finding trivial, quickly drawn and repetitive details removed from the heart of the painting, such as ears, hands, grass, leaves, or even horses' manes, legs or hooves. But beware, the method doesn't work if the illustrator himself is mindful that this detail has become his own secret signature. Mustaches won't work, for instance, because many artists are aware how freely they're drawn as a sort of signature anyway. But eyebrows are a possibility: No one pays much attention to them. Come now, let's see which young masters have brought their brushes and reed pens to bear upon late Enishte's illustrations."

Thus we brought together the pages of two illustrated manuscripts, one that was being completed secretly and the other openly, two books with different stories and subjects, illustrated in two distinct styles; that is, deceased Enishte's book and the *Book of Festivities* recounting our prince's circumcision ceremony, whose creation was under my control. Black and I looked intently wherever I moved my magnifying lens:

1. In the pages of the *Book of Festivities,* we first studied the open mouth of the fox whose pelt a master of the furrier's guild, in a red caftan and purple sash, held on his lap as the guild passed before Our Sultan, watching the parade from a loge made specifically for the event. Unmistakably, Olive had made both the fox's teeth, which were individually distinguishable, and the teeth in Enishte's illustration of Satan, an ominous creature, half-demon and half-giant, that appeared to have come from Samarkand.

2. On a particularly joyous day of the festivities, below Our Sultan's loge overlooking the Hippodrome, a division of impoverished frontier ghazis appeared in tattered clothes. One of their lot made a plea: "My Exalted Sultan, we, your heroic soldiers, fell captive as we fought the infidel in the name of our religion and were only able to gain our freedom by leaving a number of our brethren behind as hostages; that is, we were set free in order to amass ransom. However, when we arrived back in Istanbul, we found everything so expensive that we've been unable to collect the money to save our brethren who languish as prisoners of the kaffirs. We're at the mercy of your aid. Please grant us gold or slaves that we might take back to exchange for their freedom." Stork clearly made the nails of the lazy dog off to the side—glaring with one open eye at Our Sultan, at our poor, destitute ghazis and at the Persian and Tatar ambassadors in the Hippodrome—as well as the nails of the dog occupying a corner of the scene depicting the adventures of the Gold Coin in Enishte's book.

3. Among the jugglers spinning eggs on pieces of wood and turning somersaults before Our Sultan was a bald man with bare calves wearing a purple vest, who played a tambourine as he sat off to one side on a red carpet; this man held the instrument exactly the same way the woman held a large brass serving tray in the illustration of Red in Enishte's book: doubtless the work of Olive.

4. As the cooks' guild pushed past Our Sultan, they were cooking stuffed cabbage with meat and onions in a cauldron resting on a stove in their cart. The master cooks accompanying the cart stood

on pink earth resting their stew pots on blue stones; these stones were rendered by the same artist who made the red ones on dark-blue earth above which floated the half-ghostly creature in the illustration that Enishte called Death: the unmistakable work of Butterfly.

5. Mounted Tatar messengers brought word that the Persian Shah's armies had begun to mobilize for another campaign against the Ottomans, who thereupon razed to the ground the exquisite observation kiosk of the Persian ambassador who'd repeatedly affirmed to Our Sultan, Refuge of the World, in a cascade of pleasantries, that the Shah was His friend and harbored nothing but brotherly affection for Him. During this episode of wrath and destruction, water bearers ran out to settle the dust raised in the Hippodrome, and a group of men appeared shouldering leather sacks full of linseed oil to pour over a mob ready to attack the ambassador, in hopes of pacifying it. The raised feet of the water bearers and of the men carrying sacks of linseed oil were made by the same artist who painted the raised feet of charging soldiers in the depiction of Red: also the work of Butterfly.

I wasn't the one who made this last discovery as I directed our search for clues, moving the magnifying lens right and left, to that picture then this one; rather it was Black, who opened his eyes wide and scarcely blinked gripped by the fear of torture and the hope of returning to his wife who awaited him at home. Using the "courtesan method," it took an entire afternoon to sort out which of our miniaturists worked on each of the nine pictures left by the late Enishte, and later, to interpret that information.

Black's late Enishte didn't limit any single page to the artistic talent of just one miniaturist; all three of my master miniaturists worked on most of the illustrations. This meant that the pictures were moved from house to house with great frequency. In addition to the work I recognized, I noticed the amateurish strokes of a fifth artist, but as I grew angry at the dearth of talent shown by this disgraceful murderer, Black determined from the cautious brush strokes that it was indeed the work of his Enishte—thereby saving us from following a false lead. If we discounted poor Elegant Effendi, who'd done almost the same gilding for Enishte's book and our *Book of Festivities* (yes, this of course broke my heart) and who, I gathered, had occasionally lowered his brush to execute a few walls, leaves and clouds, it was evident that only my three most brilliant master miniaturists had contributed to these illustrations. They were the darlings I'd lovingly trained since their apprenticeships, my three beloved talents: Olive, Butterfly and Stork.

Discussing their talents, mastery and temperaments to the end of finding the clue we were looking for inevitably led to a discussion of my own life as well:

The Attributes of Olive

His given name was Velijan. If he had a nickname besides the one I'd given him, I don't know it, because I never saw him sign any of his work. When he was an apprentice, he'd come get me from my home on Tuesday mornings. He was very proud, and so if he ever lowered himself to sign his work, he'd want this signature to be plain and recognizable; he wouldn't try to conceal it anywhere. Allah had quite generously endowed him with excess ability. He could readily and easily do anything from gilding to ruling and his work was superb. He was the workshop's most brilliant creator of trees, animals and the human face. Velijan's father, who brought him to Istanbul when he was, I believe, ten years old, was trained by Siyavush, the famous illustrator specializing in faces in the Persian Shah's Tabriz workshop. He hails from a long line of masters whose genealogy goes back to the Mongols, and just like the elderly masters who bore a Mongol-Chinese influence and settled in Samarkand, Bukhara and Herat 150 years ago, he rendered moon-faced young lovers as if they were Chinese. Neither during his apprenticeship nor during his time as a master was I able to lead this stubborn artist to other styles. How I would've liked him to transcend the styles and models of the Mongol, Chinese and Herat masters billeted deep in his soul, or even for him to forget about them entirely. When I told him this, he replied that like many miniaturists who'd moved from workshop to workshop and country to country, he'd forgotten these old styles, if he'd ever actually learned them. Though the value of many miniaturists resides precisely in the splendid models of form they've committed to memory, had Velijan truly forgotten them, he'd have become an even greater illustrator. Still, there were two benefits, of which he wasn't even aware, to harboring the teachings of his mentors in the depths of his soul like a pair of unconfessed sins: 1. For such a gifted miniaturist, clinging to old forms inevitably stirred feelings of guilt and alienation that would spur his talent to maturity. 2. In a moment of difficulty, he could always recall what he claimed to have forgotten, and thus, he could successfully complete any new subject, history or scene by recourse to one of the old Herat models. With his keen eye, he knew how to harmonize what he'd learned from the old forms and Shah Tahmasp's old masters in new pictures. Herat painting and Istanbul ornamentation happily merged in Olive.

As with all of my miniaturists, I once paid an unannounced visit to his home. Unlike my work area and that of many other master miniaturists, his was a filthy confusion of paints, brushes, burnishing shells, his folding worktable and other objects. It was a mystery to me, but he wasn't even embarrassed by it. He took no outside jobs to earn a few extra silver coins. After I related these facts, Black said it was Olive who showed the most enthusiasm for and the most ease with the styles of the Frankish masters admired by his late Enishte. I understood this to be praise from the deceased fool's point of view, mistaken though it was. I can't say whether Olive was more deeply and secretly bound to the Herat styles—which went back to his father's mentor Siyavush and Siyavush's mentor Muzaffer, back to the era of Bihzad and the old masters—than he appeared to be, but it always made me wonder whether Olive harbored other hidden tendencies. Of my miniaturists (I told myself spontaneously), he was the most quiet and sensitive, but also the most guilty and traitorous, and by far the most devious. When I thought about the Commander's torture chambers, he was the first to come to mind. (I both wanted and didn't want him to be tortured.) He had the eyes of a jinn; he noticed and took account of everything, including my own shortcomings; however, with the reserve of an exile able to accommodate himself to any situation, he'd rarely open his mouth to point out mistakes. He was wily, yes, but not in my opinion a murderer. (I didn't tell Black this.) Olive didn't believe in anything. He had no faith in money, but he'd nervously squirrel it away. Contrary to what is commonly believed, all murderers are men of extreme faith rather than unbelievers. Manuscript illumination leads to painting, and painting, in turn, leads to—God forbid—challenging Allah. Everybody knows this. Therefore, to judge by his lack of faith, Olive is a genuine artist. Nevertheless, I believe that his God-given gifts fall short of Butterfly's, or even Stork's. I would've wanted Olive to be my son. As I said this, I wanted to incur Black's jealousy, but he only responded by opening his dark eyes and staring with childlike curiosity. Then I said Olive was magnificent when he worked in black ink, when he rendered, for pasting in albums, warriors, hunting scenes, Chinese-inspired landscapes full of storks and cranes, pretty boys gathered beneath a tree reciting verse and playing lutes, and when he depicted the sorrow of legendary lovers, the wrath of a sword-bearing, enraged shah, and a hero's expression of fear as he dodged the attack of a dragon.

"Perhaps Enishte wanted Olive to do the last picture that would show in great detail, in the style of the Europeans, Our Sultan's face and manner of sitting," Black said.

Was he trying to confuse me?

"Supposing this were the case, after Olive killed Enishte, why would he abscond with a picture he was already familiar with?" I said. "Or, if you like, why would he murder Enishte in order to see that picture?"

We both pondered these questions for a while.

"Because there's something missing in that painting," said Black. "Or because he regrets something he did and is scared by it. Or even . . ." he thought for a while. "Or, having killed Enishte, he might've taken the painting to do further harm, for the sake of having a memento, or even for no reason at all. Olive is, after all, a great illustrator who'd naturally have a lot of respect for a beautiful painting."

"We've already discussed in what ways Olive is a great illustrator," I said, growing angry. "But none of Enishte's illustrations is beautiful."

"We haven't yet seen the last painting," Black said boldly.

The Attributes of Butterfly

He is known as Hasan Chelebi from the Gunpowder Factory district, but to me he's always been "Butterfly." This nickname always reminds me of the beauty of his boyhood and youth: He was so handsome that those who saw him didn't believe their eyes and wanted a second look. I've always been astonished by the miracle of his being as talented as he is handsome. He's a master of color and this is his greatest strength; he painted passionately, reeling with the pleasure of applying color. But I cautioned Black that Butterfly was flighty, aimless and indecisive. Anxious to be just, I added: He's a genuine miniaturist who paints from the heart. If the arts of ornamentation are not meant to cater to intelligence, to speak to the animal within us, or to bolster the pride of the Sultan; that is, if this art is meant to be only a festival for the eyes, then Butterfly is indeed a true miniaturist. He makes wide, easy, blithe curves, as if he'd taken lessons from the masters of Kazvin forty years ago; he confidently applies his bright, pure colors, and there's always a gentle circularity hidden in the arrangement of his paintings; but I'm the one who trained him, not those long-dead masters of Kazvin. Maybe it's for this reason that I love him like a son, nay, more than a son—but I never felt any awe toward him. As with all of my apprentices, in his boyhood and adolescence, I beat him freely with brush handles, rulers and even pieces of wood, but this doesn't mean I don't respect him. Though I beat Stork frequently with rulers, I respect him too. In contrast to what the casual onlooker might assume, a master's beating doesn't rid the young apprentice of jinns of talent and the Devil, but only suppresses them temporarily. If it happens to be a good beating, and deserved, later on the jinns and the Devil will rise up and stimulate the developing miniaturist's resolve to work. As for the beatings I administered to Butterfly, they shaped him into a content and obedient artist.

I at once felt the need to praise him to Black: "Butterfly's artistry," I said, "is solid proof that the picture of bliss, which the celebrated poet ponders in his masnawi, is only possible through a God-given gift for understanding and applying color. When I realized this, I also realized what Butterfly lacked: He hadn't known that momentary loss of faith that Jami refers to in his poetry as 'the dark night of the soul.' Like an illustrator painting in the great happiness of Heaven, he sets to his work with conviction and contentment, believing that he can make a blissful painting, which he does succeed in doing. Our armies besieging Doppio castle, the Hungarian ambassador kissing the feet of Our Sultan, Our Prophet ascending through the seven heavens, these are of course all inherently happy scenes, but rendered by Butterfly, they become flights of ecstasy springing from the page. In an illustration of mine, if the darkness of death or the seriousness of a government session weighs heavy, I'll tell Butterfly to 'color it as you see fit,' and thereupon, the outfits, leaves, flags and sea that lay there muted as if sprinkled with dirt meant to fill a grave begin to ripple in the breeze. There are times when I think Allah wants the world to be seen the way Butterfly illustrates it, that He wants life to be jubilation. Indeed, this is a realm where colors harmoniously recite magnificent ghazals to each other, where time stops, where the Devil never appears."

However, even Butterfly knows this isn't enough. Someone must have quite rightly—yes, in good measure—whispered to him that in his work everything was as joyous as a holiday, but devoid of depth. Child princes and senile old harem women on the verge of death enjoy his paintings, not men of the world forced to struggle with evil. Because Butterfly is well aware of these criticisms, poor man, he at times grows jealous of average miniaturists who though much less talented than he are possessed of demons and jinns. What he mistakenly believes to be devilry and the work of jinns is more often than not straightforward evil and envy.

He aggravates me because when he paints, he doesn't lose himself in that wondrous world, surrendering to its ecstasy, but only reaches that height when he imagines his work will please others. He aggravates me because he thinks about the money he'll earn. It's another of life's ironies: There are many artists with much less talent yet more able than Butterfly to surrender themselves to their art.

In his need to make up for his shortcomings, Butterfly is preoccupied with proving that he has sacrificed himself to art. Like those birdbrained miniaturists who paint on fingernails and pieces of rice, pictures almost invisible to the naked eye, he's engrossed with minute and delicate craftsmanship. I'd once asked him whether he gave himself over to this ambition, which has blinded many illustrators at an early age, because he was ashamed of the excessive talent Allah had granted him. Only inept miniaturists paint each leaf of a tree they've drawn on a grain of rice to make an easy name for themselves and to gain importance in the eyes of dense patrons.

Butterfly's inclination to design and illustrate for other people's pleasure rather than for his own, his uncontrollable need to please others, made him, more than any of the others, a slave to praise. And so it follows that an uncertain Butterfly wants to ensure his standing by becoming Head Illuminator. It was Black who had raised this subject.

"Yes," I said, "I know he's been scheming to succeed me after I die."

"Do you think this would drive him to murder his miniaturist brethren?"

"It might. He's a great master, but he's not aware of this, and he can't leave the world behind when he paints."

I said this, whereupon I grasped that in truth I, too, wanted Butterfly to assume leadership of the workshop after me. I couldn't trust Olive, and in the end Stork would unwittingly become slave to the Venetian style. Butterfly's need to be admired—I was upset at the thought that he could take a life—would be vital in handling both the workshop and the Sultan. Only Butterfly's sensitivity and faith in his own palette could resist the Venetian artistry that duped the viewer by trying to depict reality itself rather than its representation, in all its detail: pictures, shadows included, of cardinals, bridges, rowboats, candlesticks, churches and stables, oxen and carriage wheels, as if all of them were of the same importance to Allah.

MY NAME IS RED

"Was there ever a time when you visited him unannounced as you had with the others?"

"Whosoever looks upon Butterfly's work will quickly sense that he understands the value of love as well as the meaning of heartfelt joy and sorrow. But as with all lovers of color, he gets carried away with his emotions and is fickle. Because I was so enamored of his God-given and miraculous talent, of his sensitivity to color, I paid close attention to him in his youth and know everything there is to know about him. Of course, in such situations, the other miniaturists quickly become jealous and the master-disciple relationship becomes strained and damaged. There were many moments of love during which Butterfly did not fear what others might say. Recently, since he married the neighborhood fruit seller's pretty daughter, I've neither felt the desire to go see him, nor have I had the chance."

"Rumor has it that he's in league with the followers of the Hoja from Erzurum," Black said. "They say he stands to gain a lot if the Hoja and his men declare certain works incompatible with religion, and thereby, outlaw our books—which depict battles, weapons, bloody scenes and routine ceremonies, not to mention parades including everyone from chefs to magicians, dervishes to boy dancers, and kebab makers to locksmiths—and confine us to the subjects and forms of the old Persian masters."

"Even if we returned skillfully and victoriously to those wondrous paintings of Tamerlane's time, even if we returned to that life and vocation in all its minutia—as bright Stork would best be able to do after me—in the final analysis, all of it'll be forgotten," I said mercilessly, "because everybody will want to paint like the Europeans."

Did I actually believe these words of damnation?

"My Enishte believed the same," Black confessed meekly, "yet it filled him with hope."

The Attributes of Stork

I've seen him sign his name as the Sinning Painter Mustafa Chelebi. Without paying any mind to whether he had or ought to have a style, whether it should be identified with a signature or, like the old masters, remain anonymous, or whether or not a humble bearing required one to do so, he'd just sign his name with a smile and a victorious flourish.

He continued bravely down the path I'd set him on and committed to paper what none before him had been able to. Like myself, he too would watch master glassblowers turning their rods and blowing glass melted in ovens to make blue pitchers and green bottles; he saw the leather, needles and wooden molds of the shoemakers who bent with rapt attention over the shoes and boots they made; a horse swing tracing a graceful arc during a holiday festival; a press squeezing oil from seeds; the firing of our cannon at the enemy; and the screws and the barrels of our guns. He saw these things and painted them without objecting that the old masters of Tamerlane's time, or the legendary illustrators of Tabriz and Kazvin, hadn't lowered themselves to do so. He was the first Muslim miniaturist to go to war and return safe and sound, in preparation for the *Book of Victories* that he would later illustrate. He was the first to eagerly study enemy fortresses, cannon, armies, horses with bleeding wounds, injured soldiers struggling for their lives and corpses—all with the intent to paint.

I recognize his work from his subject matter more than his style and from his attention to obscure details more than his subject matter. I could entrust him with complete peace of mind to execute all aspects of a painting, from the arrangement of pages and their composition to the coloring of the most trivial details. In this regard, he has the right to succeed me as Head Illuminator. But he's so ambitious and conceited, and so condescending toward the other illustrators that he could never manage so many men, and would end up losing them all. Actually, if it were left to him, with his incredible industriousness, he'd simply make all the illustrations in the workshop himself. If he put his mind to such a task, he could in fact succeed. He's a great master. He knows his craft. He admires himself. How nice for him.

When I visited him unannounced once, I caught him at work. Resting upon folding worktables, desks and cushions were all the pages he was working on: illustrations for Our Sultan's books, for me, for miserable costume books that he dashed off for foolish European travelers eager to belittle us, one page of a triptych he was making for a pasha who thought highly of himself, images to be pasted in albums, pages made for his own pleasure and even a vulgar rendition of coitus. Tall, thin Stork was flitting from one illustration to the next like a bee among flowers, singing folk songs, tweaking the cheek of his apprentice who was mixing paint and adding a comic twist to the painting he was working on before showing it to me with a smug chuckle. Unlike my other miniaturists, he didn't stop working in a ceremonial show of respect when I arrived; on the contrary, he happily exhibited the swift exercise of his God-given talent and the skill he'd acquired through hard work (he could do the work of seven or eight miniaturists at the same time). Now, I catch myself secretly thinking that if the vile murderer is one of my three master miniaturists, I hope to God it's Stork. During his apprenticeship, the sight of him at my door on Friday mornings didn't excite me the way Butterfly did on his day.

Since he paid equal attention to every odd detail, with no basis of discrimination except that it be visible, his aesthetic approach resembled that of the Venetian masters. But unlike them, my ambitious Stork neither saw nor depicted people's faces as individual or distinct. I assume, since he either openly or secretly belittled everyone, that he didn't consider faces important. I'm certain deceased Enishte didn't appoint him to draw Our Sultan's face.

Even when depicting a subject of the utmost importance, he couldn't keep from situating a skeptical dog somewhere at some distance from the event, or drawing a disgraceful beggar whose misery demeaned the wealth and extravagance of a ceremony. He had enough self-confidence to mock whatever illustration he made, its subject and himself.

"Elegant Effendi's murder resembles the way Joseph's brothers tossed him into a well out of jealousy," said Black. "And my Enishte's death resembles the unforeseen murder of Hüsrev at the hands of his son who had his heart set on Hüsrev's wife, Shirin. Everyone says that Stork loved to paint scenes of war and gruesome depictions of death."

"Anyone who thinks an illuminator resembles the subject of the picture he paints doesn't understand me or my master miniaturists. What exposes us is not the subject, which others have commissioned from us—these are always the same anyway—but the hidden sensibilities we include in the painting as we render that subject: A light that seems to radiate from within the picture, a palpable hesitancy or anger one notices in the composition of figures, horses and trees, the desire and sorrow emanating from a cypress as it reaches to the heavens, the pious resignation and patience that we introduce into the illustration when we ornament wall tiles with a fervor that tempts blindness . . . Yes, these are our hidden traces, not those identical horses all in a row. When a painter renders the fury and speed of a horse, he doesn't paint his own fury and speed; by trying to make the perfect horse, he reveals his love for the richness of this world and its creator, displaying the colors of a passion for life—only that and nothing more."

It Is I, Master Osman

CHAPTER 42

I AM CALLED BLACK

Various manuscript pages lay before me and the great Master Osman—some with calligraphed texts and ready to be bound, some not yet colored or otherwise unfinished for whatever reason—as we spent an entire afternoon evaluating the master miniaturists and the pages of my Enishte's book, keeping charts of our assessments. We thought we'd seen the last of the Commander's respectful but crude men, who'd brought us the pages collected from the miniaturists and calligraphers whose homes they raided and searched (some pieces had nothing whatsoever to do with either of our two books and some pages confirmed that the calligraphers, as well, were secretly accepting work from outside the palace for the sake of a few extra coins), when the most brash of them stepped over to the exalted master and removed a piece of paper from his sash.

I paid no mind at first, thinking it was one of those petitions from a father seeking an apprenticeship for his son by approaching as many division heads and group captains as possible. I could tell that the morning sun had vanished by the pale light that filtered inside. To rest my eyes, I was doing an exercise the old masters of Shiraz recommended miniaturists do to stave off premature blindness, that is, I was trying to look emptily into the distance without focusing. That's when I recognized with a thrill the sweet color and heart-stopping folds of the paper which my master held and stared at with an expression of disbelief. This matched exactly the letters that Shekure had sent me via Esther. I was about to say, "What a coincidence" like an idiot, when I noticed that, like Shekure's first letter, it was accompanied by a painting on coarse paper!

Master Osman kept the painting to himself. He handed me the letter that I just then embarrassingly realized was from Shekure.

My Dear Husband Black. I sent Esther to sound out late Elegant Effendi's widow, Kalbiye. While there, Kalbiye showed Esther this illustrated page, which I'm sending to you. Later, I went to Kalbiye's house, doing everything within my power to persuade her that it was in her best interest to give me the picture. This page was on poor

Elegant Effendi's body when he was removed from the well. Kalbiye swears that nobody had commissioned her husband, may he rest in divine light, to draw horses. So then, who made them? The Commander's men searched the house. I'm sending this note because this matter must have significance to the investigation. The children kiss your hands respectfully. Your wife, Shekure.

I carefully read the last three words of this beautiful note thrice as if staring at three wondrous red roses in a garden. I leaned over the page that Master Osman was scrutinizing, magnifying lens in hand. I straightaway noticed that the shapes whose ink had bled were horses sketched in a single motion as the old masters would do to accustom the hand.

Master Osman, who read Shekure's note without comment, voiced a question: "Who drew this?" He then answered himself, "Of course, the same miniaturist who drew the late Enishte's horse."

Could he be so certain? Moreover, we weren't at all sure who'd drawn the horse for the book. We removed the horse from among the nine pages and began to examine it.

It was a handsome, simple, chestnut horse that you couldn't take your eyes off of. Was I being truthful when I said this? I had plenty of time to look at this horse with my Enishte, and later, when I was left alone with these illustrations, but I hadn't given it much thought then. It was a beautiful, but ordinary horse: It was so ordinary that we weren't even able to determine who'd drawn it. It wasn't a true chestnut, but more bay-colored; there was a faint hint of red in its coat as well. It was a horse that I'd seen so often in other books and other illustrations that I knew it'd been drawn by rote without the miniaturist's stopping to give it any consideration at all.

We stared at the horse this way until we discovered it concealed a secret. Now, however, I could see a beauty in the horse that shimmered like heat rising before my eyes and within it a force that roused a zest for life, learning and embracing the world. I asked myself, "Who's the miniaturist with the magic touch that depicted this horse the way Allah would see it?" as if having forgotten suddenly that he was also nothing but a base murderer. The horse stood before me as if it were a real horse, but somewhere in my mind I also knew it was an illustration; being caught between these two thoughts was enchanting and aroused in me a sense of wholeness and perfection.

For a time, we compared the blurred horses drawn for practice with the horse made for my Enishte's book, determining finally that they'd been

I Am Called Black 265

made by the same hand. The proud stances of those strong and elegant studs bespoke stillness rather than motion. I was in awe of the horse of Enishte's book.

"This is such a spectacular horse," I said, "it gives one the urge to pull out a piece of paper and copy it, and then to draw every last thing."

"The greatest compliment you can pay a painter is to say that his work has stimulated your own enthusiasm to illustrate," said Master Osman. "But now let's forget about his talent and try to uncover this devil's identity. Had Enishte Effendi, may he rest in peace, ever mentioned the kind of story this picture was meant to accompany?"

"No. According to him, this was one of the horses that lived in the lands that our powerful Sultan rules. It is a handsome horse: a horse of the Ottoman line. It is a symbol that would demonstrate to the Venetian Doge Our Sultan's wealth and the regions under his control. But on the other hand, as with everything the Venetian masters depict, this horse was also to be more lifelike than a horse born of God's vision, more like a horse that lived in a particular stable with a particular groom in Istanbul so that the Venetian Doge might say to himself, 'Just as the Ottoman miniaturists have come to see the world like us, so have the Ottomans themselves come to resemble us,' in turn, accepting Our Sultan's power and friendship. For if you begin to draw a horse differently, you begin to see the world differently. Despite its peculiarities, this horse was rendered in the manner of the old masters."

The more we deliberated over the horse, the more beautiful and precious it became in my eyes. His mouth was slightly open, his tongue visible from between his teeth. His eyes shone bright. His legs were strong and elegant. Did a painting become legendary for what it was or for what was said about it? Master Osman was ever so slowly moving the magnifying lens over the animal.

"What is it that this horse is trying to convey?" I said with naive enthusiasm. "Why does this horse exist? Why this horse! What about this horse? Why does this horse excite me?"

"The pictures as well as the books commissioned by sultans, shahs and pashas proclaim their power," said Master Osman. "The patrons find these works beautiful, with their extensive gold leaf and lavish expenditures of labor and eyesight because they are proof of the ruler's wealth. An illustration's beauty is significant because it is proof that a miniaturist's talent is rare and expensive just like the gold used in the picture's creation. Others find the picture of a horse beautiful because it resembles a horse, is a horse of God's vision or is a purely imaginary horse; the effect of verisimilitude is attributed to talent. As for us, beauty in illustration begins with subtlety and profusion of meaning. Of course, to discover that this horse reveals not merely itself, but the hand of the murderer, the mark of that devil, this would augment the meaning of the picture. Then there's finding out that it's not the image of the horse, but the horse itself that's beautiful; that is, seeing the illustration of the horse not as an illustration, but as a true horse."

"If you looked at this illustration as if you were looking at a horse, what would you see there?"

"Looking at the size of this horse, I could say that this wasn't a pony but, judging from the length and curve of its neck, a good racehorse and that the flatness of its back would make it suitable for long trips. From its delicate legs we might infer that it was agile and clever like an Arabian, but its body is too long and large to be one. The elegance of its legs suggests what the Bukharan scholar Fadlan said of worthy horses in his *Book of Equines*, that were it to happen upon a river it'd easily jump it without being startled and spooked. I know by heart the wonderful things written about the choicest horses in the *Book of Equines* translated so beautifully by our royal veterinarian Fuyuzi, and I can tell you that every word applies to the chestnut horse before us: A good horse should have a pretty face and the eyes of a gazelle; its ears should be straight as reeds with a good distance between them; a good horse should have small teeth, a rounded forehead and slight eyebrows; it should be tall, long-haired, have a short waist, small nose, small shoulders and a broad flat back; it should be full-thighed, long-necked, broadchested, with a broad rump and meaty inner thighs. The beast should be proud and elegant and when it saunters, it should move as though it were greeting those on either side."

"That's our chestnut horse exactly," I said, looking at the image of the horse in astonishment.

"We've discovered our horse," said Master Osman with the same ironic smile, "but unfortunately this doesn't do us any good when it comes to the identity of the miniaturist, because I know that no miniaturist in his right mind would depict a horse using a real horse as a model. My miniaturists, naturally, would draw a horse from memory in one motion. As proof, let me remind you that most of them begin drawing the outline of the horse from the tip of one of its hooves."

"Isn't this done so the horse can be depicted standing firmly on the ground?" I said apologetically.

"As Jemalettin of Kazvin wrote in his *The Illustration of Horses*, one can properly complete a picture of a horse beginning from its hoof only if he carries the entire horse in his memory. Obviously, to render a horse through excessive thought and recollection, or even more ridiculous, by repeatedly looking at a real horse, one would have to move from head to neck and then neck to body. I hear there are certain Venetian illustrators who are happy to sell tailors and butchers such pictures of your average street packhorse drawn indecisively by trial and error. Such an illustration has nothing whatsoever to do with the meaning of the world or with the beauty of God's creation. But I'm convinced that even mediocre artists must know a genuine illustration isn't drawn according to what the eye sees at any particular moment, but according to what the hand remembers and is accustomed to. The painter is always alone before the page. Solely for this reason he's always dependent on memory. Now, there's nothing left for us to do but use the 'courtesan method' to uncover the hidden signature borne by our horse, which has been drawn from memory through the quick and skillful movement of the hand. Take a careful look here."

He was ever so slowly moving the magnifying lens over the spectacular horse as if he were trying to discover the location of a treasure on an old map meticulously rendered on calfskin.

"Yes," I said, like a disciple overcome by the pressure to make a quick and brilliant discovery that would impress his master. "We could compare the colors and embroidery of the saddle blanket to those in the other pictures."

"My master miniaturists wouldn't even deign to lower a brush to these designs. Apprentices draw the clothes, carpets and blankets in the pictures. Perhaps the late Elegant Effendi might've done them. Forget them."

"What about the ears?" I said in a fluster. "The ears of the horses . . ."

"No. These ears haven't changed form since the time of Tamerlane; they're just like the leaves of reeds, which we well know."

I was about to say, "What about the braiding of the mane and the depiction of every strand of its hair," but I fell silent, not at all amused by this master-apprentice game. If I'm the apprentice, I ought to know my place.

"Take a look here," said Master Osman with the distressed yet attentive air of a doctor pointing out a plague pustule to a colleague. "Do you see it?"

He'd moved the magnifying lens over the horse's head and was slowly pulling it away from the surface of the picture. I lowered my head to better see what was being enlarged through the lens.

The horse's nose was peculiar: its nostrils.

"Do you see it?" said Master Osman.

To be certain of what I saw, I thought I should center myself right behind the lens. When Master Osman did likewise, we met cheek to cheek just behind the lens that was now quite a distance from the picture. It momentarily alarmed me to feel the harshness of the master's dry beard and the coolness of his cheek on my face.

A silence. It was as if something wondrous were happening within the picture a handspan away from my weary eyes, and we were witnessing it with respect and awe.

"What's wrong with the nose?" I was able to whisper much later.

"He's drawn the nose oddly," said Master Osman without taking his eyes off the page.

"Did his hand slip, perhaps? Is this a mistake?"

We were still examining the peculiar, unique rendering of the nose.

"Is this the Venetian-inspired 'style' everyone, the great masters of China included, has begun talking about?" asked Master Osman mockingly.

I succumbed to resentment, thinking that he was mocking my late Enishte: "My Enishte, may he rest in peace, used to say that any fault arising not from lack of ability or talent, but from the depths of the miniaturist's soul, ought not be deemed fault but style."

However it came about, whether by the miniaturist's own hand or the horse itself, there was no clue other than this nose as to the identity of the blackguard who murdered my Enishte. For, let alone making out the nostrils, we were having difficulty identifying the noses of the smudged horses on the page found with poor Elegant Effendi.

We spent much time searching for horse pictures that Master Osman's beloved miniaturists had made for various books in recent years, looking for the same irregularity in the horse's nostrils. Because the *Book of Festivities*, still being completed, depicted the societies and guilds marching on foot before Our Sultan, there were few horses among its 250 illustrations. Men were dispatched to the book-arts workshop, where certain figure books, some notebooks of standard forms and newly finished volumes were stored, as well as to the private rooms of the Sultan, and the harem so that they could bring back any books that hadn't been securely locked up and hidden in the palace treasury, all of this, naturally, with the permission of Our Sultan.

In a double-leaf illustration from a *Book of Victories* found in the quarters of a young prince, which showed the funeral ceremonies of Sultan Süleyman the Magnificent who'd died during the siege of Szegetvar,

I Am Called Black

we first examined the chestnut horse with a white blaze, the gazelle-eyed gray pulling the funeral carriage and the other melancholy horses fitted with spectacular saddle blankets and gold embroidered saddles. Butterfly, Olive and Stork had illustrated all these horses. Whether the horses were pulling the large-wheeled funeral carriage or standing at attention with watery eyes trained on their master's body covered with a red cloth, all stood with the same elegant stance borrowed from the old masters of Herat, that is, with one foreleg proudly extended and the other firmly planted on the ground beside it. All their necks were long and curved, their tails bound up and their manes trimmed and combed, but none of the noses had the peculiarity we sought. Neither was this peculiarity evident in any of the hundreds of horses that bore commanders, scholars and hojas, who'd participated in the funeral ceremony and now stood at attention on the surrounding hilltops in honor of the late Sultan Süleyman.

Something of the sadness of this melancholy funeral passed to us as well. It upset us to see that this illustrated manuscript, upon which Master Osman and his miniaturists labored so much, had been ill-treated, and that women of the harem, playing games with princes, had scribbled and marked various places on the pages. Beside a tree under which Our Sultan's grandfather hunted, written in a bad hand were the words, "My Exalted Effendi, I love you and am waiting for you with the patience of this tree." So, it was with our hearts full of defeat and sorrow that we pored over the legendary books, whose creation I'd heard about, but none of which I'd ever seen.

In the second volume of the *Book of Skills,* which had seen the brush strokes of all three master miniaturists, we saw, behind the roaring cannon and the foot soldiers, hundreds of horses of every hue including chestnuts, grays and blues, clattering along in mail and full panoply, bearing their glorious scimitar-wielding spahi cavalrymen, as they crossed over pink hilltops in an orderly advance, but none of their noses was flawed. "And what is a flaw after all!" Master Osman said later, while examining a page in the same book, which depicted the Royal Outer Gate and the parade ground where we happened to be at that very moment. We also failed to discover the mark we were searching for on the noses of the horses of various hues mounted by guards, heralds and Secretaries of the Divan Council of State in this illustration, which depicted the hospital off to the right, the Sultan's Royal Audience Hall, and the trees in the courtyard on a scale small enough to fit into the frame yet grand enough to match their importance in our minds. We watched Our Sultan's great-grandfather Sultan Selim the

Grim, during the time he declared war on the ruler of the Dhulkadirids, erect the imperial tent along the banks of the Küskün river and hunt scurrying red-tailed black greyhounds, gazelle fawns with rumps in the air and frightened rabbits, before leaving a leopard lying in a pool of red blood, its spots blooming like flowers. Neither the Sultan's chestnut horse with the white blaze nor the horses upon which the falconers waited, their birds at the ready on their forearms, had the mark we were looking for.

Till dusk, we pored over hundreds of horses that had issued from the brushes of Olive, Butterfly and Stork over the last four or five years: the Crimean Khan Mehmet Giray's elegant-eared chestnut palomino; black and golden horses; pinkish and gray-colored horses whose heads and necks alone could be seen behind a hilltop during battle; the horses of Haydar Pasha who recaptured the Halkul-Vad fortress from the Spanish infidels in Tunisia and the Spaniards' reddish-chestnut and pistachio-green horses, one of which had tumbled headlong, as they fled from him; a black horse that caused Master Osman to remark, "I overlooked this one. I wonder who did such careless work?"; a red horse who politely turned his ears to the lute that a royal pageboy was strumming under a tree; Shirin's horse, Shebdiz, as bashful and elegant as she, waiting for her while she bathed in a lake by moonlight; the lively horses used in javelin jousts; the tempestlike horse and its beautiful groom that for some reason caused Master Osman to remark, "I loved him dearly in my youth, I'm very tired"; the sun-colored, golden, winged horse which Allah sent to the prophet Elijah to protect him from an attack by the pagans—whose wings had been mistakenly drawn on Elijah; Sultan Süleyman the Magnificent's gray thoroughbred with the small head and large body, which stared sorrowfully at the young and lovable prince; enraged horses; horses at full gallop; weary horses; beautiful horses; horses that nobody noticed; horses that would never leave these pages; and horses that leapt over gilded borders escaping their confinement.

Not one of them bore the signature we were looking for.

Even so, we were able to maintain a persistent excitement in the face of the weariness and melancholy that descended upon us: A couple of times we forgot about the horse and lost ourselves to the beauty of a picture, to colors that forced a momentary surrender. Master Osman always looked at the pictures—most of which he himself had created, supervised or ornamented—more out of nostalgic enthusiasm than wonder. "These are by Kasım from the Kasım Pasha district!" he said once, pointing out the little purple flowers at the base of the red war tent of Our Sultan's grandfather Sultan Süleyman. "He was by no means a master, but for forty years he filled the dead space of pictures with these five-leaf, single-blossom flowers, before he unexpectedly died two years ago. I always assigned him to draw this small flower because he could do it better than anyone." He fell silent for a moment, then exclaimed, "It's a pity, a pity!" With all my soul, I sensed that these words signified the end of an era.

Darkness had nearly overtaken us, when a light flooded the room. There was a commotion. My heart, which had begun to beat like a drum, comprehended immediately: The Ruler of the World, His Excellency Our Sultan had abruptly entered. I threw myself at His feet. I kissed the hem of His robe. My head spun. I couldn't look Him in the eye.

He'd long since begun speaking with Head Illuminator Master Osman anyway. It filled me with fiery pride to witness Him speak to the man with whom I'd only moments ago been sitting knee to knee looking at pictures. Unbelievable; His Excellency Our Sultan was now sitting where I'd been earlier and He was listening attentively to what my master was explaining, as I had done. The Head Treasurer, who was at his side and the Agha of the Falconers and a few others whose identities I couldn't make out were keeping close guard over Him and gazing at the open pages of books with rapt attention. I gathered all my courage and looked at length at the face and eyes of the Sovereign Ruler of the World, albeit with a sidelong glance. How handsome He was! How upright and proper! My heart no longer beat excitedly. At that moment, our eyes met.

"How much I loved your Enishte, may he rest in peace," He said. Yes, He was speaking to me. In my excitement, I missed some of what He was saying.

". . . I was quite aggrieved. However, it's quite a comfort to see that each of these pictures he made is a masterpiece. When the Venetian giaour sees these, he will be stunned and fear my wisdom. You shall determine who the accursed miniaturist is by this horse's nose. Otherwise, however merciless, it'll be necessary to torture all the master miniaturists."

"Sovereign Refuge of the World Your Excellency My Sultan," said Master Osman. "Perhaps we can better catch the man responsible for this slip of the brush, if my master miniaturists are forced to draw a horse on a blank sheet of paper, quickly, without any story in mind."

"Only, of course, if this is really a slip of the brush and not an actual nose," said Our Sultan shrewdly.

"My Sultan," said Master Osman, "to this end, if a competition by express command of Your Highness were announced tonight; if a guard were to visit Your miniaturists, requesting them to draw a horse quickly on a blank sheet for this contest . . ."

Our Sultan looked at the Commander of the Imperial Guard with an expression that said, "Did you hear that?" Then he said, "Do you know which of the Poet Nizami's stories of rivalry I like best of all?"

Some of us said, "We know." Some said, "Which one?" Some, including myself, fell silent.

"I'm not fond of the contest of poets or the story about the contest between Chinese and Western painters and the mirror," said the handsome Sultan. "I like best the contest of doctors who compete to the death."

After He'd said this, He abruptly took leave of us for His evening prayers.

Later, as the evening azan was being called, in the half dark, after exiting the gates of the palace, I hurried toward my neighborhood happily imagining Shekure, the boys and our house, when I recalled with horror the story of the contest of doctors:

One of the two doctors competing in the presence of their sultan—the one often depicted in pink—made a poison green pill strong enough to fell an elephant, which he gave to the other doctor, the one in the navy-blue caftan. That doctor first swallowed the poisonous pill, and afterward, swallowed a navy-blue antidote that he'd just made. As could be understood from his gentle laughter, nothing at all happened to him. Furthermore, it was now his turn to give his rival a whiff of death. Moving ever so deliberately, savoring the pleasure of taking his turn, he plucked a pink rose from the garden, and bringing it to his lips, inaudibly whispered a mysterious poem into its petals. Next, with gestures that bespoke extreme confidence, he extended the rose to his rival so he might take in its bouquet. The force of the whispered poem so agitated the doctor in pink that upon bringing the flower to his nose, which bore nothing but its regular scent, he collapsed out of fear and died.

CHAPTER 43

I AM CALLED "OLIVE"

Prior to the evening prayers, there came a knock at the door and I opened it without ceremony: It was one of the Commander's men from the palace, a clean, handsome, cheerful and becoming youth. In addition to paper and a writing board, he carried an oil lamp in his hand, which cast shadows over his face rather than illuminating it. He quickly apprised me of the situation: Our Sultan had declared a contest among the master miniaturists to see who could draw the best horse in the shortest time. I was asked to sit on the floor, arrange paper on the board and the board on my knees and quickly depict the world's most beautiful horse in the space indicated within the borders of the page.

I invited my guest inside. I ran and fetched my ink and the finest of my brushes made from hair clipped from a cat's ear. I sat down on the floor and froze! Might this contest be a ruse or ploy that I'd end up paying for with my blood or my head? Perhaps! But hadn't all the legendary illustrations by the old masters of Herat been drawn with fine lines that ran between death and beauty?

I was filled with the desire to illustrate, yet I was seemingly afraid to draw exactly like the old masters, and I restrained myself.

Looking at the blank sheet of paper, I paused so that my soul might rid itself of apprehension. I ought to have focused solely on the beautiful horse I was about to render; I ought to have mustered my strength and concentration.

All the horses I'd ever drawn and seen began to gallop before my eyes. Yet one was the most flawless of all. I was presently going to render this horse which nobody had been able to draw before. Decisively, I pictured it in my mind's eye. The world faded away, as if I'd suddenly forgotten myself, forgotten that I was sitting here, and even that I was about to draw. My hand dipped the brush into the inkwell of its own accord, taking up just the right amount. Come now, my good hand, bring the wonderful horse of my imagination into this world! The horse and I had seemingly become one and we were about to appear.

Following my intuition, I searched for the appropriate place within the bordered blank page. I imagined the horse standing there, and suddenly:

Even before I was able to think, my hand set forth decisively of its own volition—see how gracefully—curling quickly from the hoof, it rendered that beautiful thin lower leg, and moved upward. As it curved with the same decisiveness past the knee and rose quickly to the base of the chest, I grew elated! Arching from here, it moved victoriously higher: How beautiful the animal's chest was! The chest tapered to form the neck, exactly like that of the horse in my mind's eye. Without lifting my brush, I came down from the cheek, reaching the powerful mouth, which I'd left open after a moment's thought; I entered the mouth—this is how it's going to be then, open your mouth wider now, horsey—and I brought out its tongue.

I slowly turned out the nose—no room for indecision! Angling up steadily, I looked momentarily at the whole image, and when I saw that I'd made my line exactly as I'd imagined it, I forgot entirely what I was drawing, and the ears and the magnificent curve of the spectacular neck were rendered by my hand alone. As I drew the backside from memory, my hand stopped on its own to let the bristles of the brush sip from the inkwell. I was quite content while rendering the rump, and the forceful and protruding hindquarters; I was completely engrossed in the picture. I seemed to be standing beside the horse I was drawing as I joyously began the tail. This was a war steed, a racehorse; making a knot of its tail and winding it around, I exuberantly moved upward; as I was drawing the dock and buttocks I felt a pleasant coolness on my own ass and anus. Pleased by that feeling, I gleefully completed the splendid softness of the rump, the left hind leg that was slightly behind the right, and then the hooves. I was astonished by the horse I'd drawn and by my hand, which had rendered the elegant positioning of the left foreleg exactly as I had conceived it.

I lifted my hand from the page and quickly drew the fiery, sorrowful eyes; with but a moment's hesitation, I made the nostrils and the saddle blanket. I hatched in the mane strand by strand, as if tenderly combing it with my fingers. I fitted the beast with stirrups, added a white blaze to his forehead and finished him off properly by eagerly, measuredly, yet in full proportion drawing his balls and cock.

When I draw a magnificent horse, I become that magnificent horse.

CHAPTER 44

I AM CALLED "BUTTERFLY"

I believe it was about the time of the evening prayer. Someone was at the door. He explained that the Sultan had announced a competition. As you command, my dear Sultan; indeed, who could draw a more beautiful horse than I?

It gave me pause, however, when I learned that the picture was to be made without color in the black-ink style. Why no colors? Because I happen to be the best in the selection and application of them? Who would judge which illustration was best? I tried to get more information out of the broad-shouldered, pink-lipped, pretty boy who'd come from the palace, and was able to infer that Head Illuminator Master Osman was behind this contest. Master Osman, without a doubt, knows my talent and likes me the best of all the masters.

So, as I gazed at the empty page, the stance, look and demeanor of a horse that would please both the Sultan and Master Osman came to life before my eyes. The horse ought to be lively, but serious, like the horses Master Osman made ten years ago, and it should be rearing, in the way that always pleased Our Sultan, so that both of them would concur on the horse's beauty. How many gold pieces are they offering, I wonder? How would Mir Musavvir make this picture? How would Bihzad?

Suddenly, the beast entered my thoughts with such speed, that by the time I understood what it was, my damnable hand grabbed the brush and began to draw a miraculous horse beyond anyone's conception, starting from the raised left foreleg. After quickly joining the leg to the body, I made two arcs swiftly, pleasurably and confidently—had you seen them, you would've said this artist is no illustrator, but a calligrapher. I was gazing at my hand with awe, while it moved as if it belonged to another. These spectacular arcs became the horse's ample stomach, solid chest and swanlike neck. The illustration might've been considered complete. Oh, the talent of which I am possessed! Meanwhile, I looked to see that my hand had traced out the nose and open mouth of the strong and joyful horse and laid down the intelligent forehead and ears. Next, once again, look Mother, how beautiful, I merrily drew another arc as if scripting a letter, and I was moved to the verge of laughter. I swooped down in a perfect arc from the neck of my rearing horse to its saddle. My hand occupied itself with the saddle as I proudly regarded my horse, now coming into being, with a robust, rounded body not unlike my own: Everyone will be stunned by this horse. I thought about the sweet comments Our Sultan would make when I won the prize; He'd present me with a purse of gold coins; and I had the urge to laugh again as I imagined how I'd count them at home. Just then, my hand, which I gazed at out of the corner of my eye, finished with the saddle and took my brush to the inkwell and back before I began the horse's rump with a chuckle as though I'd told a joke. I briskly outlined the tail. How gentle and curvaceous I made the rear end, lovingly wishing to cup it in my hands like the gentle butt of a boy I was about to violate. As I smiled, my clever hand finished with the hind legs, and my brush stopped: This was the finest rearing horse the world had ever known. I was overcome with joy, happily thinking about how much they would like my horse, how they would declare me the most talented of miniaturists and even how they would announce at once that I was to become Head Illuminator; but then I considered what else those idiots would say: "How quickly and joyfully he's drawn this!" For this reason alone, I was worried they wouldn't take my wonderful illustration seriously. Therefore, I meticulously rendered the mane, nostrils, teeth, strands of horsetail and saddle blanket in minute detail so there would be no doubt that I had indeed labored over the illustration. From this position, that is, the rear lateral view, the horse's testicles should've been visible, but I left them out because they might unduly preoccupy the women. Proudly, I studied my horse: rearing, moving like a tempest, strong and powerful! It was as if a wind had kicked up and set elliptical brush strokes in motion, like the letters in a line of script, yet the animal was also poised. They'd praise the magnificent miniaturist who drew this illustration as if praising a Bihzad or a Mir Musavvir, and then, I, too, would be like them.

When I draw a magnificent horse, I become a great master of old drawing that horse.

CHAPTER 45

I AM CALLED "STORK"

After the evening prayers I intended to go to the coffeehouse, but they told me there was a visitor at the door. Good tidings, I hoped. I went to discover a messenger from the palace. He described the Sultan's contest. Fine, the world's most beautiful horse. You tell me how much you'll offer for each, and I'll quickly draw you five or six of them.

Rather than say any such thing, I maintained my reserve, and simply invited the boy waiting at the door inside. I thought for a moment: The world's most beautiful horse doesn't even exist that I might draw it. I can draw war steeds, large Mongolian horses, noble Arabians, heroic, writhing chargers covered in blood, or even luckless packhorses pulling a cartfull of stone to a building site, but no one would call any of them the world's most beautiful horse. Naturally, by "the world's most beautiful horse," I knew that Our Sultan meant the most splendid of the horses that had been depicted thousands of times in Persia, in keeping with all of the formulas, models and poses of yore. But why?

Of course, there were those who didn't want me to win the purse of gold. If they'd told me to draw your average horse, it's common knowledge that nobody's picture could compete with mine. Who was it that had duped Our Sultan? Our Sovereign, despite the endless gossip of all of those jealous artists, knows full well that I am the most talented of His miniaturists. He admires my illustrations.

My hand abruptly and angrily sprang to action as if wanting to rise above all of these vexing considerations, and in one concentrated effort, I drew a true horse beginning from the tip of its hoof. You might see one like this on the street or in battle. Weary, but controlled . . . Next, in the same fit of anger, I dashed off a spahi cavalryman's horse, and this one was even better. None of the miniaturists of the book arts workshop could draw such beautiful animals. I was about to draw another from memory when the boy from the palace said, "One is enough."

He was about to grab the sheet and leave, but I restrained him because I knew full well, as I know my own name, that these scoundrels would be giving up a purse of gold coins for these horses.

If I illustrate the way I want to, they won't give me the gold! If I can't win the gold, my name will be tarnished forever. I stopped to think. "Just wait," I said to the boy. I went inside and returned with two incredibly shiny counterfeit Venetian gold pieces, which I proceeded to give to the boy: He was afraid, his eyes widened. "You're as brave as a lion," I said.

I removed one of the notebooks of forms that I kept hidden from the eyes of the world. This is where I secretly made copies of the most beautiful illustrations that I'd seen over the years. Not to mention the copies that the chief of the dwarfs, Jafer, in the treasury would make of the best trees, dragons, birds, hunters and warriors from the pages of volumes locked away; that is, if you gave him ten gold pieces, the rogue. My notebook is excellent, not for those who want to see the actual world in which they live through pictures and decoration, but for those who want to recall the fables of old.

Flipping through the pages while showing the images to the pageboy, I selected the best of the horses. I briskly poked holes over the lines of that picture with a needle. Next, I placed a clean sheet of paper under the stencil. I gradually sprinkled a liberal amount of coal dust on top, then shook it so the dust would pass through the holes. I lifted the stencil. The coal dust, dot by dot, had transferred the beautiful horse's entire shape to the sheet below. It was a pleasure to behold.

I grabbed my pen. With an inspiration that suddenly welled up within me, I elegantly connected the dots with quick and decisive strokes, such that as I was drawing the horse's belly, graceful neck, nose and rump, I lovingly felt the horse within me. "There it is," I said. "The world's most beautiful horse. Not one of those fools could draw this."

So the boy from the palace would believe this as well, and so he wouldn't explain to Our Sultan how I'd been inspired to draw this picture, I gave him three more counterfeit coins. I implied that I would give him even more if I ended up winning the gold. Furthermore, he also imagined, I believe, that he might soon be able to catch sight of my wife once again, whom he'd leered at open-mouthed. There are many who believe you can tell a good miniaturist by the horse he draws; however, to be the best miniaturist, it's not enough to make the best horse, you must also convince Our Sultan and His circle of sycophants that you are indeed the best miniaturist.

When I draw a magnificent horse, I am who I am, nothing more.

CHAPTER 46

I WILL BE CALLED A MURDERER

Were you able to determine who I am from the way I sketched a horse?

As soon as I heard I was invited to make a horse, I knew this was no competition. They wanted to catch me through my illustration. I'm perfectly aware that the horse sketches I'd drawn on rough paper were found on poor Elegant Effendi's body. But I have no fault or style by which they might discover me through the horses I've made. Though I was as certain of this as I could be, I was in a panic while rendering the horse. Had I done something incriminating when I made the horse for Enishte? I had to depict a new horse this time. I thought of completely different things. I "restrained" myself and became another.

But who am I? Am I an artist who would suppress the masterpieces I was capable of in order to fit the style of the workshop or an artist who would one day triumphantly depict the horse deep within himself?

Suddenly and with terror, I felt the existence of that triumphant miniaturist within me. It was as if I were being watched by another soul, and, in short, I was ashamed.

I quickly knew that I wouldn't be able to remain at home, and bolting outside, I walked briskly down the darkened streets. As Sheikh Osman Baba wrote in his *Lives of the Saints*, in order for a genuine wandering dervish to escape the devil within, he must roam his entire life without remaining anywhere too long. After roaming from city to city for sixty-seven years, he tired of running and surrendered to the Devil. This is the age when master miniaturists attain blindness, or the darkness of Allah, the age when they involuntarily achieve a style, while freeing themselves of all intimations of style.

I wandered through the Chicken-Sellers Market in Bayazid, through the empty square of the slave market, amid the pleasant aromas of soup and pudding shops, as if searching. I passed the closed doors of barber-shops, clothes pressers, an old bread baker who was counting his money and looking at me in surprise; I passed a grocer's shop smelling of pickles and salted fish, and since my eyes were taken only by colors, I walked into a herbs and notions shop where something was being weighed, and in the light of a lamp, stared passionately, the way one looks at one's beloved, at the sacks of coffee, ginger, saffron and cinnamon, the colorful cans of gum mastic, the aniseed whose scent wafted from the counter, and at mounds of brown and black cumin. Sometimes I want to put everything into my mouth; sometimes I want to fill a page with a picture of all creation.

I walked into the place where I'd filled my stomach twice before in the last week, which I'd personally named the "soup kitchen of the downtrodden"—actually, of the "miserable" would've been more appropriate. It was open until midnight to those who knew about it. Inside were a few unfortunates dressed like horse thieves or like men who'd escaped the gallows; a couple of pathetic characters whose sorrow and hopelessness caused their sights to slip from this world to distant paradises, as happens with opium addicts; two beggars who were at pains to follow even basic guild etiquette; and a young gentleman who'd seated himself in a corner at a distance from this crowd. I gave the Aleppan cook a graceful greeting. Heaping the meat-filled cabbage dolma into my bowl, I covered it with yogurt and topped it off with handfuls of hot red pepper flakes before taking a seat beside the young gentleman.

Every night a sorrow overwhelms me, a misery descends upon me. Oh, my brothers, my dear brothers, we're being poisoned, we're rotting, dying, we're exhausting ourselves as we live, we've sunk up to our necks in misery . . . Some nights, I dream that he emerges from the well and comes after me, but I know we've buried him deeply beneath plenty of earth. He couldn't possibly rise from the grave.

The gentleman, who I thought had buried his nose in his soup and forgotten the whole world, opened the door to a conversation. Was this a sign from Allah? "Yes," I answered, "they've ground the meat to the right consistency, my stuffed cabbage is quite to my liking." I asked about him: He'd recently graduated from a miserable twenty-coin college and been taken into Arifi Pasha's patronage as a clerk. I didn't ask him why, at this hour of the night, he wasn't at the Pasha's estate, at the mosque or at home in the arms of his beloved wife, but chose instead to be at this street kitchen teeming with unmarried thugs. He asked me where I'd come from and who I was. I thought for a moment.

"My name is Bihzad. I've come from Herat and Tabriz. I've painted the most magnificent pictures, the most incredible masterpieces. In Persia and Arabia, in every Muslim book arts workshop where illustrations are made, they've said this about me for hundreds of years: It looks real, just like the work of Bihzad."

Of course, this isn't the issue. My paintings reveal what the mind, not the eye, sees. But painting, as you know quite well, is a feast for the eyes. If you combine these two thoughts, my world will emerge. That is:

ALIF: Painting brings to life what the mind sees, as a feast for the eyes.
LAM: What the eye sees in the world enters the painting to the degree that it serves the mind.
MIM: Consequently, beauty is the eye discovering in our world what the mind already knows.

Did the graduate of the miserable college understand this logic, which I'd extracted with lightning inspiration from the depths of my soul? Not at all. Why? Because, though you've spent three years seated at the foot of a hoja who gives lessons in an out-of-the-way neighborhood religious school for twenty silver coins a day—today you can buy twenty loaves of bread with that amount—you still wouldn't know who the hell Bihzad was. It was obvious that the twenty-coin Hoja Effendi didn't know who Bihzad was either. All right then, let me explain. I said:

"I've painted everything, absolutely everything: Our Prophet at the mosque before the green prayer niche seated together with his four caliphs; in another book, the Apostle and Prophet of God ascending the seven heavens on the night of the Ascension; Alexander on his way to China banging on the drum of a seaside temple to scare off a monster stirring up the ocean with storms; a masturbating sultan spying on the beauties of his harem swimming naked in his pool while listening to a lute; a young wrestler sure of victory after learning all his mentor's moves, only to be defeated in the presence of the Sultan at the hands of his mentor who had yet one last trick up his sleeve; Leyla and Mejnun as children kneeling in a schoolroom with exquisitely decorated walls, falling in love while reciting the Glorious Koran; the inability of lovers, from the most embarrassed to the most crass, to look at each other; the stone by stone construction of palaces; the punishment by torture of the guilty; the flight of eagles; playful rabbits; treacherous tigers; cypress and plane trees that held magpies; Death; competing poets; feasts to commemorate victory; and men like you who see nothing but the soup before them."

The reserved clerk was no longer afraid, he even found me entertaining and was smiling.

"Your Hoja Effendi must've had you read this, you'll know it," I continued. "There's a story I love from Sadi's *Garden*. You know the one, King Darius becomes separated from the crowd during a hunt and goes off to roam the hills. Unexpectedly, a dangerous-looking stranger with a goatee appears before him. The king falls into a panic and reaches for the bow on his horse, whereupon the man begs, 'My king, hold off from shooting your arrow. How is it that you haven't recognized me? Am I not the loyal groom to whom you've entrusted a hundred horses and foals? How many times have we seen each other? I know each of your hundred horses by temperament and disposition, nay, by color even. So then, how is it you pay no attention to us, the servants under your command, even those like myself whom you encounter with such frequency?'"

When I depict this scene, I render the black, chestnut and white horses—so tenderly cared for by the groom in a heavenly green pasture covered with flowers of every imaginable color—with such happiness and calm that even the dullest of readers would understand the moral of Sadi's story: The beauty and mystery of this world only emerges through affection, attention, interest and compassion; if you want to live in that paradise where happy mares and stallions live, open your eyes wide and actually see this world by attending to its colors, details and irony.

This progeny of the twenty-coin hoja was at once entertained and frightened by me. He wanted to drop his spoon and flee, but I didn't give him the chance.

"This is how the master of masters Bihzad depicted the king, his groom and the horses in that picture," I said. "For a hundred years miniaturists haven't stopped imitating those horses. Each horse rendered out of Bihzad's imagination and heart has become a model of form. Hundreds of miniaturists, including myself, can draw those horses from memory. Have you ever seen a picture of a horse?"

"I once saw a winged horse in an enchanting book that a great teacher, a scholar of scholars, had presented to my late hoja."

I didn't know whether I should push the head of this clown into his soup, who, along with his teacher, had taken *Strange Creatures* seriously, and drown him or leave him to describe in glowing terms the only horse picture he'd ever seen in his life—in who knows how poor a manuscript copy. I came up with a third alternative, and that was to drop my spoon and quit the shop. After walking for a long while I entered the abandoned dervish lodge, where I was overcome with a sense of peace. I tidied up and without doing anything else, I listened to the silence.

Later, I removed the mirror from where I kept it hidden and set it upon the low worktable. Next, I placed the two-page illustration and the drawing board on my lap. When I could see my face in the mirror from where I sat, I attempted to draw my portrait in charcoal. I drew for a long time, patiently. Much later, when I saw that once again the face on the page didn't resemble my face in the mirror, I was filled with such misery that tears welled in my eyes. How did the Venetian painters that Enishte described with such flourish do it? I then imagined myself to be one of them, thinking that if I illustrated in that state of mind, I could perhaps make a convincing self-portrait.

Later still, I cursed the European painters and Enishte both, erased what I'd done and began looking into the mirror anew to begin another drawing.

Ultimately, I found myself wandering the streets again, and then, here, at this despicable coffeehouse. I wasn't even sure how I happened to come here. As I entered, I felt such embarrassment about mingling with these miserable miniaturists and calligraphers that sweat accumulated on my forehead.

I sensed that they were watching me, alerting each other of my presence with their elbows, and laughing—all right, I could plainly see them doing it. I seated myself in the corner, trying to behave naturally. At the same time my eyes sought the other masters, my dear brethren with whom, at one time, I'd served as Master Osman's apprentice. I was certain each of them was also asked to draw a horse this evening and that they'd each expended great desperate efforts, taking the contest arranged by these idiots quite seriously.

The storyteller effendi hadn't yet begun his performance. The picture hadn't even been hung up yet. I was forced to socialize with the coffeehouse crowd.

So be it then, let me be frank with you: Like everyone else I, too, made jokes, told indecent stories, kissed my companions on the cheeks with exaggerated gestures, spoke in double entendres, innuendos and puns, asked how the young assistant masters were doing, and like everybody else, mercilessly needled our common enemies; and after I really warmed up, I went so far as to roughhouse and kiss men on the neck. Yet, knowing that a part of my soul remained mercilessly silent when I involved myself in such behavior caused me unbearable torment.

Nonetheless, before long, I not only succeeded in using figurative language to compare my own cock, and those of others that were much-talked about, to brushes, reeds, coffeehouse pillars, flutes, newel posts, door knockers, leeks, minarets, lady fingers in heavy syrup, pine trees, and twice, to the world itself, I was equally successful in comparing the asses of much-discussed pretty boys to oranges, figs, small haycocklike pastries, pillows and also to tiny anthills. Meanwhile, the most conceited of the calligraphers my age was only able to compare his own tool—quite amateurishly and without any self-confidence I might add—to a ship's mast and a porter's pole. Furthermore, I made allusions to old miniaturists' dicks that would no longer rise; the cherry-colored lips of new apprentices; master calligraphers who hoarded their money (as did I) in a certain place ("the most disgusting nook"); how perhaps opium had been put into the wine I was drinking instead of rose petals; the last great masters of Tabriz and Shiraz; the mixing of coffee and wine in Aleppo; and the calligraphers and beautiful boys to be found there.

At times it seemed that one of the two spirits within me had, in the end, emerged victorious, leaving the other behind, and that I'd finally forgotten that silent and loveless aspect of myself. At these times I remembered the holiday celebrations of my childhood during which I was able to be myself along with my kith and kin. Despite all these jokes, kisses and embraces, there was still a silence within me that left me suffering and isolated in the heart of the crowd.

Who had endowed me with this silent and merciless spirit—it was not a spirit but a jinn—which always chided me and cut me off from others? Satan? But the silence within me was eased, not by the crass mischief instigated by Satan, on the contrary, by the most pure and simple stories that drove into one's soul. Under the influence of wine, I told two stories, hoping that this would grant me peace. A tall, pale, yet pinkish-complected calligrapher's apprentice focused his green eyes onto mine and was listening to me with rapt attention.

Two Stories on Blindness and Style the Miniaturist Told to Ease the Loneliness in His Soul

ALIF

Contrary to what is assumed, making drawings of horses by looking at actual horses wasn't a discovery of European masters. The original idea belonged to the great master Jemalettin of Kazvin. After Tall Hasan, the Khan of the Whitesheep, conquered Kazvin, the old master Jemalettin was not content to simply join the book-arts workshop of the victorious khan; instead he headed out on campaign with him, claiming that he wanted to embellish the khan's *History* with scenes of war he'd witnessed himself. So this great master, who for sixty-two years had made pictures of horses, cavalry charges and battles without ever having seen a battle, went to war for the first time. But before he could even see the thunderous and violent clash of sweating horses, he lost his hands and his eyesight to enemy cannon-fire. The old master, like all genuine virtuosos, had in any case been awaiting blindness as though it were Allah's blessing, and neither did he treat the loss of his hands as a great deficiency. He maintained that the memory of a miniaturist was located not in the hand, as some insisted, but in the intellect and the heart, and furthermore, now that he was blind, he declared that he could see the true pictures, scenery and essential and flawless horses that Allah commanded be seen. To share these wonders with lovers of art, he hired a tall, pale-skinned, pink-complected, green-eyed calligrapher's apprentice to whom he dictated exactly how to draw the marvelous horses that appeared to him in God's divine darkness—as he would've drawn them had he been able to hold a brush in his hands. After the master's death, his account of how to draw 303 horses beginning from the left foreleg was collected by the handsome calligrapher's apprentice into three volumes respectively entitled *The Depiction of Horses*, *The Flow of Horses* and *The Love of Horses*, which were quite widely liked and sought after for a time in the regions where the Whitesheep ruled. Though they appeared in a variety of new editions and copies, were memorized by illustrators, apprentices and their students and were used as practice books, after Tall Hasan's Whitesheep nation was obliterated and the Herat style of illustration overtook all of Persia, Jemalettin and his manuscripts were forgotten. Doubtless, the logic behind Kemalettin Rıza of Herat's violent criticism of these three volumes in his book *The Blindman's Horses*, and his conclusion that they ought to be burned, had figured in this turn of events. Kemalettin Rıza claimed that none of the horses described by Jemalettin of Kazvin in his three volumes

I Will Be Called a Murderer 285

could be a horse of God's vision—because none of them were "immaculate," since the old master had described them after he'd witnessed an actual battle scene, no matter how briefly. Since the treasures of Tall Hasan of the Whitesheep had been plundered by Sultan Mehmet the Conqueror and brought to Istanbul, it should come as no surprise that occasionally certain of these 303 stories appear in other manuscripts in Istanbul and even that some horses are drawn as instructed therein.

LAM

In Herat and Shiraz, when a master miniaturist nearing the end of his days went blind from a lifetime of excessive labor, it would not only be taken as a sign of that master's determination, but would be commended as God's acknowledgment of the great master's work and talent. There was even a time in Herat when masters who hadn't gone blind despite having grown old were regarded with suspicion, a situation that compelled quite a few of them to actually induce blindness in their old age. There was a long period during which men reverently recalled artists who blinded themselves, following in the path of those legendary masters who'd done so rather than work for another monarch or change their styles. And it was during this age that Abu Said, Tamerlane's grandson from the Miran Shah line of descent, introduced a further twist in his workshop after he'd conquered Tashkent and Samarkand: The practice of paying greater homage to the imitation of blindness than to blindness itself. Black Veli, the old artisan who inspired Abu Said, had confirmed that a blind miniaturist could see the horses of God's vision from within the darkness; however, true talent resided in a sighted miniaturist who could regard the world like a blind man. At the age of sixty-seven he proved his point by dashing off a horse that came to the tip of his brush without so much as a glance at the paper, even as his eyes remained all the while open and fixed on the page. At the end of this artistic ceremony for which Miran Shah had deaf musicians play lutes and mute storytellers recite stories to support the legendary master's efforts, the splendid horse that Black Veli had drawn was compared at length with other horses he'd made: There was no difference whatsoever among them, much to Miran Shah's irritation; thereafter, the legendary master declared that a miniaturist possessed of talent, regardless of whether his eyes are open or closed, will always and only see horses in one way, that is, the way that Allah perceives them. And among great master miniaturists, there is no difference between the blind and the sighted: The hand would always draw the same horse because there was as yet no such thing as the Frankish innovation called "style." The horses made by the great master Black Veli have been imitated by all Muslim miniaturists for 110 years. As for Black Veli himself, after the defeat of Abu Said and the dispersal of his workshop, he moved from Samarkand to Kazvin, where two years later he was condemned for his spiteful attempts to refute the verse in the Glorious Koran that declares, "The blind and the seeing are not equal." For this, he was first blinded, then killed by young Nizam Shah's soldiers.

I was on the verge of telling a third story, describing to the pretty-eyed calligrapher's apprentice how the great master Bihzad had blinded himself, how he never wanted to leave Herat, why he never painted again after being taken forcibly to Tabriz, how a miniaturist's style was really the style of the workshop in which he worked and other tales I'd heard from Master Osman, but I became preoccupied with the storyteller. How had I known that he was going to tell Satan's story tonight?

I had the urge to say, "It was Satan who first said 'I'! It was Satan who adopted a style. It was Satan who separated East from West."

I closed my eyes and drew Satan on the storyteller's rough sheet of paper as my heart desired. As I drew, the storyteller and his assistant, other artists and curious onlookers giggled and goaded me on.

Pray, do you think I have my own style, or do I owe it to the wine?

CHAPTER 47

I, SATAN

I am fond of the smell of red peppers frying in olive oil, rain falling into a calm sea at dawn, the unexpected appearance of a woman at an open window, silences, thought and patience. I believe in myself, and, most of the time, pay no mind to what's been said about me. Tonight, however, I've come to this coffeehouse to set my miniaturist and calligrapher brethren straight about certain gossip, lies and rumors.

Of course, because I'm the one speaking, you're already prepared to believe the exact opposite of what I say. But you're smart enough to sense that the opposite of what I say is not always true, and though you might doubt me, you're astute enough to take an interest in my words: You're well aware that my name, which appears in the Glorious Koran fifty-two times, is one of the most frequently cited.

All right then, let me begin with God's book, the Glorious Koran. Everything about me in there is the truth. Let it be known that when I say this, I do so with the utmost humility. For there's also the issue of style. It has always caused me great pain that I'm belittled in the Glorious Koran. But this pain is my way of life. This is simply the way it is.

It's true, God created man before the eyes of us angels. Then He wanted us to prostrate ourselves before this creation. Yes, it happened the way it's written in "The Heights" chapter: While all the other angels bowed before man, I refused. I reminded all that Adam was made from mud, whereas I was created from fire, a superior element as all of you are familiar. So I didn't bow before man. And God found my behavior, well, "proud."

"Lower yourself from these heavens," He said. "It's beyond the likes of you to scheme for greatness here."

"Permit me to live until Judgment Day," I said, "until the dead arise."

He granted His permission. I promised that during this entire time I would tempt the descendents of Adam, who'd been the cause of my punishment, and He said He'd send to Hell those I'd successfully corrupted. I don't have to tell you that we've each remained true to his word. I have nothing more to say about the matter.

As some will claim, at that time Almighty God and I made a pact. According to them, I was helping to test the Almighty's subjects by attempting to destroy their faith: The good, possessed of sound judgment, would not be led astray, while the evil, giving into their carnal desires, would sin, to later fill the depths of Hell. Therefore, what I did was quite important: If all men went to Heaven, no one would ever be frightened, and the world and its governments could never function on virtue alone; for in our world evil is as necessary as virtue and sin as necessary as rectitude. Given that I am to thank for the genesis of Allah's worldly order—with His permission no less (why else would He allow me to live until Judgment Day?)—to be branded "evil" and never be granted my due is my hidden torment. Men like the mystic Mansur, the wool carder, or the famous Imam Gazzali's younger brother Ahmet Gazzali, have taken this line of reasoning so far as to conclude in their writings that if the sins I caused are actually committed through God's permission and will, then they are what God desires; furthermore, they maintain that good and evil do not exist because everything emerges from God, and even I am a part of Him.

Some of these mindless men have quite appropriately been burned to death with their books. Of course, good and evil do exist, and the responsibility for drawing a line between the two falls to each of us. I am not Allah, God forbid, and I was not the one who planted such absurdities into the heads of these dimwits; they came up with it all by themselves.

This brings me to my second complaint: I am not the source of all the evil and sin in the world. Many people sin out of their own blind ambition, lust, lack of willpower, baseness, and most often, out of their own idiocy without any instigation, deception or temptation on my part. However absurd the efforts of certain learned mystics to absolve me of any evil might be, so too is the assumption that I am the source of all of it, which also contradicts the Glorious Koran. I'm not the one who tempts every fruit monger who craftily foists rotten apples upon his customers, every child who tells a lie, every fawning sycophant, every old man who has obscene daydreams or every boy who jacks off. Even the Almighty couldn't find anything evil in passing wind or jacking off. Sure, I work very hard so you might commit grave sins. But some hojas claim that all of you who gape, sneeze or even fart are my dupes, which tells me they haven't understood me in the least.

Let them misunderstand you, so you can dupe them all the more easily, you might suggest. True. But let me remind you, I have my pride, which is what caused me to fall out with the Almighty in the first place. Even though I can assume every imaginable form, and though it's been recorded in numerous books tens of thousands of times that I've successfully tempted the pious, especially in the lust-kindling guise of a beautiful woman, can the miniaturist brethren before me tonight please explain why they persist in picturing me as a misshapen, horned, long-tailed and gruesome creature with a face covered with protruding moles?

Like so, we arrive at the heart of the matter: figurative painting. An Istanbul street mob incited by a preacher whose name I won't mention so he won't bother you later on, condemns the following as being contrary to the word of God: the calling of the azan like a song; the gathering of men in dervish lodges, sitting in each other's laps, and chanting with abandon to the accompaniment of musical instruments; and the drinking of coffee. I've heard that some of the miniaturists among us who fear this preacher and his mob claim that I'm the one behind all this painting in the Frankish style. For centuries, countless accusations have been leveled at me, but none so far from the truth.

Let's start from the beginning. Everybody gets caught up in my provoking Eve to eat of the forbidden fruit and forgets about how this whole matter began. No, it doesn't begin with my hubris before the Almighty, either. Before anything else, there's the matter of His presenting man to us and expecting us to bow down to him, which met with my quite appropriate and decisive refusal—though the other angels obeyed. Do you think it fitting that, after creating me from fire, He require me to bow before man, whom He created out of the crudest mud? Oh my brethren, speak the truth of your conscience. All right, then, I know you've been thinking about it and fear that anything said here will not just remain between us: He will hear it all and one day He'll call you to account. Fine, never mind why He's provided you with that conscience in the first instance; I agree, you're justified in being afraid, and I'll forget about this question and the mud-versus-fire debate. But there's something I'll never forget—yes indeed, something I'll always be proud of: I never bowed down before man.

This, however, is precisely what the new European masters are doing, and they're not satisfied with merely depicting and displaying every single detail down to the eye color, complexion, curvy lips, forehead wrinkles, rings and disgusting ear hair of gentlemen, priests, wealthy merchants and even women—including the lovely shadows that fall between their breasts. These artists also dare to situate their subjects in the center of the page, as if man were meant to be worshiped, and display these portraits like idols before which we should prostrate ourselves. Is man important enough to warrant being drawn in every detail, including his shadow? If the houses on a street were rendered according to man's false perception that they gradually diminish in size as they recede into the distance, wouldn't man then effectively be usurping Allah's place at the center of the world? Well, Allah, almighty and omnipotent, would know better than I. But surely it's absurd on the face of it to credit me with the idea of these portraits; I, who having refused to prostrate myself before man suffered untold pain and isolation; I, who fell from God's grace to become the subject of curses. It would be more reasonable to hold me responsible, as some mullahs and preachers do, for all the children who play with themselves and everyone who farts.

I have one last comment on this subject, but my words aren't for men who can't think beyond their eagerness to show off, their carnal desires, lust for money or other absurd passions! Only God, in His infinite wisdom, will understand me: Was it not You who instilled man with pride by making the angels bow before him? Now they regard themselves as Your angels were made to regard them; men are worshiping themselves, placing themselves at the center of the world. Even your most devoted servants want to be depicted in the style of the Frankish masters. I know it as well as I know my own name that this narcissism will end in their forgetting You entirely. And I'm the one who'll be blamed.

How might I convince you that I don't take all of this to heart? Naturally, by standing firmly on my own two feet despite centuries of merciless stonings, curses, damnings and denouncements. If only my angry and shallow enemies, who never tire of condemning me, would remember that it was the Almighty Himself who granted me life until Judgment Day, while allotting them no more than sixty or seventy years. If I were to advise them that they could extend this period by drinking coffee, I know quite well that some, because it was Satan speaking, would do the exact opposite and refuse coffee entirely, or worse yet, stand on their heads and try pouring it into their asses.

Don't laugh. It's not the content, but the form of thought that counts. It's not what a miniaturist paints, but his style. Yet these things should be subtle. I was going to conclude with a love story, but it's gotten quite late. The honey-tongued master storyteller who's given me voice tonight promises to tell this story of love when he hangs up the picture of a woman the day after tomorrow, on Wednesday night.

CHAPTER 48

I, SHEKURE

I dreamed that my father was telling me incomprehensible things, and it was so terrifying that I woke up. Shevket and Orhan were clinging tightly to me on either side, and their warmth made me sweat. Shevket had his hand on my stomach. Orhan was resting his sweaty head on my bosom. Somehow, I was able to get out of bed and leave the room without waking them.

I crossed the wide hallway and silently opened Black's door. In the light cast by my candle, I couldn't see him, only the edge of his white mattress which lay like a shrouded body in the middle of the dark, cold room. The candlelight seemed unable to reach the mattress.

When I brought my hand even closer, the reddish-orange light of the candle struck Black's weary, unshaven face and naked shoulders. I drew near to him. Just as Orhan did, he slept curled up like a pill bug, and he wore the expression of a sleeping maiden.

"This is my husband," I said to myself. He seemed so distant, so much a stranger, that I was filled with sorrow. If I'd had a dagger with me, I would've murdered him—no, I didn't actually want to do such a thing; I was only wondering, the way children do, how it'd be if I killed him. I didn't believe he'd lived for years through thoughts of me, neither in his innocent childlike expression.

Prodding his shoulder with the edge of my bare foot, I woke him. When he saw me, he was startled more than enchanted and excited, if only for a moment, just as I'd hoped. Before he'd completely come to his senses, I said:

"I dreamed I saw my father. He confided something horrible to me: You were the one who killed him . . ."

"Weren't we together when your father was murdered?"

"I'm aware of this," I said. "But you knew that my father would be at home all alone."

"I did not. You were the one who sent the children out with Hayriye. Only Hayriye, and perhaps Esther, knew about it. And as for whoever else might've known, you'd have a better idea than I."

"There are times I feel an inner voice is about to tell me why everything has gone so badly, the secret of all of our misfortune. I open my mouth so that voice might speak, but as in a dream, I make no sound. You're no longer the good and naive Black of my childhood."

"That naive Black was driven away by you and your father."

"If you've married me to take revenge on my father, you've accomplished your goal. Maybe this is why the children don't like you."

"I know," he said without sorrow. "Before going to bed you were downstairs for a while. They were chanting 'Black, Black, my ass's crack,' loud enough so I could hear."

"You should've given them a beating," I said, at first half-wishing he'd done so. Then I added in a panic, "If you raise a hand against them, I'll kill you."

"Get into bed," he said. "Or you'll freeze to death."

"Maybe I'll never get into your bed. Maybe we've made a mistake by getting married. They say our ceremony has no legitimacy before the law. Do you know I heard Hasan's footsteps before I fell asleep? It's not surprising, when I was living in the house of my late husband, I heard Hasan's footsteps for years. The children like him. And he's merciless, that one. He has a red sword, take care to guard yourself against it."

I saw something so weary and so stern in Black's eyes that I knew I wouldn't be able to scare him.

"Of the two of us, you're the one with more hope and the one with more sadness," I said. "I'm just struggling not to be unhappy and to protect my children, whereas you're stubbornly trying to prove yourself. It's not because you love me."

He went on at length about how much he loved me, how he always thought only of me in desolate caravansaries, on barren mountains and during snowy nights. If he hadn't said these things, I would've awakened the children and returned to my former husband's house. Because I had the urge, I said the following:

"Sometimes it seems that my former husband might return at any time. It's not that I fear being caught in the middle of the night with you or being caught by the children, I'm afraid that as soon as we embrace he'll come knocking on the door."

We heard the wailing of cats fighting for their lives just outside the courtyard gate. This was followed by a long silence. I thought I might sob. I could neither set my candle holder down on the end table nor turn around and head to my room to be with my sons. I told myself that I wouldn't leave this room until I was absolutely convinced that Black had nothing whatsoever to do with my father's death.

"You belittle us," I said to Black. "You've grown haughty since you married me. You clearly looked down on us because my husband was missing, and now that my father's been killed you find us even more pitiful."

"My respected Shekure," he said cautiously. It pleased me that he'd begun this way. "You yourself know that none of this is true. I'd do anything for you."

"Then get out of bed, and wait with me on your feet."

Why had I said that I was waiting?

"I cannot," he said, and in embarrassment, gestured to the quilt and his nightgown.

He was right, but it annoyed me anyway that he wasn't heeding my request.

"Before my father was murdered, you entered this house cowering like a cat who'd spilled milk," I said. "But now when you address me as 'My respected Shekure' it seems empty—as though you want us to know it is."

I was trembling, not out of anger, but because of the icy cold that seized my legs, back and neck.

"Get into bed and be my wife," he said.

"How will the villain who killed my father ever be found?" I said. "If it's going to take some time before he's found, it's not right for me to stay in this house with you."

"Thanks to you and Esther, Master Osman has focused all his attention on the horses."

"Master Osman was the sworn enemy of my father, may he rest in peace. Now my poor father can see from above that you're depending on Master Osman to find his murderer. It must be causing him great agony."

He abruptly leapt out of bed and came toward me. I couldn't even move. But contrary to what I expected, he just snuffed out my candle with his hand and stood there. We were in pitch blackness.

"Your father can no longer see us," he whispered. "We're both alone. Tell me now, Shekure: You gave me the impression, when I returned after twelve years, that you'd be able to love me, that you'd be able to make room in your heart for me. Then we married. Since then you've been running away from loving me."

"I had to marry you," I whispered.

There, in the dark, without pity, I sensed how my words were driving into his flesh like nails—as the poet Fuzuli had once put it.

"If I could love you, I would've loved you when I was a child," I whispered again.

"Tell me then, fair beauty of the darkness," he said. "You must've spied on all those miniaturists who frequented your house and come to know them. In your opinion, which one is the murderer?"

I was pleased that he could still keep this good humor. He was, after all, my husband.

"I'm cold."

Did I actually say this, I can't remember. We began to kiss. Embracing him in the dark, still holding the candle in one hand, I took his velvety tongue into my mouth, and my tears, my hair, my nightgown, my trembling and even his body were full of wonder. Warming my nose against his hot cheek was also pleasant; but this timid Shekure restrained herself. As I was kissing him, I didn't let myself go or drop the candle, but thought of my father, who was watching me, and of my former husband, and my children asleep in bed.

"There's somebody in the house," I shouted. I pushed Black away and went out into the hall.

CHAPTER 49

I AM CALLED BLACK

Silent and unseen, under cover of early morning darkness, I left like a guilty houseguest and walked tirelessly through the muddy backstreets. At Bayazid, I performed my ablution in the courtyard, entered the mosque and prayed. Inside, there was no one but the Imam Effendi and an old man who could sleep as he prayed—a talent only rarely achieved after a lifetime of practice. You know how there are moments in our sleepy dreams and sad memories when we feel Allah has taken notice of us and we pray with the hopeful anticipation of one who's managed to thrust a petition into the Sultan's hand: Thus did I beg Allah to grant me a cheerful home filled with loving people.

When I'd reached Master Osman's house, I knew that within a week's time he'd gradually usurped my late Enishte's place in my thoughts. He was more contrary and more distant, but his belief in manuscript illumination was more profound. He resembled an introspective elderly dervish more than the great master who'd kicked up tempests of fear, awe and love among the miniaturists for so many years.

As we traveled from the master's house to the palace—he mounted on a horse and hunched slightly, I on foot and likewise hunched forward—we must've recalled the elderly dervish and aspiring disciple in those cheap illustrations that accompany old fables.

At the palace, we found the Commander of the Imperial Guard and his men even more eager and ready than we. Our Sultan was certain that once we'd looked at the three masters' horse drawings this morning we could, in a trice, determine who among them was the accursed murderer; and so, He'd ordered that the criminal be quickly put to torture without even allowing him to answer the accusation. We were taken not to the executioners' fountain where everyone could see and take warning, but to that small slapdash house in the sheltered seclusion of the Sultan's Private Garden, which was preferred for interrogation, torture and strangling.

A youth, who seemed too elegant and polite to be one of the Commander's men, authoritatively placed three sheets of paper on a worktable.

Master Osman took out his magnifying lens and my heart began to pound. Like an eagle gliding elegantly over a tract of land, his eye, which he maintained at a constant distance from the lens, passed ever so slowly over the three marvelous horse illustrations. And like that eagle catching sight of the baby gazelle which would be its prey, he slowed over each of the horses' noses and focused on it intently and calmly.

"It's not here," he said coldly after a time.

"What isn't here?" asked the Commander.

I'd assumed the great master would work with deliberation, scrutinizing every aspect of the horses from mane to hoof.

"The damned painter hasn't left a single trace," said Master Osman. "We won't be able to determine who illustrated the chestnut horse from these pictures."

Taking up the magnifying lens he'd put aside, I looked at the horses' nostrils. The master was correct; there was nothing in the three horses resembling the peculiar nostrils of the chestnut horse drawn for my Enishte's manuscript. Just then, my attention turned to the torturers waiting outside with an implement whose purpose I couldn't fathom. As I was trying to observe them through the half-opened door, I saw somebody scuttle quickly backward as if possessed by a jinn, seeking shelter behind one of the mulberry trees.

At that moment, like an ethereal light that illuminated the leaden morning, His Excellency Our Sultan, the Foundation of the World, entered the room.

Master Osman confessed to Him that he hadn't been able to determine anything from the illustrations. Nevertheless, he couldn't refrain from drawing Our Sultan's attention to the horses in these magnificent paintings: the way one reared, the delicate stance of the next and, in the third, a dignity and pride matching the content of ancient books. Meanwhile, he speculated about which artist had made each picture, and the pageboy who'd gone door to door to the artists' houses confirmed what Master Osman said.

"My Sovereign, don't be surprised that I know my painters like the back of my hand," said the master. "What bewilders me is how one of these men, whom I indeed know like the back of my hand, could make a completely unfamiliar mark. For even the flaw of a master miniaturist has its origins."

"You mean to say?" said Our Sultan.

"Your Excellency, Prosperous Sultan and Refuge of the World, in my opinion, this concealed signature, evident here in the nostrils of this chestnut horse, is not simply the meaningless and absurd mistake of a painter, but a sign whose roots reach into the distant past to other pictures, other techniques, other styles and perhaps even other horses. If we were allowed to examine the marvelous pages of centuries-old books that You keep under lock and key in the cellars, iron chests, and cabinets of the Inner Treasury, we might be able to identify as technique what we now see as mistake; then, we could attribute it to the brush of one of the three miniaturists."

"You wish to enter my Treasury?" said the Sultan in amazement.

"That is my wish," said my master.

This was a request as brazen as asking to enter the harem. Just then, I understood that in as much as the harem and the Treasury occupied the two prettiest spots in the courtyard of the Private Paradise of Our Sultan's Palace, they also occupied the two dearest spots in Our Sultan's heart.

I was trying to read what would happen from Our Sultan's beautiful face, which I could now look upon without fear, but He suddenly vanished. Had He been incensed and offended? Would we, or even the miniaturists as a whole, be punished on account of my master's impudence?

Looking at the three horses before me, I imagined that I would be killed before seeing Shekure again, without ever sharing her bed. Despite the immediacy of all their beautiful attributes, these magnificent horses now seemed to have emerged from a quite distant world.

I thoroughly realized during this horrifying silence that just as being taken into the heart of the palace as a child, being raised here and living here meant serving Our Sultan and perhaps dying for Him, so being a miniaturist meant serving God and dying for the sake of His beauty.

Much later, when the Head Treasurer's men brought us up toward the Middle Gate, death occupied my mind, the silence of death. But, as I passed through the gate where countless pashas had been executed, the guards acted as if they didn't even see us. The Divan Square, which yesterday had dazzled me as if it were Heaven itself, the tower and the peacocks didn't affect me in the least, for I knew that we were being taken further inside, to the heart of Our Sultan's secret world, to the Private Quarters of the Enderun.

We passed through doors barred even to the Grand Viziers. Like a child who'd entered a fairy tale, I kept my eyes trained on the ground to avoid coming face-to-face with the wonders and creatures that might confront me. I couldn't even look at the chamber where the Sultan held audiences. But my gaze happened to fall momentarily on the walls of the harem near an ordinary plane tree, one no different from other trees, and on a tall man in a caftan of shimmering blue silk. We passed among towering columns. Finally, we stopped before a portal, larger and more imposing than the rest, framed in ornate stalactite patterns. At its threshold stood Treasury chiefs in glimmering caftans; one of them was bending to open the lock.

Staring directly into our eyes, the Head Treasurer said: "You are truly blessed by fortune, His Excellency Our Sultan has granted you permission to enter the treasury of the Enderun. There, you will examine books that no one else has seen; you will gaze upon incredible pictures and pages of gold, and like hunters, you will track the spoor of your prey, the murderer. My Sultan bade me remind you that good Master Osman has three days—one of which is now over—until Thursday noon, in which to name the culprit in the miniaturists' midst; failing that, the matter shall be turned over to the Commander of the Imperial Guard to be resolved by torture."

First, they removed the cloth sheath around the padlock, sealed to ensure no key entered the keyhole without permission. The Doorkeeper of the Treasury and the two chiefs confirmed the seal was intact, signaling with a nod. The seal was broken, and when the key was introduced, the lock opened with a clatter that filled the pervasive silence. Master Osman suddenly turned an ashen gray. When one wing of the heavy, embellished-wood double door was opened, his face was struck by a dark radiance that seemed a remnant of ancient days.

"My Sultan didn't want the scribal chiefs and the secretaries who keep inventory records to enter unnecessarily," said the Head Treasurer. "The Royal Librarian has passed away and there's no one to look after the books in his stead. For this reason, My Sultan has commanded that Jezmi Agha alone should accompany you within."

Jezmi Agha was a dwarf with bright, shining eyes who appeared to be at least seventy years old. His headdress, which resembled a sail, was even more peculiar than he.

"Jezmi Agha knows the interior of the treasury like his own house; he knows the locations of books and all else better than anyone."

The aging dwarf displayed no pride in this. He was running an eye over the silver-legged heating brazier, the chamber pot with a mother-of-pearl inlaid handle, the oil lamp and the candlesticks that the palace pages were carrying.

The Head Treasurer announced that the door would again be locked behind us and sealed with the seventy-year-old signet of Sultan Selim the Grim. After the evening prayers, at sunset, the seal would again be broken, before the witness of the attendant crowd of Treasury chiefs. Moreover, we should exercise great caution that nothing whatsoever "mistakenly" found its way into our clothes, pockets or sashes: we would be searched down to our undergarments upon exiting.

We entered, passing between chiefs standing at either side. Inside, it was ice cold. When the door closed behind us, we were enveloped in blackness. I smelled a combination of mildew, dust and humidity that drove deep into my nasal passages. Everywhere the clutter of objects, chests and helmets intermingled in a huge chaotic jumble. I had the feeling that I was witness to a great battle.

My eyes adjusted to the odd light that fell over the entire space, which filtered through the thick bars of the high windows, through the balustrades of the stairs along the high walls and the railing of the second-floor wooden walkways. This chamber was red, tinged with the color of the velvet cloth, carpets and kilims hanging on the walls. With due reverence, I considered how the accumulation of all this wealth was the consequence of wars waged, blood spilt and cities and treasuries plundered.

"Frightened?" asked the elderly dwarf, giving voice to my feelings. "Everybody is frightened on their first visit. At night the spirits of these objects whisper to each other."

What was frightening was the silence in which this abundance of incredible objects was interred. Behind us we heard the clattering of the seal being affixed to the lock on the door, and we looked around in awe, motionless.

I saw swords, elephant tusks, caftans, silver candlesticks and satin banners. I saw mother-of-pearl inlaid boxes, iron trunks, Chinese vases, belts, long-necked lutes, armor, silk cushions, model globes, boots, furs, rhinoceros horns, ornamented ostrich eggs, rifles, arrows, maces and cabinets. There were heaps of carpets, cloth and satin everywhere, seemingly cascading over me from the wood-paneled upper floors, from the balustrades, the built-in closets and small storage cells built into the walls. A strange light, the likes of which I'd never seen, shone on the cloth, the boxes, the caftans of sultans, swords, the huge pink candles, the wound turbans, pillows embroidered with pearls, gold filigree saddles, diamond-handled scimitars, ruby-handled maces, quilted turbans, turban plumes, curious clocks, ewers and daggers, ivory statues of horses and elephants, narghiles with diamond-studded tops, mother-of-pearl chests of drawers, horse aigrettes, strands of large prayer beads, and helmets adorned with rubies and turquoise. This light, which filtered faintly down from the high windows, illuminated floating dust particles in the half-darkened room like the summer sunlight that streams in from the glass skylight atop the dome of a mosque—but this wasn't sunlight. In this peculiar light, the air had become palpable and all the objects appeared as if made from the same material. After we apprehensively experienced the silence in the room for a while longer, I knew it was as much the light as the dust covering everything that dimmed the red color reigning in the cold room, melding all the objects into an arcane sameness. And as the eye swam over these strange and indistinct items, unable to distinguish one from another at even the second or third glance, this great profusion of objects became even more terrifying. What I thought was a chest, I later decided was a folding worktable, and later still, some strange Frankish device. I saw that the mother-of-pearl inlaid chest among the caftans and plumes pulled out of their boxes and hastily tossed hither and yon was actually an exotic cabinet sent by the Muscovite Czar.

Jezmi Agha placed the brazier in the fire niche that had been cut into the wall.

"Where are the books located?" whispered Master Osman.

"Which books?" said the dwarf. "The ones from Arabia, the Kufic Korans, those that His Excellency Sultan Selim the Grim, Denizen of Paradise, brought back from Tabriz, the books of pashas whose property was seized when they were condemned to death, the gift volumes brought by the Venetian ambassador to Our Sultan's grandfather, or the Christian books from the time of Sultan Mehmet the Conqueror?"

"The books that Shah Tahmasp sent His Excellency Sultan Selim, Denizen of Paradise, as a present twenty-five years ago," said Master Osman.

The dwarf brought us to a large wooden cabinet. Master Osman grew impatient as he opened the doors and cast his eyes on the volumes before him. He opened one, read its colophon and leafed through its pages. Together, we gazed in astonishment at the carefully drawn illustrations of khans with slightly slanted eyes.

"'Genghis Khan, Chagatai Khan, Tuluy Khan and Kublai Khan the Ruler of China,'" read Master Osman before closing the book and taking up another.

We came across an incredibly beautiful illustration depicting the scene in which Ferhad, empowered by love, carries his beloved Shirin and her horse away on his shoulder. To convey the passion and woe of the lovers, the rocks on the mountain, the clouds and the three noble cypresses witnessing Ferhad's act of love were drawn with a trembling grief-stricken hand in such agony that Master Osman and I were instantly affected by the taste of tears and sorrow in the falling leaves. This touching moment had been depicted—as the great masters intended—not to signify Ferhad's muscular strength, but rather to convey how the pain of his love was felt at once throughout the entire world.

"A Bihzad imitation made in Tabriz eighty years ago," Master Osman said as he replaced the volume and opened another.

This was a picture that showed the forced friendship between the cat and the mouse from *Kelile and Dimne*. Out in the fields, a poor mouse, caught between the attacks of a marten on the ground and a hawk in the air, finds his salvation in an unfortunate cat caught in a hunter's trap. They come to an agreement: The cat, pretending to be the mouse's friend, licks him, thereby scaring away the marten and the hawk. In turn, the mouse cautiously frees the cat from the snare. Even before I could understand the painter's sensibility, the master had stuffed the book back beside the other volumes and had randomly opened another.

This was a pleasant picture of a mysterious woman and a man: The woman had elegantly opened one hand while asking a question, holding her knee with the other over her green cloak, as the man turned to her and listened intently. I looked at the picture avidly, jealous of the intimacy, love and friendship between them.

Putting that book down, Master Osman opened to a page from another book. The cavalry of Persian and Turanian armies, eternal enemies, had donned their full panoply of armor, helmets, greaves, bows, quivers and arrows and had mounted those magnificent, legendary and fully armored horses. Before they engaged one another in a battle to the death, they were arrayed in orderly ranks facing each other on a dusty yellow steppe holding the tips of their lances upright, bedecked in an array of colors and patiently watching their commanders, who'd rushed to the fore and begun to fight. I was about to tell myself that regardless of whether the illustration was made today or a hundred years ago, whether it's a depiction of war or love, what the artist of absolute faith actually paints and conveys is a battle with his will and his love for painting; I was going to declare further that the miniaturist actually paints his own patience, when Master Osman said:

"It's not here either," and shut the heavy tome.

In the pages of an album we saw high mountains interwoven with curling clouds in a landscape illustration that seemed to go on forever. I thought how painting meant seeing this world yet depicting it as if it were the Otherworld. Master Osman recounted how this Chinese illustration might've traveled from Bukhara to Herat, from Herat to Tabriz, and at last, from Tabriz to Our Sultan's palace, moving from book to book along the way, bound and unbound, finally to be rebound with other paintings at the end of the journey from China to Istanbul.

We saw pictures of war and death, each more frightening and more expertly done than the next: Rüstem together with Shah Mazenderan; Rüstem attacking Afrasiyab's army; and Rüstem, disguised in armor, a mysterious and unidentified hero warrior... In another album we saw dismembered corpses, daggers drenched in red blood, sorrowful soldiers in whose eyes the light of death gleamed and warriors cutting each other down like reeds, as fabled armies, which we could not name, clashed mercilessly. Master Osman—for who knows how many thousandth time—looked upon Hüsrev spying on Shirin bathing in a lake by moonlight, upon the lovers Leyla and Mejnun fainting as they beheld each other after an extended separation, and a spirited picture, all aflutter with birds, trees and flowers, of Salaman and Absal as they fled the entire world and lived together on an isle of bliss. Like a true great master, he couldn't help drawing my attention to some oddity in a corner of even the worst painting, perhaps having to do with an oversight on the part of the illuminator or perhaps with the conversation of colors: As might be expected, Hüsrev and Shirin are listening to a charming recital by her ladies-in-waiting, but see there, what kind of sad and spiteful painter had needlessly perched that ominous owl on a tree branch?; who had included that lovely boy dressed in woman's garb among the Egyptian women who cut their fingers trying to peel tasty oranges while gazing upon the beauty of handsome Joseph?; could the miniaturist who painted İsfendiyar's blinding with an arrow foresee that later on he, too, would be blinded?

We saw the angels accompanying Our Exalted Prophet during his Ascension; the dark-skinned, six-armed, long-white-bearded old man symbolizing Saturn; and baby Rüstem sleeping peacefully in his mother-of-pearl-inlaid cradle beneath the watchful eyes of his mother and nursemaids. We saw the way Darius died an agonizing death in Alexander's arms, how Behram Gür withdrew to the red room with his Russian princess, how Siyavush passed through fire mounted on a black horse whose nostrils bore no peculiarity, and the woeful funeral procession of Hüsrev, murdered by his own son. As Master Osman rapidly picked out the volumes and set them aside, he would at times recognize an artist and show me, or winkle out an illustrator's signature humbly hidden among flowers growing in the seclusion of a ruined building, or hiding in a black well along with a jinn. By comparing signatures and colophons, he could determine who'd taken what from whom. He'd flip through certain books exhaustively in hope of finding a series of pictures. Long silences passed wherein nothing but the faint susurrus of turning pages could be heard. Occasionally, Master Osman would cry out "Aha!" but I kept my peace, unable to understand what had excited him. At times he would remind me that we'd already encountered the page composition or arrangement of trees and mounted soldiers of a particular illustration in other books, in different scenes of completely different stories, and he'd point out these pictures again to jog my memory. He compared a picture in a version of Nizami's *Quintet* from the time of Tamerlane's son Shah Rıza—that is, from nearly two hundred years ago—with another picture he said was made in Tabriz seventy or eighty years earlier, and then go on to ask me what we could learn from the fact that two miniaturists had created the same picture without having seen each other's work. He answered the question himself:

"To paint is to remember."

Opening and shutting old illuminated manuscripts, Master Osman would sink his face with sorrow into the wondrous artwork (because nobody could paint this way anymore) and then become animated with joy before poorly executed pieces (for all miniaturists were brethren!)—and he'd show me what the artist had remembered, that is, old pictures of trees, angels, parasols, tigers, tents, dragons and melancholy princes, and in the process, what he hinted at was this: There was a time when Allah looked upon the world in all its uniqueness, and believing in the beauty of what he saw, bequeathed his creation to us, his servants. The duty of illustrators and of those who, loving art, gaze upon the world, is to remember the magnificence that Allah beheld and left to us. The greatest masters in each generation of painters, expending their lives and toiling until blind, strove with great effort and inspiration to attain and record the wondrous dream that Allah commanded us to see. Their work resembled Mankind recalling his own golden memories from the very beginning. Unfortunately, even the greatest masters, just like tired old men or great miniaturists gone blind from their labors, were only vaguely able to recollect random parts of that magnificent vision. This was the mysterious wisdom behind the phenomenon of old masters who miraculously drew a tree, a bird, the pose of a prince washing himself in the public baths or a sad young woman at a window in exactly the same way despite never having seen each other's work and despite the hundreds of years that separated them.

Long afterward, once the red light of the Treasury had dimmed and it became evident that the cabinet contained none of the gift books that Shah Tahmasp had sent to Our Sultan's grandfather, Master Osman revisited the same logic:

"At times, a bird's wing, the way a leaf holds to a tree, the curves of eaves, the way a cloud floats or the laugh of a woman is preserved for centuries by passing from master to disciple and being shown, taught and memorized over generations. Having learned this detail from his master, the miniaturist believes it to be a perfect form, and is as convinced of its immutability as he is of the glorious Koran's, and just as he memorizes the Koran, he'll never forget this detail indelibly painted in his memory. However, never forgetting does not mean the master artist will always use this detail. The customs of the workshop wherein he extinguishes the light of his eyes, the habits and taste for color of the ornery master beside him or the whims of his sultan will, at times, prevent him from painting that detail, and he'll draw a bird's wing, or the way a woman laughs—"

"Or the nostrils of a horse."

"—or the nostrils of a horse," said a stone-faced Master Osman, "not the way it's been ingrained in the depths of his soul, but according to the custom of the workshop where he presently finds himself, just like the others there. Do you understand me?"

From a page in Nizami's *Hüsrev and Shirin,* quite a few versions of which we'd thumbed through already, in a picture depicting Shirin seated on her throne, Master Osman read aloud an inscription engraved on two stone plates above the palace walls: EXALTED ALLAH PRESERVE THE POWER OF THE VICTORIOUS SON OF TAMERLANE KHAN, OUR NOBLE SULTAN, OUR JUST KHAN, PROTECT HIS SOVEREIGNTY AND DOMAINS SO HE MAY FOREVER BE CONTENTED (the leftmost stone read) AND WEALTHY (the rightmost stone read).

Later, I asked, "Where might we find illustrations wherein the miniaturist has rendered a horse's nostrils in the same way they were etched upon his memory?"

"We must locate the legendary *Book of Kings* volume that Shah Tahmasp sent as a gift," said Master Osman. "We must revisit those glorious old days of legend, when Allah had a hand in the painting of miniatures. We have many more books yet to examine."

It crossed my mind that, just perhaps, Master Osman's main goal was not to find horses with peculiarly drawn noses, but to scrutinize as much as possible these spectacular pictures that had slept quietly for years in this Treasury safe from prying eyes. I grew so impatient to find the clues that would unite me with Shekure, who awaited me at the house, that I'd been loath to believe that the great master might want to stay in the icy Treasury as long as possible.

Thus did we persist in opening other cabinets, other chests shown us by the aged dwarf, to examine the pictures therein. Periodically, I'd get fed up with the pictures, which all looked alike, and wish never again to watch Hüsrev visit Shirin under the castle window; I'd leave the master's side—without even a glance at the nostrils of the horse Hüsrev rode—and try to warm myself at the brazier or I'd walk respectfully and awestruck among the heaps of cloth, gold, weapons, armor and plunder in the adjacent rooms of the Treasury. At times, prompted by an abrupt cry and hand gesture by Master Osman, I'd imagine that a new masterpiece had been found or, yes, at last a horse with a curious nose, and running to his side, I'd look at the picture the master was holding with his hand slightly atremble as he sat curled up on an Ushak carpet dating from the time of Sultan Mehmed the Conqueror, only to encounter an illustration, the likes of which I'd never before seen, depicting, say, Satan slyly boarding Noah's ark.

We watched as hundreds of shahs, kings, sultans and khans—who'd ruled from the thrones of various kingdoms and empires from the time of Tamerlane to Sultan Süleyman the Magnificent—happily and excitedly hunted gazelles, lions and rabbits. We saw how even the Devil bit his finger and recoiled in embarrassment at the shameless man who stood upon scraps of wood tied to the back legs of a camel so he could violate the poor animal. In an Arabic book that had come by way of Baghdad, we watched the flight of the merchant who clung to the feet of a mythical bird as he spanned the seas. In the next volume, which opened by itself to the first page, we saw the scene that Shekure and I loved the most, in which Shirin beheld Hüsrev's picture hanging from a branch and fell in love with him. Then, looking at an illustration that brought to life the inner workings of a complicated clock made from bobbins and metal balls, birds and Arabic statuettes seated on the back of an elephant, we remembered time.

I don't know how much more time we spent examining book after book and illustration after illustration in this manner. It was as if the unchanging, frozen golden time revealed in the pictures and stories we viewed had thoroughly mingled with the damp and moldy time we experienced in the Treasury. It seemed that these illuminated pages, created over the centuries by the lavish expenditure of eyesight in the workshops of countless shahs, khans and sultans, would come to life, as would the objects that seemed to besiege us: The helmets, scimitars, daggers with diamond-studded handles, armor, porcelain cups from China, dusty and delicate lutes, and the pearl-embellished cushions and kilims—the likes of which we'd seen in countless illustrations.

"I now understand that by furtively and gradually re-creating the same pictures for hundreds and hundreds of years, thousands of artists had cunningly depicted the gradual transformation of their world into another."

I'll be first to admit that I didn't completely understand what the great master meant. But the close attention my master had shown to the thousands of pictures made over the last two hundred years from Bukhara to Herat, from Tabriz to Baghdad and all the way to Istanbul, had far exceeded the search for a clue in the depiction of some horse's nostrils. We'd participated in a kind of melancholy elegy to the inspiration, talent and patience of all the masters who'd painted and illuminated in these lands over the years.

For this reason, when the doors of the Treasury were opened at the time of the evening prayer and Master Osman explained to me that he had no desire whatsoever to leave, and that furthermore, only by remaining here until morning examining pictures by the light of oil lamps and candles could he execute properly Our Sultan's charge, my first response, as I informed him, was to remain here with him and the dwarf.

However, when the door was opened and my master conveyed our wish to the waiting chiefs and asked permission of the Head Treasurer, immediately regretted my decision. I longed for Shekure and our house. I grew increasingly restless as I wondered how she would manage, spending the night alone with the children and how she would batten down the now-repaired shutters of the windows.

Through the opened half of the Treasury portal, I was beckoned to the magnificence of life outside by the large damp plane trees in the courtyard of the Enderun—now under a hint of fog—and by the gestures of two royal pages, speaking to each other in a sign language so as not to disturb the peace of Our Sultan; but I remained where I was, frozen by embarrassment and guilt.

CHAPTER 50

WE TWO DERVISHES

Yea, the rumor that our picture was among the pages from China, Samarkand and Herat comprising an album hidden away in the remotest corner of the Treasury filled with the plunder of hundreds of countries over hundreds of years by the ancestors of His Excellency, Our Sultan, was most probably spread to the miniaturists' division by the dwarf Jezmi Agha. If we might now recount our own story in our own fashion—the will of God be with us—we hope that none of the crowd in this fine coffeehouse will take offense.

One hundred and ten years have passed since our deaths, forty since the closing of our irredeemable, Persia-partisan dervish lodges, those dens of heresy and nests of devilry, but see for yourselves, here we are before you. How could this be? I'll tell you how: We were rendered in the Venetian style! As this illustration indicates, one day we two dervishes were tramping through Our Sultan's domains from one city to the next.

We were barefoot, our heads were shaven, and we were half naked; each of us was wearing a vest and the hide of a deer, a belt around our waists and we were holding our walking sticks, our begging bowls dangling from our necks by a chain; one of us was carrying an axe for cutting wood, and the other a spoon to eat whatever food God had blessed us with.

At that moment, standing before a caravansary beside a fountain, my dear friend, nay, my beloved, nay, my brother and I had given ourselves over to the usual argument: "You first please, no you first," we were noisily deferring to each other as to who'd be the first to take up the spoon and eat from the bowl, when a Frank traveler, a strange man, stopped us, gave us each a silver Venetian coin and began to draw our picture.

He was a Frank; of course, he was weird. He situated us right in the center of the page as if we were the very tent of the Sultan, and was depicting us in our half-naked state when I shared with my companion a thought that had just then dawned upon me: To appear like a pair of truly impoverished Kalenderi beggar dervishes, we should roll our eyes back so our pupils look inward, the whites of our eyes facing the world like blind men—and that's exactly what we proceeded to do. In this situation, it's the nature of a dervish to behold the world in his head rather than the world outside; since our heads were full of hashish, the landscape of our minds was more pleasant than what the Frank painter saw.

Meanwhile, the scene outside had grown even worse; we heard the ranting of a Hoja Effendi.

Pray, let us not give the wrong idea. We've now made mention of the respected "Hoja Effendi," but last week in this fine coffeehouse there was a great misunderstanding: This respected "Hoja Effendi" of whom we speak has nothing whatsoever to do with His Excellency Nusret Hoja the cleric from Erzurum, nor with the bastard Husret Hoja, nor with the hoja from Sivas who made it with the Devil atop a tree. Those who interpret everything negatively have said that if His Excellency Hoja Effendi

We Two Dervishes

becomes a target of reproach here once again, they'll cut out the storyteller's tongue and lower this coffeehouse about his head.

One hundred and twenty years ago, there being no coffee then, the respected Hoja, whose story we've begun, was simply steaming with rage.

"Hey, Frank infidel, why are you drawing these two?" he was saying. "These wretched Kalenderi dervishes wander around thieving and begging, they take hashish, drink wine, bugger each other, and as is evident from the way they look, know nothing of performing or reciting prayers, nothing of house, or home, or family; they're nothing but the dregs of this good world of ours. And you, why are you painting this picture of disgrace when there's so much beauty in this great country? Is it to disgrace us?"

"Not at all, it's simply because illustrations of your bad side bring in more money," said the infidel. We two dervishes were dumbfounded at the soundness of the painter's reasoning.

"If it brought you more money, would you paint the Devil in a favorable light?" the Hoja Effendi said, coyly trying to start an argument, but as you can see from this picture, the Venetian was a genuine artist, and he'd focused upon the work before him and the money it'd bring rather than heeding the Hoja's empty prattle.

He did indeed paint us, and then slid us into the leather portfolio on the back of his horse's saddle, and returned to his infidel city. Soon afterward, the victorious armies of the Ottomans conquered and plundered that city on the banks of the Danube, and the two of us ended up coming back this way to Istanbul and the Royal Treasury. From there, copied over and over, we moved from one secret book to another, and finally arrived at this joyous coffeehouse where coffee is drunk like a rejuvenating, invigorating elixir. Now then:

A Brief Treatise on Painting, Death and Our Place in the World

The Hoja Effendi from Konya, whom we've just mentioned, has made the following claim somewhere in one of his sermons, which are written out and collected in a thick tome: Kalenderi dervishes are the unnecessary dross of the world because they don't belong to any of the four categories into which men are divided: 1. notables, 2. merchants, 3. farmers and 4. artists; thus, they are superfluous.

Additionally, he said the following: "These two always tramp about as a pair and always argue about which of them will be the first to eat with their only spoon, and those who don't know that this is a sly allusion to their true concern—who'll be the first to bugger the other—find it amusing and laugh. His Excellency Please-Don't-Take-It-Wrong Hoja has uncovered our secret because he, along with us, the pretty young boys, apprentices and miniaturists, are all fellow travelers on the same path."

The Real Secret

However, the real secret is this: While the Frank infidel was making our picture, he gazed at us so sweetly and with such attention to detail that we took a liking to him and enjoyed being depicted by him. But, he was committing the error of looking at the world with his naked eye and rendering what he saw. Thus, he drew us as if we were blind although we could see just fine, but we didn't mind. Now, we're quite content, indeed. According to the Hoja, we're in Hell; according to some unbelievers we're nothing but decayed corpses and according to you, the intelligent society of miniaturists gathered here, we're a picture, and because we're a picture, we stand here before you as though we were alive and well. After our run-in with the respected Hoja Effendi and after walking from Konya to Sivas in three nights, through eight villages, begging all the way, one night we were beset by such cold and snow that we two dervishes, hugging each other tightly, fell asleep and froze to death. Just before dying I had a dream: I was the subject of a painting that entered Heaven after thousands and thousands of years.

CHAPTER 51

IT IS I, MASTER OSMAN

They tell a story in Bukhara that dates back to the time of Abdullah Khan. This Uzbek Khan was a suspicious ruler, and though he didn't object to more than one artist's brush contributing to the same illustration, he was opposed to painters copying from one another's pages—because this made it impossible to determine which of the artists brazenly copying from one another was to blame for an error. More importantly, after a time, instead of pushing themselves to seek out God's memories within the darkness, pilfering miniaturists would lazily seek out whatever they saw over the shoulder of the artist beside them. For this reason, the Uzbek Khan joyously welcomed two great masters, one from Shiraz in the South, the other from Samarkand in the East, who'd fled from war and cruel shahs to the shelter of his court; however, he forbade the two celebrated talents to look at each other's work, and separated them by giving them small workrooms on opposite ends of his palace, as far from each other as possible. Thus, for exactly thirty-seven years and four months, as if listening to a legend, these two great masters each listened to Abdullah Khan recount the magnificence of the other's never-to-be-seen work, how it differed from or was oddly similar to the other's. Meanwhile, they both lived dying of curiosity about each other's paintings. After the Uzbek Khan's life had run its long tortoiselike course, the two old artists ran to each other's rooms to see the paintings. Later still, sitting upon either edge of a large cushion, holding each other's books on their laps and looking at the pictures that they recognized from Abdullah Khan's fables, both the miniaturists were overcome with great disappointment because the illustrations they saw weren't nearly as spectacular as those they'd anticipated from the stories they'd heard, but instead appeared, much like all the pictures they'd seen in recent years, rather ordinary, pale and hazy. The two great masters didn't then realize that the reason for this haziness was the blindness that had begun to descend upon them, nor did they realize it after both had gone completely blind, rather they attributed the haziness to having been duped by the Khan, and hence they died believing dreams were more beautiful than pictures.

In the dead of night in the cold Treasury room, as I turned pages with frozen fingers and gazed upon the pictures in books that I'd dreamed of for forty years, I knew I was much happier than the artists in this pitiless story from Bukhara. It gave me such a thrill to know, before going blind and passing into the Hereafter, that I was handling the very books whose legends I'd heard about my whole life, and at times I would murmur, "Thank you, God, thank you" when I saw that one of pages I was turning was even more marvelous than its legend.

For instance, eighty years ago Shah Ismail crossed the river and by the sword reconquered Herat and all of Khorasan from the Uzbeks, whereupon he appointed his brother Sam Mirza governor of Herat; to celebrate this joyous occasion, his brother, in turn, had a manuscript prepared, an illuminated version of a book entitled *The Convergence of the Stars,* which recounted a story as witnessed by Emir Hüsrev in the palace of Delhi. According to legend, one illustration in this book showed the two rulers meeting on the banks of a river where they celebrated their victory. Their faces resembled the Sultan of Delhi, Keykubad, and his father, Bughra Khan, the Ruler of Bengal, who were the subjects of the book; but they also resembled the faces of Shah Ismail and his brother Sam Mirza, the men responsible for the book's creation. I was absolutely certain that the heroes of whichever story I conjured while looking at the page would appear there in the sultan's tent, and I thanked God for giving me the chance to see this miraculous page.

In an illustration by Sheikh Muhammad, one of the great masters of the same legendary era, a poor subject whose awe and affection for his sultan had reached the level of pure love was desperately hoping, as he watched the sultan play polo, that the ball would roll toward him so he could grab it and present it to his sovereign. After he'd waited long and patiently, the ball did indeed come to him, and he was depicted handing it to the sultan. As had been described to me thousands of times, the love, awe and submission that a poor subject aptly feels toward a great khan or an exalted monarch, or that a handsome young apprentice feels toward his master, was rendered here with such delicacy and deep compassion, from the extension of the subject's fingers holding the ball to his inability to summon the courage to look at the sovereign's face, that while looking at this page, I knew there was no greater joy in the world than to be apprentice to a great master, and that such submissiveness verging on servility was no less a pleasure than being master to a young, pretty and intelligent apprentice—and I grieved for those who would never know this truth.

I turned the pages, gazing hurriedly but with rapt attention upon thousands of birds, horses, soldiers, lovers, camels, trees and clouds, while the Treasury's happy dwarf, like a shah of elder days given the opportunity to exhibit his riches and wealth, proudly and undauntedly removed volume after volume from chests and placed them before me. From two separate corners of an iron chest stuffed with amazing tomes, common books and disorderly albums, there emerged two extraordinary volumes—one bound in the Shiraz style with a burgundy cover, the other bound in Herat and finished with a dark lacquer in the Chinese fashion—which contained pages so resembling each other that at first I thought they were copies. While I was trying to determine which book was the original and which the copy, I examined the names of the calligraphers on the colophons, looked for hidden signatures, and finally came to the realization, with a shudder, that these two volumes of Nizami were the legendary books that Master Sheikh Ali of Tabriz had made, one for the Khan of the Blacksheep, Jihan Shah, and the other for the Khan of the Whitesheep, Tall Hasan. After he was blinded by the Blacksheep shah to prevent him from making another version of the first volume, the great master artist took refuge with the Whitesheep khan and created a superior copy from memory. To see that the pictures in the second of the legendary books, made when he was blind, were simpler and purer, while the colors in the first volume were more lively and invigorating, reminded me that the memory of the blind exposes the merciless simplicity of life but also deadens its vigor.

Since I myself am a genuine great master, so acknowledged by Almighty Allah, who sees and knows all, I knew that one day I would go blind, but is this what I wanted now? Since His presence could be sensed quite nearby in the exquisite and terrifying darkness of the cluttered Treasury, like a condemned man who wishes to look upon the world one last time before he is beheaded, I asked Him: "Allow me to see all these illustrations and have my fill of them."

As I turned the pages, by the force of God's inscrutable wisdom, I frequently came across legends and matters of blindness. In the famous scene showing Shirin on a countryside outing falling in love with Hüsrev after seeing his picture on the branch of a plane tree, Sheikh Ali Rıza from Shiraz had drawn distinctly all the leaves of the tree one by one so they filled the entire sky. In answer to a fool who saw the work and commented that the true subject of the illustration wasn't the plane tree, Sheikh Ali replied that the true subject wasn't the passion of the beautiful young maiden either, it was the passion of the artist, and to proudly prove his point he attempted to paint the same plane tree with all its leaves on a grain of rice. If the signature hidden beneath the beautiful feet of Shirin's darling lady attendants hadn't misled me, I was of course seeing the magnificent tree made by the blind master on paper—not the tree made on a grain of rice, which he left half finished, having gone blind seven years and three months after he started the task. On another page, Rüstem blinding Alexander with his forked arrow was depicted in the manner of artists who knew the Indian style, so vivaciously and colorfully, that blindness, the ageless sorrow and secret desire of the genuine miniaturist, appeared to the observer as the prologue to a joyous celebration.

My eyes wandered over these pictures and volumes, no less with the excitement of one who wanted to behold for himself these legends he'd heard about for years than with the worry of an old man who sensed he would soon enough never see anything more. There, in the cold Treasury room suffused with a dark red that I'd never seen before—caused by the color of the cloth and dust within the peculiar light of the candles—I would occasionally cry out in admiration, whereupon Black and the dwarf would rush to my side and look over my shoulder at the magnificent page before me. Unable to restrain myself, I'd begin to explain:

"This color red belongs to the great master Mirza Baba Imami from Tabriz, the secret of which he took with him to the grave. He's used it for the edges of the carpet, the red of Alevi allegiance on the Persian Shah's turban, and look, it's here on the belly of the lion on this page and on this pretty boy's caftan. Allah never directly revealed this fine red except when He let the blood of his subjects flow. So that we might wearily strive to find this variety of red that is only visible to the naked eye on man-made cloth and in the pictures of the greatest of masters, God did, however, consign its secret to the rarest of insects living beneath stones," I said and added, "Thanks be to Him who has now revealed it to us."

"Look at this," I said much later, once again unable to refrain from showing them a masterpiece—this one could've belonged in any collection of ghazals, which spoke of love, friendship, spring and happiness. We looked at the trees of springtime blooming in an array of color, the cypresses in a garden reminiscent of Heaven and the elation of the beloveds reclining in that garden as they drank wine and recited poetry; it was as if we in the moldy, dusty and icy Treasury could also smell those spring blossoms and the delicately scented skin of the joyous revelers. "Notice how the same artist who rendered the forearms of the lovers, their beautiful naked feet, the elegance of their stances and the lazy delight of the birds fluttering about them with such sincerity, also made the crude shape of the cypress in the background!" I said, "This is the work of Lütfi of Bukhara whose ill-temper and belligerence caused him to leave each of his illustrations half finished; he fought with every shah and khan claiming that they understood nothing of painting, and he never remained in one city for long. This great master went from one shah's palace to another, from city to city, quarreling all the way, never able to find a ruler whose book was deserving of his talents, until he ended up in the workshop of an inconsequential chieftain who ruled over nothing but bare mountaintops. Claiming that 'the khan's dominions might be small but he knows painting,' he spent the remaining twenty-five years of his life there. Whether he ever knew that this inconsequential lord was blind remains, even today, a subject of conjecture and a source of humor."

"Do you see this page?" I said well into the night, and this time they both rushed to my side, candlesticks aloft. "From the time of Tamerlane's grandchildren to the present, this volume has seen ten owners on its way here from Herat over a span of one hundred fifty years." Using my magnifying lens, the three of us read the signatures, dedications, historical information and names of sultans—who'd strangled one another—filling every corner of the colophon page, pinched together, between and on top of each other: "This volume was completed in Herat, with the help of God, by the hand of Calligrapher Sultan Veli, son of Muzaffer of Herat, in the year of the Hegira 849 for Ismet-üd Dünya, the wife of Muhammad Juki the victorious brother of the Ruler of the World, Baysungur." Later still, we read that the book had passed into the possession of the Whitesheep Sultan Halil, thence to his son Yakup Bey, and thence to the Uzbek sultans in the North, each of whom happily amused himself with the book for a time, removing or adding one or two pictures; beginning with the first owner, they added the faces of their beautiful wives to the illustrations and appended their names proudly to the colophon page; afterward, it passed to Sam Mirza who'd conquered Herat, and he made a present of it, with a separate dedication, for his elder brother, Shah Ismail, who in turn brought it to Tabriz and had it prepared as a gift with yet another dedication. When the denizen of paradise Sultan Selim the Grim defeated Shah Ismail at Chaldiran and plundered the Seven Heavens Palace in Tabriz, the book ended up here in this Treasury in Istanbul, after traveling across deserts, mountains and rivers along with the victorious sultan's soldiers.

How much of an aging master's interest and excitement did Black and the dwarf share? As I opened new volumes and turned their pages, I sensed the profound sorrow of thousands of illustrators from hundreds of cities large and small, each with a distinctive temperament, each painting under the patronage of a different cruel shah, khan or chieftain, each displaying his talent and succumbing to blindness. I felt the pain of the beatings we all received during our long apprenticeships, the blows inflicted with rulers, until our cheeks turned bright red, or with marble polishing stones upon our shaven heads, as I flipped—with humiliation—through the pages of a primitive book that displayed methods and implements of torture. I had no idea what this miserable book was doing in the Ottoman Treasury: Instead of seeing torture as a necessary practice administered before the supervision of a judge to ensure Allah's justice in the world, infidel travelers would convince their coreligionists of our cruelty and evil-heartedness by having dishonorable miniaturists abase themselves and dash off these pictures in exchange for a few gold pieces. I was embarrassed at the obvious depraved pleasure with which this miniaturist had drawn pictures of bastinados, beatings, crucifixions, hangings by the neck or the feet, hookings, impalings, firings from cannon, nailings, stranglings, the cutting of throats, feedings to hungry dogs, whippings, baggings, pressings, soakings in cold water, the plucking of hair, the breaking of fingers, the delicate flayings, the cutting off of noses and the removal of eyes. Only true artists like us who'd suffered throughout our apprenticeships merciless bastinados, random pummelings and fists so that the irritable master who drew a line incorrectly might feel better—not to mention hours of blows from sticks and rulers so that the devil within us would perish to be reborn as the jinn of inspiration—only we could feel such extreme joy by depicting bastinados and tortures, only we could color these implements with the gaiety of coloring a child's kite.

Hundreds of years hence, men looking at our world through the illustrations we've made won't understand anything. Desiring to take a closer look, yet lacking the patience, they might feel the embarrassment, the joy, the deep pain and pleasure of observation I now feel as I examine pictures in this freezing Treasury—but they'll never truly know. As I turned the pages with my old fingers numbed from the cold, my trusty mother-of-pearl-handled magnifying lens and my left eye passed over the pictures like an old stork traversing the earth, little surprised by the view below, yet still astonished to see new things. From these pages withheld from us for years, some of them legendary, I came to know which artist had learned what from whom, in which workshop under which shah's patronage the thing we now call "style" first took shape, which fabled master had worked for whom, and how, for example, the curling Chinese clouds I knew had spread throughout Persia from Herat under Chinese influence were also used in Kazvin. I would occasionally allow myself an exhausted "Aha!"; but an agony lurked deeper within me, a melancholy and regret I can scarcely share with you for the belittled, tormented, pretty, moon-faced, gazelle-eyed, sapling-thin painters—battered by masters—who suffered for their art, yet remained full of excitement and hope, enjoying the affection that developed between them and their masters and their shared love of painting, before succumbing to anonymity and blindness after long years of toil.

It was with such melancholy and regret that I entered this world of fine and delicate feelings, the possibility of whose depiction my soul had quietly forgotten over years of rendering wars and celebrations for Our Sultan. In an album of collected pictures I saw a red-lipped, thin-waisted Persian boy holding a book on his lap exactly as I was holding one at that moment, and it reminded me of what shahs with a weakness for gold and power always forget: The world's beauty belongs to Allah. On the page of another album drawn by a young master from Isfahan, with tears in my eyes, I beheld two marvelous youths in love with each other, and was reminded of the love my own handsome apprentices nourished for painting. A tiny-footed, transparent-skinned, weak and girlish youth had bared a delicate forearm, which aroused in one the desire to kiss it and die, while a cherry-lipped, almond-eyed, sapling-thin, button-nosed beauty of a maiden gazed with wonder—as though viewing three lovely flowers—upon the three small, deep marks of passion the youth had burned onto the inside of that adorable arm to demonstrate the strength of his love and his attachment to her.

Oddly, my heart began to quicken and pound. As had happened sixty years ago in my early apprenticeship, while I was looking at some rather indecent illustrations of handsome marble-skinned boys and slim small-breasted maidens drawn in the black-ink style of Tabriz, beads of sweat accumulated on my forehead. I recalled the passion for painting I felt and the depth of thought I experienced when, a few years after I'd married and taken my first steps toward master status, I saw a lovely angel-faced, almond-eyed, rose-petal-skinned youth brought in as an apprentice candidate. For a moment, I had the strong feeling that painting was not about melancholy and regret but about this desire I felt and that it was the talent of the master artist that first transformed this desire into a love of God and then into a love of the world as God saw it; so strong was this feeling that it caused me to relive with ecstatic delight all the years I'd spent over the drawing board until my back was hunched, all the beatings I'd endured while learning my craft, my dedication to courting blindness through illustration and all the agonies of painting I'd suffered and made others suffer. As if running my eyes over something forbidden, I stared long and silently at this wondrous illustration with the same delight. Much later I was still staring. A teardrop slid from my eye over my cheek into my beard.

When I noticed that one of the candlesticks slowly floating through the Treasury was approaching me, I put the album away and randomly opened one of the volumes the dwarf had recently set beside me. This was a special album prepared for shahs: I saw two deer at the edge of a green copse enamored of each other, with jackals watching them in hostile envy. I turned the page: Chestnut and bay horses that could've been the work of only one of the old masters of Herat—how spectacular they were! I turned the page: A confidently seated governmental official greeted me from a seventy-year-old picture; I couldn't determine who it was from the face because he looked like anybody, or so I thought, yet the air of the painting, the seated man's beard painted in various hues recalled something. My heart beat quickly as I recognized the execution of the magnificent hand in the piece. My heart knew before I did, only he could've drawn such a splendid hand: This was the work of Bihzad. It was as if light were gushing from the painting to my face.

I had seen pictures drawn by the Great Master Bihzad a few times before; perhaps because I hadn't looked at them alone, but in a group of former masters years ago, perhaps because we couldn't be certain whether it was indeed the work of the great Bihzad, I hadn't been as taken as I was now.

The heavy moldy darkness of the Treasury chamber seemed to brighten. This beautifully drawn hand merged in my mind with that thin, magnificent arm branded with signs of love, which I'd just now seen. Again, I praised God for showing me such spectacular beauty before I went blind. How do I know I'll soon be blind? I don't know! I sensed that I could share this intuition of mine with Black, who'd sidled up to me holding a candle and was looking at the page, but something else came out of my mouth.

"Behold the remarkable rendering of the hand," I said. "It's Bihzad."

My hand went of its own will to hold Black's, as if it were holding the hand of one of those soft, velvet-skinned, beautiful apprentice boys, each of whom I'd loved in my youth. His hand was smooth and firm, warmer than my own, delicate and broad, and I was thrilled by the veined side of his wrist. When I was young, I would take an apprentice child's hand into my palm and, before telling him how to hold the brush, I'd gaze with affection into his sweet, frightened eyes. That's how I looked at Black. Reflected in his pupils, I saw the flame of the candle he held aloft. "We miniaturists are brethren," I said, "but now everything is coming to an end."

"How do you mean?"

I said, "Everything is coming to an end" like a great master who longs for blindness, having devoted his years to a lord or a prince, having created masterpieces in his workshop in the style of the ancients, having even ensured that this workshop had its own style, a great master who knows, whenever his patron lord loses his last battle, that new lords will come in the wake of the plundering enemy, disband the workshop, tear apart bound volumes leaving the pages in disarray and belittle and destroy what remains, including the fine details that he long believed in, that were of his own discovery and that he loved like his own children. But I needed to explain this to Black differently.

"This illustration is of the great Poet Abdullah Hatifi," I said. "Hatifi was such a great poet that he simply stayed home while everybody else rushed out and toadied up to Shah Ismail after the king took Herat. In response,

Shah Ismail personally went all the way to his house on the outskirts of the city to see him. We know this is Hatifi, not from Bihzad's rendering of Hatifi's face, but from the writing beneath the illustration, don't we?"

Black looked at me, indicating "yes" with his pretty eyes. "When we look at the face of the poet in the painting," I said, "we see that it could be a face like any other face. If Abdullah Hatifi were here, God rest his soul, we could never hope to recognize him from the face in this picture. However, we could do so relying on the illustration in its entirety: There's something in the manner of the composition, in Hatifi's pose, in the colors, the gilding and the stunning hand rendered by Master Bihzad that at once indicates the picture is of a poet. Meaning precedes form in the world of our art. As we begin to paint in imitation of the Frankish and Venetian masters, as in the book that Our Sultan had commissioned from your Enishte, the domain of meaning ends and the domain of form begins. However, with the Venetian methods . . ."

"My Enishte, may he rest in eternal peace, was murdered," Black said rudely.

I caressed Black's hand, which rested within my own, as if respectfully stroking the tiny hand of a young apprentice who might one day indeed illustrate masterpieces. Quietly and reverently we looked at Bihzad's masterpiece for a time. Later, Black withdrew his hand from mine.

"We passed quickly over the chestnut horses on the previous page without examining their noses," he said.

"There's nothing to them," I said, and turned back to the previous page so he might see for himself: There was nothing extraordinary about the nostrils of the horses.

"When shall we find the horses with peculiar noses?" Black asked like a child.

But, in the middle of the night, toward morning, when we found Shah Tahmasp's legendary *Book of Kings* in an iron chest beneath piles of various shades of green watered silk and drew it forth, Black was curled up fast asleep on a red Ushak carpet, with his well-formed head lying on a velvet pillow embroidered with pearls. Meanwhile, as soon as I laid eyes upon the legendary tome again after so many years, I quickly understood that the day had only just begun for me.

The legendary volume I'd seen only from afar twenty-five years ago was so large and heavy that Jezmi Agha and I had difficulty lifting and carrying it. When I touched the binding, I knew there was wood within the leather. Twenty-five years ago, upon the death of Sultan Süleyman the Magnificent, Shah Tahmasp was so elated to be finally rid of this sultan who'd occupied Tabriz three times, that along with the gift-laden camels he sent to Süleyman's successor, Sultan Selim, he included a spectacular Koran and this volume, the most beautiful of the books in his treasury. First, a Persian ambassadorial delegation three hundred strong took the tome to Edirne where the new sultan spent the winter hunting; after it arrived here in Istanbul along with the other presents carried on camels and mules, Head Illuminator Black Memi and we three young masters went to see the book before it was locked up in the Treasury. Just like the Istanbulites who would rush to see an elephant brought from Hindustan or a giraffe from Africa, we hurried to the palace where I learned from Master Black Memi that the great Master Bihzad, who'd left Herat for Tabriz in his old age, hadn't contributed to this book because he'd gone blind.

For Ottoman miniaturists like us who were astonished by ordinary books with seven or eight illustrations, looking through this volume, which contained 250 large illustrations, was like roaming through an exquisite palace while its inhabitants slept. We stared at the incredibly rich pages with a quiet pious reverence as if beholding the Gardens of Paradise that had appeared miraculously for a fleeting moment. And for the following twenty-five years we discussed this book which remained locked in the Treasury.

I silently opened the thick cover of the *Book of Kings* as if opening a huge palace door. As I turned the pages, each of which made a pleasant rustle, I was overcome by melancholy more than awe.

1. Mindful of the stories suggesting that all the master miniaturists of Istanbul had stolen images from the pages of this book, I couldn't give my full attention to the pictures.
2. Thinking that I might chance upon a hand drawn by Bihzad in some corner, I couldn't devote myself wholeheartedly to the masterpieces that appeared in one of every five or six pictures (how decisively and with what grace did Tahmuras lower his mace upon the heads of the demons and giants, who later, in a time of peace, would teach him the alphabet, Greek and various other languages!).
3. The noses of horses and the presence of Black and the dwarf prevented me from surrendering myself to what I saw.

Naturally, I was disappointed to find myself observing more with my mind than with my heart, despite the great luck of having Allah, in His munificence, grant me the chance to have my fill of this legendary book before the velvet curtain of darkness descended over my eyes—the divine grace bestowed upon all great miniaturists. By the time the light of dawn reached the Treasury, which had gradually begun to resemble an icy tomb, I'd gazed upon each of the 259 pictures in this superlative book. Since I looked with my mind, allow me once more to categorize, as if I were an Arab scholar interested only in reasoning:

1. Nowhere could I locate a horse with nostrils that resembled what the wretched murderer had drawn: Not among the variously colored horses that Rüstem encountered while pursuing horse thieves in Turan; not among Feridun Shah's extraordinary horses which swam the Tigris after the Arab Sultan had denied him permission to do so; not among the gray horses sorrowfully watching Tur's treachery in beheading his younger brother Iraj, of whom he was jealous because their father, while doling out his territory, gave the best country, Persia, and far away China to Iraj, while leaving only the western lands to Tur; not among the horses of the heroic armies of Alexander that included Khazars, Egyptians, Berbers and Arabs, all equipped with armor, iron shields, indestructible swords and glimmering helmets; not the fabled horse that killed Shah Yazdgird—whose nose bled perpetually as a result of the divine punishment for rebelling against God's fate—by trampling him on the shores of the green lake whose restorative waters eased his affliction; and not among the hundreds of mythical and perfect horses all drawn by six or seven miniaturists. Yet, there was still more than one entire day ahead of me in which to examine the other books in the Treasury.

2. There's a claim that has been a persistent topic of gossip among master illuminators for the last twenty-five years: With the express permission of the Sultan, an illustrator entered this forbidden Treasury, found this spectacular book, opened it and by candlelight copied into his sketchbook examples of a number of exquisite horses, trees, clouds, flowers, birds, gardens and scenes of war and love for later use in his work . . . Whenever an artist created an amazing and exceptional piece, jealousy prompted such gossip from the others, who sought to belittle the picture as nothing but Persian work from Tabriz. Back then, Tabriz was not Ottoman territory. When such slander was directed at me, I felt justifiably angry, yet secretly proud; but when I heard the same accusation about others, I believed it. Now, I sadly realized that in

some strange way the four of us miniaturists who'd looked at this book once twenty-five years ago ingrained its images into our memories, and since then, we've recalled, transformed, altered and painted them into the books of Our Sultan. My spirits were dampened not by the mercilessness of overly suspicious sultans who wouldn't take such books out of their treasuries and show them to us, but by the narrowness of our own world of painting. Whether it be the great masters of Herat or the new masters of Tabriz, Persian artists had made more extraordinary illustrations, more masterpieces, than we Ottomans.

Like a lightning flash, it occurred to me how appropriate it'd be if two days hence all my miniaturists and I were put to torture; using the point of my penknife I ruthlessly scraped away the eyes beneath my hand in the picture that lay open before me. It was the account of the Persian scholar who learned chess simply by looking at a chess set brought by the ambassador from Hindustan, before defeating the Hindu master at his own game! A Persian lie! One by one, I scraped away the eyes of the chess players and of the shah and his men who were watching them. Flipping back through the pages, I also pitilessly gouged out the eyes of the shahs who battled mercilessly, of the soldiers of imposing armies bedecked in magnificent armor and of severed heads lying on the ground. After doing the same to three pages, I slid my penknife back into my sash.

My hands trembled, but I didn't feel so bad. Did I now feel what so many lunatics felt after committing this strange act whose results I encountered frequently during my fifty-year tenure as a painter? I wanted nothing more than blood to flow onto the pages of this book from the eyes I had blinded.

3. This brings me to the torment and consolation awaiting me at the end of my life. No part of this excellent book, which Shah Tahmasp had completed by spurring Persia's most masterful artists for ten years, had seen the touch of the great Bihzad's pen, and his excellent rendering of hands was nowhere to be found. This fact confirmed that Bihzad was blind in the last years of his life, when he fled from Herat—then a city out of favor—to Tabriz. So, I once again decided happily that after he attained the perfection of the old masters by working his entire life, the great master blinded himself to avoid tainting his painting with the desires of any other workshop or shah.

Just then, Black and the dwarf opened a thick volume they were carrying and placed it before me.

"No, this isn't it," I said without being contrary. "This is a Mongol *Book of Kings*: The iron horses of Alexander's iron cavalry were filled with naphtha and set aflame like lamps, before being set against the enemy with flames shooting from their nostrils."

We stared at the flaming army of iron copied from Chinese paintings.

"Jezmi Agha," I said, "we later depicted in the *Chronicle of Sultan Selim* the gifts that Shah Tahmasp's Persian ambassadors, who also presented this book, brought with them twenty-five years ago . . ."

He swiftly located the *Chronicle of Sultan Selim* and placed it in front of me. Paired with the vibrantly colored page that showed the ambassadors presenting the *Book of Kings* along with the other gifts to Sultan Selim, my eyes found, among the gifts which were listed one by one, what I'd long ago read but had forgotten because it was so incredible:

> *The turquoise-and-mother-of-pearl-handled golden plume needle which the Venerated Talent of Herat, Master of Master Illuminators Bihzad, used in the act of blinding his exalted self.*

I asked the dwarf where he found the *Chronicle of Sultan Selim*. I followed him through the dusty darkness of the Treasury, meandering between chests, piles of cloth and carpet, cabinets and beneath stairways. I noticed how our shadows, now shrinking, now enlarging, slipped over shields, elephant tusks and tiger skins. In one of the adjoining rooms, this one also suffused with the same strange redness of cloth and velvet, beside the iron chest whence emerged the *Book of Kings*, amid other volumes, cloth sheets embroidered with silver and gold wire, raw and unpolished Ceylon stone, and ruby-studded daggers, I saw some of the other gifts that Shah Tahmasp had sent: silk carpets from Isfahan, an ivory chess set and an object that immediately caught my attention—a pen case decorated with Chinese dragons and branches with a mother-of-pearl-inlaid rosette obviously from the time of Tamerlane. I opened the case and out came the subtle scent of burned paper and rosewater; within rested the turquoise-and-mother-of-pearl-handled golden needle used to fasten plumes to turbans. I took up the needle and returned to my spot like a specter.

Alone again, I placed the needle that Master Bihzad had used to blind himself upon the open page of the *Book of Kings* and gazed at it. It wasn't the needle he'd blinded himself with that made me shudder, but seeing an object he'd taken into his miraculous hands.

Why did Shah Tahmasp send this terrifying needle with the book he'd presented to Sultan Selim? Was it because this Shah, who as a child was a student of Bihzad's and a patron of artists in his youth, had changed in his old age, distancing poets and artists from his inner circle and giving himself over entirely to faith and worship? Was this the reason he was willing to relinquish this exquisite book, which the greatest of masters had labored over for ten years? Had he sent this needle so all would know that the great artist was blinded of his own volition or, as was rumored for a time, to make the statement that whosoever beheld the pages of this book even once would no longer wish to see anything else in this world? In any event, this volume was no longer considered a masterpiece by the Shah, who felt poignant regret, afraid that he'd committed a sacrilege through his youthful love of illustrating, as happened with many rulers in their old age.

I was reminded of stories told by spiteful illuminators who'd grown old to find their dreams unfulfilled: As the armies of the Blacksheep ruler, Jihan Shah, were poised to enter Shiraz, Ibn Hüsam, the city's legendary Head Illuminator, declared, "I refuse to paint in any other way," and had his apprentice blind him with a hot iron. Among the miniaturists that the armies of Sultan Selim the Grim brought back to Istanbul after the defeat of Shah Ismail, the capture of Tabriz and the plunder of the Seven Heavens Palace was an old Persian master who it was rumored blinded himself with medicines because he believed he could never bring himself to paint in the Ottoman style—not as the result of an illness he'd had on the road as some claimed. To set an example for them, I used to tell my illuminators in their moments of frustration how Bihzad had blinded himself.

Was there no other recourse? If a master miniaturist made use of the new methods here and there in out-of-the-way places, couldn't he then, if only a little, save the entire workshop and the styles of the old masters?

There was a dark stain on the extremely sharp point of the elegantly tapered plume needle, yet my weary eyes couldn't determine whether it was blood or not. Lowering the magnifying lens, as if beholding a melancholy depiction of love with a matching sense of melancholy, I looked at the needle for a long time. I tried to imagine how Bihzad could've done it. I'd heard that one doesn't go blind immediately; the velvety darkness descends slowly, sometimes after days, sometimes after months, as with old men who go blind naturally.

I'd caught sight of it while passing into the next room; I stood and looked, yes, there it was: an ivory mirror with a twisted handle and thick ebony frame, its length nicely embellished with script. I sat down again and gazed at my own eyes. How beautifully the flame of the candle danced in my pupils—which had witnessed my hand paint for sixty years.

"How had Master Bihzad done it?" I asked myself once more.

Never once taking my eyes off the mirror, with the practiced movements of a woman applying kohl to her eyelids, my hand found the needle on its own. Without hesitation, as if making a hole at the end of an ostrich egg soon to be embellished, I bravely, calmly and firmly pressed the needle into the pupil of my right eye. My innards sank, not because I felt what I was doing, but because I saw what I was doing. I pushed the needle into my eye to the depth of a quarter the length of a finger, then removed it.

In the couplet worked into the frame of the mirror, the poet had wished the observer eternal beauty and wisdom—and eternal life to the mirror itself.

Smiling, I did the same to my other eye.

For a long while I didn't move. I stared at the world—at everything.

As I'd surmised, the colors of the world did not darken, but seemed to bleed ever so gently into one another. I could still more or less see.

The pale light of the sun fell over the red and oxblood cloth of the Treasury. In the accustomed ceremony, the Head Treasurer and his men broke the seal and opened the lock and the door. Jezmi Agha changed the chamber pots, lamps and brazier, brought in fresh bread and dried mulberries and announced to the others that we would continue searching for the horses with oddly drawn nostrils within Our Sultan's books. What could be more exquisite than looking at the world's most beautiful pictures while trying to recollect God's vision of the world?

CHAPTER 52

I AM CALLED BLACK

When the Head Treasurer and the chief officers opened the portal with great ceremony my eyes were so accustomed to the velvety red aura of the Treasury rooms that the early morning winter sunlight filtering in from the courtyard of the Royal Private Quarters of the Enderun seemed terrifying. I stood dead still, as did Master Osman himself: If I moved, it seemed, the clues we sought in the moldy, dusty and tangible air of the Treasury might escape.

With curious amazement, as if seeing some magnificent object for the first time, Master Osman stared at the light cascading toward us between the heads of the Treasury chiefs lined up in rows on either side of the open portal.

The night before, I watched him as he turned the pages of the *Book of Kings*. I noticed this same expression of astonishment pass over his face as his shadow, cast upon the wall, trembled faintly, his head carefully sank down toward his magnifying lens, and his lips first contorted delicately, as if preparing to reveal a pleasant secret, then twitched as he gazed in awe at an illustration.

After the portal was shut again, I wandered impatiently between rooms ever more restless; I thought nervously that we wouldn't have time to cull enough information from the books in the Treasury. I sensed that Master Osman couldn't focus adequately on his task, and I confessed my misgivings to him.

Like a genuine master grown accustomed to caressing his apprentices, he held my hand in a pleasing way. "Men like us have no choice but to try to see the world the way God does and to resign ourselves to His justice," he said. "And here, among these pictures and possessions, I have the strong sensation that these two things are beginning to converge: As we approach God's vision of the world, His justice approaches us. See here, the needle Master Bihzad blinded himself with..."

Master Osman callously told the story of the needle, and I scrutinized the extremely sharp point of this disagreeable object beneath the magnifying glass which he lowered so I might better see; a pinkish film covered its tip.

"The old masters," Master Osman said, "would suffer pangs of conscience about changing their talent, colors and methods. They'd consider it dishonorable to see the world one day as an Eastern shah commanded, the next, as a Western ruler did—which is what the artists of our day do."

His eyes were neither trained on mine nor upon the pages in front of him. It seemed as though he were gazing at a distant unattainable whiteness. In a page of the *Book of Kings* lying open before him, Persian and Turanian armies clashed with all their force. As horses fought shoulder to shoulder, enraged heroic warriors drew their swords and slaughtered one another with the color and joy of a festival, their armor pierced by the lances of the cavalry, their heads and arms severed, their bodies hacked apart or cloven in two, strewn all over the field.

"When the great masters of old were forced to adopt the styles of victors and imitate their miniaturists, they preserved their honor by using a needle to heroically bring on the blindness that the labors of painting would've caused in time. Yes, before the pureness of God's darkness fell over their eyes like a divine reward, they'd stare at a masterpiece ceaselessly for hours or even days, and because they stubbornly stared out of bowed heads, the meaning and world of those pictures—spotted with blood dripping from their eyes—would take the place of all the evil they suffered, and as their eyes ever so slowly clouded over they'd approach blindness in peace. Do you have any idea which illustration I'd want to stare at till I'd attained the divine blackness of the blind?"

Like a man trying to recall a childhood memory, he fixed his eyes, whose pupils seemed to shrink as their whites expanded, on a distant place beyond the walls of the Treasury.

"The scene, rendered in the style of the old masters of Herat, wherein Hüsrev, burning madly with love, rides his horse to the foot of Shirin's summer palace and waits!"

Perhaps he'd now go on to describe that picture as if reciting a melancholy poem eulogizing the blindness of the old masters. "My great master, my dear sire," on a strange impulse, I interrupted him, "what I want to stare at for all eternity is my beloved's delicate face. It's been three days since we wed. I've thought of her longingly for twelve years. The scene wherein Shirin falls in love with Hüsrev after seeing his picture reminds me of none other than her."

There was a wealth of expression on Master Osman's face, curiosity perhaps, but it had to do neither with my story nor with the bloody battle scene before him. He seemed to be expecting good news in which he could gradually take comfort. When I was sure he wasn't looking at me, I abruptly grabbed the plume needle and walked away.

In a dark part of the third of the Treasury rooms, the one abutting the baths, there was a corner cluttered with hundreds of strange clocks sent as presents from Frankish kings and sovereigns; when they stopped working, as they usually did within a short time, they were set aside here. Withdrawing to this room, I carefully scrutinized the needle that Master Osman claimed Bihzad had used to blind himself.

By the red daylight filtering inside, reflecting off the casings, crystal faces and diamonds of the dusty and broken clocks, the golden tip of the needle, coated with a pinkish liquid, occasionally shimmered. Had the legendary Master Bihzad actually blinded himself with this implement? Had Master Osman done the same terrible thing to himself? The expression of an impish Moroccan, the size of a finger and colorfully painted, attached to the mechanism of one of the large clocks, seemed to say "Yes!" Evidently, when the clock was working, this man in the Ottoman turban would merrily nod his head as the hour tolled—a small joke on the part of the Hapsburg king who sent it, and his skillful clockmaker, for the amusement of Our Sultan and the women of His harem.

I looked through quite a few very mediocre books: As the dwarf confirmed, these were among the effects of pashas whose properties and belongings were confiscated after they were beheaded. So many pashas had been executed that these volumes were without number. With a pitiless joy, the dwarf declared that any pasha so intoxicated by his own wealth and power as to forget he was a subject of the Sultan and to have a book made in his own honor, illuminated with gold leaf as if he were a monarch or a shah, well deserved to be executed and have his possessions expropriated. Even in these volumes, some of which were albums, illuminated manuscripts or illustrated collections of poetry, whenever I came across a version of Shirin falling in love with Hüsrev's picture, I stopped and stared.

The picture within a picture, that is, the picture of Hüsrev which Shirin encountered during her countryside outing, was never rendered in detail, not because miniaturists couldn't adequately depict something so small—many had the dexterity and finesse to paint upon fingernails, grains of rice or even strands of hair. Why then hadn't they drawn the face and features of Hüsrev—the object of Shirin's love—in enough detail so that he might be recognized? Sometime in the afternoon, perhaps to forget my hopelessness, and thinking, as I leafed through a disorderly album I'd chanced upon, that I'd broach such questions to Master Osman, I was struck by the image of a horse in a picture of a bridal procession painted on cloth. My heart skipped a beat.

There before me was a horse with peculiar nostrils carrying a coquettish bride. The beast was looking at me out of the picture. It was as though the magical horse were on the verge of whispering a secret to me. As if in a dream, I wanted to shout, but my voice was silent.

In one continuous movement, I collected up the volume and ran among the objects and chests to Master Osman, laying the page open before him.

He looked down at the picture.

When no spark of recognition appeared on his face, I grew impatient. "The nostrils of the horse are exactly like those made for my Enishte's book," I exclaimed.

He lowered his magnifying lens over the horse. He bent down so far, bringing his eye to the lens and picture, that his nose nearly touched the page.

I Am Called Black

I couldn't stand the silence. "As you can see, this isn't a horse made in the style and method of the horse drawn for my Enishte's book," I said, "but the nose is the same. The artist attempted to see the world the way the Chinese do." I fell quiet. "It's a wedding procession. It resembles a Chinese picture, but the figures aren't Chinese, they're our people."

The master's lens seemed to be flat against the page, and his nose was flat against the lens. In order to see, he made use of not only his eyes, but his head, the muscles of his neck, his aged back and his shoulders with all his might. Silence.

"The nostrils of the horse are cut open," he said later, breathless.

I leaned my head against his. Cheek to cheek we stared at the nostrils for a long long time. I sadly realized that not only were the horse's nostrils cut, but Master Osman was having difficulty seeing them.

"You do see it, don't you?"

"Only very little," he said. "Describe the picture."

"If you ask me, this is a melancholy bride," I said mournfully. "She's mounted on a gray horse with its nostrils cut open, she's on her way to be wed, with her companions and an escort of guards who are strangers to her. The faces of the guards, their harsh expressions, intimidating black beards, furrowed eyebrows, long thick mustaches, heavy frames, robes of simple thin cloth, thin shoes, headdresses of bear fur, their battle-axes and scimitars indicate that they belong to the Whitesheep Turkmen of Transoxiana. Perhaps the pretty bride—who appears to be on a long journey to judge by the fact she's traveling with her bridesmaid at night by the light of oil lamps and torches—is a melancholy Chinese princess."

"Or perhaps we only think the bride is Chinese now, because the miniaturist, to emphasize her flawless beauty, whitened her face as the Chinese do and painted her with slanted eyes," said Master Osman.

"Whoever she might be, my heart aches for this sad beauty, traveling the steppe in the middle of the night accompanied by grim-faced foreign guards, heading to a strange land and a husband she's never seen," I said. Then I immediately added, "How shall we determine who our miniaturist is from the clipped nostrils of the horse she rides?"

"Turn the pages of the album and tell me what you see," said Master Osman.

Just then, we were joined by the dwarf whom I'd seen sitting on the chamber pot as I was running to bring the volume to Master Osman; the three of us looked at the pages together.

We saw strikingly beautiful Chinese maidens depicted in the style of our melancholy bride gathered together in a garden playing a peculiar-looking lute. We saw Chinese houses, morose-looking caravans heading out on long journeys, vistas of the steppes as beautiful as old memories. We saw gnarled trees rendered in the Chinese style, their spring blossoms in full bloom, and nightingales tipsy with elation perched on their branches. We saw princes in the Khorasan style seated in their tents holding forth on poetry, wine and love; spectacular gardens; and handsome nobles, with magnificent falcons clutching their forearms, hunting bolt upright astride their exquisite horses. Then, it was as if the Devil had passed into the pages; we could sense that the evil in the illustrations was most often reason itself. Had the miniaturist added an ironic touch to the actions of the heroic prince who slew the dragon with his gigantic lance? Had he gloated at the poverty of the unfortunate peasants expecting comfort from the sheikh in their midst? Was it more pleasurable for him to draw the sad, empty eyes of dogs locked in coitus or to apply a devilish red to the open mouths of the women laughing scornfully at the poor beasts? Then we saw the miniaturist's devils themselves: These weird creatures resembled the jinns and giants the old masters of Herat and the artists of the *Book of Kings* drew frequently; yet the sardonic talent of the miniaturist made them more sinister, aggressive and human in form. We laughed watching these terrifying devils, the size of a man yet with misshapen bodies, branching horns and feline tails. As I turned the pages, these naked devils with bushy brows, round faces, bulging eyes, pointed teeth, sharp nails and the dark wrinkled skin of old men began to beat each other and wrestle, to steal a great horse and sacrifice it to their gods, to leap and play, to cut down trees, to spirit away beautiful princesses in their palanquins and to capture dragons and sack treasuries. I mentioned that in this volume, which had seen the touch of many different brushes, the miniaturist known as Black Pen, who'd made the devils, also drew Kalenderi dervishes with shaved heads, ragged clothes, iron chains and staffs, and Master Osman had me one by one repeat their similarities, listening closely to what I said.

"Cutting open the nostrils of horses so they might breathe easier and travel farther is a centuries-old Mongol custom," he said later. "Hulagu Khan's armies conquered all of Arabia, Persia and China with their horses. When they entered Baghdad, put its inhabitants to the sword, plundered it and tossed all its books into the Tigris, as we know, the famous calligrapher, and later, illuminator Ibn Shakir fled the city and the slaughter, heading north on the road by which the Mongol horsemen had come, instead of south along with everyone else. At that time, no one made illustrations because the Koran forbade them, and painters weren't taken seriously. We owe the greatest secrets of our noble occupation to Ibn Shakir, the patron saint and master of all miniaturists: the vision of the world from a minaret, the persistence of a horizon line visible or invisible, and the depiction of all things from clouds to insects the way the Chinese envisaged them, in curling, lively and optimistic colors. I've heard that he studied the nostrils of horses in order to keep himself moving northward during that legendary journey into the heartland of the Mongol hordes. However, as far as I've seen and heard, none of the horses he drew in Samarkand, which he reached after a year's travel on foot undaunted by snow and severe weather, had clipped nostrils. For him, perfect dream horses were not the sturdy, powerful, victorious horses of the Mongols that he came to know in his adulthood; they were the elegant Arab horses that he'd sorrowfully left behind in his happy youth. This is why for me the strange nose of the horse made for Enishte's book brought to mind neither Mongol horses nor this custom the Mongols spread to Khorasan and Samarkand."

As he spoke, Master Osman looked now at the book and now at us, as if he could see only those things he conjured in his mind's eye.

"Besides horses with clipped noses and Chinese painting, the devils in this book are another thing brought with the Mongol hordes to Persia and thence all the way here to Istanbul. You've probably heard how these demons are ambassadors of evil dispatched by dark forces from deep beneath the ground to snatch away human lives and whatever we deem valuable and how they're bent on carrying us off to their underworld of blackness and death. In this underground realm everything, whether cloud, tree, object, dog or book, has a soul and speaks."

"Quite so," said the elderly dwarf. "As Allah is my witness, some nights when I'm locked in here, not only the spirits of the clocks, the Chinese plates and the crystal bowls that chime constantly anyway, but the spirits of all the rifles, swords, shields and bloody helmets grow restless and begin to converse in such a ruckus that the Treasury becomes the swarming field of an apocalyptic battle."

"The Kalenderi dervishes, whose pictures we've seen, brought this belief from Khorasan to Persia, and later all the way to Istanbul," said Master Osman. "As Sultan Selim the Grim was plundering the Seven Heavens Palace after defeating Shah Ismail, Bediüzzaman Mirza—a descendant of Tamerlane—betrayed Shah Ismail and together with the Kalenderis that constituted his followers, joined the Ottomans. In the train of the Denizen of Paradise, Sultan Selim, as he returned through winter cold and snow to Istanbul, were two wives of Shah Ismail, whom he'd routed at Chaldiran. They were lovely women with white skin and slanting almond eyes, and with them came all the books preserved in the Seven Heavens Palace library, books left by the former masters of Tabriz, the Mongols, the Inkhanids, the Jelayirids and the Blacksheep, and taken as plunder by the defeated shah from the Uzbeks, the Persians and the Timurids. I shall stare at these books until Our Sultan and the Head Treasurer remove me from here."

Yet by now his eyes showed the same lack of direction that one sees in the blind. He held his mother-of-pearl-handled magnifying glass more out of habit than to see. We fell silent. Master Osman requested that the dwarf, who listened to his entire account as though to some bitter tale, once again locate and bring him a volume whose binding he described in detail. Once the dwarf had gone away, I naively asked my master:

"So then, who's responsible for the horse illustration in my Enishte's book?"

"Both the horses in question have clipped nostrils," he said, "regardless of whether it was done in Samarkand or, as I said, in Transoxiana, the one you've found in this album is rendered in the Chinese style. As for the beautiful horse of Enishte's book, that was made in the Persian style like the wondrous horses drawn by the masters of Herat. Indeed, it is an elegant illustration whose equal would be difficult to find anywhere! It's a horse of artistry, not a Mongol horse."

"But its nostrils are cut open like a genuine Mongol horse," I whispered.

"It's apparent that two hundred years ago when the Mongols retreated and the reign of Tamerlane and his descendants began, one of the old masters in Herat drew an exquisite horse whose nostrils were indeed cut open—influenced either by a Mongol horse that he'd seen or by another miniaturist who'd made a Mongol horse with clipped nostrils. No one knows for certain on which page in which book and for which shah it was made. But I'm sure that the book and picture were greatly admired and praised—who knows, maybe by the sultan's favorite in the harem—and that they were legendary for a time! I'm also convinced that for this very reason all the mediocre miniaturists, muttering enviously to themselves, imitated this horse and multiplied its image. In this fashion, the wonderful horse with its nostrils gradually became a model of form ingrained in the minds of the artists in that workshop. Years later, after their rulers were defeated in battle, these painters, like somber women headed to other harems, found new shahs and princes to work for in new countries, and carried with them, stowed in their memories, the image of horses whose nostrils were elegantly cut open. Perhaps under the influence of different styles and different masters in different workshops, many of the artists never made use of and eventually forgot this unusual image which nonetheless remained preserved in a corner of their minds. Others, however, in the new workshops they joined, not only drew elegant clipped-nosed horses, they also taught their pretty apprentices to do the same with the encouragement that 'this is how the old masters used to do it.' So then, in this manner, even after the Mongols and their hardy horses retreated from the lands of the Persians and Arabs, even centuries after new lives had begun in ravaged and burned cities, some painters continued drawing horses this way, believing it was a standard form. I'm also sure that others still, completely unaware of the conquering Mongol cavalry and the clipped noses of their steeds, draw horses the way we do in our workshop, insisting that this too is 'a standard form.'"

"My dear master," I said, overwhelmed with awe, "as we hoped, your 'courtesan method' truly did produce an answer. It seems that each artist also bears his own hidden signature."

"Not each artist, but each workshop," he said with pride. "And not even each workshop. In certain miserable workshops, as in certain miserable families, everyone speaks in a different voice for years without acknowledging that happiness is born of harmony, and that as a matter of course, harmony becomes happiness. Some painters try to illustrate like the Chinese, some like the Turkmen and some like they do in Shiraz, fighting for years on end, never attaining a happy union—like a discontented husband and wife."

I saw that pride quite definitely ruled his face; the cross expression of a man who wanted to be all powerful had now replaced the look of the morose, pitiable old man that I'd seen him wear for so long.

"My dear master," I said, "over a period of twenty years here in Istanbul, you've united various artists from the four corners of the world, men of all natures and temperaments, in such harmony that you've ended up creating and defining the Ottoman style."

Why did the awe that I'd felt wholeheartedly only a short time ago give way to hypocrisy as I voiced my feelings? For our praise of a man, whose talent and mastery genuinely astounds us, to be sincere, must he lose most of his authority and influence and become slightly pathetic?

"Now then, where's that dwarf hiding?" he said.

He said this the way powerful men who are pleased by flattery and praise but recollect vaguely that they ought not be would—as though he wished to change the subject.

"Despite being a great master of Persian legends and styles, you've created a distinct world of illustration worthy of Ottoman glory and strength," I whispered. "You're the one who brought to art the power of the Ottoman sword, the optimistic colors of Ottoman victory, the interest in and attention to objects and implements, and the freedom of a comfortable lifestyle. My dear master, it's been the greatest honor of my life to look at these masterpieces by the old legendary masters with you . . ."

For a long time I whispered on in this manner. Within the icy darkness and cluttered disarray of the Treasury, which resembled a recently abandoned battlefield, our bodies were so close that my whispering became an expression of intimacy.

Later, as with certain blind men who can't control their facial expressions, Master Osman's eyes assumed the look of an old man lost in pleasure. I praised the old master at length, now with heartfelt emotion, now shuddering with the inner revulsion I felt toward the blind.

He held my hand with his cold fingers, caressed my forearm and touched my face. His strength and age seemed to pass through his fingers into me. I, again, thought of Shekure who awaited me at home.

Standing still that way for a time, pages opened before us, it was as if my lavish praise and his self-admiration and self-pity had so fatigued us that we were resting. We'd become embarrassed of each other.

"Where's that dwarf gone to?" he asked again.

I was certain that the wily dwarf was hiding in some niche watching us. As if I were searching him out, I turned my shoulders right and left, but kept my eyes trained attentively on Master Osman. Was he truly blind or was he trying to convince the world, including himself, that he was blind? I'd heard that some untalented and incompetent old masters from Shiraz feigned blindness in their old age to curry respect and to prevent others from mentioning their failures.

"I would like to die here," he said.

"My great master, my dear sir," I fawned, "in this age when value is placed not on painting but on the money one can earn from it, not on the old masters but on imitators of the Franks, I so well understand what you're saying that it brings tears to my eyes. Yet it is also your duty to protect your master illustrators from their enemies. Please tell me, what conclusions have you drawn from the 'courtesan method'? Who is the miniaturist who painted that horse?"

I Am Called Black

"Olive."

He'd said this with such ease that I had no chance to be surprised.

He fell silent.

"But I'm also certain that Olive wasn't the one who murdered your Enishte or unfortunate Elegant Effendi," he said calmly. "I believe that Olive drew the horse because he's the one who's most bound to the old masters, who knows most intimately the legends and styles of Herat and whose master-apprentice genealogy stretches back to Samarkand. Now I know you won't ask me, 'Why haven't we encountered these nostrils in the other horses that Olive drew over the years?' since I've already mentioned how at times a detail—the wing of a bird, the way a leaf is attached to a tree—can be preserved in memory for generations, passing from master to apprentice, and yet might not manifest on the page due to the influence of a moody or rigid master or on account of the particular tastes and whims of a particular workshop or sultan. So then, this is the horse that dear Olive, in his childhood, learned directly from the Persian masters without ever being able to forget it. The fact that the horse suddenly appeared for the sake of Enishte's book is a cruel trick of Allah's. Hadn't all of us taken the old masters of Herat as our models? Just like the Turkmen illustrators for whom the face of a beautiful woman meant one with Chinese features, didn't we think exclusively of the masterpieces of Herat when we thought of well-executed pictures? We are all their devoted admirers. Nourishing all great art is the Herat of Bihzad, and supporting this Herat are the Mongol horsemen and the Chinese. Why should Olive, thoroughly bound to the legends of Herat, murder poor Elegant Effendi, who was even more bound—even blindly devoted—to the same old methods?"

"Who then?" I said. "Butterfly?"

"Stork!" he said. "This is what I know in my heart of hearts, for I am well acquainted with his greed and fury. Listen, in all probability while gilding for your Enishte, who foolishly and clumsily imitated Frankish methods, poor Elegant Effendi came to believe that this venture might somehow be dangerous. Since he was enough of a dolt to listen earnestly to the drivel of that foolish preacher from Erzurum—unfortunately, masters of gilding, though closer to God than painters, are also boring and stupid—and moreover, because he knew your silly Enishte's book was an important project of the Sultan, his fears and doubts clashed: Should he believe in his Sultan or in the preacher from Erzurum? Any other time this unfortunate child, whom I knew like the back of my hand, would've come to me about a dilemma that was eating away at him. But even he, with his bird brain, knew very well that the act of gilding for your Enishte, that mimic of the Franks, amounted to a betrayal of me and our guild; and so he sought another confidant. He confided in the wily and ambitious Stork and made the mistake of letting himself be awed by the intellect and morality of a man whose talent impressed him. I've seen plenty of times how Stork manipulated Elegant Effendi by taking advantage of the poor gilder's admiration. Whatever argument took place between them, it resulted in Elegant Effendi's murder at Stork's hands. And since the deceased long ago confided his worries to the Erzurumis, they, in a fit of vengeance and to demonstrate their power, went on to kill your Frankophile Enishte, whom they held responsible for the death of their companion. I can't say that I'm all that sorry about the whole matter. Years ago, your Enishte duped Our Sultan into having a Venetian painter—his name was Sebastiano—make a portrait of His Excellency in the Frankish style as if He were an infidel king. Not satisfied with that, in a disgraceful affront to my dignity, he had this shameful work given to me as a model to be copied; and out of dire fear of Our Sultan, I dishonorably copied that picture which was made using infidel methods. Had I not been forced to do that, perhaps I could grieve for your Enishte, and today help find the scoundrel who killed him. But my concern is not for your Enishte, it's for my workshop. Your Enishte is responsible for the way my master miniaturists—whom I love more than if they were my own children, whom I trained with doting attention for twenty-five years—betrayed me and our entire artistic tradition; he's to blame for their enthusiastic imitation of European masters with the justification that 'it is the will of Our Sultan.' Each of those disgraceful masters deserves nothing but torture! If we, the society of miniaturists, learn to serve foremost our own talent and art instead of Our Sultan who provides us with work, we shall have earned entry through the Gates of Heaven. Now then, I'd like to study this book alone."

Master Osman uttered this last statement like the last wish of a disconsolate weary pasha who was responsible for military defeat and condemned to beheading. He opened the book Jezmi Agha placed before him and in a scolding voice ordered the dwarf to turn to the pages he wanted. With this accusatory tone, he instantly became the Head Illuminator with whom the entire workshop was familiar.

I withdrew into a corner among cushions embroidered with pearls, rusty-barreled rifles with jewel-studded butts and cabinets, and began eyeing Master Osman. The doubt gnawing away at me spread throughout my entire being: If he wished to stop the creation of Our Sultan's book, it made perfect sense that Master Osman might've orchestrated the murders of poor Elegant Effendi and, afterward, of my Enishte—I reprimanded myself for just now feeling such awe toward him. On the other hand, I couldn't restrain myself from feeling profound respect for this great master who now gave himself over to the picture before him and, blind or half blind, was peering at it closely as if looking with the countless wrinkles of his old face. It dawned on me that to preserve the old style and the regimen of the miniaturists' workshop, to rid himself of Enishte's book and to become again the Sultan's only favorite, he would gladly surrender any one of his master miniaturists, and me as well, to the torturers of the Commander of the Imperial Guard. I furiously began to think of freeing myself from the love that bound me to him over the last two days.

Much later, I was still completely confused. I stared randomly at the illuminated pages of the volumes I extracted from chests solely to appease the demons that had risen within me and to distract my jinns of indecision.

How many men and women had fingers in their mouths! This was used as a gesture of surprise in all the workshops from Samarkand to Baghdad over the last two hundred years. As the hero Keyhüsrev, cornered by his enemies, safely crossed the rushing Oxus River aided by his black charger and Allah, the wretched raftsman and his oarsman, who refused to offer him safe passage on their raft each had a finger in his mouth. An astonished Hüsrev's finger remained in his mouth as he saw for the first time the beauty of Shirin, whose skin was like moonlight as she bathed in the once glimmering lake whose silver leaf had tarnished. I spent even more time carefully examining the gorgeous women of the harem who, with fingers in their mouths, stood behind half-opened palace doors, at the inaccessible windows of castle towers and peered from behind curtains. As Tejav, defeated by the armies of Persia to lose his crown, was fleeing the battlefield, Espinuy, a beauty of beauties and his harem favorite, watched with sorrow and shock from a palace window, finger in mouth, begging him with her eyes not to abandon her to the enemy. As Joseph, arrested under Züleyha's false accusation that he raped her, was being taken to his cell, she stared from her window, a finger in her beautiful mouth in a show of devilishness and lust rather than bewilderment. As happy yet somber lovers who emerged as if from a love poem were carried away by the force of passion and wine in a garden reminiscent of Paradise, a malicious lady servant spied on them with an envious finger in her red mouth.

Despite its being a standard image recorded in the notebooks and memories of all miniaturists, the long finger sliding into a beautiful woman's mouth had a different elegance each time.

How much did these illustrations comfort me? As dusk fell, I went to Master Osman and said the following:

"My dear master, when the portal is opened once again, with your permission, I shall quit the Treasury."

"How do you mean!" he said. "We still have one night and one morning. How quickly your eyes have had their fill of the greatest illustrations the world has ever known!"

As he said this, he hadn't turned his face away from the page before him, yet the paleness in his pupils confirmed he was indeed gradually going blind.

"We've learned the secret of the horse's nostrils," I said confidently.

"Ha!" he said. "Yes! The rest is up to Our Sultan and the Head Treasurer. Perhaps they will pardon us all."

Would he name Stork as the murderer? I couldn't even ask out of fear, for I worried he wouldn't allow me to leave. Even worse, I had the recurring thought that he might accuse me.

"The plume needle Bihzad used to blind himself is missing," he said.

"In all probability the dwarf put it back in its place," I said. "The page before you is so magnificent!"

His face lit up like a child's, and he smiled. "Hüsrev, burning with love, as he waits astride his horse for Shirin before her palace in the middle of the night," he said. "Rendered in the style of the old masters of Herat."

He was now gazing at the picture as if he could see it, but he hadn't even taken the magnifying glass into his hand.

"Can you see the splendor in the leaves of the trees in the nighttime darkness, appearing one by one as if illuminated from within like stars or spring flowers, the humble patience implied by the wall ornamentation, the refinement in the use of gold leaf and the delicate balance in the entire painting's composition? Handsome Hüsrev's horse is as graceful and elegant as a woman. His beloved Shirin waits at the window above him, her neck bowed, but her face proud. It's as if the lovers are to remain here eternally within the light emanating from the painting's texture, skin and subtle colors which were applied lovingly by the miniaturist. You can see how their faces are turned ever so slightly toward one another while their bodies are half-turned toward us—for they know they're in a painting and thus visible to us. This is why they don't try to resemble exactly those figures which we see around us. Quite to the contrary, they signify that they've emerged from Allah's memory. This is why time has stopped for them within that picture. No matter how fast the pace of the story they tell in the picture, they themselves will remain for all eternity there, like well-bred, polite, shy young maidens, without making any sudden gestures with their hands, arms, slight bodies or even eyes. For them, everything within the navy-blue night is frozen: The bird flies through the darkness, among the stars, with a fluttering like the racing hearts of the lovers themselves, and at the same time, remains fixed for all eternity as if nailed to the sky in this matchless moment. The old masters of Herat, who knew that God's velvet blackness was lowering over their eyes like a curtain, also knew that if they went blind while staring motionless at such an illustration for days and weeks on end, their souls would at last mingle with the eternity of the picture."

At the time of the evening prayer, when the portal of the Treasury was opened with the same ceremony and under the gaze of the same throng, Master Osman was still staring intently at the page before him, at the bird that floated motionless in the sky. But if you noticed the paleness in his pupils you'd also realize that he stared at the page quite oddly, as blind men sometimes incorrectly orient themselves to the food before them.

The officers of the Treasury detail, learning that Master Osman would stay inside and that Jezmi Agha was at the door, neglected to search me thoroughly and never found the plume needle I hid in my undergarment. When I emerged onto the streets of Istanbul from the palace courtyard, I slipped into a passageway and removed the terrifying object, with which the legendary Bihzad had blinded himself, from where it was, and stuck it into my sash. I practically ran through the streets.

The cold of the Treasury chambers had so penetrated my bones that it seemed as though the gentle weather of an early spring had settled over the city streets. As I passed the grocer, barber, herbalist, fruit and vegetable shop and firewood shop of the Old Caravansary Bazaar, which were shutting down one by one for the night, I slowed my pace and carefully examined the casks, cloth sheets, carrots and jars in the warm shops lit by oil lamps.

My Enishte's street (I still couldn't say "Shekure's street" let alone "my street") appeared even stranger and more distant after my two-day absence. But the joy of being reunited safe and sound with my Shekure, and the thought that I'd be able to enter my beloved's bed tonight—since the murderer was as good as caught—made me feel so intimate with the whole world that upon seeing the pomegranate tree and the repaired and closed shutters, I had to restrain myself from shouting like a farmer hollering to someone across a stream. When I saw Shekure, I wanted the first words out of my mouth to be, "We know who the wretched murderer is!"

I opened the courtyard gate. I'm not sure if it was from the squeak of the gate, the carefree way the sparrow drank water from the well bucket, or the darkness of the house, but with the wolflike prescience of a man who'd lived alone for twelve years, I understood at once that nobody was home. Even bitterly realizing that one's been left to his own devices, one will still open and close all of the doors, the cabinets and even lift the lids of pots, and that's just what I did. I even looked inside the chests.

In this silence, the only sound I heard was the thudding of my own racing heart. Like an old man who's done everything he will ever do, I felt consoled when I abruptly girded my sword, which I'd kept hidden at the bottom of the most out of the way chest. It was this ivory-handled sword which always provided me with inner peace and balance during all those years I worked with the pen. Books, which we mistake for consolation, only add depth to our sorrow.

I went down to the courtyard. The sparrow had flown away. As if abandoning a sinking ship, I left the house to the silence of an impending darkness.

My heart, now more confident, told me to run and find them. I ran, but I slowed through crowded places and the mosque courtyards where dogs picked up my trail and joyously followed, anticipating some kind of amusement.

CHAPTER 53

I AM ESTHER

I was putting lentil soup on the boil for our evening meal when Nesim said, "There's a visitor at the door." I replied, "Make sure the soup doesn't burn," handing him the spoon and giving it a couple of turns in the pot while holding his aged hand. If you don't show them, they'll stand there for hours idly holding the spoon in the pot.

When I saw Black at the door I felt nothing but pity for him. There was such an expression on his face I was afraid to ask what had happened.

"Don't bother to come inside," I said, "I'll be out as soon as I change clothes."

I donned the pink and yellow garments that I wear when I'm invited to Ramadan festivities, wealthy banquets and lengthy weddings, and took up my holiday satchel. "I'll have my soup when I get back," I said to poor Nesim.

Black and I had crossed one street in my little Jewish neighborhood whose chimneys labor to expel their smoke, the way our kettles force out their steam, and I said:

"Shekure's former husband is back."

Black fell silent and stayed that way until we left the neighborhood. His face was ashen, the color of the waning day.

"Where are they?" he asked sometime later.

From this question I guessed that Shekure and her children weren't at home. "They're at their house," I said. Because I meant Shekure's previous home, and knew at once that this would singe Black's heart, I opened a door of hope for him by tacking the word "probably" onto the end of my statement.

"Have you seen her newly returned husband?" he asked me, looking deep into my eyes.

"I haven't seen him, neither did I see Shekure's flight from the house."

"How did you know they'd left?"

"From your face."

"Tell me everything," he said decisively.

Black was so troubled he didn't understand that Esther—her eye eternally at the window, her ear eternally to the ground—could never "tell everything" if she wanted to continue to be the Esther who found husbands for so many dreamy maidens and knocked on the doors of so many unhappy homes.

"What I've heard," I said, "is that the brother of Shekure's former husband, Hasan, visited your house"—it heartened him when I said "your house"—"and told Shevket that his father was on his way home from war, that he would arrive around midafternoon, and that if he didn't find Shevket's mother and brother in their rightful home, he'd be very upset. Shevket told this to his mother, who acted cautiously, but couldn't come to a decision. Toward midafternoon, Shevket left the house to be with his Uncle Hasan and his grandfather."

"Where did you learn these things?"

"Hasn't Shekure told you about Hasan's schemes over the last two years to get her back to his house? There was a time when Hasan sent letters to Shekure through me."

"Did she ever respond to them?"

"I know all the varieties of women in Istanbul," I said proudly, "there's no one who's as bound to her house, her husband and her honor as Shekure is."

"But I am her husband now."

His voice bore that typically male uncertainty that always depressed me. Amazingly, to whichever side Shekure fled, the other side went to pieces.

"Hasan wrote a note and gave it to me to deliver to Shekure. It described how Shevket had come home to await the return of his father, how Shekure had been married in an illegitimate ceremony, how Shevket was very unhappy on account of the false husband who was supposed to be his new father and how he was never going back."

"How did Shekure respond?"

"She waited for you all through the night with poor Orhan."

"What about Hayriye?"

"Hayriye's been waiting for years for the opportunity to drown your beautiful wife in a spoonful of water. This was why she began sleeping with your Enishte, may he rest in peace. When Hasan saw that Shekure was spending the night alone in fear of murderers and ghosts, he sent along another note through me."

"What did he write?"

Thanks be to God that your unfortunate Esther can't read or write, because when irate Effendis and irritable fathers ask this question, she can say: "I couldn't read the letter, only the face of the beautiful maiden reading the letter."

"What did you read in Shekure's face?"

"Helplessness."

For a long time we didn't speak. Awaiting nightfall, an owl was perched on the dome of a small Greek church; runny-nosed neighborhood kids laughed at my clothes and bundle, and a mangy dog happily scratching himself loped down from the cemetery lined with cypresses to greet the night.

"Slow down!" I shouted at Black later, "I can't get up these hills the way you can. Where are you taking me with my satchel like this?"

"Before you bring me to Hasan's house, I'm taking you to some generous and brave young men so you can spread out your bundle and sell them some flowery handkerchiefs, silk sashes and purses with silver embroidery for their secret lovers."

It was a good sign that Black could still make jokes in his pitiable state, but I could fathom the seriousness behind his mirth. "If you're going

I Am Esther

to gather a posse, I'll never take you to Hasan's house," I said. "I'm frightened to death of fights and brawls."

"If you continue to be the intelligent Esther you've always been," he said, "there'll be neither fight nor brawl."

We passed through Aksaray and entered the road heading back, straight toward the Langa gardens. On the upper part of the muddy road, in a neighborhood that had seen happier days, Black walked into a barbershop that was still open. I saw him talking to the master barber being shaved by an honest-looking boy with lovely hands by the light of an oil lamp. Before long, the barber, his handsome apprentice, and later, two more of his men joined up with us at Aksaray. They carried swords and axes. At a side street in Shehzadebashı, a theology student, whom I couldn't picture involved in such rough affairs, joined us in the darkness, sword in hand.

"Do you plan on raiding a house in the middle of the city in broad daylight?" I said.

"It's not day, it's night," said Black in a tone more pleased than joking.

"Don't be so confident just because you've put together a gang," I said. "Let's hope the Janissaries don't catch sight of this fully equipped little army wandering around."

"No one will catch sight of us."

"Yesterday the Erzurumis first raided a tavern and then the dervish house at Sağırkapı, beating up everyone they found in both places. An elderly man who took a blow to his head with a stick died. In this pitch blackness, they might think you're of their lot."

"I hear you went to dearly departed Elegant Effendi's house, saw his wife, God bless her, and the horse sketches with the smeared ink before relaying it all to Shekure. Had Elegant Effendi been spending a lot of time with the henchmen of the preacher from Erzurum?"

"If I sounded out Elegant Effendi's wife, it was because I thought it might ultimately help my poor Shekure," I said. "Anyway, I'd gone there to show her the latest cloth which had come off the Flemish ship, not to involve myself in your legal and political affairs—which my poor brain couldn't fathom anyway."

As we entered the street, which ran behind Charshıkapı, my heart quickened with fear. The bare, wet branches of the chestnut and mulberry trees glimmered in the pale light of the half-moon. A breeze kicked up by jinns and the living dead rippled the laced edging of my satchel, whistled through the trees and carried the scent of our group to neighborhood dogs lying in wait. As they began to bark one by one, I pointed out the house to Black. We stared quietly at its dark roof and shutters. Black had the men take positions around the house: in the empty garden, on either side of the courtyard gate and behind the fig trees in back.

"In that entryway over there is a vile Tatar beggar," I said. "He's blind, but he'll know who's come and gone along this street better than the neighborhood headman does. He continually plays with himself as if he were one of the Sultan's vulgar monkeys. Without letting your hand touch his, give him eight or ten silver pieces and he'll tell you everything he knows."

From a distance, I watched Black hand over the coins, then lay his sword against the throat of the beggar and begin to pressure him with questions. Next, I'm not sure how it happened, the barber's apprentice, who I thought was simply watching the house, began to beat the Tatar with the butt of his axe. I watched for a while, thinking it wouldn't last, but the Tatar was wailing. I ran over and pulled the beggar away before they killed him.

"He cursed my mother," said the apprentice.

"He says that Hasan isn't home," Black said. "Can we trust what this blind man says?" He handed me a note that he'd quickly written. "Take this, bring it to the house, give it to Hasan, and if he's not there, give it to his father," he said.

"Haven't you written anything for Shekure?" I asked as I took the note.

"If I send her a separate note, it'll incite the men of the house even more," Black said. "Tell her I've found her father's vile murderer."

"Is this true?"

"Just tell her."

Chastising the Tatar, who was still crying and complaining, I quieted him down. "Don't forget what I've done for you," I said, coming to the realization that I'd drawn out the incident so I wouldn't have to leave.

Why had I stuck my nose into this affair? Two years ago in the Edirne Gate neighborhood they'd killed a clothes peddlar—after cutting off her ears—because the maiden she'd promised to one man married another. My grandmother used to tell me that Turks would often kill a man for no reason. I longed to be with my dearest Nesim, at home having lentil soup. Even though my feet resisted, I thought about how Shekure would be there, and walked to the house. Curiosity was eating at me.

"Clothierrr! I have new Chinese silks for holiday outfits."

I sensed the orangish light filtering out between the shutters move. The door opened. Hasan's polite father invited me inside. The house was warm, like the houses of the rich. When Shekure, who was seated at a low dining table with her boys saw me, she rose to her feet.

"Shekure," I said, "your husband's here."

"Which one?"

"The newer," I said. "He's surrounded the house with his band of armed men. They're prepared to fight Hasan."

"Hasan isn't here," said the polite father-in-law.

"How fortunate. Take a look at this," I said, giving him Black's note like a proud ambassador of the Sultan executing His merciless will.

As the gentlemanly father-in-law read the note, Shekure said, "Esther, come and let me pour you a bowl of lentil soup to warm you up."

"I don't like lentil soup," I said at first. I didn't like the way she spoke as if she were mistress of the house. But when I understood that she wanted to be alone with me, I grabbed the spoon and rushed after her.

"Tell Black that it's all because of Shevket," she whispered. "Last night I waited all night alone with Orhan deathly afraid of the murderer. Orhan trembled with fright until morning. My children had been separated! What kind of mother could remain apart from her child? When Black failed to come back, they told me that Our Sultan's torturers had made him talk and that he'd a hand in my father's death."

"Wasn't Black with you when your father was being killed?"

"Esther," she said, opening her beautiful black eyes wide, "I beg of you, help me."

"Then tell me why you've come back here so I might understand and help."

"Do you think I know why I've returned?" she said. She seemed on the verge of tears. "Black was rough with my poor Shevket," she said. "And when Hasan said that the children's real father had returned, I believed him."

But I could tell from her eyes that she was lying, and she knew I could tell. "I was duped by Hasan!" she whispered, and I sensed that she wanted me to infer from this that she loved Hasan. But did Shekure realize that she was thinking more and more about Hasan because she had married Black?

The door opened and Hayriye entered carrying freshly baked bread whose aroma was irresistible. When she caught sight of me, I could tell from her expression of displeasure that after the death of Enishte Effendi, the poor thing—she couldn't be sold, couldn't be dismissed—had become a legacy of misery for Shekure. The scent of fresh bread filled the room, and I understood the truth of the matter as Shekure faced the children: Whether it be their real father, Hasan or Black, her problem wasn't finding a husband she could love, her challenge was to find a father who would love these boys, both of whom were wide-eyed with fear. Shekure was ready, with the best of intentions, to love any good husband.

"You're seeking what you want with your heart," I said unthinkingly, "whereas you need to be making decisions with your mind."

"I'm prepared to go back to Black immediately with the children," she said, "but I have certain conditions!" She fell quiet. "He must treat Shevket and Orhan well. He shan't inquire about my reasons for coming here. Above all, he must abide by our original conditions of marriage—he'll know what I'm talking about. He left me all alone to fend for myself last night against murderers, thieves and Hasan."

"He hasn't yet found your father's murderer, but he told me to tell you he has."

"Should I go to him?"

Before I could answer, the former father-in-law, who'd long since finished reading the note, said, "Tell Black Effendi I can't take the responsibility of handing over my daughter-in-law without my son being present."

"Which son?" I said for the sake of being shrewish, but softly.

"Hasan," he said. Since he was a man of etiquette, he blushed. "My oldest son is on his way back from Persia; there are witnesses."

"Where's Hasan?" I asked. I ate two spoonfuls of the soup Shekure had offered me.

"He went to gather the clerks, porters and other men of the Customs Office," he said in the childish manner of decent yet dull men who cannot lie. "After what the Erzurumis did yesterday, the Janissaries are certain to be on the streets tonight."

"We didn't see anything of the sort," I said as I walked toward the door. "Is this all you have to say?"

I asked this question of the father-in-law to intimidate him, but Shekure knew full well that I was really addressing her. Was her head truly this befuddled or was she hiding something; for example, was she awaiting the return of Hasan and his men? Oddly, I sensed that I liked her indecisiveness.

"We don't want Black," Shevket said confidently. "And make this your last visit, fat lady."

"But then who'll bring around the lace tablecloths, the handkerchiefs embroidered with flowers and birds that your pretty mother likes, and your favorite red shirt cloth?" I said, leaving my bundle in the middle of the room. "Until I return, you can open it up and take a look, try on, alter and sew whatever you like."

I Am Esther

I was saddened as I left. I'd never seen Shekure's eyes so wet with tears. As soon as I adjusted to the cold outside, Black stopped me on the muddy road, sword in hand.

"Hasan's not home," I said. "Perhaps he's gone to the market to buy wine to celebrate Shekure's return. Perhaps he'll soon be back with his men. In that case you'll come to blows, because he's crazy. And if he takes up that red sword of his, there's no telling what he'll do."

"What did Shekure say?"

"The father-in-law said absolutely not, I won't give up my daughter-in-law, but if I were you I wouldn't worry about him, worry about Shekure. Your wife is confused. If you ask me, she took refuge here two days after her father perished for fear of the murderer, because of Hasan's threats and your disappearance without a word. She knew she couldn't spend another night in that same house plagued by the same fears. They also told her that you had a hand in her father's death. But her first husband hasn't come back or anything like that. Shevket, and it seems the father-in-law, believed Hasan's lie. She wants to return to you, but she has certain conditions."

Staring directly into Black's eyes, I listed her conditions. He accepted at once with an official air as if he were speaking with a genuine ambassador.

"I, too, have a condition," I said. "I'm heading back into the house again." I pointed out the shutters of the window behind which the father-in-law sat. "In a little while attack from there and the front door. When I scream, that'll be the signal for you to stop. If Hasan arrives, don't hesitate to attack him."

My words, of course, did not befit an ambassador, to whom no harm should come, but I let myself get carried away, you see. This time, as soon as I yelled "Clothierrr," the door opened. I went directly to the father-in-law.

"The entire neighborhood, and the judge who presides over these parts, that is everyone, knows that Shekure has long been divorced and properly remarried in keeping with the dictates of the Koran," I said. "Even if your son, who has long since passed away, came back to life and returned here to you from Heaven in the company of the Prophet Moses, it'd be of no use for he's divorced from Shekure. You've abducted a married woman and are holding her here against her will. Black requested that I tell you he and his men will see to your punishment for this crime before the judge can."

"Then he will have made a grave mistake," said the father-in-law delicately. "We didn't abduct Shekure at all! I'm the grandfather of these children, praise be to God. Hasan is their uncle. When Shekure was left all alone, what choice did she have but to seek shelter here? If she wants, she can leave now and take her children with her. But never forget that this is her first home, where she gave birth to her children and happily raised them."

"Shekure," I said unthinkingly, "do you want to return to your father's house?"

She'd begun to cry on account of the "happy hearth" speech. "I have no father," she said, or was that how I heard it? Her children first embraced her legs, then sat her down and hugged her; the three of them hugged one another in a large ball and wept. But Esther is no idiot: I knew full well that Shekure's tears were meant to appease both sides without her having to make a decision. But I also knew they were genuine tears, because they moved me to cry, too. A while later, I noticed that Hayriye, that snake, was also crying.

As if to pay back the green-eyed father-in-law for being the sole person in the room who wasn't crying, Black and his men began their attack on the house that very moment by banging on the shutters and forcing the door. Two men were at the front door with a battering ram whose blows sounded like cannonfire through the house.

"You're an experienced and dignified man," I said, encouraged by my own tears, "open the door and tell those rabid mongrels out there that Shekure is on her way."

"Would you send an unprotected woman, your daughter-in-law no less, who'd taken refuge in your house, out onto the streets with those dogs?"

"She herself wants to go," I said. With my purple handkerchief I wiped my nose, which had stuffed up from crying.

"In that case she's free to open the door and leave," he said.

I sat down beside Shekure and her children. At each new blow, the terrifying noise made by the men forcing the door became yet another excuse for yet more tears, the children began to cry louder, which in turn increased Shekure's wailing and mine as well. Still, even taking into account the threatening cries from outside and the blows of the battering ram that seemed on the verge of destroying the house, both of us knew we were crying to gain time.

"My beautiful Shekure," I said, "your father-in-law has given you permission and your husband Black has accepted all of your terms, he's waiting for you lovingly, you no longer have any business in this house. Put on your cloak, don your veil, take your belongings and your children, and open the door so we can go quietly back to your house."

I Am Esther

This statement of mine made the children wail even more, and caused Shekure to open her eyes in shock.

"I'm afraid of Hasan," she said, "his revenge will be horrible. He's wild. Remember, I came here on my own."

"This doesn't cancel out your new marriage," I said. "You were left helpless, of course you were going to take refuge somewhere. Your husband's forgiven you, he's prepared to take you back. As for Hasan, we'll deal with him the way we have for years." I smiled.

"But I'm not going to open the door," she said, "because then I'll have returned to him of my own free will."

"My dearest Shekure, I cannot open the door either," I said. "You know as well as I that this would mean I've meddled in your affairs. They'd bitterly avenge such meddling."

I could see from her eyes that she understood. "Then no one will open the door," she said. "Let's wait for them to break it down and take us by force."

I knew at once this would be the best alternative for Shekure and her children, and I was afraid. "But that means blood will be spilled," I said. "If the judge isn't involved in this affair, blood will flow, and a blood feud will last for years. No honorable man could stand by and watch as his house was broken into and raided to abduct a woman residing there."

I once again understood regretfully how deceptive and calculating this Shekure was as she embraced her two boys and wailed with all her being rather than answer. A voice was telling me to forget everything and leave, but I could no longer walk back through the door, which was being battered to the breaking point. Actually, I was afraid of both what would happen if they broke down the door and came through and what would happen if they didn't; I kept thinking that Black's men, who trusted in me, were worried about going too far and might retreat at any moment, which would, in turn, embolden the father-in-law. When he went to Shekure's side, I knew he'd begun to cry fake tears, but what's worse, he was trembling in a way that couldn't be feigned.

Stepping toward the door, I screamed with all my strength, "Stop, that's enough!"

The commotion outside and the wailing inside ended in a heartbeat.

"Mother, have Orhan open the door," I said in a moment of inspiration and in a sweet voice, as if I were speaking to the boy. "He wants to go home, no one will take issue with that."

The words had hardly left my mouth when Orhan freed himself from his mother's loosening arms, and like somebody who'd lived here for years, slid open the bolt, lifted the wooden bar, then unfastened the latch, and moved backward two steps. The cold from outside entered as the door yawned open. There was such a silence that all of us heard a lazy dog bark off in the distance. Shekure kissed Orhan, who was back in his mother's lap, and Shevket said, "I'm going to tell Uncle Hasan."

I saw Shekure stand, take up her cloak and prepare her bundle to leave, and I was so greatly relieved, I was afraid I might laugh. I seated myself and had two more spoonfuls of the lentil soup.

Black was intelligent enough not to come anywhere near the door of the house. For a time, Shevket locked himself in his late father's room, and even though we called for Black's help, neither he nor his men came. After Shekure agreed to let Shevket take along his Uncle Hasan's ruby-handled dagger, the boy was willing to leave the house with us.

"Be afraid of Hasan and his red sword," said the father-in-law with genuine worry rather than an air of defeat and vengeance. He kissed each of his grandchildren, sniffing their heads. He also whispered into Shekure's ear.

When I saw Shekure gazing one last time at the door, walls and stove of the house, I remembered once again how this was where she spent the happiest years of her life with her first husband. But could she also tell that this same house was the refuge of two miserable and lonely men, and that it bore the stench of death? I didn't walk with her on the way back for she had broken my heart by coming back here.

It wasn't the cold and blackness of the night that brought together the two fatherless children and three women—one servant, one Jewess and one widow—it was the strange neighborhoods, the nearly impassable streets and the fear of Hasan. Our crowded company was under the protection of Black's men, and just like a caravan carrying treasure, we walked over out-of-the-way roads, backstreets and solitary, seldom-visited neighborhoods, so as to avoid running into guards, Janissaries, curious neighborhood thugs, thieves or Hasan. At times, through blackness in which you couldn't see your hand before your face, we groped our way, perpetually bumping against each other and the walls. We walked clinging to one another, overcome by the sensation that the living dead, jinns and demons would surely emerge from underground and abduct us into the night. Just behind the walls and closed shutters, which we felt blindly with our hands, we heard the snoring and coughing of people in the nighttime cold as well as the lowing of beasts in their stables.

Even Esther, no stranger to the poorest and worst districts, who'd walked all the streets of Istanbul—that is excluding those neighborhoods wherein migrants and the members of various unfortunate communities congregated—occasionally felt that we would vanish on these streets, which twisted and turned without end through an endless blackness. Yet I could still make out certain street corners that I'd patiently passed in the daytime toting my satchel; for example, I recognized the walls of Head Tailor's Street, the sharp smell of manure—which for some reason reminded me of cinnamon—coming from the stable adjacent to Nurullah Hoja's property, the fire-ravaged sites on Acrobats Street and the Falconers Arcade that led into the square with the Blind Haji Fountain, and thus I knew we weren't heading toward the house of Shekure's late father at all, but to some other, mysterious destination.

There was no telling what Hasan would do if angered, and I knew Black had found another place to hide his family from him—and from that devil of a murderer. If I could've made out where that place was, I would tell you, now, and Hasan tomorrow morning—not out of spite, but because I'm convinced that Shekure will again want to have Hasan's interest. But Black, intelligent as he was, no longer trusted me.

We were walking down a dark street behind the slave market when a commotion of cries and wails erupted at the far end of the street. We heard the sounds of a scuffle, and I recognized with fear the clamorous start of a fight: the clash of axes, swords and sticks and the bellow of bitter pain.

Black handed his own large sword to one of his most trusted men, forcibly took the dagger from Shevket, causing the boy to cry, and had the barber's apprentice and two other men move Shekure, Hayriye and the children a safe distance away. The theology student told me he'd take me home by way of a shortcut; that is, he didn't let me stay with the others. Was this a twist of fate or some cunning attempt to keep secret the whereabouts of their hideout?

There was a shop, which I understood to be a coffeehouse, at the end of this narrow street we were passing down. Perhaps the swordfight stopped as soon as it'd begun. Crowds of men were hooting as they entered and left; at first I thought they were looting, but no, they were destroying the coffeehouse. They carefully took out all of the ceramic cups, brass pots, glasses and low tables under the light of the torches of the onlookers and destroyed them all as a warning. They roughed up a man who tried to stop them, but he was able to get away. Originally, I thought their target was only coffee, as they themselves claimed. They were condemning its ill effects, how it harmed the sight and the stomach, how it dulled the intellect and caused men to lose their faith, how it was the poison of the Franks and how Exalted Muhammad had turned down coffee even though it was offered to him by a beautiful woman—Satan in disguise. It was as if this were the theatrics for a night of instruction in moral etiquette, and if I finally made it home, I thought I might even scold Nesim, warning him not to drink too much of that poison.

Since there were quite a few rooming houses and cheap inns nearby, a curious crowd formed in no time, made up of idle wanderers, homeless men and no-good mongrels who'd snuck illegally into the city, and they emboldened these enemies of coffee. It was then I understood that these men were the henchmen of Preacher Nusret Hoja of Erzurum. They intended to clean up all the dens of wine, prostitution and coffee in Istanbul and punish severely those who veered from the path of Exalted Muhammad; those who, for example, used dervish ceremonies as an excuse for belly-dancing to music. They railed against the enemies of religion, men who collaborated with the Devil, pagans, unbelievers and illustrators. I suddenly recalled this was the coffeehouse on whose walls drawings were hung, where religion and the hoja from Erzurum were maligned and where disrespect knew no bounds.

A coffee maker's apprentice, his face spattered with blood, emerged from inside, and I thought he might collapse, but he wiped the blood from his forehead and cheeks with the cuff of his shirt, melded in with our group and began to watch the raid. The crowd pulled back a little out of fear. I noticed Black recognize somebody and hesitate. By the way the Erzurumis began to collect together, I knew that the Janissaries or some other band armed with clubs was on its way. The torches were extinguished and the crowd became a confused mob.

Black grabbed me by the arm and had the theology student take me away. "Go by way of the backstreets," he said. "He'll see you to your house." The student wanted to slip away as soon as possible and we were almost running as we departed. My thoughts were with Black, but if Esther's taken out of the scene, she can't possibly continue with the story, can she now?

CHAPTER 54

I AM A WOMAN

I can hear your objections already: "My dear Storyteller Effendi, you might be able to imitate anyone or anything, but never a woman!" Yet I beg to differ. True, I've wandered from city to city, imitating everything into the wee hours of the night at weddings, festivals and coffeehouses until my voice gave out, and thus it was never my lot to marry, but this doesn't mean I'm unacquainted with womenfolk.

I know women quite well; in fact, I've known four personally, seen their faces and spoken with them: 1. my mother, may she rest in eternal peace; 2. my beloved aunt; 3. the wife of my brother (he always beat me), who said "Get out!" on one of those rare occasions when I saw her—she was the first woman I fell in love with; and 4. a lady I saw suddenly at an open window in Konya during my travels. Despite never having spoken with her, I've nursed feelings of lust toward her for years and still do. Perhaps, by now, she's passed away.

Seeing a woman's bare face, speaking to her, and witnessing her humanity opens the way to both pangs of lust and deep spiritual pain in us men, and thus the best of all alternatives is not to lay eyes on women, especially pretty women, without first being lawfully wed, as our noble faith dictates. The sole remedy for carnal desires is to seek out the friendship of beautiful boys, a satisfactory surrogate for females, and in due time, this, too, becomes a sweet habit. In the cities of the European Franks, women roam about exposing not only their faces, but also their brightly shining hair (after their necks, their most attractive feature), their arms, their beautiful throats, and even, if what I've heard is true, a portion of their gorgeous legs; as a result, the men of those cities walk about with great difficulty, embarrassed and in extreme pain, because, you see, their front sides are always erect and this fact naturally leads to the paralysis of their society. Undoubtedly, this is why each day the Frank infidel surrenders another fortress to us Ottomans.

After realizing, while still a youth, that the best recipe for my spiritual happiness and contentment was to live far from beautiful women, I grew increasingly curious about these creatures. At that time, since I hadn't seen any women besides my mother and my aunt, my curiosity assumed a mystical quality, my head seemed to tingle, and I knew that I could only learn how women felt if I did what they did, ate what they ate, said what they said, imitated their behavior and, yes, only if I wore their clothes. Therefore, one Friday, when my mother, father, older brother and aunt went to my grandfather's rose garden on the shores of the Fahreng, I told them I was feeling ill and stayed at home.

"Come along. Look, you'll entertain us by mimicking the dogs, trees and horses in the country. What'll you do here all alone, anyway?" said my mother, may she rest in peace.

"I'm going to put on your dresses and become a woman, dear mother," was an impossible answer. So I said, "My stomach hurts."

"Don't be such a coward," said my father. "Come along and we'll wrestle."

I shall now describe to you, my painter and calligrapher brethren, exactly what I felt once they'd left and I donned the underclothes and dresses belonging to my now dearly departed mother and aunt, as well as the secrets I learned that day about being a woman. Let me first state forthright that contrary to what we've often read in books and heard from preachers, when you are a woman, you don't feel like the Devil.

Not at all! When I pulled on my mother's rose-embroidered wool underclothes, a gentle sense of well-being spread over me and I felt as sensitive as she. The touch against my bare skin of my aunt's pistachio-green silk shirt, which she could never bring herself to wear, made me feel an irrepressible affection toward all children, including myself. I wanted to nurse everybody and cook for the whole world. After I understood to some extent what it was like to have breasts, I stuffed my chest with whatever I could find—socks and washcloths—so I might understand what really made me curious: how it felt to be a large-breasted woman. When I saw these huge protrusions, yes, I admit it, I was as proud as Satan. I understood at once that men, merely catching sight of the shadow of my overabundant breasts, would chase after them and strive to take them into their mouths; I felt quite powerful, but is that what I wanted? I was befuddled: I wanted both to be powerful and to be the object of pity; I wanted a rich, powerful and intelligent man, whom I didn't know from Adam, to fall madly in love with me; yet I also feared such a man. Sliding on the bracelets made of twisted gold that my mother hid at the bottom of her trousseau chest next to the sheets embroidered with leafy designs, in lavender-scented wool socks, applying the rouge with which she brightened her cheeks on the way back from the public baths, donning my aunt's evergreen cloak and putting on the thin veil of the same color after gathering up my hair, I stared at myself in the mirror with the mother-of-pearl frame, and shuddered. Although I hadn't touched them, my eyes and eyelashes had become those of a woman. Only my eyes and cheeks were exposed, but I was an extraordinarily attractive woman and this made me very happy. My manliness, which took note of this fact before even I had, was erect. Naturally, this upset me.

In the hand mirror I held, I watched a teardrop slide from my lovely eye and just then, a poem painfully came to mind. I've never been able to forget it, because at that same moment, inspired by the Almighty, I sang that poem rhythmically like a song, trying to forget my woes:

> *My fickle heart longs for the West when I'm in the East and for the*
> *East when I'm in the West.*
> *My other parts insist I be a woman when I'm a man and a man*
> *when I'm a woman.*
> *How difficult it is being human, even worse is living a human's life.*
> *I only want to amuse myself frontside and backside, to be Eastern*
> *and Western both.*

I was going to say, "Let's hope our Erzurumi brethren don't hear the song issuing from my heart," for they'll be cross. But why should I be afraid? Perhaps they won't be angry at all. Listen, I'm not saying this for the sake of gossip, but I've learned how that famous preacher the Exalted Not-Husret-by-a-Longshot Effendi, despite being married, prefers handsome boys to us women just as you sensitive painters do. I'm just telling you what I've heard. But I pay no mind to any of this because I find him repulsive besides, and he's so old. His teeth have fallen out and as the young boys who get close to him say, his mouth stinks, excuse the expression, like a bear's ass.

All right then, I'm holding off on the hearsay to return to the real issue at hand: As soon as I saw how beautiful I was, I no longer wanted to wash clothes and dishes and parade about the streets like a slave. Poverty, tears, sorrow, gazing forlornly at a mirror of disappointment and crying are the lot of sad and ugly women. I must find a husband who'll put me on a pedestal, but who might that be?

That was why I began spying through a peephole on the sons of pashas and notables, whom my late father had invited to our house under various pretexts. I wanted my predicament to resemble that of the petite-mouthed beauty with two children whom all the miniaturists love. Perhaps it'd be best for me to describe to you poor Shekure's story. But wait a minute, I'd promised to recount the following story tonight:

The Love Story Told by a Woman Prompted by the Devil

It's quite simple actually. The story takes place in Kemerüstü, one of the poorer neighborhoods of Istanbul. A prominent inhabitant of the neighborhood, Chelebi Ahmet, secretary to Vasıf Pasha, was a married gentleman with two children who kept to himself. One day, through an open window, he catches sight of a black-haired, black-eyed, silver-skinned, tall and thin Bosnian beauty, and is smitten. But, the woman is married, has no interest whatsoever in the Chelebi, and is devoted to her handsome husband. The hapless Chelebi refuses to confide his woes to anybody, and reduced by love to skin and bone, takes to wine he's bought from a Greek, yet ultimately he cannot hide his love from the neighborhood. At first, because the neighbors adore such love stories and admire and respect the Chelebi, they honor his love, making a passing joke or two about it and letting life take its course. But the Chelebi, who can't control his incurable agony, begins to get drunk each night and sit at the doorstep of the house wherein the silver-skinned beauty lives happily with her husband, crying for hours on end like a child. In the end this alarms the neighbors. Each night as the lover cries in agony, they are able neither to beat him and drive him away nor to comfort him. The Chelebi, as suited a gentleman, learns to cry inwardly without lashing out or annoying anybody. But gradually, his hopeless grief works its way into the neighborhood, becoming the sorrow and grief of all; the residents lose their sense of well-being, and like the fountain which flows mournfully in the square, the Chelebi himself became a font of sorrow. Initially, the talk of misery spreads throughout the neighborhood, becoming in turn the rumor of ill-fortune and later the certainty of doom. Some move away, some experience a spate of bad luck and some are unable to practice their craft, because they've lost the will to work. After the neighborhood empties out, one day the lovelorn Chelebi also moves away with his wife and children, leaving the silver-skinned beauty and her husband all alone. This misfortune, of which they are the focus, douses the flames of their love and causes them to drift apart. Though they live together for the rest of their lives, they're never again able to be happy.

* * *

I was on the verge of saying how much I liked this story because it showed the pitfulls of love and women, when for Heaven's sake, I'd forgotten that I'd lost my capacity to reason. Since I'm now a woman, I'm going to say something else entirely. All right then, it's something like this:

Oh, how wonderful love is!

Now then, who are those strangers bursting through the door?

CHAPTER 55

I AM CALLED "BUTTERFLY"

I saw the mob and knew the Erzurumis had begun slaying us witty miniaturists.

Black was also in the crowd watching the attack. I saw him holding a dagger accompanied by a group of odd-looking men, the well-known Esther the clothier and other women carrying cloth sacks. I had an urge to flee after seeing the establishment cruelly wrecked and the coffeehouse-goers beaten mercilessly as they tried to leave. Later, another mob, perhaps the Janissaries, arrived. The Erzurumis snuffed out their torches and fled.

There was nobody at the dark entrance of the coffeehouse, and no one was looking. I walked inside. Everything was in shambles. I stepped on the shattered cups, plates, glasses and bowls. An oil lamp hanging from a nail high on the wall hadn't died out during the turmoil but only illuminated the soot marks on the ceiling, leaving in darkness the floor strewn with the boards of wrecked wood benches, broken low tables and other debris.

Stacking long cushions atop one another, I reached up and grabbed hold of the oil lamp. Within its circle of light, I noticed bodies lying on the floor. When I saw that one face was covered in blood, I turned away, and went to the next. The second body was moaning, and upon seeing my lamp, made a childlike noise.

Someone else entered. At first I was alarmed, though I could sense it was Black. The both of us leaned over the third body sprawled on the floor. As I lowered the lamp to his head, we saw what we'd suspected: They'd killed the storyteller.

There was no trace of blood on his face, which was made up like a woman's, but his chin, brow and rouge-covered mouth were battered, and judging by his neck, covered in bruises, he'd been throttled. His hands were cast backward over his head on either side. It wasn't difficult to figure out that one of them held the old man's arms behind his back while the others beat him in the face before strangling him. I wonder, had they said, "Cut out his tongue so he never again slanders his Excellency the Preacher Hoja Effendi," and then set about doing so?

"Bring the lamp here," said Black. Near the stove, the light of the lamp struck broken coffee grinders, sieves, scales and pieces of broken coffee cups lying in the mud of spilled coffee. In the corner where the storyteller hung his pictures each night, Black was searching for the performer's props, sash, magician's handkerchief and popping stick. Black said he was after the pictures and held the lamp he'd taken from me to my face: Yes, of course I'd drawn two of them out of a sense of fraternity. We could find nothing but the Persian skullcap that the deceased wore over his perfectly shaved head.

Seeing no one else, we exited into the blackness of night through a narrow passageway that led away from the back door. During the raid much of the crowd and the artists within probably escaped through this door, but the knocked-over planters and bags of coffee strewn everywhere indicated that there was a struggle here as well.

The fact that the coffeehouse was raided and the master storyteller murdered, coupled with the terrifying blackness of night, brought Black and I closer together. This was also what caused the silence between us. We passed two more streets. Black handed the lamp back to me, then he drew his dagger and pressed it to my throat.

"We're going to your house," he said. "I want to search it so I can put my mind at ease."

"It's already been searched."

Rather than be offended by him, I had the urge to tease him. Didn't Black's belief in the disgraceful rumors about me simply prove he was also jealous of me? He held the dagger without much confidence.

My house was opposite the direction we were heading along the road leading away from the coffeehouse. We tacked right and left down neighborhood streets and passed through empty gardens that bore the depressing scent of damp and lonely trees as we traced a wide arc back toward my house. We'd covered more than half the route, when Black stopped and said:

"For two days, Master Osman and I examined the masterpieces of the legendary masters in the Treasury."

Much later, nearly screaming, I said, "After a certain age, even if a painter shares a worktable with Bihzad, what he sees may please his eyes and bring contentment and excitement to his soul, but it won't enhance his talent, because one paints with the hand, not the eyes, and the hand at my age, let alone at Master Osman's, does not easily learn new things."

Assured my beautiful wife was waiting for me, I spoke at the top of my voice to let her know I wasn't alone so she might hide herself from Black—not that I took this pathetic dagger-wielding fool seriously.

We passed through the courtyard gate, and I thought I saw the light of a lamp moving in the house, but thank God all was in darkness now. It was such a merciless rape of my privacy for this knife-wielding beast to force his way into my heavenly home, where I spent my days, indeed all my time, seeking out and painting Allah's memories until my eyes tired—whereupon I'd make love to my beloved, the most beautiful woman in the world—that I swore to take revenge upon him.

Lowering the lamp, he examined my papers, a page I was in the midst of completing—condemned prisoners pleading to the Sultan to be relieved of their chains of debt and receiving His benevolence—my paints, my worktables, my knives, my reed-cutting boards, my brushes, everything around my writing table, my papers again, my burnishing stones, my penknives and the spaces between my pen and paper boxes; he looked in cabinets, chests, beneath cushions, at one of my paper scissors, and beneath a soft red cushion and a carpet before going back, bringing the lamp closer and closer to each object and examining the same places once again. As he said when he first drew his weapon, he wouldn't search my entire house, only my atelier. Indeed, couldn't I conceal my wife—the only thing I wanted to hide—in the room from which she was now spying on us?

"There's a final picture that belonged to the book my Enishte was having made," he said. "Whoever killed him also stole that picture."

"It was different from the others," I said immediately. "Your Enishte, may he rest in peace, made me draw a tree in one corner of the page. In the background somewhere . . . and in the middle of the page, in the foreground, was to be someone's picture, probably a portrait of Our Sultan. That space, quite large if I might add, was awaiting its picture. Because the objects in the background were to be smaller, as in the European style, he wanted me to make the tree smaller. As the picture developed, it gave the impression of being a view of this world from a window, nothing like an illustration at all. It was then I comprehended that in a picture made with the perspectival methods of the Franks, the borders and gilding took the place of a window frame."

"Elegant Effendi was responsible for the borders and the gilding."

"If that's what you're asking, I already told you I didn't murder him."

"A murderer never admits to his crime," he said quickly, then asked me what I was doing at the coffeehouse during the raid.

He placed the oil lamp just beside the cushion upon which I was seated, in a way that would illuminate my face along with my papers and the pages I was illuminating. He himself was scurrying about the room like a shadow in the dark.

Besides telling him what I've told you, that I actually was an infrequent visitor to the coffeehouse and just happened to be passing by, I also repeated that I made two of the pictures which were hung on the wall there—although I actually disapproved of the goings-on at the coffeehouse. "Because," I added, "the art of painting only ends up condemning and punishing itself when it derives its strength from the desire to condemn and punish the evils of life rather than from the painter's own skill, love of his art and desire to embrace Allah . . . regardless of whether it's the preacher from Erzurum or Satan himself that's denounced. More importantly, if that coffeehouse crowd hadn't targeted the Erzurumis, it might not have been raided tonight."

"Even so, you would go there," said the wretch.

"Yes, because I enjoyed myself there." Had he an inkling of how honest I was being? I added, "Despite knowing how ugly and wrong something is, we descendants of Adam might still derive considerable pleasure from it. And I'm embarrassed to say I was also entertained by those cheap illustrations, the mimicry and those stories about Satan, the gold coin and the dog, which the storyteller told crudely without meter or rhyme."

"Even so, why would you even step foot in that den of unbelievers?"

"Fine then," I said resigning myself to an inner voice, "at times there's also a worm of doubt that gnaws at me: Ever since I was openly recognized as the most talented and most proficient among the masters of the workshop, not only by Master Osman, but by Our Sultan as well, I began to be so terrified of the envy of the others that I tried, if only at times, to go where they went, to befriend them and to resemble them so they wouldn't turn on me in a sudden fit of vengeance. Do you understand? And since they've begun labeling me an 'Erzurumi,' I've been going to that den of vile unbelievers so others might discount this rumor."

"Master Osman said you often acted as if apologizing for your talent and proficiency."

"What else did he say about me?"

"That you'd paint absurd, minute pictures on grains of rice and fingernails so that others would be convinced you'd forsaken life for art. He said you were always trying to please others because you were embarrassed by the great gifts Allah had bestowed upon you."

"Master Osman is on Bihzad's level," I said with sincerity. "What else?"

"He listed your faults without the slightest hesitation," said the wretch.

"Let's hear my faults then."

"He said that despite your prodigious talent, you painted not for the love of art but to ingratiate yourself. Supposedly, what most motivated you while painting was imagining the pleasure an observer would feel; whereas, you should've painted for the pleasure of painting itself."

It singed my heart that Master Osman so brazenly revealed what he thought about me to a man of such diminished spirit, one who devoted his life, not to art, but to being a clerk, writing letters and hollow flattery. Black continued:

"The great masters of old, Master Osman claimed, would never renounce the styles and methods they cultivated through self-sacrifice to art just for the sake of a new shah's authority, the whims of a new prince or the tastes of a new age; thus, to avoid being forced to alter their styles and methods, they'd heroically blind themselves. Meanwhile, you've enthusiastically and dishonorably imitated the European masters for the pages of my Enishte's book, with the excuse that it's the will of Our Sultan."

"The great Head Illuminator Master Osman most certainly meant no evil by this," I said. "Allow me to put some linden tea on the boil for you, my dear guest."

I passed into the adjoining room. My beloved tossed over my head the nightgown of Chinese silk she was wearing, which she'd purchased from Esther the clothier, then mockingly parroted me, "Allow me to put some linden tea on the boil for you, my dear guest," and placed her hand on my cock.

I took out the agate-handled sword hidden among rose-scented sheets at the bottom of the chest on the floor nearest our roll-up mattress, which she'd hopefully spread out, and drew the weapon from its sheath. Its edge was so sharp that if you tossed a silk handkerchief over it, the sword would easily cut through it; if you placed a sheet of gold leaf upon it, the edges of the resulting pieces would be as straight as any cut with a ruler.

Concealing the sword as best I could, I returned to my atelier. Black Effendi was so pleased with his interrogation of me that he was still circling the red cushion, dagger in hand. I placed a half-finished illustration upon the cushion. "Take a look at this," I said. He knelt out of curiosity, trying to understand the picture.

I stepped behind him, drew my sword and in one motion lowered him to the ground, pinning him with my weight. His dagger fell away. Grabbing him by the hair, I pushed his head against the ground and pressed my sword to his neck from below. I flattened out Black's delicate body and pressed him facedown beneath my heavy body, using my chin and one free hand to push his head so it nearly touched the sharp point of the sword. My one hand was full of his dirty hair, the other held the sword to the delicate skin of his throat. Wisely, he didn't move at all, because I could have finished him then and there. Being this close to his curly hair, to the nape of his neck—which might've invited an insulting slap at another time—and to his ugly ears enraged me all the more. "I'm using all my restraint to keep from doing away with you this instant," I whispered into his ear as if divulging a secret.

That he listened to me like an obedient child without making a peep pleased me: "You'll recognize this legend from the *Book of Kings*," I whispered. "Feridun Shah, in error, bequeaths the worst of his lands to his two older sons and the best, Persia, to Iraj, the youngest. Tur, bent on revenge, dupes his younger brother, Iraj, of whom he is jealous; before he cuts Iraj's throat, he grabs his hair just as I am doing now and lies on top of him with all his weight. Do you feel the weight of my body?"

He gave no answer, but from his eyes, which stared blankly like those of a sacrificial lamb, I could tell that he was listening, and I was struck with inspiration: "I'm not only faithful to Persian styles and methods in painting, but also in beheadings. I've also seen another version of this much loved scene that describes Shah Siyavush's death."

I explained to Black, who listened silently, how Siyavush made preparations for avenging his brothers, how he burned down his entire palace, all his belongings and property, how he forgivingly parted from his wife, mounted his steed and went to war, how he lost the battle and was dragged by his hair along the ground before being laid out facedown "just as you are now," and how a knife was pressed against his throat, how there erupted an argument between his friends and enemies over whether they should kill him or let him free and how the defeated king, his face in the dirt, listened to his captors. Then I asked him, "Are you fond of that illustration? Geruy comes up behind Siyavush, as I have to you, gets on top of him, rests his sword against his neck, grabs a fistful of hair and cuts his throat. Your red blood, soon to flow, makes black dust rise from the dry earth, where later still, a flower will bloom."

I fell quiet and from distant streets we could hear the Erzurumis screaming as they ran. The terror outside at once brought the two of us, lying one on top of the other, closer.

"But in all those pictures," I added, pulling harder on Black's hair, "one can sense the difficulty of elegantly drawing two men who despise each other yet whose bodies, like ours, have become as one. It's as if the chaos of treachery, envy and battle that comes just before the magical and magnificent moment of beheading has too fully permeated those pictures. Even the greatest masters of Kazvin would have difficulty drawing two men on top of each other; they'd confuse everything. Whereas you and I, see for yourself, we're much more tidy and elegant."

"The blade is cutting," he whimpered.

"I'm much obliged for your polite words, my dear man, but it's doing no such thing. I'm being quite careful. I wouldn't do anything to ruin the beauty of our pose. In the scenes of love, death and war, wherein the great masters of old rendered intertwined bodies as if they were one, they were able to elicit only our tears. See for yourself: My head rests upon the nape of your neck as if it were a part of your body. I can smell your hair and the scent of your neck. My legs, on either side of yours, are stretched out in such harmony with yours, that an onlooker might mistake us for an elegant four-legged beast. Do you feel the balance of my weight on your back and buttocks?" Another silence, but I didn't press the sword upward, because it would indeed have cut his throat. "If you're not going to speak, I might be provoked to bite your ear," I said, whispering into that very ear.

When I noticed in his eyes that he was prepared to speak, I asked the same question again: "Do you feel the balance of my weight upon your body?"

"Aye."

"Do you like it?" I said. "Are we beautiful?" I asked. "Are we as beautiful as the legendary heroes who slay each other with such elegance in the masterpieces of the old masters?"

"I don't know," said Black, "I can't see us in the mirror."

When I imagined how my wife saw us from the other room in the light cast by the coffeehouse's oil lamp resting on the floor only a short distance away, I thought I might actually bite Black's ear out of excitement.

"Black Effendi, you, who have forced your way into my home and have disturbed my privacy, dagger in hand, in order to interrogate me," I said, "do you now feel my strength?"

"Yes, I also sense that you're truly in the right."

"Then proceed, once again, to ask me what you want to know."

"Describe how Master Osman would caress you."

"As an apprentice, I was much more lithe, delicate and beautiful than I am now, and he would mount me then the way I have mounted you. He would caress my arms, at times he would even hurt me, but because I was in awe of his knowledge, his talent and strength, what he did pleased me, and I never harbored any ill will toward him, because I loved him. Loving Master Osman enabled me to love art, colors, paper, the beauty of painting and illumination and everything that was painted, and thereby to love the world itself and God. Master Osman is more than a father to me."

"Would he beat you often?" he asked.

"In the role of a father, he beat me with an appropriate sense of justice; as a master, he beat me painfully so that I might learn from the punishment. Thanks to the pain and the fear of a ruler whacking my fingernails I learned many things better and faster than I would've alone. So he wouldn't grab me by my hair and bang my head against the wall when I was an apprentice, I'd never spill paint, never waste his gold wash, would quickly memorize, for example, the curve of a horse's foreleg, cover up the mistakes of the master limner, clean my brushes regularly and focus my attention and spirit on the page before me. Since I owe my talent and mastery to the beatings I received, I, in turn, beat my own apprentices without a guilty conscience. What's more, I know that even a beating given without just cause, if it doesn't break the spirit of the apprentice, will ultimately benefit him."

"Even so, you understand that while drubbing a handsome-faced, sweet-eyed, angelic apprentice, now and then, you get carried away by the sheer pleasure of it, and you know that Master Osman probably experienced the same sensation with you, don't you?"

"Sometimes he'd take a marble burnishing stone and strike me with such force behind the ear that my ear would ring for days, and I'd walk around half stunned. Sometimes he'd slap me so hard that for weeks my cheek would ache, enough to bring continual tears to my eyes. I shall never forget, yet I still love my mentor."

"Nay," said Black, "you were furious with him. You took revenge for the anger that silently accumulated deep within you by making illustrations for my Enishte's Frankish-imitation book."

"The opposite is true. The beatings that a young miniaturist receives from his master bind him to his master with a profound respect until the day he dies."

"The cruel and treacherous cutting of the throats of Iraj and Siyavush from behind, as you are doing to me, arose out of sibling rivalry, and sibling rivalry, as in the *Book of Kings,* is always provoked by an unjust father."

"True."

"The unjust father of you master miniaturists, the one who set you at each other's throats, is now preparing to betray you," he said brazenly. "Ahh, I beg of you, it is cutting," he whimpered. He cried in agony a bit longer. Then he went on, "True, cutting my throat and spilling my blood like a sacrificial lamb would be but the work of an instant, but if you do this without listening to what I'm about to explain—I don't think you'll do it anyway, ahh, please, enough—you'll forever wonder what I was going to say. Please, move the blade away slightly." I did so. "Master Osman, who followed your every step and your every breath since childhood, who happily watched your God-given talent bloom into artistry like a spring flower under his care, has now turned his back on you in order to save his workshop and its style, to which he has devoted his entire life."

"I recounted three parables to you the day we buried Elegant Effendi so you might know how disgusting this thing they call 'style' truly is."

"Those stories pertained to a miniaturist's individual style," said Black carefully, "whereas Master Osman is concerned with preserving the style of the entire workshop."

He explained how the Sultan attached great importance to finding the murderer of Elegant Effendi and his Enishte, how He'd even let them inspect the Royal Treasury to this end, and how Master Osman was using this opportunity to sabotage his Enishte's book and punish those who betrayed him by imitating the Europeans. Black added that based on style, Master Osman suspected Olive was responsible for the horse with the clipped nostrils, but as Head Illuminator, he was convinced of Stork's guilt and would turn him over to the executioners. I could sense he was telling the truth under the pressure of my sword, and I felt like kissing him because he gave himself over to what he was saying like a child. What I heard didn't worry me, having Stork out of the way meant I'd become Head Illuminator after Master Osman's death—may God grant him long life.

I wasn't disturbed that what he said might happen, but by the possibility that it might not. Reading between the lines of Black's account, I was able to glean that Master Osman was willing not only to sacrifice Stork, but me as well. Considering this incredible possibility made my heart quicken and drew me toward the horror of complete abandonment felt by a child who's suddenly lost his father. Each time this came to mind, I had to restrain myself from cutting Black's throat. I didn't attempt to argue the point with Black or myself: Why should the fact that we made a few foolish illustrations inspired by European masters lower us to the level of traitors? Once again, I thought that behind Elegant's death stood Stork and Olive and their schemes against me. I removed the sword from Black's throat.

"Let's go to Olive's house together, and search it from top to bottom," I said. "If the last picture is with him, at least we'll know whom to fear. If not, we'll take him with us as support and go on to raid Stork's house."

I told him to trust me and that his dagger was enough weaponry for the two of us. I apologized for not even having offered him a glass of linden tea. As I lifted the oil lamp from the floor, we both stared meaningfully at the cushion upon which I'd flattened him. I approached him with the lamp in my hand and told him how the ever-so-faint cut on his throat would be a mark of our friendship. He bled only slightly.

The commotion made by the Erzurumis and those pursuing them could still be heard on the streets, but no one noticed us. We were quick to arrive at Olive's house. We knocked on the courtyard door, the door of the house, and impatiently upon the shutters. Nobody was home; we made so much noise that we were certain he wasn't sleeping. Black gave voice to what we both were thinking: "Shall we go inside?"

I twisted the metal loop of the door lock using the blunt edge of Black's dagger, then inserting it into the space between door and jamb and levering it with all our weight, we broke the lock. We were met by the stench of dampness, dirt and loneliness, which had accumulated over years. By the light of the lamp, we noticed an unmade bed, sashes tossed randomly upon cushions, vests, two turbans, undershirts, Nimetullah Effendi the Nakshibendi's Persian dictionary, a wooden turban stand, broadcloth, needle and thread, a small copper pan full of apple peels, quite a few cushions, a velvet bedspread, his paints, his brushes and all of his supplies. I was on the verge of rifling through the writing paper, the layer upon layer of carefully trimmed Hindustan paper, and the illuminated pages on his small desk, but I restrained myself both because Black was more enthusiastic than I, and because I knew full well how a master miniaturist would incur nothing but bad luck if he went through the belongings of a less talented miniaturist. Olive is not as talented as is assumed, he's merely eager. He tries to cover up for his lack of talent with adoration of the old masters. The old legends, however, only rouse an artist's imagination; it's the hand that does the painting.

As Black was searching meticulously through all the chests and boxes, going as far as to check the bottoms of laundry baskets, without touching anything I glanced at Olive's Bursa towels, his ebony comb, his dirty bath hand towel, his rosewater bottles, a ridiculous waist cloth with an Indian block-print pattern, quilted jackets, a heavy, dirty women's robe with a slit, a dented copper tray, filthy carpets and other furnishings too cheap and slovenly for the money he earned. Olive was either very stingy and salting his money away or he was squandering it somehow . . .

"The house of a murderer, precisely," I said later. "There isn't even a prayer rug." But this wasn't what I was thinking. I concentrated. "These are the belongings of a man who doesn't know how to be happy . . ." I said. Yet, in a corner of my mind, I thought sadly about how misery and proximity to the Devil nursed painting.

"Despite knowing what it takes to be content, a man might still be unhappy," said Black.

He placed before me a series of pictures drawn on coarse Samarkand paper, backed with heavy sheets, which he'd removed from the depths of a chest. We studied the pictures: a delightful Satan all the way from Khorasan that had emerged from beneath the ground, a tree, a beautiful woman, a dog and the picture of Death I myself had drawn. These were the illustrations that the murdered storyteller hung up each night he told one of his disgraceful stories. Prompted by Black's question, I pointed out the picture of Death I had drawn.

"The same pictures are in my Enishte's book," he said.

"Both the storyteller and the proprietor of the coffeehouse realized the wisdom of having the miniaturists render the illustrations each night. The storyteller would have one of us quickly dash off an illustration on one of these coarse sheets, ask us a little about the story and about our in jokes and then, adding some of his own material, he'd start the evening's performance."

"Why did you make the same picture of Death for him that you made for my Enishte's book?"

"Upon the request of the storyteller, it was a lone figure on the page. But I didn't draw it with attention and effort the way I had for Enishte's book; I drew it quickly, the way my hand felt like drawing it. The others too, perhaps trying to be witty, drew for the storyteller in a cruder and simpler manner what they had made for that secret book."

"Who made the horse," he asked, "with the slit nostrils?"

Lowering the lamp we watched the horse in wonder. It resembled the horse made for Enishte's book, but it was quicker, more careless and catered to a simpler taste, as if somebody had not only paid the illustrator less money and made him work faster, but also forced him to make a rougher and, I suppose precisely for this reason, more realistic horse.

"Stork would know best who made this horse," I said. "He's a conceited fool who can't last a day without listening to the gossip of miniaturists, that's why he visits the coffeehouse every night. Yes, most certainly, Stork drew this horse."

CHAPTER 56

I AM CALLED "STORK"

Butterfly and Black arrived in the middle of the night; they spread the pictures on the floor before me, and asked me to tell them who'd made which illustration. It reminded me of the game "Whose Turban" we used to play when we were children: You'd draw the various headdresses of a hoja, a cavalryman, a judge, an executioner, a head treasurer and secretary and try to match them with the corresponding names written on other face-down sheets.

I told them I'd made the dog myself. We'd told its story to the storyteller. I said that gentle Butterfly, who held a dagger to my throat, must've drawn Death, over which the light of the lamp wavered pleasantly. I remembered that Olive had rendered Satan with great enthusiasm, whose story was spun entirely by the dearly departed storyteller. I'd started the tree whose leaves were drawn by all of us who came to the coffeehouse that night. We came up with the story as well. So it was with Red, too: Some red ink had splattered onto a page and the stingy storyteller asked if we could make a picture of it. We dribbled some more red ink onto the page, then each of us sketched the image of something red in a corner and told the story of his image so the storyteller might recount it. Olive made this exquisite horse here—praised be his talent—and I think it was Butterfly who drew the melancholy woman. Just then Butterfly removed the dagger from my throat and told Black that, yes, he now remembered how he'd drawn the woman. We all contributed to the gold coin in the bazaar, and Olive, a descendant of Kalenderis himself, drew the two dervishes. The sect of the Kalenderis is based on buggering young boys and begging and their sheikh, Evhad-üd Dini Kirmani wrote the sect's sacred book 250 years ago, revealing in verse that he'd seen God's perfection manifested in beautiful faces.

I asked the forgiveness of my master artist brethren for the disheveled state of our house, offering the excuse that we'd been caught unprepared, and I told them how sorry I was that we could offer them neither fragrant coffee nor sweet oranges because my wife was still asleep in the inner room. I said this so they wouldn't barge in there and I wouldn't have to wreak bloody havoc upon them when they didn't find what they were looking for among the canvas, drawstring cloth, summer sashes of Indian silk and fine muslin, Persian prints and dolmans in the baskets and trunks they eagerly rummaged through, under the carpets and cushions, among the illuminated pages I'd prepared for various books, and within the pages of bound volumes.

Nevertheless, I must confess that it gave me a certain pleasure to behave as if I were afraid of them. An artist's skill depends on carefully attending to the beauty of the present moment, taking everything down to the minutest detail seriously while, at the same time, stepping back from the world, which takes itself too seriously, and as if looking into a mirror, allowing for the distance and eloquence of a jest.

Accordingly, upon their asking, I said that, yes, when the Erzurumis began their raid, there was, as on most evenings, a crowd of about forty in the coffeehouse, which included, besides myself, Olive, Nasır the Limner, Jemal the calligrapher, two young assistant illustrators, the young calligraphers who were now spending their days and nights with them, Rahmi the apprentice of unsurpassed beauty, other handsome novices, six or seven men belonging to the lot of poets, drunks, hashish addicts and dervishes and others who cunningly charmed the proprietor into allowing them to join this mirthful and witty group. I explained how confusion reigned as soon as the raid began. When the crowd of onlookers gathered by the proprietor for some bawdy entertainment began to leave in a panic, no one thought to mount a defense of the establishment or of the poor old storyteller dressed as a woman. Did I grieve over this calamity? "Yes! I, Mustafa the Painter, also known as 'Stork,' who have truly devoted my entire life to illumination, find it necessary, each night, to sit together with my artist brethren and converse, joke, ridicule, pay compliments, recite poems and speak in innuendos," I confessed, looking directly into the eyes of dim-witted Butterfly, shrouded in the air of a plump, moist-eyed boy plagued by envy. Even as an apprentice, this Butterfly of ours, whose eyes were still as lovely as a child's, was a sensitive, fine-skinned beauty.

Again, upon their asking me, I described how on the second day that the storyteller, may his soul find peace in Heaven, wandering the city and neighborhoods began plying his trade in the coffeehouse, one of the miniaturists, perhaps under the influence of coffee, hung a picture on the wall to be amusing; the glib storyteller took notice and, as a joke of his own, began a monologue as if he were the dog in the picture, which met with great success; thenceforth, every night he continued to feature pictures drawn by the master miniaturists and to tell witty tales they whispered into his ear. Because the jibes at the preacher from Erzurum at once exhilarated the artists, who lived in terror of the preacher's wrath, and drew more customers to the coffeehouse, the proprietor from Edirne encouraged the performances.

They asked me my interpretation of the pictures the storyteller hung up behind himself each night, the ones they found during their raid of brother Olive's empty house. I explained that there was no need for interpretation because the proprietor, like Olive himself, was a begging, thieving, wild wretch of a Kalenderi dervish. The simple-minded Elegant Effendi, terrified of Hoja Effendi's exhortations, and especially of his fire-and-brimstone Friday sermons, must've complained of them to the Erzurumis. Or even more probable, when Elegant warned them to stop in their mischief, the proprietor and Olive, both of the same temperament, conspired to cruelly do away with the ill-fated gilder. The Erzurumis, incited by Elegant's murder, and perhaps because Elegant Effendi had described Enishte's book to them, held Enishte responsible for the murder and killed him; and, they must've raided the coffeehouse to complete their revenge.

How much attention were chubby Butterfly and grave Black (he was like a ghost) paying to what I said as they ransacked my possessions, gleefully lifting every lid and leaving not a stone unturned? When they came across my boots, armor and warrior's equipage in the embellished walnut trunk, a look of envy blossomed on Butterfly's childish face, and I once again declared what everybody already knew quite well. I was the first Muslim illustrator to set out on campaign with the army and the first to carefully study and depict what I'd witnessed in various victory *Chronicles*—the firing of cannon, the towers of enemy castles, the colors of infidel soldiers' uniforms, the sprawl of corpses, the piles of severed heads along riverbanks and the order and charge of armored cavalry!

When Butterfly asked me to show him how I donned my armor, I forthwith and without embarrassment took off my overshirt, my black rabbit-fur-lined undershirt, my trousers and my underwear. Pleased with the way they watched me by the light of the stove, I pulled on my clean long underwear, the thick shirt of red broadcloth worn under armor in cold weather, woolen socks, the boots of yellow leather, and over them, my gaiters. Removing it from its case, I was delighted to put on my breastplate, then I turned my back toward Butterfly and as if ordering a pageboy, had him do up the laces of the armor tightly and ordered him to attach my shoulder plates. As I was putting on my vambraces, gloves, the camel hair sword belt and finally the gold-worked helmet that I wore for ceremonies, I proudly declared that henceforth battle scenes would never again be depicted as they'd been in days of old. "It is no longer permissible to depict the cavalries of two opposing armies uniformly using the same pattern as a guide and simply flipping it over to draw the enemy's forces," I said. "From now on, the battle scenes made in the workshops of the Ottomans will be drawn the way I've seen them and drawn them: a tumult of armies, horses, armor-clad warriors and bloodied bodies!"

Seized by envy, Butterfly said, "The illuminator draws not what he sees, but what Allah sees."

"Yes," I said, "however, exalted Allah certainly sees everything we see."

"Of course, Allah sees what we see, but He doesn't perceive it the way we do," said Butterfly as if chastising me. "The confused battle scene that we perceive in our bewilderment, He perceives in His omniscience as two opposing armies in an orderly array."

Naturally, I had a response. I wanted to say, "It falls to us to believe in Allah and to depict only what He reveals to us, not what He conceals," but I held my peace. And I hadn't kept quiet because Butterfly would otherwise accuse me of imitating the Europeans or because he was relentlessly striking one end of his dagger against my helmet and back, supposedly to test my armor, but because I calculated that only if I restrained myself and won over Black and this pretty-eyed oaf could we deliver ourselves from Olive's scheming.

Once they knew they wouldn't find what they were looking for here, they told me what they were after. There was a picture that the unspeakable murderer had absconded with . . . I said that my house was already searched for the same reason; as a result, the wise murderer most certainly would've hid that picture where nobody could ever find it (I was thinking of Olive), but did they heed my words? Black explained the horse drawn with clipped nostrils and how the three-day period Our Sultan had granted Master Osman was well nigh over. When I inquired further about the significance of the clipped nostrils, Black told me, looking straight into my eyes, how Master Osman, analyzing them as a clue, linked them to Olive, although he suspected me even more, being no stranger to my ambitions.

At first, it appeared they'd come here prepared to believe that I was the murderer and to find proof of it, but in my opinion, this wasn't the sole reason for their visit. They'd also come knocking at my door out of loneliness and desperation. When I opened the door, the dagger that Butterfly pointed at me shook in his hand. Not only were they terrified, thinking that the despicable murderer, whose identity they were at such pains to uncover, might corner them in the darkness, smiling like an old friend, and swiftly cut their throats, they were also losing sleep for fear that Master Osman might conspire with Our Sultan and the Head Treasurer to turn them over to the torturer—not to mention the mob of Erzurumis roaming the streets, which demoralized them. In short, they desired my friendship. But Master Osman had instilled in them the opposite notion. It was my present obligation to show them sincerely how Master Osman was mistaken, which is what they'd hoped for deep down anyway.

Simply declaring that the great master was mistaken and that he'd become senile would surely arouse Butterfly's enmity. For in the watery eyes of the handsome illuminator, whose eyelashes fluttered like the insect he was named for as he banged upon my armor with his dagger, I could still make out the pale fire of love he felt for the great master, whose favorite he had been. In my youth, the closeness of those two, master and apprentice, was enviously ridiculed by the others; but they themselves paid no mind, they'd stare into each other's eyes at length and fondle each other in front of everybody; later still, Master Osman would declare tactlessly that Butterfly was possessed of the most agile pen and the most mature color brush. This declaration—often quite true—became the source of endless puns among the jealous miniaturists using pens, brushes, inkpots and pen boxes in vulgar allusions, devilish comparisons and indecent metaphors. For this reason, I'm not the only one who senses that Master Osman wants Butterfly to succeed him as head of the workshop. I've long understood from the way he talks to others about my belligerence, incompatibility and stubbornness that this is what the great master has hidden in the back of his mind. He thinks, justifiably, that I tend far more toward the European methods than Olive or Butterfly, and could never resist Our Sultan's new desires by saying, "The great masters of old would never paint this way."

I knew I'd be able to cooperate closely with Black because our eager new groom must've wanted to complete his deceased Enishte's book, not only to conquer beautiful Shekure's heart and show her that he could fill her father's shoes, but also, most probably, to ingratiate himself with Our Sultan by the quickest means possible.

Therefore, I introduced the matter quite unexpectedly by saying that Enishte's book was a blissful miracle without equal in the world. When this masterpiece was completed, in keeping with Our Sultan's decree and the late Enishte Effendi's desire, the whole world would marvel over the Ottoman Sultan's power and wealth as well as the talent, elegance and ability of us, His master miniaturists. Not only would they fear us, our power and our relentlessness, they'd be bewildered, seeing how we laughed and cried, how we stole from the Frankish masters, how we saw the most buoyant colors and the minutest of details; and ultimately, they would acknowledge with terror what only the most intelligent sultans understood: that we were situated both within the world of our paintings and far far away in the company of the old masters.

Butterfly had been striking me all along, first like a child eager to determine whether or not my armor was genuine; next, like a friend who wanted to test its strength; and finally, like an incorrigible and jealous foe who wanted to do me harm. In truth, he understood that I was more talented than he; even worse, he probably sensed that Master Osman knew this too. With his God-given talent, Butterfly was a superb master, and his envy made me prouder: Unlike him, I became a master through the strength of my own "reed," not by holding my master's, and I sensed that I could force him to accept my superiority.

Raising my voice, I explained how pitiful it was that there were men who wanted to undermine Our Sultan and the late Enishte's miraculous book. Master Osman was like a father to us all; he was everyone's superior; we learned everything from him! Yet, after tracing the clues in Our Sultan's Treasury, for some unknown reason, Master Osman tried to conceal his realization that Olive was the despicable murderer. I said I was certain that Olive, who couldn't be found at home, was hiding away in the deserted Kalenderi dervish house near the Phanar Gate. This dervish lodge was closed during the reign of Our Sultan's grandfather, not because it was a den of degradation and immorality, but rather, as a result of the endless wars with the Persians, and, I added, there was even a time when Olive boasted that he was keeping guard over the forbidden dervish lodge. If they didn't trust me, suspecting some ruse behind my words, the dagger was in their hands, they were free to mete out my punishment then and there.

Butterfly landed two more heavy blows of the dagger that most armor could not have withstood. He turned to Black, who believed what I told them, and screamed at him childishly. I came up from behind, put my armor-plated arm around Butterfly's neck and drew him toward me. Bending his other arm back with my free hand, I made him drop the dagger. We weren't quite struggling, nor were we entirely playing. I recounted a similar, little-known scene in the *Book of Kings*.

"On the third day of a confrontation between Persian and Turanian armies fully equipped in armor and weaponry and arrayed at the foot of Mount Hamaran, the Turanians sent the wily Shengil into the field to learn the identity of a mysterious Persian who'd killed a great Turanian warrior on each of the previous two days," I began. "Shengil challenged the mysterious warrior, and he accepted. The armies, their armor glimmering brightly in the afternoon sun, watched with bated breath. The armored horses of the two warriors engaged each other with such speed that sparks flying from the clash of metal singed the hides of the horses which gave off smoke. The fight was a lengthy one. The Turanian shot arrows; the Persian maneuvered his sword and horse skillfully; and finally, the mysterious Persian felled the Turanian after catching him by the tail of his steed. He then chased after Shengil who was trying to escape, and grabbed him by his armor from behind before taking him by the neck. As he accepted his defeat, the Turanian, still curious about the identity of the mysterious warrior, asked without hope what everybody had wondered for days, 'Who are you?' 'To you,' replied the mysterious warrior, 'my name is Death.' Tell me then, my friends, who was he?"

"The legendary Rüstem," said Butterfly with childlike glee.

I kissed him on the neck. "We've all betrayed Master Osman," I said. "Before he metes out his punishment, we must find Olive, rid ourselves of this venom in our midst and come to an agreement so we can stand strong against the eternal enemies of art and those who long to send us directly to dungeons of torture. Perhaps, when we arrive at Olive's abandoned dervish house, we'll learn that the cruel murderer isn't even one of our lot."

Poor Butterfly uttered not a sound. Regardless of how talented, confident or well supported he might be, just like all illuminators who sought one another's company depite their mutual loathing and envy, he was deathly afraid of being left alone in this world and of going to Hell.

On the route to the Phanar Gate, there was an eerie greenish-yellow light above us, but it wasn't the light of the moon. In this light, the old, faithful nighttime appearance of Istanbul comprised of cypress trees, leaden domes, stone walls, wooden houses and tracts ravaged by fire was overtaken by an unfamiliarity such as might be caused by an enemy fortress. As we ascended the hill, in the distance we saw the fire that burned somewhere beyond the Bayazid Mosque.

In the heavy darkness, we came across an oxcart half-loaded with sacks of flour heading toward the city walls, and parting with two silver coins, we procured a ride. Black had the pictures with him, and he sat down carefully. As I lay back and watched the low clouds glow from the fire, two raindrops fell upon my helmet.

After a long journey, as we searched for the deserted dervish lodge we roused all the dogs in the neighborhood which, in the middle of the night, seemed to be abandoned. Although we saw that lamps were now burning in a few stone houses in response to our clamor, it was only the fourth door we knocked upon that opened to us, and a man in skullcap, gaping at us by the light of his lamp as if we were the living dead, gave us directions to the deserted dervish lodge without even sticking his nose out into the quickening rain—merrily adding that once there, we'd have no peace from the evils of jinns, demons and ghosts.

In the garden of the dervish lodge we were greeted by the calm of proud cypresses, indifferent to the rain and the stench of rotting leaves. I brought my eye up to one of the cracks between the wooden planks of the dervish-lodge walls, and later, to the shutter of a small window, whereupon, by the light of an oil lamp, I saw the menacing shadow of a man performing his prayers—or perhaps, a man pretending, for our sake, to pray.

CHAPTER 57

I AM CALLED "OLIVE"

Was it more fitting for me to abandon my prayers, spring to my feet and open the door for them or to keep them waiting in the rain until I'd finished? When I realized they were watching me, I completed my prayers in a somewhat distracted state. I opened the door, and there they were—Butterfly, Stork and Black. I gave a cry of joy and embraced Butterfly.

"Alas, what we've had to bear of late!" I lamented, burying my head into his shoulder. "What do they want from us? Why are they killing us?"

Each of them displayed the panic of being separated from the herd, which I'd seen from time to time in every master painter over the span of my life. Even here in the lodge, they were loath to separate from one another.

"We can safely take refuge here for days."

"We worry," Black said, "that the person we should fear is perhaps in our very midst."

"I, too, grow anxious," I said. "For I have heard such rumors as well."

There were rumors, spreading from the officers of the Imperial Guard to the division of miniaturists, claiming that the mystery about the murderer of Elegant Effendi and late Enishte was solved: He was one of us who'd labored over that book.

Black inquired as to how many pictures I'd drawn for Enishte's book.

"The first one I made was Satan. It was of the variety of underground demon common to the old masters in the workshops of the Whitesheep. The storyteller and I were of the same Sufi path; that's why I made the two dervishes. I was the one who suggested to Enishte that he include them in his book, convincing him that there was a special place for these dervishes in the lands of the Ottomans."

"Is that all?" asked Black.

When I told him, "Yes, that's all," he went to the door with the superior air of a master who caught an apprentice stealing; he brought in a roll of paper untouched by the rain, and placed it before us three artists like a mother cat bringing a wounded bird to her kittens.

I recognized the pages while they were still under his arm: They were the illustrations I'd rescued from the coffeehouse during the raid. I didn't deign to ask how these men had entered my house and located them. Nevertheless, Butterfly, Stork and I each placidly owned up to the pictures we made for the storyteller, may he rest in peace. Afterward, only the horse, an exquisite horse, remained unclaimed off to the side, its head lowered. Believe me, I didn't even realize that a horse had been drawn.

"You weren't the one who made this horse?" said Black like a teacher holding a switch.

"I wasn't," I said.

"What about the one in my Enishte's book?"

"I didn't make that one either."

"Based on the style of the horse, however, it's been determined that you're the one who drew it," he said. "Furthermore, it was Master Osman who came to this conclusion."

"But I have no style whatsoever," I said. "I'm not saying this out of pride to counter the latest tastes. Neither am I saying so to prove my innocence. For me, having a style would be worse than being a murderer."

"You have a distinct quality that distinguishes you from the old masters and the others," said Black.

I Am Called "Olive"

I smiled at him. He started to relate things that I'm sure you all know by now. I listened intently to how Our Sultan, in consultation with the Head Treasurer, sought a solution to the murders, to the matter of Master Osman's three days, to the "courtesan method," to the peculiarity in the noses of the horses and to Black's miraculous admittance to the Royal Private Quarters for the sake of actually examining those superlative books. There are moments in all our lives when we realize, even as we experience them, that we are living through events we will never forget, even long afterward. A melancholy rain was falling. As if upset by the rain, Butterfly mournfully gripped his dagger. Olive, the backside of whose armor was white with flour, was courageously forging into the heart of the dervish lodge, lamp in hand. These master artists, whose shadows roamed the walls like ghosts, were my brethren, and how I loved them! I was delighted to be a miniaturist.

"Could you appreciate your good fortune as you gazed at the great works of the old masters for days on end with Master Osman at your side?" I asked Black. "Did he kiss you? Did he caress your handsome face? Did he hold your hand? Were you awed by his talent and knowledge?"

"There among the great works of the old masters he showed me how you had a style," said Black. "He taught me how the hidden fault of 'style' isn't something the artist selects of his own volition, but is determined by the artist's past and his forgotten memories. He also showed me how these secret faults, weaknesses and defects, at one time such a source of shame they were concealed so we wouldn't be estranged from the old masters, will henceforth emerge to be praised as 'personal characteristics' or 'style,' because the European masters have spread them over the world. Henceforth, thanks to fools who take pride in their own shortcomings, the world will be a more colorful and more stupid and, of course, a much more imperfect place."

The fact that Black confidently believed in what he said proved that he was one of the new breed of fools.

"Was Master Osman able to explain why, for years, I drew hundreds of horses with regular nostrils in Our Sultan's books?" I asked.

"It was due to the love and beatings he gave all of you in your childhood. Because he was both father and beloved to you all, he doesn't see that he associates all of you with himself and each of you with the others. He didn't want you each to have a style of your own, he wanted the royal atelier as a whole to have a style. Because of the awesome shadow he cast over all of you, you forgot what came from within, the imperfections, the elements and differences that fell outside the confines of standard forms. Only when you painted for other books and other pages, which Master Osman's eyes would never see, did you draw the horse that had lain within you all those years."

"My mother, may she rest in peace, was more intelligent than my father," I said. "One night I was at home, in tears, determined never again to return to the workshop because I was daunted not only by Master Osman's beatings, but by those of the other harsh and irritable masters and by those of the division head who always intimidated us with a ruler. In consolation, my dearly departed mother advised me that there were two types of people in the world: those who were cowed and crushed by their childhood beatings, forever downtrodden, she said, because the beatings had the desired effect of killing the inner devils; and those fortunate ones for whom the beatings frightened and tamed the devil within without killing him off. Though the latter group would never forget these painful childhood memories—she'd warned me not to tell this to anybody—the beatings would in time enable them to develop cunning, to fathom the unknown, to make friends, to identify enemies, to sense plots being hatched behind their backs and, let me hasten to add, to paint better than anyone else. Because I wasn't able to draw the branches of a tree harmoniously, Master Osman would slap me so hard that, amid bitter tears, forests would burgeon before me. After angrily striking me in the head because I couldn't see the errors at the bottoms of pages, he lovingly took up a mirror and placed it before the page so I could see the work as if for the first time. Then pressing his cheek to mine, he so lovingly identified the mistakes that magically appeared in the mirror image of the picture that I never forgot either the love or the ritual. The morning after a night spent weeping in my bed, my pride violated because he chastised me with a ruler before everyone, he came and kissed my arms so tenderly that I passionately knew I'd one day become a legendary miniaturist. Nay, it was not I who drew that horse."

"We," Black was referring to Stork and himself, "will search the dervish house for the last picture which was stolen by the accursed man who murdered my Enishte. Did you ever see that last picture?"

"It is nothing that could be accepted by Our Sultan, illuminators like us bound to the old masters or by Muslims bound to their faith," I said and fell silent.

My statement made him more eager. He and Stork began their search of the premises, turning the whole place upside down. A few times, simply to make their work easier, I went to them. In one of the dervish cells with a leaky ceiling, I pointed out the hole in the floor so they wouldn't fall and could search it if they so desired. I gave them the large key to the small room in which the sheikh lived thirty years ago, before the adherents of this lodge joined up with the Bektashis and dispersed. They entered eagerly, but when they saw that an entire wall was missing and the room was open to the rain, they didn't even bother to search it.

It pleased me that Butterfly wasn't with them, but if evidence implicating me were found, he, too, would join their ranks. Stork was of the same mind as Black, who was afraid that Master Osman would turn us over to the torturers, and maintained that we must support one another and must be united in confronting the Head Treasurer. I sensed Black was not only motivated by the desire to give Shekure a genuine wedding present by finding his Enishte's murderer, he also intended to set Ottoman miniaturists on the path of European masters by paying them with the Sultan's money in order to finish his Enishte's book in imitation of the Franks (which was not only sacrilegious, but ridiculous). I also understood, with some certainty, that at the root of this scheme was Stork's desire to be rid of us and even of Master Osman, for he dreamt of being Head Illuminator and (since everyone guessed that Master Osman preferred Butterfly) he was prepared to try anything to increase his chances. I was momentarily confused. Listening to the rain, I deliberated at length. Next, like a man who breaks away from the crowd and struggles to give his petition to the sovereign and grand vizier as they pass on horseback, I had the sudden inspiration to endear myself to Stork and Black. Leading them through a dark hallway and large portal, I took them to a frightening room that was once the kitchen. I asked them if they were able to find anything here among the ruins. Of course, they hadn't. There was no trace of the kettles, the pots and pans and the bellows that were once used to prepare food for the forsaken and the poor. I never even attempted to clean up this ghastly room covered in cobwebs, dust, mud, debris and the excrement of dogs and cats. As always, a strong wind, rising up as if out of nowhere, dimmed the lamp—making our shadows now lighter, now darker.

"You searched and searched but you couldn't find my hidden treasure," I said.

Out of habit, I used the back of my hand as a broom to sweep away the ashes in what used to be a hearth and when an old stove emerged, I lifted up its iron lid with a creak. I held the lamp to the small mouth of the stove. I shall never forget how Stork leapt forward and greedily grabbed the leather pouches within before Black could act. He was about to open the pouches right there in the mouth of the oven, but as I had returned to the large salon, followed by Black who was afraid of remaining here, Stork bounded after us on his long thin legs.

When they saw that one pouch contained a pair of clean woolen socks, my drawstring trousers, my red underwear, the nicest of my undershirts, my silk shirt, my straight razor, my comb and other belongings, they were momentarily at a loss. Out of the other pouch, which Black opened, emerged fifty-three Venetian gold coins, pieces of gold leaf that I'd stolen from the workshop in recent years, my sketchbook of model forms which I concealed from everybody, more stolen gold leaf hidden between the pages, indecent pictures—some of which I'd drawn myself and some I'd collected—a keepsake agate ring from my dear mother along with a lock of her white hair, and my best pens and brushes.

"If I were truly a murderer as you suspect," I said with stupid pride, "the final picture would've emerged from my secret treasury, not these things."

"Why these things?" asked Stork.

"When the Imperial Guard searched my house, as they did yours, they shamelessly pilfered two of these gold pieces that I've spent my entire life collecting. I thought about how we'd be searched again on account of this wretched murderer—and I was right. If that last picture were with me, it would be here."

It was a mistake to utter this last sentence; nevertheless, I could sense that they were put at ease and no longer afraid that I'd strangle them in a dark corner of the lodge. Have I gained your trust as well?

At this time, however, I was overwhelmed by a severe restlessness; no, it wasn't that my illuminator friends, whom I'd known since childhood, saw how I'd been greedily squirreling money away for years, how I bought and saved gold, or even that they learned about my sketchbooks and obscene pictures. In truth, I regretted having shown them all of these things in a moment of panic. Only the mysteries of a man who lived quite aimlessly could be exposed so easily.

"Nonetheless," said Black much later, "we must come to a consensus about what we will say under torture if Master Osman happens to turn us over without any forewarning."

A hollowness and depression descended upon us. In the pale light of the lamp, Stork and Butterfly were staring at the vulgar pictures in my sketchbook. They displayed an air of complete indifference; in fact, they were even happy in some horrid way. I had a strong urge to look at the picture—I could very well surmise which one it was; I rose and circled around behind them, gazing silently at the obscene picture I'd painted, thrilled as though I were recalling a now distant yet blissful memory. Black joined us. For whatever reason, that the four of us were looking at that illustration relieved me.

"Could the blind and the seeing ever be equal?" said Stork much later. Was he implying that even though what we saw was obscene, the pleasure of sight that Allah had bestowed upon us was glorious? Nay, what would Stork know of such matters? He never read the Koran. I knew that the old masters of Herat would frequently recite this verse. The great masters used this verse as a response to enemies of painting who warned that illustrating was forbidden by our faith and that painters would be sent to Hell on Judgment Day. Until that magical moment, however, I'd never even once heard from Butterfly those words that now emerged from his mouth as if on their own:

"I'd like to depict how the blind and the seeing are not equal!"

"Who are the blind and the seeing?" Black said naively.

"The blind and the seeing are not equal, it's what *'ve ma yestevil'ama ve'l basiru'nun* means," Butterfly said and continued:

"... *nor are the darkness and the light.*
The shade and the heat are not equal,
nor are the living and the dead."

I shuddered for an instant, thinking of the fates of Elegant Effendi, Enishte and our storyteller brother who was killed tonight. Were the others as frightened as I? Nobody moved for a time. Stork was still holding my book open, but seemed not to see the vulgarity I'd painted though we were all still staring at it!

"I'd want to paint Judgment Day," said Stork. "The resurrection of the dead, and the separation of the guilty from the innocent. Why is it that we cannot depict the Sacred Word of our faith?"

In our youth, working together in the same room of our workshop, we would periodically lift our faces from our work boards and tables, just as the aging masters would do to rest their eyes, and begin talking about any topic that happened to enter our minds. Back then, just as we now did while looking at the book open before us, we didn't look at one another as we chatted. For our eyes would be turned toward some distant spot outside an open window. I'm not sure if it was the excitement of recalling something remarkably beautiful from my halcyon apprenticeship days, or the sincere regret I felt at that moment because I hadn't read the Koran for so long, or the horror of the crime I'd seen at the coffeehouse that night, but when my turn came to speak, I grew confused, my heart quickened as if I'd come under the threat of some danger, and as nothing else came to mind, I simply said the following:

"You remember those verses at the end of 'The Cow' chapter? I'd want most of all to depict them: 'Oh God, judge us not by what we've forgotten and by our mistakes. Oh God, burden us not with a weight we cannot bear, as with those who have gone before us. Forgive and absolve us of our transgressions and sins! Treat us with mercy, my dear God.'" My voice broke and I was embarrassed by the tears I shed unexpectedly—perhaps because I was wary of the sarcasm that we always kept at the ready during our apprenticeships to protect ourselves and to avoid exposing our sensitivities.

I thought my tears would quickly abate, but unable to restrain myself, I began to cry in great sobs. As I wept, I could sense that each of the others was overcome by feelings of fraternity, devastation and sorrow. From now on, the European style would be preeminent in Our Sultan's workshop; the styles and books to which we'd devoted our entire lives would slowly be forgotten—yes, in fact, the whole venture would come to an end, and if the Erzurumis didn't throttle us and finish us off, the Sultan's torturers would leave us maimed... But as I cried, sobbed and sighed—even though I continued to listen to the sad patter of the rain—a part of my mind sensed that these were not the things I was actually crying about. To what extent were the others aware of this? I felt vaguely guilty for my tears, which were at once genuine and false.

Butterfly came up beside me, placed his arm upon my shoulder, stroked my hair, kissed my cheek and comforted me with honeyed words. This show of friendship made me cry with even more sincerity and guilt. I couldn't see his face but, for some reason, I incorrectly thought he too was crying. We sat down.

We recalled how we'd started our workshop apprenticeships in the same year, the strange sadness of being torn away from our mothers to suddenly begin a new life, the pain of beatings we received from the first day, the joy of the first gifts from the Head Treasurer, and the days we went back home, running the whole way. At first, only he talked while I listened sorrowfully, but later, when Stork and, sometime afterward, Black—who came to the workshop for a time and left it, during our early apprenticeship years—joined our mournful conversation, I forgot that I'd just been crying and began to talk and laugh freely with them.

We reminisced about winter mornings when we would wake early, light the stove in the largest room of the workshop and mop the floors with hot water. We recalled an old "master," may he rest in peace, who was so uninspired and cautious that he could draw only a single leaf of a single tree during the span of a single day and who, when he saw that we were again looking at the lush green leaves of the springtime trees through the open window rather than at the leaf he drew, without striking us, would chastise us for the hundredth time: "Not out there, in here!" We recalled the wailing, which could be heard throughout the entire atelier, of the scrawny apprentice who walked toward the door, satchel in hand, having been sent back home because the intensity of the work caused one of his eyes to wander. Next, we imagined how we watched (with pleasure because it wasn't our fault) the slow spread of a deadly red seeping from a bronze inkpot that had cracked over a page three illuminators had labored on for three months (it depicted the Ottoman army on the banks of the Kınık River en route to Shirvan, overcoming the threat of starvation by occupying Eresh and filling their stomachs). In a refined and respectful manner, we talked about how the three of us together made love to and together fell in love with a Circasian lady, the most beautiful of the wives of a seventy-year-old pasha who—in consideration of his conquests, strength and wealth—wanted ceiling ornamentation in his home made in imitation of the designs in Our Sultan's hunting lodge. Then, we longingly recalled how on winter mornings we would have our lentil soup on the threshold of the yawning door so its steam wouldn't soften the paper. We also lamented being separated from workshop friends and masters when the latter compelled us to travel to distant places to serve as journeymen. For a time, the sweetness of my dear Butterfly in his sixteenth year appeared before my eyes: He was burnishing paper to a high gloss by rubbing it quickly with a smooth seashell as the sunlight, coming through an open window on a summer's day, struck his naked honey-colored forearms. For a moment he stopped what he was so absentmindedly doing and carefully lowered his face to the page to examine a blemish. After making a few passes over the offending spot with the burnishing shell using different motions, he returned to his former pattern, moving his hand back and forth as he stared out of the window into the distance, losing himself in daydreams. I shall never forget how before looking outside again, he briefly gazed into my eyes—as I would later do to others. This dolorous look has only one meaning, which all apprentices know quite well: Time doesn't flow if you don't dream.

CHAPTER 58

I WILL BE CALLED A MURDERER

You'd forgotten about me, hadn't you? Why should I conceal my presence from you any longer? For speaking in this voice, which is gradually getting stronger and stronger, has become irresistible for me. At times, I restrain myself only with great effort, and I'm afraid that the strain in my voice will give me away. At times, I let myself go completely unchecked, and that's when those words, signs of my second character, which you might recognize, spill from my lips; my hands begin to tremble, beads of sweat collect on my forehead and I realize at once that these little whispers of my body, in turn, will furnish new clues.

Yet I'm so very content here! As we console ourselves with twenty-five years of memories we're reminded not of the animosities, but of the beauties and the pleasures of painting. There's also something in our sitting here with a sense of the impending end of the world, caressing each other with tear-filled eyes as we remember the beauty of bygone days, that recalls harem women.

I've taken this comparison from Abu Said of Kirman who included the stories of the old masters of Shiraz and Herat in his *History* of the sons of Tamerlane. Thirty years ago, Jihan Shah, ruler of the Blacksheep, came to the East where he routed the small armies and ravaged the lands of the Timurid khans and shahs who were fighting among themselves. With his victorious Turkmen hordes, he passed through the whole of Persia into the East; finally, at Astarabad, he defeated Ibrahim, the grandson of Shah Ruh who was Tamerlane's son; he then took Gorgan and sent his armies against the fortress of Herat. According to the historian from Kirman, this devastation, not only to Persia, but to the heretofore undefeated power of the House of Tamerlane, which had ruled over half the world from Hindustan to Byzantium for half a century, caused such a tempest of destruction that pandemonium reigned over the men and women in the besieged fortress of Herat. The historian Abu Said reminds the reader with perverse pleasure how Jihan Shah of the Blacksheep mercilessly killed everyone who was a descendant of Tamerlane in the fortresses he conquered; how he selectively culled women from the harems of shahs and princes and added them to his own harem; and how he pitilessly separated miniaturist from miniaturist and cruelly forced most of them to serve as apprentices to his own master illuminators. At this point in his *History*, he turns his attentions from the shah and his warriors who tried to repel the enemy from the crenellated towers of the fortress, to the miniaturists among their pens and paints in the workshop awaiting the terrifying culmination of the siege whose outcome was long evident. He lists the names of the artists, declaring one after another how they were world-renowned and would never be forgotten, and these illuminators, all of whom, like the women of the shah's harem, have since been forgotten, embraced each other and wept, unable to do anything but recall their former days of bliss.

We too, like melancholy harem women, reminisced about the gifts of fur-lined caftans and purses full of money that the Sultan would present to us in reciprocation for the colorful decorated boxes, mirrors and plates, embellished ostrich eggs, cut-paper work, single-leaf pictures, amusing albums, playing cards and books we'd offer him on holidays. Where were the hardworking, long-suffering, elderly artists of that day who were satisfied with so little? They'd never sequester themselves at home and jealously hide their methods from others, dreading that their moonlighting would be found out, but would come to the workshop every day without fail. Where were the old miniaturists who humbly devoted their entire lives to drawing intricate designs on castle walls, cypress leaves whose uniqueness was discernible only after close scrutiny and the seven-leaf steppe grasses used to fill empty spaces? Where were the uninspired masters who never grew jealous, having accepted the wisdom and justice inherent in God's bestowal of talent and ability upon some artists and patience and pious resignation upon others? We recalled these fatherly masters, some of whom were hunched and perpetually smiling, others dreamy and drunk and still others intent upon foisting off a spinster daughter; and as we recollected, we attempted to resurrect the forgotten details of the workshop as it had been during our apprentice and early mastership years.

Do you remember the limner who stuck his tongue into his cheek when he ruled pages—to the left side if the line he drew headed right, and to the right side if the line went left; the small, thin artist who laughed to himself, chortling and mumbling "patience, patience, patience" when he dribbled paint; the septuagenarian master gilder who spent hour upon hour talking to the binder's apprentices downstairs and claimed that red ink applied to the forehead stopped aging; the ornery master who relied on an unsuspecting apprentice or even randomly stopped anyone passing by to test the consistency of paint upon their fingernails after his own nails were completely filled; and the portly artist who made us laugh as he caressed his beard with the furry rabbit's foot used to collect the excess flecks of gold dust used in gilding? Where were they all?

Where were the burnishing boards which were used so much they became a part of the apprentices' bodies and then just tossed aside, and the long paper scissors that the apprentices dulled by playing "swordsman"? Where were the writing boards inscribed with the names of the great masters so they wouldn't get mixed up, the aroma of China ink and the faint rattle of coffeepots aboil in the silence? Where were the various brushes we made of hairs from the necks and inner ears of kittens born to our tabby cats each summer, and the great sheaves of Indian paper given to us so, in idle moments, we could practice our artistry the way calligraphers did? Where was the ugly steel-handled penknife whose use required permission from the Head Illuminator, thus providing a deterrent to the entire workshop when we had to scrape away large mistakes; and what happened to the rituals that surrounded these mistakes?

We also agreed that it was wrong for the Sultan to allow the master miniaturists to work at home. We recalled the marvelous warm halva that came to us from the palace kitchen on early winter evenings after we'd worked with aching eyes by the light of oil lamps and candles. Laughing and with tears in our eyes, we remembered how the elderly and senile master gilder, who was stricken with chronic trembling and could take up neither pen nor paper, on his monthly workshop visits brought fried dough-balls in heavy syrup that his daughter had made for us apprentices. We talked about the exquisite pages rendered by the dearly departed Black Memi, Head Illuminator before Master Osman, discovered in his room, which remained empty for days after his funeral, within the portfolio found beneath the light mattress he'd spread out and use for catnaps in the afternoons.

We talked about and named the pages we took pride in and would want to take out and look at now and again if we had copies of them, the way Master Black Memi had. They explained how the sky on the upper half of the palace picture made for the *Book of Skills*, illuminated with gold wash, foreshadowed the end of the world, not due to the gold itself, but due to its tone between towers, domes and cypresses—the way gold ought to be used in a polite rendition.

They described a portrayal of Our Exalted Prophet's bewilderment and ticklishness, as angels seized him by his underarms during his ascension to Heaven from the top of a minaret; a picture of such grave colors that even children, upon seeing the blessed scene, would first tremble with pious awe and then laugh respectfully as if they themselves were being tickled. I explained how along one edge of a page I'd commemorated the previous Grand Vizier's suppression of rebels who'd taken to the mountains by delicately and respectfully arranging the heads he'd severed, tastefully drawing each one, not as an ordinary corpse's head, but as an individual and unique face in the manner of a Frankish portraitist, furrowing their brows before death, dabbing red onto their necks, making their sorrowful lips inquire after the meaning of life, opening their nostrils to one final, desperate breath, and shutting their eyes to this world; and thus, I'd imbued the painting with a terrifying aura of mystery.

As if they were our own unforgettable and unattainable memories, we wistfully discussed our favorite scenes of love and war, recalling their most magnificent wonders and tear-inducing subtleties. Isolated and mysterious gardens where lovers met on starry nights passed before our eyes: spring trees, fantastic birds, frozen time . . . We imagined bloody battles as immediate and alarming as our own nightmares, bodies torn in two, chargers with blood-spattered armor, beautiful men stabbing each other with daggers, the small-mouthed, small-handed, slanted-eye, bowed women watching events from barely open windows . . . We recalled pretty boys who were haughty and conceited, and handsome shahs and khans, their power and palaces long lost to history. Just like the women who wept together in the harems of those shahs, we now knew we were passing from life into memory, but were we passing from history into legend as they had? To avoid being drawn further into a realm of horror by the lengthening shadows of the fear of being forgotten—even more terrifying than the fear of dying—we asked each other about our favorite scenes of death.

The first thing to come to mind was the way Satan duped Dehhak into killing his father. At the time of that legend, which is described in the beginning of the *Book of Kings*, the world had been newly created, and everything was so basic that nothing needed explanation. If you wanted milk, you simply milked a goat and drank; you'd say "horse," then mount it and ride away; you'd contemplate "evil" and Satan would appear and convince you of the beauty of murdering your own father. Dehhak's murder of Merdas, his father of Arab descent, was beautiful, both because it was unprovoked and because it occurred at night in a magnificent palace garden while golden stars gently illuminated cypresses and colorful spring flowers.

Next, we recalled legendary Rüstem, who unknowingly killed his son Suhrab, commander of the enemy army that Rüstem had battled for three days. There was something that touched us all in the way Rüstem beat his breast in tearful anguish when he saw the armband he had given the boy's mother years ago and recognized as his own son the enemy whose chest he'd ravished with thrusts of the sword.

What was that something?

The rain continued its patter on the roof of the dervish lodge and I paced back and forth. Suddenly I said the following:

"Either our father, Master Osman, will betray and kill us, or we shall betray and kill him."

We were stricken with horror because what I said rang absolutely true; we fell silent. Still pacing, and panicked by the thought that everything would revert to its former state, I told myself the following: "Tell the story of Afrasiyab's murder of Siyavush to change the subject. But that's a betrayal such as fails to frighten me. Recount the death of Hüsrev." All right then, but should it be the version told by Firdusi in the *Book of Kings* or the one told by Nizami in *Hüsrev and Shirin*? The pathos of the account in the *Book of Kings* rests in Hüsrev's tearful realization of the identity of the murderer intruding in his bedroom chamber! As a last resort, saying that he wants to perform his prayers, Hüsrev sends the servant boy attending him to fetch water, soap, clean clothes and his prayer rug; the naive boy, without understanding that his master has sent him for help, goes to gather the requested items. Once alone with Hüsrev, the murderer's first task is to lock the door from the inside. In this scene at the end of the *Book of Kings,* the man whom the conspirators found to enact the murder is described by Firdusi with disgust: He is foul smelling, hairy and pot-bellied.

I paced to and fro, my head swarmed with words, but as in a dream, my voice would not take.

Just then I sensed that the others were whispering among themselves, maligning me.

They were so quick to take out my legs that the four of us collapsed to the floor. There was a struggle and fight on the ground, but it was brief. I lay faceup on the floor beneath the three of them.

One of them sat on my knees. Another on my right arm.

Black pressed a knee into each of my shoulders; he firmly situated his weight between my stomach and chest, and sat on me. I was completely immobilized. All of us were stunned and breathing hard. This is what I remembered:

My late uncle had a rogue son two years older than me—I hope he's been caught in the act of raiding caravans and has long since been beheaded. This jealous beast, realizing I knew more than he and was also more intelligent and refined, would find any excuse to pick a fight, or else he'd insist that we wrestle, and after quickly pinning me, he'd hold me down with his knees on my shoulders in this same way; he'd stare into my eyes, the way Black was now doing, and let a string of saliva hang down, slowly directing it toward my eyes as it gained mass, and he'd be greatly entertained as I tried to avoid it by turning my head to the right and to the left.

Black told me not to hide anything. Where was the last picture? Confess!

I felt suffocating regret and anger for two reasons: First, I'd said everything I had for naught, unaware that they'd come to an agreement beforehand; secondly, I hadn't fled, unable to imagine that their envy would reach this level.

Black threatened to cut my throat if I didn't produce the last picture.

How very ridiculous. I firmly closed my lips, as if the truth would escape if I opened my mouth. Part of me also thought that there was nothing left for me to do. If they came to an agreement among themselves and turned me over to the Head Treasurer as the murderer, they'd end up saving their own hides. My only hope lay with Master Osman, who might point out another suspect or another clue; but then, could I be certain what Black said about him was correct? He could kill me here and now, and later place the onus on me, couldn't he?

They rested the dagger against my throat, and I saw at once how this gave Black a pleasure that he could not conceal. They slapped me. Was the dagger cutting my skin? They slapped me again.

I was able to work through the following logic: If I held my peace, nothing would happen! This gave me strength. They could no longer hide the fact that since the days of our apprenticeships they'd been jealous of me; I, who quite evidently applied paint in the best manner, drew the steadiest line and made the best illuminations. I loved them for their extreme envy. I smiled upon my beloved brethren.

One of them, I don't want you to know which of them was responsible for this disgrace, passionately kissed me as if he were kissing the beloved he'd long desired. The others watched by the light of the oil lamp that they brought near to us. I could not but respond in kind to this kiss from my beloved brother. If we're nearing the end of everything, let it be known that I do the best illuminating. Find my pages and see for yourselves.

He began to beat me angrily, as if I'd enraged him by answering his kiss with a kiss. But the others restrained him. They experienced a moment of indecision. Black was upset that there was a scuffle among them. It was as if they weren't angry with me, but with the direction in which their lives were headed, and as a result, they wanted to take their revenge against the entire world.

Black removed an object from his sash: a needle with a sharpened point. In an instant, he brought it to my face and made a gesture as if to plunge it into my eyes.

"Eighty years ago, the great Bihzad, master of masters, understood that everything was coming to an end with the fall of Herat, and honorably blinded himself so nobody would force him to paint in another way," he said. "A short while after he deliberately inserted this plume needle into his own eye and removed it, God's exquisite darkness slowly descended over His beloved servant, this artist with the miraculous hand. This needle which came from Herat to Tabriz with the now drunk and blind Bihzad, was sent as a present by Shah Tahmasp to Our Sultan's father, along with that legendary *Book of Kings*. At first, Master Osman was unable to determine why this object was sent. But today, he was able to see the ill will and just logic behind this cruel present. After Master Osman understood that Our Sultan wanted to have His own portrait made in the style of the European masters and that you all, whom he loved more than his own children, had betrayed him, he stuck this needle into each of his eyes last night in the Treasury—in imitation of Bihzad. Now, if I were to blind you, the accursed man responsible for bringing to ruin the workshop Master Osman established at the expense of his entire life, what of it?"

"Whether or not you blind me, in the end, we'll no longer be able to find a place for ourselves here," I said. "If Master Osman truly goes blind, or passes away, and we paint the way we feel like painting, embracing our faults and individuality under the influence of the Franks so we might possess a style, we might resemble ourselves, but we won't be ourselves. No, even if we were to agree to paint like the old masters, reasoning that only in this way could we be ourselves, Our Sultan, who's turned His back even on Master Osman, will find others to replace us. No one will look at us anymore, we shall only incur pity. The raiding of the coffeehouse merely rubs salt into our wounds, because half the blame for this incident will fall to us miniaturists, who've slandered the respected preacher."

Although I tried at length to persuade them that it would work quite against us to quarrel, it was to no avail. They had no intention of listening to me. They were panicked. If they could only decide quickly, before morning, right or wrong, which of their lot was guilty, they were convinced they could save themselves; be delivered from torture and that everything having to do with the workshop would persist for years to come as it always had.

Nevertheless, what Black threatened to do didn't please the other two. What if it became evident that somebody else was guilty and Our Sultan learned they blinded me for no reason whatsoever? They were terrified both of Black's closeness to Master Osman and his insolence toward him. They tried to pull back the needle which Black, in blind rage, persisted in holding before my eyes.

Black fell into a panic, as if they were taking the plume needle from his hand, as if we'd taken sides against him. There was another scuffle. All I could do was tilt my head upward to escape the struggle over the needle, which was happening perilously close to my eyes.

Everything occurred so fast that I couldn't make out what happened at first. I felt a sharp but limited pain in my right eye; a passing numbness seized my forehead. Then everything was as it had been, yet a horror had already taken root within me. The oil lamp had been withdrawn, but I could still clearly see the figure before me decisively thrust the needle, this time into my left eye. He'd taken the needle from Black only moments before, and was more careful and meticulous now. When I understood that the needle effortlessly penetrated my eye, I lay dead still, though I felt the same burning sensation. The numbness in my forehead seemed to spread over my entire head, but ceased when the needle was removed. They were looking at the needle and then at my eyes in turn. It was as if they weren't certain what had transpired. When everybody fully understood the misfortune that had befallen me, the commotion stopped and the weight upon my arms eased.

I began to scream, nearly howling. Not from the pain, but from the terror of comprehending fully what had been done to me.

At first, I sensed that my wailing put not only me at ease, but them as well. My voice brought us together.

Even so, as my screaming persisted, their nervousness increased. I could no longer feel any pain. All I could think was that my eyes had been pierced with a needle.

I was not yet blind. Thank goodness I could still see them watching me in terror and sorrow, I could still see their shadows moving aimlessly on the ceiling of the lodge. This at once pleased and alarmed me. "Unhand me," I screamed. "Unhand me so I can see everything once more, I implore you."

"Quickly, tell us," said Black. "How did you meet up with Elegant Effendi that night? Then we'll unhand you."

"I was returning home from the coffeehouse. Poor Elegant Effendi accosted me. He was frenzied and very agitated. I pitied him at first. But leave me be now and I shall later recount it all. My eyes are fading."

"They won't fade right away," said Black with determination. "Believe me, Master Osman could still identify the horses with cut-open nostrils after his eyes had been pierced."

"Hapless Elegant Effendi said he wanted to talk to me and that I was the only person he could trust."

Yet it wasn't him I pitied, but myself now.

"If you tell us before the blood clots in your eyes, in the morning you can look upon the world to your heart's content one last time," said Black. "See, the rain has eased."

"'Let's go back to the coffeehouse,' I said to Elegant, but sensed at once that he didn't like it there, and even that it frightened him. This was how I first knew Elegant Effendi had broken from us completely and had gone his separate way after painting with us for twenty-five years. In the last eight or ten years, after he married, I'd see him at the workshop, but I didn't even know what he was occupied with . . . He told me he saw the last picture, how it contained a sin so grave we'd never live it down. As a consequence, he maintained, we'd all burn in Hell. He was agitated and possessed by fear, overcome with the sense of devastation felt by a man who'd unwittingly committed heresy."

"What heresy?"

"When I asked him this very question, he opened his eyes wide in surprise as if to say, You mean you don't know? It was then I thought how our friend had aged, as have we all. He said unfortunate Enishte had brazenly used the perspectival method in the last picture. In this picture, objects weren't depicted according to their importance in Allah's mind, but as they appeared to the naked eye—the way the Franks painted. This was the first transgression. The second was depicting Our Sultan, the Caliph of Islam, the same size as a dog. The third transgression also involved rendering Satan the same size, and in an endearing light. But what surpassed them all—a natural result of introducing this Frankish understanding into our painting—was drawing Our Sultan's picture as large as life and his face in all its detail! Just like the idolators do . . . Or just like the 'portraits' that Christians, who couldn't save themselves from their inherent idolatrous tendencies, painted upon their church walls and worshiped. Elegant Effendi, who learned of portraits from your Enishte, knew this quite well, and believed correctly that portraiture was the greatest of sins, and would be the downfall of Muslim painting. As we

I Will Be Called a Murderer

hadn't gone to the coffeehouse, where, he claimed, our exalted Preacher Effendi and our religion were being maligned, he explained all this to me while we walked down the street. Occasionally, he'd stop, as though seeking help, ask me whether all of this was indeed correct, whether there wasn't any recourse and whether we'd truly burn in Hell. He suffered fits of regret and beat his breast in remorse, but I was unpersuaded. He was an imposter who feigned regret."

"How did you know this?"

"We've known Elegant Effendi since childhood. He's very orderly, quiet, ordinary and colorless, like his gilding. It was as if the man standing before me then was dumber, more naive, more devout, yet more superficial than the Elegant we knew."

"I hear he'd also become quite close to the Erzurumis," said Black.

"No Muslim would ever feel such torment and regret for inadvertently committing a sin," I said. "A good Muslim knows God is just and reasonable enough to consider the intent of His servants. Only pea-brained ignoramuses believe they'll go to Hell for eating pork unawares. Anyway, a genuine Muslim knows the fear of damnation serves to frighten others, not himself. This is what Elegant Effendi was doing, you see, he wanted to scare me. It was your Enishte who taught him that he might do such a thing; and it was then I knew that this was indeed the case. Now, tell me in complete honesty, my dear illuminator brethren, has the blood begun to clot in my eyes, have my eyes lost their color?"

They brought the lamp toward my face and gazed at it, displaying the care and compassion of surgeons.

"Nothing seems to have changed."

Were these three, staring into my eyes, the last sight I'd see in this world? I knew I'd never forget these moments until the end of my life, and I related what follows, because despite my regret, I also felt hope:

"Your Enishte taught Elegant Effendi that he was involved in some forbidden project by covering up the final picture, by revealing only a specific spot to each of us and having us draw something there—by giving the picture an air of mystery and secrecy, it was Enishte himself who instilled the fear of heresy. He, not the Erzurumis who've never seen an illuminated manuscript in their lives, was the first to spread the frenzy and panic about sin that infected us. Meanwhile, what would an artist with a clear conscience have to fear?"

"There's much that an artist with a clear conscience has to fear in our day," said Black smugly. "Indeed, no one has anything to say against decoration, but pictures are forbidden by our faith. Because the illustrations of the Persian masters and even the masterpieces of the greatest masters of Herat are ultimately seen as an extension of border ornamentation, no one would take issue with them, reasoning that they enhanced the beauty of writing and the magnificence of calligraphy. And who sees our painting anyway? However, as we make use of the methods of the Franks, our painting is becoming less focused on ornamentation and intricate design and more on straightforward representation. This is what the Glorious Koran forbids and what displeased Our Prophet. Both Our Sultan and my Enishte knew this quite well. This was the reason for my Enishte's murder."

"Your Enishte was murdered because he was afraid," I said. "Just like you, he'd begun to claim that illustration, which he was doing himself, wasn't contrary to the religion or the sacred book . . . This was exactly the pretext sought by the Erzurumis, who were desperate to find an aspect contrary to the religion. Elegant Effendi and your Enishte were a perfect match for each other."

"And you're the one who killed them both, isn't that so?" said Black.

I thought for a moment that he would hit me, and in that instant, I also knew beautiful Shekure's new husband really had nothing to complain about in the murder of his Enishte. He wouldn't strike me, and even if he did, it made no difference to me any longer.

"In actuality, as much as Our Sultan wanted to have a book prepared under the influence of the Frankish artists," I continued stubbornly, "your Enishte wanted to prepare a provocative book whose taint of illicitness would feed his own pride. He felt a slavish awe toward the pictures of the Frankish masters he'd seen during his travels, and he'd fallen completely for the artistry that he regaled us about for days on end—you too must have heard that nonsense about perspective and portraiture. If you ask me, there was nothing damaging or sacrilegious in the book we were preparing . . . Since he was well aware of this, he pretended that he was preparing a forbidden book and this gave him great satisfaction . . . Being involved in such a dangerous venture with the Sultan's personal permission was as important to him as the pictures of the Frankish masters. True, if we'd made a painting with the intent of exhibiting it, that would've been sacrilege. Yet in none of those pieces could I sense anything contrary to religion, any faithlessness, impiety or even the vaguest illicitness. Did you sense anything of the sort?"

My eyes had almost imperceptibly lost strength, but thank God, I could see enough to know that my question gave them pause.

"You cannot be certain, can you?" I said, gloating. "Even if you secretly believe that the blemish of blasphemy or the shadow of sacrilege exists in

I Will Be Called a Murderer

the pictures we've made, you could never accept this belief and express it, because this would be equivalent to giving credence to the zealots and Erzurumis who oppose and accuse you. On the other hand, you cannot claim with any conviction that you're as innocent as freshly fallen snow, because this would mean giving up both the dizzying pride and refined self-congratulation of engaging in a secretive, mysterious and forbidden act. Do you know how I became aware that I was behaving pretentiously in this way? By bringing poor Elegant Effendi to this dervish lodge in the middle of the night! I brought him here with the excuse that we'd nearly frozen walking the streets so long. In actuality, it pleased me to show him I was a free-thinking Kalenderi throwback, or worse yet, that I aspired to be a Kalenderi. When Elegant understood I was the last of the followers of a dervish order based on pederasty, hashish consumption, vagrancy and all manner of aberrant behavior, I thought he'd fear and respect me even more, and in turn, be intimidated into silence. As fate would have it, the exact opposite happened. Our dim-witted boyhood friend disliked it here, and he quickly decided the accusations of blasphemy he'd learned from your Enishte were quite on the mark. So, our beloved apprenticeship companion, who'd at first implored, 'Help me, convince me that we won't go to Hell so I might sleep in peace tonight,' in a newfound, threatening tone, began to insist that 'this will end in nothing but evil.' He was convinced the preacher hoja from Erzurum would hear the rumors that in the final picture we'd veered from the orders of Our Sultan, who'd never forgive this transgression. Convincing him everything was clear skies and sunshine was nearly impossible. He'd tell all to the preacher's dull congregation, exaggerating Enishte's absurdities, the anxieties about affronts to the religion and rendering the Devil in a favorable light, and they'd naturally believe every slanderous word. I don't have to tell you how, not only the artisans, but the entire society of craftsmen have grown jealous of us since we've become the intense focus of Our Sultan's attention. Now all of them will gleefully declare in unison 'the miniaturists are mired in heresy.' Furthermore, the cooperation between Enishte and Elegant Effendi would prove this slander true. I say 'slander' because I don't believe in what my brother Elegant said about the book and the last picture. Even then, I would hear nothing against your late Enishte. I found it quite appropriate that Our Sultan turn his favors from Master Osman to Enishte Effendi, and I even believed, if not to the same degree, what Enishte described to me at length about the Frankish masters and their artistry. I used to believe quite sincerely that we Ottoman artists could comfortably take from this or that aspect of the Frankish methods as much as our hearts desired or as much as could be seen during a visit abroad—without bartering with the Devil or bringing any great harm upon us. Life was easy; your Enishte, may he rest in peace, had succeeded Master Osman, and was a new father to me in this new life."

"Let's not discuss that point yet," said Black. "First describe how you murdered Elegant."

"This deed," I said, recognizing that I couldn't use the word "murder," "I committed this deed not only for us, to save us, but for the salvation of the entire workshop. Elegant Effendi knew he posed a powerful threat. I prayed to Almighty God, begging him to give me a sign showing me how despicable this scoundrel really was. My prayers were answered when I offered Elegant money. God had shown me how wretched he really was. These gold pieces came to mind, but by divine inspiration, I lied. I said the gold pieces weren't here in the lodge, but I'd hidden them elsewhere. We went out. I walked him through empty streets and out-of-the-way neighborhoods without any consideration for where we were going. I had no idea what I would do, and in short, I was afraid. At the end of our wandering, after we'd come to a street we'd passed earlier, our brother Elegant Effendi the gilder, who devoted his entire life to form and repetition, grew suspicious. But God provided me with an empty lot ravaged by fire, and nearby, a dry well."

At this point I knew I couldn't go on and I told them so. "If you were in my shoes, you would've considered the salvation of your artist brethren and done the same thing," I said confidently.

When I heard them agree with me, I felt like crying. I was going to say it was because their compassion, which I hardly deserved, softened my heart, but no. I was going to say it was because I again heard the thud of his body hitting the bottom of the well wherein I dropped him after killing him, but no. I was going to say it was because I remembered how happy I was before becoming a murderer, how I'd been like everybody else, but no. The blind man who used to pass through our neighborhood in my childhood appeared in my mind's eye: He'd take a dirty metal water dipper out of his even dirtier clothes, and would call out to us neighborhood kids who watched him from a distance, there by the local water fountain, "My children, which of you will fill this blind old man's drinking cup with water from the fountain?" When no one went to his aid, he'd say, "It'd be a good turn, my children, a pious deed!" The color of his irises had faded and they were nearly the same color as the whites of his eyes.

Agitated by the thought of resembling that blind old man, I confessed how I did away with Enishte Effendi hurriedly, without savoring any of it.

I was neither too honest nor too insincere with them: I found a medium consistency, such that the story wouldn't trouble my heart too much, and they'd be assured I hadn't gone to Enishte's house to murder him. I wanted to make clear that it wasn't a premeditated murder, which intent they gathered when I reminded them of the following while trying to absolve myself: "Without harboring bad intentions, one never goes to Hell."

"After surrendering Elegant Effendi to the Angels of Allah," I said thoughtfully, "what the dearly departed expressed to me in his last moments started to gnaw at me like a worm. Having caused me to bloody my hands, the final painting loomed larger in my mind, and so, resolving to see it, I went to your Enishte, who no longer summoned any of us to his house. Not only did he refuse to reveal the painting, he behaved as if nothing were the matter. There was, he sniffled, neither a painting nor anything else so mysterious that it called for murder! To preempt further humiliation, and to get his attention, I thereupon confessed that I was the one who killed Elegant Effendi and tossed him into a well. Yes, then he took me more seriously, but he continued to humiliate me all the same. How could a man who humiliates his son be a father? Great Master Osman would become irate with us, he'd beat us, but he never once humiliated us. Oh my brothers, we've made a grave mistake by betraying him."

I smiled at my brethren whose attention was focused upon my eyes, listening to me as though I lay on my deathbed. Just as a dying man would, I saw them growing increasingly blurry and moving away from me.

"I murdered your Enishte for two reasons. First, because he shamelessly forced the great Master Osman into aping the Venetian artist, Sebastiano. Second, because in a moment of weakness, I lowered myself to ask him whether I had a style of my own."

"How did he respond?"

"It seems I am possessed of a style. But coming from him, of course, this was not an insult. I remembered wondering, in my shame, if this were indeed praise: I considered style to be a variety of rootlessness and dishonor, but doubt was eating at me. I wanted nothing to do with style, but the Devil was tempting me and I was, furthermore, curious."

"Everybody secretly desires to have a style," said Black smartly. "Everybody also desires to have his portrait made, just as Our Sultan did."

"Is this affliction impossible to resist?" I said. "As this plague spreads, none of us will be able to stand against the methods of the Europeans."

No one was listening to me, however. Black was recounting the story of a sad Turkmen chieftain who was sent off on a twelve-year exile to China because he'd prematurely expressed his love for the daughter of the shah. Since he didn't have a portrait of his beloved, of whom he dreamed for a dozen years, he forgot her face amid the Chinese beauties, and his lovelorn suffering was transformed into a profound trial willed by Allah.

"Thanks to your Enishte, we've all learned the meaning of 'portrait,'" I said. "God willing, one day, we'll fearlessly tell the story of our own lives the way we actually live them."

"All fables are everybody's fables," said Black.

"All illumination is God's illumination too," I said, completing the verse by the poet Hatifi of Herat. "But as the methods of the Europeans spread, everyone will consider it a special talent to tell other men's stories as if they were one's own."

"This is nothing but the will of Satan."

"Unhand me now," I shouted. "Let me look upon the world one last time."

They were terrified, and a new confidence rose within me.

"Will you take out the final picture?" Black said.

I gave Black such a look that he was quick to understand I'd do so and he released me. My heart began to beat rapidly.

I'm certain you've long ago discovered my identity, which I've been trying to conceal. Even so, don't be surprised that I'm behaving like the old masters of Herat, for they would conceal their signatures not to hide their identities, but out of principle and respect for their masters. Excitedly, I walked through the pitch-black rooms of the lodge, oil lamp in hand, making way for my own pale shadow. Had the curtain of blackness begun to fall over my eyes, or were these rooms and hallways truly this dark? How many days and weeks, how much time did I have before going blind? My shadow and I stopped among the ghosts in the kitchen and lifted up the pages from the clean corner of a dusty cabinet before quickly heading back. Black had followed me as a precaution, but he'd neglected to bring his dagger. Would I, perchance, consider taking up that dagger and blinding him before I myself went blind?

"I'm pleased that I will see this once again before going blind," I said with pride. "I want you all to see it as well. Look here."

Under the light of the oil lamp, I showed them the final picture, which I'd taken from Enishte's house the day I killed him. At first, I watched their curious and timid expressions as they looked at the double-leaf picture. I circled around and joined them, and I was ever so faintly trembling as I stared. The lancing of my eyes, or perhaps a sudden rapture, made me feverish.

I Will Be Called a Murderer

The pictures we made on various parts of the two pages over the past year—tree, horse, Satan, Death, dog and woman—were arranged, large and small, according to Enishte's albeit inept new method of composition, in such a way that the dearly departed Elegant Effendi's gilding and borders made us feel we were no longer looking at a page from a book but at the world seen through a window. In the center of this world, where Our Sultan should've been, was my own portrait, which I briefly observed with pride. I was somewhat unsatisfied with it because after laboring in vain for days, looking into a mirror and erasing and reworking, I was unable to achieve a good resemblance; still, I felt unbridled elation because the picture not only situated me at the center of a vast world, but for some unaccountable and diabolic reason, it made me appear more profound, complicated and mysterious than I actually was. I wanted only that my artist brethren recognize, understand and share in my exuberance. I was both the center of everything, like a sultan or a king, and, at the same time, myself. The situation fed my pride as it increased my embarrassment. Finally these two feelings balanced each other, and I was able to relax and take dizzying pleasure in the picture. But for this pleasure to be complete, I knew every mark on my face and shirt, all of the wrinkles, shadows, moles and boils, every detail from my whiskers to the weave of my clothes and all their colors in all their shades had to be perfect, down to the minutest details, as much as the skill of Frankish painters would allow.

I noted in the faces of my old companions fear, bewilderment and the inescapable feeling devouring us all: jealousy. Along with the angry revulsion they felt toward a man hopelessly mired in sin, they were also envious.

"During the nights I spent here staring at this picture by the light of an oil lamp, I felt for the first time that God had forsaken me and only Satan would befriend me in my isolation," I said. "I know that even if I were truly the center of the world—and each time I looked at the picture this is precisely what I wanted—despite the splendor of the red that ruled the painting, despite being surrounded by all of these things I loved, including my dervish companions and the woman who resembled beautiful Shekure, I'd still be lonely. I'm not afraid of possessing character and individuality, nor do I fear others bowing down and worshiping me; on the contrary, this is what I desire."

"You mean to say that you feel no remorse?" said Stork like a man who'd just left a Friday sermon.

"I feel like the Devil not because I've murdered two men, but because my portrait has been made in this fashion. I suspect that I did away with them so I could make this picture. But now the isolation I feel terrifies me. Imitating the Frankish masters without having attained their expertise makes a miniaturist even more of a slave. Now I'm desperate to escape this trap. Of course, all of you know: After all is said and done, I killed them both so the workshop might persist as it always has, and Allah certainly knows this too."

"Yet this will bring even greater trouble upon us," said my beloved Butterfly.

I abruptly grabbed the wrist of that fool Black, who was still looking at the picture, and with all my strength, digging my nails into his flesh, I angrily squeezed and twisted it. The dagger that he rather timidly held dropped from his hand. I grabbed it from the ground.

"But now you won't be able to resolve your troubles by handing me over to the torturer," I said. As if to poke out his eye, I brought the point of the dagger toward Black's face. "Give me the plume needle."

He took it out and handed it to me with his good hand, and I stuck it into my sash. I focused my gaze into his lamblike eyes.

"I pity beautiful Shekure because she had no alternative but to marry you," I said. "If I hadn't been forced to kill Elegant Effendi to save you all from ruin, she would've married me and been happy. Indeed, I was the one who most fully understood the tales and talents of the Europeans as her father recounted them to us. So, listen carefully to the last of what I will tell you: There is no longer any place here in Istanbul for us master miniaturists who wish to live by skill and honor alone. Yes, this is what I've realized. If we're reduced to imitating the Frankish masters, as the late Enishte and Our Sultan desired, we will be restrained, if not by the Ezurumis and those like Elegant Effendi, then by the justified cowardice within us, and we won't be able to continue. If we fall sway to the Devil and continue, betraying everything that has come before in a futile attempt to attain a style and European character, we will still fail—just as I failed in making this self-portrait despite all my proficiency and knowledge. This primitive picture I've made, without even achieving a fair resemblance of myself, revealed to me what we've know all along without admitting it: The proficiency of the Franks will take centuries to attain. Had Enishte Effendi's book been completed and sent to them; the Venetian masters would've smirked, and their ridicule would've reached the Venetian Doge—that is all. They'd have quipped that the Ottomans have given up being Ottoman and would no longer fear us. How wonderful it would be if we could persist on the path of the old masters! But no one wants this, neither His Excellency Our Sultan, nor Black Effendi—who is melancholy because he has no portrait of his precious Shekure. In that case, sit yourselves down and do nothing but ape the Europeans century after century! Proudly sign your names to your imitation paintings. The old masters of Herat tried to depict the world the way God saw it, and to conceal their individuality they never signed their names. You, however, are condemned to signing your names to conceal your lack of individuality. But there is an alternative. Each of you has perhaps been summoned, and if so, you're hiding it from me: Akbar, Sultan of Hindustan, is strewing about money and blandishments, trying to gather in his court the most talented artists in the world. It's quite apparent that the book to be completed for the thousandth year of Islam will not be prepared here in Istanbul, but in the workshops of Agra."

"Must an artist first become a murderer to be as high and mighty as you?" asked Stork.

"Nay, it's enough to be the most gifted and the most talented," I said heedlessly.

A proud cockerel crowed twice in the distance. I gathered my bundle and my gold pieces, my notebook of forms, and put my illustrations into my portfolio. I considered how I might kill each of them one by one with the dagger, whose point I held at Black's throat, but I felt nothing but affection for my boyhood friends—including Stork, who'd stuck the plume needle into my eyes.

I screamed at Butterfly, who had stood up, and thus scared him into sitting back down. Now, confident I'd be able to escape the lodge safely, I hastened toward the door; and at the threshold, I impatiently uttered the momentous words I'd been planning to say:

"My flight from Istanbul shall resemble Ibn Shakir's flight from Baghdad under Mongol occupation."

"In that case, you must head West instead of East," said jealous Stork.

"*To God belongs the East and the West*," I said in Arabic like the late Enishte.

"But East is east and West is west," said Black.

"An artist should never succumb to hubris of any kind," said Butterfly, "he should simply paint the way he sees fit rather than troubling over East or West."

"So very true," I said to beloved Butterfly. "Accept my kiss."

I'd hardly taken two steps toward him when Black dutifully pounced upon me. In one hand I held my satchel containing my clothes and gold coins, and under my other arm, the portfolio filled with pictures. Taking care to protect my belongings, I failed to protect myself. I couldn't prevent him from grabbing the forearm of the hand that held the dagger. But luck did not shine upon him, either; he tripped slightly over a low worktable and momentarily lost his balance. Instead of taking control of my arm, he ended up hanging by it. Kicking him with all my might and biting his fingers, I freed myself. He howled, fearing for his life. Then, I stepped on the same hand, causing him great pain. Brandishing the dagger before the other two, I shouted:

"Halt!"

They stayed seated where they were. I stuck the point of the dagger into one of Black's nostrils, the way Keykavus had done in the legend. When it began to bleed, bitter tears flowed from his imploring eyes.

"Now, tell me then," I said, "shall I go blind?"

"According to legend, blood clots in the eyes of some and not in others. If Allah is pleased with your artistry, he'll bestow His own magnificent blackness upon you and take you under His care. In that case, you shall behold not this wretched world, but the exquisite vistas that He sees. If He is displeased, you shall continue to see the world the way you now do."

"I shall practice genuine artistry in Hindustan," I said. "I've yet to make the picture Allah will judge me by."

"Don't nourish the illusion over much that you'll be able to escape Frankish methods," said Black. "Did you know that Akbar Khan encourages all his artists to sign their work? The Jesuit priests of Portugal long ago introduced European painting and methods there. They are everywhere now."

"There's always work for the artist who wants to remain pure, there's always a place to find shelter," I said.

"Aye," said Stork, "going blind and fleeing to nonexistent countries."

"Why is it that you want to remain pure?" said Black. "Stay here with us."

"For the rest of your lives you'll do nothing but emulate the Franks for the sake of an individual style," I said. "But precisely because you emulate the Franks you'll never attain individual style."

"There's nothing else left to do," said Black dishonorably.

Of course, it wasn't artistry but beautiful Shekure that was his sole source of happiness. I removed the bloodstained dagger from Black's bleeding nose and raised it over his head like the sword of an executioner preparing to behead a condemned man.

I Will Be Called a Murderer 401

"If I so desired, I could cut off your head this instant," I said, announcing what was already apparent. "But I'm prepared to spare you for the sake of Shekure's children and her happiness. Be good to her and don't act crudely and ignorantly toward her. Promise me!"

"I give my word," he said.

"I hereby grant you Shekure," I said.

Yet my arm acted of its own accord, heedless of my words. I drove the dagger down upon Black with all my might.

At the last moment, both because Black moved and because I altered the path of my blow, the dagger struck his shoulder, not his neck. I watched in terror, the deed enacted by my arm alone. Once I removed the dagger, sunk to its handle in Black's flesh, the spot bloomed a pure red. What I'd done both frightened and shamed me. But if I went blind on the ship, perhaps on the Arabian seas, I knew that I could not then take revenge upon any of my miniaturist brethren.

Stork, afraid that his turn had come, and justifiably so, fled into the blackened rooms within. Holding the lamp aloft, I went after him, but soon grew frightened and turned back. My last gesture was to kiss Butterfly, and saying farewell, to take my leave of him. Since the tang of blood had come between us, I couldn't kiss him to my heart's content. But he noticed that tears flowed from my eyes.

I left the lodge within a kind of deathly silence punctuated by Black's moaning. Nearly running, I fled the wet and muddy garden, the dark neighborhood. The ship that was to take me to Akbar Khan's workshop would depart after the morning azan; at that hour the last rowboat would leave for the ship from Galleon Harbor. As I ran, tears poured from my eyes.

As I passed through Aksaray like a thief, I could faintly make out the first light of day on the horizon. Opposite the first neighborhood fountain I encountered, among the side streets, narrow passages and walls, was the stone house in which I'd spent the night of my first day in Istanbul twenty-five years ago. There, through the yawning courtyard gate, I saw once again the well into which I wished to hurl myself in the middle of the night, tormented by guilt for having at the age of eleven wet the mattress that a distant relative spread out for me in a show of kind and generous hospitality. By the time I reached Bayazid, the watchmaker's shop (where I often came to fix the mechanism of my broken clock), the bottle seller's shop (where I purchased the empty crystal lamps and sherbet cups I embellished and the little bottles I decorated with floral designs and secretly sold to the gentry) and the public baths (where my feet went out of habit for a time because it was both inexpensive and empty) were all respectfully standing at attention before me and my tearful eyes.

There was nobody in the vicinity of the ravaged and burned coffeehouse, nor anyone at the house of beautiful Shekure and her new husband, who was perhaps in the throes of death at this very moment. I heartily wished them nothing but happiness. While roaming the streets in the days after I'd tainted my hands with blood, all of Istanbul's dogs, its shadowy trees, shuttered windows, black chimneys, ghosts and hardworking, unhappy early risers hurrying toward mosques to perform their morning prayers always stared at me with animosity; yet, from the moment I confessed my crimes and resolved to abandon the only city I'd ever known, they all regarded me with friendship.

After passing the Bayazid Mosque, I watched the Golden Horn from a promontory: The horizon was brightening, yet the water was still black. Ever so slowly bobbing in invisible waves, two fishermen's rowboats, freight ships with their sails furled and an abandoned galleon repeatedly insisted that I not leave. Were the tears flowing from my eyes caused by the needle? I told myself to dream of the splendid life I would live in Hindustan off the splendid works my talent would create!

I left the road, ran through two muddy gardens and took shelter beneath an old stone house surrounded by greenery. This was the house where I came each Tuesday as an apprentice to get Master Osman and followed two paces behind him carrying his bag, portfolio, pen box and writing board on our way to the workshop. Nothing had changed here, except the plane trees in the yard and along the street had grown so large that an aura of grandeur, power and wealth hearkening back to the time of Sultan Süleyman had settled over the house and street.

Since the road leading to the harbor was near, I succumbed to the Devil's temptation, and was overcome by the excitement of seeing the arches of the workshop building where I'd spent a quarter century. This was how I ended up tracing the path that I'd take as an apprentice following Master Osman: down Archer's Street which smelled dizzyingly of linden blossoms in the spring, past the bakery where my master would buy round meat pasties, up the hill lined with beggars and quince and chestnut trees, past the closed shutters of the new market and the barber whom my master greeted each morning, alongside the empty field where acrobats would set up their tents in summer and perform, in front of the foul-smelling rooming houses for bachelors, beneath moldy-smelling Byzantine arches, before İbrahim Pasha's palace and the column made up of three coiling snakes, which I'd drawn hundreds of times, past the plane tree, which we depicted a different way each time, emerging into the Hippodrome and under the chestnut and mulberry trees wherein sparrows and magpies alighted and chirped madly in the mornings.

The heavy door of the workshop was closed. There was nobody at the entrance or under the arched portico above. I was able to look up only momentarily at the shuttered small windows from which, as apprentices stifled by boredom, we used to stare at the trees, before I was accosted.

He had a shrill voice that clawed at one's ears. He said that the bloody ruby-handled dagger in my hand belonged to him and that his nephew, Shevket, and Shekure had conspired to steal it from his house. This was apparently proof enough that I was one of Black's men who raided his house at night to abduct Shekure. This arrogant, shrill-voiced, irate man also knew Black's artist friends and that they would return to the workshop. He brandished a long sword that shimmered brightly with a strange red and indicated that he had a number of accounts that, for whatever reason, he meant to settle with me. I considered telling him that there was some misunderstanding, but I saw the incredible anger on his face. I could read in his expression that he was about to launch a sudden murderous assault on me. How I would've liked to say, "I beg of you, stop."

But he'd already acted.

I wasn't even able to raise my dagger, I simply lifted the hand in which I held my satchel.

The satchel dropped. In one smooth motion, without losing speed, the sword cut first through my hand and then clear through my neck, lopping off my head.

I knew I'd been beheaded from the two odd steps taken by my poor body which had left me behind in its confusion, from the stupid manner in which my hand waved the dagger and from the way my lonely body collapsed, blood spraying from the neck like a fountain. My poor feet, which continued to move as though still walking, kicked uselessly like the legs of a dying horse.

From the muddy ground upon which my head had fallen, I could neither see my murderer nor my satchel full of gold pieces and pictures, which I still wanted to cling to tightly. These things were behind me, in the direction of the hill leading down to the sea and Galleon Harbor which I would never reach. My head would never again turn and see them, or the rest of the world. I forgot about them and let my thoughts take me away.

This is what occurred to me the moment before I was beheaded: The ship shall depart from the harbor; this was joined in my mind with a command to hurry; it was the way my mother would say "hurry" when I was a child. Mother, my neck aches and all is still.

This is what they call death.

But I knew that I wasn't dead yet. My punctured pupils were motionless, but I could still see quite well through my open eyes.

What I saw from ground level filled my thoughts: The road inclining slightly upward, the wall, the arch, the roof of the workshop, the sky . . . this is how the picture receded.

It seemed as if this moment of observation went on and on and I realized seeing had become a variety of memory. I was reminded of what I thought when staring for hours at a beautiful picture: If you stare long enough your mind enters the time of the painting.

All time had now become this time.

It seemed as if no one would see me, as my thoughts faded away, my mud-covered head would go on staring at this melancholy incline, the stone wall and the nearby yet unattainable mulberry and chestnut trees for years.

This endless waiting suddenly assumed such bitter and tedious proportions, I wanted nothing more than to quit this time.

CHAPTER 59

I, SHEKURE

Black had hidden us away in the house of a distant relative, where I spent a sleepless night. In the bed where I curled up with Hayriye and the children, I was occasionally able to nod off amid the sounds of snoring and coughing, but in my restless dreams, I saw strange creatures and women whose arms and legs had been severed and randomly reattached; they wouldn't stop chasing me and continually woke me. Toward morning, the cold roused me and I covered Shevket and Orhan, embracing them, kissing their heads and begging Allah for pleasant dreams, such as I'd enjoyed during the blissful days when I slept in peace under my late father's roof.

I couldn't sleep, however. After the morning prayers, looking out on the street through the shutters of the window in the small, dark room, I saw what I'd always seen in my happy dreams: A ghostly man, exhausted from warring and the wounds he'd received, brandishing a stick as if it were a sword, longingly approach me with familiar steps. In my dream, whenever I was on the verge of embracing this man, I'd awake in tears. When I saw the man in the street was Black, the scream that would never leave my throat in dreams sounded.

I ran and opened the door.

His face was swollen and bruised purple from fighting. His nose was mangled and covered in blood. He had a large gash from his shoulder to his neck. His shirt had turned bright red from the blood. Like the husband of my dreams, Black smiled at me faintly because he had, in the end, successfully returned.

"Get inside," I said.

"Call for the children," he said. "We're going home."

"You're in no condition to return home."

"There's no reason to fear him anymore," he said. "The murderer is Velijan Effendi, the Persian."

"Olive . . ." I said. "Did you kill that miserable rogue?"

"He's fled to India on the ship that departed from Galleon Harbor," he said and avoided my eyes, knowing that he hadn't properly accomplished his task.

"Will you be able to walk back to our house?" I said. "Shall we have them bring a horse for you?"

I sensed that he would die upon arriving home and I pitied him. Not because he would die alone, but because he'd never known any true happiness. I could see from the sorrow and determination in his eyes that he wished not to be in this strange house, and that he actually wanted to disappear without being seen by anybody in this horrible state. With some difficulty, they mounted him on a horse.

During our trip back, as we passed through side streets clinging to our bundles, the children were at first too frightened to look Black in the face. But from astride the slowly ambling horse, Black was still able to describe how he foiled the schemes of the wretched murderer who'd killed their grandfather and how he challenged him to a sword fight. I could see that the children had warmed up to him somewhat, and I prayed to Allah: Please, don't let him die!

When we reached the house, Orhan shouted, "We're home!" with such joy I had the intuition that Azrael, the Angel of Death, pitied us and Allah would grant Black more time. But I knew from experience that one could never tell when exalted Allah would take one's soul, and I wasn't overly hopeful.

We helped Black down from the horse. We brought him upstairs, and settled him into the bed in my father's room, the one with the blue door.

Hayriye boiled water and brought it upstairs. Hayriye and I undressed him, tearing his clothes and cutting them with scissors, removing the bloodied shirt stuck to his flesh, his sash, his shoes and his underclothes. When we opened the shutters, the soft winter sunlight playing on the branches in the garden filled the room, reflected off the ewers, pots, glue boxes, inkwells, pieces of glass and penknives, and illuminated Black's deathly pale skin, and his flesh- and sour-cherry-colored wounds.

I soaked pieces of bedding in hot water and rubbed them with soap. Then I wiped clean Black's body, carefully as though cleaning a valuable antique carpet, and affectionately and eagerly as though caring for one of my boys. Without pressing on the bruises that covered his face, without jarring the cut in his nostril, I cleansed the horrible wound on his shoulder as a doctor might. As I'd do when bathing the children when they were babies, I cooed to him in a singsong voice. There were cuts on his chest and arms as well. The fingers of his left hand were purple from being bitten. The rags I used to wipe his body were soon bloodsoaked. I touched his chest; I felt the softness of his abdomen with my hand; I looked at his cock for a long time. The sounds of the children were coming from the courtyard below. Why did some poets call this thing a "reed pen"?

I could hear Esther enter the kitchen with that joyous voice and mysterious air she adopted when she brought news, and I went down to greet her.

She was so excited she began without embracing or kissing me: Olive's severed head was found in front of the workshop; the pictures proving his guilt in the crimes and his satchel had also been recovered. He was intending to flee to Hindustan, but had decided first to call at the workshop one last time.

There were witnesses to the ordeal: Hasan, encountering Olive, had drawn his red sword and cut off Olive's head in a single stroke.

As she recounted, I thought about where my unfortunate father was. Learning that the murderer had received his due punishment at first put my fears to rest. And revenge lent me a feeling of comfort and justice. At that instant, I wondered intensely whether my now-dead father could experience this feeling; suddenly, it seemed to me that the entire world was like a palace with countless rooms whose doors opened into one another. We were able to pass from one room to the next only by exercising our memories and imaginations, but most of us, in our laziness, rarely exercised these capacities, and forever remained in the same room.

"Don't cry, my dear," said Esther. "You see, in the end everything has turned out fine."

I, Shekure

I gave her four gold coins. She took them, one at a time, into her mouth and bit down upon them crudely with eagerness and longing.

"Coins counterfeited by the Venetians are everywhere," she said, smiling.

As soon as she'd left, I warned Hayriye not to let the children upstairs. I went up to the room where Black lay, locked the door behind me and cuddled up eagerly next to Black's naked body. Then, more out of curiosity than desire, more out of care than fear, I did what Black wanted me to do in the house of the Hanged Jew the night my poor father was killed.

I can't say I completely understood why Persian poets, who for centuries had likened that male tool to a reed pen, also compared the mouths of us women to inkwells, or what lay behind such comparisons whose origins had been forgotten through rote repetition—was it the smallness of the mouth? The arcane silence of the inkwell? Was it that God Himself was an illuminator? Love, however, must be understood, not through the logic of a woman like me who continually racks her brain to protect herself, but through its illogic.

So, let me tell you a secret: There, in that room that smelled of death, it wasn't the object in my mouth that delighted me. What delighted me then, lying there with the entire world throbbing between my lips, was the happy twittering of my sons cursing and roughhousing with each other in the courtyard.

While my mouth was thus occupied, my eyes could make out Black looking at me in a completely different way. He said he'd never again forget my face and my mouth. As with some of my father's old books, his skin smelled of moldy paper, and the scent of the Treasury's dust and cloth had saturated his hair. As I let myself go and caressed his wounds, his cuts and swellings, he groaned like a child, moving further and further away from death, and it was then I understood I would become even more attached to him. Like a solemn ship that gains speed as its sails swell with wind, our gradually quickening lovemaking took us boldly into unfamiliar seas.

I could tell by the way he was able to navigate these waters, even on his deathbed, that Black had plied these seas many times before with who knows what manner of indecent women. While I was confused as to whether the forearm I kissed was my own or his, whether I was sucking my own finger or an entire life, he stared out of one half-opened eye, nearly intoxicated by his wounds and pleasure, checking where the world was taking him, and from time to time, he would hold my head delicately in his hands, and stare at my face astounded, now looking as if at a picture, now as if at a Mingerian whore.

At the peak of pleasure, he cried out like the legendary heroes cut clear in half with a single stroke of the sword in fabled pictures that immortalized the clash of Persian and Turanian armies; the fact that this cry could be heard throughout the neighborhood frightened me. Like a genuine master miniaturist at the moment of greatest inspiration, holding his reed under the direct guidance of Allah, yet still able to take into consideration the form and composition of the entire page, Black continued to direct our place in the world from a corner of his mind even through his highest excitement.

"You can tell them you were spreading salve onto my wounds," he said breathlessly.

These words not only constituted the color of our love—which settled into a bottleneck between life and death, prohibition and paradise, hopelessness and shame—they also were the excuse for our love. For the next twenty-six years, until my beloved husband Black collapsed next to the well one morning to die of a bad heart, each afternoon, as the sunlight filtered into the room through the slats of the shutters, and for the first few years, to the sounds of Shevket and Orhan playing, we made love, always referring to it as "spreading salve onto wounds." This was how my jealous sons, whom I didn't want to suffer beatings at the jealous whims of a rough and melancholy father, were able to continue sleeping in the same bed with me for years. All sensible women know how it's much nicer to sleep curled up with one's children than with a melancholy husband who's been beaten down by life.

We, my children and I, were happy, but Black couldn't be. The most obvious reason for this was the wound on his shoulder and neck that never completely healed; my beloved husband was left "crippled," as I heard him described by others. But this didn't disrupt his life, other than in its appearance. There were even times when I heard other women, who'd seen my husband from a distance, describe him as handsome. But Black's right shoulder was lower than the left and his neck remained oddly cocked. I also heard gossip to the effect that a woman like myself could only marry a husband whom she felt was beneath her, and how as much as Black's wound was the cause of his discontent, it was also the secret source of our shared happiness.

As with all gossip, there is perhaps an element of truth in this as well. However deprived and destitute I felt at not being able to pass down the streets of Istanbul mounted tall on an exceptionally beautiful horse, surrounded by slaves, lady servants and attendants—what Esther always thought I deserved—I also occasionally longed for a brave and spirited husband who held his head high and looked at the world with a sense of victory.

Whatever the cause, Black always remained melancholy. Because I knew that his sadness had nothing to do with his shoulder, I believed that somewhere in a secret corner of his soul he was possessed by a jinn of sorrow that dampened his mood even during our most exhilarating moments of lovemaking. To appease that jinn, at times he'd drink wine, at times stare at illustrations in books and take an interest in art, at times he'd even spend his days and nights with miniaturists chasing after pretty boys. There were periods when he entertained himself in the company of painters, calligraphers and poets in orgies of puns, double entendres, innuendos, metaphors and games of flattery, and there were periods when he forgot everything and surrendered himself to secretarial duties and a governmental clerkship under Hunched Süleyman Pasha, into whose service he'd managed to enter. Four years later, when Our Sultan died, and with the ascension of Sultan Mehmed, who turned his back entirely on all artistry, Black's enthusiasm for illumination and painting turned from an openly celebrated pleasure into a private secret pursued behind closed doors. There were times when he'd open one of the books left to us by my father, and stare, guilty and sad, at an illustration made during the era of Tamerlane's sons in Herat—yes, Shirin falling in love with Hüsrev after seeing his picture—not as if it were part of a happy game of talent still being played in palace circles, but as if he were dwelling upon a sweet secret long surrendered to memory.

In the third year of Our Sultan's reign, the Queen of England sent His Excellency a miraculous clock that contained a musical instrument with a bellows. An English delegation assembled this enormous clock after weeks of toil with various pieces, cogs, pictures and statuettes that they brought with them from England, erecting it on a slope of the Royal Private Garden facing the Golden Horn. The crowds that collected on the slopes of the Golden Horn or came in caïques to watch, astonished and awed, saw how the life-size statues and ornaments spun around each other purposefully when the huge clock played its noisy and terrifying music, how they danced elegantly and meaningfully by themselves in time to the melody as if they were creations of God rather than of His servants, and how the clock announced the time to all Istanbul with a chime that resembled the sounding of a bell.

Black and Esther told me on different occasions how the clock, as well as being the focus of endless astonishment on the part of Istanbul's riffraff and dull-witted mobs, was understandably a source of discomfort to the pious and to Our Sultan because it symbolized the power of the infidel. In a time when rumors of this sort abounded, Sultan Ahmed, the subsequent sovereign, woke up in the middle of the night under Allah's instigation, seized His mace and descended from the harem to the Private Garden where He shattered the clock and its statues to pieces. Those who brought us the news and the rumors explained how as Our Sultan slept, He saw the sacred face of Our Exalted Prophet bathed in holy light and how the Apostle of God warned Him: If Our Sultan allowed his subjects to be awed by pictures and, worse yet, by objects that mimicked Mankind and thus competed with Allah's creations, the sovereign would be diverging from divine will. They also added that Our Sultan had taken up His mace while still dreaming. This was more or less how Our Sultan dictated the event to His faithful historian. He had this book, entitled *The Quintessence of Histories*, prepared by calligraphers, upon whom He lavished purses full of gold, though He forbade its illustration by miniaturists.

Thus withered the red rose of the joy of painting and illumination that had bloomed for a century in Istanbul, nurtured by inspiration from the lands of Persia. The conflict between the methods of the old masters of Herat and the Frankish masters that paved the way for quarrels among artists and endless quandries was never resolved. For painting itself was abandoned; artists painted neither like Easterners nor Westerners. The miniaturists did not grow angry and revolt, but like old men who quietly succumb to an illness, they gradually accepted the situation with humble grief and resignation. They were neither curious about nor dreamed about the work of the great masters of Herat and Tabriz, whom they once followed with awe, or the Frankish masters, whose innovative methods they aspired to, caught indecisively between envy and hatred. Just as the doors of houses are closed of an evening and the city is left to darkness, painting was also abandoned. It was mercilessly forgotten that we'd once looked upon our world quite differently.

My father's book, sadly, remained unfinished. From where Hasan scattered the completed pages on the ground, they were transferred to the Treasury; there, an efficient and fastidious librarian had them bound together with other unrelated illustrations belonging to the workshop, and thus they were separated into several bound albums. Hasan fled Istanbul, and disappeared, never to be heard from again. Shevket and Orhan never forgot that it wasn't Black but their Uncle Hasan who was the one who killed my father's murderer.

In place of Master Osman, who died two years after going blind, Stork became Head Illuminator. Butterfly, who was also quite in awe of my late father's talents, devoted the rest of his life to drawing ornamental designs for carpets, cloths and tents. The young assistant masters of the workshop gave themselves over to similar work. No one behaved as though abandoning illustration were any great loss. Perhaps because nobody had ever seen his own face done justice on the page.

My whole life, I've secretly very much wanted two paintings made, which I've never mentioned to anybody:

1. My own portrait; but I knew however hard the Sultan's miniaturists tried, they'd fail, because even if they could see my beauty, woefully, none of them would believe a woman's face was beautiful without depicting her eyes and lips like a Chinese woman's. Had they represented me as a Chinese beauty, the way the old masters of Herat would've, perhaps those who saw it and recognized me could discern my face behind the face of that Chinese beauty. But later generations, even if they realized my eyes weren't really slanted, could never determine what my face truly looked like. How happy I'd be today, in my old age—which I live out through the comfort of my children— if I had a youthful portrait of myself!

2. A picture of bliss: What the poet Blond Nazım of Ran had pondered in one of his verses. I know quite well how this painting ought to be made. Imagine the picture of a mother with her two children; the younger one, whom she cradles in her arms, nursing him as she smiles, suckles happily at her bountiful breast, smiling as well. The eyes of the slightly jealous older brother and those of the mother should be locked. I'd like to be the mother in that picture. I'd want the bird in the sky to be depicted as if flying, and at the same time, happily and eternally suspended there, in the style of the old masters of Herat who were able to stop time. I know it's not easy.

My son Orhan, who's foolish enough to be logical in all matters, reminds me on the one hand that the time-halting masters of Herat could never depict me as I am, and on the other hand, that the Frankish masters

MY NAME IS RED

who perpetually painted mother-with-child portraits could never stop time. He's been insisting for years that my picture of bliss could never be painted anyhow.

Perhaps he's right. In actuality, we don't look for smiles in pictures of bliss, but rather, for the happiness in life itself. Painters know this, but this is precisely what they cannot depict. That's why they substitute the joy of seeing for the joy of life.

In the hopes that he might pen this story, which is beyond depiction, I've told it to my son Orhan. Without hesitation I gave him the letters Hasan and Black sent me, along with the rough horse illustrations with the smeared ink, which were found on poor Elegant Effendi. Above all, don't be taken in by Orhan if he's drawn Black more absentminded than he is, made our lives harder than they are, Shevket worse and me prettier and harsher than I am. For the sake of a delightful and convincing story, there isn't a lie Orhan wouldn't design to tell.

1990–92, 1994–98

CHRONOLOGY

336–330 B.C.: **Darius** ruled in Persia. He was the last king of the Achaemenids, losing his empire to Alexander the Great.

336–323 B.C.: **Alexander the Great** established his empire. He conquered Persia and invaded India. His exploits as hero and monarch were legendary throughout the Islamic world even until modern times.

622: **The Hegira.** The emigration of the Prophet Muhammad from Mecca to Medina, and the beginning of the Muslim calendar.

1010: **Firdusi's *Book of Kings*.** The Persian poet Firdusi (lived circa 935–1020) presented his *Book of Kings* to Sultan Mahmud of Ghazni. Its episodes on Persian myth and history—including Alexander's invasion, tales of the hero Rüstem and the struggle between Persia and Turan—have inspired miniaturists since the fourteenth century.

1206–1227: The reign of Mongol ruler **Genghis Khan.** He invaded Persia, Russia and China, and extended his empire from Mongolia to Europe.

c. 1141–1209: The Persian poet **Nizami** lived. He wrote the romantic epic the *Quintet*, comprised of the following stories, all of which have inspired miniaturist painters: *The Treasury of Mysteries, Hüsrev and Shirin, Leyla and Mejnun, The Seven Beauties* and *The Book of Alexander the Great.*

1258: **The Sack of Baghdad.** Hulagu (reigned 1251–1265), the grandson of Genghis Khan, conquered Baghdad.

1300–1922: **The Ottoman Empire,** a Sunni Muslim power, ruled southeastern Europe, the Middle East and North Africa. At its greatest extent, the empire reached the gates of Vienna and Persia.

1370–1405: Reign of the Turkic ruler **Tamerlane.** Subdued the areas that the Blacksheep ruled in Persia. Tamerlane conquered areas from Mongolia to the Mediterranean including parts of Russia, India, Afghanistan, Iran, Iraq and Anatolia (where he defeated the Ottoman Sultan Bayazid I in 1402).

1370–1526: **The Timurid Dynasty,** established by Tamerlane, fostered a brilliant revival of artistic and intellectual life, and ruled in Persia, central Asia and Transoxiana. The schools of miniature painting at Shiraz, Tabriz and Herat flourished under the Timurids. In the early fifteenth century Herat was the center of painting in the Islamic world and home to the great master Bihzad.

1375–1467: **The Blacksheep,** a Turkmen tribal federation, ruled over parts of Iraq, eastern Anatolia and Iran. Jihan Shah (reigned 1438–67), the last Blacksheep ruler, was defeated by the Whitesheep Tall Hasan in 1467.

1378–1502: **The Whitesheep** federation of Turkmen tribes ruled northern Iraq, Azerbaijan and eastern Anatolia. Whitesheep ruler Tall Hasan (reigned 1452–78) failed in his attempts to contain the eastward expansion of the Ottomans, but he defeated the Blacksheep Jihan Shah in 1467 and the Timurid Abu Said in 1468, extending his dominions to Baghdad, Herat, and the Persian Gulf.

1453: Ottoman Sultan **Mehmet the Conqueror** took Istanbul. Demise of the Byzantine Empire. Sultan Mehmet later commissioned his portrait from Bellini.

1501–1736: **The Safavid Empire** ruled in Persia. The establishment of Shia Islam as the state religion helped unify the empire. The seat of the empire was at first located in Tabriz, then moved to Kazvin, and later, to Isfahan. The first Safavid ruler, Shah Ismail (reigned 1501–24), subdued the areas that the Whitesheep ruled in Azerbaijan and Persia. Persia weakened appreciably during the rule of Shah Tahmasp I (reigned 1524–76).

1512: **The Flight of Bihzad.** The great miniaturist Bihzad emigrated from Herat to Tabriz.

1514: **The Plunder of the Seven Heavens Palace.** The Ottoman Sultan Selim the Grim, after defeating the Safavid army at Chaldiran, plundered the Seven Heavens Palace in Tabriz. He returned to Istanbul with an exquisite collection of Persian miniatures and books.

1520–66: **Süleyman the Magnificent and the Golden Age of Ottoman Culture.** The reign of Ottoman Sultan Süleyman the Magnificent. Important conquests expanded the empire to the east and the west, including the first seige of Vienna (1529) and the capture of Baghdad from the Safavids (1535).

1556–1605: Reign of **Akbar, Emperor of Hindustan,** a descendant of Tamerlane and Genghis Khan. He established miniaturists' workshops in Agra.

1566–74: The reign of Ottoman **Sultan Selim II.** Peace treaties signed with Austria and Persia.

1571: **The Battle of Lepanto.** A four-hour naval battle between allied Christian forces and the Ottomans subsequent to the Ottoman invasion of Cyprus (1570). Though the Ottomans were defeated, Venice surrendered Cyprus to the Ottomans in 1573. The battle had great impact on European morale and was the subject of paintings by Titian, Tintoretto and Veronese.

1574–95: The reign of Ottoman **Sultan Murat III** (during whose rule the events of our novel take place). His rule witnessed a series of struggles between 1578–90 known as the Ottoman-Safavid wars. He was the Ottoman sultan most interested in miniatures and books, and he had the *Book of Skills,* the *Book of Festivities* and the *Book of Victories* produced in Istanbul. The most prominent Ottoman miniaturists, including Osman the Miniaturist (Master Osman) and his disciples, contributed to them.

1576: **Shah Tahmasp's Peace Offering to the Ottomans.** After decades of hostility, Safavid Shah Tahmasp made a present to the Ottoman Sultan Selim II upon the death of Süleyman the Magnificent in an attempt to foster future peace. Among the gifts sent to Edirne is an exceptional copy of the *Book of Kings,* produced over a period of twenty-five years. The book was later transferred to the Treasury in the Topkapi Palace.

1583: The Persian miniaturist **Velijan (Olive)**, about ten years after coming to Istanbul, is commissioned to work for the Ottoman court.

1587–1629: Reign of the Safavid Persian ruler **Shah Abbas I,** begins with the deposition of his father Muhammad Khodabandeh. Shah Abbas reduced Turkmen power in Persia by moving the capital from Kazvin to Isfahan. He made peace with the Ottomans in 1590.

1591: **The Story of Black and the Ottoman Court Painters.** A year before the thousandth anniversary (calculated in lunar years) of the Hegira, Black returns to Istanbul from the east, beginning the events recounted in the novel.

1603–17: The reign of Ottoman **Sultan Ahmet I,** who destroyed the large clock with statuary sent to the sultan as a present by Queen Elizabeth I.

New from

Orhan Pamuk

The Museum of Innocence

Pamuk's first novel since winning the Nobel Prize—emotionally charged, culturally illuminating, set in the last decades of 20th-century Istanbul. Kemal's obsessive, frustrated love for Füsun, a poor relation, comes to take form in a collection of objects stolen from her house, eventually making him famous—and a laughingstock—in Istanbul society. And when a final chance at happiness is ripped away, he will have only this hoard to console him: the museum of his and Füsun's innocence, the map of one man's broken heart.

Available October 2009 in hardcover from Knopf
$26.95 • 544 pages • 978-0-307-26676-7

Please visit www.aaknopf.com